Bantam Books by John Crowley

Three Novels by John Crowley:
The Deep
Beasts
Engine Summer

Little, Big

Ægypt

LOVE & SLEEP

JOHN CROWLEY

BANTAM BOOKS
NEW YORK TORONTO LONDON
SYDNEY AUCKLAND

LOVE & SLEEP
A Bantam Book / September 1994

Library of Congress Cataloging-in-Publication Data
Crowley, John.
Love & sleep / John Crowley.
p. cm.
ISBN 0-553-09642-7
1. Title. II. Title: Love and sleep.
PS3553.R597L68 1994
813'.54—dc20   93-44430
                                                    CIP
Published simultaneously in the United States and Canada

Bantam Books are published by Bantam Books, a division of Bantam
Doubleday Dell Publishing Group, Inc. Its trademark, consisting of the
words "Bantam Books" and the portrayal of a rooster, is Registered in
U.S. Patent and Trademark Office and in other countries. Marca Regis-
trada. Bantam Books, 1540 Broadway, New York, New York 10036.

PRINTED IN THE UNITED STATES OF AMERICA

BVG   0 9 8 7 6 5 4 3 2 1

Thou wouldst not think how ill all's here about my heart.

—Hamlet

LOVE & SLEEP

PROLOGUE

TO THE
SUMMER
QUATERNARY

nce, the world was not as it has since become.

Once it worked in a way different from the way it works now; its very flesh and bones, the physical laws that governed it, were ever so slightly different from the ones we know. It had a different history, too, from the history we know the world to have had, a history that implied a different future from the one that has actually come to be, our present.

In that age (not really long ago in time, but long ago in other bridges crossed, which we shall not return by again) certain things were possible that are not now; and contrariwise, things we know not to have happened indubitably had then; and there were other differences large and small, none able now to be studied, because this is now, and that was then.

Actually, the world ("the world;" all this; time and space; past, present, future; memory, stars, correspondences, physics; possibilities and impossibilities) has undergone such an agony more than once, many times maybe within the span of human life on earth, as we measure that life now in our age. And whenever it does happen, there comes a brief moment—a moment just as the world turns from what it has all along been into what it will from then on be—a brief time when every possible kind of universe, all possible extensions of Being in space or time, can be felt, poised on the threshold of becoming: and then the corner is turned, one path is taken, and all of those possibilities return into nonexistence again, except for one, this one. The world is as we know it now to be, and always has been: everyone forgets that it could be, or ever was, other than the way it is now.

If this were so—if it were really so—would you be able to tell?

Even if you somehow came to imagine that it was so; if—seized by some brief ecstasy in a summer garden, or on a mountain road in winter—you found yourself certain it was so, what evidence or proof could you ever adduce?

Suppose a man has crossed over from one such age of the world into the next (for the passage-time might not be long, not centuries; a life begun in the former time might well reach across the divide into the succeeding one, and a soul that first appeared under certain terms might come of age and die under others). Suppose that, standing on the farther shore, such a man turns back, troubled or wondering, toward where he once was: wouldn't he be able to perceive—in the memories of his own body's life, the contents of his own being—this secret history?

Maybe not; for his new world would seem to have in it all that he remembers the old world to have had; all the people and places, the cities, towns and roads, the dogs, stars, stones and roses just the same or apparently the same, and the history likewise that it once had, the voyages and inventions and empires, all that he can remember or discover.

Like a mirror shaken in a storm, in the time of passage memory would shiver what it reflects into unrecognizability, and then, when the storm was past, would restore it, not the same but almost the same.

Oh there would be small differences, possibly, probably, differences no greater than those little alterations—whimsical geographies, pretend books, names of nonexistent commercial products—that a novelist introduces, to distinguish the world he makes from the diurnal real, which his readers supposedly all share: differences almost too small to be discovered by memory, and who nowadays trusts memory anyway, imperious, corrosive memory, continuously grinding away or actually forcing into being the very things it pretends only to shelter and preserve.

No: Only in the very moment of that passage from one kind of world to the next kind is it ever possible to discover this oddity of time's economy. In that moment (months long? years?) we are like the man who comes down around the bend into his hometown and discerns, rising beyond the low familiar hills, a new range of snowy alps. Brilliant, heart-taking, steep! No they are clouds, of course they are, just cast momentarily for some reason of the wind's and weather's into imitation mountains, so real you could climb them, this is just what your homeland would be if its hills were their foothills. But no, the blue lake up on those slopes, reflecting the sky, *is* the sky seen through a rent, you will never drink from it; the central pass you could take upward, upward, is already beginning to tatter and part.

Pierce Moffett (standing on a winter mountain road, in his thirty-sixth year, unable just for the moment to move either onward or back, but able to feel the earthball beneath his feet roll forward in its flight) remembered how when he was a boy in the Cumberland Mountains of Kentucky he and his cousins had taken in a she-wolf cub, and kept it hidden in their rooms, and tried to tame it.

Now had he really done such a thing? How could he even ask this question of himself, when he could remember the touch of it, how he had cared for it, fed it, baptized it?

He remembered how in those days he had known the way to turn a lump of coal into the diamond that it secretly is, and had done it, too, once; remembered how he had discovered a country beneath the earth, which could be reached through an abandoned mine. He remembered the librarian of the Kentucky State Library in Lexington (Pierce could just then see her clearly, within her walls of dark books, a chain on her glasses), how she had set him a quest when he was a boy, a quest he had embarked on willingly, knowing nothing, not how far it would take him, nor what it would cost him. A quest he was sure now he would not ever complete.

He had once set a forest on fire, so that a woman he loved could see it burn, a woman who loved fire. Hadn't he?

O God had he actually once for her sake killed his only son?

But just then the road upward began to unroll again, and took Pierce's feet along with it; and he mounted a little farther toward the summit, where there was a monument he had heard of, but hadn't ever seen. The sun rose, in a new sign. Looking down at his feet, Pierce saw in wonder and dread that he was wearing mismatched shoes, almost the same but not the same. He had walked a couple of miles and more from home without noticing.

———

But it might be felt differently; indeed it would have to be felt differently, the last age ending and the new coming into being, felt differently by every person who passes through the gates.

Or it might not be felt at all. It might not be easy to notice, and our attention is anyway consumed almost all the time by the lives we have found to lead; we would probably just press on into the future as we have always done, even as the unnoticed scenery alters around us, feeling per-haps a little more sharply than usual that sense of loss or of hope, that conviction that, year by year, things are getting better and better, or worse and worse.

What Winnie Oliphant Moffett found was that she had solved the problem of forking paths.

She had not, before, very much needed a solution to this prob-lem. She had never been a person who pondered the choices she might have made, or suffered regrets; she had, usually, been glad to find that a path of any kind had continued to unfold before her, for her to take.

Like her choice to sell the house in Kentucky where she had lived with her brother Sam and his children until Sam's death, where she had raised her son Pierce; and with the money to go in on this Florida motel with Doris, whom she hardly knew: she had followed the path that had come to be before her, and here she was.

Only in this winter she had come to think that she might have done something else entirely, not just about Doris and the tourist cabins but earlier, far back, choice upon choice; she couldn't imagine clearly what she might have done, but the possibility was suddenly real to her, and troubling. She could see, or feel, herself in another life, the one she had not led, and could imagine, with an awful tug of poignancy sometimes, that that was her real life, abandoned, still waiting in the past for her to live it.

"It's just your time of life," Doris told her. "Your climacteric. I had funny feelings too. Oh I wept buckets."

What Winnie learned at last, the solution she arrived at, was that we must always choose exactly the path we most want to take.

Doris said to her that people *always* think the way they didn't take was the way they should have taken. The grass is always greener,

Doris said. We are always supposing that the path we didn't take was our real destiny; we think it must have been, because we think that this one, which we *did* take, certainly isn't.

But we will always feel that way, Winnie saw no matter what path we choose. And so if we *had* taken that other way, then we would surely by now be harking after *this* way, and yearning for its consequences, and knowing *it* was the one we should have taken: and we *did* take it, this is it.

So we have always taken the path we most wanted, the path that, if we had not taken it, we would now be longing to have taken. And we did. We took the right path. We always do.

A deep calm entered her with this solution, and a solemn sense of privilege, as she sat smoking an Old Gold and combing her wet hair in the sun of the back deck. Whether it had been entirely happy or not, and it hadn't, or very successful, and it wasn't, she was here living the life she would have tried to imagine if she had not lived it; the real life she wanted to lead.

She tried out her solution on Doris, who didn't seem to grasp it; but she thought she would describe it to Pierce when he came, if she could remember it, because he was surely a person who needed to know it.

But it was already departing, leaving only a shadow of absurd satisfaction in her spirit, on the day the service bell rang, and Winnie opened the door to find Pierce standing there: seeming to be in more trouble than she had thought him to be when he had called to say he was coming, and looking disordered and startled too, as though he had just been blown here by a sudden wind.

I

GENITOR

1

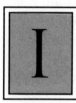n 1952 when he was nine years old, Pierce Moffett did
start a forest fire in the Cumberland Mountains of Ken-
tucky. The fire burned from Saturday morning till Sun-
day night, from the hillside beyond Pierce's house over the hills to the
No Name River in the east, where it stopped.

Every Saturday it was a chore of Pierce's and his younger cousins'
to carry the week's trash from the house to a burned and bare spot
near a disused garage. Why a garage stood there, far from the house
and without even a driveway leading to it, puzzled Pierce in those
days, but one was there, and beside it two corroded wire baskets too
small for a week's worth of litter. When the baskets were filled the
rest was piled between them.

It fell to Pierce to light the matches that set fire to the heap, which
is why he thought of himself as the one who set the forest on fire,
though all of them were present—Hildy, Bird and Warren. Hildy, a
year older than Pierce, was the one who first went for water.

Most Saturdays the pile burned uneventfully. Pierce's uncle Sam,
after a lifetime of shaving cream in tubes, had begun to buy cream in
aerosol cans, and when one or two of these were to be burned, the
children buried them at the bottom of the pyre, and after Pierce had
got the fire going well, they all retired to the old garage (Warren
would have already run laughing to hide there) and from the chinks
between its weather-shrunk boards, they watched till the cans one by
one imploded. When they had all been fired (sending showers of

sparks and burning detritus a good distance sometimes) then it was safe to come out again.

It wasn't one of these, though, that started the fire. That morning was dry and windy, a premonitory burnt and ashy smell was in the air, and the brush and weeds were high all around: there was milk-weed and yarrow and goldenrod, mullein and pigweed. At the edge of the open patch was a dry creek and a line of brushy poplars that Kentuckians called bummagillies; beyond them, the hillside and the forest. The wind blew that way.

Was it a page of *Collier's* or a *Look* that the fire was leafing through (blackening the pages as it touched and turned them one by one) or a sheet from an *Our Sunday Visitor,* or the dusty wax paper that lined a box of Kix? It was a big burning ash of something that arose not suddenly but gracefully from the fire as Pierce poked the burning mass with a rake. He tried to snare it as it rose, but it got away from him, and, black wings undulating, set out across the field as the transfixed children watched. Not far off it struck tall weeds and set-tled, dispersing. That's that. No, it's not: one tall weed had caught, and was burning down its length like a fuse toward the ground.

What you had to do then was to rush to the spot and stamp out the starting fire, sneakering it wholly out, then back to work. But on this Saturday the runaway had already started a fire, black ground salted with white ash, before they could reach the spot and begin their stamping. Pierce, Bird and Hildy chased along one arc of its progress, stamp stamp stamp, until Warren called out, and they turned to see that behind them it had bitten a big circle of meadow, tall weeds were igniting at their bases and firing like torches: and they knew it was not going to go out. That was when Hildy set off toward home for water.

Even as he felt the knowledge thrust on him that something terrible and irreversible had happened, Pierce was able to apprehend the interesting logic of fire, a logic he could have imagined in advance but hadn't: how it worked in a perfect circle from where it began, outward in all directions as it found new fuel at its edges and left the consumed places behind. He could see how the circle would just grow larger as long as fuel was found. Fire burned once, and left behind the place where it had burned, and went on; and there was no reason for it ever to stop.

Bird had run home now following Hildy, and Warren crying

following Bird. The soles of Pierce's sneakers were hot, hotter than when he stood long in an asphalt roadway in the summer sun: too hot. He set out after the others.

Hildy was already on her way back with a small bucket in one hand and a watering can in the other when Pierce reached the yard of the house. Off-balance and hurrying, she was spilling most of what she carried. The sight of her fierce face, her urgent willingness, and the thrashing hose she had left running behind her where she had filled her futile buckets, paralyzed Pierce. He understood that the emergency had reached that point when grownups must be alerted. He stood trying to think whether his uncle Sam was in the house, or rather he waited while vivid imaginings of his uncle in the house, not in the house, in the house, came and went within him. He hadn't made up his mind when his mother put her head out the door and called to him. Pierce what's the matter. And Pierce's fire was instantly in others' hands.

"It's probably nothing, isn't it?" she said; she tossed down her cigarette and stepped on it carefully. And went with Pierce out to the top of the yard, from where the field beyond could be seen. Bird and Warren came up after her.

"Oh hell," she said.

A long time afterward, Pierce asked his cousin Bird if she thought they had really set a forest on fire, or whether only a few acres of brush had burned.

"I think it was big," she said. "Sure it was. It must have burned a hundred acres at least. I know it burned all the way up over Yokun's place, because it burned up his fence, and he wanted Daddy to buy him a new fence. But his was an old broken-down rail fence that he never fixed anyway, and he wanted a new fence with like nice posts and bobwire! And it burned all the way to the river. I remember them saying there was no way to stop it, but that it would stop anyway when it got to the river. I guess it did.

"There were always fires in those days. You remember. The sun in the summer if it was dry was a lot of times hazy and red. Smoke from some fire, somewhere."

In the years of the postwar mining boom the prop-cutters sent out by the mine-owners cut over thousands of acres; paid by the piece, the cutters had pulled out what was easy and left the rest—cut tops and shattered detritus and good long logs as well, too hard to extract and left behind. The woods beyond Sam Oliphant's hillside were a weird wilderness of cull and old stumps, the hollers filled with tumbled logs like great dropped jackstraws, dryrotting to tinder, awaiting Pierce's match. Bird remembered—though Pierce didn't— how after the red sun set she and Hildy and Joe Boyd (Bird and Hildy's older brother, who hadn't been at the fire's birth) climbed out onto the roof through the window of the second-story closet—a window in a closet, Pierce had wondered when he was first shown this trick, but why—and sat in the ashy-tasting dark watching the slow crawl of their fire through the holler and over the mountain.

If it was a forest fire it didn't look like one; didn't look like the fire that devastated Bambi's home, and drove the frightened animals before it. It wasn't a space of living orange flame but a line, a dull-russet smoking frontier between the burned and the unburned: not different really from the fire in the grass where it had started.

"Your daddy's going to have to pay for that," Joe Boyd said to Pierce, smug in the security of innocence, burning trash not being one of his chores.

"That's not fair," Hildy said.

"It's true," said Joe Boyd. "When a little kid does something, or something? The little kid can't pay, but his daddy is responsible. He has to pay."

Pierce said nothing, unable to imagine the cost Joe Boyd meant. A mountain, two mountains? They seemed to Pierce's mind either invaluable or valueless.

"It wasn't *his* fault," Bird said, though often enough when Joe Boyd announced awful facts like that he turned out to be right; Bambi's mother (though Bird covered her ears not to hear him whisper it to her) had really died. "Besides, his father's in New York. And he's poor."

She didn't add that it wasn't Pierce alone who set the fire, but all of them: the Invisible College, working together, pledged to one another. And that being so, Joe Boyd was guilty of it too: for Joe Boyd was himself Permanent President of this Kentucky branch of the College, duly elected by the membership. Bird didn't say any of that, because saying it meant revealing to Joe Boyd the existence of the

College and the secret of his Presidency: and that was the deepest of the many secrets the Invisible College was sworn to keep.

"Not my daddy," Joe Boyd said, to be sure no mistake would be made about this. "*Your* daddy."

Pierce Moffett's wasn't the only fire burning that night in the mountains, nor the only one not put out. The Cumberlands had been burning for years, and there had never been anyone to put them out. Not only the trees that covered them: once the mountains themselves had used to burn, set afire by the dynamite used to loosen the seams of coal like teeth; the seams would ignite, and the mountain burned, smoking out of fissures, parching its earth. A hot bitter breath could be felt coming from the mine's driftmouth then, and on the mountain's back the stones under bare feet were warm as flesh.

Slate dumps built beside the coal-tipples used to burn too: fires starting deep down from the pressure of tons of rock on the coal fragments and dust, and issuing up through fault lines in the slate and shale, to spit and smoke in long creeping veins. Now and then the bosses would set teams of men to following these fire-lines and smothering them with ashes; the men worked a day or two days, climbing over the heap like attendant devils in a little hell, only putting fires out and not stirring them. It didn't work for long; the fire only crept elsewhere, and found other outlets. Some of the slate fires burned for years; some that were burning in 1936 when Sam Oliphant, newly Dr. Oliphant, first came to the Cumberlands were still burning when he brought his family back there after the war.

His was a family of doctors. When old Doc Oliphant had died, Sam's older brothers had taken over his practice, leaving Sam to find a practice of his own. Instead, and without giving it a lot of thought, Sam had answered an ad for Public Health doctors in Kentucky, was accepted gratefully, and set out South in his father's Olds, part of his share of a small estate. In this car he came to ride a wide circuit, like a traveling preacher; in a country of old Fords it earned him both respect and suspicion, until it had acquired a few dents and the dusty roads had permanently dulled its lacquer.

Wild, wild and strange he found the mountain country to be, his circuit of towns and coal camps with their simple utilitarian names,

Cut Shin Creek, Stinking Creek, Black Mountain, Big Sandy River—
names having been given only to places that needed them, and not
out of any ambition of permanence or glory, no classical evocations,
no biblical names either, no Bethel, Goshen, Beulah: maybe because
the founders were unlearned even in the Bible, or maybe because
however beautiful and vast their mountains were they had not believed this was God's country, nor ever mistaken it for the Promised
Land. The people Dr. Oliphant preached to (how was it they didn't
know how to build a proper privy, or how to put food safely by?)
filled him with stories that his Westchester relatives would find hard
to swallow; Sam refined them and polished them over the years, and
his children refined them further in their own retellings. Sam on his
first tour, examining a girl of fourteen, who's feeling peaked. His
consternation: the girl's clearly pregnant.

Child, did you know you're going to have a baby?

Wide eyes astonished: Ain't so!

Well it is. Do you know how it happened? How you get a baby?

A solemn nod, reckon I do.

Well, what happened? You can tell me. Were you raped?

Oh doctor (a sigh of cheerful resignation) it's been nothn but rape
rape rape all summer long.

His people, their lives harsh and poignant as their fiddle laments;
his dawn journeys along pea-vine roads that skirted deep glens and
crossed crackling brooks (hollers and cricks, he would learn to say);
the morning smoke of hidden rivers rising through the timberlands,
drifting with the soft curl of smoke from cabin chimneys; even the
smell of his Olds and its upholstery, the taste of his Camels and his
coffee, all of it came soon to be colored for Sam with love. Love would
be the reason he remembered it so fondly, and why, when a widower
with no reason to remain, he lived there till he died.

Opal Boyd was a schoolteacher, a child of the Western farmlands
of the state and like Sam a recruit of the decade's hopes for progress.
She wore her ash-blond hair in two long braids wound on her head in
a pale tiara; she wore cotton shirtwaist dresses with woven belts,
which she bought on a yearly trip to Louisville or Chicago. In her
rented room in the house of the county clerk there was a tennis racket
in a wooden press. Hopeful and useless and brave in that valley, the
tennis racket too was touched for Sam with love.

When Opal married Sam and conceived a child, she began to see the ravaged mountains differently. They went North to have the baby, they went to the great World's Fair in New York and saw the future, they decided not to go back. But the established practice on Long Island that Sam bought into with all of his and Opal's savings proved to be not very large or very lucrative, and by the time he returned to it after four years of war, he found that it had in effect disestablished itself, divided among two doctors who had elected to remain at their necessary work rather than enlist as Sam had done. In the same medical journal where he had once found the ad wanting Public Health doctors in Kentucky, Sam saw that a small Catholic mission hospital in the town of Bondieu, Breshy County (a town he could not remember ever having passed through), was offering a good salary for a chief physician, more by quite a bit than he ever seemed likely to make among the potato farmers and oystermen; and some ten years after he and Opal Boyd had left the Cumberlands they came back, with four children, not to stay forever but only long enough to build a little capital for starting over elsewhere.

"I suppose it was a sudden decision, and I suppose it wasn't a very smart one," he wrote to his daughter Hildy a long time after, in the last months of his life. Hildy was the child he could talk to most easily, but even she was surprised when she began getting letters from him, and she started laying plans to get home quickly. "I'm sorry that I never made much money, or accumulated much of an estate to leave you and the others. Doctors now are assumed to be well off, and I guess I should be ashamed I'm not; but you know in the years when I went to medical school we really *didn't* expect to make a lot of money. Most of us did in the end—things changed in medicine—but we didn't expect it, like the med students now do. So I don't feel so much like a failure that I didn't. Only I *am* sorry for this damned impulsiveness I've always had, that I never thought through the big decisions. I think maybe I've passed that on, with the no money that goes with it. Any talent for good sense you'll have to thank your mother for."

Opal hadn't liked Long Island; she thought maybe it was the salt fogs that brought on her headaches. Sam believed, though he didn't say, that she brought on her headaches herself: and though he knew himself to be a good doctor, and knew also not to charge himself with failure if he'd done all that his knowledge and skill could do, he was sorry ever after that he had thought so. They had just set up house in Bondieu—in the largest house in town, the old Hazelton place, bought for them by the hospital—when Opal's tumor was discovered.

Pierce, who had been eight years old that year, always remembered—perhaps because it was the first time he had ever seen her weeping openly—coming upon his mother, Sam's sister, with Sam's letter crushed in her hand, in the kitchen of their Brooklyn apartment. Ailanthus grew so close to the windows of that kitchen that sometimes it came right in, as though to look. "Poor Sam," his mother was saying, her eyes squeezed shut and fist pressed against her brow. "Poor Sam. Poor, poor children." And even after long acquaintance with Sam and with his children, all tough nuts and not always friends of his, the memory of Winnie's tears for them could raise a lump of awful pity in Pierce's throat.

One year later, Winnie put Pierce aboard a bus and took him with her to Pikeville, Kentucky, the town nearest to Bondieu for which she could get a ticket. There Sam picked them up in his huge Nash bought not long before for the big trip South, and brought them to Bondieu, and Winnie settled in to be his housekeeper and stepmother to his four children. She had always loved, even worshipped, her older brother, and she did deeply grieve for the children: but those weren't her reasons for leaving her husband in Brooklyn forever. And despite the abiding antipathy she felt for Bondieu, her never-shaken sense of the unlikelihood of her being there for good, she had not regretted her decision: she had had nowhere else to go.

"It wasn't like now, then," Winnie said to Pierce in Florida. Pierce sat with his feet up on the rail of the deck, a can of soda warming in his hands. "Now you'd have so many ways to proceed, ways to feel about it. So many. Then you only had a few. So you picked among the ones you had, and were glad for the safety. I couldn't get a divorce, and couldn't have made a living by myself—anyway I didn't think I could. I guess I'm trying to explain. I won't apologize.

"It's hard to imagine now, how shocked you could be, now when it seems so ordinary a thing. I mean look at Key West for heaven's sake. But it wasn't ordinary then; it was like—well it was like finding a breach in nature. I couldn't share a bed with him then, could I? And

I had to get *you* away from him; that just seemed self-evident, like snatching you away from a fire.

"But you know, the sad thing," Winnie said. She laughed, chagrined. "He really was such a good father, in his way. I'm sorry, Pierce."

2

_____

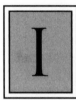t had been fall when Pierce came to Bondieu to live. It happened that about the time he and Winnie settled in, the storm windows were taken out of the garage and piled on the porch to be put up; nobody finished the chore, though, and for a long time the storm windows lay there on the porch in two rows of two. For a reason he could not afterward remember (he could only occasionally remember the interesting sensation of it, which was perhaps itself the only reason) Pierce had carefully and deliberately stepped in every pane of these windows, each of which bore his weight for a moment before crashing like thin ice over a dried puddle. When what he had done was discovered, he denied having done it, though it was obvious enough to Sam that it had been he. There was no real proof, though, and Pierce didn't feel he needed to confess without it. He was made to anyway.

And hadn't he always been a denier of what he had done, a denier too of what had become of him; a liar in fact? Had his mother actually been a denier too, only with the handy quality of actually forgetting the things she had done, and being left only with the reasons, the good reasons, she had done them?

He thought that what had made it so hard for him to admit what he had done was that Sam's next question would have been Why, as in many later instances it was; _Why_, not unkindly meant, but leaving Pierce no recourse at all, because he didn't know why. He had no reason. When later on he carried Sam's tools into the woods and left them there to rust, unable to remember that he'd borrowed them; when one winter afternoon he cut the telephone line into Sam's bedroom with his knife; when he took from Sam's bureau drawer his dead wife's engagement ring: he had known (at the time, anyway) why he had done so—crises faced by the Invisible College had demanded it. But his lies in those instances had the same logic as the first instance, the storm windows, that if he confessed to what he'd done he'd be asked why. And he couldn't answer. So he denied he'd done it.

"What on earth were you thinking of?" Sam asked, holding Pierce's shoulder, pointing his nephew's head down at the shatter and ruin.

"I didn't."

"You *did*! Don't insult my intelligence. I just want to know *why*."

"I didn't."

Sam always insisted (and Pierce doubted) that Pierce's offenses bothered him less than Pierce's willingness to outface him. He devised mild but ingenious punishments for Pierce designed to impress on him the unreasonableness of his lying, punishments that Pierce took, though deeply aggrieved that Sam thought he had the right to inflict them. But they didn't change him.

Had he really thought he could get away with the outrageous lies he told? It was as though he thought he really *was* invisible, that he left no trail others could follow, that nothing could be pinned on him because he wasn't really there at all.

"Lives in a world of his own," Sam said to Winnie; though the opposite always seemed as true to Winnie, who knew him better: that Pierce lived in a world not his at all.

The house built on a rise above the town of Bondieu by old man Hazelton (himself a doctor around the time of the First World War, then a politician, then a speculator in coal leases, then a bankrupt, then a suicide) had two distinct parts: a big, square two-story place of dingy clapboard with a pillared front porch, and a low bungalow of four rooms in a row, connected to the big house by a trellised breezeway. Bird told Pierce that the little house had been built as a gift for the Hazeltons' only daughter and her husband, so that she wouldn't leave home, a motive that Pierce could not then credit. Bird had the first of the four rooms for herself, and Hildy the second; the third was the daughter's kitchen, and the fourth a tiny windowed sitting-room or sun-porch where an old couch moldered.

Upstairs in the big house Sam and Opal Boyd had had their bedroom, and a small connecting room was Warren's. Joe Boyd had another to himself, and a fourth was empty. That was the one Winnie took. Into it went her marble-topped dresser, and atop the dresser the silver-backed brushes and mirror she never actually used, and the silver-framed photographs of her parents; into it too, borne in somehow on these things, went an odor of Brooklyn and his infancy that Pierce could detect there even years later.

Where was Pierce to go? The first plan was that he would share with Joe Boyd, but Joe Boyd set himself so adamantly against this that no one, not Sam, not Winnie, not Pierce certainly, wanted to try converting him. So Hildy moved in with Bird, and Pierce took her room next to the kitchen of the bungalow. (When Joe Boyd at length left home, Pierce was offered his room in the big house next to Sam's; but he preferred his room in the girls' wing. Hildy took it instead.)

Sam had supposed that one thing he was providing for Pierce under his roof was a sort of older brother, someone who might counteract any bent that being his father's son might have left him with—no, that was too strongly put, Sam knew, but still he thought that Joe Boyd could be mentor, guide, friend for Pierce, all that Sam's own older brothers had been for him. Sam was sure enough of this that he paid less careful attention to Pierce than he might have. To Pierce, though, Joe Boyd with his sad, minatory eyes and jailbird haircut remained just what he had always seemed, the viceroy or dark archangel of Sam, the one who brought him Sam's wishes and instructions moral or practical, lessons Pierce could never learn.

That spring Joe Boyd had organized his sisters and his brother into a club, with passwords and offices and swearings-in. Joe Boyd's club was called the Retrievers, in imitation of the animal lodges he had known of back North, Elks, Moose, Lions; his was named in honor of the breed of dog he most admired and would never own. The Retrievers had their headquarters in a long-disused chicken house up the steep hillside from the big house; its chief activity was the impossible job of cleaning this place of its accumulation of guano and pinfeathers and crushed eggshell: the job being done by the younger members at Joe Boyd's direction.

Pierce, hands in his jacket pockets, stood at the door watching the distasteful work go on, never having seen or smelled such a place before. He hadn't been invited to be a Retriever by the only Retriever able to issue the invitation, Joe Boyd, and he couldn't bring himself to ask for admission either. He had come to realize, though, that he wouldn't be able to spend the rest of his childhood in his room, as he had opined to his mother he might; he'd have to come to accommodation.

"Whatcha doing?"

"What's it look like?"

Shrug. He asked what anyway the place was, with its boxes of whitened screening and strawdusty air. Joe Boyd took exception to his superior tone, which Pierce hadn't intended.

"Not good enough for you?"

"Well we don't exactly have chicken houses in Brooklyn."

"Yeah? Well."

Without knowing where he was headed, Pierce allowed himself to be drawn into a debate with Joe Boyd about the relative merits of New York and Kentucky. It was never in doubt who would win this debate; Joe Boyd, though loyal to his mother's state, the state where he had been conceived, could not himself name enough virtues in it to keep up.

"Name a hero who came from Kentucky."

"Daniel Boone."

"Name another." Joe Boyd didn't name Abraham Lincoln, though Pierce had counterclaims if he had.

"Well name one from New York," Joe Boyd said.

"Peter Minuit. He had a peg leg. Peter Stuyvesant. Alexander Hamilton. Joe DiMaggio. Thomas E. Dewey."

"Who?"

At length Joe Boyd chose another way to settle the matter. It wasn't so unfair a match as it seemed, as it seemed to Hildy who pointed out that Joe Boyd was two years older: for Pierce had already begun the weedlike, apelike (so he would one day think it) burgeoning that would take him to a thick six feet, and Joe Boyd took after his light-boned and delicate mother. Joe Boyd still won handily, being less afraid of giving and getting pain than his cousin, and more willing to fight to conclusive victory. Pierce face down in the odorous dust of the floor was made to admit that Kentucky, the state where he now lived, was a better state of the United States than New York, the state where he had lived with his father and mother, but where he lived no more.

"Wanna go again? Two out of three."

"No."

"Say uncle."

"What?"

"Say uncle."

Pierce, not ever having been forced to this formula of surrender, made his own sense of it. "Uncle," he said.

For a long time after he let Pierce rise, Joe Boyd sat with his arm around Pierce's shoulders, Pierce shy to shake him off; and after this meeting of the lodge was over, and supper eaten, Joe Boyd took Pierce up to his room to show him his treasures.

Unnerved by the sudden intensity of his comradeship, Pierce looked in silence at Joe Boyd's beautifully preserved comic books and his Long Island seashells. A branch on which real stuffed birds perched with real bird feet, jay, cardinal, robin. Snake's skin and deer's skull. His plated six-guns, which hung in their holsters over the bedposts, little worn these days. An engraving of Robert E. Lee, which Joe Boyd had begged as a souvenir from Arlington when the Oliphants had visited there on their way South: something in the sad-eyed noble-dog figure, gloved and sashed, had touched him.

Lastly he drew out from its box and opened to Pierce his latest project.

"It's a battle," he said.

It was a tall roll of smooth white paper such as Pierce had never seen before, which Joe Boyd called "shelf paper." He unrolled a foot of it, revealing pencil-drawn figures, tiny ones, many of them. They were in fact engaged in a struggle; each little stick man had a stick-gun which he fired, or aimed, or lay dead gripping. Dotted lines showed the trajectories of these guns' bullets toward a facing crowd of armed figures, which Joe Boyd now revealed farther along the scroll.

"I can draw better people," he said. "But this is the quick way to draw lots."

He'd said it was a battle, but it wasn't really; there were no massed formations maneuvering, no regiments or officers. The dozens on each side fought independently over the crudely-drawn landscape, aimed from behind rocks and stumps, fired and died alone in dozens of carefully-conceived attitudes. Some bled tiny penciled puddles.

"But look at this," Joe Boyd said. He unrolled the shelf paper further, revealing that the opponents of the first bunch were themselves being attacked in the rear by a third group; some had already turned to face them. It was evident that this new band would be vulnerable too, though Joe Boyd hadn't got that far yet. There was no reason for it ever to stop.

"I'm going to do more," Joe Boyd said, rolling it up. "Lots more."

No, Joe Boyd would never be his mentor, nor ever entirely his friend, whatever Sam hoped. And though Pierce would anyway show no trace of Axel's inclinations, would soon begin accumulating evidence that his nature contained none, still one among his secret heroes would always be Georgie Porgie, puddn and pie, who kissed the girls and made them cry:

> But when the Boys came out to play
> Georgie Porgie ran away.

Still Pierce wasn't offered membership in the Retrievers; perhaps Joe Boyd sensed in him some remaining reluctance about fellowship, or the work it entailed, that might be a source of disaffection. "I don't care anyway," Pierce said to Bird and Hildy in their bungalow at night. "I already have a club. Sort of."

The three of them were gathered at the brown gas heater, big as a chest of drawers, that stood in Pierce's room and heated the whole of the little house. It took all three of them to light it: Hildy to direct operations, and turn on the gas; Pierce to light the match; Bird, afraid of lighting matches but not afraid of the heater as Pierce was, to thrust the lit match into the hole in the heater's side.

"What's your club?"

"Well, it's secret." He readied himself with match and box next to Bird at the touch-hole. Hildy crouched at the gas cock. "It's a secret club of my father's."

"They let little kids in?"

"Some."

"What's the name of it?"

"I can't tell you. It's secret." He saw his father's face, binding him in an imaginary but suddenly vivid past to secrecy.

"Ready?" said Hildy impatiently, whose skinny legs trembled with cold.

"Okay."

"Okay."

Pierce, after a few misfires, got the match to flame, turning it in his fingers. Hildy had opened the cock already, too soon; Bird fumbled for the match in Pierce's fingers, each of them trying to keep farthest from the flame. She half-thrust half-threw the match within the hole and turned away. Gas built up within the chamber ignited with an impatient *whump,* not as loud as on some nights when the process took even longer.

"Who's all are members?" Hildy asked. "Can we be?"

"Maybe," Pierce said.

"Can Warren be?"

Pierce shrugged.

"Can Joe Boyd be?"

There was no reason to exclude him. There was also no reason, and Pierce felt no compulsion, to inform him that he was eligible for membership; or that his membership had been considered. And accepted. The taste of triumph, like the taste of the burned gas, was in the back of Pierce's throat. "Sure," he said. "Sure he can."

Later, in bed, his two cousins tried to guess the name of Pierce's secret lodge, or wheedle it from him. They guessed birds and beasts noble and ridiculous ("The Lizards Club! The Bugs Club!") until they got the giggles; they asked Pierce for the initials, the number of letters, the sounds-like. Pierce wasn't telling, though; he didn't yet know himself. He only knew that he was a member, inducted long ago (he with so little long-ago, that had recently come to seem so much to him), the brothers robed and smiling to welcome him, rank on rank. His heart was full of a wicked glee, that he wasn't alone here as they had all thought him to be, but one of a company, invisible for now but coming clearer to him all the time.

The Retrievers soon passed out of existence, its clubhouse still un-cleaned, as Joe Boyd turned his hungry heart elsewhere. Pierce couldn't later remember if he was ever formally sworn in, but Bird said sure he had been, didn't he remember, there were outings and official business that included him, and dues extracted. It would later surprise Pierce how much more his younger cousin could remember, of things they had both experienced, than he could himself. That first year he came to Bondieu must, he thought, have been so full of shifting challenges and things hard to understand that like the succes-sive crises of a long dream they couldn't be retained in memory afterwards: only the umbrageous colors, and the sense of a struggle.

"I can't even really tell you how we *got* there," Winnie in Florida said to him, "with all our things, our trunks and clothes and the beds and things."

"The marble-topped dresser," Pierce said—locating it suddenly, vividly, just as it was on the point of departing, got *you* at least. "The spool bed."

"Did Axel send them on?" Winnie wondered. "I guess he must have, because they were all there later on, weren't they? Sure they were. Well, I was in a state, I know it."

Pierce never blamed Winnie for his exile. Of Axel his father he had been deeply, inarticulately ashamed; on those nights when Axel had used to call to talk to him, he would listen almost without speak-ing to Axel's anyway unbreakable stream of sentiments (always a sound in the background of these calls, a tinkle and sea-murmur of voices and music) which inevitably grew maudlin, sorry, filled with moist pauses, while the Oliphants watched and Pierce's cheeks grew hot. But he didn't blame Axel for what had become of him either, because Winnie didn't or didn't seem to. She never complained of Axel; she seemed to bear him no grudge; she rarely spoke of him at all. Maybe it was because Winnie was able not to notice things, be-cause she sought so diligently for a space of rest for herself untouched by the consequences of things, maybe because she loved Pierce so much and never questioned him either, that Pierce had always found in her room not the reasons for his exile but a respite from it.

Take care of your mother, Axel had commissioned him, his words drowned in tears, that last morning in Brooklyn before Pierce set out with Winnie, in a cab filled with their swollen suitcases, toward the bus station. *Be a good knight,* he had said.

Be a good knight. Axel, quixotic lover of romances, chivalry, and vows of service, had also suffered a quixotic harm to the brain from them. Pierce in Kentucky remembered his injunction, but he didn't feel burdened by it, not then anyway. Axel grew dim to Pierce in Kentucky, insubstantial, which judging from Winnie's behavior he was supposed to do, evaporate, melt into nothing like a snowman in the advancing of Pierce's seasons. But Pierce *was* his mother's knight, and would remain; she had rescued him from the dark wood of the Brooklyn apartment where his father was lost (Why dark? Why lost?) and now she was his alone, installed over in the upper story of the main house, in the bedroom next to Sam's. There he served her, there he waited on her, laughed with her, capered before her; he poured himself endlessly into the vacancy that was her, teasing her with questions that would last forever because they had no answers: What if everything suddenly got twice as big as it is? Could you tell? What if the stars are really small and close overhead, just a little ways, a thousand miles, and only seem to be far away? What if seeming-to-be-far-away is just the way they are, and you could really reach them easily in a jet? Why is everything the way it is, and not some different way instead? Why is there space? Why is there anything, anything at all, and not just nothing?

3

utumn rains slaked the ash of the hillside and the holler; for a long time the smell of things burned and then wetted reached the nose on every wind, but more cold rain washed the air. In spring the burnt-over land would only be the more fertile because of the rich ash the children had laid on it; burning and then planting, after all, was how Cumberland crops had long been grown. Pierce turned a leaf of *Collier's* magazine and saw an ad for the Plywood Association: an emerald sprout of fir, sheltered like a flame by rough caring hands, first growth of a new forest in the colorless blasted land all around.

The school year hadn't yet started for the Oliphants. Every autumn since they had come school had started late, and this year Father Midnight's sister, who had been the children's tutor, went away to a distant hospital just as the process of setting up school in the kitchen and sitting room of the little bungalow was to begin. What sort of hospital she went away to, and for what reason, wasn't described to the children, which left them free to imagine reasons and outcomes more drastic than any the real case warranted. They hadn't loved Miss Martha, Father Midnight's sister, but she was vague and easily fooled, and they hadn't feared her.

(It was Hildy who had first seen that their parish priest was a replica of the unheroic hero on TV, who, whatever deeds he might once have done in some other medium somewhere else, on their Saturdays now merely introduced ancient cowboy movies from behind a desk, and in the intervals sold a hot drink the children had never drunk and could not imagine. The priest was he exactly, but in phony eyeglasses and liturgical gear: Father Midnight. Warren had to be strictly schooled never to call him that.)

It wasn't conceivable that the children should attend the local grammar school. There was one, a square brick building not in the town of Bondieu but in the town of Good Luck, a mile or so distant. Like the square brick hospital, like the rows of gritty cabins along the railroad track, the school was a beneficence of the Good Luck Coal and Coke Company in the early years of the century. Now it was the property of the state, and all the children of Bondieu who went to school went there, just as almost all the fathers who worked had once worked for Good Luck Coal and Coke. Dr. Hazelton himself had dispensed pills to miners and miners' wives at the Good Luck hospital, which had just closed its doors for good. "Good luck for the patients," Sam said.

Sam's arrangement with his hospital had from the beginning included provision of a tutor for his children; Opal Boyd had seen too many schools like the Good Luck school, and had known their teachers. So Miss Martha, who had trained as a teacher though she had only briefly been one, had been hired, and Opal had done the rest, until her headaches got too bad; and now Miss Martha too was gone. September ran into October. The children lived within an unwonted freedom that could end any day; they got used to it. Summer's games continued. They were like the mountain children they knew of but rarely encountered, shoeless wraiths invisible to teacher or to principal.

They did read, though. There wasn't one of them, not even Joe Boyd, who didn't. They read through meals and chores and car-trips; they hogged the bathroom, unwilling to leave the pot where they sat reading. Hildy could read and listen to the radio at the same time, and miss nothing either of Nancy Drew or of Sky King. Sam read the novels that Winnie finished, as he had read Opal's.

They got their books by writing to the State Library in Lexington and asking for them; there was no public library for mountain miles in any direction from Bondieu. Once a month a big box of them arrived in a sort of laundry case with canvas belts that could be done up when the books had been read (or not read) and were to be sent back. What books were received depended on what was asked for, who received the order, and what the library had, which wasn't Everything though it seemed bottomless from Bondieu. If Bird asked for a book about horses, she was as likely to get dense volumes on equine anatomy or ranch management as she was to get another book like *Black Beauty,* which was what she wanted. Joe Boyd knew what he wanted, but not how to describe it: he wanted books full of facts, strange but true, things which he could ask others if they knew and be certain they would not: the number of peepers that could sit side by side on a single pencil, the number of pencils that could be made from a single cedar tree. If the facts were disgusting as well as obscure, that was all the better.

It was Joe Boyd's description of this category, however he had phrased it, that had once brought him a big book whose end-papers showed a mass of ruins, and whose double-columned pages were filled with tenebrous illustration. Or maybe it had been put in just to fill up the box, as the best and worst books the family got often were. Anyway Joe Boyd claimed it, and looked through it for a while, enjoying the images of monstrous gods, witches at their sabbats, and heretics aflame. Then Pierce took it up: *A Dictionary of Deities, Devils and Dæmons of Mankind,* by Alexis Payne de St.-Phalle, a name that Sam would have had fun with if Pierce had ever shown him the book, which he never did. Whenever it arrived (and Pierce ordered it again and again after the first time) it would immediately be removed to Pierce's room, to the shelf where he kept things important to him: the missal his father had given him, his photo album, his crystal of quartz and his souvenir sheath-knife from Bear Mountain, his bookends in the form of two hemispheres of the world, beneath which on either side little sculpted boys and girls read books of unimaginable facts.

"This one again?" Winnie asked him when she opened the case that October. Pierce only took it from her, without apology: he knew how much there was in it yet to read, or to reread. Winnie distributed the other books. Hildy's allotment of Nancy Drew and Cherry Ames (Hildy played it safe, and ordered her books in named series: the only danger then was getting the same one twice, which after the passage of a little time she didn't notice). Winnie's own novels, dense and pictureless. Bird's horses and Warren's, his surmounted by cowboys. They all went their separate ways then with their piles, like starvelings, to consume them in private.

Abraxas. Adocentyn. Apollyon. Ariel. Ars Notoria. Azael. In the

Angelic Conversations of Doctor DEE (*q.v.*), *Azael* is the Interpreter of God. What did "q.v." mean? The first thing to do after staring again long into the vast ruins pictured on the end-papers front and back—broken antique torsos, huge headstones covered in clearly cut but unintelligible words, toppled pillars sunken in tufts of grass, arches, urns, capitals, obelisks—was to turn to the page whereon he had found the name of his secret lodge or club, the one Joe Boyd was now President of (though he didn't know it). It wasn't far from the front, in an entry on Alchemy (the dictionary was broader than its name suggested, almost any odd name or notion could get an entry); the book almost fell open there, so stared at was the page.

There were the row of small dark etchings, the creatures brought forth from the base matter by alchemical processes, but how: the Red Man and the White Woman, the Green Lion, the Child of the Philosopher, the Androgyne (one breast, one half a beard, convolute privates too ill-drawn to study). Below them, a picture of the Alchemist, in bathrobe and complex hat, the smoke of his cauldron and the flames of his fire drawn with the same harshly cut black lines as the pleats of his robe. Too absorbed in his mysteries to notice a crowd of long-nailed curly-tusked bat-winged devils swarming through his window, glad to see him at the work that would damn him. Below him, another picture: a miniature castle, its drawbridge drawn up, the inhabitants within at work on tasks of transformation or studying big books or firing guns or arrows out the windows.

Only this castle moved, or was supposed to have moved, on four spindly cartwheels at its corners. It looked comically little, insufficient, like Humphrey Pennyworth's house in the funnies, and yet grave and minatory: not a joke. A finger from heaven pointed to it, and a wind from there filled the sails by which it traveled. It was, said Alexis Payne de St.-Phalle in a caption almost too small to read, the Invisible College of the Rose Cross Brothers, and it was evident from the dress of the people, both the wise men within and the ignorant outside, that the moving college had gone its way long ago, in the past. It was certainly gone now, if it had ever truly been; gone with the past wherein it had existed, wherein the other beings listed here in their alphabetical order had also existed, the people and events and the facts strange but true.

The past: these ruins.

In the past, once, somewhere, somewhen, kings and gods had gone naked: armed and crowned and shod sometimes, but naked where it mattered, filled maybe with the same grave elation that filled Pierce when in private games he as liberator, as ancient king come home again into his own kingdom, would order his people to throw off their garments, and be as they had been—he leading the way, putting aside his (bath) robe and reclining in easeful nakedness, a Royal Crown in his hand and magnanimity in his heart, the world returned to antique gaiety. In the past there had been a Golden Age.

"This was before Columbus," Hildy said.

"This was the Old World," said Pierce.

In the past, in the Old World, there had been empires whose geographies were now lost, the maps no longer had room for them, filled up as they were with classroom countries; empires still somehow in existence though beyond the demarcated globe, undersea or underground. Pierce committed to memory lists of their interchangeable gods and godlets, the air and water had been crowded with them then, potent but not omnipotent—a comfort somehow, they were strong friends or difficult enemies but not all-seeing, not everywhere at once; the wise could compel them, back then (or maybe that was sometime later, when they had grown smaller): could bring them to mirrors, draw them into statues, talk with them. *Magi*, said Alexis Payne de St.-Phalle, a word from PERSIA (*q.v.*).

"This was before Jesus," said Hildy. "They would have believed in Jesus." As all the good and wise who had not heard of Him no doubt would have if they had had the chance, Invincibly Ignorant because of when they lived, and where were they now? Limbo.

Maybe, Pierce said, but he couldn't himself fix his empires in time, they were under or over or occurring elsewhere, undecidably; in the dates AD that grow smaller toward the beginning or in the mirror-dates BC proceeding the other way and growing larger with distance, Bronze Age, Iron Age, Stone Age. When Jesus came the gods had died or hidden, the air had emptied; and at that time too, though maybe not all at once, and not because of His coming but only because the existence of a new order somehow canceled out the other even retroactively (a wind blowing backward through time that brought down

the colonnades and temples and the groves of oak) those empires had
Fallen. Persia had Fallen. Rome Fell. Byzantium Fell. Pierce looked
again into the ruins inside the Dictionary's cover: Fallen. One sad
square of split marble half-engulfed in forgetful earth bore a single
deep-incised word: ÆGYPT.

From empire to fallen empire they wandered, in exile, alone but for
each other; their weapons were resourcefulness in invention, the
pledge they had made to one another, and a pot of medicine carried
from their unforgotten motherland, a medicine so powerful it could
raise the dead if the soul had not yet departed: these, and their
invisibility, which like Mandrake's wasn't real invisibility so much as
a kind of exalted anonymity that clouded men's eyes to their presence. They had swords too. "And guns," Warren said, unwilling to
give up his own.

     When Warren played, the game was an endless series of fights,
subterfuges, challenges and escapes; Bird, mild and willing, would be
set upon, imprisoned, rescued, defended in age upon age. Their enemies were imaginary, for there was no one to embody them, but three
Invisibles could represent any number, up to migratory thousands,
crossing out of their home places and into Old Worlds endlessly
unfolding. Hildy disdained pretend (though she loved theatricals,
pageants, the reenactment of saints' lives and the founding of nations)
and so she would be the dying king or prophet who handed out
commissions, urged crusades, bound the Brothers with oaths. What
the younger ones did with her instructions she didn't know. Now and
then as she sat reading she would see them go by outside, caped and
armed, intent on their errands; Warren would return to report, in
garbled notions real to him, their progress.

     Pierce would forget, as all adults forget, the effort required of
children making believe, the concentration, no expansion, of the will,
the conscious effort to erase the conscious decision to pretend (which
kids tend to do one kid at a time, mesmerizing the ones who find the
trick hard, bullying the holdouts if necessary); and then the constant
pruning and tending of the products of the imagination—cancel the
contradictions without a thought, discard the used adventures, roll

the ball ever into the undiscovered. When those gardens were all shut up in him, those wells capped, Pierce would not remember how good he had been at it. Through the limbo of that hot October, he and Warren and Bird quested daily at Hildy's direction over the hills burned or yellow (the ragweed, astonishingly, sprouting again in the ashes they had made), furthering the story at both ends until they could no longer find one another in the gathering dark.

"They have this city," he said to Bird and Hildy, they in their beds, he in his, long after lights-out; "this city underground . . ."

"How can you build a city underground?"

"It used to be aboveground," said Pierce, "but then it Fell. Now it's underground."

"But they can get in it."

"They know how to get into it, because there's entrances in lots of places. Where you think it's just, like, a cave mouth or a space in the rocks; then you go in, and it leads to this city."

Pursued by badguys (because of their jewels, their secrets, their medicines) the little band enters in.

"Joe too," said Bird.

"Joe too."

Push away the rock, thrust a torch within: hollow drip of water, flare of firelight on stone; but after a few stumbling steps you come upon stairs, cut into the living rock, stairs leading down. Generations have passed and all knowledge of the way has been lost; in wonder the Invisibles (Joe Boyd too) follow the carved figures sideways-walking down the walls. The chambers are growing larger, the way lit from unseen sources. They could not now find their way back again, but they feel no fear. Down there: the dim glow brightens, and there are sounds of life and labor. Step out onto the belvedere overlooking the vast inward space, the ravaged ruined city half-rebuilt, the bustle of folks at unimaginable duties in the artificial sunlight that warms it.

Adocentyn. Safe now. In the center of the center a machine, under construction for decades, silver disc perfect but immobile, waiting only for the jewel we have brought, the jewel the badguys wanted, the jewel for which we have risked everything, not knowing its worth. The gowned mage, beard white as milk, grave eyes glad, takes it and places it in the starship's heart. The mountains open up above them to the night sky spangled with stars.

Like Mount Palomar which Pierce had seen on TV, mountain and observatory conflated in his memory. His cousins were asleep now, and Pierce himself would not remember these conclusions tomorrow, but it didn't matter, there were more where they came from. In that city they had imagined Joe Boyd's investiture as President to have taken place too, the wand of power given him, the password and the ring, only they couldn't resist elaborating the ceremonies into absurdity, getting the giggles irrefusably as Joe Boyd was loaded with special hats and shoes, was put through endless rituals, was read to out of great books and scrolls, made to swear, swear again, chivvied from altar to throne as the girls and Pierce shrieked with laughter imagining it.

What Joe Boyd did not have that the others had, though, was a mark.

Warren and Hildy and Bird believed Pierce had invented the mark himself, though they were willing to listen to Pierce's story (that it was the actual hieroglyph of the last of the just Ægyptians, cast by them to know each other by) as Pierce drew it for each of them on their bodies with a ballpoint: on Hildy's shoulder and on the wing of Bird's back and, at Warren's insistence, on Warren's grubby stomach:

"Oh Warren," Winnie said, scrubbing him. "I wish you wouldn't draw on yourself."

"I didn't."

"What is it?"

"I don't know." Staring down at himself in wonder, as though the sign had just then appeared, a blue-black spider stigma, how do you like that.

"Well it's not coming off. Don't do that again."

Secretly, as the others did, he refreshed it when it faded, marveling with Winnie at its strange persistence; and finding himself able, years later, to reproduce it on a cocktail napkin or a phone pad, and ponder it.

The last Sunday of the month, and Pierce sat in the living room curled in a chair of black canvas and bony iron, writing his monthly letter to his father. He had started well, confident that with the big fire he'd be able to fill a few pages before becoming baffled and bored, but at the bottom of the first sheet (his words already dipping precipitously toward the bottom corner like soldiers marching off a cliff) he'd remembered what Joe Boyd had said: *Your* daddy. He didn't believe it, but it made him pause, caught in conflicting impulses to exaggerate the splendid damage on the one hand and dismiss it on the other: and after a while he gave up. He twisted in the batlike chair, feeling beneath it for the comic book he knew was there.

The television turned from *The Christophers* to *The Big Picture*: from the earnest young priest in his study to an earnest Army officer at his desk. Flags on poles stood at his left and right, and slanting bars of light fell across the wall behind him from an unseen half-closed Venetian blind. Then tanks began streaming left to right across the screen. Joe Boyd, lying on the floor, raised his head from the sofa's lip and took notice. *Over these ancient plains of Europe a thousand armies have marched and countermarched, toppling kings and emperors.* The tanks clambered over bare hills, fired at imaginary enemies. *Today your Army takes a hand in Europe's defense against the kings of the East.*

Pierce looked away. Better to light one candle than curse the darkness. Badguys had somehow got hold of a huge lump of acid-green Kryptonite, and its effect on Clark Kent was dreadful: a leaden, sinking weakness, coma, near-death. *Got to—got to—get OUT of here* . . . Awaking then in a squalid alley much later—days? Weeks?—with his superstrengths not yet returned, he remembers nothing, not his true nature, nor his fictional one either; not his lost home planet, nor his father Jor-El, nor his kindly step-parents in Smallville. Wanders the mean streets with his hat pulled down and his collar turned up. *Who am I? How do I come to be here?*

"I thought you were writing to your father," Winnie said to him, come in to find her sweater, and in her sweater pocket her cigarettes.

"I was. I am. I will be."

"What were you writing about?"

"The fire."

A tremendous energy, discovered at the heart of matter, puts into your

Army's hands new weapons for the defense of freedom. Joe Boyd—and Pierce and Hildy too, it was impossible not to look—watched the weird cloud-flower unfold, low-rumbling. Fading in over it was a legend, *E=mc²,* the mystic reason for it. *Matter, energy, light: all manifestations of one Creation. How shall we use this knowledge wisely? To what uses shall we put it?*

"You really can turn lead into gold," Joe Boyd said. "You can smash their atoms." GIs in dark goggles also watched the transformation, whitened as a wave of bomblight struck them. Winnie alighted on the piano bench, and lit an Old Gold; not really here and attending, but also caught.

Like the black chair her son sat curled in, the blond piano had been bought for the Long Island ranch house that Sam and Opal had bought unbuilt the year before they left, and which they moved out of not long after it was finished. The rest of the furnishings of that long low house were gathered here too, the red-plastic-covered club chairs with black peg legs, the wrought-iron magazine rack, the pole lamp with ovoid aluminum fruit growing from it, the banana-leaf drapes and the fire tools with brass handles like flames. Crowded against one wall, never to fit exactly no matter how it was disposed, were the nubby puce units of the sectional sofa ("The sexual sofa," Joe Boyd joked, shocking prim Pierce). They had all seemed terribly sad to Winnie when she found them all still here, divorced from their picture window, their fieldstone fireplace, exiled with their owners to this dowdy place with its gumwood china cabinets and cabbage-rose wallpaper. But it was a long time before she suggested changing them. Not that Sam took much notice of them: that being just the point, as Winnie knew. Sam now came in and took the only large armchair in the room, his chair, which anyone else sitting in would have vacated at his approach. Sam looked as out of place seated in any other chair there as he did seated anywhere in his car except behind the wheel.

"So what was that about?" Winnie asked him. Sam had been called down to the hospital, as he often was on Sunday mornings, usually to repair the survivors of mountain Saturday nights.

"A child with a high fever who's had a seizure," Sam said, and Winnie winced in pity. "I think it's just a febrile seizure—some kids get them with spiking fevers. Can't tell till he's over the fever."

"What if it's not?"

Sam shrugged, watching the set. "We'll try phenobarbital. Send him to Lexington for observation, if his mother'll go. It doesn't help any that the kid's pretty undernourished." He laughed, remembering: "I asked what she'd been feeding him. She said, 'Oh, same as ever, titty and taters.'"

"Sam!" Winnie said. The children pretended not to hear. A white-coated scientist thrust a length of two-by-four into the focus of a huge dish antenna: the board burst into flame. A carful of miners descended into tunneled darkness; one white black-smeared face turned back to grin. *The energy of the sun; the energy brought up out of the sunless realms.*

"Did you know," Joe Boyd said, "that diamonds are really just coal in another form? You can make diamonds out of coal. If you put enough heat and pressure on them."

"*Did* you *know*," Hildy mocked, "that sixty peepers can sit side by side on a pencil?"

"Diamonds *are* coal," Joe Boyd said, staring at her. "Just coal."

"I didn't say they weren't," Hildy said, bringing her own face, unafraid, closer to his. "Anyway I knew that."

"I bet," said Joe.

"*And,*" said Sam, "I have more news." He waited to gather their attention, which he got, though their eyes didn't leave the screen. "I ran into Sister Mary Eglantine." His boss, the hospital's Director. "And she said she's found a sister who can be released for tutoring."

"Released?" Winnie asked laughing.

"'Released' is the word she used. I don't know where she's been kept."

Except for Warren, all of them had been schooled by nuns before, in Brooklyn or Long Island. The silence of their watching altered from absorption to foreboding.

"Sister Mary Philomel," said Sam gravely. "Seems very qualified, just fine. Taught third grade for years in Cincinnati or somewhere. Sounds fine."

"Well I'd like to meet her," Winnie said. "At least."

"Sure," Sam said. "She says she can start tomorrow."

"*Tomorrow!* Well but Sam . . ."

"Sooner the better. Get this show on the road."

He reached down for the Sunday paper lying in tents around his chair. Winnie contained her objections. Hildy slipped from the sofa and faded from the room—lots to do, if school was really starting

tomorrow—and Winnie soon went out too. Joe Boyd stayed for the
end of *The Big Picture*.

"Dad, were you in the Army or the Air Force?"

"Both."

"No, which?"

"Both. I was in the Army Air Corps, before it was a separate arm.
As they say."

Joe Boyd mulled, pondering his own choice, fly or ride. The show
was over: tanks crawled unstoppably forward in ranks; men marched;
planes in vigilant formation soared above. When Joe Boyd too left the
room, Pierce was alone with his uncle.

"Shut that off, will you, Pierce."

Sam Oliphant possessed within his household an unquestionable
kind of authority that he did not ponder, not how he came by it nor
whether he should exercise it. He was subject to infrequent bitter
moods, which he thought he had a right to; he could be rageful
sometimes and easily exasperated, as though unable to reconcile himself to the fact that after the disaster that had befallen him, and after
the efforts he had made not to be crushed by it, he should still be
subject to the daily irritations and dissatisfactions of physical life. The
rest of the family tried to make up for it, and Sam got his way and his
comforts around the house without difficulty most of the time. But
still he thought of himself as good-natured and forthcoming, on the
whole, and it would have grieved him to know that his nephew found
it impossible to remain alone in the same room with him for more
than a few minutes.

Pierce found the funnies at his uncle's feet and stretched out on
the floor with them. Sam shook the sheets of the front section. Pierce
squirmed uncomfortably, flipped the colored pages. Peter Pain (a
cucumber-green demon not in the *Dictionary*) bound a sufferer's head
with iron bands, pounded plugs into his nostrils: rout him with Ben-
Gay. Sam glanced at Pierce over the tops of his glasses.

Pierce rose; sighed; felt Sam's look but did not return it; and
without offensive haste, as though he had nothing particular to do
elsewhere but no real interest in staying in this room either, he left.

It had grown colder; beyond the window that Hildy looked out
of, and the one Pierce looked out of, wind was snatching colored
leaves from the trees, reminding Hildy of calendar pages rapidly

blown away in a movie scene. Upstairs in the big house, Winnie sought in the closets for the store of schoolbooks she had sent away for months before, standard texts for the children's grades this year, which she had hidden so that the kids wouldn't have read them all before school started.

4

---

ister Mary Philomel's guardian angel awoke her before dawn, as she had asked it specially to do: her eyes opened at 4:24 (according to the luminous hands of the minute wristwatch propped on her bedside table, a gift from her father on the occasion of her final vows). She lay unmoving on the narrow bed and silently spoke the Magnificat. She would have got up to kneel, but she wanted not to disturb the sisters beyond the white curtains on either side of her, nurses who needed every second of the sleep they got.

When the dormitory began to bustle and the curtains first on this side then on that to move slightly with the movements of the sisters beyond, Sister Mary Philomel got up, and knelt on the tile floor (so much colder somehow than the wooden floors of the convent in Washington) to ask for help and strength and wisdom in the new task to which she had been called. And she did feel something like strength flow into her, like the light growing stronger in the window beyond her bed.

She found when she went to sit on the toilet that her menstrual flow had ceased, which was gratifying; she could take a shower today, as she had been unable to do for the previous days, and cleanse cleanse cleanse. The dank shower stall even felt less penitential than usual today, though the water smelled, as always, faintly sulfurous; completely natural, Sisters, mountain springs, said Sister Mary Eglantine, but it wasn't Sister Mary Philomel alone who thought of pollution, mine tailings, the coal cars that passed endlessly along the tracks beyond the hospital grounds.

While she dressed—with special care this morning—she repeated the Magnificat. My soul magnifies the Lord. She thought of the long way up to the Hazelton house on the hill. She had not yet been able to find the materials, the little workbooks and readers and flashcards and teacher's guides, that she had used in Washington when she had taught there; she had prayed hard that she might be shown where in the hospital or its outbuildings they had been put, but she had not been shown. The wooden statue of St. Wenceslaus—the only object in her partition besides the crucifix and the dresser—stood still with his face turned to the wall, having been no help at all despite Sister's specific requests, no help with her school materials or with her stomach either. Well he could just stand there a little longer.

In the halls the nuns moved together toward the chapel, hands within their sleeves and veils drawn over, turtle-private, snail-self-sufficient, though cheerful looks were exchanged. They took their places in the little chapel, and Sister Mary Eglantine led them in a Litany while they awaited the priest:

Queen of the Angels.
Pray for us.
Mountain of Mercy.
Pray for us.
Cave of adamant.
Pray for us.
Temple of Ivory.
Pray for us.
Wisdom of Egypt.
Pray for us.
Gates of the Moon.
Pray for us.

The tiny chapel with its miniature appointments always reminded Sister Mary Philomel of the little castles and throne-rooms of old art, jeweled closets where the Virgin or the saints just fit, elbow almost out the arched window, foot touching the doorstep. But no matter where, here or St. Peter's, the mystery proceeded identically, soothing and rhythmic, like a bandage rapidly and firmly wrapped. Incarna-

tion Passion Resurrection Ascension. *Hoc est enim Corpus Meum.* Sister
Mary Philomel took the food on her tongue, sweet water filled her
mouth, and she nearly fell asleep again.

At breakfast downstairs though, faced with her earthly cereal, she
was once again unable. She took a few infinitesimal bites, willing
herself to be cheerful and brisk, but she could do no more. Heck. And
with the long long morning ahead too. She cleaned up her dishes,
hoping the wasted Wheaties would not be noticed. The saintliest
Mother Superior in the history of their Order had been granted the
gift of inedia: she didn't eat, or need to eat, for three months, or was it
years. And since she didn't eat she didn't, you know, and she ceased
to have her menstrual flow as well, which right there would be a
blessing. Sister Mary Philomel doubted that her own inability to eat
breakfast was a gift of grace. It was too queasy a feeling, too cold in
her innards.

She went out of the kitchen the back way, where one of the
kitchen sisters was punching out Communion wafers with a sort of
waffle iron to send over to the church; the white rounds with their
embossed letters (IHS) were stacked up in piles, reminding Sister
Mary Philomel of her father's celluloid poker chips, beautiful rounds
colored and white which she had used to play with. Strange the
things you think of. She could remember the taste of those poker
chips.

There was no time to look further for the cardboard boxes that
contained her old profession. She hurried up the back stairs, never
hurry, Sisters, and down the central hall of the hospital to the dormitory stairs. In the hall, lying odd as a dragon's corpse or an execu-
tioner's mask and axe on this tile floor, against this light veneered
paneling, was the Old Chest: a great worm-holed beeswax-blackened
carved chest from the Old World, one of the things that had come
over with the sisters, one of the things parceled out among the
branches of the Order like the shares of an old immigrant's useless
inheritance, to be dragged through woods and over water, never forget. Among the sisters it was said that anything lost was in the Old
Chest, which was a joke since the key or keys had long been lost, and
its dozen drawers and doors would not open; the sisters used it for
nothing but to put a great vase of flowers on, always fresh, rising from
it as from a grave. Sister Mary Philomel stopped her hurry to smell
them.

No luck again in the bathroom either.

In her partition, she noticed that Wenceslaus had turned a shy and hopeful half-turn away from the wall where she had stood him. Oh no you don't, Sister Mary Philomel thought, not if *that's* the best you can do. She took the saint firmly by the shoulders and turned him back again.

The nuns of Our Lady of the Way Hospital ("Our Lady in the Way," Warren had first innocently called it; now all the Oliphants did, among themselves) were an Austrian order, established in the seventeenth century in the Czech lands of the Hapsburg Empire, which had just then been newly reconverted to the Catholic faith. Theirs was a teaching order from the first, entrusted by the Emperor with the care of the infants of Bohemian noble houses, many of them recently Protestant. (Pierce and the Oliphant children would commit to memory a fairy-tale version of this history as part of their lessons.) The order's full name was the Pacific Order of the Most Holy Infant, and they professed a special devotion to that manifestation of Jesus witnessed in Prague, a pretty child dressed in miniature crown and royal robes. In the tart-smelling entrance hall of the hospital, the Infant of Prague stood on a pedestal beneath a bell jar in his lace and silk ("like a collection doll," said Hildy); and beyond Him, His Mother.

The mission of the Infantines was still what it had been, to establish the Faith in Protestant lands, though they no longer proselytized, and had mostly turned to Works instead at the suggestion of Our Lady (communicated to that nineteenth-century Mother Superior now in the toils of the beatification process). Still it might have been the old Imperial connection that drew them to Bondieu, for the first inhabitants of the tidy rows of houses built by Good Luck Coal & Coke had been (along with the mountain men drawn from all over the county) a band of Bohemian miners, recruited by company agents in the coalfields of Pennsylvania. It was for these men and their families (called variously Dutchmen or Polacks by the others) that a priest had first been sent to Bondieu, who with the help of the men had built the clapboard church in the holler, Blessed Sacrament, the odd one out among the seven churches of the town.

Pierce would sometimes in later years have a hard time account-

ing for his childhood circumstances, to himself and others: the extremes were too disparate, nuns and hillbillies, and his own and the
Oliphants' presence among them too anomalous. On Sundays from
their hilltop they could hear the loudspeakers of the Full Gospel
Church of God in Christ, which broadcast its service (songs and
hectoring and indeterminate cries and moaning) to all the town. The
volume was too high, the accents too strong, the theology too extreme
for the children to understand more than a few words: still, Hildy
wondered if listening weren't a violation of the rule that forbade
Catholics to attend the church services of others.

"Anyway what right do they have to make everybody else listen?"

Pierce thought that what could be done was to get a helicopter,
and equip it with a big loudspeaker at the end of a long wire; then on
an overcast day (one of those days, say, when high-piled volumes of
cloud fill the sky, parting now and then to let religious beams of
sunlight fan out on earth) fly the copter out from some hidden place,
then up above the clouds, high up where its engine couldn't be heard.
Then the loudspeaker, dangling far down, could suddenly announce
itself as the voice of God speaking, and tell everybody to be Catholics.

"They'd believe that," Joe Boyd said. "Oh sure."

"Anyway," Hildy said, "it wouldn't be the same if you fooled them
into it."

Pierce didn't see it that way. It seemed to him that once gathered
into the one true flock, by whatever means, they could then come
gradually to see the obvious rightness of its doctrines; in the meantime they wouldn't be in danger of dying outside the Church. It
would have to be a helicopter, because helicopters can hover in one
place. A job for the Invisibles.

"Anyway," Hildy said, "if God wanted that he could do it himself,
and he doesn't, so he doesn't want to." Hildy thought it was silly to
imagine God as a sort of busybody continually interfering in the
quotidian: the natural order of rules and their consequences had been
set up at the beginning, and they functioned now by themselves,
accessible to any thinking person of good will. Mary might appear to
children here and there with messages, for reasons of her own, but
God didn't bother with those sorts of miracles. What Hildy most
appreciated about God the Father was his clear if impersonal realism.
It's what she most appreciated in her own father too.

Living far from institutional checks, Sam Oliphant had grown heterodox, Pelagian; unwittingly he fell into the heretical doctrine of two churches, one for children and the ignorant, in which all the stories were true as given, unquestionable; and another for the smart, who knew better. Like an eighteenth-century deist, Sam took it that his ground of faith was simply the conclusions of reason, and every layer of liturgy or dogma or ritual compliance laid over that ground was made acceptable, if not actually justifiable, by the initial irreducible sensibleness. You met all your varied obligations in the big church to the letter, but you believed only what reason agreed to; in fact if reason demanded it, then it was dogma. The world itself was the product of reason, of evolution progressing, making sense, of people getting smarter and seeing the sense the world made. The sense the world made was truth; God had made it, and His Church wasn't going to contradict it. Like fraternity secrets or team mascots, the absurdities of faith didn't bother Sam, because this was his side, they were his absurdities.

"Daddy, did you ever baptize anybody?"

"Not that I remember."

"Well because Sister said that everybody and especially doctors should know how to baptize somebody, in case you find somebody dying who wants to be baptized. Especially doctors."

"In case I'm about to lose one, huh? I should get them to heaven if I can't keep 'em on earth."

"You don't need a priest or holy water. You just do it."

"What if you don't have any water?"

"It has to be *mostly* water. You could use muddy water."

"*Mostly water*! You know your own body is mostly water? Sixty-five percent. A *woodchuck* is mostly water! Am I allowed to baptize people by hitting them with a woodchuck?"

"Daddy!"

In the fights he liked to pick with his children or with Winnie over religious punctilio (to which he brought a gleeful sophistry) Sam seemed often to be actually addressing someone else, or intending someone else to overhear and be amused, some other version of himself; he said things the child couldn't be expected to get or even to notice were supposed to be funny. Pierce could sometimes tell when he did it to Warren, so he could assume Sam was doing it to him as well, when he couldn't tell.

Irony doesn't come naturally to children; brutal sarcasm ("*Now

48 LOVE & SLEEP

are you satisfied?") they can recognize and deplore, but—especially in religion—they are dogmatists, not ironists; Sam's teasing left them in difficulties he seemed not to feel, and mortified. They all caught on to the trick eventually, and made it their own, as they did Sam's heresy of Two Churches, which came to seem only common sense to them; but it generated within them a kind of double life, lived differently by each of them. It was a harsh training, and Hildy only survived it in the end by reversing the terms, Sam's terms, which were outward observance ironized by inward demur: Hildy's outward jokey familiarity would approach contempt, and get her in some hot water with her Order and its superiors, but it expressed an inward allegiance deeper than any words.

Sister Mary Philomel's was a different deity from Sam's, more manifold and perplexing, more nearby too.

"Children," she said to them. "In the little garden in the middle of the hospital, right in the middle of the garden where the pathways cross, there is a birdbath, do you know? And right in the middle of that birdbath there is a silver ball. Isn't there?"

"Yesstr."

"Now if you look into that silver ball you see that it reflects everything at once, up, down, below, above, near, far. Doesn't it?"

"Yesstr."

"Yes. You can see the walls curving all around and every window and even yourself sitting there looking in. And when I sit and look into that ball I think, That is what the eye of God is like, looking at everything at once."

Under Sister Mary Philomel's tutelage the Oliphant kids and Pierce were enmeshed again in the old net of observances and scruples, and provided again with the ritual objects, scapulars, holy cards, Miraculous Medals, which under Miss Martha they had been without. Now for their parents' birthdays or for Thanksgiving or Christmas gifts they were each to prepare a Spiritual Bouquet: a cluster of prayers said, Masses heard, Communions taken, rosaries told— even tiny prayers whispered throughout the day, scattered in the Bouquet like baby's-breath, Ejaculations.

"Jesus Mary and Joseph!" said Hildy. "That's an Ejaculation."

"Or Oh my God!" said Sam, whom she was instructing in this prayer type, not understanding why he had laughed at her offering of One Thousand Ejaculations.

"You can make Ejaculations all day long," she said. "Wherever you are."

"Yes," said Sam, still laughing. "I see."

Sister Mary Philomel was their daily instructrix in such pieties; she was the great pythoness of their cult, the guardian of the gate into the land of the dead: it was she who taught them what prayers the Church had determined would, if said at Mass on All Souls' Day, free a soul from its salutary torments in Purgatory and get it (still sore and trembling) right into Heaven; she who all on her own gathered them up on that November morning, next day after All Saints', bitter damp day with the smell of coal fires and dung sharp in the air, and got them to church to do the work. Two, four, six souls released by their prayers, and Hildy wanted to stay longer and do more, imagining the grateful dead freed by the prayers of conscientious children like herself worldwide, winging upward by tens and hundreds like autumn blackbirds rising to migrate.

It was she also who convinced Pierce (and Winnie and Sam too) that Pierce was fit to take up liturgical duties himself; she touched his vanity and his taste for the hieratic as well as his good nature and willingness to assent, and she brought him to Father Midnight to be instructed. Now (she said) it would be easy for him to make a daily Communion; now he could begin accumulating the special benefits that accrue to those who volunteer in God's service. Joe Boyd snorted, amazed that Pierce would volunteer for duties he could have wriggled out of, but Pierce didn't mind; he learned his lines by rote, he took his place beyond the altar rail with Father Midnight. And long after, when the words he had committed to memory were no longer said anywhere, not anyway in the dead language Pierce had learned them in, they would now and then return spontaneously to him like the jingles of old ads, heard by an inner ear in the mnemonic rhythms he had bent them into, their absurd dago-American pronunciation. *Soosheepiat Dominus sacrafeechium d'manibus tooies.* Touching him with an inexplicable poignancy in the street or on the stair.

In some ways dealing with Sister Mary Philomel was like dealing with a smart and powerful child, a Warren able to make a grownup's case for his fear of the dark or his theory that badguys came into his room at night while he was asleep and messed up his things. If Sister Mary Philomel opened a closet door in search of her umbrella and found it not there, and then not much later (after asking God's help in finding it) she opened the same closet again and there it was, her first thought was not that she had overlooked it the first time. Saints and angels, when compelled by the proper invocations, interceded on the petitioner's behalf with the remoter divine figures, who then altered the weather or the natural order, sped mailmen on their way, and of course healed the sick and saved the lost or the endangered.

The Oliphant children weren't equipped to argue with claims which Sister Mary Philomel had after all a large authority to make. She told them Jesus had promised: if you asked it would be given to you, period. If you asked for bread, God wouldn't give you a stone.

"But if you ask for a real gun or a hundred pounds of candy you won't get it," Hildy warned Warren and the others after school. "God won't give you what's not good for you. Just try it."

Which cut out almost everything you might want to apply for, especially since the decision about whether the item was or wasn't good for you wasn't yours to make: it never was. And yet His promises remained; Sister Mary Philomel took as given that they were to be acted on, and when she prayed for His aid with the intercession of His Saints it wasn't in the self-mocking way that Winnie sang out:

Dear St. Anthony
Please find my keys for me
Or I won't get to the grocer-ee.

So they all wore their itchy and unmanageable phylacteries and their tin medals on ten-cent beaded chains (Where did she get this stuff, Pierce later wondered, did she spend her own pin money on it or did it just come naturally out of her concealed and bottomless pockets?) and for a week Pierce worked on believing that a dim ectoplasmic glow somehow generated in the corner of his room was a vision of the Virgin, or maybe the Holy Ghost, come to answer his prayer that Joe Boyd quit trying to pick fights with him; and Hildy learned to ask her Guardian Angel to wake her up in the morning so that she would have time to bathe and dress more carefully than she was accustomed to, and in a way more pleasing to Sister: and it worked. Sam thought that was funny too.

It wasn't unlike the commitments of make-believe: it required the same division into a proposing and an accepting self, the same quick discarding of unrewarding instances, the same communal intensity of effort. It was like wishing, too, the objects more restricted, but requiring the same surrender to desire, the willingness to accept provisionally (for as long anyway as the wish, or the prayer, filled up the heart) the primacy of desire over common reality. Sister Mary Philomel called it Faith.

From the beginning she felt a special responsibility had been placed on her for these smart wild children. Miss Martha had come at nine and left at noon, having handed out assignments she might or might not remember to ask for next day. Sister Mary Philomel left at noon, a dark frigate under sail, walking down the hill toward the hospital and her lunch; and then at two, to the children's horror, she sailed back again, her arms full of papers and projects, to pester her charges for an indeterminate length of the afternoon. She had no real commission for this; she said she was there only to "tidy up" in the schoolroom and prepare for the next day (prepare what?) but the very ambiguity of her afternoon presence within the compound gave her scope Miss Martha would not have dared take. There were plenty of things active children could be set to doing instead of watching Garry Moore on television.

What Sister Mary Philomel couldn't know was that her fuss-budgeting disrupted more than idleness. The Invisible College had business, Pierce had far-ranging researches to complete. He experienced an anxiety almost unendurable to know that the nun was nearby, even if not actively interfering; anxiety that she would put her black-shod foot through the thin fabric he and the others had woven. His faith was not as strong as hers.

When he came later on in life to study history, unavoidably learning something of the history of the Church in which he had been raised, Pierce would experience a definite but unnameable thrill when (usually by chance) he would happen upon one of his own old beliefs just coming into being, some practice or complication of ritual which he had used to assume was somehow pre-existent, eternal, given: Ember Days and Rogation Days, feasts and fasts and the reason for them, the divisions of the next world and its inhabitants. The cult of the Sacred Heart (gruesome Jesus with effulgent exposed organ wrapped in thorns) swept the Church in the early nineteenth century; the choirs of the angels (Thrones Powers Virtues Dominations and the rest) came into being in the late second. It was a pleasure like and unlike the pleasure of opening an old school reader (*Roads and Highways*) and finding it full of tales of dirigibles and Pullman cars, organ-grinders and circus-wagons, Arbor Day and Armistice Day: what he had then taken for the whole great world shown to be only a trans-verse section, worldwide maybe but decade-thin, and gone by, now, with those who had issued it.

"What would you think, children," asked Sister Mary Philomel, "if a rich man at dinner heard of a beggar at his door, who had nothing, and sent out to the beggar some food? That would be good of him, wouldn't it? And what if this rich man sent the poor beggar his own dinner? Wouldn't you think he was a good man? And children what if the man sent the beggar *his own arm to eat*? That would be wonderful charity, wouldn't it? Well Jesus gives us not only His arm or just a part of Him for us to eat but His whole Body. Now think of that." And they did think of it, only a little horror-struck, unaware that (as Pierce would read years later, and hoot with amazement and triumph to read) Sister Mary Philomel had retailed a common trope of Baroque piety, dating from the years when embattled Catholics were pulling out all the stops on transubstantiation, the years when Sister Mary Philomel's own order was being founded.

For all that she lived in a world malleable by belief and desire, still Sister paid close attention to mundane reasons, and the daily manage-ment of life; Pierce would think of her when his favorite teacher at college, the historian Frank Walker Barr, pointed out how even if the primitive hunter believes his prayers and his magic are what guide his spear to his prey, still he knows he has to sharpen the spear, and learn to aim and throw it.

"Will God help us if we ask Him?"

"Yesster."

"Will God help us if we do nothing for ourselves?"

"Nosster."

"God helps those who help themselves."

"Yesster."

It was easy enough for Sister to assume her unchallengeable ascendancy over the younger children. Pierce at yellow-brick St. Simon Cyrenean in Brooklyn (separate doors for Boys and Girls) and the Oliphants in a new long low concrete-block and plate-glass St. Longinus on Long Island had learned unbreakable habits of deference. They could make no objection, wronged as they felt themselves to be, when Sister Mary Philomel organized them into after-school work details, to clean the fishbowl her fat carp swam in, to cut out turkeys and shamrocks and lilies green and white to festoon her walls at the proper seasons, not even when she took it on herself to have them mop their bedroom floors and remake their beds, like prison trusties.

But Joe Boyd was a harder case. It was apparent he was too old for the miniature classroom and its cutouts and flashcards. As much as she could Sister Mary Philomel set Joe Boyd problems and readings to be done by himself in the cold but at least private windowed room beyond the kitchen. Though she was cautious with Joe Boyd, she wasn't afraid of him; she chose carefully the instances when she would try conclusions with him, and almost always she won, gracious if unbending in victory and including him in that teacher's "we" that cut him too deep for words: Are we ready to start on our assignment now?

He was one of those spirits Pierce would always marvel at, supposing them to be rare: those who grant no absolute authority to anyone, who assume that all proscriptions are *ad hoc* and negotiable and that those in power are mere men, more or less like themselves. Pierce might do all he could to avoid being subject to the power of others, of rule-makers and -enforcers, but he neither thought to question their right to enforce their own rules, nor supposed their rules were bendable. Joe Boyd always did.

"You don't have to do that," he said to Bird, who was busy mulching and tidying a bare spot that Sister Mary Philomel had decided would be a flower garden in the spring. "Just because she says so."

"I don't mind."

"This isn't *her* place," Joe Boyd said. "This isn't her property."

"I don't mind."

"Are you going to do everything she says? Would you jump in the river if she said?"

"That's dumb."

"You're dumb."

Their father, about to sit on the toilet of the bathroom beneath whose window the garden was being laid out, overheard this, and came out.

"Joe. Why are you pestering her?"

"I'm not." He thrust his hands in his pockets defensively as Sam approached him.

"Huh? Why are you taunting her? She's doing something useful and beautiful, and you're doing nothing."

"I wasn't."

"You can just leave her alone. Go find something to do yourself. I can think of several things if you don't have any ideas."

He turned to go, putting his magazine under his arm; Joe Boyd went off, but as he did so he tossed a final sneer at Bird for her submission: Teacher's pet.

Sam heard him, and rounded on him.

Sam never hit his children, and almost never raised his voice to them: he had never needed to. Bird watched now in horror as he seized Joe Boyd by the collar with both hands and thrust him hard against the wall.

"*Did you hear what I just said?*" His nose inches from Joe Boyd's face. "Did you hear me tell you to leave her alone? Why did you just turn right around and insult her? *Huh?*"

There was no answer, and Joe Boyd knew better than to make one: and yet even looking into Sam's furious face his gray eyes were unflinching, unafraid, alert to possibility. Bird, scandalized, dismayed to have been the occasion for this outrage, wouldn't forget his courage or his cool.

Pierce that afternoon was hiding in the attic with a book.

5

---

*WEREWOLF: Men (more rarely women) who occasionally
have the form of wolves are Werewolves. The greatest question
concerning Werewolves, and one debated since the Middle Ages by
learned writers and doctors, is whether Werewolves can actually
change their forms, or only think they have changed them;
whether, as a result of their nature or through the power of the
DEVIL (q.v.,) they are actually capable of transformation, or
rather suffer from a delusion (Lycanthropy) in which they believe
themselves to be so transformed, though they remain human. The
psychological explanation came to predominate, though it explains
far fewer recorded instances than the physiological.*

Across one end of the cool dusty-gray attic Pierce had run a rope, and
on the rope had hung four old drapes he had found there, flowered
with maroon roses; behind them, lit by the pointed attic window, was
the clubhouse of the Invisible College—not of the physical chapter,
but of the other, the one that consisted of Pierce alone. Sometimes the
adventures that the College undertook up here were told of in the
regular nighttime meetings: sometimes not.

*Augustine thought that what is transformed is the phantasticum,
a sort of spectral double that goes out in a form able to be seen,
while the sleeping person dreams its experiences. More than one
Werewolf, however, has claimed that his wolf's pelt is a real part*

*of him, only turned inward like a hairshirt (versipilis). One Were-
wolf who claimed that his hair was inside was so badly cut by the
surgeons trying his claim that he died. That was not, seemingly,
the "inside" of which he spoke.*

Pierce shuddered, but not from cold. He put his finger on the page,
and looked up, hearing voices calling to him from below: Joe Boyd,
Warren. They would wait.

*Werewolves were known to antiquity, of course, and appear both
in literature and medical texts, where the condition is described as
Morbus lupinus and is always understood as a delusion, as it
would not later be. There are Werewolves all through the Dark
Ages as well, but there is a sudden and distinct increase in reported sightings and depredations of Werewolves in the later 16th
C. and the early 17th. In Burgundy, in Hungary, in Bohemia, in
Moldavia, men and women are charged with being Werewolves,
the deaths of domestic animals and children are blamed on them.
Great wolf-hunts are licensed and organized; Werewolves are captured and sentenced to horrifying deaths. These are also the years
in which WITCHES (q.v.) also are discovered everywhere, tried,
tortured and burned in vast numbers. Bodin the encyclopædist
believed the plague of witches was due to the operations of the
overreaching magicians of his day, who irresponsibly let loose
crowds of dæmons that then seized upon and possessed the unwary.*

Suddenly struck with the presence of that double letter, "æ," which
he saw often in this book and in the pages of his missal, and nowhere
else. Was a dæmon a demon? What was the difference? Where was
Ægypt?

*We typically think of Werewolves as creatures of evil, despoilers of
the herds and of the herders too, who are able to take on animal
form as witches took on the forms of cats or mice. But there is
evidence that the Werewolves may not, or may not always, have
thought of themselves in that way. There took place in Jurgensburg
in 1692 the trial of a certain Thiess, a man in his eighties, who
confessed to being a Werewolf, and astonished his judges by claim-*

ing that his kind, so far from being witches, were the natural enemies of witches. The witches, he told them, are the despoilers; they seize the new-planted seed-grains and seedlings from the earth, they steal the ripening harvest, and carry them off to Hell. In the Ember Days of the year, the Werewolves gather at night to pursue and do battle with them, to rescue the grain, and the livestock too and other fruits of the earth which the witches have stolen, and return them safely to the fields. If they fail, if they delay their pursuit, they find the gates of Hell locked against them; and the harvest that year will fail, fish in the sea hide themselves away, the young stock die. Nor were the Livonian Werewolves singular: the Russian and the German Werewolves fought witches in the same way. Thiess was punished for witchcraft despite his story of the enmity of witches and Werewolves, a secret history within the history of witchcraft.

What if it were true. It could not be: but what if it were. Strange but true.

A sudden partisanship arose within Pierce's heart, a longing so deep and simple that he could not even be puzzled by it: a longing indistinguishable from grief, that the story ought to be true, and could not be.

He thought of their sufferings: To be one thing on the outside, another on the inside; to seem nothing and no one, to be despised and ignored, unseen, and yet to be somebody on whom the welfare of everybody depends, even though they don't know it.

Pierce thought, in those days, that his attraction to the wrong sides, to the losing armies in historical struggles, was a motion of his spirit to take the part of the underdog, a kind of noble motion, like Joe Boyd's attraction to the dove-gray Confederacy: but it wasn't. Often enough the losers he was drawn to weren't the underdogs at all (Pierce leaned to the Tory side of the American Revolution as well as to the South, though he knew as well as Joe Boyd did who had been right in both those quarrels and who wrong). It wasn't taking the underdog's side: it was simply a sneaking desire to reverse the sides, to experience the story as though it had a secret inner logic the opposite of its usual one, the goodguys now the others, bearing the other flag: it couldn't be true, but what if it was.

The game gave him an inexplicable satisfaction, the same he felt when he lay on his back in bed hanging his head downward over the bed's edge, and by an act of will convinced his eyes that the floor was a dark dusty ceiling over his head, and the ceiling a white floor, with lamps sprouting upward from it: and a house different but the same, empty of furniture, extending outward room upon room over the tall thresholds of the open doors.

He enlisted the Invisibles, recklessly, in the secret struggles he recounted to himself; they were themselves losers, from a no longer existent time, and could be imagined to be takers of the wrong, the doomed side, the side History would leave behind. Anyway (he thought) he couldn't ever really alter the outcomes by taking the sides he took, for the right side always had to win—according to all the histories Pierce had read or been made to study it always had, in the end—and so Pierce's secret allegiances were moot: but still, into these adventures the others were not invited.

And the battle of the angels: which side then?

That afternoon, as they did every Saturday, Joe Boyd and Pierce went together with Warren to the Bondieu theater to see the cowboy movie always shown: walking each with his hands in the pockets of his denim jacket, each corduroy collar turned up, Warren alone of them wearing guns. On the stretch of sidewalk before the theater the boys of the town milled, waiting to be let in, eying the Oliphant boys and Pierce. One or two no older than Pierce smoked cigarettes with casual assurance. Sam said smoking stunted your growth; it certainly seemed to have stunted these guys'.

The picture was ten years old, but they neither knew that nor cared; and after it came a cartoon, or a comedy as the Kentuckians called it, rapid rituals of destruction and revival; and then the familiar urgent music of the serial. The announcer's doomladen voice hurried through the events of ten weeks to the present moment while snatches of scenes flew by carried on the runaway music. How Gene found the deserted mineshaft leading to the underground empire; how he had gone down to struggle with the powerful subterraneans and their plans of conquest. He was left at the end of every episode in mortal danger, as good as dead in fact, only to be seen at the begin-

ning of the next episode to have survived: the cliff over which he had
been shoved had a projecting ledge to cling to that had not been there
last week, the careening truck had missed him, he had leapt out of its
path though it was clearly impossible that he could have: as though
the drastic and the final softened, between one Saturday and the next,
into something less final.

Not this time though. The X-ray bomb that Gene had deflected
from the upper regions and his own innocent ranch had gone haywire, blown up Gene himself. "They can't get out of *that* one," Joe
Boyd last Saturday had said, with a certain satisfaction too: and they
had not. Gene was still dead. The empress of the underworld looks
down on him lifeless and still, the toes of his pointed boots turned
up. But she is secretly his ally. She convinces her dark Vizier (Father
Midnight, now in high-collared cape and cuffed gloves) that the
secrets Gene knows must not be lost. Very well, Majesty: there are
ways. By techniques of science which the upper regions will not learn
for centuries, or have for as long forgotten, Gene is brought to life.

—*Hurry, oh hurry.*

—*Have patience, Majesty. Death is strong.*

He stirs on the shimmering operating table, beneath the reviving
lamps. From his mouth comes a gout of language in a voice not his.

—*What does he say?*

—*It is the language of the dead, Majesty. They often speak it on
returning; but they soon forget.*

"Oh good grief," said Joe Boyd. "Oh lordy."

After they left the movie, Joe Boyd insisted they stop at the dark and
odorous variety store where magazines and comics were sold; while
Joe Boyd, jaws working over a wad of Bazooka, looked through the
new issue of *Guns and Ammo*, Warren and Pierce mooched among the
comics, never holding any one too long, the embittered and watchful
storekeeper whom Joe Boyd alone of them did not fear could decide
suddenly that it was soiled and thus sold.

The vengeful dead, rising from the rotten plush beds of their
coffins, dragging their decaying cerements after them. You could tell
the girl skeletons because their hair, white and fine, still clung to their

yellow skulls. Did it really? Warren would not touch or even approach the horror ones, looking at the covers only with one eye shut and his face turned away.

Outside the store they parted. Pierce was to serve an early Mass next day, and ought (he thought) to take Communion too; when he served a later Mass he could be excused, a growing boy who needed his breakfast. And if he went to Communion, then he needed to go now to confession. Joe Boyd saluted him, grinning around his gum, and Warren followed his big brother toward home.

Blessed Sacrament was like no church Pierce had known in Brooklyn, not like smoky-black St. Simon Cyrenean, nor like St. Basil's where Axel had used to go to hear the music, all pink and blue paint within. It looked like a house: small and dirty white, clapboarded and square-windowed, with a little porch. It even had a picket fence running in front of its square of grass and up its cement front walk. There was a miniature steeple, though, and an electric bell inside it.

The story was that once the priest (Father Midnight's predecessor) had built it himself, with the men of the parish, collar off and sleeves rolled up. Pierce thought of this often as he sat in it, noting small details of its construction, wondering if it had been the priest who had failed to make the moldings meet squarely at that corner, the priest who had made the dollhouse altar of white-painted wood. IHS. *In hoc signo.* Beneath the stone let into the altar's surface were the relics of a saint, Pierce knew, for every altar had to have some. Relics: bits and pieces, unrecognizable. Not a skull with floating hair.

He knelt, hands still in his jacket pockets, guessing which among the six or eight old women and the single man there were in line to be absolved, which were already scrolling through their penances. The man knelt with his hands over his eyes, hands like great worn-out tools, as though he had clawed rock all his life or broken trees with them. What had he done, what had he unburdened himself of here?

His own conscience, when he regarded it, was dingy but not really marked, like his underwear; the problem was finding enough nameable faults to make it worth bending Father Midnight's ear. Pierce knew that to conceal a sin you knew about would make the sacrament inefficacious, would be a sin in itself actually, and Pierce was not tempted to conceal sins; he was tempted to make them up. Envy. Anger. Pride. Lust.

His turn. In the dark of the booth he waited, hearing the delicate murmur of the priest's voice speaking to the sinner on his other side. Then the window slid shut on that side, and the window on Pierce's side slid open. Father Midnight dim behind the violet screen. Father forgive me for I have sinned. Decades later Pierce would read about the invention of the double confession booth, by the Jesuits in the sixteenth century, and would see it then as others must who had not grown up with it: a construction weird as a bathing-machine, as fraught as a guillotine.

"Father, I started a fire."

A silence in the violet dimness. Pierce fully believed himself to be anonymous here, unrecognizable voice of an unknown sinner; later he would grow less certain.

"Did you start the fire on purpose, son?"

"No, Father. It was an accident."

"Well. In order for something to be a sin, there has to be an intention. You can't commit a sin by accident."

Pierce said nothing.

"Can you try to make restitution for the damage you caused?"

"I don't know."

"Ask and see. But you shouldn't think it was a sin. Now for any carelessness you may have been guilty of, make a good act of contrition."

Pierce bent his head to the padded lip of the prie-dieu and whispered through the prayer with mnemonic haste, feeling strangely privileged: to have been the cause of wide destruction, and at the same time to be officially innocent.

Why (he wondered, making his miniature penance) do we ever do anything but pray? If we know life is short, not even an eye-blink compared to All Eternity, then why do we take the chance of living a life? Obviously it was best just to kneel, hands clasped, wrapped in adoration until the (quick) end. Then bang right into your endless happiness. That he was not tempted to do this himself, that he found the argument self-evident but not somehow convincing, suggested a flaw somewhere, a flaw maybe inside himself; and maybe not.

It was evening when he came out, the year heading toward its darkness, old age of the Sun. When he came in sight of the big square house atop the rise at the end of town, lamplight was already shining in the windows, in the kitchen and in Joe Boyd's room upstairs:

yellow lamplight that warned him away. He turned from the road and climbed the gullied bank at a place he knew of. And on silent feet up through the scrubby trees into the brown field above. Night was falling, and the mild beings of the day hid themselves away.

He felt the black melancholy burden of his nature, turned outside in now and warming him for his task. He was as he was and not different: and that was all right. The harvest was cut and in the barns; the flocks—sensing him pass, perhaps—hurried quick into their byres. With the wind on his cheek he entered the pines at the top of the hill where it was night already (night, and the moon full, and the world aghast) and climbed along the ridge above the house and its outbuildings.

Which was harder, he wondered: to make your home in a strange far place, or to be a stranger in your own home place?

Superb in his loneliness he looked down on the human habitations. Let them eat and drink in peace: they need not know of his passage near them, on his way somewhere they could not imagine. It's all right.

He turned his steps away, toward the far side of the ridge and the path downward, toward the battle. He would be there; his kind would know him: he would not be alone.

6

————

n Christmas night that year there was a sudden drop in the temperature, and beneath the bungalow the pipes running unprotected through the crawlspace froze, as they did once almost every winter. Most of Christmas morning Sam and Joe Boyd poured hot water on them from kettles and wrapped them in hot rags, Sam in his overcoat and fedora. "They think they live in the South around here," Sam muttered. "The sunny South."

That was the Christmas that Bird learned there was no Santa Claus, or was anyway officially informed of it, which left Warren alone in the dark, or the light. Bird got a camera from Santa anyway, which she loved and quickly mastered. Hawkeye. One of the first pictures she took was of the drive that led down to the highway from their house, a picture that ended up much later among Pierce's possessions, and seemed to him to distill an entire Cumberland winter in a single shiny square: the black undergrown trees slick with rain, the winter-exposed trash caught in the claws of the bushes; a scrawny chicken; broken barbed wire. Down at the end of the drive, across the highway, the little store could be seen, propped on posts over the clay banks of the Little No Name River, or the crick as everybody called it. A turtleback Chevy and a Hudson parked outside; no folks. In that store, besides numberless Nehis and Sky Bars, Pierce bought the first tobacco he ever smoked.

That happened in February of the new year, when Sam and Winnie were in Florida. They decided to go—Sam decided—in the sudden and exasperated way he tended to make up his mind to indulge himself in something, a new car, a vacation. He stunned Winnie somewhat with the news, and she stunned the children. Two weeks. They would be taken care of in that time by a housekeeper (couldn't say babysitter in Joe Boyd's hearing) who would see to their every need. And Sister Mary Philomel would come extra-long, to help.

What housekeeper? Sam asked around at the hospital and among his patients, and Winnie asked at the store, and they came up with a name or two, and Winnie interviewed them a little awkwardly.

"You have children of your own?"

"Yes, ma'am. Three."

"Won't they be needing you?"

"Jes Baby Henry, ma'am. T'other's growed. She's married now."

"Oh. How old is she?"

"Sixteen. And t'other's in heaven."

"Oh."

"Phthisic."

"Oh."

Mousie (not a nickname, but all the name she had been given) was a big soft woman with big soft arms freckled orange, the same orange as her hair and her pale lashes. The children were to call her Mrs. Calton, not Mousie, and she let them do so even though it was evident in her milk-white face that she found it funny, funnier than being called Mousie.

"Why did they name you Mousie?" Bird asked her at last.

"Cause when I was born? My momma thought I looked just like a little mouse. That's what Momma says."

After the horror of being left in this woman's care had worn off, of seeing Sam and Winnie drive off South alone in the Nash, the children came to appreciate Mousie, and never stopped marveling at her. She turned on the television first thing in the morning, when there was nothing to see but a man with a picture of a farm behind him, who talked about tobacco and beans, and she let it run unceasing through *Ding Dong School* and *A World Elsewhere* to the capering puppets and varnished-haired newscasters, not closing its eye even at dinnertime, when a man at a church organ played mild favorites for half an hour without interruption, only occasionally gazing sweetly into the room where the Oliphants and Mousie and Baby Henry ate their dinner.

Winnie had done her best making lists of bedtime hours, house rules, and bad habits, but she forgot a lot, and what she did remember was cast in language so odd to a Bondieu ear that much of it didn't catch. "Caint make out her meaning," said Mousie, pondering Winnie's dashing blue-black hand when Winnie was far away. When Winnie's menus and the frozen store of Winnie's bread ran out, Mousie began giving them the same meals she ate herself, sandwiches of white bread ("like Kleenex," Hildy said) filled with pale cold Spam, lettuce and margarine; these accompanied by unchilled strawberry pop and blocks of ice cream striped pink, white and brown.

She did give them each their spoonful of vitamins every morning, as Sam directed, a viscous yellow-green stuff that could still be tasted hours later, years later too in memory. But she also gave them Alka-Seltzer if they complained of stomach-aches (which Hildy often did because she liked the acrid foaming stuff, liked especially to watch the tablets dissolving as though in ecstasy, leaping and spinning and bumping into each other). She gave Baby Henry something for his teething that kept him mild and placid (or maybe he inherited these qualities from Mousie) and fun for Bird to dress, put to sleep, take for trips, bury.

They were used to being left alone and paid little attention to, but Mousie (probably assuming rightly that there were realms of trouble it wouldn't occur to these children to get into) hardly gave them an order during the whole of her stay, unless it was one she was relaying from Winnie's instructions. "Your momma says warsh your har Saturday night, so git now." To Joe Boyd she was particularly deferential, and together they settled into an easy joky relationship that seemed to come automatically to both. She simply treated Joe Boyd as a grown man, as all the boys his age whom she knew were treated; his right to his indolence and his occupations understood. Man of the family. Joe Boyd would not forget.

The Oliphant children had rarely ventured beyond the limits of the Hazelton place on its hillside, except inside the Nash. Hildy sometimes visited the daughters of the people who kept the store at the bottom of the hill, or they came up and solemnly played cards or Parcheesi now and then; there was a little boy down the hill who would tag after the Invisibles sometimes, ignoring the cries of his mother calling him: *Johnnie Ray-ee? Johnnie Ray-ee?* with endless patience. Mousie now brought into their ken not only Baby Henry but her married daughter as well, and her baby and her husband too (Mousie's own husband was in Deetroit gettn rich makn cars, and would be back with the money soon). The daughter was on Well Far, and her husband never came into the house; instead, while his wife visited with her mother, he opened the hood of his Ford or crawled under it to tinker. Inevitably Joe Boyd drew near.

"Reach me that wrench, will you, son?"

"That one?"

"Nope. The littly. Next over but one."

Joe Boyd knelt to choose among the tools that lay on an oily rag on the ground beside the Ford. Mousie's daughter's husband smoked as he worked, cigarette stuck to his lip and his eye squinted against the rising smoke. If there were Kentucky kinds of destinies, then Joe Boyd had just then met one, and found it his.

Nor was that the sum of Mousie's family.

"Mrs. Calton, there's a little girl on the porch who won't come in and won't go away."

Hildy watched from the hall as Mousie went out. The girl whom Hildy had found there backed away a cautious step from Mousie but didn't flee.

"Now *what* are you doin here?" Mousie demanded, and then the two of them began talking at once, both with arms indignantly akimbo, each trying to overtop the other, spooling out their complaints and commands too quickly for Hildy to follow. Then they stopped. Mousie fanned a hand at the child. "Gwan. Git. Go home to your daddy."

"Ain't my daddy." She was about Bird's age, Hildy thought, skinny and cold-looking, with a round doll's face and thick untidy ringlets. She wore an overcoat with a matted collar, pretend fur; the buttons were buttoned wrong.

"He's your daddy now."

"Ain't."

"Gwan home."

"Won't."

Mousie crossed her plump arms across her breast, stumped. "How'd you get here, anyways?"

"Walked."

"Well, you can walk back then."

"My feet hurt." Her shoes were cracked patent leather; her anklets were walked down in back beneath her heels in a way painful to look at.

"More'n that'll hurt when you get home."

The girl's eyes narrowed. "You big fat," she said.

This made Mousie's mind up, and she went and took the girl by her fur collar. She walked her down the length of the porch, down the steps, out onto the drive leading down. Now Pierce and Bird (carrying out trash for Sister Mary Philomel from the bungalow) saw the encounter, and watched too. Mousie set the girl on the drive, facing downward, and gave her a small push. The girl, head down, took a few small steps down the hill, but as soon as Mousie turned to go back to the house, the girl spun around and started back.

"Now gwan!"

Mousie bent to the dirt and made as if to pick up a stone: just the gesture Sam had taught the children to use in scaring off strange dogs. It worked as well, too: the girl turned on her heel, and deliberately but without haste walked away. Maybe, like the dogs, she was used to having stones thrown at her.

Mousie looked around herself then, and saw that she was being stared at in wonder by the three children. "Oughten never to have come so far," she said. "Wild child." And nothing more.

Through that day, Pierce or Hildy glimpsed the girl, far off, who had not really left after all. Once they saw her through the tangle of trees along the road at the bottom of the hill; she seemed to be looking for thrown-away bottles along the shoulder, as the Oliphants did too sometimes, to return for the deposit. Then later on Bird saw her away up the hill beyond the chicken house, eating something, maybe a candy bar bought with the bottle money.

Without agreeing among themselves to do so, they said nothing to Mousie about what they'd seen.

At bedtime Pierce in his pajamas went into the bathroom, to open the faucets a little as Sam had told them to do if it might freeze. The trick was to get them to run in a standing stream as thin as possible, a thread of water, which would not break up into sleep-destroying ticktock drops. He was making the necessary fine adjustments when his eye, then his mind, caught a face in the bathroom window: half a face, from the nose up. When he had yelped in surprise and truly looked, the face was gone.

He knew who it had been.

"What should we do?" he asked the girls.

"What if she freezes?" Hildy asked. They were sitting on Bird's bed, talking for some reason in whispers.

"Mousie won't let her in," Bird said.

"Maybe if we asked."

"No," said Hildy.

They looked up then, as one, because the girl they talked about was at the bedroom window, looking in.

Hildy went to the window and called softly through the glass: "*Go down* to the *back door.*" She pointed several times toward the far end of the bungalow. Then, with Pierce and Bird following, she went down the hall and through the dark schoolroom to the sun-porch door and opened it.

The girl was larger in the house than she had seemed to them outside; as soon as she had come in, they knew they had done something extraordinary in bringing her in, something anarchic almost, as though they had brought in one of the half-wild bristle-back dogs that lived around the holler, to have for a pet. They stood for a long moment just looking, inhaling the odor of her cold wool and her person. Then Bird remembered her manners, and asked the proper first question of a kids' colloquy.

"What's your name?"

"Bobby."

Hildy in her nightgown had begun to shiver, and Bobby did too, as though she could release herself enough now in the warmth of the bungalow to allow tremors to wrack her thinness; her knees vibrated and her chin began to tremble. "Come on," Hildy said, and they guided the girl, with small touches as though she were blind, back through the schoolroom and the hall into Pierce's room where the heater was.

"Is this y'all's house?"

"This is our part."

"What's that Mousie's livn in?"

"That's the rest of it."

She had ceased shivering, and looked warily around herself, arms hugged tightly and protectively across her middle. "Huh," she said.

"We must have the same name," Bird said. "Roberta. My name's Roberta, they just call me Bird."

"Nope. Jes Bobby."

This was nearly as bad as Mousie. "Well you can't just be baptized Bobby," Bird said mildly. "It's not a real name."

"Ain't baptized," said Bobby. "What's his name?"

"Pierce," said Bird.

She smiled at him. "That's a nice name," she said. "Sounds like Pee-ears."

Pierce blushed hotly, and Bobby watched him do so with interest.

"Do you want to see Mrs. Calton?" Hildy asked.

Bobby shook her head.

"Is she your relative?"

"Nope. She's jes kin."

"Why did she make you go away?"

Bobby shrugged, a quick lift of one shoulder. "Cause she's a pismire."

"Why don't you want to go home?"

"Got no home."

"Mousie—Mrs. Calton—told you to go home to your daddy."

"Ain't my daddy."

"Why did she say that?"

"Ain't my daddy. He's my grandpap."

"Oh."

"He adopted me. So he says now he's my daddy, and I'm spose to call him daddy, but I don't."

She pushed the dark ringlets of untended hair from her face and folded her small plump hands in her lap, unconscious that she had said something so odd that the others didn't even know what question to ask next.

"She'll let you stay here," Pierce said, magnanimous. "We'll tell her to."

"No!" said Bird.

"She has to!" Pierce said. "She works for us, doesn't she?"

No one could dispute that, but no one really knew how to act on it either. Bobby gave them no help, neither asking to stay nor making any motion to go. She only sat by the heater, gradually ceasing to shiver, looking from one to another of them as frankly as a cat.

What they decided, then, by default, was that she would stay in the bungalow with them, and Mousie wouldn't be told. She would sleep on the couch in the windowed sitting room. Pierce volunteered to go for food, which they decided (Bobby listening unoffended to them discussing her) she must need.

"Milk," Hildy said.

"No milk," Bobby said. "Milk's like a pizen to me."

Pierce tied his bathrobe tightly around himself and found his slippers. Through the glass of the bungalow's front door he could see that lights were still on in the big house.

Pee-ears. A nun at Saint Simon Cyrenean had once told him that Pierce wasn't a saint's name, and that every Catholic child should have a saint's name. Not long after he had come to Kentucky he told this fact solemnly at dinner, and Hildy said it was okay, he could pick a new name for Confirmation, and Sam said Sure and went to the shelf for his Book of Saints to look for a good one. The kids made some suggestions, the general favorites—Francis, Joseph, Anthony— but Sam scoffed, too tame. He leafed through the book. Waldo, how about Waldo. No? My god, look at some of these. St. Pancras, a great railroad station. St. Qoudvultdeus, what on earth. Now they were all laughing. "Blessed Dodo," cried Sam, tears of laughter in his eyes. "Locally famous for practicing astonishing austerities. Oh Lord." And Pierce had laughed too.

Night wind blew across the breezeway between the houses, cold and odorous.

The first room of the big house he entered was the summer kitchen, winter mudroom, where an old refrigerator stood, and piles of boots. Then the kitchen. Beyond, the TV murmured, programs he had never seen. If he was caught he would Come To, act astonished, and pretend he had been sleepwalking. He opened the refrigerator, got out the box of Velveeta and some of the Kleenex bread kept there, a carrot and a Nehi orange soda. And got back across the breezeway undetected.

Bobby had taken off her coat but hadn't moved from her place by the heater. Her dress was thin figured cotton, a summer dress; the sweater she wore over it was gray and far too small. "But why did he adopt you?" Hildy was asking. "Are your parents dead?" The books she read were full of girls whose mothers were dead, who had been adopted by kindly aunts or rich uncles.

Bobby looked shocked. "No! They're in Deetroit."

"Then why are you adopted?"

"I was base-born," Bobby said. "My daddy wronged my mam, in Deetroit. Then she come back and we lived in Clay County where I growed up, and my grandpap adopted me, cause of gettn benefitted. Now my mam's went back to Deetroit to look for my daddy and my grandpap says he's my daddy now but he ain't."

Pierce and his cousins had listened intently, but for all they understood it might as well have been glossolalia.

"Anyways I ain't gone live with him. Gone find my mam."

They had no knife to cut the cheese, so they used a thin wire coat hanger. Bobby ate slice after slice with bread, watching the orange block even as she ate, as though it might disappear before she'd had her fill. The soda they opened on the opener that was screwed into the bathroom doorjamb, as in a motel, but why. They shut the lights off in Hildy and Bird's room and talked in whispers though Mousie was far away: the consequences of Mousie finding Bobby among them eating cheese were incalculable. Then they took an extra blanket from the closet in the hall (Indian stripes, diamonds and triangles) and Hildy's long dress coat too.

They guided Bobby back to the cheerless sitting room, Hildy with blanket and coat. The heater seemed far away. But Hildy insisted (sticking to the convention by which these things happened in books, orphans taken in and put to bed on sofas), and so Bobby lay down on the couch in her clothes, hands crossed over her breast like a corpse, and they put the bedclothes on her.

"Okay."

"Okay."

"You okay?"

"I reckon."

"Okay."

Later though, long after they were asleep in their own beds, she got up, and—passing through Pierce's room and maybe through his dream as well—she went into the front room, slipped off her shoes but not the summer dress and baby's sweater, crawled into Bird's bed without waking her, and slept there till morning almost without moving.

7

———

Pierce awoke with the conviction that something altogether new, something both dangerous and valuable, lay in the bungalow with them, but couldn't at first remember what it was. When he did remember he also remembered that Winnie no Mousie would in a moment come in to see if they were up, and call them to breakfast, and that not long after that Sister Mary Philomel would be arriving, who could not, must not see Bobby.

"Pierce! She's in here!"

He got out of bed, too late, the front door had opened and Mousie was talking. Come on now git y'all's grits. Fore they's cold. And the door closed as she left.

He looked into Bird and Hildy's room just as Bobby uncovered herself, having made herself small amid an artful tumble of bedclothes on Bird's bed. She climbed out, refreshed, unapologetic, pulling at her tangled locks with both hands: their charge now, and satisfied to be so it seemed, though still wary in the depths of her closed face.

While they dressed and washed, they tried to lay plans, but Pierce's were so outrageous—involving disguises, illusions, huge lies rapidly changed—that Hildy said she wouldn't be part of it, and Bobby got nervous and cried out over their altercation Y'all don't tell don't tell don't TELL, which they had no intention of doing: she was amid expert secret-keepers, and safe.

At breakfast they filled their pockets with bread and fruit as Hildy told them to do, which Mousie did notice but didn't ponder; there was no time for Bobby to eat it, though, for Sister was on her way.

"Whose sister?"

"Sister. From the hospital."

"But whose?"

They got her into her coat and filled her pockets from theirs, and Pierce tugged her by the hand out through the schoolroom and out the back door. Just in time, for as they crept along the far side of the bungalow ducking under the windows (Gene and Smiley did it that away, duck beneath the windows, peek up to see the badguys unaware within), they heard Sister Mary Philomel arriving, and Mousie delivering Warren to be schooled.

A dash across the open space of the breezeway and around the backside of the house, Pierce afraid to let go of her hot hand for fear she'd bolt, and to the bulkhead doors leading to the cellar.

"Ain't gone go down there."

"It's just for a *second*," Pierce said. "We'll go up inside."

She looked around her, up the hillside, cold smoke coming from her mouth. She had nowhere to go. She went down the bulkhead stairs into darkness with Pierce.

Base-born, born in a basement? At St. Simon Cyrenean the toilets had been in the basement, and a request to go to the basement elicited giggles. Sister may I go to the Basement, thighs shut tight together.

His daddy too had wronged his mam, somehow; Pierce didn't know how or why, but somehow.

The light switch was near the interior stairs, so they crossed the cellar in the dark, she willingly holding his hand now and silent. She froze when the automatic stoker spilled coal into the furnace—the automatic stoker which it was Joe Boyd's job to fill daily with coal, he'd be coming down here any minute.

"It's nothing."

"Somebody shoveled."

"No, it's nothing. Come on."

They climbed the narrow stair pressed close together, Pierce half aware of Bobby's strange strong odor, rough as her speech. What Axel called a *hum*. Pierce opened the door an inch.

The house was silent. Mousie might have gone back to bed, or gone out, or into the bathroom with Baby Henry. Pierce pulled Bobby unwilling out the door and around to the stairs upward. Once in the house, though, Bobby wanted to linger and see things, and Pierce had to whisper urgently to her; even more than in the bungalow, Bobby seemed uncontrollable, a source of catastrophe here, in Sam's house. Sam, though, was gone.

Gone.

He pushed her up the stairs, his ears huge to hear Mousie with Henry. Nothing. He urged Bobby over against the hallway wall, showing her where to step along the outermost floorboards that didn't creak.

"Go on. Go *on*."

At length she pushed back, having had enough, and turned to look at him in defiant contempt, arms akimbo. Pierce made urgent hand signals: that door, that one. Bobby walked to it with deliberate steps, on her own, a guest here.

Sam's bedroom was more silent than the silent house. Pierce's heart beat hard, conscious of the outrage he was committing. "Stay here," he said to Bobby, who was looking around the room from the threshold, her eyes alone moving, almost unwilling to step up on the carpet. "Just *stay here*." He pointed to the little clock on the bedside table, next to the phone that now and then woke Sam in the middle of the night. "When it says *twelve*, I'll come back. *Twelve*."

For a long time after he closed the door on her (she watched the knob turned carefully so as to make no noise) she only stood hugging herself; but she grew braver. She took wadded bread from her pocket and ate it as she looked over Sam's furnishings. There were two beds, or really one bed split into two, joined behind by shelves of gray grained wood, she ran her hand over its glassy unwoodlike surface. She looked into the broad mirror over a dresser made of the same wood, burned by a cigarette here, a little wound that would never heal: she put her finger into it.

When she had lost her fear of the room she dared open the door and peek out. She heard voices, Mousie's and a male voice she didn't know (it was Joe Boyd), and closed the door again. She tried a chair —it had a wooden coat hanger affixed to the top of it, with a coat draped over it, and big shoes on a rack below: a chair wearing clothes. She went to the bed and lay down on one side of it, listening to the hum of the clock (which she couldn't read) and smelling the familiar male smell of the pillow, like her grandpap's. When she got up, she noted that an impression of herself remained on the bed and the pillow.

She opened Sam's drawers, and marveled at the black eggs of his rolled socks; she looked at huge glossy issues of *Esquire* magazine that Sam prudishly stashed there, at pictures of cars and bottles of amber whiskey and elongated women the color of biscuits. She found the furry humpbacked box that held Opal's wedding rings: she opened it, and watched the tiny stone color the light that entered it, her thighs tight together and her hand pressed between her legs.

She had seen the commode in the little house where the children lived and thought there might be another one in here too, but where. She bent to look under the bed for the pot, one side, the other side, wetting her pants. No pot. At length she lifted a ginger jar off the headboard of the bed, and used that as well as she could, watering the flocked rug too. She rolled up her damp pants and tossed them deep under the bed where no one could ever find them; she capped the jar and put it back. Later she could ask where to empty it.

She forgot it, though, when she saw the knob of the door turn, and Pierce's anxious white face looked in: and though Winnie eventually found the pants, still for a long time Sam would smell in his room the tang of stale urine, and not know why.

"Come on," Pierce whispered.

"There's a diamond ring there," she said.

"Come on." He had sat all day in Sister Mary Philomel's classroom burdened with his knowledge that she was in the house, knowledge that at once filled and shrank his heart; now when he opened the door and saw her, she seemed to be a different person than the one he had been thinking of, denser, more problematic, renewing his fear and wonder.

"I'm hungry," she said.

Could it really have been (Pierce wondered, having cause to ponder these things again) that they had kept Bobby to themselves for many days, a week at least, without Mousie knowing? Maybe there were enough children in the house that Mousie hadn't detected an extra pair of feet clattering on the back stairs; maybe Sister Mary Philomel couldn't distinguish a Cumberland whisper amid the urgent whispers in the garden plot below her schoolroom window (Bobby refusing to stay in the hideaway under the house they had found for her). Anyway no one caught her. She slept with Bird, and the one time her shape under the covers was discerned by Mousie, Hildy had been in the bathroom, and Mousie thought it was she in Bird's bed.

Days she moved from room to room, or snuck up into the woods or into the chicken house or down into town with Pierce and Bird (dangerous, daring, if they hadn't felt themselves to be truly Invisible, and Bobby too as long as she was in their keeping, they would have betrayed themselves and her). She could stay preternaturally still and silent, make herself transparent to observation somehow, like a speckled toad in dead leaves; if you looked long at her (Pierce hiding out with her in the upstairs closet, waiting for a chance to run) there could seem something alien in the shape of her face, something opaque in her hard eyes, as though she only closely resembled a human girl.

She still talked about getting to Deetroit and her maw, but— though they schemed with her and stole from the kitchen and the closets to provision her—they knew, Pierce and Hildy at least, that this was like make-believe, like Joe Boyd's constant threat to run away to sea. It seemed clear that she didn't know the way, and when once they took out the volume of maps from the cabinet where the maroon Encyclopedia was kept, and found Kentucky, she couldn't follow what they did. *There*'s Clay County. There's Pikeville. There was the No Name River too and the centipede of the railroad track. Bobby watched them without interest.

It only slowly grew clear to them that she couldn't read at all. "Yes I sure can," she said defiantly, and sang out "A b c d e f g, hi jk ello mello pee," but couldn't pass the real tests Hildy quickly put to her. For her part she didn't seem to believe completely that they could read what they read, and would challenge them to read passages aloud, from pages she chose, so they couldn't cheat.

"Ophites," Pierce read from the Dictionary where her finger, tipped with a black-moon nail, pointed. "The Ophites were a sect who, like most Gnostics, regarded the Jehovah of the Jews with great abhorrence, and believed that the emancipation of human souls from his power was the great work of life. Thus they considered that the Serpent who tempted Eve to revolt was the great benefactor of the human race. They worshipped a serpent which they kept within a sanctuary, and after it had blessed (by licking with its tongue) the Eucharist bread, the communicants each kissed it on the mouth."

Bobby considered this. "Don't wonder they didn't like Jews," she said. "They kilt Jesus. My uncle took up a snake once in church, cause the Bible says if you believe, you can handle snakes, or drink pizen, and no harm come to you. He didn't kiss it though." She leafed further through the book. "Kissn snakes," she said in disgusted disbelief, and turned the page. "Who's this all?"

"Statues."

"Where's ther clothes?"

"They didn't wear them like we do."

She lifted her eyes slowly to Pierce, as though he had planted the picture of Hermes there for her to find. "This was long ago," he said, blushing. "In another country."

"What country?" she said. "I guess Bar Nekkid Land."

"No, Greece."

"Grease, huh," she said cynically, regarding the page.

What she knew and they didn't: how to light a paper match by closing the matchbook cover over the match head and the brown sandpaper strip together and then pulling the match sharply out. How to spit between her teeth, a fine straight spray like a bullet, and hit a target feet away. How to roll a cigarette with paper and loose tobacco, and smoke without choking. When Pierce bought the tobacco for her (charging it at the little store, the incurious keeper noting it on the long strip of other Oliphant charges, where it would puzzle Winnie later on amid the pop and bread and milk), they paused before the chewing tobacco displayed there: some of it tasty looking golden squares inside cellophane, another kind that was plain twists of tobacco like hanks of thick grapevine.

"You ever chew?" she asked him.

"No."

"My grandpap does. Try it," she said, and held one of the shaggy twists to his face.

"No!"

"Jes try it!" she said urgently, and when he did touch his tongue to it, and recoiled from the burning bitterness, like an awful practical joke, like everything terrible he had ever tasted by mistake, she laughed with satisfaction.

While they tried smoking the loose-rolled bundles of tobacco she made, like Saturday's bonfire, Bobby showed him another thing she knew.

"Lookit," she said. She tore out two of the paper matches from the book she carried, and with her long fingernails she pried the layers of paper apart and spread them open. Now she had two little stick-figures like the ones that warred in Joe Boyd's endless battle. Squatting by a flat rock, her sharp knees up and her dress pushed down with a fist between her knees, she laid the two figures down, one on top of the other; then, laughing low, she lit a third match in her special fashion, and with it touched the match heads of the little figures.

"See?"

They leapt when they ignited, and then their limbs began to writhe languorously together as the flame curled and blackened them, legs spreading and backs arching. Bobby watched delighted, then looked at Pierce, her opaque eyes alight with devilment.

"It's your mawn pa," she said. "Fuckn."

Then she jumped up to run, sure she had insulted him outrageously; but Pierce only looked from her to the two matchstick people, twisted as in agony, their bodies afire. Fuckn. From a distance Bobby laughed, waiting to be chased.

Nights they talked about death, God and revelation in the dark of the bungalow by the heater's glow.

"When you die," Bobby said, "you get put down in your grave, and there you lie, dead and asleep till Jesus come. Then on that day ever'body gets out of their graves alive again, and gets judged. *Then* y'all go to hell, and Christians live on earth with Jesus 'bout a thousand years, and then they go on up to heaven forever. That's all."

These certainties had come, she said, out of the Bible. Didn't they read the Bible? Her grandpap read the Bible all the time, with the Holy Spert guiden him. The Holy Spert had revealed to him a secret Gospel underneath the Gospel everybody read.

"Holy Spirit is another name for Holy Ghost," said Hildy.

"Not a ghost!" said Bobby, scandalized. "Ghosts are dead people come back, clankn ther chains or a big knife in ther backs. The Holy Sperta God."

"What about us?" Pierce said. "We're Christians."

"Ain't neither. You born again? You cept Christ?"

"What about you?"

"I ain't gone die yet."

"What about little babies? Who die, who don't get baptized? They didn't do anything wrong."

"They go to hell too."

Bird drew breath at this, shocked.

"Well to get baptized you got to cept Christ. How can a baby do that?"

"Godparents do it," said Bird, whose own sent her a present every year on her christening day. Bobby snorted in contempt, having no idea what a godparent might be but quick to put up a defense.

"When babies die without getting baptized," Hildy told Bobby, "they go to Limbo. That's not hell. It's outside heaven." Hildy thought of death as being like going into a closet or a wardrobe, the earth; only (like the one upstairs) the closet had an exit on the other side, the wardrobe was one such as magicians had, where after you were shut up in it you could be shown to have exited without having come back out: you exited into a geography that seemed to Hildy to be not in the sky or even in the earth but within death itself. Heaven. Hell. Purgatory. Limbo. When she thought of people there she always thought of them as on the move, in passage, migrating always farther within the endless interior of death. "Because they never got baptized, they can't go to heaven, but it's not *their* fault, so they go to Limbo, where everything is sort of nice, but they can't be with God. Ever."

"*But,*" Pierce said, "if you're not baptized and you grow up, and you're like bad, you still go to hell." An inequity in this struck him for the first time: it was like being able to lose in a game you didn't know you were playing, but not allowed to win.

"*Unless,*" Hildy added, raising a finger, "you have Baptism of Desire. That means you *would* have believed in God and gotten baptized and been a Catholic if only you had heard about it, only you didn't, and you did your best anyway."

Bobby sat listening, chin in her hands, in a flannel nightgown of Bird's, her own invincible ignorance (Pierce realized uncomfortably)

slipping fast away, and with it her chance for Baptism of Desire. Nor
was she an infant. Where did that leave her?

"Anyway our mother's in heaven now," said Bird.

"No she ain't," said Bobby. "She ain't yet, cause Jesus ain't come
yet. Then he'll see."

But there was only one of her, and three smart Oliphants (four
after Warren had to be let in on the secret), and she knew which side
her bread was buttered on; she listened to Hildy's catechisms, not
unpleased at the fuss made over her.

Anyway there could be no objection, Pierce thought, to the mild
dogmas they wanted to convince her of. Like Sam, the children believed that nothing which could be shown to be true could contradict
faith, not evolution or the great age of the earth or Relativity; natural
casuists, they were quick to notice and adopt any qualifications,
ecumenicisms, loopholes in the strong fortress of faith to let in the
real world, which had for them a primacy they neither perceived nor
questioned. For the Oliphants—for Pierce at least—the long story
read out in snatches at every Mass, never heard whole, endlessly
recycled, never completed, though unquestionably true, happened
somewhere elsewhere: in eternity, maybe. It was History that happened now.

But Bobby had never heard of History; she had only the one
story, her grandpap's, about the dead and their awaking and their
judgment, graphic as a horror comic, which she seemed to believe
was taking place right now, this week, this winter. She had no ritual
obligations, she didn't even go to church on Sunday, no church having the true story the Holy Spert had taughtn her grandpap; and she
knew no prayers at all.

Under the bungalow with Hildy and Bird, close around Bobby,
showing her how to pray: hands pressed palm to palm, thumbs op-
tionally crossed or side by side. Hail Mary Mother of God. At Jesus'
name Hildy tipped Bobby's head down with a finger and then released it. The fruit of thy womb. Which had what to do, exactly, with
the name of the underpants Pierce wore, it must be something,
chance alone couldn't account for such a similarity. From above their
heads (they were right below the schoolroom) they heard the sharp
strike of Sister's desk bell. They dared ignore it once.

"If you're Catholic you aren't prejudiced," Hildy said, "and you
don't have to think Negroes are worse than other people. It's a sin to

have prejudice." Colored people are no different at all from us, Opal Boyd had told them all, and Hildy believed it, though she'd known none; neither had Opal.

"Sun don't set on ther heads in Clay County," Bobby said mildly. "My ma said they better not let it."

She had begun to shiver. Sister's bell rang again. They could see it in their minds, silver, but shaped exactly like a chocolate marshmallow cookie, why. "Don't leave," Hildy said. She pressed Bobby back against the cold dry clay.

Clay County. Sam said mountain kids were sometimes given to eating clay.

In Brooklyn when he was in the second grade Pierce had dreamt, not once but several times exactly the same, that he was to be crucified alongside Mary's Son, share in His sacrifice; it was to happen on the auditorium stage of St. Simon Cyrenean's, three crucifixes set up there amid the dusty velvets before rows of kids in the fanny-polished wooden seats (Pierce himself somehow among them as well as being crucified or about to be crucified); he felt no fear or reluctance, only the grave weight of responsibility, privilege too, the same priggish satisfaction that he felt at the work of Bobby's conversion. When he recalled it—for the first time since that winter—caused him an involuntary groan of embarrassment. How could he have.

She was gone when they looked for her again under the bungalow. The empty crawlspace smelled of her and of the food they had brought for her there. A small cold rain had begun to fall.

She wasn't in the chicken house either, or in the garage out by where the trash was burned. The rain came and ceased like sniffles; Mousie called them for supper from the kitchen. Wieners and beans, sweetened with dark Karo. They ate in silence, feeling cold darkness assemble itself around them and the house.

She was in Bird's bed, rolled in the bedspread (she hadn't seemed to understand the differences, bedspread, blanket, sheet) and asleep; when Hildy touched her she writhed as though bitten, and sat up to stare at them. Her hair was wet on her forehead. When they asked where she had been, she answered in thick gobs of language they couldn't understand and crawled again into the pillow. Then she flung the spread aside and stood, her mouth open and her breath coming harsh and quick.

"Are you sick?" Hildy put her hand on Bobby's damp forehead, but Bobby shook her off and tottered toward the bathroom (the others following) and to the sink. Wet panties lay on the floor; the toilet unflushed. Bobby opened the tap, her hands shaking, and put her mouth to it to drink.

Smacking and swallowing, she pushed unseeing through them and to the bed again, and was asleep again immediately, or at least still, face turned down, labored breathing loud. The others stood by the bed, smelling the sour odor of her sickness.

"What if she dies?" Hildy said.

8

———

ll night she tossed and talked, and once again got out of bed and back in again; her frightful breathing, deep and fast like a dog's, only slowed a little toward morning. She was quiet when Pierce's alarm woke him to get to Mass.

Mousie was supposed to be up too, to pour his Cheerios and make sure his hair was brushed, but on the first morning of his week-long early-Mass duty he had gone into the still-dark kitchen and stood waiting, listening to the upstairs alarm ring, fade and die, and silence follow it. Mousie couldn't get up fast enough, apparently, and so Pierce (unwilling to disturb her and the house's sleep by making his own breakfast) just went on, stopping at the little store, already lit, to buy orange crackers filled with gray peanut butter.

On this morning he didn't stop even there, only hurried on through the sad-breaking morning, his stomach and ribcage trembling; so he was fasting, as he wasn't usually, and when Father Midnight turned to him inquiringly after ingesting his own huge Host, he could put the paten under his own chin (he and Father Midnight being the only two present at the sacrifice, two being enough, one alone being enough for that matter). With the invariable few unintelligible words Father Midnight placed the circle on his tongue. Pierce closed his eyes, left hand pressed against his bosom and right hand still holding the paten that caught falling crumbs of God (every minute fragment, every molecule being wholly God) as the almost nonexistent sweetish circle dissolved against his palate: waiting for certainty, or at least resolve, to flow into him from its dissolution.

After Mass in the vestibule the priest removed his layers of embroidered satin and white lace one after the other, his lips moving almost indetectably in silent prayer, and kissed the stole that contained his power (Mass could be said without the rest of it, but not that) before hanging it. Pierce too hung up his white surplice and black cassock among the others, his heart beating fast and still warm from the Host he had swallowed.

"Son."

"Yes, Father."

"Do you know that when you move the book from Gospel to Epistle side, it's appropriate to kiss the page?"

"Yes, Father."

"Have we discussed this?"

"Yes, Father."

"Do you have an objection to osculation?" This said in Sam's tone, as though for the amusement of some knowing hearer not actually present. Osculation: he guessed the meaning. He had no objection; it had only seemed to him weirdly forward, extravagant, like kissing elderly relatives.

"Well then," Father Midnight said.

Pierce pulled his jacket on.

"Thank you, son."

"Thank you, Father."

Back out through the empty church, hands in his jacket pockets, not forgetting a quick bend-of-knee when passing the inhabited altar: and to the font of pale stone by the door, filled with cold and faintly slimy water. Feeling along his back a horrid certainty that he would be caught, that he was being looked at even now by Father Midnight at least, he took from his pocket the aluminum cylinder (it was waterproof, meant to keep matches in on camping trips, though no matches had ever been put in it) and dipped it in the font. Brief endless moment while it gurgled full. Out then, capping the vial, into the day, which had grown up, while he was inside, into gray fullness.

Maybe the Communion he had taken hadn't been such a good idea after all. The warmth in his heart had overspread his chest and seemed no longer warm but caustic, angry, affronted maybe at his impertinence. His throat had filled with sour matter, and his head was light.

Hildy, white-faced and wide-eyed, looked out the window of the bungalow's door and then opened it a crack to admit him. "She threw up," she whispered to him in awe. "Not real throwup, but this goo."

Bird sat by Bobby in her bed, holding Bobby's hand in hers and staring at her fixedly. Bobby's face seemed coated faintly in shining slime, and she stared at Pierce unseeing with eyes clouded and pale, as though cooked, like eggs. As soon as he saw her, as soon as he breathed in the sickroom odor, Pierce knew two things: that it was all up, Mousie would have to be told; and that he was sick himself. And ever after, when the onset of fever would assemble within him all the other days of fever he had ever experienced (as though fever were a different life he only sometimes lived, with its own memories as well as its own thirsts and needs and weaknesses), this morning would be one of them.

"She's got to get better she's got to she's got to," Hildy whined softly, out of her depth and afraid.

"Okay," Pierce said. "Okay." He took out the vial of water from his pocket and put it on the rickety table beside Bird's bed, decals of bear and bunny, where wadded tissues and half-filled glasses of water were crowded.

"Please God get her better."

All they really had to do was nothing, which they agreed to do without speaking, to sit suspended in guilty trance between the obvious need to tell adults and the impossibility of telling, until at length Mousie opened the door.

Only it wasn't Mousie who first opened their door, but Sister Mary Philomel.

She was only taking seriously her promise to Doctor Oliphant to keep an eye on the kids, a promise Winnie had received without thinking much about it; she had a Saturday morning's work to do, and it could be done in her schoolroom as well as anywhere. Perhaps she sensed she might be trespassing here on this day, though, for she peeked around the half-open door of the bungalow more circumspectly than was usual for her.

Pierce remembered later that she did nothing foolish; she saw the sick child in Bird's bed, who was beginning to cough spasmodically as though shaken, and she came to help.

"Who is she?" Sister asked gently, sitting on the bed beside her. Bobby, still coughing, pushed weakly back into the corner as though she could push right through, staring at Sister, seeing who knew what in the black habit and wimple.

"Bobby," said Bird, nearly weeping with grief and relief.

"Well we'll have to get a doctor for Bobby. Won't we."

"Yesster."

"We'll take her temperature, shall we." Her pink hand pressed against Bobby's forehead, her arm around Bobby's trembling shoulders. For a moment Bobby ceased coughing; her eyes grew huge and crossed and her mouth opened in an unrefusable gag; she arched like a vomiting dog, and expelled a mass of yellowish sputum. Sister Mary Philomel tried to draw away, but a lashing of grue wetted her black habit as the children watched in deep horror, a horror each could recall with gleeful exactness when they were grownups: the time Bobby puked on Sister.

"I sicked up," Bobby said weakly, her lip flecked with foam. *"Again."*

Hildy was sent to find a thermometer in the big house. Bobby, panting and swallowing, sat immobile like a caught bird in the grip of Sister Mary Philomel. At Sister's elbow was the stolen holy water; she might sense it there, Pierce felt, recognize it by some vibration it put out; in the pocket of his jacket Pierce's hand stirred of its own accord, wanting to take it back, but then Hildy returned, having met Warren and Mousie in the summer kitchen, on their way here.

She opened the door wide, solemn, all secrets patent now, and stepped aside for Mousie to enter.

"There she is."

Mousie's hands rose slowly to her cheeks, her white fingers fencing her open mouth, looking from the child to the nun to the fouled towels on the floor and the tortuous spotted sheets where Bobby lay: more stricken even than the children could know, for she had grieved and worried ever since she had so high-handedly turned the child away, no place for such a one in the household that had been entrusted to her, afraid of the chaos Bobby might cause, nothing this bad though, what on earth.

Bobby, who had at first not even seemed to recognize Mousie, now broke at last; she seemed to arise or descend again into her body, she lifted her hands to Mousie as though they burned, she began to sob in the quick, panting rhythm of a baby.

"Now what on earth," Mousie said, sitting with her and pushing the damp hair from her brow as Bobby clung to her sobbing. "Now what on God's green earth."

She turned then, and Sister Mary Philomel did too, to Pierce, who was now, he knew, to begin the explaining; but in the moment's silence that fell came the sound of a car door slammed, so distinctly that it could only be in their own driveway.

"Daddy's here," Warren at the window said.

"Well," said Sister Mary Philomel, "well there," with a smile breaking on her face of a sort the children knew well, whose obvious import they would not at that moment have wanted to dispute: prayer answered, in so drastic a form they might have wished it not answered, but answered for sure. "The doctor's here," she said cheerfully to Bobby. "It's all right now."

Then Sam and Winnie were in the breezeway; the door opened, and the children jumped, as though they were as startled as their parents were. Sam and Winnie (their faces unwontedly orange, hands too, as though colored with movie makeup) looked around the room, and for an immeasurable time no one spoke; Pierce waited with held breath for Bobby to be instantly ordered out of the house, and maybe himself finally as well, Sam's house and his perfect right after all and Pierce with nothing to say.

"Dad!" Warren whispered. "Can we keep her?"

"Warren!" Hildy warned.

"But can we? If we don't she'll die and go to hell."

Somehow, wonderfully, they weren't ever really interrogated about Bobby, how she had come to be there, what they had done with or to her in that time; Sam and Winnie had automatically held Mousie responsible for her, and anyway she was so sick that the first thing was to see to her, and ask questions later, by which time the children had their exculpations and evasions ready.

As soon as Sam returned from fetching his black bag from the car, the two women stepped aside for him, and he concentrated solely on Bobby, calming her with quick skill and an astonishing firm gentleness even as he learned what was up with her. Pierce, seeing Sam for the first time as doctor and not as uncle, seemed to be seeing him turned inside out or reversed back to front, a different person entirely, not teasing, tired, fussy, but full of knowledge, full of compassionate regard. Bobby looked not at the instruments he used but at his eyes, and his eyes, though Pierce couldn't see them, must have reassured her, for she didn't shrink from him.

"And what about everybody else?" Sam asked, not looking away from Bobby. "All okay?"

"Okay," said Hildy.

"Okay," said Bird.

"Okay," said Warren.

"I don't feel so hot," Pierce said, "actually."

He was sent to his room, to wait for his examination, and everybody else was ordered out; and he lay afloat on his bed, no longer himself, and said in his heart over and over Thank you thank you thank you: though to whom and for what he could not have said.

Bobby got a shot—the word spread quickly from Hildy at the bungalow door to the others who had been excluded. Through the flimsy wall that separated their rooms, Pierce witnessed the procedure, which Bobby apparently didn't even know enough to protest; he heard Sam move aside the matter on the bedside table (among which was Pierce's match case and its unsuspected contents), and ready himself. Afterwards, she would be given the minute plastic box with neat snap closures in which the ampoule had come, almost recompense for the pain. Pierce, knowing he was next, lay with his buttocks clenched, waiting for the cry he knew she wouldn't be able to withhold when she was pierced.

Through that day and night he and Bobby lay quarantined in the bungalow; from far within his mounting fever Pierce heard someone, Winnie, come in and clean up in Bobby's room, and he saw Bobby pass in a nightdress of Bird's through his room to the bathroom, or maybe he imagined that.

When he closed his eyes he didn't so much dream as believe that, even as he lay in bed, he was also walking a spiral track up a featureless conical mountain, a mountain consisting of nothing but his walking up it, which he did for hours, never getting any higher; the path was like the whirling spiral on a moving barber pole that eternally ascends without progressing. Exhausted, he would start awake, damp with sweat, the room shuttered and the heater high; he would rise up on an elbow, feeling unreal, and listen to the bungalow, to Bobby's breathing; then he would fall back, and as soon as his eyes were shut, start climbing again.

Sometime after dark he at last alighted in the old world, like a magic-carpet voyager, feeling new-minted and fire-hot. He hadn't seen night begin, and so didn't know if it was young or old. He was thirsty; his chest felt solid, and his penis was stiff.

"Bobby?"

She didn't move in her bed, but her presence there was large to him. The head of her bed was pressed against the same wall where the side of his own bed ran. He rolled over against that wall and listened, but couldn't hear anything.

He slipped from his bed, sure that he was not dreaming because he was awake, but otherwise feeling just that dream compulsion, the rooms around him empty of actuality but charged with dense meaning and looking at him. The heater's grille glowed blue and orange. He went into the next room.

"Bobby?"

He could not have spoken more softly; only if he had spoken it right into her whorled ear could she have heard him, and she didn't. She had thrown off the covers in the thick heat, and lay on her back across the bed; the flannel nightdress she had been given to wear had ruched up over her thighs, and her pale legs lay together. He stood looking down at her for an immeasurable time, his own breathing in and out matching hers, and then he went back to bed.

He woke again without knowing he had slept, as though no time had passed; but day was coming on, filling up the world outside the window with a skim-milk light. If he rolled over on his bed and extended his arm as far as possible, Pierce could just reach the books in the bookcase, and he did so now, snagging by its spine the one he wanted and lifting it (feeling the volatile blood rush to his head) to his bed.

This time around he had decided to read it systematically, from beginning to end, starting with ABBA and ending with ZOROASTER, reading every entry, forgetting each one even as he dutifully ingested it. He had got to the F's.

FIRE is a God in every clime and time, and while worshipped in itself by the PARSEES (*q.v.*), it is more often personified. Fire is AGNI (*q.v.*), among the Hindus, and HEPHÆSTOS (*q.v.*), among the Greeks, who is the same as VULCAN (*q.v.*), among the Romans.

He started when his eye, in moving from one page to the next, caught movement in his doorway. Bobby watching him.

"You readn that?"

"Yes." PROMETHEUS the trickster stole fire from heaven, and bequeathed it to the human craftsmen whose patron he was; and those who have wielded fire have seemed ever since to share in divine power, and to be connected to the Gods: smiths, alchemists, torturers. There is a reason why the *auto-da-fé* is done with fire.

She came to stand beside him, to see what he studied. "Read me," she said.

"PARACELSUS (*q.v.*)," Pierce read, "supposed that as there were creatures indigenous to the elements of Earth, Water and Air, so there must be creatures of the Fire too, and he called them Salamanders."

"Push over," she said.

"There is no explaining why a humid, soft-bodied creature of the forest floor should be supposed to be fireproof, but so it has always been." He moved so that Bobby could get up on the narrow bed next to him. "Benvenuto Cellini as a boy saw the Great Salamander in his own fire, and his father gave him a great clout on the head, so that the pain would cause the memory of this rarity to stick there."

Bobby looked down at the page. There was a sort of coin or seal pictured there, with a muscle-y lizard of sorts surrounded by tongues of symbolic flame and Latin words. "What's that?"

"That's the Salamander," Pierce said. "I guess."

"My grandpap seed a Salamander once," Bobby said. "Right round chir."

"So have I. In the woods."

"Not one athem little red things," Bobby said. "A spert."

"Oh yeah," Pierce said.

"It was a mockn spert. It mocked my grandpap when he ast a question of it."

"Oh yeah?"

"Then it showed its power, and defied my grandpap. And that was the night them woods was set afar. Look at another page."

Pierce turned to other gods. Hermes in his winged construction worker's hat and Keds, very like the figure bearing flowers by wire on the back cover of the telephone book. And nothing else.

"Bar Nekkid Land," said Bobby appreciatively. "Did you ever."

"Well," said Pierce, but just then she leapt from his bed and hustled to her own, having heard, though Pierce had not, someone approaching over the dogtrot. Winnie came in the door just as Bobby pulled Bird's covers up to her neck. Winnie had breakfast for them, and she wore her New York suit (so Pierce thought of it) and her autumnal hat, fox-orange plush with the pheasant feather, and her Sunday makeup, including the perfume he inhaled as she put his toast beside him on the bedside table.

"Sam says he thinks it's best if you stay home from Mass this morning," she said. "And just rest. All right?"

Pierce nodded solemnly.

"You'll be all right?"

"Yes."

She paused by Bobby's bedside, and asked her too if she would be all right, getting the answer she expected since it was evident she would not have known what to do with any other, and said that she thought her father would be coming soon to see her.

"Not my father."

"Well a Mr. Shaftoe. Mrs. Calton told us . . ."

"Ain't my father."

"Well." She drifted away, unwilling to solve this. "We'll be back soon. Rest."

She closed the door softly behind her.

For a long time Bobby and Pierce lay silent, listening to the bustle of the family leaving the house, going to the car, someone running back for something forgotten, the car starting, shifting gears, departing. And then for a moment Pierce still lay unmoving, in the almost unbearably intense peace and silence of the empty house and his own missing of Mass, a peace pregnant with unguessable possibility, like a flame in his sternum.

He got out of bed this time, bringing the great dark book with him.

"Is she your maw?"

"Yes."

"But not thers."

"No. Theirs is dead."

"Where's your paw?"

"Brooklyn, New York."

She pulled away her covers. "Show me," she said.

"This was a long time ago," Pierce said. "In the Old World." He opened the book on the sheets of her bed: Bar Nekkid Land.

"Let's," Bobby said.

Winnie at her place in Blessed Sacrament would be kneeling now, taking out her beads to pass the time till the show started (so her face seemed to Pierce always to suggest); the pale amber beads like a string of glycerine cough drops.

"Lookit it," Bobby said. "Why's it do that?"

"I don't know," Pierce said. "It just does."

"Hang yer hat onm," Bobby said.

"You can touch it," Pierce said. "If you want."

She did, delicately, with one finger. She herself remained covered, small fingers delicately holding the mound, just as the motherly Venus on the next page of the Dictionary did. She laughed and turned half away from him when he pulled gently at her hand; then she flung herself back on the pillow, hands above her head, stretching, gleeful: the balls of her knees still tight together, though.

"You can *kiss* it," she said. "If you want."

Probably she meant that as the sort of mocking challenge he wasn't supposed to rise to, the kind she liked to throw at him; maybe he surprised her by his willingness. Osculation. Softer than its firm plumpness suggested, still fever-hot, and with an odor he would not often remember but never entirely forget, different from the sea-smell of the grown-up women whom now and then his willingness would also surprise.

Cumberland girls of eight and nine in those days either knew everything about sex or they knew nothing. Bobby knew nothing, nothing but a few scandalous words, and Pierce didn't know even that much; when his mother had found out that everything she thought she knew was wrong, she had decided the whole subject could not be spoken of, and she had not tried. So mostly he and Bobby only lay together side by side, chaste as knight and lady separated by a sword, knowing the effervescent delight of their choice to see and touch: the delight was the knowledge, the snake's knowledge brought to Adam and Eve, which the Ophites rejoiced in: they knew that they were naked.

"Your grandfather's here!" Bird called around the door into the bungalow (Pierce and Bobby again in separate beds, jammies chastely up). "He's right outside!" She watched Bobby closely to see what effect this news would have, but Bobby's face revealed nothing that Bird could read: except that for the first time Bobby looked foreign to Bird, temporary, out of place in Bird's bed and house, and in passage away.

9

is hair stood up thick and black, not gray or white like a grandfather's, but his face was lined, so deeply lined it seemed to have been gruesomely scarred, furrows running not only down his cheeks and across his forehead but diagonally too over the ridge of his brows and across his eye. He arrived in a pickup driven by someone else, who remained in the truck while Floyd got out and came up to the porch.

Sam at his Sunday dinner was called out by Winnie, who had been alerted by Warren, who had been sent in by Hildy, she having seen the truck drive up as she came out of the bungalow after bringing Pierce's and Bobby's trays. Winnie looked down from the porch at Floyd, who seemed unwilling to come closer. The engine of the truck was still running.

"Come to get my daughter."

"Well I wonder if you'd mind talking to Dr. Oliphant first."

Floyd chewed, blew impatiently, looked off into the distance.

"Just for a minute," Winnie said. "She's just been so sick."

Floyd looked back at the truck, and after a moment the driver turned off the engine. Floyd started up the steps of the porch, and as he did, Hildy ran through the kitchen, disposing of the trays and gathering Bird and Warren with her as she ran, pulling them up the back stairs and down the hall to the register where (they well knew) conversations in the room beneath could be heard.

They had missed the howdys and other careful compliments, and the ritual offer of a cigarette, which Sam made and Floyd accepted, slipping it behind his ear like a carpenter's pencil.

My legal responsibility, is what it is, Floyd was saying.

Well sure. (Sam's voice, from Sam's chair.)

Can't have her where I can't see her.

But I've got my responsibilities too, Sam said (and Hildy's breast warmed where her breath was held). She's a very sick child, and I have to be sure she's not going to get worse. Now now now. (This maybe in response to some gesture of Floyd's.) I could put her in the hospital here. I could do that.

There was a shuffling of protest or realignment of forces below that Hildy, even ear to the grate, couldn't interpret; then Warren insisted on having what had happened explained to him.

"Just hush. Just *hush* Warren. *Please.*"

Don't mean no offense to you, she heard Floyd say.

No. Sure.

You understand, Doc. What it is. We're Christian people.

Uh huh, Sam said. Hildy thought she knew what face he had when he said it.

Now yall down there. To that hospital. Yall worship the Popa Rome. Now for us thad be no different than worshippn the Devila Hell.

Scandalized, Hildy with drawn breath waited for Sam's reply, which she couldn't imagine but whose irrefutability she could sense already.

But Sam only said: Well, I'm not going to argue with you.

He rose, then, apparently, and Hildy heard him say: I tell you what. You go see her, in the little back house there, and see she's all right. And then we'll talk.

That was all. Silence fell in the room below. Hildy (while Warren pestered her, whadeesay whadeesay) had a paralyzing insight, that the world of grown people was divided from the world she knew by a gulf, and that she must one day cross it, and think and feel as they did, and not as she now did; and that only then would she know if her horror now at what Sam had done—and not done—was justified, or not: just as a person asleep and dreaming can only judge her dream when she awakes.

———

Pierce in his bed heard the bungalow door open; he heard Floyd Shaftoe studying his daughter, granddaughter—he could hear the man's breathing, while Bobby said nothing. When they did speak they spoke both at once and so low and quick that it was like foreign language.

Cmon. You ain't stayn here.

Will if I want.

You ain't sick.

I like to die.

Well you ain't sick now. Cmon.

Won't.

Floyd said nothing more for a moment. Pierce (as though his ear were huge, sensitive as an antenna) could now hear Bobby's breath: quick, angry, and the phlegm whistling faintly in her throat.

They teach you things? Floyd asked. They make you swar to things? Did they?

None your business.

You have some damn respect.

Pismire.

You're comn home.

Won't. Don't you touch me. You touch me I'll kill you. I'll cut your throat while you lie sleepn. I will.

You're a devil. They turned you on me. You're accursed.

Silence then. The door of the bungalow closed. Pierce lay unmoving while the mephitic curses the Shaftoes had loosed (the more terrible for being all constrained whispers) evaporated, and Bobby's hot breathing slowed. His own heart beat hard; it was evident to him that Bobby could never leave here, never return to where she had come from, that she had only escaped harmless from Floyd by the most terrific daring and pluck, and that to go back would be death: the wrongness of it was self-evident, and would not be permitted in the world he lived in, which Sam and Winnie managed and not Floyd.

A little later Winnie came in, and told Bobby gently that her father wanted her to rest here, with them, and get better. And that after she rested a day or two, Dr. Oliphant would take her back to her father's house.

———

That night then, in the bungalow, the Invisibles gathered (slipping out one by one on various pretend errands and across the breezeway, violating the quarantine that was anyway effectually over); they got Bobby to dress in a clean nightshirt of white, and when that was done they found the vial that Pierce had filled at the Blessed Sacrament font —it had been moved and hidden several times in the last two days, maybe losing efficacy as it was handled, but unspilled at least.

There was no question who would administer the sacrament. Sister had read out the rules from her blackbound book (pressed for the details by Hildy): An ecclesiastic, if one is present, rather than a lay person; a Catholic, rather than one not of the faith; a man, rather than a woman—though except in cases of extreme necessity, a parent should not baptize his child (but why? Hildy wondered, and wonders still).

Bobby changed her mind at the last instant, but after some forceful argument—her last chance, and surely she knew enough now to take it; they wouldn't abandon her, they would continue her instruction somehow—she consented. They had her kneel, with her sponsors on either side, Bird and Hildy, and Pierce (certain they would be interrupted any second, but by whom?) uncapped the vial of stolen theurgy. After baptism, just for a moment, just until the first venial impulse, the first wrongful desire, inevitably shadows it again, the soul is as white as God meant it to be: and if the roof were to fall in on all of them now, Bobby alone would find herself without an instant's hindrance before the throne of God. Pierce's heart filled, he poured out the dribble of oily fluid over Bobby's dark curls, she giggled at the tickling rivulets. The world turned palpably beneath them where they knelt. "*Baptiso te . . . ,*" he read from his missal.

"Bapteezo?" Warren said, struck in the funny bone.

"*Baptiso te, Roberta, in nomine + Patris et + Filii et + Spiritus Sancti.*"

"Amen," they said. And didn't know what next. Pierce, faintly sick with wonder and dread, lay down the book and vial. Bobby wiped a trickle of fluid from her ear with the shoulder of her night-gown, looking at nothing; then she got up quickly, climbed into Bird's bed, and faced the wall unmoving.

"Bapteezo," Warren said, laughing helplessly. "Bap*teezo!*"

The next day, pale and slow and all but silent, Bobby put on her flimsy print dress, more raglike now even than when she had first appeared among them, then her sweater (her fingers blindly feeling for the remaining buttons and their holes while her eyes looked elsewhere) and her fur-collared coat. In a paper bag she carried other clothes, Bird's and Hildy's, that Winnie had chosen for her, and some cans of food and a loaf of bread; and a picture-book of angels she had chosen herself from the Oliphants' books. Hildy sorted through her holy cards and selected a few that weren't favorites—then, generously, one that was, the Little Flower in soft brown robe and black hood like a nuthatch, her arms full of roses—and gave them to Bobby to have.

In the back of the Nash she sat next to the window, looking not out though but at the back of Sam's head; she took Pierce's hand in her small one and held it. Pierce said nothing either, only staring at Sam too, who had been unable or unwilling to keep Bobby, and who now kept up a patter of jokes none of them laughed at as he steered the car up the black winter mountain to Hogback, where the Shaftoes lived, to give her over to Floyd. Where a rattleboard bridge crossed the tumbling crick, and a cabin stood on a grassless yard beneath the beetle of the mountain, Sam stopped; he reached behind him to open Bobby's door. He wouldn't trust his car on that bridge, he said; she'd have to walk from here.

Floyd Shaftoe came out onto the porch of the cabin and stood, making no sign. A dog barked monotonously from the stake where he was tied. Bobby humped her bag of stuff from the car and started across the bridge, not looking back at Pierce but bearing nonetheless indelibly on her soul the sign he had put there of an inward and invisible grace.

Joe Boyd explained fuckn to him, down in the basement of the main house while he filled the automatic furnace stoker with coal. Pierce insisted that the discussion be kept on an impersonal or scientific level, using the right words, which Pierce happened to know—*penis* for boys, *pelvis* for girls. It was warm in the dim basement; coal dust clung in the damp hairs of Joe Boyd's arms and brows. He explained the mechanisms. He explained too about prostitutes, a subject that interested him; prostitutes, he said, were women who were willing to do the thing with someone if he paid, and since they got money for doing it, it was no imposition, it was all equitable and fair. Joe said there were no prostitutes in Bondieu, only in big cities like Huntington; when Joe was ready to do it, and had the money, that's where he would go, he said. He also told Pierce about the Studilac, which was a Studebaker with a Cadillac engine implanted in it, and about the fastest car on the road.

What had become of him? April had come and he felt burdened, as though he still wore his brown wool winter coat, only not on the outside but under his skin. He longed to turn entirely inside out, to be hatched, as from an egg. So silent and abstracted did he seem, staring for long periods at vacancy and drifting to a standstill in halls and doorways, that Winnie decided he must not be well yet. She brought it up to Sam, who supposed it could be so; and it was decided that every afternoon for a time he must spend an hour or two in his room, the blind drawn against the burgeoning spring, to rest, to nap better still, which he protested he wasn't capable of; still he had to lie in the semidarkness and not even read books.

He obeyed, mostly, lying with his hands behind his head and watching the sunlight cross the drawn blind, studying the curious braided ring that dangled from the string. He sang. He even fell asleep sometimes, with cataleptic suddenness, awaking after an hour with open mouth dry and forehead damp. He dreamed, too: often of the same room he lay in, which seemed a waste to him when he awoke. Once though he dreamt of Bobby: Bobby and his cousin Bird lying together in a bed not like his but more like his parents' bed in Brooklyn. Bobby and Bird were prostitutes: Pierce lay naked in the bed between them, the covers up around all their necks, they looking at him smiling and willing and presumably also naked, and the fuckn about to begin. And Pierce was filled with an immense and joyous expectation, no feeling he had ever felt before, a compound of gratitude and a leaping glee at once wholly private and wholly frank: the same unspeakable glee and gratitude he would later feel (in a fainter waking grownup form) whenever he found himself, what luck, in circumstances anything like those.

He never told Father Midnight about Bobby in confession. Not about the baptism, which he had decided could not have been a sin no matter how complicated it was to explain; nor about the Sunday morning when the Oliphants were all at church and he was home with Bobby. He had no direct information that that was a sin either; his indoctrination in the Decalogue had for the time being skipped over those numbers; but he chose not to mention it in any case, classed it somehow elsewhere in his moral books, an account that, now opened, would not ever be closed, and was nobody else's business at all.

"Certainly I remember her," Winnie said. "A little girl that woman brought in. The woman with the animal name."

"Mousie."

"And the girl had some sort of nursery rhyme name or fairy tale name herself." She glanced at Pierce, lesson done. "Well?"

Well: he had himself only in the last day and night, on the plane and the bus to his mother's house, begun to remember, or to imagine he remembered, much more than that. How he had hidden her, right there in his uncle's house, his uncle's bedroom, unbeknown ever after to Sam. How he had opened his eyes on her as though turning inside out, and for the first time entered that condition or story or situation which he would find himself entering over and over again, without ever quite exiting from it, as though the teller of an old tale had forgotten the (happy) ending and only kept idiotically repeating the opening entanglements to jog his memory.

An old tale, a fairy tale.

Not until this day, though, had Pierce connected the forest fire he had set himself with the fire which the Salamander set to show Floyd Shaftoe its power. Bobby Shaftoe's past had seemed to him at the time utterly incommensurable with his own, hers stretching behind her an untellable distance just as his did but in some entirely different dimension, unable to share parts; things that had happened to her could not also have happened to him. And when later on in the course of other researches he again came upon the connection between salamanders and fire, he had forgotten Floyd Shaftoe altogether. Only now, when Floyd came before him again, issuing out of the once-was, did he put two and two together. And now it was too late, too late to find out for sure if the fire he set had been the fire that showed Bobby's grandpap the power of the Salamander.

But even if those fires really were the same fire—if both had been the one that began at the Oliphant's trash baskets beside the old garage, in that summer of 1952—still it might have been the Salamander who started it: might have been the Salamander who snatched the burning paper from Pierce's rake, and blew it into the waiting mulleins and the milkweed. He experienced, and not for the first time this week, this winter, the sensation that he was simply creating the story backward from this moment, reasons and all. But isn't that what memory is always doing? Making bricks without straw, mortaring them in place one by one into a so-called past, a labyrinth actually, in which to hide a monster, or a monstrosity?

"But can you tell me something?" Winnie said to her son with a tentative smile. "As long as we're on the subject."

"What?"

"Why really did you take Opal's diamond ring away that time?"

"Not the ring really. Just the stone."

"Well."

"No I can't," Pierce said, feeling with dreadful sharpness the cruelty of what he had done, had surely done out of solipsistic childish necessity, but still. "I mean I remember doing it, but I'm not sure now I know why."

"Sam was so hurt," Winnie said. "That you would do that."

"Oh god," Pierce said. "Embarrassing."

The soft sky they looked at had begun to darken; a wind lifted one by one the fronds of the will-less palms, and let them go again.

"Well," Winnie said softly. "It surely doesn't matter anymore."

Pierce took from his mother's pack one of her cigarettes and lit it. The little velvet ring box, lined in rose satin, opened in his mind like a cut. He was suddenly sure—and his heart shrank to think of it—that he had taken that stone, the stone out of Opal's wedding ring, in order to give it to Floyd Shaftoe; and he knew that if he could just keep this moment from passing away, for just a moment more, he would remember why.

10

———

loyd Shaftoe was the seventh of seven sons named for the counties of the Cumberlands. That he was a seventh son gave him powers, powers he would not have known about if those he grew up with had not told him of them, and made him use them: he could draw the fire out of a burn, for one, pluck it out with his fingers and then shake it away. (His mother, as the mother of seven sons: there were things she could do as well. She could blow down the throat of a child with catarrh, who like to die, and the child would pass the matter and live.)

He had not been given his gifts for nothing; he knew that from an early age. Even now as a mature man, a Christian man and a grandfather, he did not know if he had come to the end of the meaning of his gifts or the duties they entailed.

He had been born with a caul: the granny-woman who had seen him born had saved the caul, dried it, and given it to him in a pouch to wear—and though he wouldn't do that, he had buried it carefully in a place known only to himself. And if he had thought thereby to evade a fate that the caul had carried with it, he had not succeeded. On certain nights—it might be the night of Little Christmas, or the last night of October, or when the moon was full at midsummer; less often as he grew older and the world grew worse—Floyd Shaftoe would hear his name called, not urgently but surely, at his window as he lay asleep: and he would answer. For he was one of a band, men and women born (he supposed) with the same signs as himself; and there were as many of the others, with whom his kind contended for the health and wealth of the earth: and he could no more refuse a summons to walk out against them than he could refuse to dream or die.

When he was twelve years old Floyd had seen his mother laid away, dead of her last child and first girl, dead too. There had been no preacher for her, no one to read or sing; his father made the box himself, and his brothers dug the grave.

In that summer Floyd first heard his name called at the window while he slept.

He awoke, and listened for the call to come again, while his ear remembered the sound and where it had come from. The call did not come again, but seemed to lie beyond the window, waiting. Floyd stepped out from among his sleeping brothers in the bed (somehow able not to waken them with his movements) and then lightly out the window. It was the shortest night of the year, and the moon was full; he could see as though it were day, but not the one who had called his name. Nevertheless that one led him, and though Floyd could not see him he trusted him to know the way and the reason.

Down along the cove he followed, but then felt himself to be alone, left to his own devices, set a lesson, as when his old man had showed him how to hoe a row, and then left him to do it. He walked along noiselessly on long bare feet, and at length he began to notice others on the path with him. One or two, a man, a woman: he passed them by and glanced into each face as he passed, though they took no notice of him. He overtook a tall man in a brimfallen black hat, and when he passed by him and glanced into his face, he saw it was a man he knew: his face was set in a grimace, and his breast was shot away horribly by the slug the deputy had slain him with last winter.

God bless you, Floyd said, but his neighbor answered nothing. More folk were on the path along the cove now, and the path forked in a way Floyd did not recall it doing, leading down sharply beneath the ridge. Floyd saw that they were entering a cleft in the mountain, troops of them now coming in from every footpath; some of them were bound, some were naked, some seemed to moan noiselessly, some to laugh. When Floyd found himself drawn near the cleft in the mountain, he held himself back against the tide of them, not at all wanting to enter there; and one who was just then going down in turned to look back, as though her name were called, and stared at Floyd. She had the baby that had died with her in her arms, swaddled in the shroud she wore. The others going down into the mountain jostled her, pushing past, as though eager for their beds; and at length they carried her within along with them, though her face turned back to Floyd till she was gone.

When he got back to the window of his own cabin, the sun was on the tops of the mountains. He put his foot on the sill to step in, and saw his own body asleep on the bed amid his brothers, just as it had been when he was called.

Had she beckoned him to come along with her? What would have become of him if he had? Or was she only surprised to see him there, among the dead, not knowing if he was one of them, or still quick?

He had been told that at death the person goes on away from earth to heaven, or down beneath the earth to hell. That was what his mam had said was explained in the big Bible on the dresser: but he knew she had never read it, and neither had his old man. They couldn't read at all.

Why should the dead be walking the cove, and not in their places in the earth, or above it or below? He put his hand on the brown book, shaggy and heavy as a log, thinking the answer ought to be somewhere within it.

That was the year Good Luck opened Number Two, and brought in trainloads of bricks to build the commissary and the school and the hospital, and lines of new yellow cabins cropped over the hills, smelling of creosote and tarpaper. Floyd's older brothers came down off the mountain to get theirs, and Floyd went along with them, and lived with one or another in their identical cabins. He went to school there, was taught by the company teacher to read, to sing songs about America, to write with a steel-nibbed pen. He worked hard, listening to the teacher's birdlike foreign twittering (she would catch him staring at her with unnerving intensity, his big ears seeming almost pricked up, like a fox's) and so he got his letters: and he began on the Bible, to see what he could learn. He would open it to any page and run his eyes over the congested lines of tiny print until a word leapt out at him; there he would begin to read, coming sometimes to see through the words into a truth beyond or within them, a truth he couldn't then speak, the same truth he had seen and not grasped in his mother's face and the faces of the others who walked the cove.

Good Luck Coal and Coke had bought Hogback Mountain twenty years before they opened Number Two: had bought, not the face of it that men saw, but only the rights to the minerals within it. Floyd Shaftoe's grandpap had sold the rights beneath his own fifty acres of hardscrabble hillside, fifty cents an acre, and thought he'd done well out of it; he couldn't read (signing the long form deed with a crow's-foot mark, witnessed and notarized) and so he couldn't know that he had given Good Luck not only the coal beneath the soil but the right to get it out as well, in whatever way they thought convenient. It seemed to make no never-mind then, for there was no way to get the coal out of the Cumberlands anyway: until the trains came.

The black seams lay beneath a mere hundred feet of overburden, sometimes not so much, sometimes so close that the dynamite of the track-layers brought it to light, tons of shattered midnight, the treasure-house ruptured. Even before the tracks reached Bondieu the agents of Good Luck were setting up tipples and opening driftmouths and building camps. By the time Floyd's brothers came down, a mountain of slate had already arisen beside the tipple, and the hundred-car trains wound daylong through the yard, filling with coal: nut coal, egg coal, lump coal, every fifty-cent acre of Hogback's surface yielding its thousands of tons.

The Shaftoes made more money digging it than they had ever thought possible, and they spent it as fast as they made it on things they had not known they wanted, printed curtains and linoleum, Stetson hats, store teeth, gold-filled watches, sweet-smelling flannel shirts and silk stockings. The company paid the miners for the hours they had worked whenever they asked, in shiny tin flickers marked like real money, a dime, a quarter, a dollar, five dollars, spendable at the commissary and pretty soon at the store in Bondieu as well, for white bread, boxes of made biscuits, pale corn syrup, aspirin, Coca-Cola; and out of the fat catalogues kept at the commissary they could order sets of matching dishes, electric irons, washing machines, carbines with blued barrels, huge radios with little celluloid faces. From the radio preachers on Sunday Floyd learned the name of the one who had called him out in the summer night: the Holy Spert.

He went to work first as a picker, working from before dawn in the tipple with crowds of other black-faced boys picking bone out of the endless shaking river of coal that rode the conveyors up to the loading booms. The boys weren't allowed to wear gloves, even in the coldest weather, for it made their fingers less agile; their nails were rapidly worn away to the bloody quick, and Floyd learned from the others to slip metal guards, cut from a coffee can and secured with strips of inner tube, over his forefingers when the boss looked else-where.

Bone: did they call the slate and stone that because they were the mountain's broken bones which the boys culled from the coal, its flesh? The bone, mingled with pulverized coal, went to the slate dump hundreds of feet long that lay along the creek bed; when the boys, let out from the tipple, walked along it toward school in the afternoons, they could smell the fumes of its burning deep below. In winter it steamed softly, like fresh dung.

His aunts hung out their shifts and sheets in the bitter air to dry, and after a time, long before they were old, they turned a hopeless gray and began to shred: you could put your finger right through them. They were almost not worth having, not worth washing in the acid-smelling washtubs. Greasy dust arose daylong from the tipple and the load-boom, mixing with the smoke of the slate-dump and the thousand stoves of the camp; when cloud-cover turned it back from heaven, the mixture settled again on Hogback, blistering the hopeful paint from the Good Luck cabins, peppering the snow far up the mountain. Floyd Shaftoe's father on his farm rubbed it from the handle of his ax, tasted it in his greens.

When he was eighteen, Floyd went under the hill, a miner's helper, with his tin dinner pail and his canvas hat with its carbide lamp. He rode the man-cars down the narrow throat of the mountain into the unchanging clammy coolness of its innards, and all day holp the miner drill and shoot the coal. Down here too the dust filled the air, slicking the cars, the tracks, the tools, as though they had been polished.

In the morning the miner undercut the satiny seam of coal with a pick, and Floyd pulled away the slate. The miner drilled holes along the face of the coal with a breast auger, and Floyd filled the holes with dead men—spills of paper filled with dirt—to keep the holes open. Then the company man came and set the charges, and they all went back along the corridor trailing a fuse behind them (just a line of black powder over the stone floor not long ago, said the company man, electric wire now) and he shot the coal, the whole twenty tons of it falling from the slate roof above like crockery from a shelf, lying hugely smashed and glittering in the room while black motes sparkled in the lamplight.

Then load it all into the cars all afternoon, sucking in the coal-tasty air, and send it out, a little less left in the mountain than there was at dawn; and out at last into the air and the weather, sun going down, you had almost forgotten the season.

And in all that time Floyd was not called out in the night.

With two of his aunts, he accepted Jesus Christ as his personal savior at the brand-new Full Gospel Church of God in Christ: forty-gallon Baptists who insisted on full immersion, which Floyd underwent almost prophylactically, dunked backward by the grunting preacher who clipped his nose with thumb and finger as he put him under.

Take Jesus into your heart, the preacher told them, and Floyd did so: feeling him there ever after within the spaces of his heart, smaller than a sparrow, warming him like a tiny furnace. He never went back to the pine-slab church in Bondieu.

The good times, the rich times, ended soon enough, Hoover conspiring with the millionaires and the bosses to send the country to hell. Wages fell to nothing, the company ceased to care for its dependents; Floyd's brothers could only make enough to feed their families by working the turn-around: under the hill before dawn, not out again till long past nightfall, never see the sun. Floyd, as the youngest, was sent home to the farm, where at least there would be corn and turnips to eat, and no company store to owe.

Floyd's father had worked his land hard, planting season after season of corn, making the earth bear without pause or refreshment (as he had done his wife, Floyd thought once, once only); it was far from wore out yet, though. Then in the spring of '27 he had plowed and planted as he always did, after searching his almanac for the times and the moon's age; he'd hoed it twice, and laid it by to grow. And the great flood had fallen just then on those acres of loosened weeded earth; all in a night, all through the mountains, scouring off the topsoil and vomiting it down the swollen cricks, leaving the naked yellow clay beneath that would grow nothing but broom. Even two seasons after, though Floyd's father had dunged the land and harrowed it, it wouldn't grow corn higher than a man's shoulder.

To this place, its grassless yard and its mule and its razorback hogs, its four-room cabin and its black dog beneath the porch, Floyd brought his wife, new-wed, and his wife's daughter: a woods-colt and no child of Floyd's. Which made no never-mind to Floyd: his gifts, he believed, forbade his having a woman as other men did, and his wife's daughter was the only child he would ever have.

Up Hogback on the sloping Shaftoe acres was a stand of chestnuts, a tall old tree and her striplings, whose sweet nuts fed the Shaftoe pigs in fall and winter, and which Floyd and his brothers had used to roast and eat too; in spring her white candles were filled with bees. On a November day, shortest of the year, Floyd came at evening to call home the pigs, and he saw a woman among the yellow leaves grubbing for the nuts too, and filling a poke.

She looked up, startled, mouth ajar and eyes guilty, when she felt Floyd regarding her. A rail of an old woman, articulated like a doll, in a brown soldier's coat and tongueless boots. He knew her, somehow, or thought he remembered her: she was kin to him, probably, as were all the folk along this ridge. He could see with his mind's eye the track up to her cabin.

When she saw he wouldn't upbraid her, she flung the poke over her shoulder and without a word began to hurry off. *Plenty for you,* Floyd called after her, but she didn't answer, only glanced back once at him over her shoulder as she skittered out of sight. And then he knew her pale eyes: he had been looked on by eyes like those, but not here, not in the day world.

That night, while his long body lay sleeping beside his wife,

Floyd climbed from his bed without causing the straw to rustle and set out on the track up Hogback. So many years had passed, the flood had washed away so many landmarks, so many folks had left their worn-out farms or gone down the mountain to the camps, that he might not have known the way: but it shone a little beneath his naked feet, like a snail's silver slime, and he could follow it well enough.

The door to her cabin stood open, or anyway was no barrier to him; a yellow cat shrieked at his approach and climbed the porch post to the roof. As soon as he put his bare feet on the puncheon floor, he knew the place, remembered how once he had been taken here as a child, in the grip of a fierce ague: how the woman (old then too) had taken out her madstone—ugly lump of matter, found she said in the belly of a deer—and rubbed him with it to cool the blood; how a silver coin had changed hands.

Yes I know you, Floyd Shaftoe, she said to him (keeping far from him on the other side of the cabin room). I knew then what kind you were.

You tooken somethn today belongs to me, Floyd said. I come for the return of it.

The poke full of chestnuts lay in the center of the cabin floor. They began circling it, keeping a fixed distance from each other, as though for a knife fight.

I seen you down along the cove, she said. I was among them too.

I never saw you, said Floyd.

She told him—still circling widdershins around the cabin, holding his eyes with a skinny hand raised—she told him who they were who walked the cove at night, among whom Floyd had seen his mother. They were the dead, she said, who had died before their appointed time, the murdered and the suicides and those carried off in childbirth or by mischance. Not until each one's span was up could he, could she, go lie in peace in the grave where the flesh lay, to sleep till the Judgment.

Floyd knew then what it was he had seen in the faces of those who walked that track, in the face of his mother too, for it was in the witch's eyes as well that held him like a hand at his throat, filling him with fear and pity: it was hunger.

I will tell you a trick, she said, to save your life: Iffen the flesh that now lies sleepn in your bed be turned face down, then you will not be able to get back into it when you return; and iffen you don't return in the turn of a day, you never will be able to. Then your spirit too will run with them along the cove, until your own death day.

Thankee for that, Floyd said.

You're welcome, she said: and now be on your way.

When I have the favor of the return of what's mine, Floyd said, stepping closer to the poke.

What's yours is mine, she said. She had come around to where a hickory chair stood on the floor. She grasped its pole, and quick as stirring a pot she began to whirl it around on one leg. The cat shrieked, the fire spat, Floyd leapt across the circle to grasp her.

But with the Devil's help (summoned with the hickory chair) she had changed her spirit to the likeness of a pale moth, and fluttered out of his grasp. Floyd then bent his own spirit to the spaces of his heart where Jesus held court, and with his help changed his own spirit to the likeness of a nightjar, to catch the moth.

But the witch changed her spirit into the likeness of a screech owl, and stooped at the nightjar.

But Floyd changed his spirit to the likeness of a grain of corn on the floor, and the owl could not find him. She resumed her own form, seized the poke of chestnuts, and climbed with horrid spider-like swiftness out the window with it.

But Floyd changed his spirit to the likeness of a lean timberwolf, and before she had disappeared down the moonlit track, he was after her.

She fled him down along the cove, booted feet taking unnatural great steps, hank of gray hair streaming out behind her: but he was fleet too, four-footed, great-chested. Around him as he sought for her down the track there came to be others, a crowd of others, jostling for room, standing in his way, oblivious. He knew them now: the early dead, the carried-off, the luckless; he had not known there were so many. The knife fighters and feudists and the come-by-chance children strangled at birth; the black steel-drivers and gandydancers killed by work or dope or shot by the track bosses, unable now to rest in the nigger graveyards that lay unmarked along the tracks they had laid. Hanged men and soldier boys and miners, miners crushed in slate-falls or blown up in tunnel fires or broken between coal-car and tunnel-rib or gone down with gas or chokedamp: unreconciled to death, hungry still for what the living had. The long procession of them wound through the night hollers, swept sometimes with waves of anxious longing, when they would race and stare like panicked sheep. He seemed to travel amid them for days, seeking for the face of the old woman who fled him, her eyes hungry like theirs, the poke over her shoulder.

But it wasn't days, only the space of that longest night. Toward dawn the throngs sped under the ridge to where they roosted, the rustling soft-moaning river of them, and the witch the last of them. They evaporated with the day, but she grew more distinct, and he almost had her as she turned down under the mountain. Too late: when he reached the door it was shut against him, she had gone down to hell with her spoil. He lay (his spirit lay) on the cold rock face, sobbing amid the fallen leaves with weariness and loss.

So there were those, like himself, called out by the Holy Spert; and there were others who were called out by the Devil's fiddle. The feud between them went far back, he would learn, deep and bitter as the feuds his grandpap told stories of, the feuds that arose in the Cumberlands after the War had passed through (only one war was the War in his grandpap's stories), dividing counties and clans, never entirely ended, smoldering like slate-dump fires to that day.

What's yours is mine, she had said: and in the worst year of Hoover's dearth the chestnuts died—not only on Hogback but all through the timberland, not a one left living, dead in a single season, dead as at a stroke. Floyd and his father felled the dead chestnut above their cornpatch and burned her huge corpse over the sterile clay, along with the witchbroom and the brush that alone flourished there. The ashes fed the earth, and they got a good crop of corn that year at least; after that Floyd's old man lost interest in farming, spent his time drinking whiskey and staring into the littered crick fouled with black sump from Number Two. When Assistance started, Floyd and his wife and child walked into Bondieu to get theirs.

Why they should want to harm the world he didn't know, any more than he knew why he and not another should have been chosen to give them battle; why they did harm that could bring no good to them, why they took the corn laid by in the earth to grow, took the starting farrow from the sow's belly, carried them off under the earth, though it meant no one could have them.

Like the great devil Hoover, who had brought ruin on the country, only to be turned out in disgrace himself: you wondered why.

He would come to think that their old enmity was likely just a part of nature, like the enmity fixed between owls and crows, or between the red squirrel and the gray; it might even be a part of what kept the world foursquare as it was, like the opposition of fire and water, or male and female: unless their two kinds did battle over what would grow and what would not, then nothing at all would grow.

So that would be all right, a thing in nature, and no fault of his or theirs.

But if it was not they who were sucking away the world's life, draining its goodness like a milk-snake sucking a goat's udder in the midnight, then who was it? Who? He stood with his wife and child in the giveaway lines to get the gray lard and meal, gray giveaway cotton sweaters, gray surplus of a failing world: and in the anxious faces of the folk on the lines, the hopeless hope with which they jostled each other toward the trucks, eyes fixed on the cans of meat and colorless syrup, was the same hunger he had seen in the night faces along the cove.

The world wasted, grew old; the pillars of it crumbled, like the pillars of coal left standing in the mines to hold up the hollowed hills. The money times came back to the Cumberlands with the war and after, and men fell on the ravished mountains again, and pulled out the coal—only not with pick and shovel any longer but with giant duck-bill loaders that chewed through the seam swallowing coal by the ton and spewing it straight into the gondolas to be carried into the sun. Nor was that enough to fill orders, and a thousand dog-hole mines were pushed into the mountains' backsides, the coal heaved into trucks, the trucks dumped into traincars at a thousand blackened ramps. Floyd worked the narrow gullet of a truck mine until his blacklung got so bad he couldn't do the job. He made his money, he bought his television and his refrigerator.

But they only hastened the coming-on of the world's end with their money-getting. Floyd was unsurprised when Good Luck closed Number Two for good, unable to savage it further. The same end would come to the others, even to Big Black Mountain in the end.

They had ripped out the womb of the hills; they took away too much, took away the unripe with the ripe, leaving no mother in which more could grow; they would end by leaving the mountains barren.

Nor was it only beauty and worth that were lost from the world. Floyd's father had understood the body of the year, in what part of it to plant, in what part of it to cut brush: head, arms, legs. Time's body. He'd known in what age of the moon to rive the boards for a cabin roof so they wouldn't curl; he could make a dulcimore, and play on it music of the old country, *Scotland* and *Barbrie Allen.* He who killed himself drinking busthead whiskey knew the secret of making methiglum, the old honey wine. He had learned those things from *his* father and his father's father, and then forgotten them. Now no one knew anything useful, nothing but how to get on the Well Far, and cling there: like Floyd Shaftoe himself.

He wasn't ashamed to draw. A man can look well on the outside, and have no health in him. Floyd had no Union pension—he was an old yeller dog, having had no warrant from the Holy Spert to take the Union obligation. When he adopted his granddaughter (traveling to the county seat for the first time in his life to sign the papers) a little more in food and money came in: enough. After his corn patch had been hoed twice in spring and laid by, Floyd spent most days in his chair, Bible on his lap and the television on, the same antic gray miniature life issuing from it as came through the Oliphants' television.

The world grew old, that's all; the engine of it worn out with time, like a refrigerator no longer able to keep things cold, running slower and slower, no good, throw it in the crick to rust. It had not ever been meant to last: like a snake's skin periodically shed, like a new car built to fall apart.

Floyd walked in a world that wanted to die: coruscating with dull fires, washed in filthy rain. And yet just as certainly there lay within this world a new world wanting to be born; he could feel it beneath his feet, see it before him as the new moon can be seen held within the old moon's arms. He had come to the end of his Bible, the last pages, and he knew.

How long till then? Floyd had worked out an arithmetic of his own for predicting the time, calculations using the minute red numbers that preceded the significant verses in his Bible. He put it at thirty years, more or less.

The world was slipping into its passage time, the time of signs and wonders. There was blood on the moon; monsters were bred out of the dying world as maggots are bred out of the guts of a dead dog, crawdads out of spring mud. Up on Hogback, down along the cove, Floyd had encountered beings of the promised fire, and had questioned them. Was he to live to see it? If they knew, they would not tell him; or when they spoke he could not understand them. It made no never mind. He had done all that was asked of him, and would do all that remained for him to do; and he was content to wait in silence.

11

―――――

ay is Mary's month; in Kentucky the roses bloom then, which are hers (poured from her apron upon Indian saints in Mexico, upon kneeling children in the Pyrenees; odor of roses, come to the bedsides of dying nuns in China and in Spain; roses pink as bubble-gum bordering every gold-edged blue-and-white holy card with her picture on it, crowned in stars, standing on the moon). Pierce's father Axel claimed a Special Devotion to the Virgin, and though Pierce could not do that, neither could he extract her from the springing grasses and the heavy lilacs, nor from his own stifling feelings, the Seven Joyful Mysteries.

The massy tea-rose bushes (var. Floribunda) that ranged down from the house were unkempt, more leaf and thorn than blossom, but still able to fill the air for weeks and draw ecstatic bumblebees from far away. They had reminded Opal of the gardens of home, real gardens with annual borders and tended beds, and she had worked hard over these rangy cascades to civilize them again; Winnie too, no gardener, was reminded of the life lived elsewhere, of English gardens and Westchester. And Father Midnight (who, however eternal a fixture of this place he seemed to the Oliphants to be, was himself from somewhere else) saw in the wide lawn and its roses the heartfilling ceremonies and outdoor pageantry he had participated in back in temperate Cincinnati where he had studied for the priesthood: the children in white and lace, the sodalities with their gonfalons. How wonderful it would be (he murmured to Winnie and Sam on a spring

Sunday afternoon) if Mary's month could be celebrated here, with a procession, a benediction, a rosary.

(Once Pierce had had among his souvenirs another photograph that Bird made, of himself assisting at this ceremony: large-eyed, long-necked, his own hair now shorn into Joe Boyd's fashion, in his surplice and cassock, and burdened with an immense cross surmounted by its writhen corpus of brassy gold; the day empty of color but the grasses aflame, white with sun, sun that Pierce squints his eyes against. Sun-whitened almost into nonexistence in the background, the pretty altar and his cousins in their Communion dresses: their white rosaries are drops of unfocused fire. There are Father Midnight's elbow and heel too. They only did it the once.)

On a night of May, on that night maybe, Pierce had a dream: that he and all his cousins, his mother and Sam, had died, and been consigned to Purgatory. He dreamed no death and no judgment, only the lot of them together finding themselves there. Purgatory was a burnt-over hillside under a night sky, burnt blackness and shriven trees, the ash still warm under foot. They were alone there; this was their private place, or the other sinners were maybe there but hidden in other hollers. Pierce walked beside Bird; up ahead the others went, looking side to side, awaiting the onset of the promised punishments. Purgatory was filled with that dread, at once hopeless and apprehensive, that Pierce had known in schoolyards and Little League tryouts and day camps. But he held Bird's hand firmly, determined to be brave. They became aware then of a dull continuous noise, a firestorm roaring, that came from some unimaginable somewhere not far away: and though Pierce knew that this was it, the punishment on its way, he lied to Bird, telling her it was nothing, just probably the big exhaust fan of some nearby diner.

He awoke then.

They ought to get to Bobby, he thought; they ought to, they ought to soon, it might be too late already.

So on a summer morning not long thereafter, the Invisibles gathered early in the kitchen of the big house. With Winnie's help they made sandwiches, spreading slices of Winnie's bread with peanut butter and marshmallow paste; they put milk in empty soda bottles, and corked the bottles with twists of wax paper and rubber bands. They cut carrot sticks, and for these they carried salt in another twist of wax paper. They filled up their bags with Fig Newtons, waffled sugar wafers, Saltines, and raisins in miniature boxes (Joe Boyd knew how to blow on such a box when it was empty to make an impressive hoot, but Joe Boyd wasn't coming).

Then they all swore fidelity (once again) to one another, and after Pierce and Hildy had chosen walking sticks and Warren had been shamed into leaving his guns behind, they set out and down the drive toward the highway; and at the bridge they crossed the crick, and started upward on the crumbling asphalt road into the summer.

It was a lot longer walking than it had been driving in Sam's car. They stopped often to rest, to pick wild strawberries and to argue over whether it was time to eat the lunch they had brought; they picked alder branches to swipe the deerflies from their heads.

"Warren! Those berries aren't ripe."

"They're red," Warren said.

"They're *black*berries. When they're red, they aren't ripe."

Warren looked down at his handful.

"When blackberries are red, they're green," said Pierce, and they laughed and pondered this and said it more times as they went up.

They had passed this crossroads before: they all remembered the little store that stood in the crotch of the road, but they couldn't agree on which branch of the road they had taken from here up to Hog-back. They were already much farther from home than they had ever gone before.

"Go in," Pierce said to Hildy, "and ask inside."

"You go in."

"Warren!" Pierce said. "Go in and ask which way to Hogback."

Warren, unafraid, went up to the porch, whose roof seemed to cringe under the sun's beating. This must be a store: a sign in the shape of a huge bottle cap was fixed to the wall, weeping rust at the nailholes, and the array of things on the porch and in the grassless yard could not have come to be there by chance, they must be for sale. But a yellow dog came out from under the porch to bare its teeth at Warren, growling protectively, and a store dog wouldn't do that.

Warren ignored the dog, making an automatic circle around it and climbing the porch stairs. He looked in at the tattered screen door. For some time the others watched and waited as Warren talked to whoever was within, while the dog sniffed him and Warren sidled away. Then he came back.

"What'd they say?"

"I couldn't understand their English," Warren said. But it seemed they had pointed up the left-hand way, and that was the way they all agreed they sort of remembered, and so they went leftward and up.

"Come on, Warren."

"Do dogs think they're naked?" Warren asked thoughtfully from the rear. "Or do they think they're dressed?"

They took sides on this question and argued it closely as they went up; for the time that it occupied them they didn't need to think about what exactly they were doing, nor how far from home they were getting.

How anyway was Bobby supposed to be a Catholic up here alone? How was she supposed to receive the sacraments, the others that ought to follow on the purloined one they had talked her into accepting? Pierce imagined Father Midnight in his old black Studebaker climbing this road, the Host hidden under his coat, as in the stories Sister Mary Philomel loved to tell, about priests behind the Iron Curtain. The purple stole quickly slipped over his shoulders, Bobby kneeling secretly out behind the corn-crib to receive. A hot flush of shame ran up Pierce's neck at the nunnish melodrama of it, at his own complicity in it, not now ever to be withdrawn either.

"Maybe she'll run away again," Bird said. "Maybe come live with us."

That was a story from a different book. There was another too Pierce could think of, looking into the green darkness of the pines and the holler: he and Bobby escaped together, he following her, her woodcraft and daring supplying his lack, his smarts and reasonableness hers. He could almost see their fleeing forms, hand in hand down through the clearings of the woods where sunlight fell.

They had begun to hear a constant noise from no locatable source, lower-pitched and not so various as the noise of the noontide all around. Then where the road widened for a moment and ran flat through thin woods they stopped—Pierce first, who saw it first, then Hildy behind him, then Bird—to study something inexplicable.

"Look. What happened?"

A boulder taller than Pierce stood in the woods right by the road.

It was caked in clay, like a stone troweled out of a garden plot, clay which the day had dried to pale buff on its top but which was still damp beneath in shadow. Behind it, leading a long way up the mountain out of sight, ran the path it had followed as it came down: shattered aspens and firs, crushed stone and gouged earth, a big rip down through the woods, or a long rough zipper unzipped.

What on earth. The four of them stood puzzling, then each in turn drew the same conclusion, that if by earthquake or some other agency this kingsize rock had been rooted out and thrown down the mountain, just hours ago maybe probably, then any minute another just as big might follow, and might not stop before it reached the road they walked along. What anyway was that weird noise.

They went on warily. They seemed to have ascended into a space of strange earth, unpredictable; there was a smell of raw dirt in the air. The road turned sharply upward again, crossing a tumbling crick over a bridge of cracked concrete and then climbing up beside it. The crick was brown as milky coffee, and choked with foreign stone.

The little cluster of cabins and their outhouses under the mountain appeared; the road, clinging to the spur, had brought them around to it. Hogback. The noise they had been listening to was more distinct now, and was clearly engines, big ones, the backing and attacking of an earthmover, more than one probably; and it came from up above.

"Maybe somebody building something," Warren said. "Like a school or something."

They left the main road at the turn upward, they all remembered, the last moment Sam could have turned back toward Bondieu with Bobby and hadn't, and after a sharp bend, and another bend, knowing now they were very close and drawing themselves together, they arrived, somehow suddenly.

"That's her bridge."

But across the bridge was not the same. The height of dark mountain that had stood over Shaftoe's place had collapsed, or been shattered. Pieces of it lay scattered over the sloping clearing. The green corn had been mown by tumbling stones.

"Her house got wrecked!" Warren whispered in horror.

A jagged bone of earth as big as Sam's Nash had come down the mountain on a tide of clay and stones, parting the half-grown trees of

the slope and laying them down like hair; it sat now in the bathroom
Floyd Shaftoe had added to his cabin, jammed deep in the cellar-
hole. The tarpapered roof had been lifted half off like a tipped hat, the
tub, the commode and the sink pushed out the split seam of the
house into the littered yard. A roll of toilet paper had rolled away
from the house toward the crick, leaving a zigzag white path behind
—they all noticed that.

When they had stood staring a long minute, Bird called out:
"Bobby!"

But just as she let out the name, unable to recall it (clapping her
hand too late over her mouth), Floyd Shaftoe pushed open the slack
screen door of the house and came out to stand on his canted porch.
He wore no shirt, and the children could see running over the flinty
muscle of his chest a map of white welts, scars of a long-ago rock-fall
underground. He looked at the children for a while without expression, and then went back inside.

The Invisibles looked at each other sidelong, each waiting for
another to say Oh let's forget it and go quick: but no one did. And
Bobby came banging out of the house flinging a quick stream of
invective behind her the children couldn't decipher.

She was dashing across the yard toward the bridge and the Oliphants when Floyd called to her from the house, and she stopped,
outraged by whatever she heard, and shouted back; then she stood
straight, and walked deliberately to the bridge.

"Y'all come over."

By now the Invisible College was a tight knot on the roadside,
Hildy holding Pierce's and Bird's hands, Warren behind Bird.

"*You* come over," Hildy called. "We'll stay here."

Bobby looked toward them puzzled. She seemed to be a similar
but different person from the one they had hidden in their house:
taller and stringier and duller-eyed, but more than that: at home,
usual, instead of extraordinary. "Well what'd y'all come for?"

They had no simple single answer to that, and said nothing.

"I don't think your grandfather wanted us to come over," Hildy
called.

"He says he's agoin for his gun," Bobby said sarcastically. "I don't
pay him no never mind."

"Well," Hildy said in a goodbye tone.

"No come on," Pierce said. "We said we would." He probably doesn't even *have* a gun, he thought, and it was crazy to threaten kids with one, irrational, who would.

"We can only stay a little while," Hildy called, not having actually got there yet. Her sneakers as she crossed seemed not to touch the boards of the bridge. A lot later on, Hildy would sometimes dream of crossing such a little bridge, under the impression that there was someone on the other side who needed her, but suspecting that once she was across, things would not be as she thought them—knowing absolutely with a sudden starting horror that things would be very very different on the other side—and would wake then, and for a moment know that all her life she had dreamed this dream again and again, only to forget it each time: and even then she would not know from where it had come.

"He done burned all them things you give me," Bobby said to her when she was across. "All them pitchers."

"They weren't his!" Hildy said, outraged by the unfairness.

"Said he smelt the Devil onm," Bobby said mildly. "Look," she said. She pointed behind her to the wreckage of her house, as though they might not have noticed. "Know who done that? Devil done it."

The day seemed to have darkened around Pierce, a strange hooded dusty dimness fallen over the sun.

"Got his mark on it," Bobby said. "You want to see?"

"I want to see," Warren said.

"Warren," Hildy said. "You stay."

Bobby pulled Pierce by the hand, and the others after him, to where they could look in at the rock squatting in a nest of shattered floorboards.

"See?" she said.

Someone—Floyd probably—had outlined with a burnt stick a ridgy place in the rock, to bring out its resemblance to a knuckly, three-clawed reptilian hand. It was striking without being for a second convincing.

"Wow," said Warren. "A claw."

"But it's make-believe," said Pierce. The shudder of repugnance that covered him was because someone had done this, had pretended it, had wanted it to be unnatural: make-believe for real. "Just because it's a lumpy rock."

"Devil thowed it at my grandpap account of what he knows," Bobby said. Then she shrugged one shoulder: "What *he* says. Missed him though."

"Nobody threw it," Pierce said. "It came from up there, from whatever they're building."

"Ain't buildn nothn," Bobby said. "Tearn down the mountain."

Then Bobby shrieked: the sheet hung in the rent of the wall was snatched aside, and Floyd Shaftoe stood looking at them, the whites of his eyes unnaturally huge and his pupils black.

"Let's *run!*" Bobby said, and set off away from the yard toward the woods. Pierce ran after her to stop her, having glimpsed in her face that she was almost certainly pretending, inciting their alarm for the fun of it; and Bird hurtled after him in genuine alarm, and Warren after her; Hildy last, embarrassed and afraid.

Bobby ran fast, her skinny legs scissoring rapidly; once she lost a shoe, a grownup's worn slip-on shoe too big for her, and stopped to retrieve it without missing more than a step. She led them up a track through the woods (Hildy calling from behind that they had to go home now, stop a sec) and over a hump of hill to an outcropping shelf of slate.

Panting, pleased with herself, she turned to them coming up behind. "Y'all's slow runners," she said.

"Well you didn't *have* to *run,*" Pierce said, his eyes burning with sweat or tears. "Why did you run?"

"Lookit," she said to him from up above on the outcrop. "Cmere."

He climbed up to where she stood. Warren had stumbled on the path and skinned his knee, and his sisters were comforting him. Warren he doesn't have a gun, it's illegal, don't cry or he'll hear you. Pierce looked where Bobby pointed.

He could see all the way up the holler toward the mountain top, through the flattened trees and the standing ones. There was the source of the noise and the stones and the dirt: big yellow cats, he could see one, were cutting a shelf of earth out of the mountain. He saw one backing up, could distinguish its gray smoke from the orange dust it raised. The matter of the mountain was being heaved off the shelf they were cutting, smashing the trees and growth beneath and covering the remainder with thick clay like butterscotch icing dripping down a cake's sides. Above the shelf a straight wall of exposed mountain rose.

"Strippn," Bobby said.

Like eating an ice-cream cone: push a trail along with your tongue at the perimeter of the cone, lick up the excess, while on the other side the melting blob slips over onto the cone and your fingers. Tongue comes around and cleans up. Pierce could see the dump-trucks that followed after the cats to be loaded with the coal they uncovered: heavy ribbed trucks, just like the one Warren had used to play with daylong in his own pit. Gradually the mountain would be worn away.

"The Enda Days is acomin," Bobby said in a voice not hers.

"What," Pierce said.

"Sure. My grandpa knows. Holy Sperta God tole him." She clutched her bony knees where she sat on the slate. "That's why the Devil flang that rock at us. So he don't tell the world."

"That's stupid," Pierce said desperately. "Cut it out."

"All the dead hereabouts gone break open ther graves and come on out." She gauged his response. "Not skullitons," she said. "Gone put on ther flesh."

"*Pierce.*" Hildy had had enough; the calm authority of hysteria in her voice made Pierce jump.

"My maw's maw," Bobby said. "My grandpap's maw. Ther maw too."

"We have to *go*," Hildy said. "Warren is *hurt.*"

"They's a witch lived up Hogback onct," Bobby said. "Devil tore out her house too." She clambered higher up the stones above Pierce. "Ain't gone get us, though, cause we're movn away."

"No, where," Pierce said, a sudden awful hollow opening in his heart.

"Deetroit," Bobby said. "Can't get us there."

"No," Pierce said.

"Find my mawn paw."

"No."

She stood on tiptoe on the rock ledge, and looked down the trail toward the house. "Whoops, he's acomn," she cried in mock terror. "Y'all better run."

Hildy drew Warren to his feet and grasped him, her eyes round and her mouth set in an awful bravery. "Wait," Pierce whispered, not to Hildy, not to Bobby.

"Don't go to Detroit," Bird said. "We want you to stay."

"Cain't live here," Bobby said simply. A sudden jolting bark sounded from up on the mountain, a horn of great power sounding repeatedly. Pierce realized that for some time the grinding of the cats and the trucks had ceased. Bobby danced down the outcrop to the path and took Bird's hand. "Come on," she said, and tugged Bird after her farther into the woods.

"Wait." Pierce clambered down after her. "Wait."

"Don't you hear the sigh reen?" Bobby called back to him. "Y'all's got *five minutes*."

The horn drove them along behind her down the faint trail. Where amid piles of other rubbish an old refrigerator lay fallen head-long down the slope (thrown there long ago, the refrigerator's white was stained with rust) she stopped, pointed to where the path ran down. "Git along," she said. "Down there's the road."

Now Bird was crying too, not from fear but from urgency, wring-ing her hands in a way Pierce had read of people doing and not been able to picture. "Don't go away, don't," she wept.

The siren ceased, the world for a second stopped too.

"Gwan, git," Bobby said, arms crossed against her colorless shirt.

"Come with us!" Pierce cried, knowing suddenly what the only possible solution to this was. "Run away! Come with us now!"

Bobby turned from the path and sat down in the shelter of the old refrigerator. Hildy and Warren had gone on ahead, hurrying, nearly out of sight.

"Don't stay with him," Pierce said. "Stay with us. We'll protect you. Their Dad will."

"Cain't," she said. She withdrew her gaze from Pierce, as though he had gone on already.

"It's not *true*," he called to her retreating spirit. "It's *not*!"

Bird was tugging at his shirt, weeping. Bobby closed her eyes and put her fingers in her ears.

"*Pierce!*"

He had to turn away then, with Bird, and hurry stumbling away with the others, the Invisible College in full retreat along a path that was not likely to lead anywhere but farther into the woods for good. The horn still sounding in his ears was his own heart beating, taking huge thudding turns.

"Will she be all right? Will she?" Bird wept.

The dynamite set off at the strip mine wasn't like movie explosions, mild, thunder-rumbling. It was less like a noise than like something huge that rushed with impossible speed down through the woods to whack them in the back. And then through the trees there came a dry rain of fragments pattering and dust whispering, coating the leaves and the path downward and the Invisible College too.

The road away appeared through the brush and the rubbish.

"We won't tell," Hildy said fervently, eyes on the road below. "Don't any of you ever tell."

"We won't," Bird said.

"We won't."

"Just don't," Hildy said. "Not ever ever."

12

he Sun is nine million miles from earth; it burns with an unquenchable nuclear heat, consuming its own atoms, each one a bonfire; it will burn for æons, it will become a nova or a red giant or a white dwarf in a billion years or two or ten: but it won't go out like a candle, it won't refuse to shine. She did not need to believe the things she believed; he could show her how to drop it, forget it, return into the world from it. Dinosaurs. Didn't she know there had been dinosaurs once, their bones are in museums, they lived for a million, ten million years on earth, hundreds of times longer than human beings have even been alive. When the Bible says "six days," they don't mean days, they mean ages of earth, Pleistocene, Pliocene, Eocene. Why even *have* all those years, countless years, before man if the world was just going to end? Why? Why would God be so dumb?

He sat on the steps of the breezeway thinking, thinking, for hours together, his hands and his mouth in unconscious motion, convincing Bobby that the story she thought was happening had no authority whatever to happen. The summer sky was hooded with dust, the air not refreshing but ashy, and a red sun, ghastly, going down for the last time.

"Fire somewhere," Sam at the screen door behind him said. "Criminal."

What could he do? It was as though she were going off, not to Deetroit, but into the darkness of the story's conclusion she had told, into the night of the world's end and the dead rising, whose weather Pierce sensed gathering around him as he plotted desperately to keep her from it. That the Invisibles could ever have saved her, ever have rescued her as Bird had last summer been daily rescued from the play-bonds and play-prisons that held her—Pierce knew it had only been a game, a game's dangerous and thrilling extension into somewhere beyond pretend but still a game, they were all only kids and not knights really: and yet it was *as though* it weren't a game but a true story he was caught within, a story in which he had failed to do what the hero was supposed to do, had lost his sword and his map, had no real resources after all, did not know what a hero would know, how to make the sky lighten, the dreadful magic lift.

How many nights and days did he live within the spell? He couldn't think how to ask Sam's help or even Winnie's: to ask his mother's help would have meant confessing to her how afraid he was, and thus running the risk of breaking the bond between them—the risk of bringing to her an insoluble problem that would shatter her rest, force her to fruitless action, and cost him her unqualified love.

So he turned, finally, to the one person who was outside the story and yet all unawares inside it too: he went in shame and hopeless hope to ask his President what he should do.

"So what the heck," Joe Boyd said. "She should go. Detroit's better than here."

"But it's really important she not go. Really important."

Joe Boyd looked away from the television, where with careful gravity Mr. Wizard was at work, transforming one thing into another, while his young friend watched. "Why?" he asked.

Pierce would not answer that; could not answer when he asked it of himself. In Mr. Wizard's jar a crystal grew within the fluid, many-sided, brilliant. "Just what if it was," Pierce said. "Really important."

Joe Boyd thought. "Well it's not *her* that's going. It's *him*. She's just a little kid. She doesn't have a say. So you have to keep him from going."

"How?"

That took more thought. Joe Boyd seemed to slip away entirely for a time into Mr. Wizard's garage, where now from his pocket the wizard drew gemstones. "Pay him," Joe Boyd said at last.

"What?"

"Pay him to stay. Make it worth it to him, to stay."

"But pay him what? I don't have anything to pay him with."

"It wouldn't have to be much," Joe Boyd said. "Just enough to make him think there's more. To think there's more here. Then he'll stay around."

Pierce sat confounded for a long time, waiting for more, his waiting growing increasingly burdensome to his cousin, who turned at last and asked why he had to hang around.

Just enough to make him think there's more. Drawing precious gemstones from his pocket: Look. More where this came from. In the basement he stood before the soft-roaring furnace, and with the blackened crook he opened its door. Its voice grew louder; he gazed afraid and resolute into the interior, where blue flames skittered over the coruscating lava; he swallowed its bitter breath. Into its white-hot heart he plunged the tongs (abstracted from the never-used set of fire tools beside the fireplace above) and with them grasped the centermost coal and drew it out.

Quickly, with Sam's tools and vise and with the force of his need and his knowledge, he tormented the coal until it had to give up the diamond it somehow was: there, on the charred workbench, the tiny living stone hatched from the exhausted cinder, refracting its first gasp of light.

No it was high summer and the furnace of course was cold; what he did was to go upstairs to Sam's room when Sam was far away (delivering a baby, or maybe bringing a dead man back to life as he had done once by striking him in the heart with all his might) and take from Sam's drawer the little box containing Opal's diamond ring. With Sam's needle-nose pliers he pulled away the tiny golden claws that grasped the stone, and when it was loose he shook it into his palm: smaller there than it had appeared to be in Opal's ring, and seeming likely to roll away, get lost, avoid its fate.

He put the stone into a velvet pouch no into the plastic box from which Sam had taken the ampoule of penicillin he'd injected into Pierce. Alone he went back up the road to Hogback, and when he stood in the dirt of the yard he called out to Floyd Shaftoe no to Bobby.

Show this to your father. Tell him I found it in the old Good Luck mine. Tell him that deep down in the mine, I'll tell him where, there's coal that's become diamonds. Tell him I won't tell anyone else. He won't want to go away to Detroit.

She took it no he went with her into the cabin, where Floyd shirtless and shoeless lay on the bed, the long scars white over his torso. He looked into the box that Bobby held solemnly up to him and saw the shy glowing stone within: beckoned, awed, fooled.

Or no he took the road not up to Hogback but the other way, toward Good Luck Number Two. He followed the railroad tracks along the Little No Name, through the town of Good Luck where no one lived and where the gray cabins in their rows watched him go by, and past the Good Luck school whose inside he would never know and the Good Luck hospital likewise from which Mousie said they used to throw out like cut-off arms and feet and such into the crick where you'd see them floatn.

Strike up the wooded mountainside, climb the wall of shale above which the tipple could be seen (he had seen it, once, from Sam's Nash) and up to the mouth of the mine itself, Good Luck Number Two, an arch riven into the mountain, into which the train-tracks disappeared. He had flashlight and paper and pencil, and in his pack the plastic box with Opal's stone. He began at the entrance, marking on his paper the arch of it; then he began a dotted line, mimic of his own progress in and downward.

The flashlight, topped up with Evereadies that projected an unfailing cone of light into the darkness, showed him the squat shapes of miner's cars, like placid bears asleep; the posts and beams of the low roof; the naked electric wires that Sam deplored running close overhead, but juiceless now maybe probably. At every broad room, corridors crossed, and after choosing one Pierce marked the turning on his map. And when he had turned downward and then downward again into darkness deep enough to feel and taste, where the tracks ran out, where the miners had quit forever and their picks and shovels lay abandoned, he took out the plastic box, and from it the jewel; and he placed it naked on the shelf of coal. X marks the spot.

Time to turn back then, follow the map outward, mail the map to Floyd Shaftoe no carry it to him no lose it on his farm. No.

No. Pierce on a white afternoon came up the dusty road to Good Luck Number Two, feeling his plan rapidly evanescing but willing belief in it anyway, and with the reproachful stone in his pocket. A voice that since he had come down from Bobby's place on Hogback had gone on talking to him unceasingly and so loudly he could hardly hear anything else was, if not done talking, growing at least distant and intermittent.

He should have known it. He had known it, only he had not been able to think of what to do with the knowledge, and so had refused to recognize it: The mine, the real mine, wasn't a mouth cut into the wooded mountain's face but a large and daunting industrial installation, the more daunting for being on the way to ruin. There was Absolutely No Trespassing, and violators would be prosecuted to the full extent of the law.

Well that's great, Pierce said in Winnie's voice, just great. The chainlink fence across the road stopped him a long way from the mine entrance, which was itself housed in a complex building of corrugated steel and filthy windows. A place to have an accident in, fall down, stab yourself on a rusty spike, get lockjaw. Tall structures —breakers, washers, sorters—stood up on skinny rusty legs over the endless slate dump. On the tallest of them the name Good Luck was painted, and (scrubbed almost to invisibility in the corrosive air) the company's sign, a hand of four aces neatly displayed. Good luck.

Even then he thought it was possible that if he dared climb the fence, if he dared to get to the mine and break a window and scramble in, if he could get down inside (he remembered now how on television the miners had gone down an open elevator into the depths), if he could do all that just by the strength of his needing to, then it might be that his plan could still be brought off; he might by his effort make this obdurate place the nexus of his desires. But he knew he wouldn't do it.

It was fiercely hot in the roadway, summer had already lost its sweet newness, it was an alien planet too hot for life. Why shouldn't she go to Detroit anyway.

Why shouldn't she if she wants. It's only a city.

Wake up, he thought, you dope.

He felt himself awaken, at his own command or simultaneously with it; he felt himself shed, ashamed, a game he had been playing alone, as though he had been caught at it by a mocking grownup, himself. But even as he came to, jamming his hands into his pockets and looking around himself, he went on sleepwalking away as well; and he didn't know that. It was as though, while he stood at Good

Luck's fence looking within, Pierce Moffett, who had been one up till then, came invisibly, undetectably, in two: one part of him passing into an underground river like sleep, where for years it would remain; and another part left alive aboveground, grown-up and dry-eyed, where wishes did not come true, where he did not know how plans were made, or deeds done. Not until earth at length shifted in its course, and the dark river broke from its bed, would the lost boy come forth to stand before Pierce, and claim his place: the hidden at length patent, and the inside out.

Sam soon found Opal's diamond missing, and by a combination of detective work and shrewd interrogation, concluded that Pierce had taken it. Pierce denied it.

"It's all right," Sam said, in a manner not very mollifying. "It's all right. I just want to know why. Why would you do such a thing?"

"I didn't."

"Oh come *on*."

"I didn't!"

But then he was caught virtually in the act of smuggling the tiny stone back into the ring in the box in Sam's sock drawer, and was made to confess that he had taken it; still he would not say why. Furious, baffled, at the end of his invention, Sam set Pierce to write an essay on Why I Should Not Tell Lies and to read it out to the family. And he did it, his cheeks burning with shame not so much for himself as for Winnie, who sat stricken and impotent on the red plastic club chair. The reasons he gave in his paper were all practical ones, and turned on the bad effects that being caught out in his lying had, for himself above all, his present humiliation being a good example. But he never explained.

In that summer of 1953 Sister Mary Philomel was diagnosed as having cancer of the stomach. The surgeon Sam consulted thought it was not too far gone to be operable (though she had ignored it long, and only Offered Up the pain), but Sister Mary Philomel asked for special permission to see what prayer could do, and Sister Mary Eglantine reluctantly agreed.

It was daily Communion that Sister Mary Philomel afterward believed to have been the efficacious thing. She had inquired of Father Midnight how long, exactly, the little cutout of paste remained God Himself within her stomach, and Father Midnight said that the question didn't really have an answer, though he had read speculations that after twenty minutes or so the Host had dissolved in gastric juices, and therefore God might be supposed to be within (in that special way) for at least that long; and so every morning Sister Mary Philomel—though she knew, and Sam pointed out, that pious people had died of her condition despite it—applied to the lump of cold dark pain within her the warm and brilliant poultice of Divinity, and since the two (it seemed obvious to her) could not coexist, the One gradually wore away the other as Sister Mary Philomel breathed in patience and watched the clock. In a few months it was gone.

"Well it happens," Sam said. "Ask any doctor, and if he's honest he'll tell you he's seen a miracle or two. The only thing is they seem to happen about randomly, to people who pray and people who don't, to people who believe God'll help and people who don't believe in God at all. There's no telling."

Sometime in that summer Warren began to be wakened by nightmares, or by nightmarish notions anyway, and then to be unable to return to sleep; finally to be unable to go to sleep at all without lights burning and Hildy or Winnie within calling distance. It took a long time to get from the stolid private boy what it was he feared; but at length and in fragments it came out, how it was Jesus he was afraid of: how Sister Mary Philomel had explained to him that any time of day, or any middle of night, Jesus might come to him, to take his hand and lead him away so that Warren could be with Him forever in heaven: and so (Sister Mary Philomel had no doubt concluded) Warren ought to say his prayers before he slept—just in case.

So Warren didn't want to sleep at all, in case Jesus did take it into His head to come for him, because Warren didn't want to go.

Standing shrieking on his bed in the middle of the night at a streak of watery moonlight or a gesturing curtain: not ready to go.

Sam talked to him. Took him into his room and lay on the bed with him, where the most important conversations were held, where Bird had learned there was no Santa Claus. No Jesus is not going to just show up and take you away with him. Sister's talking about dying, and you're not going to just die, son. If Jesus is ready to take you to heaven, then you're going to get real sick first, and I'll find out about it, and find out what you're sick with . . .

Like Bobby.

Like Bobby, and we'll do everything we can to get you better. And we'll keep you here with us. Okay?

Okay.

But the terrors didn't go away so easily. The others never hinted that they might not be all Sister's fault, that the nighttime meditations on Last Things with Bobby Shaftoe in the heater's glow might have contributed; instead, they suggested that they themselves might have been bent by other pronouncements of Sister's, which they had stored up for just such a moment as this and now retailed to their parents, watching Sam's and Winnie's faces for signs of dismay, incredulity and annoyance. Sister said that on Christmas Eve baby Jesus goes all around the mountains ringing a little bell. And that you can see his footprints in the snow. Sister said that Negro people have the mark of Cain on them; how does she know that?

"Good grief," said Sam. "Oh lordy."

At length he went down the hill to talk to Sister, and came home shaking his head, amused and indignant at once in a way that reminded Hildy of the way he had used to be when Opal was alive and he had talked more; but he wouldn't tell what he had said to Sister. "That woman," he called her, and the children secretly thrilled to hear him. "That woman."

New arrangements were made; the children were getting older anyhow, and home school was not going to prepare them sufficiently for the real world, the world beyond these mountains toward which in a vague way Sam still bent his attentions. So Joe Boyd, after a prolonged and delicate contest of wills, was allowed to enter a military academy in Louisville, where he would spend two miserable years before admitting his mistake; Hildy went deeper in rather than farther out, boarding at Queen of the Angels School, an Infantines establishment in Pikeville. Just then Father Midnight's sister returned from wherever she had gone off, and the younger children were given into her care again, one more year, then we'll think.

It would be twenty years before Pierce fell again under the suasion of believers of Sister Mary Philomel's powers. When he did, they would fill him not with boredom or indifference or a leftover guilty impatience to escape, but with an uncanny and nearly unbearable dread, a dread more convincing, in a way, than Sister's insistences had ever been, as convincing as a torturer's truncheon. It was as though his brief encounter with her had been the bee-sting, harmless at the time, that establishes in the secret toils of the immune system the conditions for a later fatal—well, near fatal, next to fatal it seemed to him—allergic reaction.

They never saw Bobby Shaftoe again, though she wasn't taken off to Detroit after all. Not in that year anyway.

After pondering long, Floyd decided to go up the mountain, to the offices of the company that leased from Good Luck, to ask what compensation he was to be given for the loss of his corn patch and his bathroom. In the office he chanced upon a big company man, making an inspection tour; the man heard Floyd out, nodding, and then said he wouldn't give him any compensation, for that would mean admitting that the company had done something it oughtn't by rights to have done: and the company wasn't going to do that. Instead he offered Floyd a job, off the books: night watchman for the site.

Floyd believed that God had never meant the mountain to be used the way the strippers used it, never meant coal to be got so; he thought that those who took it would not profit by it. He told the company man he would consider his offer.

Not for some time then had Floyd been called out in the night, though he did not believe he had heard that call for the last time; he thought he might have a part to play yet, in the Enda Days, though what it would be he could not guess. Once he had supposed that, come the final conflict, his kind and those with whom they had done battle for the world's health would be enrolled under opposing banners, the Beast's, the Lamb's. More often now he thought otherwise: he thought that all the night walkers were but a part of this world, which was to pass away; so when these soiled and tattered heavens were rolled up like a scroll (revealing new heavens behind, fresh as paint) they would none of them be there. They had been among those things that kept this world aworking as it did, they and the Devil too maybe; under the Lamb's rule they would not be needed, the Lamb would put paid to their long feud and together they would turn back into the past forever. They would rest.

He took the job the man offered him. He slept in the day, when the living were up and at work; he spent his nights awake, watching over the great yellow cats asleep beneath the highwall of the open cut. He sat in his little shack beneath a yellow bulb with his Bible in his lap. The silence was deep; those creatures that awake to make sounds in the night had been driven off. Even the night smell of the mountains was changed, from what it had been to plain clay, dry-dusty or wetted and sour.

While he slept through the day, Bobby stayed away; when he went to work at night she returned. Weekends they worked the cornpatch together, wary and girded for conflict. She told him nothing of her life alone; sometimes she claimed she was going to school, at other times mocked him for believing so. When he talked about the Enda Days she listened and said nothing.

What was it she did do, how did she fill her hours, what did she learn, what did she want? What did Floyd do when the strip mine began operating round the clock in shifts, lathing the mountain away nightlong under strings of blue floodlights? What became of him? What became of her? Not even Bird knew, who might have noticed Bobby in the store or on the road; gone, that's all. Over time the Oliphants and Pierce ceased to remember very well what they had done with and to her (all but Bird); sometimes they remembered that once they had taken in a mountain girl while their parents were away, but like everything else, like the dimensions of their house and the buildings of Bondieu and the length of the road that contained them, like the compunctions of their religion and its mysteries, the story shrank with distance, the details grew too small to see, the topography smoothed.

They forgot more than that; they forgot their allegiances too, and their College; Ægypt. They just forgot, as an émigré ruthlessly forgets the Old World from which he came, expunging it by an effort he does not even admit to, so that the New World, which after all holds all his chance for happiness, can have his whole soul.

13

———

n his birthday that year, Pierce was given warm socks and flannel shirts, in readiness for winter, as he had been given similar ones the year before; his birthday coming so close to Christmas, little was made of it, not when Hildy's came the week before his and Warren's the week after, crowding the schedule, too much for Winnie to rise to.

But he was also given, as he had been given the year before, the new Little Enosh, a whole year's daily comic strips collected into a stiff and tart-smelling paperback volume.

Elsewhere, in Brooklyn, in civilization, lucky people were reading Enosh every day, on the subway or at dinner, in two or three different papers. In this place to which Pierce had come, you could only get your Enosh by buying the year-end compilation, in book form, of the daily strips. This year as last year, the compilation was a present from his father—so anyway Winnie said, handing him a package gaily wrapped with suspicious care. It had always been his father who each evening had read Enosh aloud to Pierce out of the paper, or had tried to read it, often laughing so hard he could not, laughing till he cried.

Little Enosh: Lost Among the Worlds. On the book's cover Enosh's little minnow-like spaceship circled the letters of the title, emitting puffs of smoke. He had been Lost Among the Worlds from the beginning, from before the time Pierce had first asked his father what he was laughing at. Whenever he escaped from one planet on his endless journey home, he would always be captured by another, always beautiful at a distance, always the same when he landed there: a little world, a curving horizon, a desert landscape, the eternal dark sky beyond speckled with stars and ringed planets; always a banana-shaped crescent moon, whose changing expression commented on the activities below. There Little Enosh wandered in his goggles and a spacesuit that wrapped him from neck to toe in donut segments, like Tweedledum in his armor or the Michelin Man: innocent, alone, amazed.

Was he a little boy, or only little in comparison to the huge badguys, the Uthras, who thought about nothing but entrapping him, and hauling him before their Queen? The Uthras were distinguished from one another by details of costume and brutish armor, but they all wore black masks not different from their faces, with eyeslits that were the same as their eyes; and when they acted all in common, flying their smooth clamshell starships out from their hiding-places, they finished each other's threatening sentences as they crossed from panel to panel in neat formation.

What was so funny about them, was it only that they meant Little Enosh no good, and that they knew it and he *didn't* know it, and yet always failed to hurt him anyway, usually because he didn't understand they were trying to: turning away at the last moment to pluck a flower and so avoiding the net about to drop on him? *Ah* said one and *Hah!* said the other, but they had missed again. Even funnier was Little Enosh's own condensed outer-space language, unpunctuated and oddly spelt and striking Pierce as inexpressibly witty with its puns and elisions: "Oop tax," said Enosh, as he realized the wicked Uthras had strewn the path where he rode his balloon-tired car: "Owel."

And Enosh's sad plight, that was funniest of all: lost, lost, deep in the dungeons of Rutha, Queen of the Uthras, big ball and chain on his ankle, and a single far star showing in his barred window: home, maybe. "Home," said Enosh, looking out.

What Rutha wanted wasn't anything so wicked, in the end; she only went about in ways even Pierce as a boy could see were all wrong, twisted out of true by her nature and her need. All she wanted was that Enosh admit, or accept, or believe, or pretend, that he was really Rutha's little boy. He couldn't of course, because he wasn't, and the guile of pretending to be was beyond him; even when he was tempted or at least flattered by the things she offered him—caresses, icy jewels, lavish banquets with himself installed in a tall chair and the Uthras rising (one's hand deep in a pie) to toast him—still he never really understood what she wanted of him.

Anyway he already had a mother. *Somewhere in the Realms of Light:* that was what the little rumpled scroll above the panels read, periodically reintroducing Enosh's seeker and savior, Amanda D'Haye. *Where could that boy have got to?* she was always saying in the first panel, as she packed her bag to set out. Behind her, vague and vast, vague because it lacked the heavy black outlining that in comics makes things things, was a realm that was also a palace and also a gigantic doubtful impassive face that watched Amanda depart (one stripey sock always escaping from her stuffed suitcase). Who was he?

Amanda was like her boy, mild and good, and as liable to get stuck herself in the Uthras' clutches as Enosh was. That, in fact, was the invariable pattern, the artist cheerfully willing to enact and draw it again and again with subtle variations: Amanda D'Haye setting out to find Enosh, falling into the plots of Rutha which she is too innocent or simple-minded to perceive, and ending up in such trouble that in the end it is Enosh who must do the rescuing. After which he follows her dutifully toward home; and as Amanda, hands clasped in glee, imagines their imminent reunion in the Realms of Light, Enosh espies another world, pocked with craters, ringed with rings, circled by moons: his starship's track wavers, and a pretty question mark appears above his open face.

Pierce guessed, without admitting to himself that he had guessed, that it was Winnie and not Axel who bought the books of Enosh for him. Axel had not often, even in the beginning, sent much to his son, and had never actually written him a letter, being constitutionally unable to confine his thoughts within a square of white paper: but by that time he had ceased to call as well. Pierce came to suspect that his father had somehow drifted off or gone into hiding somewhere away from him, from where he could not call or write, where perhaps he was forbidden to communicate, or where, amnesiac, he could not remember how.

And he was right, as he would later come to know when after college he moved to New York City, found Axel again, and began to spend time with him. Then he would hear the stories (as Axel restaged them) of his long drunkenness in those years, of his abasement on the Bowery or somewhere like it (where they called him Doc, of course, or was it Professor), stories stark and graphic as a black-and-white movie, as comically sad as Little Enosh lost among the worlds. Axel told him that he had even dreamed in those days, or imagined in his delirium, that one day Pierce would appear, to rescue him; to take his hand (here Axel held out his own hand, a hand of human mercy, a rescuing hand) and lift him up.

"Fatherless," Pierce in Florida said to Winnie, overcome momentarily with self-pity and the consciousness of a hard fate.

"Oh I don't know," Winnie said. "I would have said rich in fathers." But then she lowered her eyes and said: "I know."

He, fatherless; and Bobby too. Axel Moffett, childless. Sam's children, motherless; Sam, wifeless. He remembered the storm of tears, wholly unexpected, that had occurred in him when Winnie called to tell him Sam was dead, tears because he knew suddenly that Sam had suffered a loss that had never been, and could not now ever be, made up to him: a flood of awful fellow-feeling, the first in his life, with those who die.

A few days after that birthday, when he came in from the schoolroom for lunch, Winnie (a little shamefaced, a little amused) said "Guess what?" and gave Pierce a package that had come for him in the mail, from Brooklyn.

A rectangular block of unmistakable heft, wrapped in brown paper pieced out from a grocery bag, tied with grubby twine and addressed in a schoolmarmishly correct yet uncertain Palmer Method script which Pierce recognized instantly (it looked a lot like his own).

"Well open it," Winnie said. Sam looked up from his sandwich. "Go ahead."

A book, of course, a hardback book with a paper jacket, one of that special class of books that had paper jackets but no library plastic covers. A novel, obviously, because of the paper jacket, and because the jacket showed a painting, a painting of an imaginary moment, chosen from the story within.

"Huh," he said, turning the book in his hands, upside down, back to front, as though he had never handled such an object before. "Wow."

Gingerly he opened it. On the empty flyleaf, an inscription in pencil had been crossed out in pen: *For Rex, who will never read it.*

Love, Sandy. The same pen that had crossed this out had written another in another corner: *My dear Son,* and below that *Love, Axel,* as though a long message were missing that should have come between. "Well," he said.

On the next page the title again, and beneath it in small italics one of those little quotations that Pierce had noticed many old books had, like a magician's distracting patter before his trick, more mysterious usually than the book that followed. He read it.

> *One met the Duke 'bout midnight, in a lane behind St. Mark's Church, with the leg of a man over his shoulder; and he howled fearfully; said he was a Wolf, only the difference was, a Wolf's skin is hairy on the outside, his on the inside; bade them take their swords, rip up his flesh, and try.*

He read it again, conscious that time's passing had slowed for him and the light had brightened, and of his mother and Sam watching him in this moment which was his; feeling spoken to, softly and intimately, not quite yet intelligibly, by all the great wide world at once.

"Gee," he said. He closed the book and looked again at the cover picture. Darkness in a city, a high-walled, narrow-laned Old World city; a black tower and a yellow moon; the only other lights a single window in the tower, and the torches of a pursuing crowd far down the twisted street: and the eyes of the one they pursued, yellow crayon-dashes, the lanterns of his eyes.

He showed it to Winnie. "Oh yes," she said.

"Have you read it?" Pierce asked in wonder.

"No," she said. "*He* liked them. There's lots more, I think. If you like that one we can send away for more."

"Huh," Pierce said, still holding the book in both hands before him, still standing in the same spot, as though rooted to it by a transmission of energy, a summoning beam coming from far away, from the future, passing through the transformer of the book into his being and out through his feet, pinning him like the poor guy who grabs the hot wire.

For a long time afterward, he didn't read the book. He kept it on top of his bookcase, with those other select books which held apart the hemispheres of cloudy Earth. He would look at its spine, there among the others (it had a little leaping wolfhound imprint at the base) and imagine what was in it—not the events so much as the paragraphs, full of print, full of meaning. He looked on it as a book which his larger self must read, the self he felt struggling to extrude itself from the strangling husk of his childhood. When at last he did open it, on a night of rainy wind, it was with a reverence and an expectation that would have surprised and abashed its author.

The Werewolf of Prague by Fellowes Kraft.

Like the rest of his *lares* and *penates* (Rockaway seashells, Bear Mountain sheath knife, the books of Enosh) he took the book with him on his later journeys—to school, to college, to the city—and somewhere along the way it had got lost. He supposed he had grieved for it, but there was a lot that got lost and trampled and left behind in those days. Anyway he did not think of it again until, in the musty library of a shuttered house in another state, he pulled it out from a row of similar ones, the author's own copies of his works, and opened it again.

"Yes," Winnie in Florida said to him. "Quite a story."

"Yes." The story that had all along lain ahead of him for him to fall into; the story that (he had come to see) every event had led him toward, beginning with the arrival of that book from Brooklyn, or beginning before that, as far back as anything can begin.

"To end up in the very same town he lived in," Winnie marveled, not for the first time. "Coming upon it, just like that, when you'd read all his books."

"Yes. You remember?"

"Well I don't actually remember you reading them. You read such a lot. But didn't you? You've told me you did."

"I did." He read them all, or all he could get from the State Library; read them one after the other, lived within each for a week or two weeks, and forgot it when the next arrived: each with its little wolfhound imprint at the base of the spine, each with its watercolor painting for a cover, gratifying and unrememberable as dreams.

"I guess that's always been a very nice area," Winnie said. "Where he lived."

"Yes. Nice." Pierce's heart and throat were filled with longing for it, as though he had not seen it in years, when in fact he had only left there yesterday: longing for the summer country he had first come to settle in, which seemed now alienated from him, maybe forever, blasted, and by more than winter.

What had he done to himself, what hurt had he done his heart, that he should think so?

"This woman, I suppose," Winnie said, as though he had spoken aloud, as perhaps he had.

"Yes."

She put her hand on his; but she shook her head too, and made a face, wry or ironic, that he knew.

A day and a half before, Pierce had awakened in darkness after a few hours' purgatorial sleep; had awakened from a dream that, though singularly dreadful, he right away recognized as cognate to a dozen others memory could lay hands on.

He spoke aloud a charm to keep him safe: "*Hypnerotomachia,*" he said. But this time it did no good; he doubted it really ever had, or ever would, for it was a charm of knowledge, and not of comfort, and knowledge was no longer any use to him, knowledge was what had hurt him.

Well by God he would not lie wide-eyed in the dark, as he had the last night and the night before that, listening to his own heart-taps and wishing. No!

So he got up, and dressed in the dark, and went out, and took the path that leads to the road that rises up the mountain; and his new demons collected to go along with him, fastened on him like Peter Pain. Everyman I will go with thee.

Up on the mountainside, he had been told, there was a place you could stand and look into three different states, north, south and east. He would climb to it, he decided. Supposedly a monument stood there too, to a man who in the last century had had a vision at that spot, a vision of—no one had been able to tell him exactly of what: peace, he thought; the unity of all religions; hope.

Salt fluid burned his eyes. He could see the monument vividly with his mind's eye, an obelisk, a cube, a sphere, a tablet to which ivy clings, neglected amid winter foliage. And a foraging deer, who looks up wide-eyed to see him approach.

He studied the earth as he went up, as though searching a loved face for some sign of help: the frosted briars, and the brown milkweed loosing its seed; the lamplit windows of a farm, the lichened stone of its fence. In the driveway a truck, waiting for its driver, breathed white smoke and rumbled patiently. All there, all the same, wasn't it? He acknowledged that it was, and still beautiful, still the same. Only he could not touch it, it was no longer for him.

A long, actually an endless, hour later, he had come no closer to the path up to the monument, if there was a path, or a monument; he had mostly stood stock still, breathing whitely, while awful crimes of omission and commission were charged to him, which he could neither quite remember nor convincingly deny.

He had done that which he should not have done; that which he should have done he had not done; and he was here again where he had been.

As though he had come around a conical mountain on a rising road, and reached the place where he had been before, only one turn higher; and looking down could see his young self below, also struggling upward, also stock still.

Then, as now, he had failed to rescue someone he had been sent to rescue (oh what had her name been, a nursery rhyme, a fairy tale, he had not thought of her in years, where was she now? What had become of her?).

And when he came around to this place again on the path above, in the new age, he would doubtless fail again, forever, until he died, if he had not already done so.

But then the sun rose, and in a new sign. Like the escaping tooth of a great clock-gear, the mountain slipped to its next notch, and rested there.

Oh you dope, Pierce thought. What are you thinking?

The hot light flooded him indoors and out. He looked down to see that he was wearing shoes from two different pairs, he had pulled them on in the dark unseeing, unfeeling too. He clutched his brow. If he was not yet mad, he would soon be thought so by his neighbors; anyway if he went on walking the roads in the pre-dawn, arguing with unseen opponents, and wearing a brown left and a black right shoe.

He laughed aloud.

Turn back, he told himself; go home, pack a bag, get out of here. He couldn't do what he had been summoned to do, not this time any more than last time; but he could cut and run.

He could go see his mom.

He turned to go back. His demons, who had risen away from him momentarily like crows startled from their roadside carrion, settled once more upon him.

"You don't really have to tell me the whole story," Winnie said to him, and touched his hand with hers. "Don't feel you have to. Really."

But he had come here just in order to tell it, the whole story, and so to cease telling it; to get from her the beginning of it, which would not be different from the end.

And would it have all been different, Pierce cried in his heart, if he had never been taken away from Brooklyn, if he had grown up instead with Axel; would he have understood it all differently, and not laid the trap for himself which he had laid, if he had not grown up with his cousins—grown up as one of them, an Oliphant, acerb, arrogant, shy—but as a different person, as the son of his father, as himself?

Was it enough, that old separation, enough to account for him, for the way he was: for the sins of avoidance and denial he had committed for twenty years, sins he had not until now even recognized as sins; for his irreparable sense that where he really belonged was always somewhere else, for a life of guilty and continual wishing? Was it enough?

A brown pelican, coasting over the cove, just then fell, as though slain, toward the water below. Belly-flopped in, and arose with a fish. Rose off the water, sailed on, shedding streams.

"Huh," Winnie said. "Did you feel that?"

"What?" His senses all pricked up, afraid.

"That."

"When?"

"Just now."

Winnie snapped her fingers, having remembered all of a sudden the thing she wanted to tell her son, the thing he needed to know, about the path not taken, and how we always choose the way we most want. Almost as suddenly she forgot again, as though her own finger-snap had been a hypnotist's, to wake her; and in the same moment Pierce discovered, in the name of his wild Kentucky girl, the name of his lost son.

The wide ripples rising on the cove dispersed. As it had now been doing for some time, the world continued to turn (at the rate of one second per second) from what it had been and into what it was to be.

"That old man is dead," Winnie said. "Is that right?"

"Boney Rasmussen," Pierce said. "This last summer."

"And of course the writer. Fellowes Kraft. What a name."

"Yes. A few years before I got there."

"Well, son." She looked at her watch, and at the evening. "I think —don't you?—that at least it's time for a drink."

14

---

n the former time, when the world was not as it has since become, wonders and unlikelihoods were more common; Coincidence, restless, constant Coincidence, was a greater engine then, though few minds or hearts perceived all that it brought about, any more than the present age is aware of its own true springs. You can't tell, when you're asleep and dreaming, that you sleep; only when you're awake can you tell the difference.

There was a highland then, the Faraway Hills, that lay a hundred miles or so away from the Cumberland counties and about as far to the west of New York City. From the top of its central massif, a weary climber could reward himself with a look into three states—north into New York, east into New Jersey, south into Pennsylvania. A good-sized river (the Blackbury) ran through these folded hills, and there were towns and villages along the river and above the river's valley. One by the river was called Fair Prospect; a road wound from Fair Prospect up into a cleft of the Faraways, to lead eventually in one direction over a hump of wooded hills and back down to the river, to the town of Blackbury Jambs; and in another direction to the smaller town of Stonykill.

Before it reached that fork, the road passed a drive, closed by a rusty chain; and down that drive, alone on a knoll like a toy castle, stood an oddly suburban little villa, red-brick Tudor style, which had been the home of Fellowes Kraft, author of *Bitten Apples* and *A Passage at* Arms and *The Werewolf of Prague* and the others Pierce read as a boy; and behind the house the garden. On a day in June, late in that age of the world, a young woman sat cross-legged on the warm earth of the garden; in the cradle of her legs was an open book, her finger on a passage, this:

> *Divine love, Giordano Bruno believed, is expressed in the endless unstinting production of things; love in man is expressed in an endless, insatiable hunger for the productions of infinity.*

The book was by Fellowes Kraft, his very first, though she had saved it for last to read; she had read all the others. Her name was Rosalind Rasmussen.

> *Giordano Bruno was the first man in Western history to conceive of the physical universe as literally infinite and unbounded, actually filled with stars that were suns around which planets like ours circled, out to infinity; and unlike Pascal in the next century the infinity never frightened or appalled him or made him feel small. He wrote in* The Expulsion of the Triumphant Beast: *"The gods take pleasure in the multiform representation of multiform things, in the multiform fruits of all talents; for they have as great pleasure in all the things that are, and in all representations made of them, as in taking care that they be, and giving order and permission that they be made." As pleased as though he were one of them himself, Bruno rejoiced in the Gods' fecundity, and thought himself large enough to contain or at least to represent all that they so generously made.*

Abashed and troubled, Rosie lifted her eyes from the page. Abashed, because she wasn't sure she understood, nor whether the sense she made of it was what Kraft had meant; troubled, because it seemed so carelessly, cheerfully voracious, and it made her feel thin and renunciatory, who could take the things of this world only one by one or a few at a time before a sort of surfeit came over her, and she had to withdraw.

"Mommy!" said her daughter Sam, blond and three years old,

who had been having her own way with the endless production of things, in this garden anyway. "Yets pick flowers."

Were they hers to pick? No one else would pick them; Fellowes Kraft was dead, and he had no heirs except a Foundation, the Rasmussen Foundation, whose employee she herself was.

"Come on yets."

"Wait hon. Let me get scissors."

It would make a great painting, she thought (Rosie was a painter, or had been or tried to be one, and would or imaginably could be one again in another time): it would show the riot of tall flowers in the June sun, realistically rendered, looking on helpless and aghast as the strong blond kid strains to break or uproot one of their number, tougher than it looks. Jaw set and bare feet firmly planted, but her hair more delicate than petals.

In Rosie's heart, or in the space within her where her heart ought to be, she felt stir into being that painful hard thing that had mysteriously come to replace it: not the muscle itself, but the other, the heart's heart.

She looked up. From where she sat, she could see the window of the little room where Kraft had used to write his books; but because of the sun on its glass casements and the black vacuity of the screen, she couldn't see inside, where Pierce Moffett was reading the pages of a book of Kraft's, his very last book, as the one Rosie read was the first.

The novelist Fellowes Kraft, though he is now known chiefly (if he is known at all) for the shelf of historical fictions that Pierce read one after the other and one after the other largely forgot, had taken a kind of pride in being good at several different kinds of literary jobbery. Amid the K's in a few dozen libraries, largely unread now for many years but still bearing unremovably their Dewey Decimal numbers, were a couple of biographies too (*Bruno's Journey,* 1931, the one Rosie Rasmussen sat reading; *The Winter King,* 1940). There was a popular history (*Elizabethan People,* 1953); there were also a children's story (*Astray,* 1959), a book of ghost stories, a couple of travel books, a hardboiled detective novel (*Scream Bloody Murder,* 1939) and even a piece of pornography (*Skin Deep,* n.d., Herm Press).

But though he thought of himself as a quick brown fox living by his wits on "the hilly country on the borderlands of literature" (where one reviewer located his works) he was actually a slow and fussy writer, who spent more time on his pages and worried more over their fate than he ever admitted. His historicals as a result were too short to truly engross fans of their genre, and his entire *ouevre* too small to support him. As he grew older, he found himself less and less able to build up the likenesses (or "likelinesses" as he used to call them) of historical personages, or to give imaginative force to their supposed actions; he wrote less and less more and more slowly, as though slipping into successively lower gears. When a small family foundation awarded him a stipend to help him continue, he seemed to stop altogether.

"The trouble is," he wrote to his new patron, Boniface Rasmussen, called Boney for more than one reason, "that all I seem capable of these days is *description,* I mean the stuff that used to be deplored in book reports when I was in high school—'I liked the story, but there was too much description.' And a novel, Boney, is like a family photo album, in this respect: that in the future, no one is going to care about your nature shots, your sunsets and distant mountains (never really satisfactory anyway, and done not so much better than many another snapshooter could do them); nor about your pictures of famous monuments or buildings. All they will care much to look at will be people, the faces of people they can recognize."

Except for a little memoir, then, privately printed (*Sorrow, Sit Down,* 1960), he produced nothing in the last years of his life; or so Pierce Moffett was given to understand when he was taken to Fellowes Kraft's house to examine his literary remains, on behalf of the Rasmussen Foundation. There in Kraft's study or office he opened a gray cardboard box on the novelist's desk, and lifted out a pile of yellow typing paper, strangely light, a large manuscript, an unfinished novel whose existence had not before been suspected; and sat down in the stillness of the dead man's house to look at it.

There was no title page. The first page had an epigraph, which was ascribed (in pencil) to Novalis, whom Pierce had never read:

I learn that I am knight Parsifal.
Parsifal learns that his quest for the Grail is the quest of all
men for the Grail.

*The Grail is just then coming into being, brought forth by a
labor of making in the whole world at once.
With a great groan the world awakes for a moment from its
slumber, to pass the Grail like a stone;
It is over; Parsifal forgets what he set out to do, I forget that I
am Parsifal, the world turns again and returns to sleep, and I
am gone.*

Pierce Moffett was then midway through the course of his thirty-fifth
year. The room was what the builders and sellers of the house would
have called a *den,* not really intending the old metaphor in the word,
the place to which a predator retreats to hide and devour what it has
caught. The chain of circumstances that had brought him there, to sit
in Fellowes Kraft's oaken swivel chair, was so long and strange it
could not but hint at the workings of Fate, even to Pierce, who didn't
believe in Fate; his coming to be there, right there in that deep den,
was as just as it was unlikely, as though his arrival were the end of a
quest, an end that could have been achieved only by singleness of
purpose and unerring Coincidence.

When he had gone down from Noate University (without getting a
doctorate, surprising everyone, including his graduate advisor Frank
Walker Barr) Pierce had taken a job teaching history and literature at
a small college in New York City. It was just at that time when
students from coast to coast (around the world too, in Paris and
Prague and even China) had begun to hear eldritch music; those who
could hear it had become transformed, almost overnight it seemed,
delighting or terrifying their teachers. Before, they had listened, or felt
obliged to pretend to listen; now they wanted to talk. The world was
not as they had been told it was, and somehow they had found out
what it *really* was, and now they were going to make their teachers
(and parents and governors) listen.

And what they wanted to tell (to tell Pierce at any rate) were
stories.

It was as though for many years people, well-educated kids in
Pierce's part of the world, had gone without stories of a certain kind,
big strange news about the meaning and direction of things, secret

true histories, the world in a parable; now suddenly they were gorging heedlessly on them, beggars at a banquet, a little of this, some of that. One of Pierce's students, quivering with emotion, had told him that once upon a time humankind had lived free on the earth, eating the fruits that came forth in their seasons, and harming nothing; but then laws and property had been invented, and that had spoiled everything.

How did they come upon such stories, who seemed to read little except bright-colored comics and the jackets of records? Pierce wondered. Did a stratum of stories lie deep in our common mentality, if we had one, that could be bent up and exposed by such geologic heavings as were then going on?

Or was it the other way around, and the periodic return of heroes (look, here they are, their stories were being told in those same comic books!) announced or even brought about the upheaval they seemed to embody?

From age to age we pass on stories, which do not seem to be inside us; we seem instead to be inside them, taking place. What if (Pierce began then to wonder) they turned out to be not primitive guesses about how things came to be, or ramparts shored up against darkness and fear, or lessons in life; what if they were true allegories (though you may not ever crack the code) about what the world is made of, why things are as they are and not some different way instead, which arise just because we are made by the same laws that made the universe?

The occult processes of physics and the history of biological evolution must be encoded in the toils of his own working brain, written there where perhaps they could be read, like a book. The Cross burning in the saint's brain might be nothing more (and therefore nothing less) than an apprehension of the foursquare carbon atom that in fact composed it.

He began then to collect stories, searching for evidence of what he had perceived, undaunted by the fact that he did not himself know what laws governed the universe, or what it was made of. While the children's crusade pressed on around him into the future, Pierce turned back, into the history he was supposed to have already learned at Noate; he struck, in wonder and delight, a thick vein of gold lying beneath the overburden of common clay and rocks he had picked over in college, and had called History and Renaissance Studies; he followed it back until it brought him, unexpectedly but inevitably, to the frontiers of a country he knew.

He never cracked the code, and gradually fell back into an old and unexamined Cartesianism (there is the world, out there, marvelously full of this and that; here am I, in here, examining it, storing up like a tourist closetsful of souvenirs of my passage through it, which retain or do not retain the smell of those places) but by then he had collected a marvelous anthology of stories, another history of the world, for there is more than one.

And all that time Fellowes Kraft in the Faraways had been accumulating the pages of a book, this book, a book unlike any other he had ever written, as though he took dictation from another voice, the same voice that tempted Pierce, and called him on.

Pierce first suggested to Boney Rasmussen that the great typescript be taken out and photocopied, so that he could read it himself if he felt incapable of coming here to sit before it (he was old and not strong); but Boney had not wanted it to leave Kraft's house, as though were it to be taken out into the sunlight it might turn to dead leaves or crumble into gravedust. So every day Rosie Rasmussen drove Pierce from his apartment in Blackbury Jambs to Kraft's house in Stonykill to read by the light of Kraft's study window (the electricity was off in the house). And since Boney Rasmussen would not come to read them he, Pierce, was going to have to tell him the story, like an ancient bard, once upon a time.

He raised his eyes to the window, where now Rosie and Sam could be seen, gathering rosebuds.

Once upon a time—say right about the time of the Christianization of the Roman Empire, or at the beginning of the Piscean age—it seems that wise men in the city of Alexandria, or maybe somewhere older and deeper in the Old World than that, made by pure thought an astonishing discovery.

They discerned that time and the world do not flow evenly forward together, but are subject to quite sudden, total, and irreversible alterations. Every now and then the observable universe passes through a sort of turnstile or baffle and comes out different on the other side—different not only in its physical extensions and the laws that govern them, but different in its past and future too: once the world was all like *this*; then it changed; now it's like *this,* and always has been.

The *magi* who thus discovered the erstwhile existence of a lost, a no-longer-findable past supposed that of course it must have been better than the past recorded in their own standard (now transmogrified) histories, and far far better than the late era they themselves lived in. In that other past, they thought, the gods had lived on earth among men, and men had possessed arts and treasures now vanished. So they bent their minds to discovering what traces of that lost past might have survived unchanged into their degraded age; and in their researches created or re-created a dozen arts and a thousand works of varying degrees of worth.

Perceiving then that their own universe was itself in the process of taking a sharp turn or transformation (perceiving, indeed, that their discovery of periodic world-overturning transformations was only possible because one was under way), the wise brotherhood set about trying to preserve something of what they had found or created: something which would bear with it, like an ark, not only the powers and arts about to be lost once again, but also the memory of falls such as they were experiencing. They guessed that the chances were slim of any one part of their world surviving unchanged into the next, and so they created several such carriers—a jewel, an elixir, a cask, a personage wrapped in changeless sleep—and, as the frame of the universe they knew shook and tottered, they went in bands out to the four corners of the earth (which did have four corners then) to preserve and conceal these treasures, and to pass on to their descendants the knowledge and the duty to keep and guard them.

Inevitably, though, one by one, corroded or fouled by the alteration of space and time, the treasures decline into useless rubbish; the guardians forget what they are guarding, and why; the new age grows old, and if the stories are remembered they are remembered as that alone, as stories.

And as that age, too, draws to its end (now we are somewhere at the end of the Renaissance) amid awful rumor and wild speculation, a new body of wise men discerns that the upheaval of their time is but the latest in a series, told of in stories and encoded in the obscurities of ancient sciences and the recipes of magic-books. The wreckage of time, they conclude, is about to bring forth the treasures that the past laid up, as an earthquake breaks open tombs; and they will be the inheritors of the jewel, the *crater,* the person wrapped in deathlike sleep with emerald tablet gripped in his white fingers; the inheritors too of the duty to preserve and transmit at least one of these alive into the unknown new age now dawning, etc., and with it the knowledge, etc., etc., as before.

All this told in approximately reverse order, not without skill, but with the unreal lightness of a film run backward, the same eerie swapping of cause and effect. Unfinished, moreover; a Möbius strip still needing to be pasted end to end in order to become endless.

And it was all true: Pierce knew the history Kraft had built on well enough to see that. Strange but true. It was only inverted, as Pierce had once himself imagined History could be inverted, the real good guys being not the textbook victors but the others, the forgotten ones, who preserved among them a secret history opposite to the history everyone else is given to learn; exiles, made to suffer unfairly through the ages by harsh authorities, though their wisdom will triumph at last and in the end.

The great coincidence, sum of all the small and apparently unimportant ones that had guided and tugged and chivvied him gently to this room in this year, was that he already knew this story of Kraft's before he sat to read it.

It *was* all true: there really had once been a country of wise priests whose magic worked, encoded in the picture-language of hieroglyphics. That was what Pierce had learned in his recent researches. It did lie far in the past, though not in the past of Egypt. It had been constructed long after the actual Egypt had declined and been buried, its mouth stopped because its language could no longer be read.

And this magic Egypt really had been discovered or invented in Alexandria around the time of the Christianization of the Roman Empire, when a Greek-speaking theosophical cult had attributed some mystical writings of their own to ancient priests of an imaginary Egyptian past of temples and speaking statues, when the gods dwelt with men. And then that imagined country really had disappeared again as those writings were lost in the course of the Christian centuries that followed.

And when they were rediscovered—during the Renaissance in Italy, along with an entire lost past—scholars believed them to be really as ancient as they purported to be. And so a new Egypt, twice different from the old original, had appeared: ancient source of knowledge, older than Moses, inspiring a wild syncretism of sunworship, obelisks, pseudo-hieroglyphs, magic and semi-Christian mysticism, which may have powered that knowledge revolution called science, the same science that would eventually discredit imaginary Egypt and its magic.

And yet even when the *real* Egypt had come to light again, the tombs broken open and the language read, the other country had persisted, though becoming only a story, a story Pierce had come upon in his boyhood and later forgot, the country he had rediscovered in the City in the days of the great Parade, when he had set out to learn the hidden history of the universe: the story he was still inside of, it seemed, inescapably.

Ægypt.

He had told his cousins when they asked him *Will we be in this story when we're grownups?* that they would, that it was a story about grownups; it wasn't make-believe, he had said, they hadn't made it up, they had discovered themselves in it. He had told them it would still be going on when they were grownups and they would be in it still. And so it had. And here again he was himself.

Pierce lifted his eyes from the eroded bluff the pile of pages made, face down on the left-hand side, face up on the right.

He had that day received his first check from the Rasmussen Foundation, made out in Rosalind Rasmussen's back-slanted left-handed script with schoolgirl circles dotting the i's, and signed in Boney Rasmussen's Palmer Method tracery. It was in his pocket.

What really was he being paid to do?

There was this huge typescript, which had been hiding so long in plain sight on Kraft's desk, which Pierce was now charged with deciding about.

There were Kraft's other papers, a dusty attic pile of liquor cartons which Pierce, heart sinking, had looked into as into another man's unwashed laundry. All through the house, floor to ceiling and in casual piles and in turnabout bookcases, were books, and he was to rummage in those, to see what of extraordinary value might turn up (his suggestion that a professional dealer be brought in to make an assessment had been dismissed gracefully, which puzzled him but pleased him too).

Above—or beneath—all these charges was another task, one that Boney Rasmussen had seemed to lay upon him without ever quite stating it: to look for something somewhere here—in the books, the book, the boxes—something that Kraft had lost or found, something which the old man (gaga maybe, probably) much desired and yet referred to in terms so delicate and tentative and shamefaced that Pierce had decided not to understand him.

And there was his own book, too, not to forget. For which another and larger check had also just arrived, signed by his agent Julie Rosengarten, the first half of an advance against the royalties of a book that was not yet half done, was not even half begun: a book that he could almost believe he need not ever actually write (he laughed a mad laugh in the hollow house) because he had found it here all done, like the shoemaker in the story; all but done, easily done, if he could only think of the right question to put to the place, and to Kraft's unlaid spirit that inhabited it.

15

hen Pierce had first left the city, where he had long lived, and moved out to the Faraway Hills not so far away but a different world for sure, it was in order to write a book of his own: not a novel but a history of sorts, for a historian (of sorts) was what he was, or what he might aspire to be called; he had certainly taught a lot of history classes, and he had never, since Kentucky, ever seriously entertained another ambition.

He had been able to picture himself—in the third person, so to speak (the only way he had ever been able to imagine his own future, or lay plans for himself)—out in the country, working and living, serene or at least quiet after a long season in the funhouse of city high life. He had not pictured himself arriving here to step directly into this story he had stepped into, which had been spooling out meantime in these hills even as he had lived his own life and thought his own thoughts elsewhere: as though you could stumble over a path you had left forever long before, here blindly by chance intersecting the one you took instead.

Blindly.

It was his friend and city neighbor Brent Spofford who had got him here. Spofford had grown up in these hills, and then had returned to them after a long sojourn in the city and the Great World, from where Pierce had continued to send him an occasional budget of news, and to hear back from Spofford about seasons and labor. Spofford had found for Pierce the fine cheap apartment on Maple Street in

Blackbury Jambs. And when Pierce's exit visa had at length been issued (that was how Pierce saw it at the time) and he was packed and prepared, Spofford came to the city in his pickup and carried Pierce and his belongings into the hills, where Pierce experienced that astonishing access of liberty and ease, in his life and in his soul, that inrush of unearned beauty that longtime city-dwellers are often whelmed by when they go to pretty country towns in the spring of the year.

He had at first supposed that he would be going back to the city regularly, unable to imagine that the little town and its environs could supply him with the excitements and possibilities he had learned to subsist on. Actually he had hardly gone back at all. But on the day after he finished reading the manuscript of Kraft's last novel, he found that he had packed an overnight bag, called his agent in the city, acquainted himself with the bus schedule, and prepared his mind to go to town.

And stood then in the middle of his little sitting room (less ready to go than he imagined himself to be, he had not got himself enough cash, he had not packed his toothbrush among other necessities, his heart was full) looking out and down into the scruffy back yard of the building whose second floor his apartment occupied, becoming aware that an old, old rose bush burdening the slat and wire fence between his and the next house's yard was in bloom.

It had been a briar patch when he arrived here in March. And now look. All by itself, untouched, unloved. He remembered the big bushes that went down the sloping lawn in Kentucky.

Something entirely different is coming.

This thought—it was not a thought but an understanding, a sudden conviction such as he had never had before, a clairvoyance distilled out of the June day and the roses and the tick of time's passing —neither surprised nor exalted him, nor made him afraid. It was a conclusion he came to, as simple and certain as a sum; only he had no idea what evidence, what multiplier or multiplicand, had been accumulating in him to be totted up just then. No idea.

Something entirely different is coming to you, that you can't imagine; and a different spirit to inhabit you, to meet it with.

He waited for more, stock still and not breathing, as though he had looked up to find a shy rare beast in his path that would flee him if he moved; but the message was done.

After a time he turned from the window, and shouldered his bag to go.

The bus (Pierce took the bus because he had no car, had never learned to drive or acquired a license) left from the little variety store on River Street, which was the main street of Blackbury Jambs, where the library and the three-story Ball Building and a bar and a coffee shop (the Donut Hole) looked out across the Blackbury River.

"Just rolling in," said the lady who sold him his ticket, and indeed just then the windows of the store were darkened by the bulk of the bus drawing up before it. Pierce bought a local paper (the Faraway *Crier*) and one of the city papers; the bus snorted and exhaled the air of its brakes; the door swung open, the cheerful driver leapt smartly out, and Pierce, though gripped momentarily by a strange reluctance, boarded.

His book, as he had at first conceived it, was a book about stories; a book about how a past world, once whole, had broken apart, and forgot itself, and yet persisted in stories, in maxims, in turns of phrase and habits of mind and childhood rhymes whose import is lost.

It was to have been about how, in the sixteenth and seventeenth centuries, a philosophical system with roots in the deep past—a system that included alchemy, astrology, the Græco-Roman pantheon, sympathetic magic, the theory of four elements and four humors, and the tall tales of a thousand years—had dominated thought in Europe. When what would become modern science began to come forth from that mental universe, it seemed at first to many to be a new and powerful extension of the same magical thinking. Science, after a struggle, established itself as different from magic, in fact the *opposite* of magic; and then it and its historians and epigones proceeded to bury its roots, paper over and deny the connections.

But the older system had not been erased, the bad brother, the secret sharer; it had persisted, in popular culture and in stories and in countless metaphors we use continually; its history was embedded in puzzles we stumble on (that Pierce had stumbled on) everywhere in the attics and basements of common thought.

Where are the four corners of the world? Who are the lily-white boys, clothed all in green-o? Why are there seven days in the week and not nine or five? Where do the little cherubs come from, that decorate Valentines, and why does love have wings? How does music have charms to soothe the savage breast? There *is* more than one history of the world: one of them patent and sensible, the other one blind, unrecognized, and yet issuing from our mouths and our actions daily, unexpungable. Why do we bless someone who sneezes? Why are there nine choirs of angels, and what are angels anyway, where did *they* come from?

Pierce knew all these things, and more. He knew why *cosmic* and *cosmetic* have the same root; he knew why you stuff a cold and starve a fever. He knew why we have always supposed that Gypsies could tell fortunes: it's because they were thought to come from Egypt, though they don't, and Egypt is preeminently the land of magic and of secret wisdom. And Pierce knew why that was too, that was a story he wanted to tell: how when he was a kid he had excavated an imaginary country that turned out not to have been imaginary at all, or not, at any rate, to have been imagined by him alone.

He had offered this book to a New York literary agent—a book about the past—and she had transformed it (page by page, lunch by lunch) into a book about the future. Pierce had not resisted, but lately when he read and endlessly reread the curling and cup-ringed pages of his proposal he had been feeling (besides the weird satisfaction he always took in the taste of his own prose) a sense of willed overstatement that had made him swallow with embarrassment.

The bus traversed back and forth down the green foothills, crossed and recrossed the river, and then entered onto the broad artery leading to the city. Across the degraded flatlands the lanes grew ever more clogged with traffic pressing toward the distant brownish towers of Dis, which for a long time seemed to grow no closer, until all the traffic rushed together into the aortic tunnel, abandon all hope, and out into the scarred old heart of it, always a surprise somehow to find it surrounding you, Heraclitean, the same but never the same.

Marveling at the filth and the crowds of wildly various humans, both more extreme than he seemed to remember (had he lost a carapace, an ability not to notice things?), Pierce went down stairs and escalators into deeper bolges with the damned throng, looking in his pockets for the address Julie Rosengarten had given him, the restaurant where she would meet him and (he hoped) buy his lunch.

Uptown. Couple of stops.

It was because he had needed badly to get out of this town and start over elsewhere, because he had needed money, needed some way to make a living other than the little college, that he had conceived of writing a book, and offered the idea to Julie Rosengarten, the owner and sole employee of the Astra Literary Agency. She listened to his stories and read the first draft of his proposal, and told him that she needed more than that to sell.

Like more what?

Well she thought it was interesting about Egypt and its shadow country, and how its magic persisted down through the centuries, only now coming to light again. What magic? She wanted more of that. She wanted Pierce not only to outline old sciences, but to intimate new ones; she wanted him to send out a call from his own potent subjectivity, newly awakened by his occult studies, to the latent powers in the souls of his readers.

She wanted—it took him a while to understand this—a book of magic, a new black book, *clavis Salmonis, ars magna.* That, she said, she could sell.

"It's a new age, Pierce," she'd said to him. "All that stuff is coming back."

Pierce had promised to try. He had many qualifications for writing such a book, and he had one serious disqualification, or drawback, or what might be construed as a drawback or maybe a sort of sidewise advantage: he did not, himself, believe in magic. Even if he could derive from his history books and his source books any exact description of what might be done, any new-old practice, he just could not bring himself to instruct anyone in it; even to make a little convincing the recipes and procedures that had been the actual endproduct of all that vast past intellection, it would be necessary to cast over them a lot of rhetorical glamour, sidestepping or mistranslating the incomprehensible physiology and the unworkable physics, in order to keep out of sight the great cæsura (Pierce at least sure felt it) between what we do, today, which at least works, and what they did, which didn't.

He actually pulled off this trick in miniature, in the scant pages of this proposal, and it had sold the book to a giant publisher of paperbacks, as Julie said it would; and then he had come to a halt, unable to think how to do it in large, in a real book. He had got no further with it when he moved to Blackbury Jambs, where at length he had come upon the box of paper on Kraft's desk. And found that Kraft had faced and satisfactorily solved the very problem Pierce could not.

Once, the world was not as it has since become, Kraft said, *or revealed, or pretended to reveal. It once worked in a different way from the way it works now; it had a different history, and thus a different future. Its very flesh and bones, the physical laws that governed it, were other than the ones we know.*

"I've never heard of this writer," Julie Rosengarten said, who faced him across the table of a calm and superior restaurant, a nicer place than she had taken him to on other occasions, maybe she was doing well. "Who is he?"

"A novelist. He was sort of popular once. He became sort of a hermit; lived alone, working on this huge . . ."

"Is it going to be published?"

"Not possible," Pierce said. "It's just an idea. One long idea. This idea."

Julie rested her chin in the cup of her hand, and the many bracelets she wore slid down along her arm with a whisper of wood and metal. "So," she said.

"So suppose it was so," Pierce said. "Think what the consequences of that would be."

"Well I guess I can't really imagine. I'm not even sure I can imagine what you're saying."

"It might mean," he said, "that once the physical laws that govern the universe were such that certain practices we read about really worked the way they were said to work, even though now they no longer do. Alchemy, for instance. Judicial astrology, or astrological medicine. Automata. Prophecy."

"Well did they? I mean *I* think they did, really. Probably. Some of them." Julie, he suspected, might now and then try a little innocent witchery, crystals, cards, *magia naturalis.*

"They didn't," Pierce said. "Or rather put it this way: either those techniques and sciences of the past did work, and ours don't; or ours do, and not theirs. If they could turn base matter into gold, then 'gold' and 'matter' weren't then what we know they are now." He drank from the glass of amber whiskey that had been put before him. "Well maybe they weren't. Maybe they weren't always what they are now. Maybe they *became* the way they are now."

"Well gee. It seems like we'd know. If this was really part of our history. Changes like that."

"No. If there were such a change, then when it was past there'd be almost no way of demonstrating that it had happened. The new laws obtain, and not the old ones. Now gold can't be made from base matter by fire, and *now it never could have been*: the laws of the universe, the nature of things, make it impossible."

He had read to this conclusion once, and then he had pondered it for a long time before he saw what he had here, which was an explanation for the history of magic that answered every need, solved every historical crux, satisfied the skeptic and the ardent seeker both, and had only the one drawback of its complete absurdity.

"It's like the old paradox: if everything suddenly got twice as big as it is, I mean atoms and all, would you be able to tell? As far as we can show by investigation, the same physical laws have always been in operation; we just haven't always known them."

"Well then how could you ever find out that it was even so? That these changes happen?"

"You can't. *You can only know they happen if you pass through one, and recognize it for what it is.* How else would you ever stumble on such a mad idea."

She crossed her arms before her, puzzlement in her dark-lashed light eyes; there was a pretty flush to her cheeks, where a few brown freckles were sown. Been to the beach, he guessed.

"So you see what that would mean," he said. "Don't you."

"*What* Pierce would it mean."

He wasn't surprised that she didn't immediately understand. He had had to rehearse it for his own inward ear periodically over the last weeks, to remember just how it went, the perfect logic of it, the satisfaction. "It means," he said, leaning toward her, "that if I, and you, and whoever else, have imagined the possibility of such changes; if we have discovered the possibility of their happening, and seen at what times in the past they might have happened; then it must be because we sense that one is under way right now."

"One?" she said.

"A change. A change in the laws by which the universe is governed."

She looked at him sidewise, out of one eye, like a bird. "Now? Right now?"

"Now when I'm telling it. Now when I'm writing this book. Now in this decade, this year."

He watched her understand this, and see what it meant for the project she was representing for him; and it was as though he could see her mind's eyes cross, and refocus.

"Not only that," Pierce said. "It seems that the souls or minds who perceive this happening—who guess that a change is under way, that old laws have lost their force, and new laws haven't yet been imposed—it seems that they can actually affect the shape of the coming world. Construct its laws and its meaning. That's what Giordano Bruno did. What Galileo and Newton did."

"They did?"

"They moved the sun," Pierce said, showing his palms, QED. "They made the earth turn."

She laughed at last, in delight he thought or hoped.

"Well but why?" she asked. "I mean why should it be just now that this change happens? If it does. Is it the stars, or . . ."

"Not the stars, apparently. There was a lot of talk in the 1590s about the stars. There were predictions of big stuff that would happen, astrologically, in 1588, and in 1600. But it wasn't the cusp of a new age, even by their own astrology. Neither is this."

"Aquarius."

"Two hundred years away. That's not it."

"Well what then."

"I don't know. It just happens, apparently. Every once in a while." A devilish exhilaration was rising in him. "Every little once in a while."

Julie looked at him, rolling a remnant of bread between her fingers, waiting for this to make sense. But this was the part of Kraft's scheme that didn't puzzle Pierce. He didn't see why the stuff of reality had to be seamless, or why the true springs of things shouldn't be blind, inaccessible to reason. He thought it likely.

"I don't know," she said. "It sounds sort of like a trick."

"It's not a trick," Pierce said. "It's a story."

He told her Kraft's story, the core of it, how twice in the last two thousand years a slip or seam, a rumple in the ground of being, had allowed observers around the world to perceive that the net of space and time is not quite stable, but like the shifting plates and molten core of Mother Earth can move beneath the feet of diurnality; can move, was moving, had moved before and would again.

He told her how only the greatest masters of the workings of the world would ever notice the subtle changes taking place, and even they would doubt themselves, and discount the evidence, blame their own tools or failing skills; if they tried to express what they knew, their contemporaries would not understand it, and the coming age would misread what they said and wrote, would take their writings for allegory or failed prophecy.

Which, when the change was past, was all they were.

He told her how, in Kraft's scheme, between the old world of things as they used to be, and the new world of things as they would be instead, there has always fallen a sort of passage time, a chaos of unformed possibility in which all sorts of manifestations could be witnessed. Then safe old theurgies and charms have suddenly turned on their practitioners and destroyed them; then huge celestial beings have been formed, born out of the assembling of smaller ones, who become the larger ones' parts and organs; then great Ægypt has been revealed again, and her children have recognized one another, by signs no one before understood.

Then the wise have forgathered, and prepared.

"Ægypt," Julie said. "Huh."

The last such a passage time happened to fall at the cusp of two centuries as well, the sixteenth and the seventeenth of our era, the time when Kraft's book took place; and hadn't Jean Bodin the encyclopædist said in those days (Pierce knew this, though he couldn't remember how he came to know it, sheep's wool caught in the great mental briar patch) that there was a sudden awful plague of evil spirits around, working all sorts of mischief? Bodin blamed it on the arrogant magicians, willing to call forth dæmons of air, fire, water, who then seized on the unwary and inhabited them. Kraft said: the passage time, breeding spirits as the sun breeds bees in the guts of dead lions. Elementals, *dæmonii,* incubi and succubi, salamanders. Look into a crystal or a dish of clear water: someone looks back at you.

"Witches," Julie said.

"Werewolves." Pierce saw in his mind a troop of gray ones, moving over burnt ground, heads looking side to side for the prey they followed.

"Then gone," Pierce said. Then gone, the time of passage past when they are possible: and all of them, or nearly all, retreat back into earth air water and fire, not only no longer existing but demonstrably never having existed; new laws, new powers just as great but different, come to be; the sky now infinite, and empty.

"And here we are," he said.

"Here we are," she said, but sounded no longer quite here; elevated slightly, exalted maybe.

"But if it's now our turn," he said, softly. "If it is."

"Then all that stuff really could be coming back," Julie said, as though she had not believed it before, when she had said it herself. "Magic *could* be done again."

"Well you don't know," Pierce said. "All you know is, what's coming will be different from, work differently from, the way things work now. It might have more magic in it. It might have less. Giordano Bruno was sure that in his time the magic of a former age was coming back again. But when the passage time was over, it hadn't. The new age brought new powers in that no one could have imagined. So will the next."

"Like what powers."

"Keep your eyes open," Pierce said. "Maybe they won't be occurring in million-dollar labs, won't be an extension of what we know now. Maybe they'll be entirely different, something we can't yet imagine. Maybe it'll be you who can have them."

He smiled teasingly at her, but his heart was in his mouth; he had not imagined that this would be as hard to say as it was turning out to be, like pushing forward a stack of chips when he held nothing but a pair of twos. One way magic really could be said to work, bad magic, was in convincing others that physical laws were bendable, even breakable, and that you knew how to do it, when you didn't at all.

And yet it was true: his myth (for that's what he was offering her, a myth, Kraft's myth) really described what happened in the sixteenth and seventeenth centuries, when systems warred and there were battles and sudden reversals and defections, and for a time the issue was in doubt.

And it was as true right now: anyway a case could be made, Pierce could make it, that the same transit was now occurring, old physics and mechanics grown feeble, unable to explain observed reality, hunger for new truths, *expectation* of new truths, intimations of renewal, of a different *paradigm* (new word the thinker could not now do without, tossed backward by ongoing Time to grow up and multiply, like Deucalion's stones), new laws, new ones to break too.

Something entirely new is coming.

"Will people believe it?" Julie said, almost a whisper.

"I don't know. I don't know if *I* do."

"How are you going to convince them? You'll have to."

"Well," Pierce said. "What if I could offer evidence. Some actual tangible evidence. What if I could find something, some sort of something somewhere, that has survived, unchanged, from the former state of things, something."

"Like what." She leaned forward to hear, and he too to speak, conspirators, their folded hands nearly touching in the middle of the table.

"Well suppose," Pierce said. "Suppose that were the story of this book. Suppose that the story of this book was the true story of how such a thing was sought for . . ."

"And found," Julie said.

"Well."

"Pierce. Do you really really know there is such a thing?"

He would not say so. But he held her eyes with his and grinned.

There was only one syllable with which she could respond to this; and when she made it, little round sound of wonder or delight, his heart rose, and he nearly laughed with tenderness and remembrance: for it returned him instantly to the railroad flat, not forty blocks from here, where a decade before he and Julie had been lovers: in the days of the great Parade, when the doors of dawn had opened, and nothing was ever to be the same again.

16

fter his lunch, Pierce went downtown on foot through the afternoon, walking without noticing where he walked, watching the unrolling of an inward movie, a movie being made even as it unrolled.

Did he really intend to suggest in his book that once-upon-a-time the useless procedures of magic had had effects, the lead had turned to gold, the dead had risen; but that then the world ("the world") had passed through some sort of cosmic turnstile and come out the other side different, so that now not only are the old magics inefficacious but *now they always were*? Was he going to say that?

He guessed he was. Certainly he was going to hint at it, utter it, assemble ambiguous evidence for it, hold his readers in suspense with a search through history for the proof of it, the one thing—event, artifact, place, word—that is still, indisputably, what it once was in the past age, as nothing else any longer is. Whatever it might be.

He was going to entertain the notion; oh more, he was going to fête it, he was going to wine and dine it; he was going to have his way with it amid the spilled cups and crushed fruit of an uproarious banquet. And he was going to father on it a notion more powerful than itself, a notion which would only be given birth to in his concluding pages: *only if we treat the past in this way, as though it was different in kind from the present, can we form any idea of how different from the present the future will be.*

The future, fast approaching now, when this passage time has ended, and all these broils and clashings are over; when the new science (*nuova scienza, novum organum, ars magna*) that we sense rising now over the horizon has been formulated, if *formulated* is how it will be made manifest; when the now-inconceivable is made conceivable, and the present, our present, can no longer be constructed intelligibly, or its technics made to work, a lost world.

He thought he could do it. For the first time he could imagine it done, could imagine the pile of manuscript, the finished book, shy and sly in its wrapper, open it and see.

He lifted his eyes from the street. He had arrived, he saw, at the Public Library, before the great stone lions, as he had after an earlier lunch with Julie, when she had first charged him to write a book about the future.

His father Axel had loved these beasts. Loved libraries and books with a chivalric passion. Often when Axel had taken him to Manhattan for some treat they had passed by here, and studied them, and read their inscriptions; Axel had told him the sculptor's name. Why are they here? Pierce asked. To keep people out, Axel answered; a joke of Little Enosh's. To keep people out. They repeated the joke every time they passed by here.

He went up the wide steps, where as always lovers and vagrants and eaters of al-fresco lunch were disposed, and through the doors. Cool and large and solemn. There were books he could look for, he had always a mental list of questions to be answered; he was at loose ends; he could turn, too, and cross town, and take the next bus home.

Home. He saw green hills in his heart.

Mounting the stairs—though still not having made a decision— he came without real surprise on his father. Axel stood beneath the big painting on the first-floor landing of Milton dictating to his (bored or transfixed) daughters. He was studying it, or might be thought to be studying it, but Pierce—not having been noticed as yet, stopped on the stairs below the landing—knew better. Axel's eyes scanned the huge dark picture, but he too watched an inward movie; his lips moved, speaking his endless monologue; his hands searched in the pockets of his blazer, and pulled out papers, which he studied with the same dreamy interest as he did Milton, and then replaced. Axel could go through whole museums in this state of semi-trance, ravished by beauty, noting great moments in Art or History, and yet borne on his own currents mostly. Pierce had been with him often thus.

Should he turn now and flee, before he was seen?

He didn't dare turn away. Axel's heart would break if he caught sight of Pierce's back, and guessed Pierce was trying to avoid him.

Nothing for it. He climbed up, and nearly had to bump into Axel before Axel focused on him.

"Good god. Well! Pierce!"

"Hello, Axel."

"I was just. Milton. I come here, you know. You remember this moment. The blind daughters. Justify God's ways to Man."

"Yes."

"Well how are you? You didn't call."

"I just decided this morning. I had some business to do."

"Well. Well." Axel Moffett looked up at his tall son, a head at least higher than himself, awed and delighted. "Your business is done?"

"Oh mostly."

"We'll have an evening then."

"Actually I was sort of thinking of going on."

"Oh no. No. Foolish. Two long bus rides in a single day. When you haven't been back in months. No, no. Come on, Pierce. We'll have a day, like we used to." He nearly danced with eagerness before Pierce. "Aw come on."

They had, actually, used to walk the city a lot, when Pierce lived here; at Axel's insistence, usually, using up Pierce's days off unless Pierce fought him off. But Pierce was also fascinated by Axel; he had turned out, when Pierce had returned to the city as an adult and had found Axel still here, to be an entirely different person from the one he remembered: not, he thought, because Axel had changed, he was a fixed entity, but because so much of him had been hidden from Pierce as a boy.

"Oh all right," he said at last, annoyed at himself for being unable to refuse; he had never been good at refusing. If he could not evade or avoid, he usually assented.

"Good, good," Axel said, mightily pleased, taking his son's arm. "Oh Pierce. Well met. Well met by moonlight."

"It's *ill* met," Pierce said. "The line is *Ill met by moonlight*."

"We'll go downtown," Axel said. "Stretch our legs. Have you ever looked into the Little Church Around the Corner? It's an interesting story."

"Yes," Pierce said. "You've told me."

Walking with Axel was a peculiar exercise, and somewhat conspicuous. Axel had a habit of spying small items on the street, papers or unrecognizable jetsam, and stooping to pick them up. Sometimes he carried what he found to a trash basket, a good citizen; more often he simply examined it and dropped it again, only to pick up another a few yards on. He had used to tell his exasperated son that he was on the lookout for money or other treasure; but had at length confessed it wasn't that at all, he just couldn't help it. He didn't cease talking while he picked and looked and discarded, and Pierce, striding ahead, had often to stop and return a pace or two. Pierce thought sometimes they must look like two silent-film comedians, the tall saturnine one, the short plump one, backing and filling in a sort of dance, or stopping in the midst of traffic to crane their necks at an unremarkable building, where Axel thought he had spied a caryatid, or a gargoyle, or a Palladian window.

"Look look, Pierce. Rustication. You see?" Axel ran his hand over the blocks of a building, carved to look roughly-quarried. "Imitating natural blocks of stone, you see? Why we might be in Rome."

"Uh huh. Rustication meant antique virtue when Roman architects used it. Then the Renaissance."

"Well yes. You see? *Rome never fell.* You see?"

Pierce hands in his pockets refrained from joining Axel in feeling the wall like a blind man. "Come on, Axel."

Had Axel got worse lately? Pierce remembered that when he was very young Axel had held a job, a real one, he had been a bookkeeper, Pierce thought. It was hard to imagine him employed now at anything except the all-but-unpaid jobs he did for Catholic charities or the temporary clerical work he sometimes got. The rents on the little building in Brooklyn he owned and lived in kept him alive. What would happen to him otherwise? Pierce thought sometimes with guilty horror of caring for him in some awful future; or refusing to.

"Your book's all about this," Axel said, who had heard Pierce's descriptions and absorbed what he chose to. "Rome. Greece. Egypt. With that little ligature."

"Well."

"*Novus ordo seclorum,*" Axel said. "The pyramid on the dollar."

"Right." Why is there a rusticated pyramid on the Great Seal of the United States, surmounted by the mystic eye? Because the Founding Fathers believed in Ægypt too.

It occurred to Pierce that perhaps his book was at bottom an explanation of Axel to himself: of the stories Axel had repeated endlessly to him, man and boy, the Story of Civilization. If every question, every history Axel loved to ponder were swept away, then only the one question would be left, naked as a needle: why did you let me go? The question little Pierce went on asking, no matter how often big Pierce told him the answer.

Axel conceived the idea of walking to Brooklyn, which was well beyond even Pierce's long legs; and somewhere downtown as evening came on they stopped in one of the low bars Axel favored, where Pierce looked into his wallet, and found it not up to a long crawl.

"Well come back to Brooklyn. We'll rustle something up. A loaf of bread, a jug of wine."

This idea appealed to Pierce so little that at length he drew out his credit card (since he could not, would not at any rate, simply send Axel home alone) and he and his father, to Axel's inexpressible delight, set themselves up in a pleasant wood-paneled restaurant, where large drinks were placed on the white cloth before them. It had struck Pierce before that he was always forced to eat lavishly when he ate on credit, since the cheap places didn't extend it.

For the remains of the evening, Axel suggested (hemming and hawing a bit, and holding out his glass for wine) that there were in this neighborhood some remarkable new clubs that had opened in recent months. Had Pierce heard of them? Axel laughed, as at the inexplicable turns of human folly. Cowboy and leather, he said, and extremes of histrionic indulgence, nothing hidden, nothing. He mentioned Tiberius's isle of Capri, and the court of Heliogabalus. Some glorious young men, though, Axel was forced to admit. There was one of these places very nearby, the Sixth Circle, Pierce caught the reference no doubt.

"Axel. Are you real familiar with these places?"

Axel managed an expression of sly indignation. It was just a phenomenon Axel thought would interest Pierce, to whom nothing human was alien, was it? Of course they would not participate, there were many who didn't. "Just stick with me," Axel said. "Like Virgil with Dante. You might learn something."

Pierce declined. He had no particular wish to look upon the incomprehensible lusts of other men. Glad as he was that Axel was getting his share of modern or latter-day fun, he wasn't sure he hadn't preferred Axel in the more repressed and guilty mode he had found him in when he had first come down from Noate, in which Axel's adventures (when described late in the night to Pierce, and probably to his own soul as well) had been rare dramas charged with tragic necessity, and not merely goods he had found on the common counter.

"Actually I'm going to try to pay a call," Pierce said. "Go visit somebody."

"Who?" Axel demanded, at once miffed and crestfallen, a look which Pierce doubted any great thespian (as Axel would have put it) could have improved on.

"A woman. Uptown."

"The one you used to. The Gypsy."

"Part Gypsy. Yes."

"Still carrying a torch? Oh Pierce."

"Oh I suppose," Pierce said, searching his pockets for a dime. "In my fashion."

"I have loved thee, Cynara! in my fashion," Axel gave out, adopting instantly a *fin-de-siècle* languor. "Flung roses, roses riotously with the throng."

" '*Been faithful to* thee,' " Pierce said, "is how it goes. I'll be back in a minute."

"*Non sum qualis eram*. I am not as I was in good Cynara's golden days," Axel went on, not to be stopped now, Pierce could hear him going on behind him as he sought the phone. "I have forgot much, Cynara! Gone with the wind . . ."

He found the phone number, written in her hand on the inside of a matchbook, her seven with the little line through the upright, where had she learned that. He had brought it with him from the Faraways though he had urged himself strongly not to use it, and perhaps he would not have if it hadn't been for the second bottle of wine.

"All night upon mine heart I felt her warm heart beat. Nightlong within mine arms in love and sleep she lay. O God."

On the day in March when he had left the city for good, Pierce had got to his knees in his emptied apartment and with absurd solemnity had made a vow: that in his new life he would spend no more of his heart's energy (to say nothing of his money and his time) on the hopeless and hurtful pursuit of love. No more.

Some men are born eunuchs, some are made eunuchs; Pierce chose celibacy for survival's sake. Love had almost killed him, and when he awoke and found the dawn was gray, he had decided to save up the little strength he felt he had left to make a life, just for himself. He was *hors de combat,* and he would shape his own ends hereafter.

She (it was just the one woman who had extracted Pierce's hopeless oath from him, he had never been a philanderer, hard as he had tried to fling his roses with the throng) had a little apartment uptown to which she had moved from Pierce's tower of steel and glass; it was an Old Law flat, he understood, in the last unrehabilitated building on a chic block, and cost near nothing. He had never been in it but he could imagine it in detail; a certain amount of his imaginative life was spent there.

"Ah but I was desolate and sick of an old passion," Axel declaimed, near tears. "Hungry for the lips of my desire."

It would be lit by candles in peculiar holders (she had not had the electricity turned on, didn't have the money for a deposit, had no desire to be officially listed anywhere, a habit left over from her days as a small dealer in cocaine, all over now as far as he knew). For a bed there would be a block of foam on pallets rescued from the street, but clothed in faded figured stuffs and piled with souvenir satin pillows where pink sunsets occurred over blue lakes and green pines. The walls too were probably hung with cloth. And everywhere there would be the things she found in rummage sales and junkshops, and resold at a profit, the advertising dolls and costume jewelry, scarves, toys, statuettes of cartoon characters, risqué party favors, plastic tortoiseshell, postcards, "smalls" as the dealers called them; they would be arranged in ever-shifting subtle combinations, tableaux, miniature dioramas, accidental-seeming but really as consciously self-referential as a modern novel. There would be (he remembered this combination from her dresser in the apartment they had shared, though perhaps it had been dispersed) a Gypsy cigarette smoker on a painted cocktail tray, offering her pack or herself or both, and a jeweled cigarette holder on the tray, along with a poison ring, an Eiffel Tower and an Empire State Building in pot metal; and a Sphinx, in plaster, which she had painted white, with rouged cheeks and cat's eyes, pink claws, and a hooker's rosebud mouth; and around its neck a little gold watch on a band.

He let the phone ring long in this place that he imagined, let it go on ringing after it was evident no one could be there; and even after he hung up it went on ringing for some time within him.

Long past midnight and far from dawn he awoke with a start in his old bedroom in Brooklyn. The wine, maybe; but what he thought of first was Julie Rosengarten, and what he had proposed to her. He felt the seducer's guilty doubt, that he had promised too much in order to win her, and had been believed; or worse, had not really been believed at all, would not be until he acted on his promises.

He rolled over in the little bed where he no longer fit, and closed his eyes; but soon opened them again and rolled back.

Why should he try to impose this shape on time? For surely he was imposing it. Wasn't he?

In the room beyond, his father snored and whistled in long classic snores out of funny movies. The old air-conditioner panted out the window, but the air was close, the smell of his old home. Pierce at length got up, and pushed open the casement.

Warm air and the street's smell; new tall apartment buildings and office towers visible above the street, still alight, having watched through the night. New gleaming futuristic streetlights. Brooklyn had been much renewed since he was a kid here; yet it looked older, worn out; when he was young it had looked fresher. So it seemed.

Frank Walker Barr, his old teacher and mentor, had once written a whole book (*Time's Body*) showing how we have always conceived time as having a shape. Maybe in this day and age (Barr had written) the only shape most of us conceive time having is a simple geometry, a big bow-tie at whose infinitesimal knot—the present moment—we stand, with past and future opening out infinitely before and behind us. But other conceptions have been potent at other periods, not only determining how people have imagined history but determining what became of them: Cortez arrives in Mexico just as an old Age (the Mexicans are sure of it) is declining and growing feeble, and a new young Age is waiting to step forth.

Why have we always supposed that time has a shape? Pierce asked the night. Couldn't it be that we believe time has a shape because it *does* have a shape?

There was that patient of some famous psychoanalyst he had read about who was tormented terribly by the delusion that he could sense time experiencing its own passing, and that the experience was intensely painful—not to him but to time. That time suffered in the birth and death of every second, the secretion of every daybreak and nightfall.

It was *not* a dumb idea, not just food for the gullible, though it was maybe not a history: it was something both more and less, a critique, an essay, it was perhaps not even actually a book at all, it was a compound monster, a mammal, a person even, himself or someone like him. Whatever it was its central trope was one rooted deeply (he thought) in the human heart, one of the unremovable ones: *An old world dying, and a new world being born; both able just for a moment to be seen at once, like the new moon seen held in the old moon's arms.*

His narrative too was an old one, that had never failed to hold readers, had once held readers through romances many volumes long: *The search for something precious, lost or in hiding, waiting to be found.* If he failed in the end to deliver it, so had those old romances sometimes, and they were still held in honor.

So he had everything in ready now, stores of weird knowledge prepared, notes piling up, pencils metaphorically sharpened.

Why then did he feel so heartsick this morning, and so unready to begin?

He was afraid, is what it was.

For it now seemed to him clear—more clear in the dry light of hangover—that in fact the passage time was over; it had come and gone, and it had left the world unchanged. More or less the same.

Yes not long ago the world had turned over in its sleep, muttering, and seemed to wake; yes he had seen it shiver, startled by the hot flashes of some sort of climacteric. He had seen it, it had passed right through the open windows of the apartment across the river which he had shared with Julie Rosengarten, when he had thought nothing would ever be the same again.

But after that—had it not grown more obvious with every passing week, every daily newspaper?—Time had just gone on continuously opening his packages; and none of them were turning out to be what he had been guessing, or was being paid to prophesy, they would be. The new was in fact looking a lot like the old; shabbier even, like the new horizon above his old home street; deeply ordinary.

And as the new passage time evanesced, the old one started to look less convincing too; the more he learned about it, the less any sort of an age it seemed to be, the less subsumable under any myth, including his new one. It was probably just history after all.

Maybe if he had been able to write his book as fast as he had conceived it. But it would be months, years, till it was done, and already it was beginning to seem shamefully belated.

What Kraft somewhere said can happen to books: their fires can go out, eternal truths whose day is over, turned to ashes, gone with the wind. It had happened to his own even before he had seen it into print, and reaped his reward, turned his trick.

No no no.

Julie still felt herself to be living in a time of manifestation, and she had said to him that lots of others did too: the time when the next age becomes visible, mankind coming out of the dark wood, finding the bright path unrolling before, the path over the hill, where the sun is rising: she had suggested such a picture for his book's cover.

But she had always stood there, for as long as he had known her she had stood just there, always expecting dawn. Pierce envied her, sometimes. She had talked to him of other books that also prophesied wonders: but he had seen that they too were already wrong.

The time was over when all things are possible. He had actually felt for a while now that, despite his luck and the happy changes he had wrought in his life, he had somehow entered onto some sort of dull plain, a featureless changeless wasteland where progress was impossible to measure. Not a wasteland *out there*; out there was still as fruitful, really, still as full of this and that; a wasteland *in here,* in his own interior country.

But if that moment of possibility was gone (was not anything but illusion now, and therefore had not ever been anything but illusion) then what was it that had come close to him in his sitting room as he looked out at the roses? What had brushed by him, and touched his cheek?

Only the wind of its passage away.

On Midsummer Day he sat once again at Kraft's little built-in desk before the pile of yellow typewritten sheets without a title page. He was reading them all again, more critically this time, and half expecting them to have changed their contents in the meantime, withdrawn the offer they had held out to him. The day beyond Kraft's mock-leaded windows was so brilliant that the darkness inside the house glowed like light, as though Pierce had thrown a switch at the door to turn it on.

In Book One the runaway Dominican monk Giordano Bruno (a real person of course, all of Kraft's characters, in this book anyway, were real persons or at least had the names and did the deeds ascribed to real persons) crosses Europe, expelled from one country after another, instructing anyone who will listen (and pay) in the Art of Memory, an obsolete mnemonics that Bruno, probably because he had a naturally tremendous memory himself, believed could revolutionize thought and bring new powers into the soul. There were close calls with the Inquisition, a trip over the Alps in snow.

In Book Two (which lay before Pierce) he would arrive in England, in the reign of Elizabeth, meet poets and magicians, and become a spy, or at least an intelligencer; and there would be plots, an execution, a severed head.

And yet in a sense there were really no people at all, no events in the book; all that was solid was thought; the characters were nothing but intimations of change in human form. The only real character was time; it was time that went through the transforming agonies of the hero, was bound, made to suffer, learned to change and arise again. Time's body.

Maybe that's why Kraft had left the book unfinished; maybe he had never intended it to be a book, a book with a plot and settings, at all. It was an abstraction, a kind of brilliant cartoon nonexistence infused with this shameful need, for the world to be able to change;

to be subject to desire. As though the whole huge drysmelling wordpacked thing, all the potent jewels and angel voices and sailing ships, castles, armor, bound books, breadloaves, pisspots, the dogs, stars, stones and roses really occurred within one instant of awful longing.

Well Pierce knew. He knew. That's why he and not another had found the book, and read it.

If it were really possible to find oneself in a story, one of that small number of stories of which the world is made, this was the only one he could have found himself in.

In a faraway land, at once green and wasted, in the sanctum of a castle on a hilltop, a foolish wise hero finds and loses again some sort of something, preserved or guarded by a priest or king at once dead and alive. And by asking the right question finally (*What is this? What is it for?*) he frees the, wins the.

No no no.

Frank Barr had once pointed out to his class in the History of History a particular feature of wastelands in myth and literature: a wasteland is made not so much of barrenness as of repetition, pointless, endless, mechanical repetition. A wasteland even if what is endlessly repeated is the story of the wasteland redeemed, and made to flower.

What he precisely was *not*, Pierce knew, was a hero. He hadn't ever felt himself to be as much at the center of things as that; did not always feel himself to be in the center even of his own existence. And anyway the moment was passed when it was possible to believe that the world is made of stories.

Pierce Moffett, lost in conflicting thoughts, mouth ajar, leaned back in Kraft's creaking and untrustworthy chair (the kind that might continue easing back until too late, and drop the sitter backward) and turned a lock of his hair in his fingers.

The powers of that age looked down upon him where he sat. They shook their great heads slowly, and tsk'd their great tongues against their teeth. Yes doubtless it would take much to forge the man into anything like a hero; he would have to pass through some sort of refining fire before he was capable of carrying any precious thing into the future. To those who have, much will be given, even to abundance; but from those who have not will be taken even the little that they have. He was likely to lose all, every knowledge, every certainty, even the companionable regard he held himself in, even the comfort he still took in the taste of his own nature.

Face front, those aged powers wanted to call out to him, in need of redemption themselves. *Wake up,* they wanted to shout. But even if they had spoken, Pierce would not have been able to hear them; for they could not, as yet, be heard.

II

NATI

1

_____

Books, like certain gems, can be fragile despite their great density and weight. As pearls darken against the skin of certain antipathetic wearers, there are books that time will darken; time will dissolve a book entirely, as vinegar will dissolve a diamond, whose name is the name of indestructibility, adamant.

Books disintegrate; their fires go out, which burned the senses of readers once, and leave only cinders: hard to see how they could ever have been read with reverent ardor. It comes to seem they were never read at all, that they were never even really written, that writers only accumulated them, covering pages with what looked like prose, numbering their chapters, marking their subsections, seeing them into print, where they started fires in the minds of those who only handled them, and dreamed of their insides. *Amphitheatrum sapientiæ æternæ. Basil Valentinus his Triumphant Chariot of Antimony. Utriusque cosmi historiæ.*

It can't really be so, that people were so very different from the way they are now, and loved and needed so much inert printed paper. So it must be that once the books were different.

Which ones, for instance?

A lover of books who walked in the yard of St. Paul's in London in the spring of the year 1583, looking among the bookstalls there for something truly new, passing up the tables of religious tracts and tales of horrible murder uncovered, and the stalls of stationers who issued almanacs and books of prophecy mostly outdated, and those who sold sober histories of the late wars of the barons or the jars in religion, would have been able to put his hand on a folio volume in Latin, no date or place of publication, though it looked like an English book. *Ars reminiscendi et in phantastico campo exarandi,* and much more on a crowded title page.

The art of remembering, and how to lay it out on an imaginary field. Wrapped in parchment covers, sewn but unbound, its pages uncut and therefore not easily searchable, *Caveat emptor.* The book lover (this one is a young Scot of good family, his name is Alexander Dicson, he is in the service of Sir Philip Sidney) has seen books of this kind before, books which seem to offer instruction in some useful art, how to remember, how to write in secret codes, how to find ores and gems in the earth, but which to the reader who persists begin to offer more, as though stirring out of bonds of sleep.

The Scot even knew of this art of remembering, though he had never practiced it: places, and things cast on them, by which the order, say, of a sermon or a lecture might be remembered. In this book the place is termed *subjectus* and the thing *adjectus.*

There was also included a book of "seals," whatever they might be, *ad omnium scientiarum et artium inventionem dispositionem et memoriam,* for discovering and arranging as well as remembering all arts and sciences. How could memory discover knowledge? Was not a seal a shutting and not an opening?

Then an Explanation of the thirty seals. Then a Seal of Seals. Last.

Per cabalam, naturalem magiam, artes magnas atque breves whispered the title page in its smallest type. By cabala, natural magic, great arts and small ones. Shifting from foot to foot Master Dicson dug through the pages, glimpsing diagrams, Hebrew letters, the Adam drawn in a square, the Adam drawn in a circle. He pulled open his purse (it was supposed to pay his month's lodgings) and raised his eyebrows inquiringly to the bookseller.

O you haunters of bookstalls and shops, you searchers in libraries; who conceive of entering in at some big title page and not thereafter ever returning—one of those title pages where wise *putti* display the bones of the heavens, the Divine Name in Hebrew sheds effulgence over Earth, Hermes puts his finger to his lips, the Seven Arts are spread over the floor (viol, compasses, chisel and mallet) and a Searcher in robes draws a triangle, gazing at the figured stars—no matter how often you are disappointed, turned back perforce into your own chair in your old cold city, there are always further books, always other doors, shake their knobs and pound for admission. Whose book anyway is this? Master Dicson turned back to the forematter. Dedication, to the French Ambassador to England. Then an address to the Vice Chancellor of Oxford and to its celebrated doctors and teachers:

> *Philotheus Jordanus Brunus Nolanus, Doctor (but of a more recondite theology), Professor (but of a pure and more innocent wisdom), noted in the best academies of Europe, a philosopher lauded and honorably received everywhere, a stranger nowhere but among the barbarous and low, waker of sleeping souls, scourge of presumptuous and obdurate ignorance, herald of a general benevolence; who does not approve the Italian more than the Briton, the male more than the female, the miter more than the crown, the senator's toga more than the general's armor, the cowled monk more than the layman, but only him who is the more peaceable, civil, faithful, useful; who cares nothing for the anointed head, the cross-thumbed forehead, the holy-water-washed hands, the circumcised member, but—what his face can indeed show—the cultured mind and soul. Who is hated by the spewers of foolishness and the hypocrites, but sought out by the honest, those willing to study . . .*

What on earth, or rather who. He shut up the big book, his now in any case, and went home through the crowds of the barbarous and the low, feeling vaguely fleeced. Who was this Bruno Nolano he had taken up, or been taken by?

He was just then (he had been other things) a gentleman servant in the household of Michel de Castelnau, Seigneur de Mauvissiere, the ambassador of King Henri III of France to the court of Elizabeth. He had been recommended to the Ambassador by the King himself, who had made Bruno his reader *extraordinaire,* and who had for a time been entranced by the Italian, by his powers, by the possibilities he shadowed forth.

So Giordano Bruno Nolano, born under a kindlier sky, had

crossed the channel and come into this country, more barbarous and dirtier than some, and closer to Thule than he had got before, closer than he liked to be. He had a room in the French Embassy on Salisbury Court, near the river, a room high up under the eaves, out whose window he could watch the river traffic, the foreign ships and the merchantmen, and see the weather come in too, gray rain and pale sun alternating.

His duties, insofar as he had any that could be named, were to be in attendance at dinner, to be amusing and learned, to fill out the Ambassador's suite when the Ambassador went to court. So much could be said aloud. He learned to read English in a few weeks' time and to understand it when it was spoken, at least as it was spoken at court. No one but the Ambassador and his children's private tutor, the Italian John Florio, knew this about the *gentiluomo servante* in the upper storey. He committed the greater part of Florio's dictionary of English and Italian to memory by transforming the words inwardly into dancers, the Italians the men, the English their ladies, so that whenever he summoned an Italian word in his mind (*tradutto,* all in black, with a poison-ring on his finger) there would come along his partner (*treachery,* her gown sewn with eyes and tongues). He never learned to say many words; he only knew them by sight, he knew their faces.

When the Ambassador and his party returned late to Salisbury Court, late from a dinner at some magnate's house on the Strand, or from an investiture or an entertainment at court, he would dismiss his other attendants, order wine brought to his private chamber, and there he and John Florio would sit and listen while the Nolan recounted what had taken place.

—The order at table, he said. Signor Leicester at the Queen's right. Signor Burleigh at the Queen's left. Milord Howard. Signor, signor, Raleigh.

He could see them all well enough, arranged by physiognomic type around the table, a menagerie of cunning and talkative gentlefolk, only the weird names he could not always say aloud. Florio prompted him, as often confusing as helping.

—At the third hour, he continued. Signor Leicester and Signor Walsingham depart for one quarter of an hour. They go out through the arras by the Queen's door.

—Had the Queen spoken yet of Sir Philip Sidney's embassy to France?

—Not then, not then. After the two returned: Signor Leicester danced. Walsingham also, not so well. A galliard. He took the Queen's hand. Then the hour struck. Four.

—So, the Ambassador said. Leicester and he spoke together. And then he had opportunity to tell the Queen. I wonder.

The Nolan only sat, not wondering, only observing the entertainment at court proceeding in the miniature galleries and halls he had constructed for them within his memory palaces, the newest therefore still the smallest of the fourteen distinct royal, civic, and ecclesiastical courts, some of them in disrepair, some shuttered, which he had had occasion to assemble in his memory as he went from country to country.

What astonished the Ambassador about his servant's accountings, besides their minute exactness, was that though he had stood in only one place or a few places at the receptions and affairs, he could tell the story as though he had been everywhere at once: when he retold the events, they seemed not to be merely remembered but to recur within him, and he could change his place in them at will. It was tedious sometimes to listen to his accounts, since he had no idea what was and what was not significant (though he was learning). It was more often illuminating. The King had suggested that it might be.

How the Nolan was able to do the thing that he did for his master (and other things that he did not choose to tell of) his master did not know. The King had described Bruno's arts in a cloudy way; when Bruno himself explained his techniques, smiling as he talked, as though a friendly demeanor could make his matter easier, the Ambassador had tried to listen. The Ambassador's childhood tutor had used the same face when he had tried to teach the boy astronomy, and Bruno got no further than that man had done. For his own part, the Ambassador remembered things by making a memorandum, or asking his secretary to make one. He had heard of men, sometimes mere children, who could do long sums in their heads almost without thinking or tell the date of Ash Wednesday in any past or future year. He supposed the Italian was a person of that sort; he did not see how mere practice in an art could accomplish what Bruno accomplished.

The Seigneur de Mauvissiere kept his strange servant awake and at work for longer than usual on this May night. He was troubled; something was afoot, something which he was not privy to and which he yet stood at the center of: that was the feeling he could not shake. He was being used, and he didn't like it. But by whom?

—The order at departing, Bruno said.

He counted backward on his fingers, starting with the smallest of the left hand. Signor Leicester, Signor Henry Sidney, Signor Raleigh. Milord Henry Howard. Signor Walsingham, who stooped to pick up your glove.

—No, said the Ambassador. That was my own servant.

—No, said Bruno.

The Nolan's head had fallen back against the chair now, and his eyes were closed, though his hands clasped before him were still alert (two raised like a steeple). Whose glove was that?

—It was a pale glove, he said. Of kid, the color of a hand.

—No, said the Ambassador.

He could see it all clearly from where he stood amid the Ambassador's suite. Walsingham the fox, Leicester the goat, the phoenix Queen. Earl Howard the goggling fish. It was fox-faced Walsingham who picked up the. No.

—It leapt when he took it from the floor. It was a severed hand. A right hand, severed for treason. You have been betrayed to Walsingham.

—Betrayed, how, by whom?

—The plot is discovered, Bruno said. No: About to be discovered. Those whom you trusted have been betrayed to the English, and will betray you in turn.

—But there is no plot, said the Ambassador.

Michel de Castelnau closed his own hands as in prayer, and then lifted them to his lips; his troubled eyes looked within, reviewing his own actions, his household. It was past midnight. In his apartment above his wife lay, sleeping he hoped, recovering from a miscarriage, her second.

—There is no plot, he said.

There was a plot. There was always a plot, the same plot, it only thickened now and then into action as men's plans and their courage hardened. It was a plot to invite Catholic troops into the country to remove the heretic Queen of England from the throne and seat there instead her cousin, Mary, formerly Queen of France and now Queen of Scotland, a Catholic whatever else she might be, and for some time now Elizabeth's prisoner.

Bernardino de Mendoza, Ambassador of the Most Catholic King of Spain; Cardinal William Allen, the exiled Englishman at the Papal court in Rome; the Pope, Sixtus V, who had forbidden Catholics to obey their heretic Queen; the Duke of Guise and the burning hearts of the Catholic League in France—this current mutation of the plot involved them all. Firm plans were being laid, numbers of troops and their dispositions and embarkation points, the names of those marked for seizure and death.

The French Ambassador had not been told of it. He was firmly Catholic, and Protestant enthusiasm frightened and disgusted him; but he had seen St. Bartholomew's Night in Paris, Protestants slain on his doorstep by Catholic fanatics, the gutters flowing with blood, and it had darkened his spirit for good. He was not reliable; too soft, too *politique,* to be entrusted with the details of a plot to murder Elizabeth and forcibly reconvert her realm to the True Faith. He didn't know that his house was used as a meeting-place, and that certain English gentlemen who took refuge in his garden, who heard Mass with him in his chapel (the English could not forbid it there) were deeply concerned in the plot.

He wrote often in cipher to Mary, in her imprisonment in Sheffield, cheering her with news of his negotiations for her release and return to her own realm of Scotland, transmitting news from her brother-in-law the King of France, sending money and jewels from devoted liegemen in England and France. He didn't know that his letters were intercepted and read before they were sent on, not always unchanged.

He didn't know that his personal secretary (a Frenchman with money troubles named Courcelles) was in the pay of Walsingham and the English, and communicated to them whatever he saw and heard and read in the Ambassador's house and papers; or that his chaplain, who said his Masses, who consecrated the Bread and placed it on the Ambassador's tongue, was also an agent of the English, and told all that he saw, all that he heard, even in the darkness of the confessional.

On the 29th, this priest wrote to Elizabeth's chief of spies, Sir Francis Walsingham: "Monsieur Throckmorton dined this night at the ambassador's house. A Catholic. He recently conveyed 1500 *ecus sol* to the Queen of Scots, on the Ambassador's account . . . At midnight the Ambassador was visited by Milord Henry Howard, a Roman Catholic and a Papist," who entered privily through the garden, and awakened the Ambassador with a handful of sand thrown against his window, to talk to him about saving a Scots Catholic who was staying in the house from being imprisoned; with such tasks the Ambassador was trusted.

The Italian *gentiluomo servante* was not mentioned in anyone's dispatches anywhere; no one attempted to recruit him. He talked too much and too loudly. The chaplain in particular avoided him: when he felt Bruno's potent attention turned on him, he made excuses, vanished, hid in his little vestry and sweated, running through in his mind every move he had made that day, looking for the slip Bruno might have noticed. But Bruno's stare was only a fascinated repulsion, frank appreciation of a specimen. For Giordano Bruno had, himself, been an Italian monk; his fingers were still consecrated, nothing could wash the chrism from them; and he knew a bad priest when he smelled one.

—You suffer fools gladly, Bruno would say to the Ambassador, late, late in the Ambassador's private chamber. I would not. I cannot.

And the narrow saint's face would smile a little.

—You are a philosopher, he would say. You see farther. Perhaps. These troubles are as nothing *sub specie æternitatis*. And yet we are flesh and blood, we are here, and the work is ours to do now. Let us talk now of the reception at court for the Prince of Laski . . .

So John Florio would pick up his pen, and Bruno would lace his fingers before him, a sarcastic smirk on his face, we will play this game if we must. There were few men the Nolan had loved as fully as his huge heart was capable of loving: the Seigneur de Mauvissiere was one of them. So he would give him now the order of the guests arriving for the reception, and the nature of the compliments given, the asides made and the faces of those who made the asides, the winners at the games and the prizes awarded them, the unspoken currents of fear, malice, unawareness and suspicion that held all of them together like a purse-seine.

The French Ambassador did not understand how Bruno was able to do what he did in the Ambassador's service; but Alexander Dicson knew. For he had read (as the Ambassador had not, to whom it was dedicated) Bruno's book on memory.

The way to remember things is to establish irremovably within your intellect a series of places, like the parts of a large building—the arches, the windows, passages, stairs, pillars, galleries and even the gardens and barns. You may commit to memory the parts of a real edifice, or you may invent a more spacious and complex one of your own. Onto the places or parts (*subjecti*) you put images (*adjecti*) of the things to be remembered, in the order in which you wish to remember them. The images are to be cast in such a way as to excite the feelings, for things that are striking or beautiful or disgusting are more easily remembered than things that are bland and uninteresting.

Very well; Dicson practiced this, using the few spaces and partitions of his room at the Ox and Pearl, and it seemed to do what was promised. Then the way grew harder.

When your memory places have all been filled with interesting and important matter that you do not wish to evict, more places can be added; on your travels collect new places, attach them with simple bridges or portals to the earlier places; or contain the old places within squares or streets of new ones. Your memory grows, and nothing is lost.

Was it possible, Dicson wondered, to use the art of memory to retain and recall the rules of the art of memory? To build houses and construct images to remind of the rules for building houses and constructing images? He had not yet even reached the Seals themselves. He got out paper and ink, to make notes, and put them away again.

The first Seal is the Field: the Field is memory itself, which is not different from the *vis imaginativa*, the power of imagination. Look out upon this Field, its many many folds and convolutions; for though it seems plain and patent we know how many hidden places it contains. In those places are the ten thousand, the virtually infinite number of things my eyes and ears and other senses have put there since I was a boy, every scene of childhood, every noble or foolish person, every dog, star, stone, rose. It is the chaos of Anaximander. I know what things are contained there but I cannot grasp any, or if I do I cannot tell what I will come away with, jewel, dog-turd, something useful, something I do not need. How will I bring order to infinite memory?

The second seal is the Chain. Dicson began to understand. All things, whether we perceive it immediately or do not, are linked, lower to higher, preceding to following, first to next to next. Aries acts on Taurus, Taurus on Gemini, Gemini on Cancer: the Zodiac is a chain; each of its links is made of smaller chains, *ad infinitum*. Everything has its place. Thus also is memory ordered.

Dicson slit the pages with his knife as he devoured bread and cheese and the text. Cut bread, cut a page. The Seals now grew more difficult.

The Peregrinator, who walks through the different chambers of the memory house, gathering what he needs from what was stored for other reasons. The Table, where twenty-three people sit, whose names begin with the letters of the alphabet. It only slowly dawned on Dicson that he was to remember individual words by means of these people, who were to change places with great rapidity, spelling out words in his mind as his tongue formed them. But the seal called the Century employed not twenty-three but one hundred boys and girls (they should be young, attractive, friends of yours, Bruno said, faces well known to you; Dicson doubted he knew a hundred people's faces) and they were to stand in the places of memory, ready to carry emblems, play parts, a laughing helpful cohort at your service always. Always. For some reason tears rose to Dicson's eyes.

There was the Garden of Circe, where the four elements mutated and changed through seven houses belonging to the planets, generating as they went not only all species of animals and plants but all the human types that resembled or shared the nature of those animals, the hot-dry sun-loving Lion, his yellow Dandelion, his planet Sol, the King whose nature and face is like his. The elemental flux of Anaximander took shape and order in the memory-artist's mind.

All things proceed from lower to higher, and beginning with the lowest we may proceed to the highest. Dicson on the stair midway to the top dared not look down; he felt with his foot for the next stair, arms out like a blind man. The twenty-second Seal was the Fountain and the Mirror. The mirror reflects the fountain: the bounty of eternity gushes forth unceasing, an uncountable tumble of this and that, but the mirror, Mind, contains every droplet exactly as it is produced. Why are we troubled, why are we confused? There is but one Knowledge, placed in one Subject.

Unable to read more than a few pages together before he had to rise, giddy and overcome; finally unable to take in more than a page, a subsection, a paragraph, before lifting his surfeited eyes, Dicson approached the Seal of Seals.

He had not waited on his patron Sir Philip for several days, had not prosecuted his family's business at court. He thought sometimes that he had fallen into the hands of one of those proud teachers who expound what they are able to do, not in order to permit you to do it too, but only to awaken your wonder, and make you certain you could never, never. Bruno alluded in these pages to other tracts he had also written, other forms of the Art of Memory he knew, systems other than this one of seals and a field: and if Alexander Dicson read his crabbed and unpleasant Latin aright, the man claimed that from them he had built for himself other artificial memories containing hundreds of thousands of items, and that he used all of them interchangeably, simultaneously, or in combination one with another.

Weary with reading what he could only partly grasp, Alexander Dicson took the round glasses that were little help to him from his nose and put them aside. When he pinched out his tallow candle, his small dark window brightened a little, and Dicson went to it. He watched candles put out in other windows, one there, one there: other late scholars, or lovers maybe.

For it was moonless midnight now, most of the stars covered up in clouds; London's lights were dim, a string of torches flaring at water-stairs, candles in windows, linkboys hurrying before belated gentlemen; and the lightless river sundering her, the river running past Dicson's window, past Salisbury Court too, and past the great houses along the Strand toward Westminster.

At that hour, not far up the river, in a room in a house in the village of Mortlake, two men knelt before a transparent globe mounted in the center of a painted table; and though candles lit the room, the globe was lit from within as well, and shone into the faces of the two who looked in. What did they see? John Dee saw nothing but the limitless depths of the stone's transparency; the other man, Edward Kelley, saw the angel Uriel.

They asked the angel: What did the vision mean, that had visited Kelley at dinner, unlooked for, sudden, of the sea, and ships covering it; and the beheading of a woman by a tall man in black?

Uriel answered. The voice he used was Kelley's, almost too soft sometimes to be heard, the voice of a man awaking from a dream or falling into one; and John Dee wrote down all that he said:

> The one did signifie the provision of forrayn powers against the welfare of this land; which they shall shortly put into practice. The other, the death of the Queene of Scotts.

—The Queen of Scots, said Dee, looking down at what he had written.

—It is not long unto it, whispered Uriel or Kelley. And John Dee wrote: It is not long unto it.

2

n Midsummer Day Doctor John Dee walked out on Mortlake field all the morning. *Beltaine* the season was called among the Welsh race from which he sprang: the other, the better half of the year. Last night on Richmond Hill with his neighbors he had made his Midsummer bonfire, the good old custom that the Puritans so much hated; there had been no trouble this year, and the Queen, who was at Richmond, had sent him a cask of Canary wine to make merry. Today there were small clouds solid and ovoid like young sheep treading the sky, summer clouds, and a sun hot and young too.

With the skirts of his long coat tucked up and his hose wet to the shins, Doctor Dee with his basket went along the brook's side, gathering this and that which he saw growing along the rushy banks. Cows stepped in and out of the stream and bent to drink, or raised their lashy eyes and swung their great calm heads toward him. There was mint here, of two kinds, for teas and comfits; some myrtle for a posy, Venus's flower, for his wife. There was comfrey, every part of it useful, root branch leaf and pale flower that the bees loved. Doctor Dee crushed mint leaves before his nose, and inhaled the summer.

He did not need to go on this walk, there were simples for sale, the woman who lived by the stile would give him all he needed for the gift of his visit to her, and she knew more of them than he. But it pleased him to gather. He thought that Galen must once have gathered: for to see those herbs that out of His bounty God through His sun's influence brought forth for man's ease and health, to see them not in jars and baskets or distilled in apothecary's liquors but unfolding in their time from earth, to know them by their leaves and colors—that made a man wise, made a doctor a good man: Doctor Dee felt that, though he might not have argued it. So—his head full of sunshine, and his eyes quartering the ground—he went around Mortlake field, humming softly and tunelessly like the bees.

Here was vervain, the shy lilac flowers upon her flimsy stalks. When you pick her—so the old woman said—if she will do good, you must pray thus, *Hail be thou, holy herb, growing on the ground; th'art good for many a sore, that healed Christ and stanched his wound; in the name of sweet Jesus, I take thee from the ground.*

And there, he had said the prayer in his remembering of her saying it, though he knew that the healing virtues of the herb were present in it naturally, and did not depend on her charm. Here were primroses, the sun's flower: keep them by you, wear gold, take the blue air, and you draw the sun into a sad Saturnian horoscope. Doctor Dee dug them for Kelley. He wrapped their roots in a spill of damp paper, and put them in his basket. Kelley's melancholy required stronger medicine, and yet these pretty blooms in his window need not be despised.

John Dee raised his eyes to the brilliant sky, wherein strange fires writhed, such as can be seen by the eye when it is raised suddenly from darkness.

He thought sometimes—not often—that perhaps he had been happier before Edward Kelley had come knocking on his door: and when he thought so his heart would contract with horror, as though the thought might have power to drive the young man away from the door on that long-past night: and Doctor Dee could not now do without him.

When he first came to Dee's Mortlake house, a year and three months ago now, a March night full of wind, Kelley had brought a book for Doctor Dee to interpret for him, a book in a code that Dee could not break, a language he could not translate. (It lay in the house still, in Master Kelley's room, beneath his pillow, from where it whispered to Kelley in his dreams.) Doctor Dee, alert as he always was for the rare sensitive soul able to look into an empty crystal sphere or empty mirror of black obsidian (or into a dish of plain water or a bead of glass) and catch faces and voices in it, had invited Master Kelley to sit before such a sphere, one that Dee had reason to believe had spirits answering to it; and the man had seen them, and heard them too. Since that night Doctor Dee had filled books with the conversations they had had, Kelley and the angels, celestial playbooks, act upon act. Doctor Dee had been greatly blessed, and so had Edward Kelley; the difference was that John Dee knew it, and praised God daily for it, and Edward Kelley did not seem to know it.

His name had not been Kelley then. His name had been Talbot. He had gone on being Talbot for some months, until on a winter day his brother had appeared at the door, and *his* name was Kelley: an evil-minded boy whose eye shifted continuously from corner to corner, looking (said Doctor Dee's wife) for something he could steal. This brother saw that Edward Talbot had got a good place, and some power over the house, and would have liked to share it, but Doctor Dee sent him away: not before the man (despite Edward's shriekings to silence him) had told all.

So Edward Talbot, Kelley, was not a learned man, nor had he a degree from Oxford as he had said; he had not journeyed in Wales but had hid in his brother's house from the magistrate's constable who sought him. He had told abominable lies, then, and seemed even now to feel no remorse; shame, perhaps, and sorrow that he had caused sorrow, but not remorse, or much embarrassment. As though to him a past were only a selection out of all possible tales, which might have changed when he next looked into it.

Knowing the truth (the coining, the ears cropped by the common hangman for wicked sorcery, which crime he still denied) had only confirmed Jane Dee's fear and dislike of Kelley. The next row had been hers with him, with much said that would be hard to unsay, much banging of doors and packing of bags. I will not stay in a house where I am not wanted. Where I am hated. I will be gone away this night. Take your hand from my coat. See to your wife.

Up the stairs to try Jane's locked door, behind which she wept, and down again to see that Kelley had not hurried away so fast as he had seemed ready to: still packing his bag, a gift of Dee's, with books of Dee's. He was a cumber to the house, he said, he dwelt here as a prisoner, he were better far to be away in the country where he could walk abroad and not be troubled with slanderous tongues. No more of the farthest room, no more of the doings there, he has got nothing by it, and must study some art by which he may live.

But have we not promises, promises, Doctor Dee had said softly, and been mocked by Kelley: Promises, promises, they have made many promises and no good come from them.

They would not be given a stone, having asked for bread: Doctor Dee was sure of it. As for money, he himself owes three hundred pounds and knows not where he shall find it, but he would walk the length of this land begging in a blanket if he could learn, or bowel out, some good thing, some godly wisdom, whereby to do God's service for His glory. Tears in his eyes. He had thought Kelley was joined with him, heart to heart, in that at least. And Kelley at length put down his bag, staring at the dark of the window, and was quiet; wept too a little.

And all those pangs had been caused by a spirit, Belmagel by name, *the firebrand that hath followed thee so long*: so the good angel Uriel next night informed them, as they knelt together again in the farthest room, before the table of practice on which the clear glass rested, wherein Kelley (though not his employer and keeper) could discern the traffic of another world.

The old woman who lived by the stile was called Mother Godefroy, though she had no children left her and lived alone in her tiny house. Her sons had lost the little living they had got from the common lands when the lands were enclosed by the lord of the manor and put to sheep-pasturage. At length the boys had left home, and now Mother Godefroy didn't know where they were: beggars or outlaws on the highway or wild men digging for roots in the waste places.

Her house by the hedge had come, over time, to be part of the hedge: the branches of locust and thorn thrust through her window in the summer, and bryony and woodbine bound her thatched roof to the hawthorns they climbed. The yellow walls were of stone patched with mud, a cave; but the yard was swept and clean, and a pot of basil and another of rosemary sunned themselves by the door; and Mother Godefroy too, on a bench there, face up to the sun.

—Good den to you, Mother, Doctor Dee said at her gate. How goes the world with you?

—Your worship's kind to ask, Mother Godefroy said. The world is as it was.

—May I come in?

—You may come in but I will stay out, said Mother Godefroy. God bless the sun.

He pushed the gate of wattles open, and stepped in. A black cat, startled by his entrance, leapt from the yard to the wall to the roof in two neat jumps.

—Hush, Spittikins, my love.

Doctor Dee sat down beside her on her bench. Her broad flat face, a moon or a pale pudding, was stubbled over with pimples; her mouth, open to let out her labored breath, showed a row of tiny sharp teeth, like a baby's.

—I've come for your advice, said Doctor Dee. And for a simple too, it may be.

—Th'art welcome to both.

The village of Mortlake could not have done without Mother Godefroy. It was she who knew the medicines that most folk could afford. The midwives came to her for calming and stupefying drugs, the young girls came to find out if they were loved—Mother Godefroy would suspend a scissors on a thread, or drop jackstraws, to find out —and, if they were not, to buy what would make them loved. She could make cows give, too; or dry them up, some said. One of her eyes was blue and clouded as a newborn baby's: blind. But some said not so blind after all.

—The young man who has come to live with me, said Doctor Dee.

—Yes, said the cunning woman. He who sees summat in a stone.

—Yes.

He did not like it well that Mother Godefroy knew this about Kelley, nor did he know how she knew it. He chose not to ask, knowing that anyway it would go no farther. She had her own reasons for keeping such matters close.

—He was to be married, said Mother Godefroy.

—He is. He is married now. Joanna Cooper her name was, of Chipping Norton. For a time after they married she stayed at home. She wrote him letters, and he visited there. Now she is here. A youngling, but eighteen years.

A good child she was, too, and willing, in a way that touched the heart, and yet with some hurt in her big fox's eyes. Jane Dee, after a single night's chiding of her beloved husband (furiously tossing the bedclothes as she rolled away from him, then back to fill his ear again) hadn't been able to be cold to the girl; the two were friends now, better friends than either was with Kelley. Kelley's new wife was dutiful and cheerful, and sat by him in the evening: though Kelley would rise up now and then, and twist himself in his clothes, as though to be rid of an annoyance.

—I think, Doctor Dee said to Mother Godefroy, I think he has not yet been with her as man to wife.

The old woman nodded, rolled her head, and put a black-nailed thumb against her chin.

—And 'tis he or she is unwilling?

—Well I know not certainly. But I think he is.

—So then, said Mother Godefroy, and placed her hands again in her great lap.

—I know you are wise, Mother. I think you may know some infusion, some herb, that might warm cold blood.

—Well I may.

She thought for a time, and Doctor Dee waited patiently.

—And will you give it him secretly, or offer it to him?

—Not secretly. None of your charms, Mother.

She smiled, and turned her good eye upon him.

—Secret does the work the best, she said.

But she would not tease him, great and good man. She got up and went into her dark small house.

Secret. Slip a posy under his pillow, she meant. Or lay a sprig of this or that on his picture, or tie it with a lock of his hair. A village girl would do so, or think of doing so, to fix her boy's affections. The charm lay in the flush it gave to her own cheek, the hope raised in her eye, when next she saw him.

A flush of shame burned the Doctor's own cheek. Look what he had been brought to: begging a cunning-woman for a drug to make a man stand. Pander. Who would have thought the work would require it of him in his age.

For it was they, the angels attendant on the glass, who had early on in their communications ordered Kelley to marry: though he protested he had no inclination to do it, nor any desire for a wife. And indeed there seemed something unformed in him, a childish way, as though he were despite his scholar's beard a boy still, who had no use for woman.

No, what the man loved, what warmed him and made him yearn (the only thing, so far as Doctor Dee knew), was gold. Not riches, gold: the yellow metal itself, sun's offspring, warm (he said) to his touch.

That time he had been sought by the officers for coining, what he had been about (he said) was no such base business but the great Work. He had had no success. If a man was to cause gold to increase and multiply, he must himself impart to it the power; no impotent or sterile man could do that (he said) and that was why (he said) the angel Michael had bade him marry, bade him swear to it on the sword of light which he held out: so that he would be fruitful. And so John Dee had set out to find him a wife, and had found one.

From whose side Kelley would bolt in the midnight, to be found asleep in his shirt in the morning curled up before the kitchen fire like a dog.

—There, said Mother Godefroy coming out.

She gave the doctor a tiny beeswax bottle.

—There is not one thing only in it but many. Melt it in a posset. Make him drink. There is a scripture to say with it.

He put it in his wallet, and (knowing she would take no money from him) gave her a small bottle of spirits of wine, which she could not make herself, for the preparing of cordials; and after he had sat and talked a time with her, he set out across the common, feeling pleased and guilty at once; the sky overhead was crowded now with clouds, and a sharp wind was rising.

He was not barren, though, Kelley was not: for he had got with child a clear cold stone empty to everyone else's eyes, a child, a girl-child. Doctor Dee had attended at the birth, and had helped the child to grow, till now when she could speak, and answer.

It was on a morning in May just past when she appeared, seemingly for the first time, as they sat talking together about the Polish prince Adelbert à Lasco, about the honor he meant to do them: how such a man's patronage might protect them from their enemies at court, of whom they had had spirit warnings. She was with them suddenly, unannounced and unforetold, "a pretty girle of 7 or 9 years, attired in a gown of Sey, changeable red and green"—Doctor

Dee wrote what Kelley saw—"and her long hair rowled up in front and hanging down very long behind," a rope of soft gold lightly braided.

She did not stay within the glass but was quickly out and moving in the Doctor's study, going in and out of the piles of books that were everywhere, Babel towers of books in several languages, open and closed: they seemed to give place to her and let her pass.

—Whose maiden are you? asked Doctor Dee.

—*Whose man are you?* she answered, like a quick schoolchild who knows a game.

—I am the servant of God, said the doctor: both by my bound duty, and—I hope—by His adoption.

She seemed pleased enough at that answer, and was about to speak herself, when there came another voice, from the corner where the great perspective glass stood:

—*You shall be beaten if you tell.*

Kelley looked up suddenly, as if stirred from a reverie, looking for whoever had spoken, and, seeing nothing, relaxed again into the strange slack posture Doctor Dee now knew so well, his hands loosely folded and held up before him but dropping ever and again slightly, as though he were passing in and out of sleep, like a torpid monk at devotions; and the child spoke again:

—*Am I not a fair maiden?*

—Do you know I cannot see you? Doctor Dee said gently. I think you must be fair, but I cannot see.

—*Let me play in your house,* she said. *My mother told me she would come here and dwell with you, she did.*

—Well, said Doctor Dee, amazed and amused, as he was before his own daughters' inventions. Well, now . . .

She seemed to lose interest in his answer then, though, and Kelley told how she went around the room, forgetting about the skryer and his master as she was absorbed in what she saw and in her own responses, as any girl might be; sometimes she sang.

—*I pray you let me stay a little while,* she said, still speaking to the unseen one, as to a careful but beloved nurse: and she laughed lightly, having got the someone's permission perhaps, and Doctor Dee, though he said he could not see her, began to know how she looked; could see her tumble of blond hair and the red of her fat cheeks, her great honey-colored eyes the only abashing thing about her, the only thing not childlike, innocent and plain as a child's but not a child's.

—Tell me who you are.

—*I pray you let me play a little with you and I will tell you who I am.*

—In the name of Jesus then, tell me.

In a play-acting voice, a story-telling voice, she said:

—*I rejoice in the name of Jesus, and I am a poor little maiden, Madimi. I am the last—but one—of my mother's children.* And in another voice, a little girl pretending: *And I have little baby children at my home.*

—Where is your home? asked Doctor Dee.

—*I dare not tell you where I dwell, I shall be beaten.*

—You shall not be beaten for telling the truth to them that love the truth, said Doctor Dee—responding immediately, as he might have to any mistaken child, not wondering then where it was she might have come from that she would be beaten for revealing to him.

—To the eternal truth (he said piously, raising a forefinger as he might have to one of his daughters) all creatures must be obedient.

—*I will be,* she said. *And I will come live with you.* And then, gaily: *My sisters all say they must come live with you too.* And Doctor Dee could hear, not with his ears, the silver of her small laughter.

So old Abbot Trithemius was wrong, wise as that holy abbot had been concerning angels, to say they never took female form. Perhaps in deference to monkish scruples they had chosen not to appear so to Trithemius.

But they could; they could be, or appear to be, women, or girl-children anyway, children changeable and full of fancies and continual invention, too young to know real from pretend, or to care to distinguish them; quick, and vain, and loving too.

They could be children: but could they also be born, and grow? Though it seemed that Madimi had never appeared to them before that white May morning, Edward Kelley then thought of the first night ever he had skryed there in Doctor Dee's upper chamber, that night in March a year before, 1582, it seemed far longer ago; how he had first knelt and after solemn prayer looked into the doctor's sphere of moleskin-colored crystal. Amid the smiling potent figures who had begun to crowd into the stone almost as soon as he looked into it he had seen one who bore a looking-glass, and in that glass there opened a window, and in that window sat a little naked girl-child, who seemed to bear a sphere of crystal in her hand: and her eyes (as he thought now) were large and honey-colored, piercing and mild, as Madimi's were.

And then on an evening later in that spring, when they had made a table of practice according to angelic instructions, and lacked only a new and virgin stone to place in its center, there had appeared in the chamber's western window, amid the ingots of dusty sunlight that the mullions cast, another naked girl-child, older by years than the first; and in her hand a globe that was (Doctor Dee wrote furiously, describing, so as not to forget) "most bright, most clere and glorious, of the bigness of an egg." The archangel Michael had pointed to the globe with his sword (a bar of light too) and spoken, bidding Doctor Dee "take it up, and let no mortal hand touch it but thine own." And the child placed it in the center of their table, in the claws of the silver frame, which were set to hold just this stone though they had not known it, this stone out of which a child of seven had now stepped, in her gown of green and red, her feet still bare.

If angels could grow from infancy to girlhood, could they be born? If they could be born, could they die? Doctor Dee had among his thousands of volumes a work of Porphyry, wherein he says that wicked spirits who live near the earth have spiritual bodies, which like ours are mortal and need to be fed.

No: she was not a child, and she had no body at all; she was not a she, no more a he. That she seemed one was no more than his and Kelley's flawed sight and darkened souls: they must needs perceive *something* sensible in the play of power concentrated in the stone, the bodiless intelligences passing by there as by a perspective glass—just as, mortal, they could not help but see faces in clouds and gesturing personages in the wind-moved leaves of trees. It was a kindness of those immortals, so to show themselves to the poor seekers who could not know them as they were, whose human senses would be burned like Isaiah's lip if once an angel covered them undisguised.

There had been other forms before Madimi, other persons coming and going within the sphere, passing in and out as though through a market gate: Michael armed and Uriel clothed with light, and others the Doctor had not before heard of, Galvah and Nalvage,

Bobogel and Il. Bobogel is sage and grave; his beard is long and a black feather nods in his velvet cap; he wears scholar's slipslop slippers. Il is a merry fellow, appareled like a Vice in an old-fashioned play, with a belly ungirded that shakes when he laughs and hose bagging at the knees. Kelley said that now and again when he knelt alone before the crystal without his master, this Il would show him bawdry, copulations, the unseen doings of airy dæmons, and laugh.

Oh, he had doubted; he had doubted Kelley, who might well know the tricks of those London friends out of whose circle Doctor Dee had rescued him—coneycatchers and blessers and quacksalvers who could cozen with throwing of the voice and a thousand other arts. He had doubted the spirits too, and so had Kelley, antic and common sometimes as a London crowd, bragging up and down, mixing their matter with gibberish and jests. But he had learned too much from them already, and he needed too badly to learn more, to believe they were evil. Only long afterward, after they had abased him and hollowed him, pithed him like a crab and left him to linger naked in his bones, would he recall what the child had said to him (she whom alone of them he had loved) when he asked how he could be sure he was not illuded here by fallen angels drawn to his stone and to his need. All the angels, she had said, are fallen angels.

All the angels are fallen angels: Neither glad nor sad at it, her light gay eyes unclouded. And he had thought it a childish riddle without meaning.

3

en may not always know that they live in a period of crisis, Time hovering at a crossroads, about to choose a way: but those living in Britain and in Europe at the end of the sixteenth century knew it.

There had fallen, just in those late years of that age of the world, a pause or halt—it could not be called a calm—in the hundred years' war of the destruction of European Christendom. Though arms had been laid down the war had not ceased; it had grown more terrible as it rested, like a dragon on his hoard, the parties ever more willing to contemplate absolute solutions to the divisions they saw around them, men ever more unable to live if it meant letting live. Even those who longed for peace and charity could imagine no peace but Perfect Peace, no reformation but the Universal Reformation of the Whole Wide World.

Nearly four centuries later, twentieth of another world, there would come a time that felt, to those who lived through it, like that one in the sixteenth. A time when one war had ended, leaving (besides the millions dead) a deep dissatisfaction, the memory of unforgivable wrongs, and a longing for absolute solutions. The hatreds and hopes of Christian sectarianism would be cold or at least harmless by then; but there would be worse hopes, and much better armed. Then as now (now, June 1583, a brilliant and blessed morning) men were either unwilling to imagine another war, or unable to think of anything else. Then as now, there were men of broad ironic sensibilities, good-humored men to whom nothing human was alien or even surprising, men who were sure that a humble skepticism was more productive of truth than angry certainties; and, push by shove, in the years fast coming, each of those men would be deprived of his liberty of mind, and forced to take a side.

Sir Philip Sidney was such a man, Protestant, knight, poet, courtier. He had been born a Catholic, under Catholic Mary; in fact the King of Spain, Mary's husband, first Catholic gentleman of the world, had stood godfather for him, and in baby Philip's name had abjured Satan and all his pomps and works—a story Sidney told with that open mirthful smile that sweetened the hearts of those he turned it on, without ever quite revealing the secrets of his own heart, nor even whether secrets were kept there.

History knows that on this morning he was already marked to die, in a Netherlandish meadow, in one of the small wars that kept the old ulcers open and bleeding till the great hemorrhage came; but he didn't know it. He was riding up the Thames road toward the University of Oxford, accompanying a visiting Polonian magnate—a Catholic, whom the French Embassy was seeing to. A young Scot in his service rode beside him, who seemed all atremble with excitement over this visit, though he would not say why. Sir Philip had nominal charge over the entertainments to be offered the Polack at Oxford, and Sir Francis Walsingham had also given him a further charge, to find out, if he could, what powers this Prince actually commanded, and what influence he had with the King there: no one knew quite what to make of him. He was not thinking about these matters as he rode, however. He was thinking about Catholics, and Atlantis, and his marriage.

Two gentlemen, Sir George Peckham and Sir Thomas Gerard (a convicted recusant and papist), had proposed a scheme that might bring peace to England, peace from her internal enemies at least, and justice to the old-religionists in their bitterness. Sir Francis Walsingham, Her Majesty's Secretary of State (and Sir Philip Sidney's father-in-law-to-be), had shown interest in the project; the Catholics of England were his constant worry. Peckham and Gerard wanted an immense grant of the New World to be given freehold to the Catholics of England, with perfect liberty to live and worship there, on condition they never returned. The more he thought about this, the more Sir Philip Sidney thought it equitable, sure, and simple. He was still quite a young man.

Sir Humphrey Gilbert had set out for the West with his fleet not two months before. Sidney's heart was with them: he had wanted to go. But he was to be married that summer instead, a different sort of journey. Gilbert, great heart, had granted to his friend Sir Philip Sidney the profits of a million acres of the New World, to which he would lay claim; Sidney had in turn granted half of it to Sir George Peckham, for his Catholic colony in Atlantis.

Atlantis: the other, mirror shore of the Atlantic. John Dee (who always called it so) had loaned Gilbert maps and given advice, and for his long support and bottomless enthusiasm Gilbert had granted Dee a patent on all lands that the expedition would lay claim to above the fiftieth parallel.

Sir Philip Sidney laughed to think of it, his old teacher lord *in absentia* over a dukedom larger than England. Alexander Dicson at his side smiled inquiringly.

—A good day to be elsewhere, said the knight.

—A good day, sir.

—I thought of Gilbert, said Sidney.

—Yes.

The doctor should have gone along himself with Gilbert, Sidney thought. He imagined the old man's white beard stirred in the winds of New-found-land: he should have been able to put his foot on the shore as Madoc the Welsh giant once did, Dee's forebear, of whom Dee had told him. By this Lord Madoc, the Welsh ancestors of Queen Elizabeth had claim to Atlantis, Dee said, and so had her glorious Majesty; and Sidney thought of Elizabeth, crowned by savages, throned in the West.

—We have got ahead of our guests, he said to Dicson. Hold up.

Dicson pulled hard at the reins of his borrowed horse, a fiery yearling.

—Hold up, he said. Hold up.

Whenever the Prince Alasco glanced back along the line of their progress, the small man in the gown of stuff seemed to have moved up a place among the riders. There was no particular reason to notice him, except for his progress toward the van; but once when the Prince looked back, the man caught his eye with a frank stare and a smile oddly intense.

—Upon arrival at the gates of the University, his secretary continued. An *oratio* by the Dean of Christchurch, a college. A concert of music, and fireworks. A gift.

—Yes, said the Prince.

—Next day, a Latin sermon at Divine Service in Your Grace's honor. *Exercitiones.* Dinner.

—Ah, said the Prince.

—In the afternoon, disputations at St. Mary's. In Divinity. Law. Physic. Natural and moral philosophy.

—Good, said the Prince. He glanced back again along the line of riders, knights, men at arms, sergeants, stewards and serving-men on foot. The man in the gown was closer to his coach.

—Next day . . .

—Enough, said the Prince. They are too kind.

The Prince à Lasco, Voivode of Sieradz in Poland, was sensible of the honor done him, and the more gratified that the Queen herself had ordered it. He was in no easy state. Unless the stars and the powers were favorable, Albertus Alascus might not be returning to Poland soon; what the good Queen no doubt intended as tribute that would make him a firm ally, Albrecht Laski himself needed as props to his claims at home. But it mattered little; Duke Laski (no one was quite sure how to style him, or what exactly he was to be called) had won everyone's good favor by his affability, his extravagant Polish manners, his wide learning, his generous heart. He had a magnificent broad white beard that grew up his cheeks almost to his eyes, and when he retired, he amused those attending by the way he spread it out across the coverlet to his shoulders.

—Who, he asked his secretary, is this gentleman riding the white mule? I have been introduced to him?

—An Italian, said his secretary (who was himself Italian). A servant of the French Ambassador. He brought Your Grace the Ambassador's greetings, such as they were. Your Grace remembers.

—Hm.

—He is down for a disputation.

—Hm, said the Prince Palatine. He rides like a friar. I wonder.

His attention was just then drawn to the view by his host and guide, Sir Philip Sidney, who had waited for the carriage to pull abreast of his blue-caparisoned horse.

—Magnificent! said the Polonian, opening his arms to the day and the river. I am deeply moved.

It was that perfect summer day (but one in a year, and that only with luck, in this country) on which the old poets began their stories, the grass high, roses blooming and nodding, airs kindly on the face, and a *spiritus* moving feelably through it all, almost able to be heard, like a concert of winds. And the country all around, not magnificent at all but little—little it seemed to him, like the scenes in a Book of Hours: men at their work, the winding road, glimpse of a castle's tower in a cleft of hills, or a great house made in the English fashion of mud and sticks. He thought of his own country.

—Around the river's bend (said the knight, leaning down to Alasco in his coach) we will see the Queen's palace at Richmond. Her favorite of all her palaces.

—And those fields, across the river, that house?

—That is Barn Elms. The house now being built by Sir Francis Walsingham. He has caught the fever of building.

And he studied the far bank, not actually supposing he would see the Secretary's daughter, whom he would marry by summer's end.

—Then, said the Prince. The town that rises there is Mortlake.

—Yes. Mortlake, between the Queen and her Secretary.

—I have visited there. The one man in your kingdom whom I knew whom I must seek out. He was well known to the Queen, who graciously sent me to him.

—I know the man you mean, said Sir Philip.

—Doctor Dee. Whose fame has reached even as far as my country.

—He has traveled widely.

—I was very well received there, said the Prince (with an air almost of awe, as though surprised to have been taken in). He lives very simply. I wonder if by his own choice.

The knight said nothing.

—Not without honor, save in his own country. That was my thought.

—He has all the honor I can give him. He was my childhood tutor.

The Polonian looked up at Sir Philip with a new respect, his face full of that generous expression that said The more I learn of you the more credit you have with me. Then he turned his gaze toward the far bank again, as though he had rather have been there than here; and started slightly when his secretary tugged at his sleeve. When Laski turned, the secretary showed him with a hand, almost apologetically, the man on the white mule, who had come up beside him.

—Permit me to present to Your Grace Signor Doctor Giordano Bruno Nolano, a philosopher, my countryman.

—A philosopher, said Laski, and lifted the hat from his head an inch.

—I am proud, the man said in Latin, to claim that name which so many have soiled by wearing it.

—Philosophy is a shield time cannot tarnish, said the Duke in Latin. Then, in Italian: If now we shed our clothes and swam to that bank, we would find more philosophy in a house there than we are likely to find in this University we make such slow progress toward.

He looked to Sir Philip then, afraid he might have offended (of course the knight knew Italian, no man of any gentility was without Italian nowadays), and saw him smiling, his face full of amusement and even wonder. He was looking, not at Duke Laski, but at the new Philosopher. Alexander Dicson beside him just then unwittingly spurred his mad steed, and was nearly thrown.

On the fifteenth of that month Doctor Dee made a note in his private diary:

About 5 of the clok cam the Polonian prince, Lord Albert Lasky, down from Bissham where he had lodged the night before, being returned from Oxford, whither he had gon of purpose to see the universitye, where he was very honorably used and enterteyned. He had in his company Lord Russell, Sir Philip Sidney, and other gentlemen: he was rowed by the Queene's men, he had the barge covered with the Queene's cloth, the Queene's trumpeters, etc. He cam of purpose to do me honor, for which God be praysed!

It happened that he was standing by his water-stairs when the two broad barges came down the Thames, and one or two small wherries beside attending on them, and pavilions raised on them to keep out the sun and rain. The barges were going down to London, heading home like old nags going to their familiar stables, but they pulled up at the house in Mortlake, trumpets blowing and silken flags lifted on the chilly river airs.

—Sent by the Queen, called out Sir Philip, smiling. To hurry us away from that Athens.

—You are welcome, gentlemen, Doctor Dee called. Your Grace is very welcome to my humble.

He hurried down the stairs to make his obeisance to the Duke, but the Duke had already leapt nimbly off the barge and swept the hat off his head. He clasped eagerly the doctor's hand, he bent close to the doctor, his white beard almost grappling with the doctor's own.

—Believe me I could not have passed these stairs and not stopped, he said. And turning to the barge which the bargemen were tying up: You know these gentlemen.

—Certain ones, yes, very well, said the doctor. He bowed to Sir Philip Sidney. Lord Russell he had seen often at Court, one of the Queen's young champions, moved by her like a chess knight in the games of chivalry they played.

They were handed out from the barges, and the other gentlemen after them; Doctor Dee showed them the stairs upward with a bow and a warning about the loose stones, then turned to send his son Arthur and Arthur's sister (who had been peeping from behind their father's skirts) to run on ahead and tell their mother who had come.

—Tell her, the last hogshead of my Christmas claret, he whispered to Arthur. Tell her, the venison pasties. A barrel of eels too.

He hurried the boy with a pat on his shoulder. This company would expect such hospitality, whether they touched it or not. Doctor Dee mounted the stairs with them.

—I trust Your Grace was honorably used at Oxford.

—Very honorably used. Much hospitality. A gift. Of gloves, he added, and raised his eyebrows, inviting Doctor Dee to share in his mild surprise at this, an article of dress and not a book, a rarity or antiquity of some kind. There were further oddities: at All Souls College the scholars had all acted in a stiff little drama of Dido, and a banquet was put on in the middle of it, where all sat down with

Æneas and Queen Dido, to hear Æneas tell the story of Troy, and then a tempest came, just as in Virgil, only the rain was rosewater, and little sweetmeats hailed down on the guests, and sugar snow fell. It had all obviously cost them a good deal of trouble, and the Prince thanked them all in his *militare Latinum* (as he said, soldier's Latin, he had never heard such neat Ciceronian periods as the Oxonians turned).

—Did you not once, sir doctor (said Sir Philip Sidney, in English, disembarking), make wonders for a show at Oxford?

—I did, said Dee, pleased to have it remembered. For Aristophanes his *Pax*, the Scarabeus flying up to Jupiter's palace, with a man and a basket of victuals on his back. There were many vain reports, by what art it was done.

—There were disputations too, said the Prince. Lectures.

He had looked forward to these, but they had been poor stuff in his opinion, as formal and rehearsed as the little play of Dido, not what Alasco meant by deep learning.

—I do not love, he said, to hear Aristotle debated.

—They love Aristotle there, said Dee. No one may graduate who has not drunk at that font. Drunk deep.

—It must flow with beer, then. Beer and not learning, for they care little there for learning.

It was the last gentleman out of the boat who said this, in Latin. John Dee turned back to see him alight and mount the stairs, lifting his scholar's gown.

—*This* gentleman, said the Prince to Dee, was not well used there. Not well used.

Doctor Dee could not tell if Laski was amused or truly scandalized at the man's ill treatment. A young Scot whom Doctor Dee knew to be in Sir Philip Sidney's service stepped to Doctor Dee's side.

—Permit me to present.

Smiling—as though they knew something which John Dee did not yet know—Sir Philip and the Prince Palatine stood aside to make room for the Doctor to bow to the Italian, and take his hand.

—I was at Oxford, Dee said. In my youth.

—They understand neither Aristotle nor anything that is not Aristotle. I call on these gentlemen to witness. And yet once it was famous for learning.

A thick-necked, stiff-backed small man, who put out his chin, perhaps to make up for its weakness. A bantam cock, expecting a fight: that's what Dee was reminded of.

—They do in some sort despise old learning there, said Dee. The learning that made the place famous. I am sorry for it.

There was more he could say. It was the Puritans at Oxford who had lately driven out the old sciences there, and decimated the libraries, pitching out any book that talked of geometry, or the heavens, or had a red letter in it, as papistical or diabolical or both. Doctor Dee had himself saved priceless things from their fires. But he would not talk of such things in this company. Sir Philip was known to lean to the Puritans; Duke Laski was newly reconverted to the Roman church; this Italian he knew nothing of. He said only:

—Come sir. All you gentlemen. Refresh yourselves. Tell me of your adventures.

At Oxford Dicson had found room to sleep with an acquaintance, Matthew Gwynne; room to stay anyway, they had slept little, sat up long in the mess of Gwynne's room amid the books and maps and piled dishes and overturned cups whereon candles melted; and late, late, they had crept out on the town like tom-cats, and collided with the watch, and had to run.

With the dawn, the creatures of night sacred to Pluto retreat into their dens, the toad, the basilisk, the owl and the witch; but the creatures of the light come forth to greet the rising, the cock, the ram, the phoenix, the lynx, eagle, lion; the lupine and the heliotrope open their cups, and turn their faces on him.

Late in the morning Dicson leapt up as though stung, thirsty and anxious. The Italian debated today.

The subject was Aristotle on Substance, and Bruno stood against the Rector of Lincoln College. A good crowd had filled the hall, Laski in the center front and Sidney beside him; Dicson crept in and stood by the wall, his spirit ready (he hoped) to receive what was said, which was to be impressed truth by truth on the places he had inwardly made ready.

Something went quickly amiss. The Rector was a careful and soft-spoken man; he spent a good deal of time silent between sentences, while the Italian squirmed and sighed in his chair, groaning once aloud, which did not hasten the Rector: then leapt out of his chair when his opponent retired, a boxer leaping into the ring, pushing up his sleeves and talking almost before he stood before them. What he had to say seemed at first to have nothing to do with substance, or with Aristotle. It was about how the heavens are ordered.

In the center of the universe, he said, the midpoint, equidistant from every point upon the outermost and ultimate sphere (beyond which is God alone), is the Earth. A great dungball, wherein are collected all the dirts, smuts, uncleannesses, heavinesses, stones, and other corporealities of all the universe: for what is heavy falls naturally to the center, and what is not heavy stays aloft, and rises to the perimeter.

There was laughter, and a rustling of academic gowns. What was the man up to? He had an odd grin fixed on his face, and his arms wove circles as he spoke.

Around this ball Earth, this insignificant fæcal mote, this *dot,* are seven or eight or nine truly gigantic spheres of some sort of crystal such as we have no experience of, spheres whose walls are thick as mountains, wherein or on the sun, moon and planets are variously implanted, impressed, plastered, knotted, glued, sculptured or painted. Outsidemost of all is the sphere of the stars, holding in all the rest and the earth too: around which in a natural spherical perfectly regular and unceasing motion it spins with incomprehensible speed, a good million miles or more in a minute. It could not be less.

The murmurings were louder now, and there were guffaws. Was he mocking them? There were cries of *Ad rem, ad rem!* The man had not yet taken up and answered a single one of the Rector's theses.

Now (said Bruno, apparently unconscious as yet of the stir) what is the first conclusion we may come to, as to this picture or image or description of the universe, which is, with many additions and qualifications, the one we are presented with by Aristotle, and on which all his physics is considered to depend?

Some unintelligible jesting answers from the hearers, which the Italian ignored.

—Come, sirs. Come. The first and most evident conclusion. Is it not that this picture of the universe is wholly and thoroughly contradictory to common reason, and could not be the universe that God in His infinite greatness and goodness made? Is it not?

Flinging out a hand, as though to show them the *mappamundi* that he had drawn there in the air:

—If the universe has a center, then the universe has a circumference. If the world has a circumference, it is finite, no it is infinitesimal, no it is in fact nothing at all compared to the incalculable, inexpressible infinity and infinite creativity of God. Aquinas knew this, though he hid it. No universe will be sufficient to the infinite creativity of God that is not itself infinite.

He folded his arms and faced them, speaking louder.

—No circumference, then. And if no circumference, no center. Is this heavy foul stationary torpid impure midden the Earth not the center? No. Neither in nature is it stable nor in logic is it immobile, as witness Copernicus, who has perfectly demonstrated it, though it is not he who first conceived it. Therefore. No circumference, no center; or since its center is no different from its circumference, we may say that the universe is all center, or that the center of the universe is everywhere and the circumference nowhere . . .

But they in the hall knew now what he was about. Loosened from the bonds of polite discourse, as the earth's bonds had been loosened in Bruno's discourse, the scholars began rising from their seats, hooting, calling out insults. Epicurean! Democritist! Schoolman! *Cheerculo! Cheercumferenchia!* He speaks Latin like a dog. Or a Dago.

Dicson could hardly hear or see. Laski had risen from the chair of honor, and had a hand cupped behind his ear. The scholars were stepping up to the dais, putting questions:

—If earth moves among the stars, and is a star, then either the earth is not corruptible, or the stars are spheres of change and corruption. Is there nowhere any perfection in your universe?

—The universe is perfect, a single, indivisible, infinite monad; and within this monad are conducted an infinite number of perfectly concluded processes of change.

—But but but. If there are no crystal spheres to carry the planets, what causes them to move in circles?

—They move in circles because they choose to. I now turn to the theses of the *doctissimus magister* . . .

But the chair was empty. The Rector of Lincoln (expecting a riot, perhaps) had left the hall.

—Good Dr. John Underhill, said Doctor Dee, and pulled at his beard to keep from smiling at the tale. I partly know the man.

—A pig, said Bruno.

—And you, sir doctor, said the Prince Alasco, turning his big head with deferential sweetness toward John Dee at the room's other end. What do you hold, concerning the opinion of my countryman, Canon Koppernigk?

—I have studied his book, said Doctor Dee carefully. His thesis accounts for the appearances. Better than does Ptolemy, who follows Aristotle.

—You agree, then, said Bruno; he was smiling his unsettling smile, the same (Dicson thought) he had smiled at the 'varsity men.

Doctor Dee did not immediately reply. The air grew heavy. It was just at this juncture that the crowd in Oxford had risen, unable to bear more. The men in Doctor Dee's chamber were still, waiting.

—I agree as to the motions.

—Then you must agree with me against Aristotle on substance. If Copernicus is right, the earth is a star, like the stars Venus Mars Jupiter Saturn that with the earth go around the Sun. And therefore of a like substance. Aristotle as he is understood says no. Copernicus confutes Aristotle on this.

—Copernicus himself does not say so.

—Copernicus did not understand what he wrote. He drew a new heavens. There must be a new earth too.

Sir Philip Sidney crossed his arms, and smiling spoke:

—All the poets will rebel. The stars must turn, the sun must rise and set, for poems to scan. Their rhymes will not bend either to these novelties.

—Then let them join those Oxford pedants. There is more matter for poetry in truth than in false seeming.

—Sir, said Laski. I sat for your disputation. I confess I could understand neither your arguments, nor how they pertain to substance, nor why you were shouted down.

—Copernicus (Bruno said airily) is not known in this country, sir; men here are not used to elucidating his hidden truths. And the doctors who once knew more even than he, who flourished long since at Oxford, their works are now despised, their bones are dug up and scattered. By these polishers of pebbles, these.

A huge spirit had arisen in the man: Doctor Dee could feel it, nearly extruding from his body, vibrating the air of the chamber, abashing and embarrassing the company. He said with great gentleness:

—You will be surprised, sir, that Copernicus's system is cried in the streets here.

The Italian turned to face him: and seemed for an instant to be replaced where he stood, by a sudden bright fulmination. Then he returned.

—Yes, said Dee, not stepping back, surprised but unalarmed. With the easy deliberate stride a man might use to approach a wary horse, he went to where the Italian stood and touched his arm.

—Cried in the streets, he said. In the almanac of my friend Master Leonard Digges. Will you read it? It will interest you. I have it here, I can find it in a moment. Do you read English?

Bruno's eyes shifted to the English lords, and away quickly.

—Not well. Not at all. This gentleman though might help me.

He meant Dicson, who stepped forward willingly. Bruno allowed Dee to guide the two of them to a corner of the chamber, where piles of books and *libelli* bound and unbound stood in unsteady piles on shelves and a deal table.

—*Of the making of books there is no end,* the doctor quoted. He rustled and rummaged among the things there; he lifted the lid of a trunk, and Bruno glimpsed manuscripts in thick blackletter; he took a book from a shelf, holding back with a hand its fellows who tried to follow it. A shabby and much-handled small book.

—*Prognostication Everlasting,* he said. To which is added a description of the heavens, by his son, Thomas, whom I have known and taught man and boy. You will see.

He laid the book upon the table, and stepped away, not however turning his back on the Italian immediately; as though (Dicson thought) he had laid a bone before a mastiff to soothe it.

Bruno opened the book. An emblem of spheres. Sun in the center.

He thought: Who is he? That English doctor had, just when Bruno's own heated spirit had been drawn out into the room, changed his image for a fountain of limpid water, his garments' folds the falling streams, face and beard the surmounting foam and spray. Just for an instant. No one else had seen.

He read:

This ball every 24 hours by wonderfull slie and smooth motion rouleth rounde, making with his period our natural daye, whereby it seems to us that the huge infinite immoveable globe should swaye and tourne about.

Dicson labored to translate this into an Italian less certain than his Latin, moving his hand beside his mouth as though to summon words out of it, *e e e* . Bruno had already absorbed the page.

The baull of ye earth wherein we move, to the common sorte seemeth greate, and yet compared with the Orbis magnus *wherein it is carried, it scarcely retaineth any sensible proportion, so merueilliously is that Orbe of Annuall motion greater than this little dark starre wherin we liue. But that* Orbis magnus *beinge but as a poynct in respect of the immensity of the immovable heaven, we may easily consider what little portion of gods frame, our* Elementare corruptible worlde *is . . .*

—Who is he? Bruno asked, and Dicson stopped his stammering to look where Bruno looked. Doctor Dee had turned away to speak privately with the Polonian. Dicson made to speak, but then was abashed, knowing no answer he had would be the answer Bruno sought. Bruno looked down again at the little universe Master Digges had drawn.

Each of the circles around the central sun was labeled: *THE ORBE OF MARS. THE ORBE OF SATURNE.* And it *was* Copernicus's scheme. The only oddity was that the ultimate sphere was not shown as a delimiting circle, as Copernicus had it, but as a scattering of stars filling out the page. This sphere was labeled too, the words arching around over the sphere of Saturn and beneath the stars: *THE ORBE OF STARRES FIXED INFINITELY VP EXTENDETH IT SELF IN AL-TITVDE SPHERICALLY, AND THEREFORE IS IMMOVABLE THE PAL-LACE OF FOELICITYE, GARNISHED WITH PERPETVAL SHININGE GLORIOVS LIGHTES INNVMERABLE, FARRE EXCEEDING OVR SVNNE BOTH IN QVANTITYE AND QVALITYE, THE VERYE COVRTE OF CELESTIALL ANGELLES, DEVOYD OF GREEFE AND REPLEN-ISHED WITH PERFITE ENDLESS JOYE THE HABITACLE FOR THE ELECT.*

He closed it.

—He errs.

Dicson, who had not done translating, closed his mouth.

—He errs, said Bruno, to say that the sun is the center of this infinite sphere. A sphere cannot be infinite, it must have a bound. Nor can an infinite sphere have a center.

He moved aside the almanac, gently, his eyes watchful now and his voice low, a hunter in a blind, or hunter's prey.

—What book is that?

It had been lying on the table with others, it must have been, and yet he had not seen it until this instant, as though it had worked its way to the surface meanwhile. Dicson shrugged, looking down. A small volume. A binding not of English work. He moved to take it up, but Bruno's hand was on it.

The title page was a pillared temple.

MONAS HIEROGLYPHICA
IONNIS DEE, LONDINENSIS

AD

MAXIMILIANVM, DEI GRATIÆ
ROMANORVM, BOHEMIÆ ET HVNGARICÆ
REGEM SAPIENTISSIMVM

And inscribed above all, like a finger to the lips:

QVI NON INTELLEGIT, AVT TACEAT, AVT DISCAT

In the center of the page, surrounded by scrolling banners bearing words, by symbols of sun and moon both weeping, by pillars labeled with the names of four elements, was drawn an egg-shaped cartouche; and in the egg, like the bones of a bird growing in there and not yet ready to be born, was drawn this sign:

For seven years Giordano Bruno of Nola had traveled the world, knocking at the gates of cities, ejected from state after kingdom, at once fleeing and pursuing, not certain what besides peace and a chance to speak he pursued: and it had happened that at certain turnings in his journey, usually just when he was choosing a path or wondering if he should turn back or stay put, someone would appear before him to point a way or open a door or take him in: and would show him, or have in his possession, or appear in conjunction with, this sign.

He was sure it was the same sign. Sure. Wasn't it? The same he had seen cut on this one's ring, drawn in the dust of that one's path, in Venice, in Genoa.

How did it come to be here? Had that English shape-shifter (who did not, it may be, even know he was a shape-shifter) carved it himself, or had someone taught it him?

—A hieroglyph, said Dicson. Hieroglyph of the monad.

The priests of Ægypt had known how to draw down from their proper realms the airy powers, by incising in the Nile mud or cutting in stone the sign of commandment, the word *Come* in the language that was before the languages of men.

Had this sign brought him out of the South and into this cold island where he would be insulted and scorned?

He asked it: Why have you brought me here?

But it answered only: If you do not understand, be silent, or learn.

—*Doctissime,* said Adelbert Laski into Doctor Dee's ear. Is it possible, do you think, that we may have some further congress with. I speak of those, those. Whom you and I and Master, Master . . .

—Kelley.

—Kelley. Those whom I was privileged to have conversation with when last I came here. Do you think . . .

—The company is too great, said Doctor Dee in a low voice. We will not have the quiet or the privacy necessary for the work.

—I will send them all away.

When the Polonian prince had first come to Mortlake, accompanied only by a servant and a guard, John Dee had taken him into the far chamber, and Kelley had besought the blessed spirits for some helpful word for the wanderer, and Laski had been troubled and amazed and fired by what he had been told. Secret enemies. Homecoming. Great victories. Blood. A crown. Through the whole tedium of his Oxford journey he had thought of little else.

—And where is Master Kelley?

Doctor Dee pulled at his beard, and looked to the window. Day was late.

—Gone fishing, he said.

For some time he had been watching a frog on a floating log, who was himself patiently angling. His great sightless-seeming eyes were open, though ever and again a kind of curtain slid over them and away again. He fished with a length of tongue as quick as the rest of him was cold and slow: a sort of spasm would shake him, and—though you had not seen it caught—he would be swallowing a long-legged fly. This often took a horrid length of time, the frog impassively ingesting while a beating wing or leg hung still outside the great mouth.

Kelley felt a tug on his line, but when he drew it toward him, it soon slackened. A fish softly broke the water, showing Kelley his backside. Taken his lobworm too.

It was Doctor Dee who had first urged this angling on his skryer, as a distraction; melancholy needs distraction, seeks it restlessly, never satisfied long with any occupation; melancholy wants at once to be engaged and to be doing nothing. Fishing is both, in some sort. But there was no medicine for his melancholy but one.

Edward Kelley had with him—he slept with it beneath his pillow, it never left his person—a stone jar stoppered with wax, within which was a minute quantity of a reddish powder, which a spirit had given him in exchange for his soul. He had told Doctor Dee that he had found the powder and the book of its use, written in unreadable characters, in a monk's grave in Glastonbury, and over time he had come to believe it himself: even though a mute dog-faced thing, the demon who had first tempted him with it, who had found the book for him, had accompanied him for years. He sat even now beside Kelley on the bank, bored and restless. Kelley even knew his name.

He had ceased angling. His eyes were open but he no longer saw. He was the fisher frog; he was the caught fly, too. When on such a day as this he sat by a slow backwater with his pole and creel, it often happened that he would sit thus for hours, a kind of curtain drawn over and drawn back from his eyes; until evening came, surprising him with its cool darkness, and returning him to the river's bank.

The young knights (with all due deference) suggested returning to London. Laski bid them adieu: he and his friend had much to say to one another, but the gentlemen should not think they must stay; let them return, he would find his own way back; he would not be swept out to sea, and the Queen hold them responsible for losing him; go go.

So Sidney bowed deeply, said he would leave his gentleman Alexander Dicson and others behind to see to the Duke; then, pulling on his gloves, he raised his brows in inquiry to the antic Italian: but he seemed to have fallen into a sort of fit, he only peeped out from behind a pile of books, a shy deer surprised, and shook his head.

—Then *buona sera, Signor,* Sidney said: and at that the strange man returned to himself, and hurried to take the knight's hand, and stare deeply into his eyes.

Laughing like schoolboys released, the gentlemen told over their adventures in Oxford and Mortlake as they went down to London. They had left behind one painted barge, the grandest; its colors limp in the still air.

The river was still bright at the ninth hour, running through the darkened land to meet the sky in the west; there the evening stars burned whitely, very near. In an upper chamber Master Dicson pushed open the tiny casement and put out his head.

—Does Earth shine then, as they do? he asked. As Mercury, Venus, Mars?

—It must, said Bruno. It is no dark star. Earth's seas are a mirror, as the seas of those worlds are too. Enlarging, and casting back, the Sun's rays.

—If we stood on Mercury . . .

—We would see Earth shine in the, the East. Now. Tonight. As they there do so see the Earth.

—They?

—The inhabitants.

Dicson turned from the window to see if the Italian was amusing himself. He stood still in the center of the room, hands behind his back, the same pugnacious thoughtful face as ever.

—If, he said, seeing Dicson's wonderment, if we are as they are, it is the same as to say, they are as we are. There may be ranks and hierarchies in this circling of the sun; maybe the best place is nearest, and maybe not; in any case there is no reason to think that those stars, as alive as ours, as quick as ours, should not be as full of, of every. As we.

—And men too?

—Beings appropriate for those stars, as we are for this one.

He went to the bed, which largely filled the room they had been given, and poked it hard with a finger.

—But but, Dicson said. The influences, the rays of those planets. How they, how they.

He stopped speaking, and stopped moving too. He felt an impulse to take hold of something firm; but, as though the room were the cabin of a ship or the inside of a swaying coach, there was nothing firm. His breast now contained two entire universes, and they kept replacing one another as he said sentences applying to the one then to the other. The old one, great Earth lying under the wheeling heavens, and the planets in their houses (mild or fierce or hot or cold) playing their lamps over her. Then, hoop-la, the other: small quick Earth, bearing all her seas mountains rivers cities states and men, taking her place in the dance amid the other great round beings who smiled upon her.

—We move among the stars, Giordano Bruno said, and we receive from each in turn its influence. So we are largely earthy, but those influences make us more like the beings of those planets. Read Ficino on drawing their good influences into our natures.

—De vita coelitus comparanda.

—And the inhabitants of those stars receive a like influence from us. They must. It might be that Earth's moist influence softens the Martian's dry choleric rage. Maybe our blue airs gladden Saturn's black melancholics.

He sat on the bed and pulled off his shoes. Dicson took the wilted ruff from his neck, laughing, giddy. Bruno said:

—These are not novelties, as that gentlemen said. Pythagoras knew these things. Palingenius. Ægypt knew this.

—Ægypt, Dicson breathed.

Bruno knit his fingers together. A net, he said. All one. E pluribus unum. Ægypt knew.

The two men had undressed to their shirts and hose. With a

practiced delicacy that came from being thrown together with strangers in inns from Venice to Paris, Bruno reached beneath his shirt, undid his points, turned his back on Dicson and made water in the chamberpot.

—What will be has been, he said. There is no new thing under the sun.

And he shed his hose, climbing into the bed at the same time. Dicson listened to the mattress crackle. Straw. With inordinate solemnity, to keep from laughing in embarrassment, an odd embarrassment he could not shed, Dicson climbed into bed on the other side.

—There is another thing you will not have thought of, said the Italian.

—Yes?

—If (and he rolled over a little, finding room, the bed was not large) if the stars, I mean the *fixed* stars, are not stuck on a sphere, but do stand at varying distances from us, out to infinity, as that Englishman's book did truthfully say, what then?

—What then?

—Well then what of their influences?

Dicson tried to think.

—The signs, Bruno said at last. The twelve.

They went away, even as Bruno said it. Of course: not twelve segments of a sphere, not twelve bands on a belt picked out like an escutcheon with nailheads: the signs were formed of stars that might stand at any distance from earth, some near, some incalculably far.

—Our senses deceive us, Bruno said, pillowing his head on his hands. What we take for pictures in the sky we have ourselves put there. Just as a one-eyed man can see no distance, and sometimes takes distant big things to be close and small.

—No pictures. No signs, Dicson said. No Aries, Taurus, Gemini. But in your book *Sigilla sigillorum*, the seal of the Chain . . .

—Those signs I wrote of are real. They are real reasons for things. We know them. It is because we know them to be real that we impose them on the sky.

He did not remark, perhaps it did not seem odd to him, that the man sharing his bed had also read his book.

—We could as well have other signs, Bruno said and yawned. Other pictures in the heavens. I have myself composed a poem of ten thousand lines, in which a congress of the Gods reforms the heavens, expels all the bad old beasts and silly furniture, signs of their own vices, and summons Virtues to rise in their stead.

—I would be very glad to read that poem.

—I have not yet written it down.

He lifted his head, and without asking leave, blew out the candle.

In the darkness the sky shone. The window was still open. Smell of candle-smoke and summer air.

—Sir I wish you a good night's sleep, Dicson said.

He did not think he would sleep. The house was quiet now, after a period of uninterpretable small noises from room and passage. He listened to the slap of river water against the stair and the barge's side. He slept.

Giordano Bruno lay still with his hands behind his head, aware of the stirrings in the house, and when they ceased, of the stirrings in the air above the house. Spirits, semhamaphores drawn down or up from their spheres or places, drawn to.

No not drawn to him. Drawn here to this house, but not, this time, to him. He felt them descend past the upper storey in which he lay (the Scotsman snoring softly beside him) and downward to where (he could feel it tug on his own nature like a lodestone) the sign was now uncovered. He would get no sleep here.

At that hour, in the small chamber at the far end of the house, Doctor Dee, Edward Kelley, and Albrecht Laski knelt as though in adoration before a small table on which a globe of clear crystal stood in a frame, reflecting from its surface (and again in its heart) the candles set around it.

Each leg of the table stood upon a seal of virgin wax, and a larger seal, the sigilla Æmeth, as the angels called it, was placed atop it: this showed a multiple cross and the letters AGAL engraved on its underside, and above, seven unsayable unreadable names of God, which had the power to bring forth the seven governors of the seven heavens above the earth: and every letter of the seven names brought forth seven daughters, every daughter another daughter, and every daughter's daughter a son, who brought forth another son.

They were not different from the names that together they composed; and out of their combination and recombination the universe was named, and so made; and by them it continues to be maintained.

Was she one of them? Youngest daughter of the powers, she would not keep to her place in the crossrow, she would be out and about, to play and tease.

—*Who is it in the house?* she said urgently and without preamble.

—Here is the noble lord Laski whom you have said you might . . .

—*Not he. The other. The great dæmon. The one I warned you of. Is he not in this house this night?*

—Was it you? Kelley said, remembering. A night that spring, the ship seen in the stone, and the man in the ship: St. Elmo's fire burning on the masts and spires.

—*It was I,* said Madimi. *You heard my voice and felt my touch and never saw me.*

—What does she speak of? Laski whispered in Latin.

—Hush, said Doctor Dee.

—*He is the traitor that turns the coat, he is the young king's usher, who is called Phoenix. He is the favorite son of the trickster God, and he will do thee mischief.*

—Those gods are false, said Kelley.

—*Blaspheme not. Know you not those great spirits who live in the stars, by whose measure all things are made? I will name them to you in Greek, Hermes, Aphrodite, Ares . . .*

—Mercury, Venus, Mars, Kelley said. These we know. Do you instruct us in the stars?

—*You may know, and you may not.*

Doctor Dee said:

—Why should we fear him?

—*Look to your house, look to your books. He has designs to steal your stone, I tell you that.*

Doctor Dee flung down the pen he wrote with, picked up a new one, dipped it, and wrote.

—What stone is it that I have?

—*I mean your picture, your letter. Old man, do you write not. Pen, mark not. Ink, be water. I will prophesy; write what I say inwardly, on your hearts.*

John Dee reluctantly laid down the pen. Duke Laski bent closer to the stone.

—*Listen*, she said. *There will come two winds. There will come the first wind, and then the second. The first wind bears in the time, and the second wind bears it away again. Noah saw water, Ægypt saw earth. Wind is as great as those.*

—Fire, said Doctor Dee.

—*Fire is not yet. Mark what I say to thee. A first wind. It will shake down towers, shake down palaces. It will shake crowns from heads. And heads too from shoulders.*

—What shall we do?

—*You were best to fly with this man. He will see to you. He will protect you.*

For a moment Doctor Dee puzzled. Were they to fly with the Italian? Then he saw that Laski was meant. Laski had invited them to return to his own country with him, where they would find honor they would not find here.

—Can we fly the wind? he said softly. Madam, if the time is come . . .

—*You are a wise old man*, she said. *His palace will not be proof against it. If it blow down in the first wind, I will rebuild it for him. If it blow down in the second wind, let him look to it himself; I will not be there.*

Now through the old house they could hear the knocks and groans that often came with the spirits, airs racing from storey to storey, putting out candles, lifting rugs along the floors; the maid weeping in the garret, head under the covers, the cat run to hide in the chimney-corner.

—The wind bloweth as it listeth, said Duke Laski beneath his breath; and he crossed himself, and kissed the nail of his thumb.

4

eptember: represent Pomona in your mind, her fruits; but blush her cheek with a chill wind, and toss her hair. The wind was sharp along the Thames.

—Mercurius, said Alexander Dicson. Theutates, who has invented letters, an art of reminding. Socrates. I make him a cackler and a pedant. Those are my speakers.

Giordano Bruno laughed. He liked to put a pedant in his own dialogues, someone who would make fatuous claims, someone to rebut.

The dialogue on Memory which Alexander Dicson was composing was based very largely on one of Bruno's own, one he had published in Paris, a titanic work of wilful and obdurate complexity which almost no one but its author could be expected to grasp in its entirety. He had given Dicson a copy, and written loving compliments in it for him.

—Mercurius, yes, said Bruno. Who is the same as Hermes. And how will you begin?

—In the night of Ægypt, said Master Dicson, and shuddered hugely.

He would tell how, before the ingenious god Theutates invented letters, which ruined the memories of men and led to endless bickering, the wise priests and living Gods of Ægypt wrote their thoughts inwardly, in a language now lost to us. Our languages—Greek, Latin, English—are nothing but the growls of beasts, roughly tamed, first used for nothing but to cry Give me, give me, or Beware, beware, and later stretched and pulled and made to imitate thought as the ape imitates man. But the words of the sacred language of Ægypt were not mere sounds or meaningless marks but were the living reflection in the soul of the things they represented.

—*Hieroglyphica,* said Bruno. Here we go down.

A door in the French Embassy's garden wall opened onto Water Lane, which led under the high wall of a mansion down to the river. There they clambered through piles of bricks and stacks of timber (the riverfront was continually in transformation, building up or tearing down, Bruno watched the work by the hour from his high window even as the same work went on in his own city within). Down to slippery Buckhurst Stairs, where a boat upriver could sometimes be hailed.

—And how will your patrons like your dialogue? he said. It seems it may not be to their taste.

—If there be true matter in it, they will welcome it, Dicson said doubtfully. I will dedicate it to Sir Philip.

—Sir Sed-Ne, Bruno said, and laughed. Sir But-No.

They were Bruno's patrons too—Sir But-No and his circle, Sir Fulke Greville, the Earl of Leicester. The Queen remotely, who knew him now by sight. The lords had got him a further course of lectures at Oxford, despite what had happened, and they were well attended at first, probably because of what had happened; still his hearers had no idea what to make of him, lecturing rapidly in his monkish Latin, raising giggles by his pronunciation, struggling with Aristotle as Jacob did with the angel; and then—unable or unwilling to hear the warning murmurs from his hearers—stepping into dangerous topics as though walking off a dock: how heaven's powers are drawn down into the soul, metempsychosis, the forging of links with airy intelligences. This was far worse than Copernicus.

They came to him privily, and charged him with plagiarism, for taking all his lectures from Ficino, which was not wholly true but was a lesser charge, and without civil penalties; and John Florio and others of his new friends (indolent Sam Daniel the sonneteer, good Matthew Gwynne) took him aside, and bade him think of the Ambassador who had been so kind to him: and so he had graciously consented to give up his lectures.

Let them know that he was a Nolan, born under a kindlier sky. Pigs.

—The tide is in, Dicson said. Beware. I have fallen in this river.

—No, Bruno said. Not this river. Another one. You can't fall in the same river twice.

Laughing, Dicson took his teacher's arm, helping him through the slob to where a very old boat awaited.

—They built that boat, Bruno said. Those two ancients in it. In the beginning of time. What river is this? Styx?

The boat, leaking and foul-bottomed, pushed out into the tidewater, borne upriver with the traffic on the swell. Two kinds of clouds sped over the hard blue, a dense and full-rigged kind, and long pale veils beyond them. Dicson negotiated a tip with the aged boatmen for the trip to Mortlake; by law the watermen were not allowed to take more than sixpence, but the wise traveler knew they had means of making the journey unpleasant for the punctilious.

Then he sat beside Bruno.

—For my Art of Memory, he said. It will be no great work such as yours is.

—We must walk before we can fly.

—I am fearful how it will be received.

—By whom?

—There are many in this country, and in the Universities especially, who do not love images. They have torn them from the churches, and from the prayer-books.

—I, too, fear those people, Bruno said. The justified. The elect who have done nothing to win election. I fear them more than death.

Dicson hesitated. He had not heard the Nolan ever say he feared anything.

—They will say, Dicson said, that to make images in the mind, and set them up in the soul, is idolatry.

Bruno laughed hugely.

—They believe they can think thoughts without them, he said. They who pretend to love Aristotle! *To think is to speculate with images.* Aristotle, Aristotle, Aristotle.

—The hieroglyphs of Ægypt, said Dicson.

—Were images.

The hieroglyphs represented to the mind the unsayable words of the Ægyptian language. They were not cut in stone as an aid to memory—the Ægyptians needed no such aid, for the signs cut in memory were more perfect, more lasting, and above all alive and capable of change: permutation, peregrination, combination and generation. The stone records were for praise, cut on obelisks pointing to the sky, lifting the heart.

—Or perhaps, said Dicson, cut to instruct a later age. When the true Ægyptian religion was forgotten.

Hermes had predicted it; Dicson had read the writings, laid down before Moses was born. Night would fall over the land, the priests would lose their powers, and barbarians would rule in their stead; the gods themselves would abandon Ægypt, and her people forget how to honor them, forget that once gods had dwelt among them, forget all: would come to believe the truths handed down in fragments of those times to be but fables, and the powers lies.

They were not lies. Philotheus Brunus Nolanus, seated beside him on the Thames, possessed them. Into the figures which he had set up within himself—seals of the natures of things, statues of the star-gods, emblems of actuality—he was able to invite the vivifying spirits who everywhere inhabit matter, who fill earth, air, water and the sky; and he bound those powers to the statues and talismans of his heart. And they spoke.

Bruno said:

—If, in the bright day of Ægypt, they possessed such powers, then in the course of things they had perforce to lose them; and we, now, who have none of those powers, in the course of things may gain them again.

Dicson thought: It's to return, then, that age, and just in time. He was not going to miss it. It was going to return in the person of this little Italian with the funny strut and the pugnacious chin. Dicson laughed, and even as he laughed grateful tears rushed to his eyes.

Ægypt, from where all knowledge comes, font from which Plato and Pythagoras had drunk. Hermes, god-man, had been a king in Ægypt. Hermes taught how Ægypt's priests had drawn down from the celestial realms the spirits of stars, airy intelligences, the guardians of the divisions of time, and caused them to take up their abode in the titanic statues of men and animals and animal-men which the priests had constructed, statues expressive of the nature of the spirits invited into them; when the priests had bound a spirit to its appropriate statue, then it could be made to speak, prophesy, tell truths of the nature of things.

He had seen so often in imagination those temples of the morning, in which vast images of gods and beasts had presided; some still stood, he had been told, buried in the sands of Ægypt; the statues broken now, the rites forgotten.

Now, now, in the greatest darkness of ignorance and strife— would it not be now that a kindly God would open men's hearts to a new revelation? Might it not be? Dawn winds rising as night turned pale; the cruel and stupid brawls of nightwalking sectarians ceasing, the ignorant fleeing from the rising sun of new knowledge, unexpected powers, vivid images. Wisdom appearing, to open men's hearts and minds, wisdom to reconcile kings and popes, to heal Christ's Body falsely and foolishly divided.

Wisdom to reconcile (O let it not be too late) the Queens of North and South, whose statues, painted in red and in green, stood in the temple of Alexander Dicson's heart: the Queen of Scotland whose subject he was, she for whom men swore to die; and the Queen of England, the Virgin Queen he served here, she for whom men swore to live.

The boatmen put them off at Mortlake village stairs, not listening when they were told another stairs farther on was the house they wanted; they were dumped in the smelly mud (the tide turning, the boat tugging at the poles to be off again downriver) and cursed to boot as they floundered to the stairs.

—*Tanchi, maester,* Bruno called back, one of the few English phrases he would say aloud, and bowed outrageously. He pulled Dicson after him up the stairs, up the village street past the church and the cross, where the gossips looked up in astonishment to hear them speak in an unknown tongue and crossed themselves when the two had passed. They asked at the low dark tavern for the way, and several drunk men looked at them with bellicose suspicion, and would not answer.

Out across the golden, laden fields, guessing the way. Crows cawed in warning. The two men were silent now, feeling a foreboding, what was it.

Doctor Dee's house. Despite the day and the warmth, the shutters were tight shut on the upper storey; but the gate gaped open. They went in. A medicinal garden where the bees were loud. Riot of flowers never tended. They banged the lion-head knocker, but no one came.

No one.

They went around the house, at loose ends now. Why was no serving girl, no boy in the house?

—The library, Bruno said.

The shutters were not shut. Dicson bent, made his hands a stirrup, and Bruno was lifted up to look.

Dim silent stillness. He cupped his hands against the glass to see better. Some shelves had been emptied; some instruments covered with cloths. Bruno sent out his spirit strongly, and the space within brightened.

There. It lay still on the table where he had read it, still open to the title page. *Monas hieroglyphica.* It burned blackly against the gray parchment page.

But he could not get at it. Could not question it.

Dicson said: Look.

He lowered Bruno. They looked off Richmond-ward. Across the fields a small crowd could be seen: reapers, it might be, with rakes. A torch. Coming this way. Not reapers.

The two men stood in the bland sunlight by the wall of the abandoned house. Bruno could hear around him the buzz and chatter of many elementals, who had been left behind like cats, unable to be taken from the earth and the house.

Dicson said: Let's be off.

Bruno, drawn back fruitlessly to this house, abandoned too, lifted empty hands.

—Gone, he said.

They had departed in the dark, all of a sudden; John Dee had put his affairs in order on Monday, signed his house and goods over to his wife's brother on the Wednesday, and on Saturday set out to meet

Prince Laski on the river, who was himself leaving in haste, under suspicion, somewhat in the way of a man letting himself out an inn-window on a knotted sheet, his bill unpaid.

They all filed down the water-stairs in the deep dark, Kelley, and Jane, and Joanna Kelley, and Kelley's brother too who had got a position not by threats exactly but after allowing that his brother might rather have him by his side than left at home in England to be questioned. Trunks and boxes bumping down the mossy steps and small children carried sleeping aboard.

And tucked down in the baggage, wrapped up in batting, stuffed inside a velvet cap, but alight in Kelley's inward eye, the crystal glass; and Madimi restless inside it.

At Barn Elms down the dark river from John Dee's house Philip Sidney that night lay for the first time with Frances, daughter of Sir Francis Walsingham. The wedding, to pay for which Sir Philip had sold his share in Humphrey Gilbert's expedition to Atlantis, had taken place in some splendor there, that very day; lights were still lit on the grounds and in the house, and a consort of music still playing, as the wherries that Prince Laski had hired for them slipped by without lights. Sidney laughed softly with his bride, learning she was wiser than he had known her to be, and wittier too; not knowing that on that night a thousand miles to westward Gilbert would go down in a storm off Newfoundland, leading his fleet through the dark in the little frigate *Squirrel*, "till soddenlye her lights were out."

Next morning Dee's party put out in a Danish double-flyboat to cross the Narrow Sea, with a boyar for Duke Alasco and his horses and men; but the wind blew them back to England, and would have sunk the ship's boat in which they returned to shore, but for Kelley, who bailed mightily with a great gauntlet (Madoc's?) that was among the luggage. The sailors carried them ashore, and Dee's children, Rowland and Arthur and Katherine, laughed to see their father dropped in the mud from the captain's back.

They set out again; prayers and a little white wizardry, and this time they got away briskly. Autumn was coming, it was in the sea wind, what makes it seem at once new and valedictory. They reached Brill, changed to a hoy of Amsterdam, changed that for scuts to sail up the cold canals. They were in Haarlem when Bruno came knocking at the door in Mortlake, and Dee heard his name suddenly called across the gray water, and looked up, to see no one there.

In November the net of evidence (much of it got from Mauvissiere's chaplain and his secretary) closed around Francis Throckmorton and Henry Howard. Walsingham had them arrested, searched Throckmorton's papers, found lists of Catholic noblemen, plans of invasion, tracts, letters to the Prince of Parma in the Netherlands. Under torture he confessed. Letters intercepted between Mary of Scotland and Mauvissiere implicated the Earl of Northumberland and the Spanish Ambassador. Elizabeth would not allow Mary to be touched, not yet if ever: but she agreed to expel Bernardino de Mendoza, because his plotting "disturbed the realm of England." He was put on a ship at Greenwich in the rain and bade good riddance. *Tell your mistress,* he shouted at them from the fly-boat's deck, *that Bernardino de Mendoza was born not to disturb kingdoms but to conquer them.*

There was already a further, a far greater plot in the making.

Northumberland committed suicide in the Tower, shooting himself in the breast with a pistol, among the first men known to history to use this means to avoid torture and disgrace. Throckmorton stayed in prison till the summer, when he was brought out of his cell in his shirt, an olive-wood rosary in his hands that had been blessed by the Pope; he vomited his last meal, a common occurrence and no shame. His head was struck off in a single blow; but because of the false vow he had once sworn in the company of so many loyal gentlemen to protect and defend the Queen, his right hand was cut off too, and Walsingham himself stooped to pick it up.

5

hat seemed remarkable to Pierce Moffett, the more re-
markable as he read it for a second time, was how much
Kraft had written here, and how little he had made up.
There was maybe not a lot of the smell or the feel or the taste of the
past, whatever those had really been like to experience; but there was
a lot in it that had really been thought and said, and very little that
hadn't, even though at the same time it was all quite impossible and
pretend, a fairy tale. This trick could certainly not have been easy,
and the achieving of it might have been amusing and even a little
thrilling, if anybody who was not well versed in the history could
have perceived him doing it.

Bruno had indeed resided at the French Embassy, doing some
sort of something, and there were really spies in the house; he had
indeed gone to Oxford to debate before the Polish magnate Laski, a
real person, and had been shouted down, though it's nowhere recorded exactly what he said. Alexander Dicson was a real person too,
a retainer of Sidney's; Sidney really had a scheme to transport the
Catholics of England to America, and really did arrange the entertainment for Laski at Oxford. Pierce happened to know.

And Laski on his way back from Oxford had dropped in on Dee.
But Pierce had never heard that Bruno came too.

Could he have?

Could Kraft have really known that John Dee and Giordano
Bruno met in England? Known from what source, how, where? Why

did it seem so likely once it was said? In his own brief biography of Bruno (*Bruno's Journey,* 1931) Kraft had said nothing about Dee, but that was no scholarly book really, and written long ago. Why *did* Dee so suddenly leave for the Continent at the end of that summer? It *was* that summer, wasn't it? Maybe it wasn't, liberties taken, times collapsed together; as far as Pierce remembered, John Dee had already left England when Bruno arrived.

He arose from his chair, Kraft's chair, and left the study where Kraft had spent so many hours; he went out through the puzzle of the little house (puzzling to one like Pierce, who could not ever reverse in his mind the way he had entered a place in order to leave it, nor always tell left from right). He stopped in the center of the faded rug in the room where Kraft had chiefly lived.

In here somewhere, he just bet.

Whenever these days Pierce found a footnote or a citation in one of his own secondary sources saying that such-and-such a fact or bit of lore could be found in such-and-such an old book, the source would lodge in his brain, alert as a dog's nose now to the traces of Kraft's track through these past woods. There were only a few sources that Pierce knew of for Dee, and they would be here, as well perhaps as other ones that he didn't know of, that might tell a longer though not necessarily a truer story.

John Dee, strange tireless man, really had written down all the conversations that he and Edward Kelley had with the angels who visited Dee's glass. He kept another record too, of all the human comings and goings at his Mortlake house. Both of these had been printed, though Pierce had never seen either one. The secret record had first been published in the seventeenth century, a very famous book ever since in some circles: *A True & Faithful Relation of what passed for many Yeers betweene Dr. John Dee, a Mathematician of Great Fame in Q. Elizabeth and King James their Reignes, and some Spirits; Tending (had it succeeded) To a General Alteration of most States and Kingdomes in the World.*

This big book was issued in 1659 by Meric Casaubon, the Huguenot refugee and Protestant polemicist. Casaubon was quite sure that Dee and Kelley had talked to spirits, and that they were wicked ones; that their relations with such spirits had damned them; that the "general alteration" would have been a frightful disaster, a demonic empire from which the world was narrowly saved: the author then "shewing the Uses that a sober Christian may make of all," as the gigantic title finally concluded, that is, the avoidance of spirits altogether: this warning issued just as the great Terror was drawing to an end, a hundred thousand or more old women, men, vagrants, priests and children having been burned, tortured, crushed, drowned and hanged for such dealings.

Puritan divines had got the book suppressed, having missed Casaubon's point, apparently, but a lot of copies had got out before then. The book could probably be got from specialists, might even turn up in shops. Kraft had more than one seventeenth-century book on his shelves, some more recondite than that one.

Where to start? Kraft's system of classifying his books was unknown to Dewey and other pedants. And yet it was, must have been, a system.

Nothing more soothing and hopeful than summer light through open windows illuminating the spines of many books. Pierce did not suppose that there were all that many who felt so. Odd duck that he was, he could remember when he was ten, twelve, how on the cool mornings of hot summer days he would sit at breakfast in the bright air and think what a good day it was to read a book, take some notes.

Well look here. Very nearly the first case he approached, the first shelf along which he ran his hand. *John Dee (1527–1608)* by Charlotte Fell Smith, Constable and Company, 1909. Nice old buckram book, deckle-edged, letterpress. On its cover this was stamped:

Your stone, Madimi said. (Kraft's Madimi had.) *I mean your picture, your letter.* Pierce lightly touched the lines. Powerless. Now.

He gazed at it for some time, feeling something in the summer and the day gather in its blankness. But he didn't remember it: didn't remember drawing it on his cousins with a Scripto, or on the flyleafs of his lost books. Memory in that age did not hold such things very well, or only some memories did; nor did the things themselves always awaken when they were looked at long and steadily enough, as sleeping children will; they had to be shaken.

Pierce opened to the index, and looked up Bruno. One brief reference. *Paracelsus had been dead but forty years. Bruno was still alive, developing his theories of God as the great unity behind the world and humanity. Copernicus was not long dead, and his new theories of the solar system were gradually becoming accepted. Galileo was still a student at Pisa, his inventions as yet slumbering in his brain.*

No more.

No meeting, then, or none in the records available in 1909, or this lady would have made much of it, it seemed to be that kind of book.

He leafed through the pages. Why had he wanted it to be true?

My my. Kraft had certainly gone through this book, and more than once; here were underlinings and brackets in several colors of ink, little wordless exclamation points beside choice bits, the whole thing marked up for repackaging, like the diagrammatic steer that butchers display. Was this an easy way to write a book, or not easy, this bricolage of facts and phrases, fixed with your own affections, given a bright coat of lifelike paint? Was it what he would have to do?

He put Miss Smith into his own bag, to study at leisure.

The thought occurred to him that Kraft's shelves were in fact the uncondensed version of his already pretty large book; or that the book was an epitome of the shelves, as though they had brought forth the book simply by their arrangement, each book a chapter, or a sentence.

What's that?

He had spotted a leather-bound folio on the next-to-top storey. To reach it he had to pull over a chair and mount it (as Kraft, he thought, must often have done); it was surprisingly light, though, and he levered it out and leapt not very featly to the floor with it.

Unreadable gold-stamped name on the spine. He took it to the window and opened it on a table there, where half-a-dozen African violets had died, thinking he knew what he would see.

Well for heaven's sake.

Not the *True & Faithful Relation*; not Dee's diary either. It was a book he knew: a polyglot edition of an Italian sort-of novel, the very edition he had struggled with one summer in college, writing a paper.

Hypnerotomachia Poliphili by Francisco Colonna, 1594 though written almost a hundred years earlier in a Dominican monastery. In Italian with French and English translations in triple columns; big woodcuts, fine light paper that crackled with a familiar sound as he turned the leaves. *Le Songe du Polifil. Poliphil's Strife of Love in a Dreame.*

Oh the cool still air of the rare book room of Noate's library, the summer vehement outside . . . The summer before his senior year, working on an Honors Thesis they called it, for which he was actually paid money, though not enough, he had washed dishes at a downtown hotel too, good Lord the things youth can put up with that age never could.

Part One, Chapter One, Poliphilo spends a bad night, tossing and turning: *altogether uncomforted and sorrowful, by meanes of my untimelie and not prosperous love, plunged into a deepe poole of bitter sorrowes.* Then, having spent some part of his wakefulness in the usual way of frustrated lovers, how well Pierce knew—*my wandering senses being wearie to feede upon unsavoury and feigned pleasures, not directly and withoute deceite, uppon the rare divine object*—toward dawn he falls asleep, and has this dream.

God he remembered: his first summer as a scholar; that splenetic dish machine. Possibility: how could a life, a time so constrained have seemed so full of it to Pierce, a banquet, not his yet but set for him as much as for any. Despite all which he had struggled to employ a disparaging irony, against love especially, against the fatuous extravagances of this book, as against his own inward parts: irony having at last been granted him, his newest weapon, sword and shield at once.

Sleeping Polifil dreams he wakes, finds himself in the usual flowery mead; stumbles in his dream into the usual dark wood, *a pritty way entered, I could not tell how to get out of it.* A long struggle, after which he escapes, hears seraphic voices, *falls asleep again,* dreams he wakes again, another flowery mead, this time with a titanic temple or shrine in the distance, toward which he makes his way.

Here was the illustration, a half-page woodcut. Pierce, a battlefield of conflicting feelings, put his hand lightly on it. Obelisk of Ægypt, flight of stairs, cube, pyramid, sphere.

He had been pointed to this book by his Senior Advisor, Frank Walker Barr, twinkle in his eye as though he knew just what trick he was playing. What Barr really thought of the book Pierce never discovered; what he liked about it himself at the time was its obdurate unlikeableness, all surface, no inside, as claustrophobic as a fancy tomb: for in those days he was drawn to the closed, the circular, the labyrinthine, maybe because he thought he knew better, was not himself caught. Ha.

Poliphilus enters the temple, attempts to mount the steps, fails, retreats; enters the cubic base of the temple instead, reads inscriptions, interprets murals, all about love, all pertinent without being in the least illuminating. New things continually happen and manage to give the impression of perfect immobility. He finds an elephant statue on whose back is carried another obelisk, cut with what the artist imagined to be hieroglyphs; he enters the body of this beast, finds tombs or statues of a naked man and woman, reads inscriptions (Pierce struggling with the elliptical Latin, never sure he understood). It was like a Dream Sequence in the black-and-white art movies he went to then, accumulations of minatory images never repeated or endlessly repeated.

More woodcuts. Little Eros in his chariot, pulled by naked girls, he lashes them with a bunch of switches, interesting. Love. No power on earth stronger. It was easy to lose track of whether a picture showed a scene Poliphil dream-witnessed, or one he dream-perceived in a mural or read about in a tablet. At the book's end he has found his beloved Polia, but then wakes to find her not there. Pierce had had only one critical insight into this hermetico-archaeoligico-crypto-romance that summer, and that was that though the hero falls asleep twice, he wakes only once.

So at the end he's still, apparently, asleep, an unusual ending among dream-books, one which Pierce in his paper had ironically maintained must have been intentional; he liked incompletion in those days too, limbos, imprisonments, the un-exitable-from. Eventually, he remembered, he lost his notes and drafts at the movies one night, and never did hand in a paper.

"Polia" could mean "many," couldn't it. Poliphilus: the lover of many, or lover of the Many.

Here was an illustration of that. Pan, Hermes' son, father of many-ness, Omniform or Pantomorph, shown surmounting a stele. Drawn clearly and hugely erect too, "ithyphallic," wasn't that the word; for this book was, also, a sort of delicate pornography. Nymphs

around him bringing him fruits, flowers, produce; a garlanded bull;
music, wine spilled, smoke of sacrifice. Bare Naked Land.

And here was winged Love, older now, a smiling boy, leading his
mother in, winged too, he had not seen that before, a winged Venus,
unusual.

A *ker,* the word tumbled into his mouth, a word out of Frank
Walker Barr's course on the Greeks, maybe, or some old book he had
had once, what book. KER, a dangerous and terrible winged being,
smiling, merciless.

Pierce's senses were suddenly alert, as though they had perceived
something, some presence, there in the bright-dark room with him.

What is it?

He, or the room he stood in, had begun to fill with some numinous something. Or was it within? His heart opened to admit the
passage of something out or in, something that seemed to him to be
at once returning to him and coming toward him from ahead.

"What," he said aloud, taut and all attention; and then "Yes," he
answered, or cried, as though jumping from a cliff, he didn't care, all
he knew was that something was nearby, in his grasp, offered him,
and he would not have long in which to assent to it.

"Yes come back," he said. Yes please come back please, listen I'm
older now, I won't waste it, I'll use it in the context of life I will; this
time I'll be wise, just don't die don't go forever.

It was not there with him anymore. Whatever it was.

He realized he had been standing unmoving for a long time,
trembling like a bowstring.

"Gone," he said.

What had been offered him? Had something? There had been a
sort of picture in his heart or mind: a woman was in it, maybe, and
and. Possibility somehow. A transforming power shown him at his
heart's root; something he recognized at the same moment he knew
how long he had been without it.

"Love," he said.

He closed the stone-dead dream-book, and mounted the chair
again to put it back into its place. Then got down. The light had
altered in the smelly old room. He could think of nothing vividly,
nothing but lunch.

It was in his bag, the stained and ragged bookbag in which he had lugged books for years, as a woodcutter might lug his fagots. In a paper sack (as they called those in Kentucky) under the borrowed book on Dee and the curled and cup-ringed pages of his proposal, the proposal that his agent Julie Rosengarten had used in selling him to Cockerel Books.

He took out the book and the lunch, went out of the library (a moment's doubt again in the hall, no one would believe he could possibly be confused here, left? right?) and out the kitchen door into the garden; sat on a stone bench there to read and eat.

He felt a return of it as he sat there, the power that had visited him, borne in the breeze that passed over his sweat-damp shirt and his hair: not so strong as before, but strong enough that he could tell for sure that it was coming and not going.

He sat stock still, sandwich in his hands, trying to make its face appear, hear its name.

Just please don't hurt me, he pleaded with whatever it was, not knowing that it could or would, and yet afraid.

6

n that Midsummer afternoon, Boney Rasmussen also sat looking out into the day, in the study of his own house, "Arcady," a brownish pile of Shingle Style whimsy and not the only house in the Faraway Hills to bear a name. On the desk behind him (he had turned his swivel chair to look out at the lawns and the oaks, under which he could now descry a small crowd of sheep taking their ease) were a messy pile of papers, and these were Fellowes Kraft's also: letters which Kraft had sent over the years to Boney. Some were formal typewritten replies, self-effacing and cagy, to Boney's first expressions of interest in his work, and to the Foundation's early and tentative offers of help. Others from later years were fuller and franker; Boney and Sandy Kraft (everyone who knew him at all well called him Sandy, his right name too much a mouthful) had become, Boney thought, fast friends at last.

Boney considered each of these letters in turn; picked it up, read the date, read the letter, and after a little thought either dropped it to the floor or filed it in order in the growing pile on his lap. The latest ones were the ones he considered the most closely, questioning through his blue-tinted glasses each sheet of airmail flimsy that trembled in his shaky grasp.

A letter from 1967, from New York apparently, about Kraft's final trip to Europe, for which the Rasmussen Foundation had paid:

"*Mon Empereur*," it began, Kraft's little joke. "I am off at dawn. Really. The ship sails at first light, after we spend a night rocking in harbor—some small problem to which they have not made us privy. Boney I know what a dreadful expense this is compared to cheap and popular air travel. I know it and *I will make it up to you.* What do you want me to bring back? Ah yes I see. But is that something we go abroad to fabled realms to seek? What we most want is, or ought to be, lying out in plain sight, isn't it; found finally in no exotic place or jeweled cabinet but right in your own backyard. Of course it is. And yet, and yet. It would be fun, Boney, wouldn't it, to find at last and finally *one* treasure that was *not* in your heart but in the world; something you could pick up in your own two unworthy hands, a splendor meant for you alone."

These two sheets Boney filed in their place in the growing pile in his lap, and took up the next. This was not the first time he had tried to read all the letters together; nor was the arrangement by date the only one he had tried. He felt sometimes, when ordering them, as he did in games of solitaire, when the cards begin turning up one after another and moving off well, and it seems certain you must go out this time, when you hit a bind, the last ace hidden under the last red queen and the last black king, hidden, hidden.

The next was from Vienna, weeks later.

"They certainly did have some nice things, the Hapsburgs. There was at one time or another in the Hofburg the seamless cloak rent or rather *not* rent by the soldiers who diced beneath the Cross; and the Spear with which Longinus pierced the side of Christ, and which like the more famous Cup has haunted German legend ever since. And— hardly least—the one single physical relic of Jesus Christ himself which we can be certain was left on earth when He ascended into Heaven. What do you suppose it is? Yes! His little foreskin, amputated by the *moyel* St. Simeon Senex, who promptly passed away, having lived a hugely long life just to do this deed. And where did it go then? Well, like the Grail itself, it comes and goes; is sought for; is seen in visions; is rumored to be inside this or that fabulous gem-encrusted reliquary. A little literature springs up around it, little compared to the Grail literature. The mystic nun Hildegarde of Bingen not only saw but tasted it in a vision; it was placed like a Host in her mouth (His Body, after all) and she said it tasted sweet like honey. I am not inventing this. Actually antiquaries say that the penis of Napoleon used to turn up now and then at auction houses, a blackened rind, labeled "a tendon" or some such thing but of course everybody knew. But which would *you* rather get hold of, *mon Empereur?* I mean: There is no question, is there?"

This, after a long moment of thought (Boney's thoughts seemed lately to arrive in his consciousness a long time after they started out, like elderly drivers driving ever more cautiously; nothing for it but to wait), he dropped to the pile at his feet.

The next was also from Vienna, from the same trip in '67 probably, though the first sheet was lost that bore the date:

". . . or an agate bowl, once in the possession of Ferdinand I, that was also supposed to be the Holy Grail. Interested? I am contemptuous, but of course there is no trouble at all in checking it out. Ferdinand was a phenomenal collector; one of his agents brought back from Constantinople the first tulips and lilacs ever seen in Europe. So says my guidebook. So it is out to the Hofburg today to see what we can see. Just let me throw on an overcoat, autumn is frigid in the Danube valley, and swallow a coffee *mit schlag.* The hunt is up."

The hunt was his game, of course, a game which had not seemed so cruel then as it did now: that the Rasmussen Foundation had sent him off to the European capitals to discover or to recognize for them the priceless and the eternal, and get possession of it somehow. They had used to laugh together, he and Sandy, about what might be found in the attics of the old empires, dusty, wrongly labeled by obtuse curators, and yet still living, still potent. A game. Boney remembered (just then remembered, old stored memories spilling, as they often did nowadays) how once, in the shabby science exhibit of his old high school, a snail shell, glued onto a card on which its Latin name was written, had one spring day, after a year or more of appearing quite dead, put out a foot, tugged itself free, and gone off across the glass of its case, leaving a starslime trail behind. Boney had seen it.

"Well it was there," Kraft had written next day, April 1, the letter arising next in Boney's pile. "Large and *luxe* and unattractive. I quote the book: 'Case V—Basin of Oriental Agate with the handles, fashioned out of what is asserted to be the largest single piece of this semiprecious stone; 75 cm in diameter; alleged that the word *Christus* is visible in the texture of the stone,' not to me. It came to the Hapsburgs as part of the dowry of Maria of Burgundy, who married Maximilian I in 1470, along with the silver baptismal utensils in Case VI and the unicorn's horn in Case VII, just a narwhal's tusk according to this wet-blanket guidebook.

"Of course it might have lost something of its numinous lustre over the centuries (the cup, Case V, I mean). It might have appeared much different two hundred or eight hundred years ago. I wonder if we don't have all this backwards, and that once the world worked differently from the way it works now, and what was then a powerful engine is now junk—like a Model T left out in the rain for half a century.

"But maybe, probably, this just isn't it. They probably never really had it; or it was with the stuff that Gustavus Adolphus took away with him to Sweden, and it lost its charm amid the snows and Lutherans. Or maybe they did have it and *still* have it only no one knows where; maybe they forgot long ago and then had only the certainty that once it really had been in their possession. I can imagine them, Duke upon Emperor, rummaging through the *kabinetten,* searching among the cups, the bezoars, the jeweled lizard's skulls, the mercury barometers, automata, magic swords, reliquaries, the petrified wood, dragon's teeth, saint's bones, perpetual motion machines, vials of Jordan water, the forty-carat emerald hollowed out for a poison ring, the mummified mermaid, the *lac lunae,* the ten thousand clocks all chiming differently. Like Fibber McGee's closet. Got to be in here somewhere."

Next letter, postmarked Praha, April 1968. Had he returned to America then from Vienna, and gone back again? Or stayed through the New Year into spring? "The visa you acquired for me with such effort seems to have worked. Am writing this on the train now between Vienna and Prague. When I was last there it was falling to the Nazis. Now the Russians may crush it. As once the armies of the Empire did. I conceived a novel there, about a werewolf let loose on the city." Out of the envelope which held this letter there fell a postcard, without a message, printed obviously long before the letter was written: The Citadel of Prague/Praha, The Hradschin, the Cathedral of St. Wenceslaus, sepia towers against the oncoming clouds.

"You know the Work *was* actually said to have been completed in Prague city, in about the year 1588. There was undoubtedly some great excitement in this city then, a huge stir, which is certainly bound up with the appearance of some sort of immensely valuable something. It's just unavoidable. Whether it was something *found,* or something *made,* or something coming into being just because the time was ripe; whether it was a process, or a treasure, or a *person,* or something entirely different—well I won't say your guess is as good as mine, else why have you gone to such generous expense to get me here; but I will say I despair of discovering it under the countless coverings of time and change, not to mention the principal players' own resolve to keep up the mumchance no matter what. And here come the greatcoats to check papers."

Another sepia postcard: "Intourist has given me a room in a former convent of the Infantines, a wonderful Baroque building built for them by the great Bohemian magnate Peter of Rosmberk (sp?). I have my own cell. I imagine myself in black, Pure, and subsumed in prayer."

Prague made him loquacious; there were many pages from that city.

"The strangely wonderful thing about Prague is that it is *untouched*. It went through the war almost without a scratch (the buildings, the stones I mean): was never shelled or bombed. And ever since it has been entombed in Socialism, which means that except for the usual atrocious concrete apartment blocks and a few statues of Uncle Joe, little has changed 'post-war' either; it hasn't been rebuilt in the International style (glass boxes) or tarted up with new shopping districts or choked with cars. (Cars are the plague of Europe now, as bad as bombs, filling every street and square, shaking down the monuments. Here there are few official Zivs with darkened windows. The rest of the populace walks, or bikes.) Look: here in the old part of town, untouched, is a street of medieval houses known as the Alchemists' Street, 'cause that's where some of the crowd of smokesellers lived and worked who were trying to produce the Elixir for the Emperor Rudolf II before their Imperial pensions ran out. One of them was Doctor Dee, with his menage of children, mediums, servants, and angelic counselors. Can his house be seen? Gotten into? I will find out, Boney, I promise you."

There was a postcard somewhere here too, Boney remembered it, of this street; sepia, empty, the cardboard brown. Had they only had antique postcards for sale in that city? Or had Kraft perhaps never actually left the United States at all, and only sent him souvenirs gathered over there in other days, had them mailed home at intervals by a confederate abroad? Were the letters and the stories and the absurdly omniscient guidebook all a game, rigged for his instruction, or for Kraft's amusement?

"Giordano Bruno was here in 1588, and the Emperor Rudolf II

gave him 300 *talari* for reasons unspecified. *Talari* is Bruno's word, 'dollars' is closer actually; the word 'dollar,' says the guidebook, comes from Tal, valley, because the great silver workings of Count Stefan Slik that supplied the Imperial mints were located in Joachimstal, near Carlsbad. The Valley of the Dollars, sort of. The Bohemians, you know, were the greatest miners of Europe. Did you know that the Czech mountains were once full of gems? Do you think of gems as being found only elsewhere, in Burma or Peru? I do. But there were lots here. Says here that Rudolf was desperately fond of jewels, and had the most extensive collection anyone had ever heard of; he had a gem-hunter *extraordinaire,* Simon Tadeus by name, who worked up in the Giant Mountains—I was up there in the 1930s, Boney, in that brief, terribly brief period when this suffering nation was free.

"The Giant Mountains! Do you see the Seven Dwarves, marching home as evening falls, picks over their shoulders, their knapsacks alight with stones? I suppose Carlsbad has some sort of accommodations still. I will speak to my guide and keeper, an unlovely and gentle youth. I have a plan."

This letter apparently continued after the interruption, or perhaps the next sheet was from another day, from the same pad of blue paper though:

"Rudolf II engages me more and more, one of those rare historical characters with whose plight you feel an instinctive sympathy. He was exactly the same age (I calculate to my astonishment) as Sir Philip Sidney! Sidney met him once when he was on a mission in Europe, a junket sort of, and found him 'extremely Spaniolated,' to his disgust. That came from his upbringing at the Spanish court of his uncle, Philip II. He always wore Spanish black and white, and had that characteristic ambivalence about his childhood that you see in people raised strict Catholics, a mixture of deep repugnance and unassuageable nostalgia. He was in some important sense not a Catholic at the end of his life, an amazing thing really at the time because he did not therefore become a Protestant either; he only abandoned, in terror, in disgust, in guilty dissatisfaction, his old religion. He is supposed to have refused the last rites.

"Of course there are a thousand portraits of him in this city he loved, to which he came I think to escape Vienna and the Jesuits; there are silver-gilt busts and equestrian portraits, etc. etc. My favorite though isn't here, it's in the Victoria and Albert Museum in London, in the deliciously horrible gallery of waxworks: a little plaque in high relief, about the size of a postcard, the Emperor in bright realistic colors, cherry cheeks, gold necklace, like a plastic souvenir; and his hand on the head of a favorite dog. He looks like a more subdued Orson Welles, but with a strange note (strange for an Emperor) of supplication in his eyes.

"You know, Boney, that when his physician—the Paracelsian iatrochemist Oswald Croll, this was—asked Rudolf why after all he longed so greatly to obtain the Elixir, the Emperor is said to have answered, That he might not die ever, and so not be judged. Is that your reason, Boney?"

The game, Boney had at length understood, had been Kraft's very sophisticated way of flattering his aged patron, repaying him for the Foundation's support by indulging him, seducing him almost it seemed at times: slyly, irresistibly persuading Boney, in the intimacy of their shared fantasy, to experience his own harmless but deep desires, his fears, his selfish hopes.

It was *not* his reason, no. He had no fear of being judged, had no fear at all of anything that he could name; he was only unable to feel the obligation to die: as though he had learned by rote the lines he would speak, ought to speak, when the scene had to be played, but now as at last it drew near, finding himself unable to speak them.

"That same Croll or Kroll, by the way (author of the Basilica Chymica), had a famous chest or trunk of some kind, containing I am not sure what, which after his sudden death (sudden for an iatrochemist) was sought for fiercely by the Emperor, who fought off the great noble Peter von Rosemberk, who also desperately wanted it. No mention of this trunk or chest after that. Where is it now? Where for that matter is the Perspective Lute, invented by Cornelius Drebbel; where is the Perpetual Motion Machine he made for the Emperor in 1610? Where is the Prophetic Automaton built in this city by Kepler's friend Jöst Burgi, the clockmaker who invented the second? And what exactly did it prophesy?"

Boney dropped the sheet from his lap, unimportant he thought, not one of those to be sequestered. He raised his eyes. The day beyond his study was summer full-charged. Summer: promise and its satisfaction, yearning and sweetness all mixed, and so palpable as not to seem to be in Boney's breast at all but in the day's and only flowing unceasingly into him through all his senses.

Now shouldn't these sensations begin to grow less intense, so that he could at least begin to resign them? He had heard his doctor say more than once that for the old and sick the world grows smaller and less dear, shrinking down to the compass of their sickrooms, its population reduced to a few or one or two (an heir, a nurse), all the rest forgotten. Which made it the easier to leave. That it was not so for him, that this summer day seemed not less but more precious than any day of any summer that had preceded it—couldn't that be a sign, a sign that he was not to surrender it?

He would not, not till it was rapt from him.

Yes, it had just been Sandy's joke, a joke intended at once to needle and to titillate: pretending to believe that the Rasmussen Foundation had sent him on this crazy errand, to bring back from the Old World an elixir against. Death.

And yet here was his last telegram, here held in Boney's brown ticking hand, from Czechoslovakia, dated 1968, one joke too many, which Boney had not dared question him about when he returned for fear of being mocked as cruelly as only Sandy could mock; and now he was dead and couldn't explain:

MON EMPEREUR STOP HAVE WHAT I PROMISED YOU STOP PACKED W/ TROUBLES IN OLD KIT BAG STOP SMILE SMILE SMILE STOP SANDY

It's six miles from Fellowes Kraft's house to Boney Rasmussen's, over a hill, through a wood, out along the open road, and down a dale. Pierce had no car, and had no way of telling Rosie Rasmussen he was done for the day and wanted to go home (his hours were very much his own) and so he'd told her that today he would walk to Arcady when he was done. Was he sure? It's a hike. Sure, he liked to walk, he needed the exercise.

So she had drawn him a map, at his insistence (he could tell that she was one of those people who almost always know where they are in relation to other places they have been or might go, as he was not; one of those who when they said "south," and pointed, really pointed south). He unfolded it now, half a long sheet of lined yellow paper, and it was indeed very simple.

He retrieved his bag from the house, locked Kraft's door carefully behind him and pocketed the brown key. If you lose it, Rosie had said

—and then no more, unable to think of consequences dire enough to threaten him with. He walked down the dusty drive.

A key, a house, a drive. Once his cousin Hildy had come home from boarding school with a game, a test actually she said, a psychological test, to be administered to each of them in private (so that one person's answers wouldn't influence the next subject's) and with a certain solemnity.

Now you must say the first thing that comes to mind, she had said. You are going to imagine you are going up the front path to a house. Not this house or somebody you know's house or any particular house. Tell me first what sort of path.

Nodding sagely at the response, no comment beyond that. Now you're going in the house. You find a key. What sort of key? Where is it? What does it open? You find a cup. What cup? Where is it?

A cup. A door. Water. He couldn't remember all the items there were, only that they were simple, and singular; and when the house had been traversed and left, the interpretations were given.

Pierce looked at his map, turning it so that it matched the way he faced. He felt again in his pocket for Kraft's key, and set off down the road rightward.

The path to the house was your past life. Was it crooked or straight, muddy or tidy? The key was knowledge, how you felt about it, how you would use it. Pierce had seen in his mind an old brown Yale key, just like the one he had just now put in his pocket; he had known, somehow, that it was the key to the door to the basement. Hildy's own key (she said) was a tiny one that unlocked a glass cabinet. The cup was love: Hildy's was a translucent china teacup, delicate as sugar; and it was locked inside the cabinet with the key. Pierce had seen a sturdy and necessary mug, and through it there ran a dreadful crack, no kidding, I mean I just instantly saw it. Joe Boyd's was a battered tin cup chained to the faucet.

The road unrolled between two rows of ancient trees, scaly-barked, lop-limbed, titanic. Had they been planted here centuries ago, or were they the remnants of a forest, left standing by the roadside to shade the traveler? Seen from within the cool vault that they made, the fields and meadows were bright as stage sets or dioramas. Pierce stopped where the road crossed a tiny brook, and stood for a time watching the water run, amid the blue flags, over coppery stones.

Meaning. You were told the meaning of the cup, the door, the water, and discovered that you had unerringly attached the right referent to each, if you had assigned any at all (Sam's house was nothing but his own house, the key his own house key, the cup his coffee cup). It was as though the meaning had come first, before there were actual cups and keys to hold it.

The first language, which cups and keys, roads and houses, dogs, stars, stones and roses had only come into existence to illustrate, the language not of denotation but of meaning.

Was *that* what Bruno had been talking about? He and all those who ransacked their vocabularies (in Latin, Italian, French, English) for words that meant what *logos* means in Greek—"word," "idea," "reason," none of them right or large enough. Maybe because they had no word such as Meaning has since become in English.

Meaning. The hidden interior light that makes things things, the light which casts a matching shadow in the mind, a picture, a glyph: not a picture of its shape or size or color, not a sign of its difference from me but of its likeness to me: of its Meaning. A glyph combinable with others in a language hot enough, powerful enough, to dissolve the distance between Inside and Outside, the fountain and the mirror, strong enough to replace the thing with its meaning. To make wishes come true.

The door of Arcady stood open, only a screen covering it, itself not completely shut. Still Pierce pulled the brass knob of the bell-pull, and waited. He was foolishly pleased to have got here without mishap.

When it appeared that no one was going to answer, he opened the screen and stepped in; and standing in the broad vestibule grew certain that there was no one at all in the house.

"Hello?"

He wouldn't be sorry to have missed Boney Rasmussen, who made him uncomfortable, the more uncomfortable the more tactful and deferential he was. But he did need a ride home.

"Hello?" he said again, only to hear the salute fade into a confirming vacuity, no human presence. He seemed to have the house to himself.

He took a few steps down to the end of the vestibule, to the threshold of a large sitting room where he had not so far ever seen anyone sit. Dark drapes over lace petticoats keep the sun from fading the rug. The cool cavern brought clammy sweat to his neck.

Rosie Rasmussen had told him that somewhere in the house Boney kept a real Renaissance crystal ball, once actually used for skrying, first owned, Boney had told her, by John Dee himself, a pedigree for which Pierce would have to see a lot of evidence before believing. He kept it, Rosie said, in a little wooden chest or drawer, locked with a key.

That one there?

A sort of commode of inlaid wood there had a top compartment, and he could see from where he stood a little key in its filigree lock.

Just as he took a step toward it, a telephone went off beside him with the force of a burglar alarm. Pierce leapt away from it, an aged black instrument on a spindly table under a lamp, probably the house's original. He almost expected when it rang again to see it rattle in its cradle, like phones in cartoons.

If someone was in the house, the ringing would cease, an extension somewhere picked up. It didn't cease. Pierce's hand reached out to still its imploring, and he drew it back. It's not for you, you dope. When it rang again, he picked it up.

"Hello?"

"Pierce? Oh I'm so glad, I didn't think you'd answer."

It was Rosie Rasmussen. Pierce grew conscious at that moment that Rosie's station wagon had not been parked outside the house.

"Something's happened," she said, sounding far away. "I can't come get you."

"What is it?" he said.

"It's Mr. Rasmussen," she said. "Some kind of attack. I found him, he was on the floor. He got a little better, but."

The black receiver was cold against his ear, and as heavy as marble. "Heart?" he asked.

"They don't know. He's in Intensive Care. Anyway. Pierce. If you could think of some way to get home."

"Sure. Sure. Listen don't worry about it at all."

"It's the housekeeper's day off . . ."

"I'll think of something. I can always hitch."

"Oh!" she said suddenly. "Spofford will be coming by to feed his sheep."

Pierce had seen the sheep when he came in the gate, standing in the shade of Arcady's oaks. "Oh. Okay. Fine."

"What?" she said, but not to him, to someone beside her there where she was, the hospital; someone with news maybe. "Pierce I gotta go," she said, and the phone was silent before he had said goodbye.

7

—

ove," said Val the Faraways astrologer to Rosie Rasmussen, and held out a fried-chicken wing to Rosie's daughter Sam, who shook her head. "If they were making up the houses of the Zodiac now, there would have to be one house that's the House of Love."

"There isn't?" Rosie said.

"No. It's amazing." Val stripped the meat from the wing herself with one practiced motion of fingers and teeth as Sam watched wide-eyed. "There's *Nati,* that's the fifth house, and that's the house of Children basically: it sort of includes sex, or at least procreation, but it's got to cover wills and legacies and inheritance too. And there's *Uxor,* the seventh house, the Wife. Marriage, and partnership, and like relationships. But hey, I don't have to tell *you*: that's just not quite love."

"Hm," said Rosie. Rosie was a single mother, in the process of getting divorced from Sam's father.

"But Love is what everybody wants to know about. After money and health. No *before* money, anyway if they're young. Love is oh Christ half my business. And there's not really a House of Love. Weird, huh?"

Rosie examined the Pu Pu Platter she and Sam and Val were sharing for lunch, and chose a fried dumpling. "Weird," she said. But in fact she didn't herself just then see the need, or feel the press of questions about love and the prospect of love that needed answering.

It was true, what Val said, that it was a big question for most people, but it had ceased to be one for Rosie. She felt herself to be (though she hadn't always been) outside or beyond the preoccupation, as she was outside other things that occupied lots of people—oh sports, or politics.

It wasn't the same, though.

"So there's houses of Health and Money?" she asked.

"Sure," Val said. "*Lucrum* is all about money and property and stuff. And *Valetudo,* the sixth house, is about Sickness. Diseases. So is *Mors*: that's Death."

"How about politics? Sports?"

Val drew back her head, affronted, the wingbone still held between thumb and medicus. "You trying to make a farce out of this?"

"We have sports in *my* house," Sam said, nodding.

"Yes?" Val said.

"In my ode house."

"Oh. Hey, okay."

"Her old house," Rosie said. "Some kids have imaginary friends. She has an imaginary old house. The house where she used to live, she says. She always had it. Since she could talk."

"Well sure," said Val. "So do you, if you could only remember it."

Rosie tried to explain about Love. "As though it were all happening someplace else, somewhere I'm not—as though I'm seeing it all through a screen or a glass, and I can't hear very well. And what I *do* hear makes me afraid. Like football: I don't know how it's played, and everybody roars with excitement, *into* it, and I feel like I'm the only one who thinks it's just dangerous and somebody's going to get killed."

"Well is it real surprising?" Val said gently. "When you've just gone through what you've gone through? I mean Christ."

Of course that made sense. It made really too much sense; it accounted for what had happened to Rosie without explaining it. She dipped the dumpling in cold dark sauce.

"Mommy I said let's GO," said Sam, who had in fact been saying it, and had been heard but ignored now for some little time by the two grownups.

"God I didn't tell you," Rosie said. "We had a time the other night. Sam. She was sleepwalking. Yes. I was in my bed, and something woke me—you know how you can wake up from someone's standing there? And there was Sam by the bed."

Realizing that Sam was in fact asleep, blind, though her eyes were open, had caused Rosie's back hair to thrill. To be looking at someone apparently present who was actually absent in the land of sleep.

"You won't believe this. She came to the bed, and held something out. For me. Know what it was? An egg."

"An egg?"

"She had I guess gone all the way down the stairs. In the dark, alone. And back up with this egg. She put it in my hand."

"What did you do?"

"I took it. I said—Thank you." Rosie wondered at it now.

"Did she wake up?"

"Nope. She turned and went. I got out of bed and followed her. She went back to her room and got in bed again. Pulled up the covers. Asleep."

Sam, whose head alone came up above the table in the booth, looked up at the two grownups who marveled at her; not pleased or proud but not embarrassed either, content to hear herself described.

"You really don't want to come with us?" Rosie said to Val. "I'm sure Boney would like a visit. And if he's too sick for you to visit, then I won't be able to stay long."

"I can't. I can't leave her."

"She'll be all right. I can drive you in tomorrow." "She" was Val's aged Beetle, undergoing routine surgery at a shop next down along the Strip from the Volcano where they sat.

"Nope," said Val. "I don't mind waiting." She lifted her drink, showing it to Rosie. "And reading matter. Look at this book I got out of the library."

From the big sloppy crewel bag she was never without, Val pulled a large and old-looking volume—not ancient-looking, just old. "I've been doing some research on love myself. Filling in the gaps. I'm finding some insane stuff, I mean anyway it's been a help to me." Rosie noticed the distinctive white paint of the librarian who had long ago carefully lettered the call numbers on the spine, and was for a moment touched. Not many people took out books with such numbers on them.

"Check out the author's name," Val said. "Isn't that wild? Like the villain in some bondage book. Not that *you'd* know."

She opened the book, hardly room for it in the little booth with Sam and big Val; Sam clambered to her knees to look. "Listen," she said. "It's like a dictionary or an encyclopedia. You look things up. When I looked up Love it sent me to Eros, who's the you know the Cupid guy, with the arrows. Eros in Greek. Here's what he says:

" 'According to Diotima'—whoever he is—'Contrivance, the son of Invention, got drunk on nectar at Aphrodite's birthday, and Poverty took advantage of this to seduce him and bear him a child: Eros.' " She lowered the book. "Isn't that a hoot? All these words have capital letters, so they're like people, carrying on. The son of Poverty and Contrivance: I love it."

Rosie laughed too, but she had begun to notice a familiar tightening in her breast, right beneath the sternum, but why.

" 'Plato says'—hey, Plato, there's a name I know—'Plato says that Eros is not to be confused with the beautiful beloved, though men often make this mistake,' women too I bet. 'Rather his appearance presages the appearance of the beloved; he is the spirit who inspires love, who makes love unrefusable, who gives the lover his divine madness.' "

"Divine madness," said Rosie. "Uh huh."

" 'Far from being sensitive and beautiful, says Plato, he is hard and weather-beaten, always poor, a beggar shoeless and homeless, always sleeping out for want of a bed, on the ground, on doorsteps, and in the street . . . But as he is the son of his father Hermes, he schemes continually to get for himself whatever is beautiful and good; he is bold and forward and strenuous, always devising tricks like a cunning huntsman; he yearns after knowledge and is resourceful and a lover of wisdom, a skillful magician too, an alchemist.' " She lowered the book. "Didn't know all that, did you?"

"Tough life for a kid."

"Hey, love is tough." She laughed her deep rough laugh. "But we knew that." She found her place again. " 'To the oldest poets he was a dangerous winged spirit, like the winged personifications of Old Age and Plague: a *Ker* that disrupted ordered society, and did harm to living people. Later poets invented a dozen genealogies for him in addition to those given above, while some argued that he was the first of the gods and without a parent, since without him none of the others could be born.' Now why is that? Oh, I get it."

"Makes the world go round." Rosie drank down her Mai Tai, more quickly and thirstily than she had intended to. "Speaking of legacies," she said.

"Huh?"

"Didn't you say legacies and inheritances? In the house about love?"

"Oh. I guess."

"Boney," Rosie said. "I've been trying to get Boney to think about all that stuff. You know I don't think he's even got a real will?"

Val closed the dictionary, and pushed it away.

"I hate to pester him," Rosie said. "I mean it's not really my business, in a way, but I'm sort of his secretary. And then Allan Butterman wants to know." Allan Butterman was Boney Rasmussen's lawyer, counsel too to the Foundation.

"Uh-huh." Val had put on the pursed mouth and knitted brows she used to signify attention, or maybe used to compel her own attention when her mind wanted to head elsewhere. "Hm."

"When I finally asked him about it, what he was going to do—I mean I thought for days how to put it—he said Oh he'd decided he was going to leave everything to an old girlfriend named Una Knox."

Now Val was paying and not pretending to pay attention. "Who?"

"He said: My old girlfriend Una Knox. But he was smiling. A joke, maybe. He wouldn't tell me any more." She saw Val's disappointment. "Well I wasn't going to grill him," she said.

Val felt absently within her bag for her cigarettes. It was hard to tell from her face whether what Rosie had told her meant something to her, or nothing at all; but Rosie thought she could see Val trying to find a place for this fact (if it was a fact) amid the store of secrets shameful and silly, humdrum and drastic, of the inward shop she kept.

"Una Knox," Val said aloud.

"Are we going to see Boney now?"

"Yep." Val reached across Sam's lap to pull shut the door of the big old Bison station wagon she drove. She had an unreasoning fear of car doors and the crushing of small fingers; she thought maybe it had happened once, to someone she knew, but she couldn't think who it might have been.

"Why doesn't Val come?"

"I don't know." Why didn't she come? Usually she liked a look into other people's dramas. Rosie wondered.

"It's not scary."

"No, it isn't."

Rosie Rasmussen was Boney Rasmussen's great-niece, daughter of his brother's son. She had come to live at "Arcady" when she left her husband, Mike Mucho, and began the process of getting a divorce, which she had recently been granted; rather, she had been granted a "decree *nisi,*" which her lawyer assured her was virtually a divorce but which made her a little uneasy. "Nisi" meant "unless," and nobody could tell her unless what, if anything; but not till six months after it would she have a real divorce. In the meantime she was neither divorced nor not: so she saw it. She had also been given custody of her daughter Samantha by the court. Unless.

"What's that, Ma?"

"What, hon?"

"All around that store."

A car dealership in early fig for the Fourth of July. "It's bunting," said Rosie.

Sam turned in her seat to look back as they passed it. The wind lifted wisps of her hair from her delicate skull. "Well it isn't doing it," she said.

"Isn't doing what?"

"Bunting."

Rosie laughed. God if she could only remember the things Sam said. But she never did.

The dark disease (as she thought of it) that had invaded her feelings, which she had tried to describe to Val and hadn't described, had not touched her feelings for Sam, not yet at least, though like advancing frostbite it might yet; it might get everything. Every day almost she felt astonished to find herself still living with this beautiful, cheerful, passionate, fastidious person. Even as she grew daily more impatient with the (after all not really very awful) duties of washing dressing feeding amusing her, dreading the early hour of her waking, though often enough Rosie was herself already awake—even so she grew more dependent on Sam's being there; needed like food or drink the sensible flow of Sam's being into her own as she sat beside her, or watched her bathe, or fought with her, or traded inanities with her in bed in the morning.

What it was, what she had tried to say to Val, was that she had found herself no longer on the side of love. That's what she should have said: Not on love's side. She had been all her life on love's side without thinking about it, because who isn't? How could you even understand stories or life at all if you weren't? Sam already knew why Cinderella stayed late at the ball, why the Prince searched the kingdom for her; the soaps that Boney's housekeeper Mrs. Pisky watched would shrivel up to nothing without love, without the people watching being for love, somehow, automatically.

Rosie wasn't. She had once been so, and now she wasn't, and she didn't know why. She went to the movies now and watched Her meet Him, and felt not mild approval or even ordinary impatience but a dark lassitude, an unwillingness to consent that made everything that followed meaningless. Worse when there was danger, or pain; when He and She couldn't help it, followed each other into the dark, cheated on their barren worried bitter busy spouses, driven into each other's arms by what seemed to Rosie to be a violent sickness. What's the matter with you? Go home and make up. Lovers had come to appear to her as people turned into puppets, their sinews pulled by this insensate power, an artificial fire burning in their hearts.

Depression, said Mike, a psychotherapist, never at a loss for a name for black feelings. But it might just as well be wisdom; her friend Beau Brachman said it was, wisdom entering the soul to realize that the things we have wanted so long enchain or burden us, that the pain of wanting isn't ever healed by having; it's a relief, he said, like the throbbing noise of some endless engine outside your window suddenly ceasing, and silence and the world surging softly in.

It didn't feel like relief, though, like escape from difficulty; it felt like waking up from a dream or delusion of possibility, and finding yourself in prison, without possibility; becalmed on the dull sea or stranded in the desert of not wanting things.

No it wasn't wisdom. But it might not be willfulness or wickedness either. It might not even be psychological, a block or a hangup. Maybe she was under a curse.

She laughed, softly, and struck the wheel of the station wagon. Sam looked up and laughed too, always ready for a joke.

A curse, or maybe a spell; sure, maybe it wasn't her at all, maybe it was the whole world under a spell. That's actually how she felt it, not as a bend or constriction of her own heart but as something she knew about the world, something she knew and others didn't, not most of them anyway, not yet. They were still all feeling things, wanting to feel more things, their feelings pumped up with sports and art and politics. And love. Till one by one they dried up too.

But if it was the world gone wrong and not just Rosie's heart, then she couldn't hope to fix it. So she'd better not believe that.

"Is that the hospital?"

"Yes. How did you guess?"

"I saw an ambliance."

"Ambulance."

"Yep."

It was a rambling, low brick building, neither new nor old, and somehow not discouraging; it hadn't seemed to Rosie to be the sort of place people were likely to die in. It was a place for births and operations and get-well fruit baskets. The nurses were dressed unseriously in tees and tennis shoes; the voice over the intercom was sweetly hesitant.

Sitting nightlong in the waiting room of the Coronary Care Unit she had overheard real disasters unfold, though; had watched doctors in green operating clothes, feet sometimes still shod in paper boots, come out to explain in weary undertones what had happened to a husband or a father (all the patients seemed to be males, most of the expectant waiters women). She saw families gather, whisper together. *But he seemed so good. They said he passed a good night. And now.*

In the space of a few hours she acquired the rudiments of a new language. *He's holding his own,* the doctor would say. *They said he's holding his own,* the wife would say to her sister, to his sister, to her son. "Holding his own" seemed to mean desperately sick but not getting worse right now. *He's not out of the woods yet,* the doctor would tell someone; Rosie would see in her mind the prostrate patient, hooked to blinking machines, while his absent spirit wandered in dark undergrowth.

No common bond like the nearness of death; no fellowship like mortality. Private as their griefs were, those gathered in the room, nowhere else to go, voyagers alone together, shared Kleenex and magazines, asked careful questions, sat fanny by fanny in the fiberglass chairs. It seemed to Rosie that every kind of person there was in the Faraways appeared in the room just in that night; tall delicate-featured aristo gent in seersucker jacket and pipe; lots of blue-rinsed frightened ladies with chains on their glasses; lots of ordinary shapeless sweatshirted working people. It surprised Rosie that a majority—she had time to count—were seriously fat. Maybe you got a high percentage in Coronary Care.

It had not really been necessary for her to stay late into the night there, far from wherever they were doing whatever to Boney, but she stayed, afraid partly that he might take a sudden turn for the worse, frail as he was, and have to check out without anyone at all he knew nearby (she didn't feel sure that she herself was the one he would want to look last upon, but just about everybody else he knew was dead already; there were far more ready to welcome him on the other side than to say goodbye). And she was captured by the front-line atmosphere of the room, where people found themselves in the gravest circumstances it was likely they would encounter in a peaceful world, and rose to them or didn't. Once she came back from the nurse's station to find a whole crew of bikers in the hall and the waiting room; one of their number in critical condition apparently; they sat on the floor tearfully hand in hand or hugged each other fiercely, thumping backs with leatherbound fists. Supportive. The others there looked at them askance, their own more private responses, be brave, pushed aside by the gang's grieving rituals.

They were still there today, some of them anyway, their buddy apparently not out of the woods. Sam sat down amid their litter of munchies bags and soda cans, watching them with interest. Rosie was suddenly sorry she had brought Sam; she wouldn't have if there had been any place to leave her, or if Sam had not wanted so much to see Boney, in whom she took an absorbing interest, her fabulous monster.

"We ask that young children not be brought to the floor, actually," the nurse said who came to bring her to Boney's room.

"Well we just wanted to peek in," Rosie said.

"You're a daughter?" said the nurse.

"Well sort of." She looked straight ahead. "By adoption."

"Well," said the nurse. "If he's active. Let's see."

Beyond the heavy door of the "semi-private" room (what would that mean anywhere else in the world?) was one empty bed wrapped in tight sheets like a package; and the drawn curtain, beyond which was Boney's bed. The nurse looked around it and greeted him heartily. Folks here to see you. Want me to run you up?

Sam (not having said a word yet, clutching tightly the bouquet she had picked for him and the get-well card she had made) watched Boney's head slowly arise from prone as the bed bent in the middle.

"Neat, huh?" Rosie said. "Hi, Boney."

He looked ashen and small, but not necessarily near death; not as bad as he had looked when Rosie had looked in on him near dawn. He fumbled his glasses on and blinked at Rosie and Sam. "Well. Well, how nice."

"How are you?"

Boney raised both his hands slightly, as though to exhibit himself; in the loose mottled skin of one hand, bandages held an IV which trailed away to a bottle.

"Still all there, huh?" Rosie said. "What do they say?"

"Well they're going to send me home," Boney said. "I don't think that's a good sign."

"Why not?"

"Well I think. I think it means they're giving up on me. They're not even going to try to fix me. That's what it means. That it's not worth trying."

"Oh I bet not," Rosie said, alarmed.

"Let me go home and die. That's what they think. Hello, sweetheart."

"You want to give him your stuff?" Rosie pushed Sam gently forward, but Sam turned instead, and would not go near him. Rosie touched her hair and looked into her face. Sam was furious.

"What is it, hon?"

Sam stamped her foot. "Why is he like that?"

"Like what?"

"What is it in his hand?"

"That helps him get better. Hon . . ."

Sam crossed her arms and marched from the room, her feet striking hard.

"What is it?" Boney asked.

"God, sorry Boney."

She went out into the hall and caught up with her daughter, who had stopped suddenly when confronted with the somber length of the hall, where now a man trundled a walker with painful steps, an oxygen tube over his nose, white hair mussed.

"Sam?" Rosie knelt beside her to talk. "Did you get scared?"

"I don't like what they *did* to him."

"Well won't you come back in?"

"No." Sam stood arms akimbo, resolute against pain and disease, unreconciled. Afraid though actually, maybe, probably; alarmed, certainly.

"He shouldn't *be* like that," she said.

"But he's getting better," Rosie said. "Did you hear? He's coming home. If you give him your card, he can look at it, and it might make him so cheerful he'll get better faster."

She put her arm around Sam where she knelt in the hallway, herself wrapped in a sudden awful pity, but for whom? The little hospital seemed shadowed momentarily as by a dark wing, a shadow she knew. "I think he's lonely in there," she said.

Still Sam wouldn't move when Rosie gently tugged on her hand; angry tears rose in her eyes, and she crossed her arms tightly before her. Another shuffler with toothless gasping mouth (too much trouble to put in the teeth yet, it seemed) went past them.

"Okay?" Rosie said, afraid she might weep herself.

"Oh *kay*," Sam said fiercely. They went together back toward Boney's room.

"Here we are again," he said faintly.

Sam approached him. His ticking hand lay on the sheet, bruised blue where the IV needle had gone in. "Why did they tie you to this?" she demanded.

"So I wouldn't slip away," Boney said. "But I won't."

She gave him her card, accepting it from Rosie as a dignitary accepts from his aide the tribute he passes to the hero; and then the bouquet. Boney in return gave her the miniature chocolate pudding that had come with his lunch.

"Rosie," he said. He had sunk back on the bed, looking mummified. She came close to hear. "That young fellow, why can I never remember his name."

"Pierce?"

"Yes. Has he said anything to you, how it's going there . . ."

"Boney, you don't have to think about that stuff."

"I don't think about anything else."

"Well except I'm not sure he entirely understands what . . ."

"He does. He does. He may not say so to you."

"Okay," she said softly. "Okay." Did it always do this, the near-ness of death, strip away the courtesies? She would have thought they were part of Boney's nature; it was odd hearing him talk as though to himself. Was death going to do that, take away everything from him bit by bit, and leave him naked of everything but this crazy wish or want?

He lifted himself off the bed on one elbow, laboring somewhat for breath. "Congestion," he said. "Supposed to bring it up." He tried to clear his lungs, but couldn't.

"Pound his back," said Sam, busy with the pudding.

"You want me to?" Rosie said. She approached him gingerly. The open back of his hospital johnny, loosely tied, revealed a weird eroded landscape of skin and muscle. She patted while Boney harked weakly.

"Like that?"

"Good. Thank you." He hunched forward, arms draped over his knees. "I've been thinking," he said. "Once upon a time the Founda-tion used to give out grants. To individuals. Research things, or study grants. They were a little hard to fit into our, our." He waved vaguely, trying to think of a word like *mission* or *statement of goals* and not finding it. "Anyway we did give out a few, nothing very large. I would like to establish that again. A small program of study grants. Study abroad."

"Okay," Rosie said tentatively, unwilling to ask for details here and now. What he had said had emptied him like a cup, and now panting slightly he waited to refill.

"Soon though," he said.

"Well sure."

"Tell him," he said, and Rosie had to think who. "That I have to know it meant nothing. That it was only a game. I have to know or I can't, I won't . . . Oh Rosie." He lay again, but not to rest. "I have to be sure."

She felt his forehead; it was hot, filmed with icy sweat. He tried to rise again, seeming unable to breathe, and Rosie pressed the nurse's call button. "Just a sec, okay?" she whispered. "Just a sec." She held his head up and he made a spectral groan. Rosie looked down to see Sam looking up at them with interest.

The nurse hustled the visitors out, looking at the two of them slightly aggrieved, and then tore the curtains rapidly around Boney's bed. The rattle of the rings, the shroud lifting outward on the air of its quick passage, a wing of white enveloping silence: Rosie watching it, watching Boney covered, remembered again, something she could not name.

"The nurse was mean."

"No she wasn't, hon. She just wanted Boney not to get too tired." Rosie backed the Bison out of its spot in the parking lot.

"She stepped on my card." A tear welled in her eye, always amazing to watch how quick they came. *Welled.*

"Oh hey now. He was real glad to see you. He liked your card. *And* your flowers."

"Will he die when he gets home?"

"No," she said.

"He said he would."

"Well." The day had turned blindingly hot, dusted as with silver powder, and mirages of water trembled in the hollows of the road ahead. "He's real old, Sam. And finally when you're real old."

"I know Mommy. I do know." Resigned, resigned and sad. Offering her mother the comfort of her wisdom and acceptance. Rosie marveled. Was all knowledge of life maybe nothing more than the right imitation of knowledge? Then Sam knew as much as she did herself.

"Hey listen," Rosie said, change the subject, as much for her own sake as Sam's. "You want to get the car washed?"

"Car washed?"

"Sure. There's a place just up here. We ought to."

"What," Sam said suspiciously, thinking maybe her leg was being pulled.

"Wash the car. With big brushes and water. You'll see."

Had Sam ever been through a carwash? Rosie tried to remember. Maybe once, too young to wonder. Rosie didn't wash the big Bison station wagon often, it seemed a little pretentious to drive such a heap through those ministrations, old biddy giving herself the beauty treatment. Mike shook his head over it, it had always been clean when he had owned it.

"Right here," she said. "See?"

Sam withheld judgment.

"Roll up the window real tight, can you. Tight tight."

"Why?"

"So the water won't come in." She paid her dollar, engaged her wheel with the track, and let go of the steering wheel. Sam looked from the abandoned wheel, moving slightly by itself, to the dark tunnel ahead, to her mother's face: not reassured by it. "I don't want to," she said.

"It's fun," Rosie said. "Wait till you see."

"I don't *want* to."

"Well you can't get out now, hon. Got to go on through to the other side. Come sit with me."

With startling suddenness the water jets opened, thundering on the roof and hood, and Sam leapt to her mother's side. "I dowanto I dowanto!"

"Watch watch," Rosie said. She had always loved carwashes herself, the letting go of the wheel, the torrential drenching. Out of your hands.

Was he going to die? Was she going to be with him? She wondered what Boney thought happened to you after you died. She had not asked and certainly would not, but it would be easier, she thought, if she knew what he expected. Or feared. If there was anything he feared, anything but the shut door itself.

So afraid.

Sam held tight to her arm as things happened one after another, each more astonishing and alarming than the last if you had never seen them before. After the water *bardo* came the *bardo* of brushes: huge furry animals fell on them, spinning like dervishes, bright blue for some reason, and Sam stared at them in disbelief. This was not the reason anyone ever had a kid, but it turned out to be one of the greatest gratifications of it, and one that no one ever described to you: to see in them the amazing world experienced, and so experience it again yourself as for the first time. Unless it was what greeting cards meant by the Wonder In the Eyes of a Child and all that.

Next came Flapper Monsters, black hundred-armed whirlers that slapped them side and top, the roaring and clattering of the machines and water never ceasing, nor the slow purgatorial crawl forward of the car. Sam flinched from them, but laughing now at last, getting it. Last and funniest of all the Sucker Creatures, slit-mouths at the end of flexible yellow necks, drinking the excess water from the car as hot air blew and droplets chased one another across the windows. And now the end of their trials visible, the cave-mouth and the day, and then they had emerged from their funhouse into the quiet and the sunlight, rain-dappled, clean.

"Let's go again," Sam said, a convert now.

"We can't go again right away," Rosie said. "Now we're clean. We have to wait till we get dirty again."

"We'll get dirty again?"

"Oh we will," Rosie said. "We will."

8

———

oving back toward Blackbury Jambs with the evening
traffic hurrying toward home and supper. Was there a
new noise down within the Bison's workings, far away
along the drive train? Almost not worth fixing; but then what?

"Look, it's Pierce," said Sam.

No one Rosie could see anywhere. "No it's not, hon."

"Tis too," Sam said, pointing, and now Rosie did see the back of a
tall person, a white shirt luffing in the evening breeze, who was
toiling along the roadside where not much provision had been made
for walkers, and carrying two full shopping bags, from the supermarket she had just passed probably.

"See?" Sam said, still pointing.

"Sharp eyes," Rosie said. She pulled over to the shoulder as carefully as she could given that her car had no rear-view mirror stuck on
the windshield. She waved back to Pierce, who took a long time to
notice her, seeming hypnotized by the noise and the traffic's progress.

"Thanks, thanks," he said, as he clambered with his crackling
bags into the back. "Road was getting a little long."

"I would think so," Rosie said.

"What did you buy?" Sam wanted to know.

"Unnecessarily heavy food," Pierce said. Sam laughed; Pierce had
learned to amuse her by using big words and a grownup tone.
"Things in metal cans and glass jars. I should have bought light
things. Sponge cake. Sponges. Wonder Bread."

"Balloons," said Sam.

"Bubbles," Pierce said. "Which are heavy till you blow them, though."

"You," said Sam, with a weirdly grown-up gesture of coquettish dismissal. "You are so *silly*."

"What you *should* do," Rosie said, "is get a car. Isn't there at least a bus from the store to town?"

"Well I noticed there was," Pierce said. "It picks people up at a bench there. But everyone waiting for it seemed to have a good reason for taking it. Extreme old age. Feeble-mindedness. Bad eyesight. Real poverty. You know. I felt I might be unwelcome. A guy who obviously has no reason not to be driving."

"Now," Rosie said to Sam, "he is being silly."

Pierce really had intended, without exactly foreseeing the process, eventually to learn to drive and then acquire a car. He had arrived at his present age unlicensed in part because he had not very often or very badly needed to drive—he had gone to a private prep school from which egress was largely forbidden during the school terms, and at Noate, his university, only upperclassmen were allowed cars. By then a distaste for cars and driving had become a feature of the eccentric character he was assembling for himself like a suit of home-made armor, and in the city no one drove anyway, no one Pierce knew.

But there was an abiding and aboriginal fear too, that had kept him from ever being tempted; where cars had been to Joe Boyd and the boys of the Cumberlands heart-filling personifications (even named, often) of freedom and power and heat, to Pierce they had been like the dogs chained to stakes outside Cumberland cabins, or encountered roaming free in the hollers: big beasts, minding their own business but to be dealt with gingerly or not at all. He still sometimes dreamed of such dogs, but filled with mindless malevolence, their chains giving way like twine; and he had dreams too of finding himself inexplicably at the wheel, under way and the pedals useless, the car speeding willfully toward ruin.

Anyway so many bodies had been broken, so many cars demolished in those years by the boys of Kentucky, so many boys themselves slain too (crushed like nutmeats within their huge old Hornets or new Hawks or Impalas, boot still on the accelerator, cigarette tucked behind the ear) that the insurance premium on such drivers was fearsome; Sam decided that Pierce and Joe Boyd would have to raise the extra themselves in order to get their learner's permits, which Joe Boyd somehow did quickly and easily and Pierce never tried very hard to do. His female cousins had no such impediment, and got their licenses early on (Hildy even learned under Sam's instruction, a mortification she felt earned her millennia of credit hereafter). So Pierce wangled rides with them.

"It's not that I have something against cars," he said to Rosie. "I have fond feelings for some. I lost my virginity in a car."

"Oh yes?"

"A Lark," Pierce said. "A now-forgotten kind. I would be one of very few, I would think."

"Are you going to get a license?"

"I have every intention. I have a learner's permit. My lifetime third. The others went stale before I learned."

"Oh right. Val drove you in. To get the permit."

"It was remarkable," Pierce said. "A dozen teenagers, one widow suddenly on her own, and me."

"Did you pass?"

"That was the most remarkable part. You were set ten questions to answer, but you only needed to get eight right. *Only eight.* Which seems to mean that you could be under the impression, for instance, that the red octagon sign is the sign for Caution and not Stop, and still be allowed to take the wheel."

"Oh everybody knows." Rosie pushed the Bison around a broad traffic circle, heading for the exit into Blackbury Jambs. A sign directed her to Merge. Now how exactly (Pierce wondered) do you Merge? Are there rules? Not explained in his learner's manual. Just sort of ease in apparently. Everybody knows.

"I saw Boney today," Rosie told him.

"How is he?"

"Well. He's coming home."

"He's not sick anymore," Sam said.

"Good," said Pierce.

"Well," Rosie warned. Pierce asked no more.

They entered onto the bridge across the somnolent summer river, and the ridges of its surface thrummed beneath the Bison.

"When you see him again," Pierce said, "tell him I've found some interesting things. Not," he cautioned, "like *astonishing*. But. Kraft did own some nice books."

"I bet."

He told her about the *Hypnerotomachia Poliphili*.

"The what," Rosie said, in exasperated wonderment. "Good lord."

"Say it again," Sam said laughing.

Pierce split the words: "Hypn. Eroto. Machia. Poliphili. That's: Sleep. Love. Struggle. Of Poliphilus. You might say: The Love-struggle of Poliphilus in a Dream. *Hypnerotomachia Poliphili*." He looked back at Sam and laughed aloud with her. "Absolutely one of the great strange unreadable books of all time."

"But you've read it."

"Well. *In* it. There is a fabulously valuable first edition with illustrations by Botticelli. This isn't that one."

"No, well."

"But it is a real nice sixteenth-century edition with wood engravings. Weird ones too. From the great days of weird book illustration."

They had come to a stop on River Street, by the variety store down from the library, at the corner of Hill Street, up which Pierce's street was.

"Valuable?" Rosie asked.

"Yes."

"But not really . . ."

"Not. No."

A little red Asp sports car was wiggling into a small parking space across the street from the library. It had several small dents and primed spots on it, as though it were accustomed to tangling with other cars. It just fit, finally, with its shapely rear end somewhat protruding.

"Say it *again*," said Sam.

"Hypnerotomachia Poliphili," said Pierce.

A long-legged woman climbed from the car, her dark loosely-braided hair aswing; Pierce thought he saw her notice their station-wagon, and then take no notice.

"You know," Pierce said to Rosie, "I once thought she was you."

"I know."

"I mean I once thought she was Sam's mother, and. Because of."

"Yes."

He had thought for a time that this dark woman—Rose Ryder, pulling a big bag from the Asp's rear space and hooking it over her bare tanned shoulder—was the Rosie who was Sam's mother, Mike Mucho's soon-to-be-ex wife, and his old friend Spofford's passion: she, and not carrot-topped Rosie here with him. Rose Ryder crossed the street to the library with a smooth pardlike stride that Pierce enjoyed watching.

"Hey. It's Rose," Sam said pointing. "Where's Daddy?"

"I don't know, hon. At work, I guess."

"Are they still," Pierce asked. Sam's father Mike was also Rose Ryder's lover, which had added to Pierce's confusion.

"I don't hear," Rosie said, a little curtly. "I think it's mostly over."

"Huh," Pierce said contemplatively.

"Are you getting out here," Rosie said, "or do you want delivery to your door?"

Pierce unlatched and swung open the heavy door of the wagon, which scraped horridly against the sidewalk. "She was very, when I talked to her last," he said, climbing out with his bags. "She seemed, and I was wondering what she would do if I."

"I think," Rosie said, "that she'd do anything the right man asked her to do."

"Anything?" Pierce said in mock scandalized astonishment. "*Anything?*"

Rosie put the car purposefully in gear, and motioned Pierce to shut the door. It groaned and creaked on its hinges before shutting with the patented thump that was intended to signify solidity and worth.

"Rose didn't say hi," Sam said, miffed.

"She didn't see us, I guess." Jeez what tact, Rosie thought: to ask her about some other woman's availability, and that one of all women. Still she felt instantly ashamed of herself for saying what she had said to Pierce about Rose, for revealing what she had revealed, if indeed she had really revealed anything: felt disloyal, somehow, having told something that no woman should tell a man about another woman, something which Rosie ought not to have known anyway, though she did know it.

Disloyal! Rosie lurched out into River Street more summarily than she had intended to, and Sam beside her laughed with glee to be rolled around.

Pierce had, in any case, no business to be making such inquiries. And as he put away his groceries in the kitchen cupboards of his second-floor apartment on Maple Street, he felt a curious lassitude in the contemplation, even, of pursuit; the lassitude maybe felt by the mountaineer who by squeezing from himself every drop of willingness and cheer has achieved a dozen subsidiary peaks, and finds himself now still snowbound, with only another and its joys ahead of him. The bear went over the mountain.

For a long time he had used to credit a malign fate with the disasters of his heart; he after all had always been willing, single-minded in his devotion, bound by his word and his need: it was *they* who always took off, wounding him atrociously, unforgivably, but he forgave them, all of them. At length he had come to understand that he had, after all, selected these women and not others out of the available population; they had not been brought him by a genie; he had selected them by his receptivity to their charms, whatever those exactly were, volatility, restless hotness, availability; huntresses, unaware themselves. He had chosen them (had acceded, at any rate, in their choosing of him) for exactly what had made it unlikely they would stay. And that was a sort of insight, he thought, not nothing anyway: his histrionic vow had probably only reflected a reality his soul had come silently to face, that he was not the marrying kind, that he was bent out of true and unsuited to a wife 'n' kids.

He had forgotten to buy capers, with which he had intended to dress his steak tartare, bachelor's indulgence, why not a dish of oysters too you dope. And a half-bottle of dregs.

It was not as though the old dynamos row on row within him had been disengaged, he could not think how to disengage them even if he wanted to; if he was not constantly on the boil as he had been in the city, that was probably only because there was no daylong night-long parade passing before him here as there had been there, the illusion of endless supply. Here in Smallville there was the other danger, fixation on the one or two who roughly match the inner template, scarcity confused with Fate's special election.

That panther's walk. He had actually embraced her once, kissed her deeply too, in a deserted summer-house on a branch of the Blackbury River. She hadn't resisted him. Her unresistance had been complete, so complete as to be unnerving, at least to Pierce; as unnerving as insistent seduction.

That was last summer, when he had first visited this country (by mistake, he had been headed elsewhere) and bumped into Spofford, and thought of coming here to live. In the confusions of a night he had come to suppose this Rose was Rosie Mucho and therefore his friend Spofford's beloved. For that reason he had gone no farther; for that reason, and because of a sudden alarm he had felt, a species of holy dread such as might come over a poor traveler who has unexpectedly entered a lost temple, and finds himself before the idol, above whose awful altar a lamp is still burning.

He finished the wine.

It might be, he thought, that his flaw lay in the stars of his birth. Pierce had recently applied to Val for his horoscope, as nearly everyone he knew in the Faraways had done, and then had listened to her analysis with attention in spite of a small unwipeable smirk on his face. We will always pay attention to vatic statements about our own natures, no matter how baseless. His own case was even less decidable than most, because of an uncertainty about his birth hour; he knew the year and the day, lucky Sunday ha ha, and when he asked Winnie for the hour she said she remembered five o'clock distinctly, but not whether it was morning or evening, and of course the whole heavens had swung around between the one hour and the other. Twilight Sleep, she said; she couldn't remember much.

So Val made a stab at two different charts (perhaps not as thorough as she usually tried to be, she wasn't getting paid double for this) and she found many little things different, and some big things the same no matter what the hour. In both, a basically cheerful and sagacious Sagittarian nature was overborne by the leaden weight of Saturn, weepy Neptune too, a planet unknown to the science when it *was* a science. In the evening option, Saturn and the Moon, coupling joylessly in the House of Death, opposed poor Venus dejected in the wrong house: Did Pierce maybe have trouble with relationships? The big difference between the morning and the evening views, said Val, was their likely outcomes, the better or the worse.

Death or life?

Maybe not that drastic. Easy oppositions or hard ones. Val suggested (maybe it was too simple an out, but not unwise) that Pierce just go with the morning chart, and by acting on it make it his.

That put Saturn in the first house, imparting to the forming body and nature his own cold sad dry qualities, predisposing the child to melancholy, to which Pierce was certainly subject. Any doctor of the sixteenth century could have pegged him as Saturnian at a glance; he would only have had to note the signs. Pierce stood before his books (where else, at evening's end) and leafed through one. Here: a Doctor Johannes of Hasfurt, standard medieval authority, lists them: "A broad ugly face," check. "Small eyes downcast, one larger than the other and having a spot or deformity," check if you looked closely. "Connecting eyebrows, bristly black hair shaggy and slightly wavy," check and check. "His beard, if he has one, is sparse, but his body— especially his chest—is hairy." Check, this was getting a little much. Legs long, hands and feet deformed with a cleft heel, well no. Body "not too big" (Pierce's was, he thought) and "honey-colored" (that would be nicer than his own untannable pallor) and "smelling like a goat," hey now.

Clap that book shut, pull out another. There was always another to consult. He had offered some of these to Val, who said she'd rather listen, it sank in better. Here was Burton: bad luck to say "melancholy" without saying "Burton" right after. He carried the *Anatomy* to the bed, and lay down with it.

Third Partition, Section Two, Member One, Subsection One. Heroical love causing melancholy. His Pedigree, Power, and Extent. No power on earth found stronger than love. The part affected in men is the liver, and therefore called heroical, because commonly Gallants, Noblemen and the most generous spirits are possessed with it.

Nice, but a doubtful etymology.

Heroical love, *Amor hereos,* that disease of the mind and members that melancholic Saturnian natures take for love itself, unable to hatch any other kind in their cold dry hearts. Doctors of the sixteenth century, medieval monks too, were quite sure you could die of heroical love.

Member Two, Subsection One. The causes of heroical love: Temperature, full Diet, Idleness, Place, Climate, &c. Of all causes the remotest are the stars. When Venus and Mercury are in conjunction, Mercury in the ascendant, I am so urged with thoughts of love that I cannot rest—so far Cardan of himself, confessing what use he made of the time allotted to study. Yet some hold with Brunus his opinion, that Saturn in the nativity, by making for melancholy, most inclines to these thoughts of lust; such spirits are endowed with imagination in overplus, and can readily conceive all sorts of delights, of which they never tire; yet they pursue the pleasures of lust for their own sake, and give no thought to propagation.

Which about hit the nail on the head.

Brunus his opinion: that was Giordano Bruno, very likely, who bragged once that he had coupled with a hundred women, who knows how truthfully.

The part affected, meanwhile (back to Burton), is the former part of the head, for want of moisture. Gordonius will have the testicles an immediate subject or cause, the liver an antecedent. Fracastorius agrees in this with Gordonius: from thence originally come the images of desire, erection, &c.; it calls for an exceeding titillation of the part, so that until the seed is put forth there is no end of frisking voluptuousness and continual remembrance of venery.

He underlined that lightly in pencil: *continual remembrance of venery.*

Of course (as Austin saith) the stars do but incline us. Saturn in the ascendant might also make for dark solitary genius, coupled especially with Sagittarian clarity and aim; Bruno knew that too. Heroical love not for phantasms of flesh but for the lasting realities perceived by the questing intellect. That was the morning view. Antisocial squalor, introspection, geezerhood, *eremita masturbans:* the evening.

He pushed Burton from his lap.

Say the telephone rings now. The unanswered phone call he had made in the city returning to him tonight. Okay.

Ring, phone.

It wasn't far from where he lay on the bed, he could pull himself roughly together and pick it up before the caller quit.

"Hello?"

Hi there. With a faintly shamefaced air of peek-a-boo.

"Oh," he said. "Well. Hello."

You busy?

"Christ no. I was just," he said, "thinking of you."

Small world, she said. He heard a jangle of bracelets as perhaps she shifted the receiver from ear to ear. *So how are you. How's the new life.*

"The new life is good."

The country bumpkin, she said.

"Haylofts," he said. "Milkmaids."

You, she said.

"And how 'bout you?" he said.

Well you know, she said, reflecting. *It's summer. It gets so crazy.*

"Hot," he said.

It's hot as hell right now, she said. *I'm sitting n-k-d with the window open.*

He could actually hear the summer city in the street below the window of her apartment, that apartment he knew, cross between a Cornell box and the Watts Towers. She on the bed.

"So," he said. "You've been good?"

I've been bad, she said, resigned to her nature, as he was not to his. *So bad.*

"Tell me."

Crazy, she said, softly, as though pondering to what extent she should indulge him. *Eduardo,* she said. *Did I tell you about Eduardo?*

"No."

I've been seeing him. Eduardo, she said, her voice lower, imparting the delightful secret, *is the first person I have ever picked up on the street. Just, you know, got the eye, gave it back—stopped to talk—oh man.*

"Good for you."

But—oh it's so. I can't tell you.

"Tell me." For he had conceived a shameful plan, which if he kept his voice level and his air insouciant, he might execute. "You can."

Well, she said. *He's fifteen years old.* Her hand shifted on the instrument. *And oh God. So sweet too. I didn't realize at first, but Pierce I think I got a cherry. I mean you just can't imagine.*

But he wouldn't need to imagine. With his gentle hints he would nudge her toward the revelations she wanted to make anyway, occupied for all he knew as he was himself; and the long telephone line would grow warm with the passage of her words toward him and his encouragements, like the wire of a busy appliance.

Continual remembrance of venery. Once upon a time back in their New York life together they had been in bed, just commencing, when the phone rang; and to his exasperation she answered it; and he had decided to proceed anyway. It was her friend Lou, the Denver cowgirl. Lou this isn't such a good time. Really really, Lou. Well do you want me to tell you what's going on? And she had laughed her deep small laugh of satisfaction, had settled down watching Pierce at work and talking meanwhile softly to Lou, telling her more, going on telling her, while Lou cooed audibly on the other end; he even spoke to her himself, hi Lou, wish you were here?

Wish you were here. He wondered if she and Lou had ever. She always hinted. Wish I could if she did. Wish I. I wish. I wish. I wish.

He fell momentarily thereupon into a shocked slumber, until his own ferocious snore awoke him.

Ugh what a mess.

The telephone squatted torpid and cold in the far corner; it had not in fact rung for days.

Hypnerotomachia Poliphili. Th'expense of spirit in a waste of shame.

That she should have become so deeply incised on his spirit, sole focus of his one-eyed Sagittarian attention, sole object of his melancholic's extravagant forebrain lust—that was no surprise; what star was it though, he wondered, what complication of the melancholic condition, which caused this tendency—he had only recently come to notice it, how entrenched it had become—to erase himself from his own imaginings? Since she did not want to be with him, he imagined her with others; and in the brief instant when he believed he could feel what she felt with another, a bright shadow of what she actually might feel or have felt, then he came.

What slippery slope had he stepped on, when? Why could he not make himself afraid of what had become of him?

The summer bloom hadn't yet left the sky, though it was after nine o'clock by the moonface of his clock. From his bed he could see the yellow oblong of his friend and neighbor Beau Brachman's window, across and down the street, alone alight in the black cutout of Beau's house. Beau the renunciatory mystagogue, who whatever he was up to would not be occupied as Pierce was.

Pierce had, himself, turned on no lights, and so needed to turn none off; he only stretched out in his shirt, pulled up the sheet, turned his face away from the kitchen where the day's dishes implored him, and fell asleep.

9

eau Brachman had in fact been imagining a coupling, too: blind, humid and hot, hot enough to turn the Androgyne inside out, and make him all male.

Beneath the lamp lit in his monkish upstairs apartment two books lay, one closed volume atop another open one, the two bound alike in maroon cloth that some tiny tropical mite had attacked, consuming the glue in speckled measle patterns all over, the consumption only stopped by the cold climate to which Beau had brought them. They had been published together by the Theosophical Publishing House in Benares, and that's where Beau had found them: *Thrice-greatest Hermes,* by G.R.S. Mead.

He had read in them for a long time this fragrant night, after not having opened them in years; the sight of the familiar print of the pages and the familiar disposition of the paragraphs on them, the little black marginal glosses like wayside shrines along a rocky path, returned him to the hot nights and days when he had read them first.

He was not reading now, though. If Pierce could have looked into, instead of merely at, Beau's window, he would have seen Beau motionless and shirtless in his armchair, a pair of headphones over his ears by which he was connected to a massy old tube amplifier (Fisher) and a turntable. He was hearing an oceanic Mahler symphony, or rather was borne on its tides without exactly hearing it, letting himself be taken up again and again by its pseudo-endless *coitus prolongatus* into or out of his own movie, for which the Mahler was the music. The script was the *Poimandres* of Hermes, thrice-great, as retold by Dr. Mead long ago.

COME UP ON: a bright roiling chaos of light, infinite mild and good, pouring itself forth out of its own unplaceable center, like the clouds that lead to or compose movie heavens.

A ROLL OF DARK DRUMS and out from the same placeless center a shadow begins to form, a darkness visible, oily and thick, the smoke of movie infernos. The white withdraws from it. It grows.

SFX: Indescribable unintelligible cries, moans, shrieks, mad laughter, gasps of horror.

A BIG VOICE speaking, not loud but large, made out of oboes and trombones:

THE LIGHT IS I MIND POIMANDRES SHEPHERD-OF-MAN WHO WAS BEFORE THE DARK WATERS.

THEN out from the agitated white cloudbreast shoots a fulmination, whiter than the white. MEANING. With the whizbang of movie lightning, MEANING shoots into the heart of the dark seethe.

The BIG VOICE:

THE MEANING THAT COMES FORTH FROM THE LIGHT IS MY SON I AM HIS FATHER WE ARE NOT DIFFERENT.

MEANING's effect on Chaos is to order it: Great bands of colored light coalesce out of the fuliginous fires, leaving the thick black stuff behind; in a great surge of viols and a big stroke of cymbals the lights begin to wheel in a rainbow race.

ANDROGYNOUS NEEDING NO PARTNER I GAVE BIRTH TO A MAKER.

A great muscle-bound inhuman, Jove or Jehovah, with knitted brow of power, big hands for shaping. Bends over the race of lights with tools: compass, stylus, mallet.

MAKER AND MEANING WORKED TOGETHER SET THE CIRCLES OF THE ARCHONS.

The lights slow, bind themselves up, take spherical form; each chooses a single color (black, red, blue, white). Seven of them. Far below their gigantic courses the elements of the chaos settle. Cold, dark, wanting, heaving.

EARTH NATURE SHE HAD NO MEANING LEFT WITH HER SHE BROUGHT FORTH HER COUNTLESS YOUNG WITHOUT MEANING.

MONTAGE: Birds of the air, fish of the sea; volcanoes, storm-clouds, wind-lashed trees; blind mole digs, tiger's cubs roll in the dirt; caribou stampede, flamingoes arise in millions from a blue lake, blocking the sun. Deer walk on the mountain, eating fallen apples; lift their heads to smell the air. Centuries pass.

Quiet.

FADE TO BLACK.

The needle ticks in the groove between movements.

CUT TO:

Far away, infinitely far away, in the sphere of Mind outside mate-riality. A Being discovered in the bosom of God: Michelangelo's Adam, huge and strong, pink as a baby, idle.

The BIG VOICE is gentler:

THE FATHER OF ALL GAVE BIRTH TO **MAN** A BEING LIKE HIMSELF AND HE TOOK DELIGHT IN MAN AS HIS OWN CHILD.

Rising, testing his wings, taking his place in the Father's sphere (huge consonance of violins, bass-powered, satisfying). Looking down through the sounding nesting rings of the planets. The weary MAKER down there resting after his labors, dusting his hands to-gether.

MAN ASKED FOR PERMISSION TO CREATE SOMETHING FOR HIMSELF AND HIS FATHER PERMITTED IT.

PAN DOWN WITH the MAN tumbling happily down through the spheres, accepting from the doting Archons the gifts each has to give, laughing though the gifts burden him absurdly, he has strength to spare. Breaking harmlessly through the orbits of Destiny, which do not apply to him. He reaches the startled Moon's sphere, accepts her gift of labile humidity.

NOW EARTH LOOK UP.

Earth looks up. Sees the beauty and form of MAN. Falls instantly, wholly, insatiably in love forever with him. She turns her swollen seas upward yearning toward the Moon's sphere. MAN sees in the mirror of the water his own divine beauty; sees the shadow of his perfect form on her lands; and falls in love himself with the form he sees, insatiably, wholly, and forever. He must dwell there with that beauty.

Down through the great clinging nets of matter he plunges, hot as hell, through fire first, through air to water and to earth; ithyphallic, arms outstretched uncaring, into the brown green blue bosom, lap, limbs of Earth. And when she has him she wraps herself around him, limbs over limbs, breast to breast. The spheres draw back in astonishment and hide their lamps. Orchestra laboring, ceaseless mounting chords, no climax large enough though, disappointment coming, modulation, withdrawal, rearousal, no end either.

PULL BACK modestly from the gigantic intercourse.

SO **MAN** WHO WAS ONE   BOTH MORTAL AND IMMORTAL FORE-EXISTING THE HEAVENS YET SUBJECT TO THEM   BECAME TWOFOLD.

HE WHO WAS ANDROGYNOUS LIKE HIS FATHER IS NEVER AGAIN WHOLE BUT IS NOW ONLY MALE OR FEMALE.

HE WHO WAS SLEEPLESS   AS HIS FATHER IS SLEEPLESS COMES TO BE BOUND UP IN LOVE & SLEEP.

Now PULL BACK, PULL BACK over seas, through mountain valleys, down silver rivers, through night groves, back through the windows of a chamber, a chamber like this one where Beau watches and listens but not this one, windows on four sides full of stars; and a sleeper, or one anyway whose body is still, in his armchair; head thrown back, eyes closed, mouth open.

The BIG VOICE has become a *small voice,* nearly a whisper, just as large as before though; a Messenger, the last and only Messenger, secreted from the bosom of God before the beginning of the story, and arriving at last, now, just now.

Listen, Man, endowed with Mind: know that you are immortal, and that the cause of death is love.

ZOOM IN ON the sleeper's face, farther, to the glitter of bright seeing eye just perceivable between upper lid and lower. A tear forms, hangs spherical on the sleeper's lid, reflecting stars; tumbles down his cheek.

And now why do you delay? You who have received all? How is it that you let them suffer who can receive this knowledge at your hands? Will you not be a guide for them?

The armchair is rising purposefully like an ascending helicopter, turning toward the open portal and the night. The cause of death is love. O Spirit, Soul, First Man, don't stay mingled forever in Nature; awaken, remember who you are, how you have come to suffer here. Turn again, remake your journey, pass at last upward again through the jealous spheres, give back to them their ambiguous and heavy gifts, saying to each one Let me pass.

Beau was borne out over the sleeping Faraways on a single so-
prano voice, singing liltingly and sorrowfully without words; borne
weightless between the sky powdered with stars and the hills' green
labial folds.

O world, planet, beautiful and strange. He loved it here, he did.
He would always remember it, too, as a tourist remembers in odd
moments the strange, the rich-smelling, the unlikely land he once
briefly visited; it would remain with him when, all his work done, he
turned, at last, toward home.

Down there, in the hills, in the woods along the Shadow River, there
was a window lit: the lamp beside Val's bed turned on, the smoke of a
cigarette rising into its double cone of light.

She couldn't sleep; she who could sleep away the winter days and
nights rarely stayed asleep through a whole night of summer. She had
turned on the light to read; and the book she turned her wakefulness
into was the big dictionary from which she had read to Rosie at the
Volcano. No reason not to continue her researches. Dennis her Pekingese slept at her feet, snoring Pekingese snores.

So. The father of little Eros was mostly, or usually, Hermes. Here
was Hermes: "He is among the oldest of the Achæan Gods, and like
all those *divi* of the Youth of Mankind, he seems to combine in himself contrary functions, as though once-upon-a-time he were the God
not of one thing but of the distinction, newly discovered by Man,
between one thing and another. Thus Hermes is the God who guides
souls down into the underworld and prevents their turning back to
the sunlight and the sky; yet he is also the God who presides over the
Anthesteria, the feast of the dead, when for a few hours those souls
are allowed out upon the earth to take a meal with the living."

See, right there, Val said to herself, noting another instance of a
general objection she had to the book: no distinction made between
what people *believed* and what actually *happened*. What was a meal
with the dead really like? How did it go on? Who washed up after?
Come on.

"He is most famously the Messenger God and thus God of speech
and the quick flow of language; but he is also a God of silence and not
speaking, who keeps to himself the arcana of the alchemists. He is the

God of merchants and commerce, and yet he is the God of thieves as well, sponsoring at once the shopkeeper who locks up his goods and the footpad who breaks the lock."

In his silvery oblong picture Hermes was just another marble hunky guy, like all of them. A child, an infant on his arm, but who. Val yawned a huge and multi-layered yawn, trying to think of a few representative people she knew who were governed by Mercury, and unable just then to locate any with certainty. No thieves that she knew of, or undertakers either.

"Hermes was long ago the male God of sexual attraction, as APHRODITE (*q.v.*) was the female; thus the little phallic *stele* set up in his honor at crossroads and marketplaces all over the ancient world, called *herms* in English, touched reverently by Pagan travelers, shunned or smashed by their Christian or Moslem supplanters. Combine Hermes' power of spell-binding speech, his thieving ways, and his sexual function, and he becomes the patron God of seducers; when the Gods combined to give life to the lifeless mannequin PANDORA (*q.v.*) Hermes granted her his own power of antic and careless seduction. He is given the epithet 'Whisperer' for his skills, an epithet he shares with Aphrodite and his own child Eros; and it is in that character that we often see him."

Often see him! There you go again, Val thought; and lifting her eyes from the page she did vividly see him for a moment, slouch hat, sweet sleepy eyes, one finger raised to his smiling lips like the Sandman. Don't make a sound.

What would it be like to have gods? To meet them? To know one had been around? Like Santa Claus maybe. The book said how Jesus was hardly the first human child for whom a divine parent was claimed; girls in trouble all over the Ancient World used that dodge. Honest, it was a God, Daddy. He had this sort of glow about him.

Down the hall her mother's door opened, and Val listened to the pat of her bare feet down the linoleum toward the john. Years since Mama could make it through the night without a trip. Val listened for the toilet's flush.

Flush. All right.

Mama padded back to her room, at her door releasing a great sigh and a muttered prayer or imprecation or both. Mama got visits from

God, pretty regular ones too. But never blamed Him for her own transgressions.

Val asked the darkness: Who is Una Knox?

Pierce awoke with a start in the same darkness out of a dream he couldn't remember; only that something precious had been taken from him, what, something he had acquired, but was it his? Anyway taken from him (he hunted, half-risen from the bed, in the deep backward for the vanishing sensations) and lost to him, and he bereft letting out an infant's bawl of loss and rage and grief, unassuageable, a howl so huge it woke him: so awful his back hair thrilled over and over again to feel just its echoes in his bosom.

He swung his legs over the bed's side. What the hell time is it anyway. He grasped the bedside clock and studied it, for a long moment unable to tell which hand was the longer one, neither of the two possible times seemed likely to him.

Quarter to one? Oh my lord, the night hardly begun.

The telephone ringing at that moment was shocking, like a sudden impalement, almost impossible to believe. Pierce pulled his shirt down modestly and hurried to answer.

"Pierce?" A timid small voice, but the one he somehow expected to hear. "You were asleep, right?"

"Actually wrong," he said. "For some reason, awake."

"How are you?"

"How are *you*." How long, he wondered, till his heart was no longer lifted on this awful wave rising in the dark every time he heard her voice, her real voice; or thought he glimpsed her, or woke from a dream of her: how long.

"Well, sick," she said. "Pains in my, under my tummy. I think an infection or something."

"Damn," he said. She had always been liable to bladder things, yeasts: Scorpio, that's where it gets you. As Dr. Johannes knew. "Sorry."

"I've been sort of out of circulation. But listen: I'm really sorry to call you so late . . ."

"Doesn't matter."

". . . only I can't think who else to call."

He sat down on the bed, phone in his hand. "Sure," he said.

"I'm in a situation," she said. "I've haven't really been able to hustle lately, you know? Because of being under the weather. And things have got really behind. And the landlord is now really impatient." She had been a different sort of dealer once, with a higher profit margin. No more. She had made abnegations too, more successful (he thought) than his own.

"Do you have electricity yet?" he asked.

"Not yet," she said. "Candlelight still. So listen. Tomorrow. Supposedly he locks the door on me."

"No."

"I just couldn't think who else to call. You know the place is rent controlled. One-fifty is all it is."

"That's all?"

"Times two." There was a pause. "I know you don't have a lot."

"I do have a lot. Comparatively. It just has to last me a long time."

"Oh god."

"It's okay," he said, and clutched his brow. "It's fine. I mean really I owe it to you."

"Pierce," she said, "you don't owe me anything."

"I know that." The hand that had clutched his brow now covered his eyes.

"It's just you're a good guy."

"I know that too." Just let her not speak tenderly to him, he couldn't bear it, he couldn't. "So, so. Can I mail you a check, or, or . . ."

There was a silence, a self-reproachful sigh. "You know I don't even have a bank account?"

He remembered, the wads of bills that would accumulate around their apartment, in the kitchen drawers, under the pillow. And now when she was legit she couldn't afford one. "Western Union," he said. "Winged messenger. Tomorrow, right? The last day."

"I'll pay you back. You know that."

"You always do."

"Tell me how you've been. How you're doing."

"Oh," he said. "Oh."

Darkness and distance between them, his night here, hers there;

they both felt it. "Well it's real late," she said. "I was up thinking. I just didn't think of you till late."

"Yes," he said. "Well, so long as you did. Think of me."

"I'm gonna let you sleep," she said.

He sat with the telephone in his lap for a time.

Sphinx he had used to call her, not only because of the hard question she had seemed to put to him, but because when in his turn he questioned her she wouldn't answer. He couldn't wish she wouldn't call, but the sound of her voice.

Like the poor dead coming forth at their festivals, all souls' eve, offered their old foods by the living, though this must only increase their hunger unbearably, reminding them that they can never touch it again. They'd be better off remaining in the abode of night, drinking their waters of forgetfulness.

Should he have a drink? That was always an awful mistake, he just didn't have the constitution for it somehow, he would pay double and quickly for the brief solace.

He got up and turned on the light, and went to the bookshelves again, where the trouble had started; ran his eyes and hands down the shelves (he still hadn't got the books in any final logical order). It was simpler, he thought, when he had had fewer, then his hand would simply, ah here it is. The year 1952. The paper spine dried and splitting but every page still there.

Little Enosh: Lost Among the Worlds.

This was the famous year (famous among devotees, of whom Pierce had come to learn he wasn't the only one) of the Thinking Contest, the Inn of the Worlds, and the Mirror Mines, and the year that introduced the Robot, Rutha's servant, a jointed riveted boiler-plate man with visibly nothing at all inside him, who liked to talk with Enosh about Higher Things. He talked in pretend math, supplemented with tiny icons of nuts and bolts.

Pierce took the little book back to his bed and clambered onto the rumpled sheets. From the darkness outside, winged things had already begun to collect against his screen. *Positive phototropism*: he heard Joe Boyd's voice.

And look at that: Down the dark street, on the opposite or left-hand side, Beau Brachman's second-story apartment was not yet dark. A bachelor, like himself, with good reason to be up and brooding no doubt. Pierce watched the mystery of the light and listened to the leaves; then he opened his book, knowing already what he would see.

So here's Amanda d'Haye looking down from the Realms of Light, and she crosses her arms and taps her foot in deep impatience; then takes out her fountain pen, which splashes tiny shiny paisleys of ink from its splayed point. She addresses a big letter, a square bond envelope brightly white:

Little Enosh

Inn of the Worlds

Care of: Rutha

And here's Little Enosh in the Inn of the Worlds (a huge collapsing place made mostly of slats). He sits in the pose that in old medical books represented a man in the grip of Melancholy: elbow on table, cheek in hand. *Snwy,* says his snore. *Snsnwy. Smnglf.* The Uthras all asleep around him, catching flies. *If that letter ever GETS there we can guess what it will say!* Pierce knew. *Now who'll she get to carry it?*

"Hermes," Val read, keeping her place in the dense column with a finger, "is identical with the Mercury of the Romans, and thus with the planet and the metal, all one thing; the fact that Mercury is the *prima materia* of the Art taught by Hermes is surely not coincidence. In the Greek mind Hermes was amalgamated with the Egyptian God THOTH (*q.v.*). In a famous passage in Plato this God is credited with the invention of writing, for which the other Gods rebuke him—he has invented an art of memory which means the end of remembering, a way of keeping secrets which will end by revealing all secrets; and he is advised not to hand it on to men, but of course he does."

Weary of night, weary of learning, weary of the ceaseless babble of the river and the frogs. Should she draw the blind?

"No doubt it is the conflation of these Gods that gives rise to Greek stories of a *Hermes Ægyptiacus* who writes books of secrets; the Greeks appended to him an Egyptian epithet of Thoth: *trismegistus,* i.e., 'thrice great.' To this figure, whether regarded as a god or a man, were later attributed dozens of writings purporting to contain secrets of cosmogony, magic, and redemption of the most profound and gnomic character, and they have been regarded with awe ever since. But—strangely—neither those who first claimed Hermes' authority for these works, nor those who later read and pondered them, ever seem to be troubled that their author is an epigone of that Whisperer, Trickster and Thief whose first recorded act was the stealing of the

cattle of his uncle Apollo and then lying his way out of the consequences."

But Val had closed the book before she reached these parts, sure
she had bored herself enough to sleep; the big book lay closed at the
bottom of her bed (she never minded sleeping with Our Friends from
Bookland as she called them) and the light was off; yet she lay still
with eyes open, hands behind her head, watching the faint bloom of
the window.

Who is Una Knox?

A joke, Rosie had said: My old girlfriend Una Knox. But who is
she? And what is she to him?

10

ut now the mystic night has passed; the cock has crowed, the goat's abroad. Black things of night, the bat, the bug, have flown away; the flowers have opened their cups to catch the sun.

There's to be a picnic. Rosie is up early and has Sam dressed and ready to be given over to her father, Mike Mucho. She and Sam sit together on the front steps at Arcady, just throne height to Sam, waiting for Mike's car to turn in at the gate.

"Do you have Brownie?" Rosie wants to know (Sam won't sleep if she has forgotten Brownie, her rag doll). "Do you have blankie? Do you have a hankie?"—until Sam laughs aloud. Yes she does. The only way Rosie can mitigate her shame and anxiety when Sam goes away with her father is to check the list over and over. She regards Sam's fat toes, peeking out beneath the straps of her sandals, and is caught by a blow of love and guilt. "Here's Daddy."

The transfer is made swiftly and without the subtle rancor that used to accompany it in the wintertime, when the separation was newer and claims were felt more sharply; and also Mike has for some reason grown nice, just in the last month, making Rosie suspicious, though she gets nothing clarifying from him when she asks why.

"Why being nice? I'm usually not?" A wide smile for Rosie's reserved one. "If there was a reason," Mike says, "would you want to hear?"

"Well."

"Uh huh," Mike says, understanding (understanding is, or ought to be, his game, he being employed at a psychotherapeutic institution up on Mount Whirligig). "Well." Sam riding his hip kicks him idly. "If you want to know."

"I'll ask," Rosie says. "I will. Really. Not now."

And they are gone away, with enough waves and goodbyes and kisses for a long journey; and Rosie sits again on the low wide warping steps in the odorous morning, chin in her hands, waiting for her lover's rattletrap truck to turn in next at the gate. A white transparent moon is going down the blue sky over the westward mountains.

First he had to check in with his sheep, as he put it: for the little flock that grazed beneath the oaks of Arcady belonged to Rosie's friend and lover Spofford, who had set them to summer here, not really having pasture for them on his own couple of mountainside acres.

"So how do they look to you? Good?" Rosie asked him.

"They're good," Spofford said, and pushed open the door for Rosie to get in. "They're unchanged. Except for being that much woollier. They seem to be running sort of wild here, which is what I expected."

"Wild and woolly." It was Rosie's dogs who actually policed the sheep under Spofford's and Rosie's supervision, two Australian sheepdogs she had acquired in the spring on an impulse she could not make sense of; Spofford had made sense of it for her, deciding on his own that Boney's grounds needed sheep to keep down the grass and that the sheep needed Rosie's dogs to keep them down in turn. Rosie thought it likely that Spofford could make sense, even profit, out of any dumb impulse she had, if she were to permit him; which is why she kept him, usually, at a long arm's length.

"Lambs getting fat," Spofford said, and touched his own belly. He was a lean big man, dark-bearded and summer-brown.

"Well the ugly one sure should be," Rosie countered, slamming the truck door. "He ate all my lettuces, your cute little fence notwithstanding."

"Ugly?" Spofford said, looking at her in mock wonderment. "*Ugly?*"

They had all clustered by now at the gate, behind the single strand of electrified fencing, to *baa* in supplication at their shepherd, grain-bringer, hoof-mender, who drove past them making calculations in his head.

"Nine lambs," he said. "I've got orders for six, and Val's two is eight . . ."

"*Val* is going to cook *lamb*?" Rosie marveled. The Faraway Lodge was known for its chicken-back cacciatore dinner, Mama's sole specialty.

"So she says."

"You talked her into that."

"The question is," he said, "are you guys going to take the other one?"

"Don't tell Sam."

"Kids," he said, "care less than you think. They don't mind eating their friends at that age. Later maybe. Now—eat, be eaten, live, die, it's all part of the fun."

She looked over at him, thinking he was probably not wrong, and wondering how he came to know that.

Not till long after they had gone did the sheep cease their calling and wander away again, coming one by two before Boney's eyes, who was sitting up in the chaise longue in the library, made up as a bed. He had moved into this room on coming home, his wheelchair, his medicines, his slippers and robe; just until he got strong enough, said Mrs. Pisky (his housekeeper, now his nurse), to go back upstairs like before. He looked out hungrily at the day, the satisfied sheep, the happy or at least uncomplaining trees, the morning slipping unceasingly away.

The moon can't be seen from the morning streets of Blackbury Jambs, for it is occluded by the big bulk of the mountains, whose heads were burning now, set afire by the climbing sun. On Maple Street where Pierce Moffett lived the robin and the wren had been long awake and were still clamorous, though the traffic of the town and a brass band somewhere nearby practicing were louder by now. Pierce, oddly cheerful considering, stood with Beau in the driveway of Beau's house, resting against the trunk of Beau's car; they were waiting for the rest of the household, those of the household who were coming on this outing, to gather themselves. (Several women always lived in the house, always a couple of them with children, maybe not always their own; Pierce sensed they had been hurt in one way or another by the world, and been taken in here; the place was a day-care center too, and a crafts factory, and tidy as a convent.)

"Like this," Beau said to Pierce. He drew a small circle in the dirt of the driveway with a twig of maple. "God," he said.

"Uh huh," said Pierce, arms crossed before him.

Beau ringed his first circle with another. "The soul," he said.

"Uh huh."

Another circle. "The spirit." And another. "The body." Beau looked down amused at his own drawing, or perhaps amusement was only suggested by the natural curve of his lips and the delicate attention of his dark eyes; Pierce often wondered. "Now I can't fit them in," Beau said, "but there should be nine circles, spheres really, between the spirit and the outside of the body . . ."

"And nine," Pierce said, for he was getting this now, "from the skin outward."

"More, actually," said Beau. "But let's just say—the world," and he circled his circles again. "Then last of all"—he drew again, a big sweeping circle that intersected the driveway's edge, the car's rear end, and a picnic basket resting by the car—"God, outside it all, outermost."

Pierce pondered. Back when he was a teacher of Western Civilization, he used to draw just such a set of nesting circles for his students, to illustrate how Dante imagined hell, the world and the heavens. *But it's not true,* he would tell them then, shake them up, get their attention. *It's really really not true.*

"So when the soul gets under way," he said now to Beau, looking up outward into the empty blue air, "then which way, which way . . ."

"It's not a map," Beau said, finishing the scratching of his circle. "It's not a *picture.* It's a plan. It's . . . did you ever study drafting?"

"A *plot,*" said Pierce, and laughed aloud.

The picnic was to take place high up on the slopes of Mount Merrow, in a spot Beau remembered but would have to find again by sense of smell; it would require some climbing, anyway, which was why they were setting off so early. Even as the women and children of Beau's household were getting into the rust-speckled Python sedan,

Rosie Rasmussen and Spofford were turning off the Shadow River road in Spofford's truck, and down a twisting way to the riverside and the Faraway Lodge where Val was waiting for them, uncharacteristically ready. Not even curtains and earplugs had returned her to sleep, and she had got up at length and deviled eggs noisily till Mama woke up and tut-tutted into the kitchen to ask for tea.

The pasture they all came to at length was high, and sloped gently down to a stone wall crossing through blueberry bushes and alders shaking the silver coins in their fingers, and there was a great beech that somehow alone had found room and root there and "spread its canopy" as Pierce insisted on saying: but Beau couldn't remember if this really was the same one as last year. They put out the plaid blanket there and laid down the baby (one of the women of Beau's household was her mother) and the lunch, and gossiped till the sun was high.

"Things are strange this year," Val said. "Stranger even than the usual summer strangeness. Do you notice like people huddled in twos and threes in like the Donut Hole or Caspar's and you get close and what they're talking about is God? You notice that? Is this new?"

"The aura balancers are in town," the child's mother put in, releasing one breast discreetly for it to have. "If I had the money."

"There was a character in the bar, I think he's at The Woods, I think a therapist," Val went on.

"Some people have been really helped."

"He starts in with God. I need this, with Mama always ready to talk about her personal experiences. And I had to say to him: What I don't understand is all the pain."

"The what?" Beau said.

"Why, if God is there and can do anything, why is there unbearable constant *pain*. Just pick up a newspaper."

"I don't think," Pierce put in, "that you're the first person in the history of monotheism to be puzzled by this."

"This?" Val said, looking around, as though for the thing Pierce had noticed. "This?"

"The problem of evil," Pierce said, crossing his arms behind his head. "If there is a God, and God is both omnipotent and good, how can he permit suffering, even if he doesn't actively cause it?"

"Well?" Val said. "Is this an easy question? Smartypants?"

"Heck no." He looked up, to contemplate the phalanx of round clouds moving overhead like a starship invasion.

"Maybe," Beau said, "the God you're talking about isn't good."

"Or maybe he isn't omnipotent," Val said. "Does his best, but."

"Or maybe," Pierce said, "he doesn't know we suffer. Since he's beyond the possibility of suffering himself, maybe he doesn't understand that certain experiences we have are painful."

"Then he's maybe omnipotent, but he's not, what's the other thing, all-knowing."

"Omniscient."

"Omniscient," said Val. "Because if he was, he'd know we suffered. Right?"

"Maybe he's even more omniscient than that," Beau said. "Maybe there is really no suffering ever, and we just delude ourselves into thinking there is; since we're made free, we're free to make that mistake; all God can do is pity us, and help try to disabuse us."

"Disabuse," said Val in a tone of foreboding.

"That's the Christian Science answer," Pierce said.

"It's the Christian answer," Beau said. "Only most Christians don't know it."

Val laughed. "Let us pray," she said. "Good bread, good meat, good God let's eat."

On the lichened rocks amid the birches up above the meadow, screened from the others, Rosie wept in the dappled shade.

"It's like this cold, hard stone," she said to Spofford, who sat on the ground below her; "a lump always there, always," and she struck her breast with her fist, once, twice, three times, in the same gesture Pierce had used to make at every confession. "Always," she said. "I get so goddamn tired of it."

Spofford plucked at the ground pine between his boots. "I never had it there."

"It's as though it's *all* I've got sometimes."

"I had it in the gut," Spofford said. "Something the same I bet. I thought for a long time I had cancer, because I could feel this cold lump of something growing bigger, and I got weaker. Never did anything about it, just waited for it to get big enough to kill me."

"What was it?"

"Nothing." He looked up at her. "Did I ever tell you about Cliff?"

"No. Yes. A little." She hadn't ever quite believed in Cliff, a vet friend of Spofford's who lived somewhere in the woods around here, whom Spofford sometimes quoted, or credited with wisdom she thought was probably Spofford's own. "Well tell me," she said now, impatient, as though he were dumbly withholding what he thought she needed, even if she didn't want it.

"I was going to say you might want to talk to him." He smiled again. "I mean he cured my cancer."

"Christ I don't know." She looked off to where the others still sat or lay around the blanket. "What do you think."

"He charges."

"He does?"

"Well sure. This is what he does, helps."

She laughed, tasting her bitter tears. "You're going to take me to some kind of homegrown guru who charges to fix you up?"

Spofford lowered his eyes to the grasses he plucked. "It's only because I don't know what else," he said.

She shook her head, done crying for the moment. "So like what did he do? To you."

"Well he works with you. Helps you to feel. Body work. It's hard to describe." He laughed at a memory. "One thing, he told me to make a list of all the things I really wanted, in every category. Like Work and Money and Love. Sex. Achievements. Anything."

"What if you don't want anything?"

"I didn't."

"So?"

"So I started a list anyway. I put down the categories. What: Money. Sex. Yes all right I would like to have sex again sometime, with somebody besides Missus Palm and her five daughters." Rosie laughed, where on earth did he get them, the chestnuts he handed her. "Okay? I wrote down: Miscellaneous. I wrote under that: Some-day I want to want things."

Rosie covered her eyes, squeezed them shut; her heart was too stony even to weep, it seemed, her very tears were dry and burned, her eyes and nose like sand or salt.

"You start by wanting," Spofford said quietly. "Even if what you want is for life to be different from what it is, the whole basic world to be different; even if you want your own"—he struck his breast, just as Rosie had done—"to be different."

"Ah," she said, in pain. "Ah."

"You can have it all. That's what Cliff said. Start by wanting."

"Like three wishes come true? Sure."

"Wanting is life, Rosie. Dreams are life. What Cliff said is: Life is dreams checked by physics."

Rosie laughed aloud, relieved by this idea somehow, which made an instant sense to her. *Life is dreams checked by physics.* "Then you sure can't have it all," she said.

"Well you'd have to see," he said, getting up, grinning at her since she was at least no longer crying. He pulled a loose scroll of paper from a birch, and a pencil from his pocket. "Because look at this, how Cliff used to picture life, or the world. Look." He spread the birchbark on the rock beside Rosie, and with the bit of blunt carpenter's pencil drew a small circle. "God," he said. "This is what Cliff said." He drew another larger circle around that. "You," he said. Another: "The world. And last"—he drew a final circle—"God again." He raised his eyes to her. "So see? Maybe you can do more than you think."

She looked down at him in wonder. "You believe in God?" she asked.

"I've always thought I could sort of imagine God, a little," Pierce said. He sipped beer. "My problem is imagining that God could imagine me."

Beau had already departed from the colloquy, too primitive for him probably, and Val was losing interest. "You'll have to write that down," she said, and yawned.

Pierce could postulate a God unaware of human suffering, a God somewhere out beyond the inconceivable frontiers of actuality, hidden for good in the paradoxes of untime and notspace; what he could not do was suppose that anything infinite—anything so large as to encompass the just-about, the as-good-as-infinite physical universe—could form any conception of something so small as himself.

There were other constructions of God that avoided this difficulty, an immanent God, a syntactical God, an aggregate God arising out of the web of human cognition, like the Skull suddenly apprehended instead of the Lady and the Mirror in the old Victorian trickpicture. But the God Beau talked about was not some artifact like that, it was a person. What person?

If you really felt the need for one, it seemed to Pierce that there were persons other than the usual one (beard, big robe, aged eye of power) that would be more congenial, more convincing too, at least to Pierce. As long as God had demonstrably no parts at all, why not assign him a different set, more consonant with his actual behavior? If you imagined God not as an old man but as say a nine-year-old girl.

As soon as, in fact almost before, he had formulated this conception, Pierce felt an unlikely satisfaction in it, a relief, as though a long-standing cramp had at last released. Sure. If the Author of the universe were nine years old, a girl-child loving and imperious and jealous. Jealous! Thou shalt have *no other gods* before me, nosirree. 'Cause I said so.

He laughed out loud. God the Daughter. Infinite God with infinite knobby knees and an infinite plaid kilt, held together with an infinite safety pin.

Infinite.

With no inward fanfare, Pierce was just then visited by, or awarded with, one of those large simple insights, logical solutions or dissolutions of a mental obstacle you had not even recognized as an obstacle, the sensation of finding that a stuck door opens inward and not out. *Infinite* had of course nothing whatever to do with size. Nothing at all. In every other context he had known this to be so: *large* followed by *very large* followed by *very very large* was not eventually followed by *infinite*. He had only not ever applied this knowledge to an infinite God.

How can God notice a tiny human soul in the vast cosmic amphitheater? Because infinity is not relative. To God, Pierce was himself not appreciably smaller than the whole universe. No difference.

And contrariwise: God did not need an infinite universe to reflect himself in; Bruno was wrong, even though he knew this himself about infinity, knew that to an infinite being a really enormous universe is no larger than a small one; the abyss of space, the titanic creatures of the abyss, nebulae, galaxies, whatever, are not to an infinite being effectively larger than atoms; dogs, stars, stones, and roses, all equivalent. Bruno still wanted a great big infinite universe for a great big infinite God, who would be insulted with anything less. And yet an infinite God is not in any sense great big.

Of course.

You got no closer to God by imagining something huge, then something huger, then something hugest. No. You might, to imagine an infinite being, get just as close by imagining not something vast but something small; makes no difference.

Something small. Something tiny, since infinitesimal is infinite too; infinite tiny spark at the core of reality. Sure. Beau had drawn the first circle of his plot—Him, Her—actually too large for infinitude; it needed to be a dot, a dimensionless point.

Had he actually been told all these things long ago, and had he only not been able to receive them? Had Sister Mary Philomel explained it to him and been unable to broach his hardened heart? God is Everywhere. Sure. He has numbered the hairs of your head. Sure. The whole of great big God the Father, condensed without loss of fullness into the human body of His Son, is condensed further and without loss into the round of Bread, sure, sure. *Veni Creator Spiritus:* Come Holy Ghost Creator Blest/And in our hearts take up Thy rest. Here, maybe, was the real functional reason for a Trinity: an approach to the paradoxical and newly understood infinitude of God by positing three persons, big, medium-size and small.

He balanced his brown bottle on a tussock of grass, where the sun struck through its heart, an amber spark. Whether or not it was what *they* had meant, he felt himself (at last and for no particular reason just at this time) admitted into the room where those who understood were gathered, those who knew that the idea of God, whatever its other merits, was not affected by cosmology. Hildy, probably, had known all along.

"I have friends who are Christians," Val said. "Jesus Freaks sort of, I guess. A lot of love: you do feel a lot of love."

There were other big problems with the old Unmoved Mover still to be solved, of course. Never mind. Pierce thought his *vis imaginativa* had had enough workout for one day. He pulled his hat across his eyes and laced his fingers over his breast.

He ought to write this down soon. Sentiments that delicate, an insight that paradoxical, were just the sort of thing he was finding it hard to retain in memory; the kind of thing that could evaporate between the turning to a clean page and the finishing of an introductory paragraph. *New thought about God today.* Now what actually had it been, pen hovering bemused over the page like a bee whose intended flower has just been plucked.

A nine-year-old girl. An infinitely tiny spark of nine-year-old girlhood ensconced at the heart of things, and therefore apprehendable by, within, his own heart as well.

Like Tinkerbell, sort of. Hm.

The afternoon was golden on his eyelids, then dark, and his ears ceased by degrees to hear.

He experienced a sort of visitation then, a remembrance of a sort he only seemed to experience just before the onset of chance sleep; not a remembrance *of* something but a recurrence, occupying his whole self, of a stored past moment, a moment he could taste and feel and recognize as past but could not further identify. Pre-puberty; indoors; not summer; close guilty preoccupation . . . gone.

A ghost of himself, haunting him momentarily, warning(?) or reminding, passing on. *Animula vagula blandula.*

That little vial of time happened to have been filled in the winter of 1953, in the upstairs closet of the house in Bondieu, with Bobby Shaftoe next to him; but that wasn't returned to him, only the drop of melancholy sweetness on his tongue. Then the earth resumed its turning; the underside of Pierce's lids brightened momentarily, and there was a brief *ritornelle,* summer and the meadow, birdsong and human voices. Then that too was gone. Pierce was asleep.

11

She knew the secret names of the seven governors of the planets, but she could not recognize a picture of King Edward VI. She could be as cruel as a child, and as dismissive, consigning people and nations to perdition in a way that made John Dee's back hair stand. She teased Kelley tirelessly, speaking to him in Greek which he did not understand; she liked to play the older man against the younger one, until Kelley would stagger to his feet furious, and break off, despite John Dee's gentle remonstrances, now now, now now.

She took Kelley's black book and said it was no puzzle to her; it was written in the language of Enoch, the language men spoke with God before the Flood. Sit, she said to them; learn and do, she said; pluck up your hearts, she said, nothing will come of nothing; I will teach you this language by which the world was made, and the names Adam gave to the animals.

She told them, too, the names of their enemies at court, which included not only Burleigh, whom Dee had always suspected, but his friend and patron Sir Francis Walsingham too. So she said. And yet she was as hard to trust as a child, as the child she was, Jesus' child whom they were enjoined to become like if they would enter the Kingdom of Heaven.

They bent their minds and their wills to understand and believe, two large bearded men kneeling to be chastised and scolded by her, her finger raised (even Doctor Dee could see it with his mind's eye) and her brow darkened. When they asked for advice about the long sudden journey they were to take with the Polonian prince, where they would stay, what would become of them, she stamped her bare foot, arms akimbo: *Thou hast no faith. He is your friend greatly and intendeth to do much for you. He is prepared to do thee good and thou art prepared to do him service. Those who are not faithful shall die a most miserable death, and shall drink of sleep everlasting.*

Just when it had been decided that they would depart with the Lord Laski, Kelley suddenly spent five pounds on a horse, saddle and boot-hose. He was grooming the animal with fierce determination when Dee (who had sought him everywhere, he needed Kelley's help in making ready, he suspected some trouble) came upon him in the dark of the stable.

—Where do you go?

—Brentford. I have been told to get clean away.

—Who has told you?

—This one, by my right shoulder. Do you see him not? I did not think you would.

He poked viciously toward his own eyes with two fingers, as though to put out his sight:

—You have not eyes to see wickedness. Even did it speak the truth.

—And when return, asked Doctor Dee. Time is short.

—If I stay here I will be hanged; if I go with the Prince I shall have my head cut off.

He turned upon Dee, pointing to him with the curry-comb:

—You mean not to keep promise with me. I release you of your promise of fifty pounds a year. And if I had a thousand pounds I would not tarry here.

Dee raised his hand, palm out, to stop the man, but his gesture only made Kelley's face stranger and more suffused with violence:

—Oh *you* need not doubt God will defend *you*. And prosper *you*. He can of the very stones raise up children to Abraham. *You* need not worry.

He turned to his horse again, and began brushing violently, as though to flay the beast and not groom it.

—And I cannot abide my wife. I love her not, nay I abhor her, and I am misliked here because I favor her no better. She is a witch and has robbed me of my powers. You have helped her I doubt not. Touch me not.

Always in these possessions he feared to be touched, even by the friend who had knelt by him hand in hand for hour upon hour. Dee bowed his head in his hands as Kelley pushed past him unseeing and stamped into the house. His wife tried to shut the door of their room against him, but he flung her aside, gathered up clothes and books and a hat and some silver-gilt spoons in a parody of packing. Joanna slipped out and down into the kitchen, where she and Jane and the scullery-girl sat together and listened to the banging and muttering above.

When he had stamped down the stairs and ridden off, Jane climbed to her husband's small study.

—Jane.

—Husband I am sorry for thee.

—Well he is gone.

It was nearly dark then. Her husband's head was in his hands, his white hair disordered. She came to take his shoulders, and could tell he wept. He said into his hands:

—I beseech Almighty God to guide him and defend him from danger and shame. Oh let him not be hurt.

—Husband, she said again, but could think of no comfort to speak to him, did not dare tell him Good riddance, did not truly think it in her own heart: that strange angry man, she wanted to take him sometimes in her own arms and shake him and hug him into silence, as she did her own sons in their anguishes and fits. There there. There there.

She guessed, too, that he was not gone for good. And he was not.

Late that night John Dee (who had not left his study, sat up writing the records of his last dealings with his spiritual visitors) heard someone mount the stairs. It was he.

A well of hot relief overflowed in his breast. He said nothing, kept writing; only looked up when Kelley stood in the study door.

—I have lent my mare, he said. And so am returned.

—It is well done.

—I have come from Brentford by boat. Those were false friends.

He sat down in the chair by John Dee's table, the chair where some sixteen months before he had first sat down, whose arms he had taken in his hands (as he did now) and thought: Now I am home.

Doctor Dee said to him:

—There are some books the Lord Laski has sent. They are meant for you. He has written in them to you.

Kelley put his hand on them. Almost immediately Madimi was there with them. (They had seen her first among books; she read to them out of books; she was a book angel, somehow.) She patted a parchment cover; John Dee heard the sound of her hand.

—Mistress you are very welcome. In God for good as I hope. What cause of your coming now?

—*To see how you do.*

Softly she said it, but not hesitantly, entering into the breach between the two friends. A sweetness entered with her.

—I know you see me often, John Dee said. But I see you only by faith and imagination.

—*That sight is perfecter than his.*

The doctor could no longer maintain his careful calm. Kelley had come back to him, the child Madimi would not be lost to him. He knitted his fingers together and asked in tears:

—O Madimi shall I have any more of these grievous pangs.

—*Cursed wives and great devils are sore companions,* she said, as though it were an old saying, as a child will utter a maxim or a jest, having the form and the lilt of it but no meaning. Doctor Dee laughed, shook his head, dabbed at his eyes with his sleeve; laughed again.

Kelley had not laughed, had grown restless, clutching the chair's arms, his curtained eyes following Madimi (Dee supposed) as she went from place to place. He said:

—Madimi. Will you lend me a hundred pounds for a fortnight?

—*I have swept all my money out of doors.*

Dee, sensing trouble, said softly that as for money, they would have what was necessary when God saw fit; but Madimi turned on the skryer.

What dost thou hunt after? Speak, man. What dost thou hunt after?

He made no reply, drawing back as though the unseen child bent over him. He loved not God, she told him, not if he broke His commandments; see, his bragging words are confounded. Faith Hope Love, these are the greatest things, if he had not these, he had hate.

Did he love silver? Did he love gold? The one is a thief, the other a murderer. Oh but he has a just God who loves him.

—*Come here,* she said to him. *Come.*

Kelley started from the chair as though pulled by the ear, a bad boy. He was made to kneel before the stone of moleskin-colored crystal, still in its frame in the study, the first glass he had ever looked into, that glass that had first summoned Madimi (though he had not then known her), a fat babe with a glass in her hands.

—*Look and tell me if you know these.*

He saw the dog-faced one, and fourteen others, herded together in the glass, like footpads and tavern haunters collected by the Queen's constables in a sweep of Cheapside. They knew him. He knew them. All their names began with B.

—*This is he who has followed thee for months,* she said. Venite Tenebrae spiritu meo. *Depart unto the last cry. Go you hither, go.*

The wicked crew looked around themselves, alarmed and trapped: a wind seemed to be stirring their brown garments; they clutched one another, open-mouthed, goggling, writhing, but they were plucked up weightless as ashes and dispersed in a whirl. He had not heard one of them speak, not one: and he was glad of it.

He knelt for a long time looking into the empty glass, feeling the dreadful relief he felt after spewing, or releasing from his bowels a mass of sickness. He raised his eyes, blinking, finding himself in the same place he had been, but a different place. Where had he been gone, where had he journeyed, these past weeks? He saw in his mind a dark slow river, a book, a horse's eye.

—How is it with you? Doctor Dee whispered.

He swallowed. It was a time before he answered.

—Methinks I am lighter than I was. Empty. Returned from. From a great amazing.

He was trembling. He held up a hand to show Doctor Dee, and laughed to see it shake.

—*Thou art eased of a great burden,* said the angel-child with satisfaction. *Now love God. Love thy friends. Love thy wife.*

John Dee had come to kneel beside him, and had begun a prayer of thanksgiving. He leadeth me beside the still waters, I shall not want, behold goodness and mercy shall follow me all the days of my life. He took Kelley's cold hand. They prayed together. They would not be parted.

She drove them out of England like geese before a goose-girl; she hurried them on across Christendom from Amsterdam to Bremen to Lübeck, though she would not tell them their final destination, nor what they were to accomplish. Then in Germany as winter came on she left them, without farewell, whether for good or not they could not know.

They still had congress with all the many others, great Gabriel and Galvah and Nalvage gowned like a king and Murifri in red like a yeoman, Il the merry player (*Jesu I had not thought to see you here,* he said to them out of the glass in Lübeck, as though it had been he traveling and not they). They had all followed the stone abroad, apparently, like bees following a dish of sugared fruits a housewife carries; and yet in Germany more and more often Kelley did not any longer need to look into the glass to see or speak to them, he met them at the top of the stair as he went down, heard them as he knelt at his prayers; he saw them from inn windows, signaling to him from the crowd in the street.

They brought news, sometimes, as pleased as gossips.

—*Your brother is clapped up in prison. How like you that? Your house-keeper I mean.*

Nicholas Fromond, Jane Dee's brother: it must be he they meant. What had happened?

—*They examine him. They say thou hast hid divers secret things. As for thy books, thou mayst go look at them at leisure.*

In horror Dee thought of his goods scattered, his books seized, he needed no glass in order to see them vividly. Why?

—*It may be that thy house will be burnt for a remembrance of thee, too. Well, if they do, so it is. I have given thee my counsel, and desired to do thee good. The choice is thine.*

What choice? What choice had they now? He felt himself to be hurrying hopelessly toward his grave, his life burning down behind him.

Hurry, hurry. There was not much time now in which the two men must get their lessons, they were told, to learn the secret purposes for which they had been chosen, and cull the message which it was theirs to deliver to all states and peoples. And yet the saving message, the whole of the new truth whose vessels they had been chosen to be—it could only be given to them in the Enochian language: and therefore they must learn it.

But it was painfully, dreadfully hard. Tables had to be constructed, of forty-nine letters square; the angels gave them numbers, and the corresponding letters were then located; words were built of these, which they were told were angels' calls, by which they could be summoned; only gradually did it become clear (to Doctor Dee, at least) that the angels who were summoned by the calls were themselves the words of the language, they had come full circle.

They talked of urgency, but they seemed not to conceive of it as mortals did; they had leisure to pause in the work to praise God at length, or prophesy, or to tell long strange stories for the two to ponder and allegorize, never sure that the meaning they arrived at and not some other might be meant. In Bremen, in Lübeck, in Emden, in the cramped bedrooms of inns and borrowed houses, Kelley and Dee set up their glass and their table (constructed now so it could be folded up on hinges, collapsed and carried) and took down further gibberish; late, late at night they waited on the angels while Rowland and Katherine and Arthur were rolled up with their mother asleep; Joanna Kelley in a chair watched with her fox's eyes her strange husband, and thought of her unthinkable fate.

Laski took them across Germany, leaving them on occasion to go wait upon some potentate, the Duke of Mecklenburg, the Bishop of Stettin, to shore up his fortunes. His star was sinking—the angels had stopped praising him—though he knew it not. He began to talk to them of gold: how it might be made easily now, with the spirits' help; why could not the question be put to them, why. A magnate of Laski's stature could live for years on credit: for years, not forever.

Winter set in, early and very hard, but they pushed on, in wagons, coaches and carts. Hurry, hurry. From Stettin to Posen (where they saw the tomb of the good king Wenceslaus) is two hundred miles, and on all of them the snow lay deep and crisp and even; the Duke hired twenty men to cut ice for two miles so their coaches could pass. Wide water-meadows, ice-locked now (little figures in the distance let down lines through the ice to catch fish), at last brought them to Lask in Poland. The Duke had been gone long. His people were not overjoyed to see him.

There by the enameled stove Kelley set up the table. And then Madimi returned, without greeting or apology, *a little wench in white* Kelley said, not at first recognizing her; she had grown.

—*I have been in England,* she said. *The Queen is sorry she hath lost her philosopher. But the Lord Treasurer answered her, and said you would come home again shortly, begging to her. Truly none can turn the Queen's heart from you.*

An awful wave of homesickness washed the old man. The Queen. He saw the loved pockmarked face. O God.

—*I have been at your house too. All is well there. I could not come into your study there, for the Queen has caused it to be sealed.*

But had not Madimi said once to them that men's locks were no hindrance to her? Doctor Dee looked into the study in his mind, not knowing what hurt had been done to it. Silence and dust.

What house, then, would they have now? How were they to live? They have been advised to go to Cracow. How shall they fare there?

—*As wise as I am I cannot tell.*

She seemed to grow dull and aimless in the foreign cold (it was their own brains, doubtless, gelid beneath their skullcaps and furs, their own contracting hearts). Kelley's breath clouded the cold stone into which he looked.

—*Sir Harry Sidney is dead,* Madimi said. *He was a secret enemy of yours.*

She was nearly asleep. The three of them bent nearer the stove. John Dee felt tears rise to his eyes. He wrote down what Madimi had said, a secret enemy. He had always loved Harry Sidney, Philip's father. There was to be nothing left of his life, nothing to return to, he would die an old man in foreign parts.

(In Prague in August, after the English news at last caught up with him, he would write a note on this page: *Sir H. Sidney was not dead in February nor March, no not in May last. So this must be considered.*)

Cracow, royal city of Great Poland, piled up in the middle of a great flat plain flooded and muddy when they crossed it in March. Kelley and the women were silent seeing it at a distance, thinking Lord the

world is huge: who would have thought great plains and cities went
on coming into being one upon another to the farthest east. And all of
Russia beyond. Doctor Dee, who had traveled widely, only groaned at
his ague, and did not look up.

Once established in a tall house near the Cathedral, John Dee
went to call on an old correspondent of his, Dr. Hannibal, a Capuchin
monk, then coming to the end of his Commentaries on the *Pimander*
of Hermes Trismegistus, many times longer than the Ægyptian book
itself.

What did they talk of for hours? Jane Dee wondered, struggling
with foreign coins and foreign foods. They talked of angels: of the
nine choirs of the angels, who are not different from the Governors
who Hermes says maintain the frame of the heavens and the distinctions and hierarchies that make things things and not mere chaos. Of
the divisions in religion, when rash unlearned ungodly men by force
and the sword impose their churches like beds of Procrustes on suffering men. How would it end? Dr. Hannibal turned the much-
marked pages of his *Pimander* and read:

> In that day not only will men neglect the worship of the gods, but
> —still more terrible—so-called laws will be enacted, which shall
> punish those who do worship them . . . In that day will men, in
> boredom, give up thinking the world worth their reverence and
> adoration, this greatest of all goods, this All . . . Then the earth
> will lose its balance, the sea no longer hold up ships, the heavens
> will not support the stars.

Was not that the state of the world now? Could not a case be made
that their own age was likewise ending in disasters? Then the out-
come was in God's hand, and Hermes foresaw that too:

> . . . a coming back of all good things, a holy and awesome
> Restoration of the Whole Wide World imposed by the Will of God
> in the course of time.

Dr. Hannibal wondered—bending his round tonsured head close to
Doctor Dee's white one and speaking in a low voice—if Christ's
church was now falling in fragments because her age was past; and

after a time of troubles would dawn a new age, the Age of the Holy Spirit, which would need no churches, no friars, no bishops, and each man would be priest to his neighbor.

—As Abbot Joachim of Flora preached, said Dee. So long ago.

—Who was condemned, said Dr. Hannibal. Let us speak no more of it.

Doctor Dee took Communion with the brave little round man at the church of the Bernardines, taking on his tongue the living God, glimpsing afterward the monk fumbling his spectacles from his face to wipe away tears (were they of joy? Gratitude?). Kelley would not receive, though Dee urged him to, though even the angels spoke to him of the Bread in wonder and adoration: *The Flesh of God is all we know of meat, His Blood of drink; he may not refuse it to us. Did you think it was yours alone? We ate and drank before the foundation of the world. If a rich man gave to you to eat, would you not praise him? If he gave you the food of his plate, would you not praise him? Be content, be joyful, He has given you the whole Flesh of His Body.*

Why did he refuse? Doctor Dee wanted to know. What holier preparation for the work they had now to do, what better.

He would not. There was a row, a row like so many others, Dee had thought they had been left behind in England but they had not been. The spirits were lying, Kelley said, they had done nothing these two years but lie, Dee was a fool to believe them, if they knew anything of worth they had not revealed it yet and would not reveal it to the mortals no though they begged them; they too were objects of the spirits' scorn and derision, he had no doubt of that, he could hear their laughter in their spheres. Look: here in Agrippa his book *De occulta philosophia*, here were all the names of the angels that govern the nations of the world, names that Kelley had spent days on his knees to be told! He would be toyed with no more. And he banged shut his door in Doctor Dee's face.

Gabriel came to him, that night, and corrected him.

Kelley would never tell his master what had been said or done that night to him, and Dee did not insist. He only knelt again with Kelley before the stone, his old kneebones crackling like broken kindling; and Gabriel, mildest and sweetest of the spirits who talked to them, joined them once again together in tears of repentance and thanksgiving: again, again, once again. On the next day Kelley received the Body of Christ in his mouth at the Church of the Bernardines.

The great plain fruited. In May, lying in bed of a morning, Kelley felt his head and breast opened as by a butcher's cleaver or an oysterer's knife, and a voice (not a voice, or a voice speaking no words) poured knowledge into the breach: why they had been chosen, what the prophecies spoke of, what the tales figured.

There was war in heaven.

Four watch-towers or castles stand in the four corners of the Earth, North South East West. Kelley started in his bedclothes as four trumpets sounded from them, and four cloths or banners rolled out vastly from the towers' tops. One as red as new-smitten blood from the East, one lily white from the South, a green one garlic-bladed like a dragon's skin from the West, one the black of raven hair or bilberry juice from the North. Then out of the towers came the hosts, colored the same, roiling and outpouring, like banners, like words from a mouth, a seeming confusion and yet no confusion, every troop with its senior, every army with its general, great captains; they march toward the center court, ranged about their ensigns, ready for a battle.

This was happening now, he knew, but not why or to what end, except that, happy as the warriors looked, splendid as their banners, the war was a desperate one, and the issue in doubt. Was it the war of the Lamb against the Beast, against the Wind that bloweth where he listeth? What Kelley could not tell was if the angelic troops moving toward one another from all directions were about to combine into a single mighty army, or whether when they met they would fall upon one another, a war of all against all. He only knew it would not be long until they met.

Still in his shirt he roused his brother, and sent him off to Dee's house in St. Stephen Street, and John the servant-boy to the Franciscan convent where Laski lay. And stood then at the window of his room trembling and gritting his teeth with a sound that made his wife in the bed draw up the covers to her neck in fear.

Past midnight that night, John Dee rose from his place by the table of practice. A mass of scribbled papers slipped from his lap to the floor, the names of angels, the order of their march. The clear sphere was empty at last, nothing but a stone; Kelley slept in his chair, his mouth open, a whinny like a sick child's coming from his lips with each breath. All the house was asleep.

He climbed the stairs past the room where his wife Jane had left a candle burning by the curtained bed. The children and their nurse were dark humps in the next room like sleeping bears, their books and pages of childish work scattered on the floor, they had got their father's vice of disorder, a small one but hard to conquer. He went silently past to a ladder at the hall's end, up it, out through a cockloft (the pigeons murmured and fluttered as he passed) and onto the house's roof. A balustrade was built there where a man could stand.

No moon, a few clouds, their hems ermine-trimmed. Stars.

The four corners of the world. Kelley had called them by the compass points but he had meant the solstices and equinoxes, the four corners of the year, the gates of time.

If the battle was being fought among the angels that govern the heavens, and the issue was in doubt—that would explain the prophecies they were continually given, that the Turk would be overthrown, that Tartary would fall, that states would alter: prophecies which changed from week to week without ever coming about. They were reports of the battle only, how it went.

Why would God allow His angels to fight over the world?

He looked up into the confusion of the stars, so many visible, so huge a horizon that he did not always recognize the old familiar constellations. The turning heavens, bound by the colures, fixed at four corners. Changeless. They were not, though: John Dee and every astronomer in Christendom (in Araby and Cathay too doubtless) had seen a new star born in Cassiopæia's chair ten years before. A new star, come forth from nothing by God's will, the first since Bethlehem.

Unless it was not new, had merely come suddenly closer to the Earth, close enough to be seen: charging from its circular course like a racehorse faulting and rushing the crowd, just because it chose to.

Because it chose to. With perfect clarity he saw the face of the little Italian who had stood in his study in Mortlake and challenged him. A new heaven: and if there was a new heaven, there must be a new earth too.

Was the war now taking place in heaven about the courses of the stars? Were the angels who turn the spheres (if there were spheres) engaged in their milliards in violently shifting the stars from their places? As though Earth and the Sun were not only to be newly *understood* as standing in each other's places, but *were even now on the move to their new places,* the one to the center, the other (Earth, our star, and we on it) out to the middle row of the planets.

An awful laughter arose in John Dee's breast, and he clutched the balustrade by which he stood. That would raise winds, that would throw down states. The Earth lose its balance, seas not hold up ships: yes.

If God meant now to roll up the heavens as a scroll, if He was now at work doing that, and a new heavens was to be revealed behind the old; if there was no longer to be lower and higher, up and down, no longer any measure by which a place in the universe could be found—no more four corners to the world—then men would have to be new, too.

Was God about to grant men new powers? Were all of John Dee's and poor Kelley's labors now to come to fruition, and all the tedious numeration they had been given to write down resolve itself, appear all at once to be the plain science of a new world? He was certain of it: not certain that he would ever live to understand or use it, but certain he had been chosen to give it to the men of the coming world, who would someday take it up, perhaps after it had lain long obscure and dusty, look into it and say *Yes yes of course, yes just so it must be.*

He thought of—he felt in his breast like the scar of an old branding—his own *Monas hieroglyphica,* child of his heart that he had never truly understood.

How would they use it? Please God they did no harm. They could not, God would not allow it to pass into their hands if their souls were not prepared for the use of it. That was why his heart shrank in his bosom when Bruno Nolano had bragged of the new powers to be had. The child Madimi had warned Dee: He has stolen fire from heaven. Like Phæton he could burn up the world.

That then was what John Dee was to do, that was the warning he had been given to issue, that was why he and not another had been chosen to issue it. He thought of words from Job: *I only am escaped to tell thee.*

He knelt on the starlit rooftop and prayed. O God let not sharp swords be put into the hands of children; let their hearts be made wise before their hands are made strong. Lead us not into temptation, but deliver us from evil. And yet Thy kingdom come, Thy will be done. World without end. Amen.

In May Adelbert of Lask set out for Transylvania, to his estates there. Before he departed he knelt before John Dee, profoundly embarrassing the doctor, and asked for his blessing, which Dee gave; Laski also asked, head bowed, that the angelic powers Dee and Kelley spoke for might aid him, in his journey, in his suit before King Stephen for relief of his debts.

They might not, he said, see them again. He would return through Prague, and if they had reached there, he might see them again, if God and His Angels willed. And if, if ever the angels spoke of him, or made any suggestion as to how his troubles might be resolved, please please do as they instructed.

He went out on a tall horse into the spring, knuckles on his sword-belt and his elbow turned proudly out. In that month King Stephen died, all of Laski's business unresolved; the angels expressed no surprise, though they had said they expected great things of Stephen: as though the right hand of God could not know what the left hand was doing.

By then John Dee and Edward Kelley and their wives and children, relations, servants, carts, furniture, books and papers had gone down into Bohemia to see the Emperor.

12

What is the one thing we inherit from the past which still retains the powers it once had?

Pierce had promised to reveal such a thing in the course of his book, and Julie said the publisher really liked the idea; a *lagniappe,* a bonus for purchasers better than a give-away record or a revealing questionnaire, oh much better. Now Pierce had actually to come up with something, pull it out of his empty fist like a string of magician's scarves.

If it were like the Stone of the alchemists, it would be lying around in plain sight, unrecognized by everyone except the fool and the wise man, the one who had never forgotten and the one who at length must learn. Though Doctor Michael Maier—who was the Emperor Rudolf's chemical doctor and knew this to be so—says that it is in the high mountains that one should search for the Stone.

It might not be a thing at all, though, Pierce thought, it might be a word, it might be a thought the mind could think by chance, sudden *conjunctio oppositorum* that starts a mental blaze.

What, what persists into this time from that near or distant past when the laws of the universe were not as they are now, but different; when such things as jewels and fire had properties they no longer have; when people witnessed, and recorded, marvels we now know to be (and believe to have always been) impossible?

Pierce thought about it. At his work at Kraft's house, at the Donut Hole, drinking alone or at Val's Faraway Lodge, he thought what in hell he could actually discover, or be seen to have discovered, that would fit the bill. On the toilet he pondered; in his bath, with the Monitor and Merrimack of the soap and sponge floating before his submerged chin; in line at the supermarket.

It could be something actual, there were a thousand possibilities for contemplation. The amulet that John Dee had supposedly cast, by means of which he raised the wind that blew away the Spanish Armada. The creepy arch-mage and blusterer Aleister Crowley (how had Pierce learned this fact or nonfact?) had actually seen this item, in the British Museum.

No no no. It would only turn out to be another of those dead things that Kraft enjoyed, Grails that were nothing but golden cups, *objets de vertu* from which the *vertu* has evaporated.

What about a journey to find such a thing? Set out to locate it, trace down the rumor, find it's worthless, but in the journey find the true magic in oh understanding, wisdom, so on.

Would he be torn apart by outraged believers if he pulled such a trick?

Something real, something simple and undeniable, not even rare; a surprise, but something you actually knew all along. Something.

As though, in the next age of the world, a cooler and a duller age than this one, somebody were to come upon a lump of radium, glowing eerily in darkness, shedding particles, decaying, showing just those properties that once upon a time in Einstein's day or Fermi's people actually believed it to have.

How could he have set himself such an insoluble problem?

He had worked on it and thought about all through one thundery stifling day, when toward evening the problem was wholly supplanted in his thinking; for an event he had been waiting for almost all his conscious life took place as he sat on the front step of Fellowes Kraft's house waiting for Rosie Rasmussen's car to pick him up. The power that had in its keeping Pierce's three wishes showed up ready to grant them to him, and Pierce had been unable afterwards to think of anything else.

If we believe, or pretend, that the world is capable of being other than it is, alterable by our desires (as perhaps more people did believe, in that age of the world, than do now), then it is likely we will spend a certain amount of our aimless mental time in imagining just how we might alter it. Pierce Moffett had never built model railroads, hadn't spent energy imagining himself into that small world, boarding the little cars at little stations, oiling the engine and driving it through the hills and over the bridges. He had never had a teddy bear who went on imaginary travels with him, or an imaginary friend, or even a dog he pretended could talk to him, not because he was refused a dog but because he seemed so unmoved by them.

But he had always, always imagined that wishes could come true; and if wishes could come true, the wisher had better be ready to make them, the right ones, the ones he most wants, at a moment's notice, when the chance is offered him. In the days when he had sat on the steps of the dogtrot in Kentucky, looking out over the shaggy hills and twisting a lock of hair in his fingers, this was what he was often about: examining his heart, testing against its unfathomable depths of need first this wish and then that, and gauging the response.

He had never completely quelled the habit.

If there were three—and most good fairies had a minimum of three to offer—then two were easy to make, foolproof wishes for Health and Money he had long ago decided on, cast in careful formulæ intended to avoid fairy ire or malevolence. We all know the cautionary tales. But the third he had not ever decided on. The older he grew the oftener it turned on reversing the consequences of choices he had made in the past, or paths anyway that he had taken in ignorance: wishing he could return to some past crux, and take the other way. But the awful implications of such a wish, if it were to in fact be granted, were vivid to him. And so (except for occasional desperate and thank-heaven unheard heart-cries in the midnight) the last wish remained unwished.

Only that day, sitting on the steps of Fellowes Kraft's house as he had once sat on the steps in Kentucky, twirling as he had then a long lock of hair in his fingers, had he discovered his need and conflated it with desire, just in time too. And having made his wish, his true last wish, he needed only to wait with patience and some tears (he was on the verge of happy tears all afternoon) for Robbie.

"Robbie," Pierce explained the next morning to a tall gray ledger that he had bought on his arrival in the Faraways in the spring, bought to record very different matters in, "is my son."

He looked at this brief sentence on the page and felt a sweetness (already familiar) rise in his throat.

"I engendered him on a thoughtless and contraceptiveless night in 1965, an early summer night that I remember very little of. I saw the girl one other time, and noted a secret smile about her, but she was a strange one, and if she knew she didn't tell me; she figured someone else, maybe—who can tell now." He could see, could smell in fact, the night streets of that neighborhood in that year, his first year down from college. "Anyway Robbie was the result. I never knew. He was raised by his grandparents (his mother was a wanderer, long gone off now to, well the coast, someplace, who knows now, vanished utterly, no surprise to me). But she told him, somehow, about me, and now he's managed to find me."

Standing on the WELCOME mat that lay before the front door of Pierce's building, having got off the bus in the wrong town and walked the rest of the way, footsore and intensely proud of himself, with nothing but a cardboard valise and his flute in its case.

"Well I was amazed of course, unbelieving," Pierce wrote, his pencil now twirling happily and more or less automatically down along the blue lines, "but he does look a lot like me, only far more beautiful than I ever was or could be, or if not beautiful so winning, so winning it doesn't matter. Apparently he just supposed that once he found me I'd just take him in. And I did."

There was a daybed on Pierce's sun-porch which he could have, the sun-porch where Pierce now sat, writing in the journal amid the complex and soothing geometries of window frame and sash, the shadows of the mullions on sills and floorboards, the golden ingots of sunlight. A narrow bed, an airy room, just right for him. Who in the sunny beams did glide.

The nature of his wish had come to Pierce as a complete surprise, not distilled out of any previous inclinations or needs that he knew of; it had simply and suddenly occurred within him whole and ready to be wished. No doubt but it was his wish, though; he had immediately recognized it as his, the wish he had so long waited to know, the one good thing he really wanted. Recognizing it was not only a necessary precondition to its coming true: the recognizing *was* the coming true. And he knew that too. He had come home from Kraft's place in a bright fog of happiness, tasting continuously this strange sweetness in the back of his throat. He had sat a long time immobile at his kitchen table admitting for the first time, yes for the first time, how much he wanted just to love and be loved, without any other conditions attached; and was possessed with dæmonic laughter to know that even if Robbie were in some trivial sense not real, Pierce could, just now, easily make him real (it would only mean going mad): and the laughter felt like the sobs that had riven him in his dream.

"So these are the fruits of renunciation," he wrote. For it came to that, it seemed: it seemed that in exchange for the vow he had taken, that foolish vow, there was to be a return. As soon as he ceased to scan the horizon, as soon as he turned back in at his own gate and shut it behind him, then there was Robbie, he who had been waiting all along within.

Something for his life to be about; someone to be clean and solvent for; a reason to go on living the life he had chosen, a reason for the abnegations he had made. There hadn't been a reason, not a good reason, and now there was.

Robbie, why that name. He had not had an imaginary friend as a child, but it must feel like this to have one; he felt *visited,* as people had once been visited by gods or godlets, sudden strong sweet friends out of the blue, dangerous too maybe, who walked with you a ways before vanishing: and he would soon, he supposed, feel the beat of departing wings. But oh not yet, not yet.

He remained all that day, and showed no signs of evanescing; in fact he grew, if not exactly more actual, more distinct. The following morning he was still there, the tiny stove still glowing merrily beneath Pierce's sternum—the same sensation (Pierce noticed) as is occasioned by finding, the day after your birthday and the day after that, that the new bike is still in the garage, its paintwork still bright, still yours.

While Pierce went on with his researches, Robbie practiced his flute, playing over and over a slow movement from the Water Music which Pierce would never after be able to hear without thinking of him, and of summer, the big maple outside the windows of the sun-porch full at last, opulent, million-handed.

(Well look at this: according to buckram-bound Miss Smith, there actually was a gap in John Dee's diaries in exactly that June and July of 1583, the summer months when Kraft pictured him and Bruno huddling, just the period that the angel Madimi told Dee not to memorialize—Kraft's Madimi, this was, there was no such interdiction in Dee's record of the conversations as far as Pierce could tell, though there wouldn't be, would there, the interdiction itself not to be written down either.)

The kid was actually a sort of musical prodigy, so it seemed to Pierce's untrained ears—to Pierce music was an arcanum as great and fast as any that he studied. A flute, for Pan's sake. Were those buds of faun-horn in the soft curls of his hair? What color hair, anyway? Gold, and the curly down of his arms and legs gold too.

(And so did this elision or absence in Dee's diary mean only that Kraft took some private pleasure in not contradicting the record, in making his inventions if not likely at least possible? Had Kraft looked up the dates, as Pierce was now doing, in the same books Pierce had, and then put his imaginary meeting in the only gap that appeared there? Yes. Of course. Any other explanation was only more complicated, only less likely. And yet.)

He whistled the Water Music as he tidied the house, and then broke out the mop and pail, no more geezerish squalor, bad example for the boy and not healthy; then lunch to make and lay on the kitchen table, sandwiches, a tall glass of milk. (And yet: Could Kraft have really known they had met? Known from what source, how, where? Why did it seem so likely once it was said? *Why* did Dee so suddenly leave for the Continent at the end of that summer?)

After their lunch, Pierce sent himself to his typewriter, time to get something concrete accomplished. Boney Rasmussen had sent to him, via Rosie, a set of questions, and Pierce had not yet sent his answers back; he was not at all sure that the answers he had were the ones the old man was looking for. Pierce felt so lucky in the Rasmussens and their Foundation that he did not dare to put too many hard queries to them; he didn't want to find himself outside again, left to his own resources: not yet.

The answers he had completed, or at least assayed, were already rolled in the typewriter, a great powder-blue electric. This machine had been accepted long ago by the Sphinx in exchange for drugs, and given for nothing, so to speak, to Pierce. He read what he had written:

1.   *No.*
2.   *Not as far as I can tell.*
3.   *The literature on Rudolf II in English is very slight. I can read German just a little, but only a university library would have the things. I don't imagine Kraft used any very exotic sources; there aren't many books at all in his library in languages other than English and Italian (and Latin, a few). So I conclude he made this up.*
4.   *It might be a powder. It might be a liquid or a stone or a jewel or almost anything. No one is going to be very specific, naturally.*

Okay. He rubbed his hands briskly together and took up the next of Boney's questions. He typed with two fingers, index of one hand, medicus of the other, he always had, but why.

5.   *Yes. In the early summer of 1588 Dee sent to Walsingham in London the news that he had in fact transmuted ordinary iron into gold, using a "powder of projection" that Kelley had long possessed. They sent Walsingham an iron pot lid, with a piece broken out of it, and they sent the matching piece, now made entirely of gold. These two items are supposedly somewhere in the British Museum.*
6.   *The stuff to be drunk, "taken internally" as the docs say now, wasn't exactly gold, it was "potable gold" (aurum potabile) which was I don't know what; like "philosophical mercury," it wasn't probably just what it seems.*

Last, a quote from a bad old magic book that Pierce had once repeated in Boney's hearing, only to have Boney turn on him and ask with interest, with too-intense interest, if Pierce could say that again, and write it down for him, and find the source.

7.   *"O Arctic Manes! O Antarctics propelled by divinity! Why do natures so great and noble seem to be enclosed in mineral spe-*

cies?" This was said or written by King Solomon, supposedly, in a
book called On the Shadows of Ideas, *a magic book which has*
since disappeared.

He couldn't recall where he had read the quote. In a book about
Bruno, maybe; Bruno's greatest book of memory magic was also
called *De umbris idearum,* on the shadows of ideas. He thought of
telling Boney this, though Bruno's book was certainly not translated
from the Latin.

Why was he afraid of Boney? He had no reason not to want to go
see him and sit with him in the pleasant study of his beautiful house,
share research with him, drink his liquor. Did he not know on which
side his bread was buttered? Sickly and slow as the old man was. Was
it that? Pierce didn't think so; he had never been embarrassed or
repelled by age, he had an odd willingness usually to indulge garru-
lous oldsters and maintain pretend conversations with them; he never
minded listening to stories he hadn't heard before, and Boney's were
of that kind for sure.

A *valetudinarian,* Pierce had called him once, talking with Rosie,
who thought he meant the complement of *salutatorian:* the other
one, the one who makes the farewell speech. No that is the *valedicto-
rian,* there is a dim linguistic connection but no real one. Valetudinar-
ians are the sickly oldsters who will not get well. *Valetudo* is health; in
Latin it could be good or bad, like luck. Good health is what valetudi-
narians don't have. It is the name of the sixth house of the Zodiac,
which is the house of Health and Sickness and also for some reason of
Servants, one of Boney's being Pierce himself.

Was it because he was afraid Boney really wanted Pierce to find a
way for him to live longer? *Skin for skin, yea all that a man has he will
give for his life.* That's what it was. Though Boney would never say
such a thing out loud. Unless Pierce were to confess a similar desire,
which he wouldn't, never yet having been conscious of fearing death:
dying, maybe, but not being dead, not yet at any rate.

That was perhaps because he hadn't yet had to think very long or
very hard about it. He had no troubling stars in that house, not in
either of his possible natal charts. Melancholy was his only sickness;
and melancholy might be mortal but was not fatal, not his kind. His
was the fiery kind that yearned and went unsatisfied. He was no
suicide. Nor would he die of boredom.

Not now, not any longer.

He had found his own medicine for melancholy, his *aurum potabile,* he had made it out of the stuff of his heart, the base matter of his need, but it would do his patron no good. Let Boney find a virgin to sleep with; every man to his own cure.

Later there came a violent thunderstorm, and he stood with Robbie at the window to watch the slew of rain across the window and the metal roof of the porch below, Robbie's head on his shoulder and Pierce's arm around his son, hand hooked in his belt. Found by the lost.

Pierce awoke after a few hours of restless sleep, erect and too hot. What had he dreamed of?

Walking, he remembered; walking night city streets (why do we walk so much in dreams, pressing on aimlessly, the walls and streets mutating around us? Why is it so often night, as though we were producing our dream-movies on the cheap, saving on scenery? Or is it only the real night in which we dream pouring softly in?). Then meeting his father, who was walking too, as he actually did walk compulsively in the city, his eyes quartering the ground continually before him as he went, searching or rather only seeming to search, and now and then stooping to pick up some oddment, a scrap of paper, only to discard it again. In the dream his father was strangely young, with glossy brown hair, and he wore a uniform (though he had never been a soldier), a Sam Browne belt, polished shoes. He was going, he told Pierce or Pierce somehow guessed, to meet Winnie, and the two of them were going to go down to the Staten Island ferry, to take a ride. World's cheapest sea cruise. Pierce saw the ferry station, and the harbor, vast antiquated works; gulls, and the machinery of the slips and docks; moonlight, wind. He wanted to pat Axel, urge him gently on to his rendezvous. He knew Axel was intending to propose marriage, hopefully, bravely, unsuited as he was for it, and thus to engender Pierce; and Pierce was grateful, knowing himself to be Axel's reason more than any other. Axel shyly admitting as much as they walked together to the subway.

Why do we awake with boners from dreams of night cities, our fathers, hope.

It was as warm as day. Pierce pushed aside the sheet that covered him, and looked up into the mirror that he had hung cantilevered over the bed, in which he was accustomed now and then to see pictures of the bed's former life in the city, pictures that, like old hand-colored photographs, grew more not less remote and unreal as he applied his tints to them. I will take it down, he thought.

The muslin curtains he had hung in the sun-porch window stirred. He noticed that, the stir of breeze. And then Robbie was beside his bed. Standing slim tall wandlike in his white undershorts over Pierce.

What is it?

I don't want to sleep out there.

What do you mean?

I don't want to sleep out there. I'd rather sleep here.

Well but, Pierce said; Robbie allowed him to stare and murmur, only smiling and possessing himself, arms wrapping his long torso; and then he placed his forefinger gently against his lips, and pulled away Pierce's sheet.

Shine of his thigh in moon- and street-light as he climbed up, still smiling, nearly laughing. When he pressed against Pierce for the first time (for they had not yet truly embraced, not wholly, shy maybe in the day) Pierce could feel the heat still emanating from him, the sun he had walked in all day to find his father.

Morning and the cicadas whine, and a light of unearthly clarity (so it seemed to Pierce, Day One in a world new-hatched) filling his apartment. He sat on the daybed with the gray ledger in his hands, wherein Robbie was chiefly kept (so far, so far).

How light but not fragile he had felt, satin-skinned and not soft: somehow like holding a bird and not a beast. The crown of his head, that one of Pierce's hands could compass; the strong vulnerable tendons of his neck. "Well I will forget a lot of things," Pierce wrote, heart a hot lump in his throat, "but I will not forget that. I wept, after, a little; and he wanted to know why, wasn't it fun? And I said it was fun, and I said I didn't know why. But I did."

He put down his pencil, vividly conscious suddenly of what

he had done, what acts; startled and shamed to see himself at them.

So. He had not, it seemed, escaped harmless from his own father's sexual tortuosities, only he had not had evidence of them till now. Robbie was doubtless nothing more than a cryptic gateway through which his inheritance had come. Maybe this was how such tendencies commonly first emerge, issuing as harmless fantasy, a Young Friend, a Chum, whose love is offered with magical swiftness and complaisance. Only then come the stalkings, the sordid crimes.

Though actually (Pierce thought) Axel wasn't bent that way; he'd often professed a horror of child molestation, had despised those he knew who confessed to or rejoiced in such tastes, and been puzzled by them too, where's the fun.

Not Axel's genes then even to blame probably. And yet even Axel might understand the love.

But how could he have, how. When the last thing he would want to do was to hurt his own son. Pierce chewed his pen's end. Can a phantasm be hurt? He would have to consult his experts. If one were, it would of course be only the creator or possessor of the phantasm who would suffer (and suffer the more as the phantasm were more present to him). That seemed obvious, and also seemed not to matter; he could not evade what he had done merely by denying the reality of his victim.

But hurt, hurt, how hurt anyway: he clapped his brow and laughed, near tears again: how hurt, when it had been Robbie who had made the invitation, who had gently mocked Pierce's inhibitions, who at morning, elbow on the pillow next to Pierce's, had looked down on him with a smile of selfless pleased godlike sweetness probably no child of thirteen had ever truly smiled. Pierce had only accepted: though he had, admittedly, elaborated and gone on elaborating the consequences of his acceptance all by himself, all that blue-and-white morning, astonished at his own ceaselessness, as though he were thirteen again himself.

For all of that had been present too in his wish from the beginning; and from the beginning he had known it, but had kept from himself the secret.

He wondered if Robbie had known it too, if it had been part of his plan, imagined as he dozed on the bus or crossed the mountain

on foot. What was it in Robbie, a natural bent, an overplus of generous feeling, what? There had been a boy at St. Guinefort's, Pierce's old
school, a charmer to whom a copulation was among the necessary
first offerings of a friendship, it was like a warm handshake, a hug, a
swap of cherished belongings.

Well: Pierce would learn in time.

"Because he's going to stay with me now, ever after," Pierce wrote
defiantly. "One of his grandparents recently died; the other is a little
gaga; so it shouldn't be hard, with my new fairy wealth, to make it all
legal. He'll love it around here, I think, away from the city, and raising
him will take all my resources, maybe some I don't yet know I have,
all right, all right. I didn't have anything else anyway to do."

He lay down the pencil then, and attended only to the rising
spring that had come forth in him, a burble of possibilities, some of
them contradictory, succeeding one another rapidly and without his
conscious participation. Robbie would grow, he would change. Of
course he would. Certainly he would love others; girls too, Pierce
thought it likely. Dates. In fact it might be that the two of them would
rarely again, would not even once more.

And yet they would not cease to be lovers, never ever, no matter
how Robbie grew or how often or for how long life parted them,
never ever.

He showered and shaved, a whole working morning having vanished away, and dressed. He stood on the steps of his building rolling
a cigarette and remembering small details of the night and morning
that had passed: thinking he knew, now, what those nuns felt who in
the night or at Mass were embraced by smiling Christ or His Angel,
made to cry aloud as they were pierced with arrows or made to take
fiery swords upon their tongues: he knew just how hard it might be
for them to make a distinction between such experiences and ones
which other fleshly people might share with them.

He walks with me and He talks with me and He tells me I am His
own. Pierce could not have imagined this solution to his difficulties in
advance, but a solution it seemed to be. Doesn't matter, doesn't matter. He stepped off purposefully down Maple Street toward Hill
Street, though he had no purpose, and needed none.

His mailbox at the Post Office was empty, except for an extremely
small package from New York City, whose handwriting and address

he didn't at first recognize. Wrapped in brown paper that had before wrapped something else. He turned it in his fingers, teasing himself with its oddness for a minute.

As he opened it the problem of who had sent it was unwrapped too in his mind, the address, her changeable hand. Oh sure.

The Sphinx in New York had sent him, inside the brown paper, a matchbox from a City restaurant; and inside that, folded absurdly small, three hundred-dollar bills. And something else: a button to pin on his shirt, gathered on a junktique hunt presumably. It bore a wreath of tiny greeting-card roses, and in churchy script the words *Be of good cheer.*

He held the little button, feeling his soul topped up with luck and love. Maybe he had been wrong, about three wishes. What if, in coming upon Robbie and making him manifest, he had not completed a triad but instead had discovered an unsuspected malleability in the whole wide world? Maybe after wishing all his life for this and that, carefully framing his wishes or moaning them out in the desperate midnight, he had somehow hit on the trick of it; just as after he had blown fruitlessly through puckered lips for weeks and months he had found himself suddenly, though doing nothing apparently different, able to whistle.

Was there, in that case, anything else he would care for? He felt beside him the smiling cosmic waiter, the long menu, not able yet to be read, but coming maybe clearer.

On River Street, he glanced sidewise at the boys on their bikes, sunstreaked moptops, golden-tanned and lithe. It might be that a nice square wrist, a frank smile, borrowed from one or another of these kids could help clothe Robbie in flesh, who remained discouragingly not quite but almost discarnate. But these real physical boys, the idea of, of. No. The approach was unthinkable, and the imagined sensation repellent, or at least weirdly unlikely, like eating snails or bathing in milk.

"Hi."

"Hi there," Pierce said. "How was the game."

"Okay."

"Hey, good." Turning away from them, seeing them try to place this tall shambling guy (teacher? parent?); laughing inwardly and blushing. No he had *not* somehow contracted a new sex perversion overnight. He didn't want a new class of bodies to handle or a new sort of thrill to stir his jaded heart: he wanted a *person,* just one, this person alive to him and with him even now.

He would walk out of town, he thought. At the end of River Street there would be two ways he could go: up the road leftward, which traveled past the better residences and out to tidy farms and thence upward, spiraling around Mount Randa; or rightward across the bridge to the Shadow River road, a poorer part of town, a steeper way upward. He thought he would choose when he got to the cross-roads. Which way, son? You pick.

But when he came to the steps of the Blackbury Jambs Library, which faces on River Street, he saw Rose Ryder just coming down them, her bookbag over her shoulder and papers in her arms. The two of them drifted to a halt together, at the bottom of the steps. The moon, almost too pale to see in the sky above the library, slipped undetectably into a new sign.

"I said I'd see you here," she said. "Eventually."

"Yes," Pierce said.

She had indeed said so, not long ago, even as she rose away from Pierce and from the earth in the basket of a hot-air balloon. That was at a festival up on Skytop, marking summer's beginning. The basket contained not only her, Rose Ryder, but Mike Mucho and his little girl as well. The balloon was a Raven, vast and black. Pierce could almost hear its burner sound on River Street.

13

———

The Blackbury Jambs Free Library was completed in 1898, a sort of Shingle Style building with a central dome and wings, paid for by the Carnegie Foundation and opened on July Fourth, wrapped in bunting. In the entranceway is a mounted slab of mud with a dinosaur's footprint embedded in it; in the children's room a frieze of North American mammals, faded now almost to ghosts and surprising the unwary child who looks up to find them there. All of Fellowes Kraft's novels are there, of course, and a couple of his other books as well; he used to look into them, surreptitiously, to see if anyone was taking them out. He used the Blackbury Jambs Library a lot, despite having so many books of his own, and Pierce was eventually to come upon several of the Library's books among his, years overdue.

Rose Ryder worked there two or three mornings a week, in the big wing to the left of the entrance. She arrived early and made her place at a long table, by a green-shaded light; she took out from her bag a big pad of graph paper, a steel ruler, a fine-pointed draftsman's pen, and a pocket calculator for the math, which otherwise defeated her. Then she got up, went to the low shelves on the north wall (beneath a portrait of George Washington) and drew out a volume of the *Dictionary of American Biography,* and carried it back to her place. There she opened it, and as though practicing a sortilege, she riffled the pages, let them fall open randomly, and with her eyes closed put her finger on a name. If the entry or the life proved too short, she took the one before or after it.

She would pick up her ruler then, and score a line across the pad's width in peacock ink (her choice). Then, carefully counting squares, she would draw sharp parabolas, up and over the line and down under it again, a sine wave. She usually did this work the night before, but not last night, too crowded with crazy incident. At the top of the first parabola she wrote the number seven; and at the tops of the others, multiples of seven: fourteen, twenty-one, twenty-eight up to the last year of the life she was charting. It looked like this:

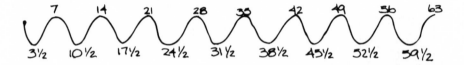

These weren't arbitrary divisions but were, according to Mike Mucho, who was the system's inventor, life's actual component units; for it was Mike's discovery that life, human life, comes in seven-year cycles of rise, climax, decline and re-arising. Rose arrayed the life she had chosen on the chart she had drawn, setting it out in seven-year parts. Early successes, breakdowns, breakthroughs, breakups; marriage, victory in battle or boardroom, illness, recovery; sudden bursts of illumination, or power, or despair: each noted in her tiniest hand on the mountains and valleys of life's journey.

When she had done this, she could begin the more subjective or judgmental part of her work, the creative part as she thought of it, the part she was good at: seeing how the life thus charted met or did not meet the predictions of the system (or of its inventor rather) about the nature and common course of life, the shaping force of its seven-year cycles. When she was all finished, and the particular life had yielded up its shape, then its accidents and incidents would be used to refine further the system's generalizations. She would have time, in the course of a morning's work, to thus dismantle and reassemble four or five lives.

Not this morning, though.

"Closed," she said to Pierce. "All day."

"Oh yes?"

"Fourth of July," she said, and somewhere nearby a string of crackers went off. Ladyfingers. "I just forgot."

"Well hell," he said. "Then come have a coffee with me."

She looked back up at the building, at its flags flying, as though it might relent and open; then back to Pierce.

"Okay," she said.

"It's a long-term project that I'm assisting someone on," she said to Pierce in the Donut Hole, settling on this formula not quite comfortably he thought. "A someone," she immediately added, "who has recently sort of lost interest."

"Oh?"

She picked up and tore in two a fragment of her pastry, looking out the front window of the little shop toward the river. She pondered what appeared from her face to be a grievance, and he waited to see if she would air it.

"It seems to me unfair," she said.

"Hm."

"When a project has gotten to a certain state, and people have worked hard to help."

"Yes."

"To just lose interest." She looked directly into Pierce's eyes. "I know how to do what I need to do. But I need some guidance."

"Sure," he said. "And this person . . ."

"A psychotherapist. The Woods Center." She sipped her coffee thirstily and brushed back the thick hair that fell forward when she drank.

"So," Pierce said. He thought he knew anyway what name she would not say. "What exactly does your part consist of?"

"Research," she said. "Compiling data, sort of, for a statistical model."

"Research on . . ."

She looked out the window, a curious twist to her mouth.

"I mean if you don't want to say," Pierce said; he well knew how fraught research can be, non-scholars would be surprised.

She considered a moment, and then took from her bag a clutch of duplicated sheets, graph paper, annotated in peacock ink.

"Lives," she said, and showed him.

Lives, beginning at zero, mount up a steady curve of learning and experience, meeting challenges, facing obstacles. At seven years children have achieved a sort of mastery; they stand on a plateau; they know what the world is and they know what they are within it, like it or not.

"Then comes a turn," said Rose, her explaining pencil taking the top of the curve.

Then comes a turn, not down so much as out (undrawable on graph paper) and new experience begins to threaten the early synthesis. Confusions and difficulties. "The Down Passage Year, here, where you cross the midline heading downward. A dangerous time." The wave overwhelms the little boat; the young life is tossed out to flounder. A nadir is reached. Rose's pencil tapped the bottom of the curve.

"Then you start up again," she said. "Slowly at first. You find out you've bottomed out."

"No place to go but up."

"Up," she said, and her pencil went up the next hill or wave. "Right *here* you cross the midline, and for the next year you are putting together this new hard stuff, working toward a new synthesis. An Up Passage Year. Kind of exciting. Until you reach a new Plateau Period, and now you know what's what again, you know who you are and what the rules are for being in the world."

"And then."

Her finger traced the way down again. "Down Passage Year." Then up to twenty-one. "Plateau Period." She looked up at him then, satisfied.

"That," Pierce said, "is absolutely remarkable."

"Now it's really just a beginning, but."

"No but I can see."

"And there is a certain, I mean. This is all supposed to be very . . ."

"My lips are sealed," Pierce said. "Absolutely. Not my field anyway," he added, looking down on her charts, which would have not puzzled any seventeenth-century doctor, though he might have envied them. "And this method is called . . ."

"Climacterics."

He laughed aloud, threw back his head and laughed. Whenever, in his ashen midnight wakings, he thought that the world really had no use any longer for the sort of practices he had promised his agent Julie Rosengarten that he could retail by the dozen, whenever he felt embarrassment or shame at his enterprise of magic, somebody would unfold to him a system for finding hidden treasure, or invite him to have his aura balanced, or define his life in mystic numbers. Climacterics!

"The Grand Climacteric . . ." she said.

"Is sixty-three. Seven years later . . ."

"You could go farther."

"You could," he said, still laughing.

She took no umbrage at his laughter, in fact she smiled too, and returned to her coffee. He looked at her, she at him. She put away her papers, and shook her long hair free of some tug somewhere.

"So," she said. "What is it that *you* do there?"

"Oh. Ah. Research too."

"Oh?"

"Well," he said. "Shouldn't I be circumspect? No, fair's fair; you told me. Actually my project is a little hard to describe. A little shocking."

"Oh come on."

"Intimate. Of course you're a professional. In a sort of allied field. So."

"So?"

"I'm doing work on magic," he said.

She lowered her cup to its saucer. "Magic," she said. "Not like, card tricks and stuff. Houdini."

"No. Not like." He said nothing more, smiling and open but not accommodating, allowing her to regard him in puzzlement. A kind of wonderful calm was in him, and an access to power in speech that he only rarely felt; he knew it was because Robbie was near, only a spiritual block away.

"Actually," he said, " 'magic' is sort of a hard word to say out loud, I think."

"Yes?"

"It is if you mean it. A little shaming to say. Like 'sex.' "

"Like sex?" She laughed.

"I mean it's a thing you want to keep at a distance. Even though it means a great deal to you, even *because* it does. It's just agreed on, under the rules of politeness. It won't be seriously discussed."

"You sound like you think it works," she said.

He leaned toward her and began to speak a little more urgently. "Magic comes in more than one kind," he said. "There's illusion, like you said; Houdini. And wonder-working, wave a wand, get what you want—that kind is restricted to stories. But there are other kinds, that were really practiced. For centuries. It doesn't seem likely that people would have gone to so much trouble for so long if what they did didn't work at all."

"Like pacts with the devil? Witchcraft?"

"No," Pierce said. "That kind wouldn't work unless there really is a devil, or was, who could help. You believe that?"

"I just got here," she said, and laughed again. "Spells?"

"Ah," Pierce said. "Ah." He brought out tobacco, and papers, and began making a cigarette. Magic *was* a hard word to say, he had always thought so, shaming by its power, its power among other things to make us look ridiculous when we take it seriously. Like sex. "Spells at least only require people. One to cast, one to receive. What's called *intersubjective* magic."

"You can resist," she said.

"Right. There are lots easier ways than magic to make you do something you don't want to do. You can refuse to be entranced; you can resist, you can deny the magician's claim to power. And if you do resist, everybody agrees the magician can't do a thing. What he can do is—knowing the secret springs of your nature, by means of his powers—he can make it very hard for you to resist."

"Yes?"

"He'd have to know first what kind of spirit yours was, and whether it was subject to magic at all. Not everyone's is."

"How would he know?"

"He'd know. He'd see," Pierce said. "In fact"—vamping now, he had never thought of these things before—"a danger for the great magician would have been that he was so sensitive himself to the projections of others. Which made his control even more heroic."

"Hm." She was paying close attention, it seemed, though perhaps not to him.

"Of course it's impossible to have perfect knowledge of somebody else's spirit. So he has to *convince* the person whose spirit he wants to bind that he does in fact have such perfect knowledge."

"Illusion? I thought you said."

"Well all magic partakes of illusion. Shared illusion." He drew the bill to his side of the table. "You have to have faith," he said. "I said so."

She seemed to ponder this silently, or maybe something else entirely, her own spell over herself; her hand, idly touching her neck and shirt, found a button that had come open, one top button too many, and her other hand moved to help button it.

"Don't," Pierce said. "Leave it."

Her hands paused in mid-task, and her eyes, into which Pierce was projecting this little command, seemed to fill with something that made them no less transparent but also somehow sightless.

Then she put her hands down on the table, looking away from him and from them, head erect though; and neither spoke for a moment.

"So tell me," Pierce said, but then only cleared his throat, having really nothing to say, speaking only to mask his awe, at his own daring, at its result. Good Lord it's true.

A rattle and bang of firecrackers, this one loud, lifting them both a millimeter. They laughed together. Moment passed. And yet the little varnished pine stall they sat in remained levitated, not much but a little, and was now turning, like a rising airship, into some sort of wind, toward somewhere; its movement too gentle even to be vertiginous, and yet definite.

Out on River Street. The Library was to the left; down to the right was another street upward, a long way round to his apartment. "So is he, are you, planning a book?"

"What?"

"Climacterics."

"Oh. Well. It's not been discussed. I mean we haven't even talked about this process *I'm* doing for *weeks*."

"It seems like a natural," he said, not missing the rancor in her voice. "Really." He could, in fact, see it on the paperback rack at the Variety Store already, in grabber colors. *Climacterics: Your New Ancient Guide to Life's Cycles*.

She turned to look at him, lips apart but not sure if she should smile or laugh, waiting for more.

"I happen," he said, "to be represented by an agent, who. This would be precisely up her alley. More than anything I."

"But it's not a book," Rose said, following him rightward. "It's a, well. A *practic*. He calls it."

"Not a book *yet*," Pierce said. "They're easily made. Listen. If you would like any help, on the historical part I mean, advice. Some books to look at. I mean it."

"Well," she said, laughing at his insistence.

"Hey," he said, guiding her toward his street with a touch on her elbow. "Research is where you find it."

Soon she stood at the door of his peculiar apartment, a string of three rooms: kitchen, little parlor, and (largest by far) the room that was both bedroom and study, where he worked: a piled messy desk, the powder-blue electric typewriter on its stand, and many books.

"You work in bed?" she asked, hands in her pockets, at the door of this room. Pierce laughed, thinking of answers to this. The bed was overlarge, brass, mounded with pillows, and clothed just now in dark Turkish-looking stuff.

"You have a sun-porch too," she noted. She pointed to the door, beyond which was Robbie's daybed, still unmade, where Pierce had spent the morning. "Nice."

"Yes," he said. "Everything I need." Was Robbie cross with him? He checked to see. No not cross. Interested, actually; even eager. Pierce felt the warmth of his interest, his wide eyes and the curve of his mouth, and he nearly laughed aloud, made of glee by now and the effervescence of certain power. Why you little.

"Books," she said.

"Books."

He watched as she passed slowly into the bedroom, her hand moving over a case of them, touching their spines with her fingertips, making him think of a diver examining a coral reef or sunken ship. A small cloud crossed the sun; the undersea wavered, and then restored itself.

"You know," he said. "I've never forgotten that river party. Last summer."

"Uh huh," she said.

"It's a funny story, actually," he said. "What I thought then. I'll tell you sometime."

She turned to face him, a look of perfect incomprehension and a dreamy lack of interest, as though it had nothing to do with her.

"Anyway I think of it often. The little cabin. Breaking in."

"Cabin?" she asked.

He studied her, as coolly as he could amid the currents already flowing between them, and an odd certainty was handed him. "You don't remember, do you?" he asked, smiling.

"Remember what?" she asked.

14

———

n that morning Rosie Rasmussen had awakened smiling, pleased, without at first knowing the reason. When Sam (who had maybe awakened her, stirring in the next room) saw that her mother was awake, she came to stand grinning up at her in her tall bed: and Rosie remembered the dream she had had, a ridiculous pornographic dream, impossible and gratifying.

"How come you're up, Mom?"

"How come *I'm* up! You just woke me up. How come *you're* up."

"That's what I *mean*."

"Oh."

She had dreamed that she lived in some mild paradisal island or planet, warm sunshot forests populated by men, well by enormous creatures who looked like men; in her memory they almost seemed more like fruit, sun-warmed and smooth-skinned, pink as babies. She herself was one of another species, female, tiny and quick and cunning, who lived with and from the men; she and her kind spent their time trying to rouse the great big baby-like males, to get them hard so they could be sucked, which was somehow not only sex and procreation for the females but nourishment as well. So slow and bland were the men, though, that it took all kinds of cosseting and teasing to get them up, they hardly noticed the little females at work on them.

She did get hers, though; she remembered his sweet sleepy smile as she watched her clamber over him and work, not minding her but not real attentive, like a cow being milked (how it was even possible for her to fit him in her hand and mouth given the disparity in their sizes the dream didn't bother explaining, it just was possible, even easy). And she remembered how at last the big thing gave up to her at last its flood, like a primed pump gushing: and the keen delight that had filled her in the dream filled her again, astonishment, accomplishment, gratification, nourishment all together. Crazy, crazy, crazy.

"The sun woke me up," Sam said. "The sun hit my eye."

"Like a big pizza pie."

Crazy, when it wasn't even anything she often elected to do in waking life, she was a good sport about it but it was he not she that got the big fun, after all. And the little dab of viscous goo, be brave, like swallowing medicine.

Not Mike, though: when it was his turn he used to dive right in.

"Is today a Daddy day?"

"Yup."

"What are you going to do?"

"Oh go someplace."

"With who?"

"What if it was by myself?"

"Is it with Spofford?"

"Maybe."

Why do men like to give Oral Sex? Why did this stump her? She had a sudden vision of the dark boulder of Mike's head lodged between her legs, of him surfacing momentarily, gazing up at her for her approval, and cross-eyed with bliss: why? She knew why she liked it, but why did he?

"Well anyway now we're both up, so get in."

"So get in," said Sam in delight.

Sam climbed laughing up and under the covers, her sleepy-warm legs tangling with Rosie's, her arms eagerly clasping Rosie's neck. And Rosie knew, hugging her, that what she had dreamed of wasn't Oral Sex or even sex at all, what she had dreamed of was breast-feeding: not sucking but suckling. With the mother transformed into the slow gentle baby-like man, and herself made the baby. She knew it, because she knew, at Sam's touch, that it had been, somehow, Sam she had dreamed of. And maybe of her own mother too: could a person remember so far back?

"Are these your breasts?" Sam asked, poking lightly with a fore-finger at one, inside Rosie's big T-shirt.

"Yes."

"I have breasts too. See?"

She lifted her own T-shirt, and pointed to the unopened buds on her chest.

"Yes. I see."

"For my little kid to get milk."

"Uh huh."

Mike always claimed he could actually remember the sensation of his mother's breast in his mouth, the pressure of the nipple against his palate; he made this claim with a particular pleased expression, quite an achievement (Rosie always thought the expression meant) for a psychotherapist.

Maybe it wasn't sex at all that men wanted, really, when they settled in that way, all smiles; maybe it was mother's milk, and they were just a little confused.

She laughed softly, and the shaking of her ribcage shook Sam, who laughed too.

"Mommy. Is Rose coming with Daddy?"

"Gee I don't know, hon. Rose is I think sort of out of the picture."

"She can do a French braid."

"Yes? I guess."

"Yets go downstairs, Mommy."

"You're not happy here? I'm happy," Rosie said, really unwilling to leave the sheets, warmed deeply at the root as you can only be by knowledge communicated in a dream.

She had learned when Sam was an infant that giving suck was like sex in a kind of a way; she had only just now thought that sex was like giving suck. No not *like* it: that was the secret, that was what the dream had told her: sex *was* it, not different from it. What she had thought to be two different things were going to turn out to be one thing: Sex, and nurture, sucking, succor, solace: all the same.

Yes!

"So yets," said Sam.

"Okay okay."

What everyone mostly felt, even the hot ones, *especially* the hot ones, and called *sex* was just the delight of solace and succor, the oblivion of nursing, the satisfaction of the watered root. That's what hotness *is*. Sex just puts that delight to its own uses, for making babies.

Making more babies who want more nurture and succor. Because if we didn't want to get and give nurture and succor, if that wasn't what we mostly wanted, to suck and give suck and get life and give life, then we wouldn't be here at all. Would we. If we didn't want it more or less continuously. Would we.

Succor, the word had come into her mind unbidden, she wasn't sure what it meant or what it had to do with sucking but she thought it was what she needed: what she had dreamed of having.

God. It was obvious, so obvious that as soon as it occurred to her she seemed to have always known it; so simple that either everyone knew it, or no one did. Probably everyone did; probably everyone just came to know it automatically as they grew up, never thought it needed pointing out, probably no one had ever seen the need to tell her.

"*This* oh *Man* he plays *One, he* plays knick-knack on my bum."

"Thumb, hon. Thumb."

Sam squealed with delight at her invention, and slid down from the bed. Rosie scrambled after her, to snatch her up, shushing and laughing. "He plays *One,*" Sam shouted out, "*he* plays knick-knack on my *BUM!*"

Piggybacking Sam through the dark of the living room, stopping at the little three-legged table where the big dictionary was.

Succor. Had a cloud come over the sun? No it was her own shadow getting between her and the day. Old familiar shadow, hi.

"What's that book?"

"Dictionary. All the words."

No: not something about sucking. Only help, aid, relief, in time of need or distress. From *Succurrere,* hurry to the help of.

Hurry, hurry.

Where would she get succor? She didn't mind giving it, she had always known how to give it, it was no credit to her especially, since it had always used to flow out of her at a touch, as from a tap, and she didn't mind. Only how was she to get it?

She thought with a spasm of dark contrary feeling: *Succor your-self.*

She didn't know how to do that, though. Maybe Cliff knew. If Cliff asked her to make a list for herself, as he had asked Spofford to do, she would put that on it.

If Rose Ryder was not out of the picture, Mike had certainly changed his habits. The vehicle that turned in at Arcady to pick up Sam was not Rose's little Asp as it had usually been in the past months, but a van from The Woods, tubby and shiny in the bee-loud morning. It came only as far as the turn-around, from where its horn was honked in a cheery beebeep, and Sam leapt up, always glad to ride in a new conveyance.

"Kiss?" said Rosie, and Sam turned back, brimful of delight, expectation, love, and gave her a happy goodbye; was this really going to turn out to be an okay way to live? When the sliding side door was opened and Mike got out to get Sam, Rosie saw that there were others in the van with him—three? Four? The tinted windows and brilliant morning made it hard to see. Mike lifted Sam into the air, higher, higher, till she shrieked; then he put her inside the dark van. Rosie watched her disappear within, and the door close behind her with a thud.

Hi, Mike, no wave hello even.

Who were those young guys? They had white shirts on, short-sleeved, and ties, but no jackets; trim haircuts. Trim smiles too. What sort of person was she reminded of, where, when? Jocks or salesmen or. She couldn't place them.

"Bye-bye," she said, and waved, not sure Sam was looking her way any longer. "Bye-bye."

The van was gone.

This was the problem, she thought: that you might sometimes want to get away from love, might try to break the bond or at least tug on it to make it slacken. Only to find. That was what was hardest, for a heart like hers, not that you could not love or give love but that you couldn't avoid it, couldn't ever get out of the standing wind of love all around you, find shelter from it. When Mike lifted Sam into his arms she knew it: the hollow in her breast was caused by love, by whatever in her had gone wrong about love. She had tried to heal it by hiding from love, but that only made it worse, because you almost couldn't escape it, no one could, even if you became a nun or a recluse you would always know you'd done it because of sex 'n' kids and avoiding all that; and anyway there would always be behind you your parents conceiving you, your father lifting you in his arms.

She thought for some reason of Pierce Moffett, so evidently hungry for someone to think about besides himself, but talking with silly pride about being reconciled to being barren, "without issue," as he said, and meantime drying up in some kind of envy he didn't even recognize; he wasn't a bad guy, he was only ignorant, ignorant of what he could not be informed about. What parents knew about love and couldn't tell other people, who thought it was a project or an enterprise, a passion, a contest you won or lost. It wasn't. It was more like a wind, a steady wind, a wind you could not stand out of.

Love. She wanted to make a painting, a painting of love, of people, a family, living and at work say, but all of them standing in that constant and invisible wind. But of course you couldn't do it. Because how could you paint an invisible wind?

And she thought then that actually it had been done, in that Giorgione painting, of the Tempest: three people, man woman and child, out in the open, under a dark and lightning-broken sky. He with his weapon apart, the two others together, the child sucking, oblivious. A family, certainly, alone together in the wind of love. Rosie's heart filled with pity, and she wept.

In the dark house behind her an alarm clock rang briefly, and ceased. Boney's, to remind him to take his morning pill. Rosie wiped her eyes on her shirt-tail. Ought to visit, see if there was anything she could do for him; and let him know (it made her feel guilty, though he would never object or even hint at an objection) that she would be away most of the day. With her lover.

She got up, went into the cool and odorous house, down the hall to Boney's office, which had been Boney's bedroom too for the last two weeks. When she knocked and entered he looked up at her, startled and trembling in a way that frightened her, she always expected him to take sudden turns for the worse, and she would have to rise to an emergency she could not imagine in advance.

"Hi," she said. "How are you?"

He appeared to ponder the question, or perhaps he hadn't even noticed it, was still trying to place her. He sat up on his chaise longue, wearing a pretty extravagant bottle-green kimono with a great snorting grinning dragon on its back, and a white towel around his throat.

"I wanted to tell you," she said. "I've made an appointment for today. Will you be all right for a while? Mrs. Pisky's going to come at noon."

"Certainly. Yes. Fine."

"Need anything now? I could . . ."

"No nothing. Rosie. I wanted to say."

She waited while he seemed to gather power; but then he only held up to show her the book he had in his lap. "Have you read this?"

She recognized it: it was Fellowes Kraft's little book of reminiscences, privately printed, that Boney had offered to let her read when she first began to work for the Foundation. It was called *Sorrow, Sit Down.*

"Well, I've read *in* it," she said, Pierce's handy formula.

He held it out to her, his hands shaking more than usual, the open book a caught bird in them. Rosie took it from him, and began to read at the first full paragraph.

It has often seemed to me that many men of the past—men of the sixteenth century anyway, men of power and responsibility—bore always in their hearts some sort of unassuageable sadness. Look into the eyes of their portraits—even official artists out to flatter them often seem to catch it, a kind of longing or incompletion. Psychiatrists now might say it's not surprising, given the atrocious childhoods most hereditary nobles had to endure, given over to wetnurses and tutors, sent to live in the houses of other magnates not always friendly to them, subject to endless ritual obligations, their parents plotted against, murdered often enough if they weren't themselves plotting against their children.

"I don't know if I got this far," Rosie said. "I don't remember this."

Perhaps it was this inadmissable sadness inside, whatever caused it, that made so many of them so fond of jewels. Jewels seemed to represent to them something longed for, they seemed to be completion itself I think. Poems and stories are full of tedious catalogues and descriptions of them. And yet no single jewel ever really healed them or stilled their restlessness, and so they were always looking for others, spending fortunes on them, little cold promises of fullness.

They were believed to grow, like living things (as indeed some crystals do grow) deep inside the mountains, bound up in a matrix or womb of base earth and stone; such jewels had grown up (from pebbles or clods I suppose) to become, finally, perfect, or almost perfect: changeless, as nothing else beneath the moon was changeless. In effect they had achieved eternal life. And perhaps what those hungry collectors thought was that one day one might be found in the mountains, or forced in the alchemical furnaces, or discovered in the plundered collections of their enemies, one fabulous something that would convey its immortality right into the heart of him who wears it.

"Well," she said, lowering the book, not understanding still his urgency. He pointed to the book.

"There's a note," he said.

She looked at the page, thinking it bore a written note, from Kraft. No he meant a footnote, in small secretive type at the right-hand page's bottom:

Of course if one knew the location or the provenance of such a jewel, one would want to be wise enough to spurn it for oneself, and not offer it or reveal it to others either. We have all read the stories. We are wiser now, or ought to be, and satisfied with our three score years and ten—extended only by the lapis lapidarum of scientific medicine. I at any rate will let my sleeping toad lie, and not take foolishly the jewel of his head.

Rosie lowered the book. It was evident that Boney was genuinely stricken, but it was not possible (Rosie thought) that it could be because of what this note of Kraft's said.

"Well so," she said gently.

"So he knew," Boney said. "He did. Even then."

"Knew what, Boney?"

He looked away then, unwilling to say. His open mouth sought for breath. Rosie thought: maybe he's going crazy. Senility. She should ask Mike. She felt a hot grief, at the unfairness of it: to have been allotted such a long life, so long that finally it goes bad.

"Did you sleep okay?" she said, fatuously, trying to fool him into dropping the subject, as Sam sometimes could be fooled.

"I don't sleep," he said. "Afraid I won't wake up." He was trying to climb from the chaise, unable to lift himself; Rosie came to help. He took her hand. No matter that he had lost mass over the last two weeks: he was heavy if you had to get him upright.

"Look," he said. "Look here."

He got to his desk. Three piles of papers covered it, and Rosie recognized Fellowes Kraft's hand, the small neat letters and long descenders. Boney rested his hand on one pile as though he meant to swear an oath on them. "There was supposed to be, somewhere there, over there I mean, some something: Kraft said he knew what it was, *where* it was anyway. Something made, or found, or. And it was that thing."

"That thing?"

"The jewel. Or something like it. He said."

Rosie watched him stare down at the piles of blue onionskin and torn envelopes. "I'll leave these here," he said. "Look at them. You'll see. He said he brought it home with him."

"Boney," Rosie said. "It's just a *story*."

"I've tried and tried, Rosie, but I just can't anymore. I hate to burden you with it, honestly. But I just." He held himself up with the desk's edge, and his arms trembled with the effort. He seemed near tears. "Why did I wait, why. Why."

"Listen," Rosie said. "Boney. Even if he really *thought* he'd found something. He was wrong."

Boney raised his head to look at her, a wild hope or fear in his eyes, good grief what should she do with him. "Because he's dead," Rosie said. It seemed obvious to her. "He got sick and died."

He laughed, and Rosie laughed too, glad to join him. He turned away from the letters on the desk, and she helped him back to the couch.

"Of course. Oh of course." He lay back again into his pillows. "Why should one old man, one old man of no special merit, why. When everyone, everyone else has gone over, as far as anyone knows. Only a fool would think there might be some, some." He lifted Kraft's book again, and it began tap tapping in his lap. "Oh I can say it, I can. But."

"But it's . . ."

"But I have to know what he meant. I have to know. Just so I can."

Die, Rosie thought. She sat down in the chair beside his couch, took the book from his lap and closed it.

A jewel to fill the hollow of your heart. How could it be that Boney could want life, just life, so much when she wanted it so little? There was the story of the woman who agreed to go down into the underworld in her husband's place, just because he didn't want to go. Once upon a time the woman's willingness had astonished Rosie, but maybe there was a story untold within the story, maybe she hadn't really minded all that much: stay, go, no difference, not so much difference anyway that she couldn't be kind to someone who cared a lot.

He spoke, not to her, too low for Rosie to hear. She bent closer. "Sorry?" she whispered. "Boney?"

"I just don't want to die," he said, and Rosie could see that tears had formed again in the reddened cups of his eyes. "I don't want to. I don't know why I have to."

He had taken her wrist in a strong grip, as though to keep himself moored on the planet. Succor. "Well are you afraid?" she asked, not knowing what else to ask, what the right question was, if there was one, that would ease him; appalled and fascinated that he should want it from her, that he didn't know it himself, that it was possible to come so close to the end of the story and still be able not to know.

"I just *don't*," he said, "I don't want to," and a shiver crossed Rosie's shoulders; his voice was eerily, terribly, like Sam's, saying she didn't want to go with Daddy, didn't want to go to sleep. All compact of hurt and desolation, and for no reason, none.

He had not released her wrist. How could she tell him to be brave? Would she be? Her own father had slipped out of life as though he were getting out of something unpleasant, doing the dishes maybe, sorry, got an appointment I can't break.

The cruel thing was that to everybody else it seemed Boney had already acquired whatever it was that kept you alive forever; it was as though he had made a deal long ago with life to avoid all that used up other people, children and marriage and a job and everything that might consume him, take up his time, so that in return his time would stretch out indefinitely; maybe he had, and like Midas had got what he wanted, and couldn't unwish it now.

He said no more. Rosie sat with him a long time in the advancing morning, holding his hand when he began to weep again or fret, until at length Spofford's truck turned in at the drive.

15

---

hree peaks ascend above the low green Faraway Hills, organizing and lending scale to them, Mount Merrow to the northeast across the Blackbury, Mount Whirligig to the west sundered by the valley of the Shadow from Mount Randa, greatest and oldest of the three and pleasingly central, like a castle keep amid its towers.

Rosie Rasmussen had been born in the Faraways, though she had been taken away when she was ten to live in the Midwest, in a place where there were no mountains and even "hill" was largely a courtesy title (Hillcrest Mall, Greenhills Estates). She was still not always aware of standing on a mountain's slopes, or ascending one, and was surprised sometimes to take a turn on a rising road, and find herself high up. Spofford always knew: where he stood, where the next valley ran and what road ran through it.

"Well, you live here all your life," he said, turning the truck's wheel with both hands through a sharp turn upward.

"But you were gone," Rosie said. "Those years."

He had spent time away: two years in the Army, two in Southeast Asia (other peaks, other river valleys), two in New York City. One or part of one (Rosie could never fit it into the bio exactly) in an institution of some kind, somewhere more drastic maybe than The Woods, but not quite a madhouse: his allusions to it were rare, and invited no questions.

"It was one of the things I found out I could do that used up the time," he said, and Rosie guessed what the time to be used up might be. "I could say All right, standing at the upper end of my orchard, what's behind me to the north, what's east, where does the road run, where does it meet another. That kind of thing. You get a map in your head. The area's still full of surprises though. Places I've never been."

They had left the tarred road upward and entered onto a dirt one.

"So where does he live?" Rosie said. "In a cave?"

"Not really."

"I'm a little nervous," Rosie said. "I guess I'm actually pretty nervous."

"Why?"

"Well some guy is about to examine my insides somehow. Doesn't the idea of that make you nervous?"

Spofford laughed. "Well I think you're imagining it wrong. Hey look."

At a turning the woods opened to the west, and Mount Randa was framed in the gap, like a postcard view: the new green of its trees, mottled in darker fir; the bald pate of rock on its height. No alp at all, only a nice heap of forested earth; old, old. Between here and there, this mountainside and that one, came the valley of the Blackbury, where the people lived, where she lived herself, with Boney and Sam. Her throat was suddenly thick with sweetness, and tears welled in her eyes. Welled. What is *with* you today, she asked herself.

"Can't see the orchard," Spofford said smiling, for on the slopes of Randa was his own old mountainside orchard, where the apple trees had long gone wild, and where now he was at work building a new house on an old foundation. He almost passed Cliff's driveway down.

"He built the house mostly himself," Spofford said.

Rosie felt alone again. Spofford had told her stories of vets he knew who had just opted out, moved into the woods, lived in the rags of their old fatigues and hunted game with an M16 smuggled out of Vietnam. She put her hand on Spofford's arm as he maneuvered down.

She wouldn't, herself, choose to live in the woods. So many trees so nearby, crowding up together to stare at you like people at an accident, resentful maybe of their sawn-off buddies in your yard. Tree-fingers coming in the windows. Inescapable damp and rot, the smell of claustrophobia. Today though brilliant and sunshot and welcoming, and the house a nice one really, ramifying in unexpected directions up a hillside, its unpainted boards and battens turning silvery, tin roofs slanting every which way and ashine, and a big window wall made of—huh, made of a row of old storm doors neatly carpentered into place.

"Nice," she said, so tentatively that Spofford laughed.

But it was also, unmistakably, uninhabited at the moment. How is it that a house can be read so certainly, some houses anyway. They both felt it, though since they had no good reason to think it, neither said anything; Spofford stopped the truck, got out, called.

"Yo. Cliff."

Confirming silence. Rosie (arms still crossed protectively before her) walked up to the house and around to the back. A garage beneath the living space where no car was but where the tools of a strenuous existence were neatly racked and hung, huge-toothed saws and a chain saw and a brush hog, axes and long shovels. A motorcycle under a blue plastic tarp. A guru with a motorcycle!

"Phooey," said Spofford behind her.

"Is it because it's the Fourth?"

"Christ," he said. "Hard to imagine."

For a while they waited in his mossy yard (Spofford said he was sure it was all right to go in, make some tea, but Rosie shook her head) and tossed pebbles at a metal drum to hear it ring. Then they stood to go.

"Well now I'm disappointed," Rosie said cheerfully. She got in the odorous truck and pulled the door shut. "Now I won't find out what he was going to do."

"We'll come back," Spofford said, downcast. "I'm sorry. Really."

"Oh, don't be. It was interesting anyway."

He pulled the truck back onto the road.

"So what *does* he do?"

"Oh. Various kinds of things. Depending."

"But what kinds of things?"

"Body stuff, mostly. It's hard to describe what kinds of things because so much of it is just Cliff seeing, or feeling I guess. He says *Get into your feet.* And you try to do that, with Cliff watching or feeling with you, even though it doesn't mean much to you at first."

"Get into your feet?"

"Try it." Spofford tried it himself, looking inward, breathing softly, and letting go, momentarily, of the truck's wheel.

"Hey."

He took the wheel again lightly, with the tips of his fingers.

"We could stop," she said.

Spofford shrugged, and turned the truck onto a logging road that just then appeared. Tender mosses filled the old wheel ruts, and its long center hump was tufted with grasses and wildflowers that tickled the truck's undercarriage. He stopped.

"Okay," said Rosie.

"Okay," said Spofford. He spread his hands on the knees of his jeans. On the back of one a pale fish was tattooed. A kind of tentative inwardness had come into his manner, as though he approached a shy animal, himself, who might flee or might hold still for a moment if he were calm with it. "Okay. We'll get into our feet."

Silence and the woods.

"See, I can't do what Cliff does," Spofford said after a time. "What he does is to guide you. He'll *tell* you if you're doing what he's asking."

"You tell me."

"I'll try."

He paid attention to her, and to the ambient actuality, in the way that Cliff did. Rosie, taking her cues from him, didn't close her eyes or assume a meditative pose; she only tried to sense her two feet.

"Yes, right," said Spofford, and in fact Rosie just then felt her appendages begin to wake; far off, across an intervening desert or silence that was the most or the rest of her.

"Huh," she said.

"Can you get into one, then the other?"

"I dunno." Left first, then Right, she could in fact make them tingle and swell in turn. Weird.

"Get them down on the ground, on the earth."

"We're not *on* the earth."

"Whatever. The bottom."

Her feet, as big now as clown's feet or bear-paws, rooted her. She laughed.

Spofford looked over at her. "See?" he said.

"I guess." She lifted her heels, and put them down again. Hello, feet. "Now what?"

"Well you might try this when you feel too light," Spofford said.

"When you feel yourself leaving your body, or feel all of you collected in your head, and disconnecting. See?"

"Um," Rosie said.

"Then there's heart," Spofford said, and touched his breast.

"Oh."

"Or your back," Spofford said. "Lower back. That's a hard one for some people."

She checked that way. Nothing stirred that she noticed. "Lower back?"

"Well"—he laughed—"yeah. Way low. The end of your tailbone, sort of. Down." His knees opened slightly, as though to allow his spirit passage. "Down," he said, or commanded, softly.

How is it we can think we have space inside us? Rosie wondered. When it's all jampacked with organs, tissues, fluids, who knows what? It feels, it felt to her just then, as she sent out her queries, like a system of caves, branching tunnels, softly alight or dark and unexplorable.

"Hm," Spofford said.

"Not so easy," she said. She backed out of her inward spaces, her Carlsbad Caverns, and returned herself to the sun-hot day and the locusts. She breathed it in, and breathed in Spofford's big presence too beside her. And at that she felt (not in herself so much as in the woods and the wide world) a shift, an aliveness, a dragon-stirring of some kind. Hello?

"So," Spofford said. His breast expanded within the T-shirt, and fell again. He scratched at a coral bugbite on his brown arm. Rosie remembered her dream. "We done?"

He turned to her smiling, not exactly embarrassed (she had seen him abashed and ashamed but she didn't think she'd ever seen him embarrassed) but done with this game.

"I don't know," Rosie said. "I think I got *too* low."

"Oh ho," Spofford said. "Big danger."

"Well," Rosie said. "Your own fault."

She shifted on the smooth leather of the truck seat, and slipped her feet (still heavy and warm) from their sandals. He still smiled at her, glad for her, happy for himself too; and Rosie was whelmed so suddenly with the fullness she had felt in her dream, fullness all glee and triumph, that she laughed aloud.

"What."

"Cmere," she said. She undid the top button of his heavy jeans, and together they worked them open, thick tough pelt protecting the soft dark parts within.

Big. Not as big though as the dream-fruit she had fed on.

"Hey," he said gently after a time. His warm hands on her cheeks and in her hair. "Careful. Unless . . ."

"Oh. Oh. Sorry," she whispered. "Getting carried away, huh."

O Summer, she thought; O big sweetness for a while, thank God, forget the rest. She let him lift her up, lift her shirt. Succor. She was flowing freely and fully, for the first time in ages.

"I *didn't* mean for this to happen," Rose Ryder said to Pierce. "Really I didn't."

It might have been an accusation, a charge, and if it were, he would not have known how to answer it; but it wasn't a charge, it was something more like an apology, and not to him either.

"Well," he said, attempting gentle gallantry, "I'm glad it did."

She didn't seem to feel deep regrets; she paid him a nice smile, searching idly amid the pillows and sheets for her clothes.

"Here," he said. He found her skimpy underthings, this one, that one. Without asking, he lifted her foot and slipped her panties over it, then the other foot, and drew them up. She made no protest; her agitated hands, though, ceased their searching, and fell still. Then the bra. He hooked it for her in the back. His own hands only lightly strayed from the work.

"Where's your, ah here."

He shook out the rumpled shirt, and she held out her arms to have it put on. Buttons: she watched his unhandy big fingers do them, and he did too, and at the successful completion of each, they lifted their eyes to meet.

When the medieval physiologists (monks, most of them, after all) pondered the strange disease of *amor hereos,* crazy love, they used to put the question: *How does a woman, who is so large, enter in through the eye, which is so small?* For unless she could get in, and thus into the temple of the soul, the contagion couldn't take hold. Actually of course they knew how; they only asked it that way in order to make clear the wonder of it, the astonishment of the transformation: a corporeal woman transformed at the frontier of the eye into a phantasm, incorporeal, made only of Meaning, which is the food of the soul, all it can ever consume.

He put her white sneakers on, and would have tied the laces too, but she withdrew from the game then and did them herself, returning the day and the scene to normal speed. She began to talk rapidly and inconsequentially: Her appointment. Her work.

"I don't even know where you live," he said.

"In Shadowland," she said. "You know?"

"Good Lord," he said. "No I don't."

"It's not even a town," she said. "Up the river toward The Woods."

"A phone?"

"Not now. Soon."

"Oh."

She let him kiss her cheek on parting, chums; but not to let her out or come with her. But then at the door she turned again to him.

"Say," she said. "Do you like fireworks?"

"You think of the strangest things," Rosie said to Spofford, and starting to laugh nearly wept instead, so full of liquid that she overflowed. In the window of Spofford's cabin, by his big lumpy bed, the sky had turned to evening green, but still bright, still day.

"Sure," he said.

What she had been thinking about as they coupled, her head apparently entirely disconnected from the rest of her and free to amuse itself, was the old tower carillon at college, which her first real lover had played. The echoey stone tower-room and the polished wood of the bell levers; the spring hills and fields you could see and own from those open windows. He grunted and sang as he pushed the levers down, they nearly lifted him off the ground in their return; he sang the songs in the hesitant *largo* which was as fast as he could play. *I come to—the gar-den—alone. When the dew is—fresh on—the roses.* Press, press, and each press answered by a huge bellboom, whose echo swallowed up the next bell's sounding and the next till the harmonics shook her ribcage and buttocks with delight.

"Oh. I've got to go, got to go," she murmured.

"Naw," he said.

She asked the transformed day What is this? How does the pressing of the big levers, becoming easier with every press, do this to things, make them translucent and welcoming, offering themselves to me, to change if I want them to, or stay the same if I want them to?

Wanting is life. Dreams are life. Only you weren't to want things to remain the same, or dream they could.

She thought: If the world really were under a dark spell, was this all it took to wake it? And if she could awaken it—from within, from inside her own self—then could she push, just a little bit, the other way, and make it sleep again?

"Christ," Spofford said, laughing lightly and regarding her absorption. "You look about stoned out of your bean."

"Well that Cliff," she said. "Some therapist, huh? Some kinda guy."

From a house down the mountain that they could not see, a rocket arose into the lucent air, drawing an uncertain line of smoke behind; then stopped, and went off with a proud little pop.

"Take me down, will you."

"Don't want to. But okay."

Another rocket, lofted from another backyard over the dark oaks of Arcady as Spofford drove in at the gate, ascended bravely, wavered, fell, went off; a handful of orange sparks fell earthward.

"Going to look in on the guys one more time," Spofford said.

"I'll walk from here," Rosie said. "See you."

"Hey. I might come knock on the back door. Get my goodnights."

"Oh don't, okay. Mrs. Pisky's here."

She slipped from the seat and started up the drive. There seemed to be no lights lit in the front of the house, usually there were by now, and the still-bright sky above made the house a blank darkness.

Now what's this. Parked in the driveway by the front door was a Beetle, unmistakably Val's: it had the plastic flower on its radio antenna by which Val found it in crowded parking lots. And the front door of the house, Rosie could see now, stood open.

She went in, the big cutout screen door swinging slowly closed behind her of its own or the breeze's volition. The front hall went straight back through the house, living room, dining room, both dark, to the library in the back. Lights were on in there.

He's dead, she thought, and she felt herself resisting her own quick progress toward the door, though her feet kept going. She pushed open the door.

Not dead. He looked at her, when she came in, with the same startled and uncomprehending look he had worn that morning. But he was different: sicker, a lot sicker.

Val sat on a straight-back chair near him; she too had looked up in guilty alarm when Rosie came in.

"What is it?" Rosie asked. "Did he have . . ."

"Don't know," Val said. "Doctor was here, I guess. Earlier. You weren't here. He wanted him to go in the hospital right away. But I guess he said no."

"Oh no really?" Rosie's heart had begun to beat faster. "Boney are you sure."

He made no response. Rosie wondered if he knew he was not alone.

"So a nurse is supposed to come," Val said. "She should be here now. The housekeeper person—"

"Mrs. Pisky."

"She went to call again."

Rosie came to the couch. "Boney," she said. He lifted a hand. He knew she was there.

"Now he says he has to pee," Val said. "Go to the bathroom. Can we? If we each get an arm."

"Well," Rosie said. "Maybe with Mrs. Pisky."

"Okay," Val said. "He was getting kind of anxious." She had put her elbow in her palm, and rested her chin on the knuckles of her hand; she looked down at Boney as the doctor in old chromos looks down on the dying child in the makeshift bed. Fading Away.

"Val," Rosie said. "Why are you here?"

She had almost not come. She had not dared to leave the Faraway Lodge that evening until the moon had exited her own sign and entered the next, afraid that in her own sign it might unsettle her or make her weep; then, after she had set out and gone a mile or two she stopped, her resolve draining away; and she had had to return to the Lodge, make tea, wait for herself to refill.

She hadn't told Mama where she was going, and when Mama looked in on her there at the kitchen table with a mug before her ("Today is the first day of the rest of your life," the mug said) Val spoke a little sharply to her, to keep her away. If Mama got it out of her (and it trembled like a drop ready to fall, just inside her) then Mama would, might, forbid her to go; and contemptuously as Val usually treated Mama's forbiddings and orders, she didn't think she could flout that one easily; and she doubted she had the stuff to decide more than once to do this.

And any day now (it might have been any day in the last five years, he was way overdue) he might die, and she'd be left without it done.

She had imagined the scene taking place in different ways depending on the shifting state of her feelings; she had imagined it in different ways since she had been a teenager, living long with a single version of it, then suddenly changing to a different one for reasons of her soul's that she often didn't understand. Years went by when she didn't think of it at all, and then months, summers, winters, when she thought of little else.

Angry, righteous, triumphant. Scornful. Sorrowful, reproachful. Needy and demanding for once in her life. Grave and judging. Cruel. What she couldn't know, what was necessary to know for the playing of each of these scenes, was how he felt, what he knew, what he had thought over the years; she could only imagine, and as her feelings underwent changes, his imagined responses did too.

Mama said that he never denied it, never spurned her or told her she couldn't prove it or that *he* could prove that it was damn unlikely and that there were a lot of other candidates; but then Mama always claimed she was highly regarded and had been treated with courtesy and kindness, not by the nobodies but by the somebodies or near- or sub-somebodies she had known over time, which included some local big men and a few entertainment celebrities so minor their very names raised giggles.

And Boney Rasmussen.

Growing up, Val had felt herself to be held within a flexible net of evasions and things poorly explained, a net which held her away from certain matters at certain ages and others later. When she was very young (Mama still pretended to believe Val made up these memories) she'd been allowed into the cabins tucked away in the pines, to help Mama clean up; the women who sort of lived there were always sleepy and glad to see her. Then she was forbidden the cabins, and a little later they were all shut. When she was a teenager and nothing Mama said mattered much to her, she went into the cabins again, and smelled the dank smell of their spavined beds, looked into drawers lined with wartime newspapers where a few hairpins lay. Meanwhile Mama had put a little effort into describing her father, lost gone absent far away, not very much more effort than she put into the Tooth Fairy or the Sandman, and Val never pressed, for fear he would turn out to be wholly imaginary. But later the net expanded: on a night when a blind date of Val's had made a cruel assumption based on ancient rumors about her past and Mama's past, Mama had finally seen that she had to be enlightened. Which didn't mean that Mama held nothing back.

How many stories had she read, or seen in the movies Mama started taking her to at five or six, in which a girl finds out her real father is a lord, a duke, a millionaire, kindly and powerful in a velvet smoking jacket, aglow in the lamplight of his dark study? Her own was not a story, he was actual, he lived down the road from her, she ran into him at crafts fairs and summer-stock shows, and since Rosie Rasmussen had returned to the Faraways and become her friend she had *gone to his house and played croquet* for Christ's sake, and nodded to him across the great green lawn.

I don't want anything from you, she would say. I know you did a little for us through the years. It was enough, it wasn't enough but never mind. I don't want anything except.

What? To be acknowledged, finally. To be told he was sorry, that he had not done all he should have, that he had been afraid, maybe even cowardly, and that he had thought of her often over the years and been sorry.

So that she could forgive him, at least, the bastard, before he died. That much at least.

And so Val had come to Arcady; had pulled up to his door, her heart full, and knocked; and no one had answered, but the lights were on, and she'd come with trepidation down the hall (just as Rosie would at day's end) and into the study at the end of the hall. Where had she got the nerve? There was no other house on this side of the Jambs, the right side, that she would dare to enter uninvited; but to this one she would not ever be invited, so. She pushed open the door, certain for some reason that this was the right room, she could see the tall bookcases, the varnished wood. Where in dreams she had always.

Mostly it was a sickroom. Sheets over the big chaise longue, an oxygen tank and a respirator. Pill bottles at hand on a folding table. At first she didn't even recognize that there was a person amid it all. He raised a hand slightly from his bed, and let it fall again.

"Mr. Rasmussen." His face didn't alter. She tried to guess if he actually saw her. He was lots worse than Rosie had said. "You know me, right?"

She came in a little farther. Still his aspect didn't alter, he watched her with the careful dull interest of a lizard on a stone. He had been a tall man, he had always seemed tall to her, and now he seemed small, tiny; she thought of the guy she had read about in the Dictionary, who got eternal life but forgot to ask for eternal youth, and finally dried up and shrank to the size of a cricket. Still alive though.

"Val," he said at last, as though the name had surprised him, turning up on his tongue. "Valerie."

O Christ let her not cry.

"I wanted to visit," she said. "I've wanted to for a long time."

He tried to lift himself from the chaise on an elbow, found he could not, and lowered himself again. "I'm afraid," he said, "I haven't been well."

"I know," she said. "I know." O why couldn't she have come earlier, why hadn't she been braver, why hadn't she listened to herself. "It's awful to put things off, put them off and off, until. But you."

He said nothing. Where had he got that silk dressing gown, like a fairy-tale emperor, it appeared actually to be empty, like a puppet's clothes. What if. No his breast just then rose and fell.

"I wanted," she said, "to ask you something, about something Rosie said to me, Rosie Mucho."

He opened his mouth, but said nothing.

"She didn't know, but I bet you can tell me. Who is Una Knox?"

She smiled when she said it, you gay dog, tell me your secrets. Boney made no sign he had heard.

"It doesn't really matter," she said. "I just wondered. Honest to

Christ it is not something I wanted to plumb." O stupid stupid tears, how irrelevant can you be, she had not meant to begin, she had *not* begun, and she would not.

"I don't," she said, "I don't *want* anything from you. It's just."

"I'm sorry," he said.

Val's heart rose into her throat, forgiveness and love ready to be poured out even before they were asked for. She stepped closer. There were tears in his eyes, unfallen.

"I'm sorry," he said again. And this time raised his hand to his ear, to cup it. "You said?"

I'm sorry, scuse me, come again: that's all he had meant. Of course. Val swallowed, trying to dislodge her unpoured heart, which was stuck painfully in her throat. "No," she said. "Nothing."

"I'm afraid," he said again. "I can't offer you anything. Mrs. Pisky."

"Well," she said. "Well listen."

Listen. But she said nothing more. He lifted himself again on his elbow, as though he had already forgotten that he couldn't do it, and settled again, a fragile thing too heavy to be lifted and so put back carefully.

"Bad day," he said.

"Yes."

She sat down on the hard chair near him. He turned his head toward her, weird object, brown-spotted and damp and absurdly small, like a doll's left out lost for years. She herself felt horribly enormous, weighty, filled up with all that she was not going to say.

Not going to say: for she had understood almost as soon as she entered here that she was not going to charge him with all that he had done, or make him acknowledge her, or ask any of the questions she had asked him in so many imaginary interviews in so many imaginary movie versions of this room. It was just too late. He had not done it and she had not been able to make him do it and now it was too late. He was only a sick old man who could think of nothing but himself and his death: as she would think of nothing else when her turn came.

"I'm sorry?" he said again.

"It's okay," she said. Even if she had demanded he listen to her, the story would still be hers to carry, no lighter. "It's nothing. Rest."

She sat by him a long time. Once she got up and with the corner

of the sheet she wiped away the tear that trickled down the crevasses
of his cheek, not shed for her or for any of his other sins, only another
gland malfunctioning, he hardly noticed. Mrs. Pisky gasped to find
her there bent over him, intruder, thief, Angel of Death in a sundress.

"So," Val said to Rosie. "I've been here helping. Cheering him up." A
sort of antic cheer had entered Val herself by then, the resolution of
no resolution, she was to be left with the self she had brought here,
but by Christ she would not imagine this room and this moment and
this man again.

"Oh, Val," said Rosie. "O god how strange."

Had he heard Val tell Rosie her story? He gave no sign. Rosie
looked on him in awe. In her eyes he had shape-shifted into something not entirely human.

She stood. Mrs. Pisky now returned from the phone, cried out
with relief to see that Rosie had come home. Boney on his sheeted
couch looked up at the three women standing over him.

"I'm afraid," he said. "I have to go."

"Well sure," Mrs. Pisky said. "When we have to go, we have to
go." Her own cheer was all worn away, transparent, seen to be the
artificial kind, no longer any mistake about it. Not at heart a cheerful
woman, stubby, strong and loud, she had always scared Rosie, who
thought Boney was afraid of her too.

They got him to his feet, at which he looked, as though uncertain
where they were placed.

"So you were just going to sneak away, I guess," Val said. "Huh?
Not a word to anybody. Well hell. Hell of a note."

Boney got to the study door, taking small uncertain steps. The
doorway was not wide enough for all of them to help Boney through
it, yet it seemed certain that he would fall over if any of them let go.

"You take his left hand," Val said to Rosie. "I'll get past and."

Maneuvering carefully, movers with an antique, they got him out
and into the hall; his throat was full, and his short breaths rattled the
phlegm.

"Sorry," he said. "I'm sorry."

"Sure," Val said. "Sure you are."

The bathroom door was not far now. Each of them was thinking the same thought, what exactly they would do when they got him standing before the toilet (which could be seen now through the open door of the bathroom, aloof and patient) when Boney all at once loosened his grip on them. The urgent tension that alone had held him upright went out of him, his wires cut. He settled backward into their arms with a grateful small exhalation.

Mrs. Pisky, who alone of them had experience of this big moment, this passage, who had experienced several in fact, made an awed moan that Boney Rasmussen didn't hear. He had not heard much of what had been said to him or in his presence during the interminable length of this day, had not always been sure that the person being talked about so gravely was himself. Anyway he had long forgotten what little he had heard.

Sorry. Sorry. It was because he had had so little time: because his time had been so short. An eyewink between the unrememberable beginning and the oblivion. How could you do anything but begin? How?

Gently he extricated himself from the women, and stood on his own. That had been a mistake, apparently, about needing to go to the bathroom. He didn't need to after all. He had thought he felt a great need, but he had been wrong.

No, no need.

He looked back once at the three women standing at the study door, puzzled and still, as though they had dropped something and hadn't yet realized it. Well he would go on. Clearly he was on his own. There was no one who could do this for him, he would have to do it himself, it had been a mistake and an injustice for him to ask and pester others so long and so fruitlessly. Not even Sandy Kraft could acquire it for him, for it was his alone, and therefore his to find.

He saw now (why had it taken him so long to see it?) that the way to proceed was simply to trace the path backward, step by step, just as you must do when you have lost anything; trace the way back until you find it. He would start from the end and go on toward the beginning, and at a turn he would come upon it, just where it ought to be, where he alone could recognize it.

First he would go to Kraft's house; he would pick up the trail within the book Kraft had left for him (yes, for him, it was quite clear, though he had not wanted to say it aloud, not even in the spaces of his heart); he would trace it backward, to Europe certainly probably, to London, Rome, Vienna. Then to Prague, too.

But Kraft's first. He knew the way well, had walked there more than once on summer nights like this one, the way illuminated by the moon. He could imagine the lights lit in the windows there, at the end of the drive, near the dark pines; could even see Sandy there within, in his armchair in the lamplight, his sweet trickster's eyes and smile. O Friend.

He took cap and stick from the hall-tree. The hall was long and strangely huge, and at its end the great door out. He would have to have strength for that. And then the night and the path. But had he forgotten something? Left something behind? It began to seem that indeed there was something left behind forgotten, that tugged at him, retarding his progress, a child ignored tugging at her father's pants-leg. What? Something done or undone, which if it weren't remembered made the whole journey pointless, the reason for setting out, the wallet, the car keys, the ticket, the something.

Though he had ceased to make any progress toward it, the door had grown larger. He *had* forgotten something back there, he had O God he had: he decided that he had to go back, he had to go back immediately. When he tried to do so, however, he found that he could not turn himself around. He could not even turn his head, not because he lacked the strength but because there was not anything, anything at all, behind him to turn to.

"Once when I was young," Pierce said to Rose Ryder, "I started a forest fire."

Below where they were parked, the surface of Nickel Lake was dashed with starlight; many cars were parked around its margins in twos and threes, and families moved down the steep banks through stands of dark fir to reach the shore, passing the little car where Pierce and Rose sat.

"It wasn't a very big one, but it was a real forest fire. I wasn't playing with matches or anything like that; I'd been doing my chores, actually. Burning trash. And it started a little brush fire."

"Yes," she said.

"I watched it for a long time, and then watched it from the roof of my uncle's house when it got dark, and watched it turn into a real fire."

"Yes."

"They didn't have the means to fight it, I guess," Pierce said. "So it just burned out of control."

"Yes," she said again. "I know."

Now and then there came a crackle of class-B fireworks, and distant laughter. Imps moved about the barge on the middle of the lake, you could see the glowing points of the punk they carried. The sheriff, the Sportsmen's Club. Catcalls for their dilatoriness.

And now at last the first rocket arose from the barge out on the lake, and burst: brilliant dandelion-moon of fire appearing full-blown, then gone, and the big whack of sound reaching them an instant after. "Oooh," she said.

The next one rose—they didn't have many, and sent them up at first singly—and they all tilted their heads back to follow its wavering trail upward. Oh! It was one of those that was all noise, the sound reflected back from the surrounding hills shaking the heart.

"Oh," she said, chuckling with deep delight and wiggling in her seat. "Oh I love those." She lifted her foot to prop it on the dashboard. "So yes?"

"That's all," Pierce said. "I just remembered. Feeling the power of it. On the roof with my cousins." Discovering how much destructive force there was in the world, pure power, neither good nor bad but only potential, and how easily it could be released.

Another bomb-burst, more complex: a fire-flower first, then sharp reports that generated whizzing devils, then the big bang at the end. Its instant of light revealed the folk in their beach chairs, kids under blankets, girls and boys on the hoods of cars, arms around one another.

"So who were all these cousins?" she asked him.

"My uncle's children. I was raised by an uncle."

"Oh." She waited to see what would become of the next one: it sent a mild scatter of blossoms in many colors. Hiss of the detritus falling into the water. "Aw," she said tenderly. "No parents?"

"Parents, sure. My mother left my father at one point and went to live with her brother."

"Sisters? Brothers?"

"No. My cousins were like brothers and sisters. Sort of."

She sipped beer, they had brought some, but her elation was not due to it. "And what about you?" she said. "Not married. No kids?"

Whack. Double globes, one inside the other, how is it done, gone before you can ponder it. *Magia naturalis.*

"I have a son," he said.

She turned to regard him.

"Twelve years old, no thirteen." Hard to fix an exact birthday, boys varied a lot; he knew just how grown-up he was, but not what age he might have attained. "Robbie," he said. Small bomb-burst in his own breast to say his name aloud; and he had said it aloud just for that purpose, just to feel it: as they both sat here now to startle and gratify themselves with the release of energy.

"Well how," she said, but another thud came from the barge; a little reaching missile arose, shedding sparks, and blossomed huge and gay, and died. Rose's hand—Pierce noticed it when he looked over at her to share delight with her—was pressed tight between her legs. Loud noises, he thought, some people can't help peeing.

Smoke from the fireworks made little thunderheads over the lake, only revealed as new bombs went off and stained them with their colors. Laughter across the dark water, and soft moans of awe from the population; all you could see of them now were the points of their cigarettes, ruddy cookfires, the flare of sparklers. Beyond, on the horizon, the real, cold clouds were still white.

"They're running out," Rose said. But then the sheriff and his merry men put out their best effort, and a half-dozen rockets arose at once, then a further triplet, *coup de théâtre,* impossible not to cry aloud at it and its foolish beauty. Then that was all. Silence and odorous smoke drifted over the lake. Already trucks were starting their engines, and the families who had passed them going down to the water passed them departing, carrying their chairs, their sleepy children.

"All over," he heard a woman near them say to her child. "All over now."

All over. And perfectly concluded, too, Pierce thought: if what they had really set out to express by gathering the townsfolk and the summer people here in the serene night and firing their lights was not splendor, or exaltation, or American glory, but the opposite, whatever that might be. Transience, maybe; the sweet brevity of life; the poignancy of things that pass away. The Triumph of Time.

"I have to tell you," Rose said. "I have a date tonight."

"Is this not tonight?" Pierce said.

"I meant later. A late date."

"Oho."

She started her car.

"I'm sorry," she said.

"No reason to be sorry. Reason to be glad." It made him, in fact, unreasonably glad. He pictured her, later, in a bar booth, on a dance floor, with an imaginable but unclear other male; he pictured her surprising this man with her restless hotness. And Pierce himself meanwhile home alone, and safe between cool sheets.

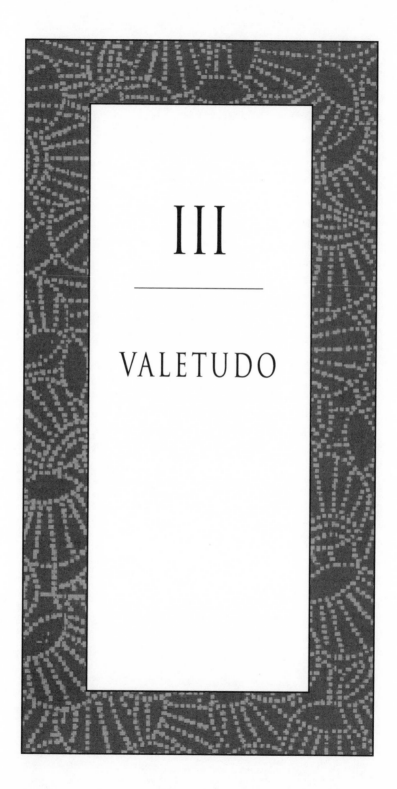

III

VALETUDO

1

oney Rasmussen hadn't wanted to be buried at all, but if he had to be, he didn't want to be buried in the common cemetery with others around him.

Like a fastidious tourist, Rosie thought, caught on a cheap tour, pretending he's not with these people. She had found and opened an envelope on which Boney had written *In the event of my death,* and she sat at Boney's desk with the brief handwritten sheet of onionskin which it contained. No embalming, no special funerary preparations; no religious service, no priest or preacher. He wanted, it seemed, to go over unattended. And he wanted to be buried on the grounds, in the ground, of his own house, he specified where: a clearing in a little stand of tall pines, amid the rhododendrons. He wanted an obelisk erected over him, which should be made of some soft stone which would begin to crumble in not too many years; and on its base he wanted these words cut: *Et in Arcadia ego.* No name, no date.

Well then why didn't you *say* so, Rosie asked of the paper, the shaky whispered words. Why didn't you *say.* She had already, with Val's and Mrs. Pisky's help, begun the process, set off in the usual way, not knowing how it was done but finding out that everyone else did, the steps were wellworn: the funeral home, the lawyer, the medical examiner, the church. It wasn't, after all, the first time it had ever happened in the world.

She called Allan Butterman, Boney's lawyer and her own.

"It doesn't really matter," Allan said. "State health regulations say you can't be buried except in a cemetery. You can't get yourself buried in your back yard."

"Health regulations? It's not going to do him any harm."

"*Our* health. The living. Not good to have dead bodies just any-where."

Hadn't Boney known that? He must have buried or seen buried dozens in his huge life. Maybe he hadn't quite meant this; maybe it was a kind of play, pretending he could have the death he wanted. If he had to have one. She felt a guilty relief that anyway she couldn't do much to get it for him.

"Here's an idea," said Allan. "Do the usual thing. Follow the rules. Do what he asked as much as possible. Then later the Foundation can put up a memorial. There where he wanted."

"He wanted no funeral though," she said. "No service." He lay already on a cool slab at the funeral home; she couldn't prevent that, nor what they had done or would do to him there.

"We'll do the minimum. The Danish Brethren isn't exactly elabo-rate. And a reception out there."

"Oh yipes," Rosie said softly. "Oh Allan."

"We'll get you through it," Allan said. "I'll tell you. It's real usual for people to leave wishes like these. The way they want things done. That can't be followed. Very usual."

Rosie thought about this, or sat anyway with it, envisioning the place in the pines that Boney meant. It was a nice place, she and Sam and he had picnicked there last summer, back when he had seemed so weirdly immortal, as though he had already died and been mum-mified.

"Okay," she said.

She called Pierce Moffett next.

"He wanted it on his, his gravestone," she said. "*Et in Arcadia ego.* It doesn't sound like it would go, if he's not going to be here. Right?"

"It's a Latin motto," Pierce said. "The 'et' means 'and' but it might mean 'also' or 'too.' So it could mean slightly different things. It could be translated *I am in Arcady too,* that is, along with all the beauty and peace. Or it could be translated *I am even in Arcady,* as well as every-where else."

"What 'I'?" Rosie asked.

"The 'I' speaking," Pierce said, "is Death."

Rosie felt in her breast and throat an uprush of tears; she wanted not to cry but they were no more to be suppressed than a shiver or a sneeze, and so she let them whelm her. She had not so far wept for Boney, not the night of his death, not the two long days that followed; now all the pity of it, of goddamn death and human impotence, came bowling up her throat.

At least he knew, she thought, he really did know, he *wasn't* crazy; for here he was admitting it, saying uncle. She couldn't stop weeping, and she couldn't hang up on Pierce, and so wept into the phone absurdly while Pierce listened and waited. O Boney: the opponent he had kept on struggling with so hopelessly had at length just inveigled him into his arms as a mother will a rebellious child, and hushed him.

"Sorry, sorry," she said at last, a squeak, all she could manage. "Okay. So. I guess we'll think of something else."

"I'll think too," Pierce said.

"Will you come? To the funeral I mean? Day after tomorrow."

"I'll come," he said.

She hung up, still wiping her eyes with her sleeve; and then she remembered Sam, who was sitting at Rosie's own old desk (a card table really, piled with Rosie's unfinished Foundation work, for whom now if for anyone would she finish it?) and coloring.

Just as it retreated back inside Sam's body, Rosie saw her daughter's soul, which had been out drinking in her mother's tears. Sam had seen her mother in tears on the phone often enough, too often, Rosie thought.

"I was just sad about Boney," she said.

"I'm not so sad now," Sam said. "Because he's not here to see."

"Yes," Rosie said. "Well. That makes a lot of sense, hon."

"Was Pierce crying too?"

"No." She got up, so much to do. "Listen I have to go get some things upstairs, can you stay here, will you . . ."

But Sam was already by her side, and Rosie thought: Let her come. She was his friend too.

"Are we going up to Boney's room?" Sam asked in some awe as they climbed the big front double staircase.

"Yep."

The funeral director had given her a list of things to bring down for the laying-out of Boney, which included a suit and a shirt and tie (but why, Rosie asked, if he's to be shut up in his box? And saw that it was as much for the director's sake as for hers or Boney's, standards to maintain). Underwear too, for heaven's sake, and socks, but not shoes.

His dentures. Weird that we go to the grave not only in our flesh but with its history too, all the accidents it's had, all the work done on it. Our pierced ears and unremovable wedding-bands, the fillings and bridges in our mouths, pins in our broken bones. Do they bury you, she wondered, with your wooden leg, your hearing aid? Flesh of your flesh by then. Why not your glasses too?

Boney's room, which neither of them had entered before, which both had peeked into, though, to see the big bed with the green velvet spread, the ancient leather slippers poking out from beneath it; the big wooden mirrored wall of closets. On his bedside table the book he had been reading when last he slept here, turned facedown at the place he had stopped. *Ill Met by Moonlight* by Fellowes Kraft, a book of ghost stories.

Sam with reverent curiosity began opening the closet doors. The closets were surprisingly full, considering how limited had been the wardrobe Boney usually wore. Never threw away anything.

"Look," Sam said, pulling out a pair of white and tan shoes. "With nails." In wonder she touched the spikes. Rosie tried to imagine a golf-playing Boney in some other decade.

There should be a crowd of descendants to do this for him, she thought; Allan said that in New York there was an aged nephew or cousin twice removed, but otherwise no one.

No one but Val.

The old bastard. Really. What an awful thing to do, enough to keep him out of heaven if there was one.

Angry at herself for being angry with him, she thought of her own father, who also snuck off, got away with it too, so that he could never be called on it, never called; waiting now for her in the future. That anyway was what Mike had always suggested: her father waiting for her to reach him, to work through her feelings, like jungle undergrowth. What would she say to him then? Mike thought he knew (she would finally admit to her love, her anger) but she did not.

Down there at the end, at the last turn of the plot, all the lost and absconded fathers waiting. Rosie's own. And Boney. Pierce's, who had been found again after years and years, apparently, and not on bad terms with his son now, she thought; and still. Kraft never mentioned his father in his memoir: lost too. She felt a clear pattern knitting itself together in the world around her, the world of lives within which she lived: a pattern like an idea for a painting, *The Lost Fathers,* a pattern that had lain all around her for a long time but which she hadn't noticed till now. A plague of dead estranged absent ignorant refusing fathers.

Was that because of the curse the world labored under? Or was that the spell itself? If it was, how was she supposed to fix it, find everyone's father for them?

She awoke then, as from a little sleep, returned to where she stood before Boney's suits, marveling at what she had just thought, which evanesced as soon as she rethought it, bearing away with it its dream-darkness.

Come on, which of these. It didn't matter at all, she should just reach in and take one, but the fact that it didn't matter at all kept her from choosing. A summer seersucker? Something dark and respectful of death's dominion? Once when she was young, an avid reader of all kinds of fictions, she had determined to her own satisfaction that ghosts are not alive for themselves, but are only creations of the persons who see them: and that was because of the clothes they wear. Where did they get them, the tattered wedding gowns, the top hats, rotted cerements, suits of armor? Were you supposed to believe the clothes were ghosts too?

She shuddered hugely in the heat, plunged her arm in among the empty male forms, which wavered, upset, at her intrusion, and abstracted one. Brown. Fine.

"Fine," Sam said gaily, enjoying this. "Now what else."

"Socks, shirt, undies."

"Okay. Can I pick out the socks?"

"Okay." Good Lord, as ready to play the game of death and burial as she was any other. But the choosing wasn't much fun, for though Boney had many pairs of socks, all rolled into neat rolls, every single pair was black.

The Danish Brethren share a plain white wooden church building on a knoll high up in Blackbury Jambs with another small denomination, neither of them having members enough to support a church of its

own. Since the Danish Brethren (among other theological and liturgical oddities) holds its weekly divine service not on Sunday but on
Saturday evening, the arrangement could be worked out.

Despite all Rosie's efforts to meet Boney's wishes and make little
of the event, the church was going to be full. Boney had lived here
and in Cascadia since the previous century, Allan Butterman reminded her; a lot of people knew him. She had filled the altar with
flowers, refusing the funeral parlor's offer of wreaths and sprays of
gladiolus ("sadiolus" she called them, and Sam laughed) and cutting
instead her own armfuls of phlox and day lilies and sweet william at
Arcady, stuffing the funeral director's vases with them not very pro-
fessionally, scattering leaves and petals underfoot where they were
crushed into the waxed wood and purplish rug.

Pierce inhaled the violent perfume. He had walked up from his
building on Maple Street, arriving too early, entering the austere
space with a sense at once of pleasure and transgression (a sin, in his
childhood, to attend services in the churches of schismatics); he had
taken a rear pew. Boney in his box of wood lay in the aisle.

Rosie at the front of the church turned and saw him (he wouldn't
have guessed from where he sat that the woman in the dark suit and
hat was she). She slipped from her pew and came down the side aisle
to him.

"Pierce." She sat to whisper to him. "Listen, I know this is a little
funny. But can I ask you a favor." There was no response he could
make to that, and he waited for her to continue. "See the guy in the
front row on the right? The sort of stooped one? That's Boney Rasmussen's cousin."

"Ah."

"He was supposed to be a whatsit, who carries the. The coffin.
Casket. Pallbearer. Only now he just told me he can't. His back or
something. So I wondered if you."

A small wave of resistant horror came over Pierce, and passed. He
hadn't been asked to help carry his uncle Sam, and couldn't remember now why he hadn't. "Um," he said. "There's nobody else to do it,
family, friends? I mean I'd be happy to, but. I hardly knew him."

"All dead," Rosie said. She looked up then, and Pierce saw her go
pale a little, a thing he didn't often actually see people do; he turned.
Val was coming uncertainly up the center aisle. She turned in at
Pierce's pew with something like relief

Not all dead, Rosie thought. "Listen," she said. "Val." Val wore a darkly dramatic swathe of a dress, not black when you looked closely but iridescent and many-colored like a grackle's plumage. And she wore dark glasses. A movie star incognito. "Do you want to help carry him?"

Val answered nothing. It took Rosie a moment to see that she had not understood and that behind the dark glasses was trying to make sense of Rosie's weird challenge.

"Be a pallbearer, I mean," Rosie said. "You know."

"Christ no," Val said.

"Sure, okay," Rosie said, and touched her shoulder. "Come on, Pierce." She took his hand, and Pierce slipped from his pew; she led him up the side aisle to sit by her, not releasing his hand but gripping it with a pressure strangely intense.

The service was as spare as the church; the minister too, a woman in a dark suit not unlike Rosie's, scrubbed cheeks and gray ash-blond hair, whose eyes and mouth were good-natured; when she rose at the service's beginning to say that the deceased had requested no eulogy or sermon and that his wishes would be respected here, she did it as gravely and eloquently as though it had been a eulogy. Then she opened her book.

> *Naked came I out of my mother's womb, and naked shall I return thither; the Lord gave, and the Lord hath taken away; blessed be the name of the Lord.*

What touched Pierce always in Christian burials, what never failed to bring surprising tears to his eyes, was when they talked of the soul coming home, to be hurt never more. Because they couldn't say it without reminding you of all that souls do suffer. Eternal rest grant unto him, O Lord. Nothing can touch him further.

It was very brief, and then Rosie nudged him, and a funeral-home functionary showed him his place and his handholds, and with Allan Butterman and four others Pierce didn't know, elders of the community, he carried Boney's box (was it light or heavy? Hard to say) down the aisle and out the door, onto the gurney of the hearse.

Then Pierce realized that he could not now turn toward home, but would have to go on to the cemetery, wherever it was, and help to get Boney into his closet in the earth, from which there is no exit.

"Ride with me," Val at his elbow said. "I'll tell you a story."

Allan had persuaded Rosie to have the reception catered, at the Foundation's expense; Mrs. Pisky, still mighty in the power of her caretaking, knew what to do, and made the arrangements as though she had been thinking about them for years; so there were long tables on the lawn laid with white cloths showing the fold-marks, like linens in Florentine paintings of dead saints, and coolers beneath them full of refreshments, and young people in white shirts behind them to serve, and even a kid to help park cars. All that early morning young people had come and gone and passed Rosie in the hall or on the lawn on their errands, asking her questions in lowered voices (though they sometimes laughed among themselves as they raised their tables and laid their cloths); and now it was done and the guests were gravely entering onto the lawns too large ever to seem crowded, and were waited on discreetly. Rosie thought: the Elysian Fields. As though they had all gone over together in their nice clothes to a stiller, calmer version of their earthly life.

She had swallowed a quick drink to fortify herself, maybe too quick, she felt she floated somewhere above the scene, able to observe keenly, but not certain she could participate. There was Allan, and the men from New York, and the weedy distant cousin. Spofford, in boots and a black suit from which his brown wrists protruded, where had he found or been keeping it; he looked more like a marshal than a mourner. As she watched, Pierce Moffett broke off his conversation with him, and moved across the lawn, to speak, apparently, to the minister, who awaited him, a nice-sized drink in her own hand.

"I wanted to ask you," Pierce said to her when they had introduced themselves. (Her name was Rhea Rasmussen, but she was no immediate relative of Boney's; they had tried hard to find the connection but had been unable to.) "When we were at the cemetery?"

"Yes."

"As we carried the, toward the, the. You asked us to stop for a moment, and you read . . ."

"Yes."

"And then we went on, a few steps, and then we stopped again."

"Yes."

Pierce had raised his eyes at this second pause (the old man was after all pretty heavy, he and his box) to see Val's Beetle, outside the gates, Val in it, her dark glasses on; she had chosen not to participate. And had not come to this reception. "Then again, three or four times more."

"Yes. Seven times in all, actually." She smiled, and her smile lightened her austere features, lit her eyes.

"Well what was . . . Oh. *Seven* times."

"There's an esoteric reason, one we don't really anymore . . ."

"The planets," said Pierce.

"Yes." She laughed a little. "You actually know? Usually it takes a lot of explaining. I sometimes hope no one will ask."

"Sort of, yes. For the leaving of earthly concerns and heaviness behind."

The soul, at death, sheds the body, but not the incorporeal or less corporeal spirit wrapping; that is only discarded as the soul ascends through the spheres that have governance over it. As the soul rises, it gives back the garment or integument that belongs to each sphere before it can go through to the next. That was neo-Platonic lore, Pierce thought, or Gnostic myth; Hermetic. How had it come to these northern Protestants?

"So we were pausing for each."

"They do the same thing in the Orthodox Jewish burial service." She shook the ice in her glass and drank. "I think we probably got it from them."

"Really?"

"Yes. Did you notice our weekly service is on Saturday? We were very ecumenical. It's an interesting story. Maybe you'd like to hear it someday."

"I would," Pierce said. "Very much." Damn if each time they

paused Boney had not in fact seemed to grow lighter. He looked into his glass, and laughed a little, imagining Boney's soul ascending through the spheres (the same spheres Beau Brachman had drawn in the dirt of his driveway), up up to the outside, wriggling out of all the heavy overcoats of earthly hurt and astral destiny. Unless of course some unfresworn attachment held him back.

Una Knox. The name tickled somewhere deep, in the wrong or unlikely part of his memory, but he couldn't reach it.

As she stood at the lawn's edge waiting for the courage to go mingle, Rosie felt a hand on her elbow.

"Oh hi, Mike."

"Rosie." He held her arm and studied her for a long moment, looking into her face with a clear frank neutrality that was probably supposed to be open and receptive but which maybe he knew was also unsettling. Then he said: "It's hard for you."

"Yep," she said.

"I guess you were there."

"Yep." She supposed she could say that Boney had died in her arms, hers and Val's and Mrs. Pisky's. She remembered the long hall, the lighted bathroom. Heat lightning or something, a rocket going off, lit the windows momentarily just then.

"You had got to be pretty close," Mike said.

"Well. Close. I don't know." She looked at Mike, who was now gazing smiling over the funeral crowd, hands loosely clasped behind his back. The beetle-browed truculent look he had worn the last months was all gone, had been gone for a while she realized, replaced by this face, sweet, wide-eyed, even gay, and somehow predatory. He appeared a stranger to her.

"You've got a lot on your mind just now," he said. "I don't want to interfere in your. In your grieving. And there've got to be a lot of business matters left over."

There were; lots. If you live denying you're going to die, you tend to not want to finish things. She said nothing, only clasped her own hands before her.

"This isn't easy to bring up," he said. "But I want to ask you a favor."

"Sure." Sure, ask: when Rosie was a kid her best friend Sylvia had explained to her that you could perfectly correctly say *Sure* when somebody said *Can I ask you a favor,* and still be able to refuse to do what was asked. Sylvia had later betrayed Rosie atrociously; she still remembered.

"Things are really changing in The Woods," Mike said. "*Really* changing. Our whole mission could change. There are major new things coming in." He shook his head in what appeared to be awe, and to Rosie it seemed his eyes were moist. "All I wanted to say," he said, "is that this would really be a terrible time for anything to happen to our funding."

She said nothing to this either. She hadn't heard that big changes were sweeping through The Woods. She wondered why Mike felt responsible for the funding that the Rasmussen Foundation supplied to The Woods, which was really a small part of their income, used for research projects she understood, Rosie hadn't ever looked closely at the paperwork.

"Well gee," she said. "I can't tell you anything, Michael."

In the middle distance toward which they both looked, a big older man in a rumpled suit stood, unattached to any group. Not someone she knew. He held a summer straw hat behind his back, and looked off placidly toward no one.

"I understand. Really. But I think if you were involved in the things that are going on there." He kicked at a harmless patch of moss that lay before his foot, testing its tenacity. "You used to be interested. In the work up there. My work."

"Climacterics," Rosie said. She wasn't going to ask about it. Mike laughed lightly, dismissively even Rosie thought, as though she had mentioned some ancient enthusiasm of his, motorbikes or stamp-collecting.

Who was that old guy? Not a local person, that was somehow evident. His big pumpkin face was astonishingly lined, his little eyes and features sunken in the expanse. "So what's the favor?" she said.

"I'd like you to meet somebody. Somebody who's been working with us at The Woods. I really wanted the old man to meet him, but."

"But," Rosie said. "Yeah. So is he a therapist?"

Mike laughed, the new little overflowing-with-unsayable-things laugh. "Um. Yes."

"What's his name? Why do you want *me* to meet him?"

"His name," Mike said. "Now don't laugh. His name is Honeybeare."

"Oh yeah?" She didn't laugh. She had actually known someone with that name, a swimming instructor, skinny and sour, under whose coaching Rosie had got to be a fair competitor.

"Raymond Honeybeare," Mike said. "I wanted you to meet him because." He stopped to choose among the reasons, which evidently clamored or contested within him. "Because he asked."

"To talk to me?"

"Well the Foundation."

"That's not me," Rosie said.

"I just think," Mike said, "that you would be very interested. I really think."

She heard that. That was Mike speaking, the little Mike inside the Mike that usually did the talking, the Mike she almost never heard anymore. "Well," she said. "Okay. Maybe sometime."

"Now would be a good time," he said, and took her elbow again.

"Now?"

"That's him," Mike said, indicating the big man holding his hat and gazing at nothing.

"Oh," Rosie said. She resisted Mike's arm pushing her gently that way. "Oh Michael no. Uh-uh."

"Just to say hello."

"There's no reason, Mike." She was quite certain she didn't want to meet, speak to, touch that man. She felt his proximity to her, his phony aloofness, with a sudden revulsion.

"Look," she said firmly, standing her ground. "Not now."

"When?"

"Make an appointment," she said. "Mike I've got things to see to."

She turned away, walking quickly and clumsily in her unaccustomed heels, and didn't look back; sorry for Mike's embarrassment, sorry she could do no other, and wondering why.

She got no farther than the veranda, where Allan Butterman sat with the people who had come out from New York, Boney's weedy cousin and the members of the Foundation's board or their lawyers or agents, who had sat up front in the church with Allan. Allan raised a shrimp on a toothpick to her in salute.

"Rosie."

"Hi, Allan." She nodded to the others, aware of their attention to her. Would this day never be over. She hoped she wouldn't have to address any of them by name; Allan had introduced her to them at the church and before that had supplied her with a list of their names, but no name had attached itself firmly to a face.

"The gentlemen have to be heading back," he said. "They wondered if they could speak to you."

"Sure," Rosie said. Allan had promised her she wouldn't be grilled about money or made to account for her stewardship, such as it was. Her heart nevertheless beat faster.

She took them into Boney's office, which Mrs. Pisky had tidied, though the oxygen tanks and breathing apparatus still stood against the wall, servants waiting to be dismissed. It was cool. Rosie could still detect Boney's odor, but the others would not recognize it.

Allan had said they wanted to talk, but he talked most; they only crossed their legs, adjusted their tie-knots, smoothed their beautiful suits, looked with firm but gentle kindness on her. Allan gave a brief history of the Rasmussen Foundation, looking now and then to one of the others for confirmation, and receiving nods; he cast his eyes over Boney's desk as he spoke, looking maybe for one of the long yellow pencils he was accustomed to manipulate as he talked, conducting his own discourse with it.

"Anyway," he said at length. "You are aware that Mr. Rasmussen died intestate. We'll take up the questions involved with that another time, they're difficult but not hopeless. What's relevant here is that he did this year do all the necessary in regard to the Foundation, naming a successor as director, signing the documents."

Rosie had seen but not studied these, beautifully printed papers with maroon covers. "Successor?" she said.

"The bylaws don't specify that a member of the family needs to hold the position, but the family's *preferences* are very clear. He didn't have a lot of people to choose from, though he could have gone some ways afield. Of course he didn't."

Of course? The certainty came over Rosie, an interpretation of Allan's face at that moment, that Boney's death was going to go on issuing surprises, things he had left unsettled and unfinished that rolling Time was going to finish up for him. "Then what . . ."

"He named you to be the Foundation's Director, Rosie." Allan looked at her, smiling, understanding. They were all smiling, as at a genteel surprise party. "I was just informed this morning. A little late, never mind, I imagine they thought Mr. Rasmussen had done this with your full knowledge and assent. No, right?"

"No." She had been filling up with a feeling that she did not immediately recognize was anger. When she did realize it she was afraid to speak.

He had known this for months before he died, and hadn't told her, or asked her; afraid probably that she might turn him down. He had just left it for her, unrefusable, unacceptable, like his letter about how his remains were to be treated.

She thought of that morning, the morning of the Fourth, the last time she had really spoken to him. *I'm sorry,* he'd said. *I hate to leave you with it.* He had meant that she should continue his search. Christ.

"Well," she said at last, all she could manage. She knew her cheeks must be aflame. "Is it legal for me to refuse?"

"Sure," Allan said. "Of course. But I would have thought."

"I guess I don't feel real qualified. For one thing."

"Boney thought you were qualified," Allan said, still smiling. She thought: They don't get it. She looked at them as though she faced a group of good-natured animals, koalas or pandas. *They* thought Boney was a kind wise mysterious old man who had left a wonderful gift for his great-niece. Not a selfish frightened egotist who wanted her to represent him among the living even when he was gone.

Oh that was too unkind, too hard. Poor foolish man, what the hell had he done.

"Well," she said again. "I have to think." She was near tears, and furious with herself because she was, and they had lost their nice smiles at last. "I was just helping out."

"I don't think the board needs an answer today," Allan said, puzzled. "Take some time. There's compensation to discuss. And there's the house, too."

The house. Where they sat. She felt it enclosing her.

The elderly Rasmussen cousin, who had been propped against Boney's desk, now pushed himself upright.

"Rosie?" he said inquiringly. "Rosie. These gentlemen might not understand. I do. I understand." He put his hands in his pockets. His dark bow tie had wilted in the heat. He reminded her a lot of Boney, but in what way, beyond a kind of gay gravity, which Boney had lost at the end.

"I don't know if you know this," he said, "but there's a large branch of the Rasmussens who belong to the Mormon church. Yes. Longtime members. Well that interested me, long ago. I went out West, I don't know why exactly now, to Utah and Salt Lake City, and spent some time with the Mormons. They have some extraordinary beliefs. They believe that the souls of the dead, like those of the living, can be saved. They spend a lot of time at it, learning the names and dates of their dead relatives, going centuries back, so that they can perform these ceremonies, which free those souls. Now it seems to me."

He paused to assemble his conclusion in his mind, and they all watched him do so. He was her cousin too, Rosie thought.

"It seems to me that it's something similar you're being asked to do here. Yes? To spend your days doing the necessary to save the souls of your dead relatives." He smiled. "Don't get me wrong," he said. "I hope you'll agree. But you're a young woman. I can see why you might want to refuse. I would in your place. In fact I did."

He picked up the cane he didn't really seem to need, strong old guy, all of the Rasmussens were long-lived, she herself too probably. The others rose at this signal. "Don't let us pressure you," he said. "You think about it. You might want to tell us no. As the Gospel says. Let the dead bury the dead."

Afternoon, and the cicadas warned from the oaks; Pierce Moffett, looking fruitlessly for the downstairs bathroom, which he had once been in, right around here somewhere, came on Rosie in the kitchen: she sat on the bottom step of the steep back stairs, her shoes off, a drink in her hand, and an unwonted cigarette.

"You," Pierce said. "You're being asked for."

She knocked ash onto the floor. "Pierce," she said. "Do you really understand what he was looking for? What it was really?"

"Well," said Pierce. "I know its name. I know what it was thought to be."

"It was so confusing," Rosie said. "He was almost embarrassed to talk about it. He always said you'd understand."

"Well." Pierce sat beside her on the stair. "In the mythology of alchemy there's supposed to be this stuff. It has many names and definitions. Nobody describes it very clearly, partly because it wasn't a very distinct idea, partly because in those days scientists and researchers—if you can call them that—spent a lot of effort keeping what they knew—what they thought they knew—secret. Big difference from now."

"But it wasn't like. Real."

"Look at it this way," Pierce said. "Transforming base, so-called base, metals into gold isn't possible. But there are several really circumstantial accounts of its being done that are hard to poke holes in. Nobody can live for years on nothing but Communion wafers. But there are nuns who were witnessed doing so."

"So."

"So." He laughed softly. "Suppose that once upon a time the world was different. Really different, in its deepest workings. And suppose one sort of something persisted from that time into this. And it happened to be that."

"That's what Boney said to me."

"It's what Kraft's book is about," Pierce said.

"He thought Fellowes Kraft knew it was so."

"Fellowes Kraft," Pierce said, "wrote fictions."

She looked into her glass, silent for a time.

"Sometimes," she said, "it sounded like a medicine. Sometimes like a metal or a jewel."

"It was a powder and a liquid too. You could say a lot about it but it seems to me what it comes down to is: it's the thing missing. The thing you don't have."

"So if you ever get it . . ."

"Then it's not it. A little parable."

Rosie felt a familiar painful absence in her breast, one that she had thought was gone. "I thought it was more like this magic medicine," she said. "To keep you alive forever."

"That was one description."

When she had played cowboys and Indians in her old neighborhood, or cops and robbers, they had used Magic Medicine (she could hear herself say it, to say it was to apply it) to revive the countless dead they produced, so that they could be slain again.

"Well you know what I think," she said. She blinked away the starting tears, the first she had shed that day. "I think it's the worst thing that a dying person can do. To lay a question on the ones left alive that they can't answer." She dropped the half-smoked cigarette into the half-full glass. "It's like a curse."

She thought: As though a departing guest were to turn back at the door, after all the farewells and compliments, to ask in sadness and anger why he had been treated so badly, and then turn away from your outstretched hand and go without another word.

"What question did he leave you with?"

"Well not me really," she said, thinking it was not even that he *put* a question but that he *was* one. "Us. You."

She climbed back into her tight shoes and took the glass to the sink. There was a sound of loud laughter far away outside, whose.

Pierce knew what the question was, of course, without asking further; it was only Boney's version of the question he imagined a lot of people put, the question he might himself ask of those unimaginable heirs and relatives who would be standing around his own bed (if he were not to die alone, putting the question to four no more communicative walls): Why must I die? Why now and not some better later time? Why not you instead of me? Why can't you, you vigorous living ones, why can't you save me?

He shuddered hugely. God save him from such a death. Which saint was it you prayed to. Nine First Fridays, guarantee of a Good Death. Not for him.

"I never did find it," he said smiling. "I looked. I did."

"Well you get to look further," she said. "Boney wanted to tell you. I was going to tell you. There was a grant set up for you. Well a sort of fellowship. A traveling fellowship he called it."

"Yes?"

"He was going to tell you how to apply. And then you'd be given it."

"Well hm," Pierce said idiotically.

"On this fellowship," Rosie said, "you were going to go to Europe for a while. Chase this thing down, whatever it is. Find out all about it. Report." She was laughing now.

"I was?"

"You still are," she said. "I guess. If you want to. I assume it's all still set up. Maybe now . . . well who knows what'll happen. But."

"When?"

"When you're ready. I suppose." She covered her mouth, stifling another laugh, this game from which Boney had cashed out was going to go on, stranger and stranger. "When you know where to look."

"Ha ha," he said, still on his seat on the step. "Okay."

"Listen I better go, they'll be wondering. I don't really know. Everything's going to be different now. We'll have to talk."

She had smoothed her wrinkled skirt as she spoke, and then she slipped out through the kitchen doors, the swinging handle-less kind such as restaurants have, which whiffed open again after she had passed through, then closed, then open again, closed.

Pierce had never been to Europe. It was a large, an embarrassing gap in his education, not the only one but one he felt deeply; he had not quite consciously worked out certain locutions to use in conversation which concealed without real prevarication the lame fact.

Now, though.

Europe. The Old World.

He laughed richly in the empty kitchen. To reach at length the land he supposedly already knew in pursuit of a dead man's wish for eternal life, in order to write a book promoting magic systems he didn't believe in. He seemed to gaze down on that land from where he sat, saw it as from a plane's window: the shores of a cold sea, fields and mountains and crowded rivers, gray cities of flint arising over the earth's curve steepled with churches and castles, where people maneuvered cars in courtyards and lanes or walked in the footsteps of their ancestors; and the unfolding ribbons of old roads leading east.

Rosie had said goodbye to the last of her guests (hers, she had not thought of them as hers but they certainly weren't Boney's, he hadn't wanted them here at all). Sam was asleep at last, after an awful bedtime battle, overtired, unable to shut off or down.

Asleep now? Yes. Rosie stood at the foot of the stairs and listened: no sound.

Outside in the drive the caterers loaded their last van. Very successful, Allan had said to her.

Successful.

The light was at last beginning to leave the big living room; the groups of chairs and sofas, shabbier and less grand than they had once been, regained their solemn formality as dusk settled on them. The long couch whose leather was webbed with fine cracks, as Boney's own skin had been; the mahogany sideboard and its bowl of china fruit that Sam longed to handle. The weird commode of inlaid wood, topped with a locked casket.

She worked her bare toes into the carpet. Never, in all her imaginings vague or vivid about where her path would take her from here, what she would have to do and to suffer along it, had she ever thought that it would take her nowhere; that she was here to stay, and it was all decided.

Well it wasn't.

She crossed the room to the impassive commode, and turned the key in its lock, as once last year Boney had done, passing to her one of the house's secrets, maybe having already decided what he was going to do. She opened the casket and took out the velvet drawstring bag inside; tugged open the bag, and let fall into her hand a sphere of quartz crystal about the size of Sam's fist.

A real magician had once owned it, Boney had said (though he hadn't said how he knew this, or how it had come to him). There were angels in it once, he said, they could be seen and spoken to, and would answer; and all their names began with A.

Heavier than she would have supposed it would be. Empty now though, as far as she could see; or maybe it was she who was empty. A thing, a something left over from the past; the thing you most need. And if you find it, that's not it.

She tried to imagine inheriting the right to send people out to find the truth, something people needed to know, something that would be a step further on the path, whatever the path was; whatever it was, it would not remain the same, learning something new would change its course in some small way and there would be no way ever to turn back.

Mike wanted to continue the Foundation's support for their research. She wondered what they were trying to find out. That weird man.

What could you really learn, she wondered. If you put all of the Foundation's money to finding out. Not Boney's nutty quest, she didn't mean that; something real, a real investigation, real knowledge.

She held the magician's cold sphere in her hand, the house's secret, but now her own as well; and it gathered the evening light like an eye.

What do you need? she asked herself. What do you want to know?

2

---

obbie had been with Pierce for a week. Each morning they rose early and did their exercises together, and sometimes walked in the humid morning, observing the fairy-coin webs on dewy lawns, the blue sky forming as the mists burned away. That case of melancholia too, it burned away every morning, his own heart sky-blue by the time they came back for breakfast.

Surely, Pierce thought, the medieval doctors were more correct about desire than latter-day therapists, who saw desire as a sort of continuous rising pressure, the psyche as a boiler needing "release," the blowing-off of steam, in danger of unseaming without it. Such a therapist (Mike Mucho? Pierce knew no therapists, and had never been treated by one) would surely say that since in some sense Robbie was occasioned by enforced chastity and sexual tension, then gratifying release with a real other person ought to cause him to evaporate. But he hadn't.

Every morning, it was true, he had to be re-created anew, Pierce working with Pygmalion's patience on the attenuated phantom until for an instant, a string of instants, he was present, a Real Presence that could be communed with. It grew no easier, but Pierce remained willing, and Robbie didn't cease coming.

He thought, sometimes, appalled, of that moment in Kraft's library, when he had felt his powers, powers to wish and to have, awaken again. *This time I won't waste it,* he had promised that gift-giver or bearer (himself?). *I'm older now, wiser, I won't waste it, I'll use it in the context of life.* He thought of the two foolish people in the story: granted three wishes, one had wished for a fat sausage; the other, outraged at this foolish waste, wished the sausage would stick to his nose; and there was but one use then they could put the last wish to.

There had not been one, not one wish since childhood that his heart had been poured into, that was not about love. If he were Boney Rasmussen, he would not search for eternal life, eternal life was an empty barrel without love, love with sex bound up in it too he meant, as intimately as dreams are bound up in sleep; he could name other kinds of love, he supposed, but had no idea what it would be like to want them this badly. Christ what a case he was. Maybe when he was Boney's age.

He thought of Rose Ryder (as he had sometimes done also, on these July mornings, while Robbie moped or evanesced). He had not heard from her since the night of Boney's death. They had watched fireworks while he died, odd conjunction, imagine how many others that night. Robbie was still here, but she had vanished into Shadowland. He had even forgotten this place's name until on a Saturday morning he saw in the Faraway *Crier,* which he had picked up on his morning constitutional, that the Shadowland Gospel Church was having a Rummage Sale today and a Healing Service tomorrow.

What he had really given thought to was Climacterics. He had mulled over the Mucho system as much as he had the rest of that afternoon's and night's events. He had drawn his own chart, insofar as he could remember the rules, and had found it astonishingly accurate, as accurate as (all it needed to be) astrology or palmistry. He discovered that he was, himself, disconcertingly, just now coming down off a big curve: he had turned thirty-five in December, had seen the wide view from the top (hadn't he? He had) and his little car would soon be gathering speed on the downward track.

He had sorted through his old inward calendars, not well kept. Finally he needed pencil and paper to work out the math.

The last time he had cycled upward had been in the flush and brilliant months when he had been a cocaine dealer's consort, when he had gone up literally: gone up in the mirrored elevator of a tower of naked concrete to a wide-windowed apartment commanding the sunset, where he and she had lived and spent.

Well he came down from there, boy, from that aerie.

He bit the pencil's eraser, studying the crude roller coaster he had drawn. In the Up Passage Year before that one, it had been not himself alone on the upward and outward move but the city and the nation, belled baubled and crying aloud. The whole world, from Paris to Prague. Almost as though . . .

Yes. Almost as though.

He saw, all in a moment, how he could make a subtle improvement or epicyclic addition to the theory of Climacterics which would increase its power tenfold, one that Mike Mucho had perhaps not thought of, or had not noticed was latent in his scheme.

What happens when the rising curve in the seven-year Cycle in a person's life (the life say of a thinker or a doer) coincides with some vague stirrings or upheavals in the common life of a society? Then the liver of that life—all those in fact who stand just then at the same point on the same cycles—will perceive a revolution of immense magnitude occurring unstoppably all around them, the Wave of History cresting, where others standing at different points on *their* cycles perceive only confusion, mess, ignorant armies.

In fact those people on the rise might *make* a revolution just because they *see* one, through the spectrum of their own rainbowing climacteric goggles, without which nothing at all can be seen.

For of course it would be natural for souls subject to these cycles to see the whole history of the world in cyclic terms, and to place their own historical moment on the cycle wherever they themselves happen just then to be standing. Cycles of ups and downs, possibilities and retreats, would account for the convictions we all have at different times in our lives—that the recent past is a dull closed book but the present is full of stirring possibility without limits, or contrariwise that this decade is jejune, a fabric of scraps and tatters, a falling off from the good old days. Cycles would account, in fact, for the oceanic and unchallengeable conviction that the world ("the world," all this, human life in aggregate) is really made up of these vast shifts, climb climax and decline, each one separating us from the older world forever, except for our altered and unreliable memories, which are part of the new world and not the old.

Yes! That's all it was, the individual life interpreting the whole life of the world in the only terms it had, and reinterpreting it as we roll along the cycle, the terms shifting from happy expectation (Up Passage Year) through confident power for change (Plateau Period) through accumulating contradiction and conflict (Down Passage Year) down to gloomy prison of repression and refusal to change (Bottom Period).

And whenever time and the soul that perceives it approach together the median line (as Pierce would soon be approaching it), that's the Passage Time: then there comes that wind of possibility, that blows always along the frontier between Then and Now, between Here and There. Along those colures new gods are born, great dæmons who assemble themselves out of the failing limbs of older and smaller ones; then appalling secrets are imparted to the soul, concealed histories of the world, the names of the Archons. Then we do magic, or fall foul of it.

God it was nothing but psychology, it was *inside* and not *outside* in the world; probably you would not even be able to imagine that once the world had worked in a different way unless you understood, however inchoately, that your own self had. As maybe Kraft had done when writing that last book, headed for death and for the Grand Climacteric at once. Maybe his last book was really a sort of autobiography. So maybe was Pierce's; not a history of the world but of the soul, its chutes and ladders, strivings and failings, taking place against the of course eternal and changeless earth and sky out there.

He rolled a cigarette, gratified, feeling the solid satisfaction of the euhemerist on reducing a myth to sense, without having to give it up.

Robbie, who sat at the daybed's other end in just his shorts, smiled at his father's happy thought; then he lifted his silver flute to his lips, and lowered his long-lashed eyes to play.

That day at midday Pierce got a call from Rose Ryder.

"I don't know about you, Moffett," she said, in a tone he could suppose was teasing but couldn't actually interpret. "I don't know about you."

"What."

"All that about magic. I don't know."

Oh all *that*. What exactly did she.

"Well. Weird dreams for one thing." She laughed lightly, low. "For the past three nights I have been having dreams about magic creatures. And these dreams are very hard to tell from reality. You know? That kind. I dream I go in to sit on the pot, and there's a little girl there, an angel sort of, and I have to brush her away in order to go. She just sort of titters at me. Others, too. Then I wake up and see them in the next room, doing things."

"You wake up and see them?"

"Well I dream I do."

"Doing things?"

"Their own business. Like mice."

"Well," Pierce said. "That's not so bad. They could be doing things to you."

"That's another thing," she said in the same probably teasing possibly accusing tone. He guessed he knew what she meant by this iteration, and he pondered some replies. Before he could choose one, she began to tell him about an incident that had taken place in The Woods, which bore or maybe didn't bear some relation to the day they had spent together and her subsequent or consequent dreams. There had been an encounter with a patient, unsettling, fatidic; her superiors hadn't understood her tricky position; someone had offered her a casual insult.

"I guess I don't completely follow," he said when her story drifted to a halt. He seemed to have been presented with a problem by her, or a difficulty, to solve or at least comment intelligently on, and he had not caught the point. The story was loosely wound up, like a skein of mismatched yarns. The conviction came to him, he seemed now to have evidence enough for it, that this Rose was a weirdo. The longer he talked to her, the more remote she grew, even her voice beginning to sound artificial and far-off, signaling more than speaking.

"Uh huh. Hm. I see."

Man, he thought. To take up this would mean many hours of tedium, only fitfully alight. "I've been thinking, by the way," he said, "about Climacterics," change the subject to one more discussable.

"O God," she said.

"It really is, you know a real old system of signposting a life. You know that."

"Oh, sure."

"Why we reach our majority at twenty-one instead of twenty."

"Sure. I think maybe people instinctively felt it."

"Seven," he said, "is the Age of Reason. In Catholic dogma. The age after which you are held responsible for sin."

"Huh," she said. "Really? Well, see, right there."

"Amid the Etruscans," he said (he had only lately remembered this, the references were turning up one after another like fruit on a slot machine), "men were considered ready for public office at thirty-five. The Romans adopted that from them. We adopted it from the Romans. Which is why you can't be president till you're seven-times-five years old."

"Really. Huh. Listen can you hold on while I get a pencil?"

"Sure."

Where was she? He could hear, faintly, birdsong on her end. The Etruscans, he thought, had actually counted in *fives,* five years to a *lustrum,* never mind.

"Say again?" she said, returning.

He did. He had thought once that he might make a living in the country by setting up a shop, dispensing history to those who needed it. As who, who after all did not. They slipped again into hesitant inconsequentialities. He wondered what he was doing, as perhaps she did herself.

They made another date, though. Closing suddenly at the end of the exchange like horse-traders who had only been pretending to talk about the weather. Pierce cradled the phone carefully, and for a long time sat not thinking of anything: sat as though with his back to a door against which many thoughts were pressing for entrance.

He had lunch at the Donut Hole, beneath the fly-stuck fan that spooned the humid air. He didn't sit in the booth he had shared with Rose Ryder on the Fourth of July, but in a booth from which that booth could be seen. Empty now.

He found he had paid his bill and left the little cafe without really participating in the process, and that he stood now in River Street facing the Blackbury. He shrugged, and walked out across the bridge that crossed to South Blackbury, the less populous shore, that ran along the river southward, lined with factories and rows of workers' houses and rusting water towers. Before this though there was a little row of two-story stores, a bar, a barber, places that seemed to be able

to live in suspended animation off the stored resources of other decades. One was a sort of department store. It had wide windows in
which a few dresses, bolts of fabric, toys were displayed, bearing
hand-lettered price tags; glass doors framed in dark wood, painted
many times, led within. Pierce didn't remember it being here before.
That was not, probably, because it had not been here before, though
indeed there were streets and houses hereabouts so gratifying to his
senses, so useless to the world, that they did seem to be of that kind
that only appear before lost travelers once in a century.

He went in.

There was but one clerk, an elderly woman with a silver chain to
her glasses, busy with her merchandise. He saw he would be alone
with her, a situation that usually made him intensely uncomfortable,
but which now did not. He walked in the coolness, soothed and
happy, around the big tables where shirts and bags and perfumes
were displayed, the overstock in the wide drawers of glossy wood
beneath.

"Hot day."

"Yes it is."

"Anything I can help you with?"

"Oh," Pierce said.

He did not need a bow tie, a pair of boxer shorts, sock suspend-
ers. Yet he would have liked to spend much time here. At last he
chose a chambray work shirt of honest blue, and brought it to the
counter.

"On sale," the woman said, as pleased as he was himself, it
seemed, to be here in the untroubled quiet.

"Oh?"

He noticed on the crowded counter a basket of colored scarves
thrown together. They were a dollar apiece. Pierce took a corner of
one at random and pulled it out. A foot square. The clerk lowered her
glasses, watching Pierce as he chose one, another, another. He could
not have said what criteria he used, but he knew which ones he did
not want. Not this one with bulldog's mugs; not this one with
yachting flags. When he had a cloudy pile of four, he handed them to
the clerk.

"Oh don't fold them," he said. "Please. Just put them in a box.
Can you."

"Sure," she said placidly, unsurprised.

He went out into the heat, the shirt and the white box in a bag; stood for a moment, surprised again to find himself where he was; and turned back toward the Jambs.

Back down River Street, past the library. He went up the stairs, thinking it was possible that Rose might be inside, at her work; then thinking it unlikely; then deciding it was unwise anyway to come upon her now. He turned back down the stairs, and nearly collided with Val, who had been coming up behind him and had not expected him to reverse direction suddenly.

"Hey," she said.

"Hey yourself. Supposed to ascend on the right."

She looked at him warily for half a moment to be sure he intended a joke, and then laughed.

They shuffled momentarily before each other, two big people in an elephant's mating dance, till Val got by.

If he had not been filled with other thoughts, Pierce might have noticed the big book she had in her arms, and glimpsed the title, but he didn't. He didn't recognize its purplish morocco binding either, for the binding on the copy the State Librarian of Kentucky, that pythoness, had sent him was bound differently, in olive buckram. Still he would have taken it from Val and discovered what it was, if he had noticed the complex hieroglyph stamped on its cover, a seal of silence and revelation that he knew.

And if he had taken it from her, and in wonder opened it, would it not very likely have fallen open (in that age of the world, when Coincidence was so strong a god) right to the page from which Val had read to Rosie in the Volcano—that verso page where Plato was quoted on Eros? *He is not to be confused with the beautiful beloved, though men often make this mistake; rather his appearance presages the appearance of the beloved. He is the spirit who inspires love, who makes love unrefusable . . .* And wouldn't he have known then what had siezed him, known it was already past escaping, and thus perhaps have escaped?

He didn't take it from her. That age was passing. Val's arm was over the hieroglyph of the Monas stamped on the book's cover, and Pierce didn't see it, and this time it didn't call to him.

She came to collect him (she was driving, of course) and they went up to a place on the mountain, and had dinner on a broad deck overlooking the confluence of the rivers (the Shadow, the Blackbury) as day turned to night with long reluctance. She talked of her youth, how she had been restless but good, and only later got a little wild.

"Wild," he said. "Now it's an odd thing, because . . ."

"Not so wild," she said. "Really. Comparatively."

"Because once, you know, in Shakespeare's time say, when a man called a woman wild—a poet anyway—it meant she was chaste."

"Oh yes?"

"Yes," he said. "Wild was chaste, like Diana's handmaids. Uncatchable. Untamed." He poured her wine. "The lover set out to tame the wild. It was the tame one who was, who came when she was called."

"Huh." She was listening carefully.

"Who came to eat from his hand. The poet's. Willing to come. To take the bit," said Pierce, and drank. "Funny, huh?"

"Funny," she said.

They talked about The Woods, a place unimaginable to Pierce. She had taken work there somewhat as an underling, earning a college credit in social work and work experience useful in counseling or teaching, where she seemed to be heading, without a lot of enthusiasm Pierce thought. And it had begun to seem that she might lose the job anyway. The Woods was not in healthy shape financially.

"Because a lot of the need for a sort of retreat like that has gone away. Not entirely. But maybe there are too many to share the business. So they've been trying to develop other resources up there."

"Like . . ."

"They offer these week-long sensitivity-training sessions for men. And self-esteem and reorientation workshops for women who are say going back into the job market."

"For men must weep and women must work," Pierce quipped.

"It's real important," she said, as though she meant "unimportant." Important, unimportant. "And then there's the special project in healing."

"The what?"

"A little core group has gotten interested in this," she said, her eyes losing focus in a certain way he was beginning to log, without being able fully to interpret; one thing he thought it sometimes re-flected was other men, passing peripherally through her thoughts, associated with the topic she spoke about. "Non-traditional ap-proaches. Or *more* traditional you might say compared to therapy."

"There are a lot of those." Pierce envisioned astrological medicine, Ficinian mood-alteration by means of solarian plants, music, colors. Surely not.

"Well that was the idea at first. But it's gotten narrowed down. Everybody's gotten real interested in this one guy. A Christian. He's come back twice."

"And he's a healer? What, Christian Science? Or faith healing?"

"Well I'm not sure," she said. "I haven't been invited to be part of it. It's just being a Christian, I think. Healing, you know, like Jesus. I mean I know he says you have to be a Christian."

"To heal or to be healed?"

"Dunno." She looked at him levelly. "Could you do that?"

"No," he said. "Not even to get healed." He rolled a cigarette. "I was raised Catholic," he said. "I think that functions as some kind of inoculation. After that it's almost impossible to become any other kind of Christian. It may immunize against other belief-systems too. I don't know."

"Magic," she said. "Don't you believe in magic?"

He inhaled tobacco smoke, and breathed it out in mystic calm. "No," he said.

"But you think it works."

He said nothing.

Rose ran her finger around the edge of her wineglass, and a faint ghostly cry arose. "If you knew a lot about it," she said, "as much as you know—I'd think you'd be tempted to try it. If I knew a lot about it I'd give it a try."

"You would?"

"Maybe I could be an apprentice. You teach me what you know."

"You could," he said. "You could sit at my feet."

She regarded him for a time, her head nodding ever so slightly first for a moment to one side, then to the other, a small smile on her lips, as though (Pierce thought) she listened first to the good angel on her right, then the bad angel on her left, unwilling to choose between them.

"The training is long," he said. "And terribly arduous."

"But you do know," she said.

He considered. He could say he didn't know. In a sense he didn't. She waited. With a sensation of stepping into dark water, he said:

"The magician does what he wants by knowing the inner workings of things. He knows the big general things that influence everybody—the stars, first of all, I mean the planets, the big forces that control us and make us what we are. He would be able to just look at me and say I was Saturnian. For instance. Under Saturn."

"How?"

"Signs. Emanations. Smells. I don't entirely . . ."

"Well you don't know me, Moffett."

He looked at her without irony, fully and frankly, and for a moment she grew still. What he knew of her had not been picked up by occult means, but only by his sensitive melancholic's antennæ pulling in the faint hint that Rosie Rasmussen dropped, and acting on it. All magic is illusion.

"What his perception gives him," Pierce went on, "is that he knows what images he should project in order to compel the soul he wants to capture."

"Images?"

"Magic pictures he constructs. Power pictures that give him inner strength. Talismans."

"Huh."

"You use them to rule the souls of others." He put out the smoke. "It's called 'binding.' The bonds you forge are called 'chains,' *vincula.*"

"But how do you project them?" she said. She lifted her hands and shot energy through her fingers like a movie sorcerer.

"Well I don't really know how *they* did it. But I don't think it was so different from what we do all the time. We can't think without images, and images have no power to work in us unless we are moved by them. What moves us most is love. Erotic power, erotic energy, desire. One magician said: *Love is magic, magic is love.* Giordano Bruno. He believed you gave life and power to the images you cast with love."

"But by that he didn't mean."

"Oh yes. He meant *love,* love: the same erotic power that binds anybody to anything, anything they desire."

"Love," she said.

"Makes the world go round," he said.

"But if we all do it all the time."

"The difference is that the magician does it *consciously*. Consciously cultivates in himself the erotic energy to animate the powerful images that will bind others."

"Cold."

"Cold love. But hot inside. And dangerous too. The master has to avoid at all costs getting enchained by these hot potent images he has created."

She was listening intently, but maybe not, he thought, to him.

"All these magicians did it, or tried to do it," he said. "They made images of the stars, or of the divine intelligences—angels, dæmons—that power the stars; sometimes they cast medallions of the planets, made of the right metal and so on, and contemplated them, to draw astral powers into themselves, make themselves bigger. Or they made them inwardly, by thought. They said: in their hearts."

She laid her hand on her own breasts lightly, as though she tried to imagine this, or feel a workshop there, where things could be made. Pierce too tried to glimpse inside, through the windows of her eyes, inward-turned and open. "So what could I learn to do?" she said. "If I studied. What things?"

"Well how about," Pierce said, "invisibility." He told her how old wonder-workers had been able, knowing the subtle and astral springs or roots of things, to churn out from their potent hearts images that could actually make them invisible. If you knew what plants, animals, stones, colors, times of day were imbued with the powers of which stars and planets, and if, say, you worked in Leo and the Sun at midday, observers would see no robed image at all but only a golden tabby cat asleep among the dandelions.

"Huh," she said. "See? Invisible." She laughed, moved and happy, making a sense out of what he had said that he could only guess at, and held out her glass for wine.

Afterwards they saw a movie, for an entrepreneur had lately taken over the big bleak grange hall in Stonykill and showed foreign films and esoterica on weekend nights. The movie was a weird and fatuous historical import, a vamp on the life of the mystic nun Hildegarde of

Bingen. Pierce tried not to laugh aloud, though in fact most of the audience was restless and talkative. Hildegarde gave herself to God: she knelt before the stern yet ember-eyed priest to have her starlet's golden tresses cut.

"Oh let's go," he said.

"Wait," she said, and he could feel her private urgency. Hildegarde, shorn and humble, held the mass of hair in her hands. In the projector's light Pierce could see the sheen of Rose's own hair, loosely braided.

In the Asp, careening down through the mountain road's dark turns toward Blackbury Jambs, Pierce expatiated on the silliness of what they had seen, about as medieval as, as; and she was silent. Only long after, when in order to save himself he was condemned to repeat in the solitude of his heart all the moments he had spent with her, would he find that film again, that night back before he understood the extent of her wondrous wiring, or what heats she endured; how she could be aroused unrefusably by, but not only by, the cutting of her hair, by sudden loud noises, by certain whispered words, by long kid gloves, by the nearness of fire.

When they sat again at his kitchen table with a glass (soda water only for her, she couldn't, she said, trust herself further with booze) he let her lead the talk for a while, looping her stories and her hopes and hurts while he listened. Then he stood, and took a flimsy white box from the counter, the sort of box old-fashioned department stores used for their wares.

"Now," he said, "I have a present for you."

He put the box in the middle of the table and waited while she stood up to open it. She unfolded the flanges of the top; the tissue parted, and she drew out the scarves, one, then another, and another. When she had seen them all, she smiled a little, and began to say Well!, but he spoke at the same time, and she stopped still.

He spoke carefully and softly, trying hard not to move, his big hands resting one atop the other on the table. "What I want you to do," he said, "is to take those in the bedroom. Take off your clothes and wait. I'll come in a while."

She didn't simper, or vamp; she said nothing, only across her features came the abstraction he had seen first in the Donut Hole, when he had told her not to button herself. He didn't need to say more. She stood motionless for a moment, as though pausing for some internal assent to come, not her own assent but an assent she awaited; then she gathered up the handful of innocent stuff and left the kitchen with her smooth swift tread.

Pierce remained.

He really hadn't known if that would work: he sat at the kitchen table, his throat thick and his skin burning, trying to gauge what an imperious coldhearted length of time might be, his heartbeats no good for counting. He hadn't ever done anything like this before; he knew not a practical thing about how to bend a woman's will, subject it to his own, *use* her for himself, the project was ludicrous. What he knew about, what he was actually good at, was service: listening for what a woman wanted, and guessing how to supply it, or some part of it, for some length of time.

Well right there it was, too, wasn't it.

He emptied his glass and rose. At the door of the bedroom he stopped, a sinister silhouette (he perceived) against the lighted kitchen behind him, for she had not dared switch on the lamp beside the bed. She had done as he had told her, and lay darkly alit on the russet bedclothes, still in her girlish knee-socks, her head lifted slightly to watch him enter; alert, expectant, a patient awaiting a novel treatment.

He went in to her, unbuckling his belt, not knowing any more than she did herself what they had embarked on. *Embarked*: the word had always had for Pierce a shadow of danger and unknowing in it, a picture in his heart of himself in his fragile boat (a *bark*) setting out in a stiff wind onto a sea of blue-black whitecaps.

She called out his name repeatedly as he worked, her cheek pressed down into the pillow by his hand, her arms and legs bound in imitation silk and unclosable. Pierce, she cried, Pierce, Pierce: and it might have been an imperative as much as a supplication. Certainly it was not a cry directed at him; it could not be, for she didn't know him. By his lies and by his histrionics, by taking the part he took with her and playing it, and not here in bed alone either, he would make certain that she couldn't know him; therefore she couldn't love him, and so could not cease loving him; and so he would be safe, having risked nothing of himself.

That was his sin, that he would try to hide himself behind his sudden and unexpected expertise at this mode, as behind a Mephisto mask or vampire makeup. He would give as good as he got, but he was determined not to be reached. It was a sin he had never tried to commit before: and he would fail at it too, in the end, as he could have guessed even on that night that he would fail.

For of course the dark bond you had to pretend to in order to play the game was going to become a real bond over time without his noticing it or assenting to it. Of course it was. There was no other way for this story to unfold but that way, at least if it was enacted by men and women of Pierce Moffett's time and not by, say, bears or angels. What I tell you three times is true. There was no excuse for not knowing it, and he did know it, he did: that there would come a time when he would try to remove the mask, wipe off the whiteface, and she would not believe the face beneath, or hear his confession, that he had never done any of those things with anyone else ever.

The blackhaired nymph Nimue apprenticed herself to Merlin, and when she had learned his secrets she turned them on him, maybe by mistake, not really knowing what she did; and shut him fast in an oak tree, from which he could not escape. Or—in one telling of the tale—in a cage of glass, where he could not even tell that he was caught. And he remains there to this day.

She left at first light, unwilling to have her car seen in front of his building by day. At the bottom of the stairs she closed the door behind her, not firmly for fear of waking sleepers elsewhere in the house; so it opened again in the dawnwind, and cool air tumbled up the stairs, into the bedroom where Pierce smelled in it the coming day.

She climbed into the Asp's embrace and powered up, feeling the thudding of the drivetrain through her seat as though for the first time; guilty, sated, at once full and empty. At the streetlight in the center of town she paused for a moment staring at its red. She brushed her mouth with the back of her hand, and then looked at it, as though her lip might have been flecked with blood; then she drove through against the light.

It was going to be a clear day, blue and green and already filling with things, with houses and tall yellow signs and the cars of early risers. She drove out across the bridge and turned up the Shadow River road and into the darkness of the firs.

3

---

he hunter Actæon steps into the forest, unafraid however dark it appears; he sends his sharp-set dogs before
him, whippets and greyhounds, far-ranging, keen-
nosed, as unafraid as their master of the forest's depths, the mountain's height. Soon they recognize their prey nearby, the Stag; they
give voice, and make pursuit. A thousand stags before have fallen to
them and to the arrows of their Master; what though this one lead
them deeper and farther than any has before, they will bring him
down.

But see where his pursuit has led Actæon: in the heart of the heart
of the forest darkness, a brilliant lucent pool reflects the blue and gold
of Apollo and the sky; and in the pool—surrounded by her chaste
nymphs, white as cloud, clear as day, naked as a needle, alabaster and
purple—Diana bathes.

Look away, Mortal! No human eye can look upon that terrible
chastity. The hounds recoil in fear and confusion, and Actæon falls to
his knees: but he will not look away. The Stag he pursued has escaped, it is of no consequence, there is only one thing he has ever
pursued in his incessant hunting, and it is this sight: he did not know
it and he knows it now. She who is both Goddess of the hunt and its
object. He will not look away.

O pitiless chaste eyes regarding him, she whom no god has
touched. Actæon senses the soul within him, satisfied and ravenous at
once, leap from his own eyes to dissolve in hers, even as her gaze

pierces him. He has already lost his own form, unwanted anyway, and grown another. He feels the heavy horns like a crown spring from his fortunate brow. And the hounds that once coursed for him turn on him, knowing their duty, and set upon him to rend him. For Actæon has become what he pursued.

Cast an emblem, or a seal; carve a statue, paint a picture, and mount it in the central chamber, the inmost circle of the maze of Memory: Actæon, the Philosopher, sending his sharp-set Thoughts in pursuit of swift-flying Truth, comes at last on Beauty bare: the untouched unknown flame of intelligential fire burning at the center of the dark world of material shadows. And on seeing it the Philosopher becomes what he pursued: dies to himself, and lives in Her.

Trembling slightly, for no reason he recognized, Giordano Bruno Nolano stood awaiting the return of Diana from her park.

The huntsmen came first, with the stag she has shot trundled on a leafy branch between them. Light applause and murmurs of approval came from the guests and the courtiers. The deer's tongue lolled from its fallen head, and its bright blood, bluer than Bruno's own, dripped thickly on the dewy grass. Next the handmaidens, all in white as they always were, he had never bothered to distinguish among them or give them names.

Last, she came out from the park on her foot-cloth horse, led by the Earl of Leicester, who carried her little crossbow too. Not naked, no, encased even for the hunt in all her manifold coverings, her redingote, forepart, cloak; petticoat, round gown, slashed sleeves; ruff, gloves, hose and boots.

Within, though, within, past the white smallclothes, she was naked, and untouched. They have all thought it.

She dismounted. His sponsors brought the Nolan forward—they were Sir Walter Raleigh and Edward Dyer, poets, devotees of Diana. She offered him her hand in its figured glove (black kid, worked with small flowers: strawberry, pansy, violet, almost too small to see, only when her hand was kissed did the eye come close enough to see the gilded fly, pismire, polished beetle in amid the thicket, where the jewels of her rings were cast away). He did not touch his lips to her person. Once he had kissed the Pope's ring so, warned not to touch it, osculation would wear it away in a thousand years.

—The gentleman wishes to offer Your Majesty a work of his own composition.

—The gentleman pays to your Majesty and her realm and people many sincere and well-wrought compliments in it.

Her smile was instant and genuine, enlisting him at once and forever in a gay army, hers. He permitted it. There was enough of himself; he could give her much, as much as she would take.

—Well let us see, she said. She took the book he proffered, and lifted him up. What is your subject?

—My subject is Love, he said in Italian. She answered him in the same language:

—Do you praise him?

—I must. There is no force on earth found greater than Love.

She laughed, as at an extravagance that pleased her, and her eye regarded him more critically. He would not look away abashed, his spirit rose to his eyes to meet hers looking in, though it was confusing to look at her in the midst of the thousand potent jewels that surrounded and protected her, cold milky pearls, hot rubies, liquid emeralds, gold, silver, adamant.

—*Eroici furores,* she said. Do you mean the frenzy of lovers? Men say they are slain by their love's eyes, that they die of love. Do you feign that? In our country we say: men may die, and worms may eat them, but not of love.

—Madam, he said. The love of which I have written is not the common love of men and women. Not even that more noble love of your courtiers and servants—of whom I name myself one—for your Majesty's sacred person.

—No?

—No. I have written, under the figures of Actæon and Diana, Phyllis and Clorinda, he and she, eyes and stars and darts and hearts, of another love than these.

—Ah, said the Queen. Does it become our servant to tell us he has another love?

For a moment Bruno (caught in a sort of stoop, so as to keep his head lower than the Queen's) felt checked. The skirt of her gown, he observed (his eyes being pointed that way) was a sea: rocks, ships, great fish coming forth, seed-pearl foam on satin waves, drowned men, treasure, pearls cast up on golden sands.

—For your sake, Madam, he said, a servant might with a flaming heart pursue Truth. Knowledge. Love himself. To bring him finally to bend the knee before Your Majesty.

Cautiously she smiled. Her forepart was worked with a forest, fountains, stubs of dead trees, moss of deep velvet pile; a forest fire too, astonishing, and animals fleeing it, ermine, squirrel, fox and hart. Water earth air and fire.

—Your master, the Ambassador, returns to France soon, she said to him. Will you go with him?

—Sadly. Unwillingly.

—In other of your books, we are told, you speak highly of our cousin of France. Henri. You promise him service, and wish more crowns for him. Is it so?

—His Majesty has favored me. I do what I can. What little.

—Yet you would serve us.

She smiled, and laid her gloved hand lightly on his wrist.

—Be our servant still when you return. Speak well of us to our cousin there. Tell him we desire his friendship against all intolerant and unjust powers whatever. Tell him that.

He could only bow. She granted him a last long entangling look, and glanced again at his book as she turned away.

—Love, she said. Love.

Love is the cause of life; no power on Earth is found stronger than love. Eros is the Great Dæmon, the little lord of this world; the strongest bond of the will is Venus' loose girdle.

Even in the Animal Kingdom Eros rules: no male will tolerate a rival, no female either; the lowliest beast will forgo food, drink and every other pleasure, even risk life itself, for love, how often we see.

Love drives old and young; it drives hot youths into one another's arms against every prohibition of priests and elders, kings and kin, drives them into love-sickness, madness, even death. Love surprises grave senators and abbesses, tormenting their old flesh with young heats, making them dance and caper to his tune.

Gigantic love turns the Earth in her socket; love for the Sun's beauty constrains her to circle forever around that lamp like a deathless moth; self-love alone, and the desire to prolong pleasure forever, keeps Earth from plunging into the beloved body and being lost in it; and even so, with every century she grows a measure closer to her love.

Love in God is endless fecundity, the continual, generous, un-stinting production of things; love in Man is the endless hunger for the products of Infinity, never satisfied.

Love is magic: able to fascinate and capture the unwary, able to make a man or a woman see what is not there and fail to see what everyone else sees, able to transform the stunted and beetle-browed swain to Hermes, the cowpoxed maid to Phyllis.

Magic is love: nothing but the power of love in the heart of the operator can move the souls of others; nothing but love can command the intelligences of the air. Magic and love will carry the hunter after truth at last beyond the chock-full caves and dens of Memory into the austere mountaintops, will allow him at last to look on Intelligential Beauty bare. Her kiss exiles his own meager soul, replacing it with her own image, material reflection of the single ultimate reality; he has ceased to be a man, he has become a God.

Without love even the simplest Art of Memory could not operate; without attraction and revulsion, what attaches the soul to images?

Poor Dicson: his little book on Memory had been fallen upon by the pedant doctors, just as he had feared it would be, *i Puritani* as he called them; one of them had issued a pamphlet showing how Dicson's Art of Memory was not only useless, it was impious, too. Just as Dicson had said: because it set up false gods within, Statues, Images. This man (he was a fellow of the other college, not the one Bruno had been evicted from) advocated instead the memory methods of Peter Ramus, arch-pedant of France, which used a schoolboy system of Specials and Generals set out on a written page, numbered and lettered.

And not only that: this ass of Cambridge had caught Dicson advising that, since the images used in memory must be of a kind to excite the feelings, the image of a beautiful woman would be very effective if established in a Memory House. Outrage and pious horror: there it was, the only sin more horrifying to those strange half-men than idolatry.

Dicson—a man of their country himself, Scotland, after all—was shocked and affronted by this charge of licentiousness, lewdness, hotness. But of course the man was right. Bruno had asked Dicson: Do your memory images make your heart beat, your breast warm, do they make your male part stand? They should; they must. If we dare not use Love ourselves, Love will use us, there is no escaping him;

hate too, revulsion, disgust, they are only the obverse of his coin, let us use them too, let us capture and not be captured.

The English gentlemen of Bruno's acquaintance—Sidney, Dyer, Fulke Greville—had laughed at the Cambridge dominie and his strictures against the Art of Memory, they seemed to think such men comical, Bruno knew better; but still they were quite capable of talking with great seriousness and wrinkled brows of Ramus and his trivialities, they could be moved by what they called Reformed Religion and the new plain style. Bruno cast in his mind the emblem: nursemaid Thames, shelterer of many orphaned children, suckles unwittingly a wolf.

The memory controversy, Bruno said to them, was easily settled. Let the gentlemen sponsor a great Tourney of Memory or Remembering Contest, in which a champion of the Great Art handed down from Ægypt through the Greeks to Albertus, Aquinas and the present would be set against a champion of the new anti-pictorial method of the Frenchman. The best man to bear away the palm. Bruno projected it to them vividly: the amphitheater, decked with myrtle and rosemary (for Apollo and Venus) and cloths of solarian blue and gold; high seats for the nobility, and one, the highest, for the Judge herself, Justice, Astræa. In the center the two lecterns, water or wine beside them; the Ramist to have reams of paper and sharpened goose-feather pens and a jug of ink if he likes. The Brunist needing nothing but heart and mind.

First problem set, the names of the inventors of all human arts and useful things. The Ramist slowly starts his cart's wheels with a General—Agriculture. A Special beneath that, Grain; a more special Special, Sowing of; and at length the name of the inventor of sowing, Triptolemus. Meanwhile the Brunist sheds the light of an inner sun out through the spheres of the planets, to the elements they inform, to the life of man on Earth, to the inventors of things rank on rank in their places, colored by the planets' colors, each holding the sign of his Art: in the circle of Saturn alone were Chiron inventor of surgery, Zoroaster of magic, Pharphacon of necromancy, Circe of fascination; under Sol Apollo there was Mirchanes who first made figures of wax, Giges who first painted pictures, Amphion who invented the musical notes; Mercury had Theut who invented writing, patron of the scribbler at the next lectern; Prometheus, Hipparchus, Atlas, dozens more, the ladies and gentlemen stare and murmur in awe; and the Brunist allows himself here one pretty jest, the name of the inventor of Re-membering by Seals and Shadows—Giordano.

The struggle goes on for hours. In the *examen* Latin histories are read, the Ramist scribbling Specials and Generals and watching his outline press relentlessly toward the right-hand margin while the Brunist only opens his great heart. Repeats the matter backward and forward while the Ramist hems and haws, searching for the gist. The Ramist does better in the *ad-libitum,* with all the propositions of Eu-clid, though the listeners grow restless; the Brunist summons to his aid the Century of Friends, and has them repeat in their galliards and gallops all the names of the ladies present, in the order of their entrance (impressed upon his memory by means of the Century as they entered and took their seats), and the crowd murmurs in delight.

More problems set, remembering the contents of ships unloaded at Wapping, inventories of the Queen of Sheba's jewels, names of the children of Deucalion and Pyrrha, the price of turnips throughout the reign of the Emperor Charles. Ramist sweats and grinds his teeth, his white bands wilting. Brunist asks for harder matter, the order of all the trees by their species in Windsor Forest, the disposition of their leaves. And now by degrees, more quickly for some than for others, a strange and wonderful motion takes place: the memory arts of the Brunist have begun to create within the souls of the ladies and gentle-men the image of a living world, a world of innumerable and endless processes producing an infinite number of things, inside every one of which is a divine spark that orders it without error or hesitation into its place in the ranks of creation from lowest to highest.

When they have begun to grasp this infinite inward world, they also begin to feel the memory artist directing their attention (he is their guide, though they know it not) to the Kingdom into which they have been born, fortunate Kingdom in the midst of the mountains, oceans, lands of Earth that rides round the Sun amid the infinite suns of creation; and to the Queen of their Kingdom, here present, to the great ardent multicolored soul within her garments, within her body, their own Sun of justice and peace. They understand. Love floods their hearts, and each renews his, her vows of fealty and duty to her.

The Brunist steps forward (the Ramist long since silent, or adding by his cackles and his paper-handling a note of hilarity) and makes his own obeisance. About them palpably the divine intelligences look on, Peace, Fecundity, Pleasure, Truth, Intellectual Delight, summoned here by his spirit's exertions. He knows by her eyes that she knows what he has accomplished for her but not only for her; and she, *unica Diana,* lifts him up. To sit by her.

Giordano Bruno looked out his high small window in the French Embassy at the winter river. Up and down the stairs behind him the serving-men went, carrying the packed trunks and *impedimenta* of the household.

Well it was not to be. He had got no forum here beyond the Ambassador's dinner table, and when he wrote a sort of Copernican comedy about a dinner party (complete with aged watermen, rude English mob, Oxford pedants, negligent noble lords) they failed also to see the fun, and failed also to see the Sun rising. A feast of ashes was his lot here.

Perhaps living isolated at the muddy end of the world had made the English dense, hard to work with; they were not unintelligent, not ignoble, but somehow unable to take any important matter seriously. His own motto had always been *In hilaritate triste, in tristitia hilare,* but the English always took him wrong, offended and affronted by his jokes, unable to believe he meant what he said in earnest. Sir Sed-Ne, with his careless smile. Who affirmed nothing, and therefore (he said) never lied.

Even the Queen, when he had sent forth his spirit to her in love and (a man must) command, was able to deflect and avoid it, turn herself to toy fortifications against which real siege was useless.

A remarkable woman, a remarkable spirit.

They said she had always had the advice of the Doctor across the river, who had cast her nativity, and taught her his arts. Treated her aches and pains too no doubt.

He (if it had been he) had made her strong, but he had made her small, too.

No matter. He did not often truly expect that kings and monarchs could understand or imagine how to use the powers he offered them. Henri of France, offered the *Shadows* and a sure method of generating potent love for his own divine person in his subject's hearts, love that would assure his Kingdom in perpetuity, had instead sent Bruno to idle here. High as they were in the order of things, they were no wiser, usually, than other men; their souls were infants in their aged hearts, squalling for praise and comfort, or dry stones that could not be struck.

So he would go on; return to France, but not stay long there. Out on the river a fat Hanseatic merchantman was being tugged into the wind by laboring galleys, her sails luffing, flags being run up.

He asked his soul: Little wanderer, where will you go now, what will become of you?

There had been talk at Court that John Dee had had audience with King Stephen of Poland, and was now resident at the Emperor's court in Prague, waited on by the wise men of that city. Making gold. So it was said.

Paracelsus, the German philosopher, had once written that he who wishes to explore Nature must tread her books with his feet. One country, one page: thus the *codex Naturæ,* thus the leaves must be turned. Alexander Dicson had told him that; Bruno had never read Paracelsus and never would, but that statement he liked. One country, one page. If kings and princes would not hear his call, perhaps an Emperor would.

He rose from the sill where he had leaned. He had, himself, little to pack; a box or two of books, cases of paper. If they were lost at sea, he could re-create them all from memory.

Set out, he thought, set out, set out.

4

---

here are many Monarchs, and many Princes, but only one Emperor. Rudolf II, King in his own right of Hungary and Bohemia, Archduke of Austria, became Emperor by election and the chrism with which the Pope had anointed his head: Singular and Universal Monarch of the Whole Wide World. Or at least his shadow.

His grandfather Charles, who had been king of all the lands Rudolf was king of, had been king of Spain too, ruler of the Netherlands and Low Countries; he was king of Savoy, lord of Naples and Sicily, he had had the Pope at his feet and sacked His City, Rome. God's scourge. Charles had had a device made for him, of all the famous devices and signs and emblems of great rulers the most famous, known and seen throughout Christendom and in lands around the world that the old emperors in Rome had never known existed. Charles's emblem showed two pillars—they were the Pillars of Hercules that stand at the Gates of the Sea, the gates to the New World. Around these two pillars ran a banner, that bore these words: *Plus oultra,* "Even farther." The emblem was cut on medals and embossed on shields and breastplates, it was engraved in wood and printed on the title pages of geographies of the New World, and it was stamped on coins made of gold that was dug on the other side of the world. This emblem was so famous that it went on being stamped on gold coins long after Charles was dead, for so long that the dies lost their detail, and the words of the motto were worn away, and still it kept being stamped on Spanish coins, though all that was left to be seen were the two pillars and the twining banner, no longer meaning "Empire" or "Charles" or "Even farther" but only "dollar":

$$ \mathbf{\$} $$

No kingdom is eternal.

Rudolf had read the histories, he had read Aurelius, he knew. Earthly empires will not last. Charles's possessions (on which the Sun could not set) he had had to divide finally among his sons, Italy, Spain, Austria, no single man great enough to hold them all in his embrace. Now the sons' sons faced each other warily across the map, as though the world were not big enough for them.

Earthly empires pass. But Rudolf's empire had been instituted by God; like Christ's Kingdom, it was not, or not entirely, of this world. No matter how his sway was challenged, no matter how many lands were hived off from it, the Empire itself could not die. It would contract for a time, shrinking like a snail; its peopled lands, governments, armies, navies, would be distilled into potent symbols small enough to be carried in procession, carved onto jewels, worn around the neck of the Emperor. Though it contracted so far, even to the compass of his own sacred person, still it contained within itself the power of sublimation, and when a new age had come it could regrow all its parts from the seeds, the jewels and the symbols, which the Emperor kept in his caskets. No matter what *they* thought, contentious bishops, princelings, reformers, nuncios, truculent populaces of walled cities, they still lived within the One Holy Roman Empire.

Meanwhile the Emperor himself, in advance of his Empire, had been withdrawing from visibility. He would not marry, despite his counselors' pleadings. He had left his city of Vienna, seat of his ancestors, and removed his court to Prague. He retreated into his castle, into his private apartments, his bedchamber, his bed often enough. Like many who suffer from melancholy, his spirit tended to become fixed on unanswerable questions. How was the essence of Empire contained in a jewel cut with an emblem? What counted more, the nature of the jewel or the construction of the emblem? And when he sought distraction from his obsessions, in his collections, his clocks, painting, metallurgy, genealogy, the distractions tended to become obsessions too. He gave more and more time to less and less.

He had lately conceived a plan for making an automaton which could replace himself at his official duties: processions, christenings, feasts, masques and Masses. Clockwork could animate it, prayers and conjurations (white ones, white ones) done in the proper times could give it a temporary intelligence. But what could be done with it so that its touch was healing, its prayers were heard by God, its blessings efficacious?

A jewel, the right jewel, carved with the right sign, enclosed in its empty heart of hearts.

The Jews of the city were rumored to be able to make a man of dirt, who would be given life when the right Hebrew letters were marked on its brow. What heart was *it* given? When its tasks were done the rabbi erased one letter of the word on its forehead (what word? The Emperor could not remember) and changed the word to Death.

He might talk to the Great Rabbi, ask him the trick of it. He had not yet, but he might. He thought about it, and waited for his gem-hunters to come back from their expeditions in the Giant Mountains. When they came back with nothing, nothing of extraordinary value, the Emperor went to bed again.

He was the most famous melancholic in Europe, and employed a dozen doctors of several nations and schools, listening to all and to none, and always ready to hear others. The regimens they prescribed appalled his torpid heart: diets, exercise, abnegations, copulation with young women, music while he slept, tiger's milk taken in wine wherein a pearl has been dissolved, a man would have to have an unappeasable lust for life to be willing to undertake all the bother of it. As the disease was obscure, ramifying, and mutable, there should be one, simple, pellucid medicine; the Emperor was certain such a medicine existed, and that it was his curse to need it, and his destiny to find it. His doctors told him that to believe so was only a further symptom of his condition; but the medicine, of course, would cure that too.

When he got John Dee's letter, and the little book of the Monad that Dee had dedicated to his father Maximilian (his secretaries had known not to delay such a letter, as they knew to delay others that might contain unsettling news or unanswerable requests) he laid the book on the table by his bed, where he might pick it up when he awakened sleepless and frightened in the night. He opened it last thing before he closed his eyes, and stared at the complex knot on its title page, which was taken apart and reassembled within. The book said it was composed of a point, which generated a line, which formed a circle, the Sun, and a Cross, which was the four elements; the seven planets were in it, the geometry of Euclid, the signs of the Zodiac, starting with Aries at the foot, Cardinal Fire, which was its *incipit* and beginning.

It was a Hieroglyph of the Work. Rudolf could see that; he had struggled with enough of them, secrets encased in an emblem, emblem wrapped in verse, verse explained in mysteries.

O thrice and four times happy, the man who attains this quasi-copulative point in the Ternary and rejects and removes that somber and superfluous part of the Quaternary, the source of obscure shadows. Thus after some time we obtain the white vestments brilliant as snow.

Change black to white, dress the Child, prepare for the Marriage, Gemaæa of Earth and Heaven. He had heard it before.

O Maximilian! May God through His mystagogy make you (or some other scion of the House of Austria) all-powerful when the time comes for me to rest in Christ, so that His potent Name may be restored amid the unbearable shadows hanging over Earth.

Unbearable shadows. If they could lift. The Emperor turned back to the page whereon the Monad was displayed. Though he stared long at it, it communicated nothing to him; yet that night he slept without waking. In the morning he sent to Dee's lodgings to call him to the Castle.

A thousand steps lead up from the Old City of Prague to the gates of the Hradschin palace, called Hradĉany in the Bohemian language. The steps are carved from the stone basis on which the Castle stands, they wind and climb and are of uneven heights and widths, the foot continually mistaking its place on the next, unable to find a rhythm. On the steps, in hovels and in caves in the stone, in tents and out in the open air, beggars and fortune-tellers cluster, and those suffering from hideous diseases and disfigurements (or those pretending to such disfigurements for alms); whores, lost children, saints who have had visions of the end; and those bringing pleas or petition to the Emperor who halfway up the endless climb (so it seemed to Doctor Dee) had abandoned their search for justice or mercy and now reclined in positions of despair, hardly able to lift an imploring hand to passers-by.

He climbed, hale old man impelled by his purpose, glad of the strength of his legs, increased by his years of clambering over the heights of Britain searching for her antiquities and sacred places. He rehearsed as he climbed the words of the Angel Uriel to them this midnight past: *If he live righteously and follow me truly I will hold up his House with pillars of hyacinth, and his chambers shall be full of modesty and comfort. I will bring the East Wind over him as a Lady of Comfort, and she shall sit upon his castles with Triumph, and he shall sleep with Joy.*

The guards and stewards at the gates seemed to have been set there to keep people out and not to let them in. Doctor Dee spent half the morning knocking at this wicket and being sent away to that one and thence to another before his *bona fides* were finally admitted, and then he was swept within joyfully, His Majesty awaits you, why have you delayed, up up we go.

The Emperor's Lord Chamberlain, Octavius Spinola, a learned courtier from whom Dee had had kind letters in extraordinary Latin, took the skirt of his robe and led him up a further titanic flight of stairs where (he said) armed men had once ridden their steeds to Mass; beneath fantastical fan vaulting spreading like laced fingers and hands, through doors opened for them, past rows of cabinets and cases where who knew what was kept, into the private apartments where the shutters were half-closed against the summer sun; through the dining chamber to the Emperor's own chamber. Full neither of modesty nor of comfort, a tall chill room, a huge table of black mahogany where the Emperor sat with a great silver service beside him, and an open casket, from which he had taken a copy of the *Monas*, bound in gilt leather: Dee recognized it.

—It was my father's, the Emperor said. I found it today.

—He was a great and a good man, said John Dee, and I honor his memory.

Was it an illusion of the unlit room, or did he see the Emperor's eyes grow moist?

—It is too hard for my understanding, he said, opening the book. But if you tell me I will listen. Take wine.

The Chamberlain poured from the huge ewer, and retired. They were alone. John Dee, who had attended the Queen of England and taught her alchemy, who had laid petitions before King Stephen of Poland, who had put into Maximilian's hand a book dedicated to him in friendship as well as duty, was silent for a time, abashed: not by the presence he stood in, but by the unseen ones, whose hard message was his to speak.

He began to speak of his childhood. His father Roland had been a servant of Henry of England. He had grown up in London near the river. He had seen extraordinary things in youth, and had heard the voices of intelligences he could not see. No more; not since he had reached man's estate. Yet he had not forgotten that everywhere, in every atom, in every region of the air, kindly ones observe us, wish for our welfare, speak on our behalf before the Throne of God.

Now they had come to speak to him directly. Not to him, though; no, he could not hear them, his ears were stoppered and his eyes were blind; but by the grace of God he had found a friend, and with him he had received the angels' news, and written it all down in twenty-eight books. Those books he had brought with him to this City, and the Emperor was invited to study them. He, like Dee, would see what they intended, what great climax the world approached, and what must now be done to meet it, and to make a new world, better than the old.

He did not hesitate to tell Rudolf that in order to realize the angels' gifts and promises, the Emperor must turn away from his sins, and repent. Christ did not fear to say so to the mighty, and speak truth to power; and Doctor Dee's commission was from Christ's Angel Uriel. So he spoke. The Emperor (who had had five children by his mistress, the wife of his favorite antiquary; who had neglected his duties to God and man, who had not opened his mail in a month, who wanted to die by his own hand or live forever) only regarded him, the untouched cup before him.

—I feign nothing, said the Doctor. Neither am I a hypocrite, or ambitious. I am not doting or dreaming. If I speak without just cause in this matter, I here forsake my salvation.

Unmoved, or at least unreadable (it was his Spanish upbringing, he could listen to anything without a change in his face, however his soul might be shaken), the Emperor at last arose from his chair.

—Do you, he asked, possess the *Steganographia* of the old Abbot of Sponheim, Trithemius?

—I do, said Doctor Dee. I copied it myself, many years ago.

—I have it. I have the Abbot's own manuscript. Somewhere. He was a confessor of the first Maximilian, my father's grandfather. The *Steganographia* tells how angels may be called. Hundreds of them.

—I tried his methods in youth, said Dee. No one came when I called. They cannot be compelled; they come when they choose. And so they did come in their time.

The Emperor clasped his hands behind his back and paced slowly. A shorter man than Dee would have guessed him to be, seeing him seated; his big head, the lantern jaw and beard.

—Maximilian once asked Trithemius, said the Emperor. Why can a wicked man get power over evil spirits, and force them to tell him secrets, get him things, when a good man can get nothing out of an angel.

Doctor Dee bowed his head.

—They have been greatly generous to us, he said. They have completed my books, that I could not see to finish; they have given us other books of wisdom that the world will not empty for a thousand years. They have given us a stone of more value than any earthly kingdom.

The Emperor ceased his slow pacing.

—A stone?

—I mean a glass, said Dee. Wherein they themselves can be seen, and spoken to.

—Hm, said the Emperor. He resumed his walk, and it brought him again to the table, and the *Monas*.

—Can you make the Stone? he asked.

Doctor Dee knew what he meant, for he had been told that the Emperor would ask; and he gave the answer he had been instructed to give by the Angel Uriel:

—Yes, he said. With the help of God and His Angels, I can make the Stone. They have told me that I can succeed.

The Emperor fixed Dee with his hurt eyes, which could be read as doubtful, or eager, or needful, like a shy child's: and John Dee understood why Uriel had spoken of Rudolf as he had.

—They intend you comfort, he said gently to the Emperor of all the earth. They do.

———————

The Stone of the Philosophers and Elixir of Life is made from philosophic gold, which is gold created out of base matter by the virtue of the Stone. The only way to make the Stone is as a product of the work of making philosophical gold; and the only agent that can make the Elixir out of the gold is the Stone. This is why the process is represented by the image of the dragon that consumes his own tail.

But the first step is to attempt the gold; and the making of gold is a simple thing.

The Earth and the world, as mother and father, make gold of baser matter, and you must do it the same way, and be mother, father and midwife to the gold you make.

First, you must have a *prima materia* such as God made from nothing. Since God went right to work on this *prima materia* he made, and changed it by addition and division and combination to become all the things that are, you must re-create it for your work: you must subtract from some existent thing the additions of this and that which make it what it is—the earth, air, fire and water present in their various degrees—and leave only the original ground of being, Substance naked, bland, indescribable. Any part of creation might be used—take shape-shifting Mercury, take lead, take horsepiss, they all have the same substance in them. This is why the wise workers have said the Stone lies all around us, in the air, in the street, in the field, unnoticed and precious.

So: when you have stripped away by degrees all that makes your base matter what it is, you need only add to it by degrees that which will give it the qualities of gold: that is, yellowness, nobility, softness, the proper weight, tastelessness, and all else gold has. How? You must put into it a seed, as a man puts a forming seed into the hot formless chaos within a woman's womb, around which collects a human child. Gold grows from a seed projected within the chaos or gas or nameless Substance you have made of nameable matter.

In the same way gold has grown for ages in the mountains from which men dig it: from a seed planted in the dark womb in the beginning of the world. Your gold will grow the same, only quicker, for you will force it, as a gardener forces plums in his greenhouse: force it by heat to quicken and put forth.

What seed, though?

Of all the simple hard parts of the easy quick way of making gold this is accounted the hardest. There is not much that maddened workers have not tried. Sulfur first for its yellowness, with salt to fix it to the naked body of the matter; antimony; cinnabar, the Sun's other metal; gold itself, then make it spread somehow throughout the corpse; or some concoction of all of these and others, calcined, distilled, fermented, coagulated or incerated. Until you have the seed of projection, the work cannot be finished; it cannot even properly be commenced.

Edward Kelley had the seed of projection. It was in a stone jar stoppered with wax, a minute quantity of a reddish powder, the powder that a spirit had given him in exchange for his soul. It might have been the demon's own concoction, made to snare him as lime snares birds; or—as Kelley thought—it might be a bit of the seed mixed within the earth at the Creation to make gold grow, which the subterranean powers had been able to catch and save.

What unclean bargaining had gone on between those earthy powers and the airy spirit that had won Kelley's soul? It didn't matter, for the dog-faced thing that had accompanied him for years had been foiled and banished, the angel Madimi had won Kelley's soul back for him: so he was twice-saved now, and could never be damned again, no matter what he did.

And he still had the demon's powder.

—Today we begin, said Doctor Dee.

The Emperor's chamberlain Spinola had arranged that they should have the house of the Emperor's senior physician, a Dr. Hajek (known by reputation to Doctor Dee), who was away on the Emperor's business. The house was well-furnished for the Work, of which Dr. Hajek was a devotee; there was a sound furnace of brick, and a collection of vessels, cucurbites, retorts, alembics; there were materials in their appropriate containers, such as picric, *aqua regia,* Mercurius, antimony, *sal cranii humani,* labeled in a neat German hand, the same hand that had spelled on the walls in the German fashion proverbs, saws and instructions concerning the Work, more distracting than helpful, as were the vessels, instruments, and rare earths, if it came to that, little of which they would need.

Firewood in quantity they had purchased and piled in the yard, sorted by size and by wood, to be used as needed to make a hotter or a slower fire, ash, oak, yew and pine each having its own heat. John, the boy, would bring what was asked for the insatiable fire to feed on, now gorging, now fasting.

When the athenor was sealed—the great egg-shaped vessel within which the agony was to take place—Kelley took the stone jar of powder from the wallet where he kept it, and gave it to John Dee. They wondered if it should be opened now, before the Work was begun, or only at that time when it was needed. With all his heart Kelley wanted to look upon it, but he would not let Dee unseal it. No: Keep it by you, he said; wait, he said, till all the rest is done; you will know when.

After two days of ablutions and abstention, when they had attended Divine Service and adored the Host and Chalice, figure and model of all transformations, and had eaten (and drunk too, in the Bohemian fashion) that Elixir of everlasting life, then the fire was lit, and the vessel put within the furnace with anxious prayers and with trepidation, as though they meant to burn alive a friend, which indeed they did mean to do. And Kelley sank to his knees before the furnace, and felt his spirit tugged out of his body toward the shut doors and the vessel within.

The Work commenced in the sign of Aries, not Aries in their own world (where it was high summer, peaches ripening against the garden wall) but the sign the Sun now entered in the very different heavens of the world-egg, the athenor, which Doctor Dee had set like a clock at the proper hour, to run through a whole year, twelve signs, twenty-eight mansions of the Moon, thirty-six decans, three hundred sixty degrees, three hundred sixty-five days and a few hours more. John Dee calculated that the alchemical year would fit within a day and a night.

They were to spell each other in tending to the fire, but when Kelley's time was done (Dee turned the great sand-glass to begin his own) he could not be roused. He had knelt continuously before the furnace for eight hours. Evening had come, and its airs came in at the windows. John Dee took the dressing-gown from his own back and put it over Kelley's trembling shoulders. And knelt to watch beside him.

Matter is a shut palace. Inside, in the inmost chamber, is the King, barren, idle, without issue; black melancholy sits in his face. His arms and feet might be shackled, he might wear a crown of obsidian bound with iron bands. Or he is sick, hurt with an old wound, and refuses all treatments, despairing; or he has armed himself against enemies and friends alike, double-locked his gates, set terrible guards, and weeps alone in anger and fear deep within.

Kelley could see the towers, beyond the border of this flowery mead, over the tops of that greening wood. Set out.

A pretty way entered the wood, but then he could not see how to get out. Yew, ash, oak and pine held him with their branches; briars plucked at his flesh (how had he come to be naked?) and fear brought tears to his eyes. Though he had been here before, had come this far on past journeys to this place, he could not remember what was to happen next. He looked around himself, and knew that he was lost.

Lost.

He felt a terrible thirst, and even as he felt it he apprehended a spring, coming forth in the dark wood, and a silver stream fed by it; and he knelt gasping in gratitude to drink.

When he was satisfied and raised his head, the wood appeared to him differently: not wild but ordered, paths he had not perceived before leading in four directions; along one the moon was setting, along another the sun rose. It was the first day of May. Along the sunward path he saw coming toward him a boy, each stride carrying him so far it seemed his feet were winged, or that he glided on the sun's beams toward Kelley.

Gratitude and gladness, like the gratitude he had felt swallowing clear water. He knew this youth, who would use him kindly, as a friend: look at his smile, that cast out care and anxiety, look at his feet and hands, winged. He would guide Kelley from the wood.

No sooner had Kelley given his heart to the youth than from the dark wood around there appeared three armed men, black grinning villains, one with a net, one with a glinting knife, one with a crossbow and cruel barbed arrow. O Christ Jesus the lad did not see them, and Kelley was mute; though he screamed soundlessly, the boy came on, and the arrow *pierced his white breast,* Kelley felt it pierce his own at the same moment. The iron huntsman with the net threw it over the shot bird. The third tested his knife's blade against his thumb. And as the beautiful youth twisted and struggled silently, his winged hands were cut off at the wrists, and his pale blood gushed to mingle with the silver water of the stream; and then his feet, their wings fluttering wildly and vainly; and all that time his eyes regarded Kelley with a plea, was it a plea to help, he could not, or a plea not to forget, he would not.

He lay still, amputated.

The murderers, still grinning wickedly with white teeth, bound him securely in the net and bore him up upon a pallet of oak. Kelley followed the bier, sole mourner; but when they reached the gates of the shut palace he was carrying the hurt boy in his arms. The door was sealed with a seal, they could not get in, but when Kelley looked closely he seemed to recognize the seal. Yes he knew it:

It was without its oval cartouche or container, he wondered why, till he knew it was all around him, *crater* or *vas Hermetis,* this world, these heavens, where now the summer constellations wheeled, the sign of Gemini, linked twins, he and the boy, in the house of Lucrum.

The door opened as he gazed at the seal on it.

He carried the boy (nestled now against him like a sleeping child) down corridors of flint and darkness, past sleeping guards, through cobwebbed doors. The crippled child began to whisper in his ear: Take me no farther. Free me. Free me and I will make gold for you. I will make you rich. Free me and I will grant your dearest wish.

But Kelley knew he must stop his ears to these pleadings. He carried him to the last inmost door, the farthest chamber, marked too with the seal, as all the doors had been. There the King sat stony and inert on his throne. Kelley set down the child on the cold floor before him. Here is your son.

The King rose, bewildered joy in his face. My son! The boy held up his poor limbs to his father, as though to show his hurts, or maybe to fend off the big king, who came to him weeping with open mouth in happiness and grief, tears squirting from the corners of his eyes. As he approached, his mouth opened wider. Very much wider. He came over to his son where he writhed unable to escape, gripped the boy and with his great frog's mouth consumed him: swallowed him whole, beginning with the head. Kelley had leisure to see the great gray molars, the shining tongue like a purple whale.

Down. Inside him. The King, astonished and goggling, held his belly and gulped. He went with burdened steps, arms extended for balance like a gravid woman, to his couch. And lay down to digest.

The sun entered Leo. It was high summer. Peaches ripened against the wall of the garden in the center of the palace. In the center of the garden was a pool, Kelley could not see the bottom. In the midday the King came forth to bathe. Oh he looked fine and young, vivified by his meal, removing his robes; like Jesus with oiled locks and soft red mouth. Kelley looked on him and knew that he was himself naked. Nymphs helped the King descend into the jeweled waters. He rolled there in delight, laving his long arms and shapely legs, rolled again, lifting his white buttocks up, now look, when he rolls back he has begun to come in two.

Looking with sweet reassurance upon Kelley, now do you see? Now do you understand? *Two.* He is with his Queen, who is himself. Look (the King-Queen seems to say) I caress and kiss her, she is mine, he too is mine. The nymphs laugh and touch each other, admiring. Kelley in the hot pour of summer sun that gilds the garden feels his own prick stand, how could it not, look how lovely, *conjunctio oppositorum,* no King no Queen but One only, they cry aloud in their clipping and coming, the waters foam in pleasure over their nakedness, O God they have sunk thrashing beneath the roiling surface of the pool, they gurgle and spit, and then are gone.

Drowned.

Kelley stared in horror. The pool's surface settled, steaming. The sun was cruel. Then the water stirred, boiled, as though reversing itself, and there climbed out, silver skin streaming, eyes laughing, the winged boy, unhurt, healed though wingless, whole and tame, more loving and wiser than before.

—Come, he said, kiss me, cease weeping. It is I.

It was dawn of the second day now. The boy John was asleep. Kelley had not moved from the cushion where he knelt, though he had slumped forward like an infant asleep, his eyes were open.

John Dee put a sooty forefinger on the natal chart he had cast for the birth and growth of the matter within the world of the athenor.

In the Houses of the Spring Quaternary they had fixed Mercury, and then combined him with old King Saturn, lead. In the fourth House, first of the Summer Quaternary, he had been sweated, and labor induced. In the fifth House (*Nati*, of children and the getting of children) they had reduced the product in a bath of Water-of-Life, and from it had generated a Monad, the Young King, who was both and neither.

Now to reduce the new substance, calcine and nigrify it, till it was indeed the first matter, without qualities.

John Dee worked his bellows judiciously, and added oakwood to the fire, king of woods, as the old Welsh said:

> *Fiercest heat-giver of all timber is green oak;*
> *From him none may escape unhurt.*
> *By love of him the head is set an-aching,*
> *By his acrid embers the eye is made sore.*

In *Valetudo* Kelley took the boy for his servant, bound him, beat him for his waywardness. He would by the gods wipe the smile from his face. In the clammy underground to which he brought him (*Uxor*) he laid the fat heavy child on a bed or table and pressed and tormented him (at his behest, at his behest) until he gave forth his gold, spewed it horribly from mouth and anus, huge piles of gold-colored mess, coated with shining slime and cold to the touch when Kelley reached for it, while the boy, laughing, relieved of his burden, ascended free and escaped.

Only to be brought back again (sublimated, condensed, sublimated again, as John Dee's fire consumed oakwood steadily) to Kelley's awful workshop, unchastened. Kelley, sweating and weeping, did not know whether he beat him, ate him, fucked him; he drew oils, acrid butters, coruscating sugars from his body as it changed from white to red to blue to black.

At last he sickened, shrank; the silver body lost form. He ceased teasing and talking as he had done through all the tortures to which he had been subjected. Grew still, reproachful, sad. Died in that darkness (*Mors*) and Kelley lay down beside him in guilty despair, O my son. O my only son. The corpse blackened and stank; then dried and hardened like a stockfish, unrecognizable, mouthless, handless, faceless, no person at all.

Done, done, all done.

By Dee's calculations the year within the athenor had now come to its shortest and darkest day, the day of the death and birth of the Sun, the cusp of Capricorn. He took the stone jar of Kelley's powder, and he broke the seal. A wondrous odor filled the chamber; the serving boy stirred and touched his lips with his tongue. Kelley now knelt erect; he opened his hands as though in adoration. John Dee went to the furnace doors and opened them.

The athenor's walls were nearly transparent in the heat; Dee could see activity within, as though he looked at a tent with a candle lit inside. With a hollow pin he punctured it, and blew the seed inside.

Kelley (the other Kelley, the Kelley who had gone out from Kelley into the athenor) bent over the formless chaos of his son. All that he had done he had also suffered, everything the boy had lost he had also lost; and when the seed of transformation entered the hot blackened mass, it entered him too. O terrible: the summons to grow and change, the struggle to move and act! The seed working in him was like a sickness not a cure, he had not imagined it could be so fearful.

But he is alive, the Sun is born. Fiery blood coursing in his veins, skin changed from black to silver to gold, he smiles and laughs as though his death and rotting had been a game, he admires his own loveliness, tests his joints and takes steps, he is alive, alive-O. Why is he so small?

No he was alive, that was what mattered, there was to be no more death ever now. Kelley would feed him, of course; feed him as the Pelican feeds her young with her heart's blood. He would grow, he would grow tall and lusty, they would gown him in red and wed him with the White Woman, his own mother, the Queen of Heaven; and *their* Son, at last, at length, would be the Elixir, *filius philosophorum,* Crown of Glory, Basilisk, Salamander, Lion of the Desert.

No. Why was he so small?

—God His grace to us be praised, he heard John Dee say. God has granted to His servants the fruit of time, the great fruit. O look, come look.

Kelley staggered to his feet. John Dee's trembling fingers held the opened athenor. The hem and sleeves of his gown were blackened and ember-eaten. His face was radiant, red, golden; a sort of wind seemed to tremble around him and the *crater* he held out.

Kelley, uncertain what room he was in, looked into the vessel.

—Look, Dee said. He was near tears with glee and gratitude.

Down at the bottom a globule of gold gave off light, a tiny bright mass like a writhen body, perhaps twenty grains in weight.

They had achieved the first stage of the Work. They had always known it to be possible but they had never been able to do it or even quite to believe it was given to them or to any man to do: and now they had done it. They had made gold, sophic, wonderful.

—Why is it so little? Kelley asked. His throat was dry, his words a croak.

—There was no Multiplication of the seed, said Doctor Dee. Some barrenness. Some lack of vigor in it somehow.

Kelley blinked, staring. This? This was the end of all their promises to him? If he had hewed wood and hauled water for as long and as eagerly as he had worked to achieve the Work, he would have earned in wages more gold than this.

—Not enough, he said.

—No, said Doctor Dee. Not enough to make the Stone. Let us therefore be patient.

O God he would have to go back into that dark fiery country of copulation, decay and death, to find and free and kill another boy, or the same boy once again. His heart fainted within him.

And the prize for which he had sold his immortal soul was gone, used up in an instant to make twenty grains of gold that would not have bought a minim of the red powder, not an atom. How would they finish the Work now?

—*Did you think there was but one Seed?* Madimi asked him, when at dawn he bent weeping to ask her help. *Foolish man, did you think that there was but one Crater, one Stone, one way of working?*

He stared open-mouthed at her. She had grown into a woman, or nearly; her breasts were full, her neck long, her golden hair afloat in some wind, the same perhaps that blew around the room, the broken athenor, the doctor's white beard.

There are small Stones and great ones, she said. *There are Stones quick to make, and Stones that have been in the making since the beginning of time. The earth is a Crater itself, and within or on it the Marriage will take place, the Son will be born. Yet even that is not the greatest Stone.*

As he watched, the woman in the glass began to undo her garment of red and white.

—*What do you want?* she asked them smiling. *I have all in my gift. Did you think I trifle with you here? I have seen the foundations laid of the Heavens and the Earth, I know where every lost thing is hidden, I know every great thing and sin and shame, there is nothing I cannot do or say or be.*

Her breasts were bare, her great dawn-colored eyes were wise and somehow lewd. She opened her skirts to him. *Are you not twice-saved?* she said to him. *Have you not had favors of God that few men have had since time began? There is no sin for you, you may do as you wish, and have what you can.*

They bowed their heads, afraid of her for the first time since she had stepped forth from the glass, a child.

—*Would you reach higher than you have done?* she said. *Would you have a Stone greater than any yet spoken of? I will find it for you, it is hidden in a place I know. Would you have gold? I will bake it as bread, you will have a surfeit if you love gold. But if you would have what I offer, you must cast away the opinions of men.*

She was near naked. Diana. Virgin. Waiting to be known.

What do you want? she asked. *Tremble not, gird up your loins. What would you know?*

5

―――

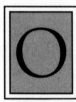n hot August days it was strangely cool inside Arcady, if you kept the drapes partly drawn and the striped canvas awnings open; it sat calmly in the shade of its trees as though with eyes heavy-lidded and half closed. At night when the air cooled Rosie went around opening the drapes, letting in the night; sat there thinking before she turned on the lights.

"What color's this?" she said to Sam, and held up to her an oblong yellow card.

"Yellow."

"Right."

"What else?" asked Sam.

Rosie turned the card over, expecting some object colored yellow on the other side, but instead there were two tiny doll-figures, and the word *two.*

"Two," she said. "See?"

"My turn," said Sam, and picked up a card from the pile. A big purple and a big yellow dot. Sam named them, and turned the card over. A scissors, cutting a string. With purple handles. Sam tossed it down without interest.

All day she'd been torpid and cranky. Rosie had tried to get her out to play, but instead she lolled daylong in the dim living room, moving from the long leather couch to the floor to the tall chairs like a seal over rocks in a sea-cave. Then hours after bedtime she'd come down the stairs, wide awake, to the living room where Rosie sat thinking, and refused to go back, complaining of vague discomforts. Rosie felt her forehead. Hot? She couldn't think where the thermometer was. Knowing she should be firm, she had not been; she let her stay.

"Now you go," Sam said.

Rosie picked another card. They were a set Mike had given Sam the week before, some sort of educational activity thing. Sam had insisted on playing with it. Rosie had glanced at the description on the box but hadn't grasped it. Colors, shapes, numbers, easy words. The one she picked up was a paintbrush spreading paint.

"What color?"

"Green."

On the back was a green tree. Okay.

"Mommy," Sam said. "Do we believe in God?"

"Well," Rosie said. "Um. I guess sort of."

"What's God?"

"Well God is sort of like Mother Nature. The reason why there are things."

"I love Mother Nature."

"So do I," Rosie said, glad to have finessed that one. "What's this?" She held up a card that showed a little house, a chimney, a picket fence, a steeply pitched roof with the same scalloped shingles that the one they sat under had. The picture was crowded with geometries to name, its secret reason, rectangle, circle, octagon, star.

"Do you love Jesus?" Sam asked.

Rosie stared at her. "What?"

Sam shrugged, withdrawing the question, and studied her next card. Three little dolls, and the word *three*. Its corner was clipped. Did that mean something?

"Mother Nature and Jesus could marry," she said. "Because Jesus is a boy."

"Sure," said Rosie. She was looking at a card that bore the word *Purple*. On the back was a circus wagon, not purple, also made of tiny geometries, diamonds, squares, ovals, triangles. Like a sign of some kind, or a shrine.

"Your turn," she said. She looked through the pile she had given herself. A lot of the cards had corners clipped; others had stripes, one or two or three, across the corner, where you might want to cut them, if you knew why you should. Some bore words, *he, do, us, go.* Sometimes a color card was all color, sometimes the paintbrush splash.

"Hon?"

"Does Daddy believe in Mother Nature?" Sam said. She held up her card. On one side a little doll walked over a bridge. On the other side, under it. "I win," she said.

"I don't know if he does," Rosie said. What the hell was with these cards, anyway? She picked up the box from the floor and looked again at the back. The Way Onward, said the box. Stimulates your child's sense of interrelationships while presenting the basic building blocks of perception. On the card she held was the word *Rectangle.* On the other side was a picture of the card that showed the little house with scalloped shingles and oval windows and diamond pickets. A picture of the card. The same little boy at the door, reduced in size, waving.

"Sam?" she asked. "You sure you want to play?"

Sam had fallen back against the pillows of the couch, her lips parted. Rosie stood, her cards spilling from her lap and came to feel Sam's forehead again. O good lord. That really is a fever. Sam's eyes seemed clouded and absent. "Hon, I think you've got a fever. I'm going to go look for the thermometer and maybe some aspirin. Okay? Chewing kind. Okay? You rest."

Rosie looked at Sam's chest, no chicken pox rash; felt under her chin, no rising lumps of mumps, which anyway she'd had a shot for, or was that measles?

Rubella, that was it, that's measles. German measles. Rosie searched in the medicine cabinet for the children's aspirin and the thermometer. Since she had become a mom she had become reacquainted with the names of childhood illnesses she had forgotten since her own childhood. Rubella. Scarlatina. Beautiful names, somehow romantic, like the names of opera heroines or *quattrocento* painters. Impetigo, roseola. Where the hell is that aspirin.

St. Joseph. Why that name. Baby Jesus in his arms in the very ancient looking picture on the label. And the thermometer right with it, neighborly, like glasses and book, pipe and tobacco, things didn't usually work out so well.

When she got back to the living room, Sam was breathing hard and staring at the rug. O please don't let it be something. She had

Sam open her mouth. What were you supposed to tell? No pains anywhere, Sam angrily brushed away her mother's hands. But she did chew the tiny pink pill, and drank water thirstily.

"Let's play," said Sam weakly.

"Oh, Sam."

Sam picked up her pile and looked down at them. "What's that?" she asked, but not of them. She lifted her eyes to Rosie, but didn't seem to see her, and down again at the cards; then she seemed to cast them away from her in spasmodic jerks, they slipped from her hands in a stream, colors, words, things, shapes and numbers. When they were all gone, her hands continued to jerk spasmodically, and then her arms and shoulders too. She seemed to have lost consciousness.

"Sam!"

Sam rolled over onto the couch face down, still twitching. Her head rolled against the fabric will-less as a doll's. Rosie tried to lift her, make her stop, but she wouldn't or couldn't, her body was rigid, intent on its spasms, unseeing.

Then it was over. Sam seemed to surface as from deep water: her released limbs made a big soft dance motion, and her eyes relit.

"What did you do, hon?" Rosie whispered. "Did you do that?"

But Sam didn't answer. She smacked her lips, and curled against her mother, an infant needing sleep.

"Hon?"

Breathing deeply, Sam slept.

Rosie lowered her to the couch. What in God's name. She felt Sam's head. Still way too hot. What was that. It had come and gone so quickly. Sam was prone to weird physical behavior, private self-involvement, inexplicable gesture. That was what it was. Was it?

She covered the sleeping child with a throw, and went to the phone. The number was where, in her book, her book was in her purse, where was her purse. Hell with it. She called Information, and only when she had the number and was dialing it did she think how late it was, and that the office would surely be closed.

Someone answered on the first ring.

"Dr. Bock's office?" she asked, surprised.

"Well no this is his service."

"Oh."

"You can leave a message and the doctor will call you. Is this an urgent matter?"

"I don't know," Rosie said. A sort of darkness seemed to be assembling around her, through which it was hard to hear what people meant. "It's my daughter, who Dr. Bock sees. Sam. She's just had the weirdest symptom."

"All right," said the voice. "Would you like me to beep the doctor."

"What?"

"I can send him a message where he is, to have him call in. Then he can call you. Can I have your number please." Rosie gave it. "He'll call you as soon as he's talked to us."

She hung up.

Sam still slept, the unwilled rising and falling of her breast quicker than usual, making her appear, even more than she usually did asleep, to be in a kind of suspended state, kept alive by outside forces that pressed her lungs to take deep breaths, while her inert body lay heedless. Sleep.

Rosie was still standing watching when the phone rang violently, still turned up loud for Boney's and Mrs. Pisky's old ears, it always made Rosie jump.

"Yes."

"This is Dr. Bock. What's the problem."

"Oh okay, Doctor." She looked around the corner at Sam still asleep. "Something weird, probably nothing," she said, the very sound of the doctor's brisk kind voice dismissed terrors; yet a strangling lump rose too in Rosie's throat. She told him what happened.

"And you had noticed her getting a fever?"

"Yes, she seemed to be. Just before."

"Any other symptoms of flu or cold? Ear infection?"

"She said she felt funny. No coughing or sneezing or anything."

"Okay," he said. "Okay."

He's going to say It's okay, it's nothing. Rosie knew it; it was as though she had already heard him say it.

"Can you bring her over to my office now?"

"Right now?"

"Yes. I can leave here shortly and meet you there. Is that all right?"

"Okay."

He was gone.

Dr. Bock's office had used to be in the Ball Building in town, but not long ago he had moved out to a featureless mini-mall on the Cascadia road, a low-roofed air-conditioned complex he shared with two other doctors and a creepy Lebanese periodontist who liked to start up pointless conversations with her in the waiting room the doctors shared.

The compound was dark when she pulled in, except for a glaring floodlight keeping watch. Dr. Bock's window was dark. She had got here first.

Sam, who had slept the whole way, soothed by the thrum of the engine (her father was the same, a danger behind the wheel), awoke, round-eyed, mouth-tasting, where am I.

"Hi, hon." She felt Sam's forehead: hot, but not feverish, probably, maybe; just the August night and the blanket Rosie had absurdly, prophylactically wrapped her in.

"Are we home?"

"Nope. Dr. Bock's."

"I don't want to."

"Only be a minute."

Sam squirmed in the blanket, beginning to seethe, in a minute she would boil. Rosie slid across the seat to her and enfolded her. "You just take it easy, hon. You want me to sing?"

"No."

"Sure." She started a song. It was a mystery which ones turned out to be soothing ones. Michael row the boat ashore. Tell me the tales that to me were so dear, long long ago, long ago. Poor Mike: for some reason he had never learned or hadn't remembered the little nonsense songs of infancy, sleeping drops or laughing gas, tried and true; when he sang to soothe her, what he came up with were old advertising jingles, maybe he had grown up minded by TV. Halo Everybody Halo. To *look* sharp, and be on the ball; to *feel* sharp, any time at all. Not that it mattered to Sam, the effect was almost the same. What would she think of them years from now when she found them in her memory along with the cow that jumped over the moon and Bobby Shaftoe gone to sea.

Asleep again, thank goodness.

What had they been thinking of, she and Mike, having a kid. Nearly impossible now to re-create the mood in which they had taken the plunge, decided to throw away the stuff, go to bed. One damn night was all it had taken, seemingly. Life and thought before Sam were out of reach now; that hospital bed had been a door, life on one side was one thing, life on the other side another.

A twist in the plot.

Where is the old fart anyway. She looked again at the radiant dial of her watch, changeless as a painted clockface. None of the lights that swept over them where they were parked slowed or changed direction; Rosie felt in her rib cage each one approach, and pass.

Before she had got pregnant, way before, she had had an idea for an art project, she thought maybe she even wrote it up once for credit in a film or photography class. What she had thought was that a willing pair of new parents could create a record like no other in the history of the world, a record that would be mysterious and awesome and even reveal something ultimate—there would be no way of knowing till it was done.

The parents would set up a camera and simple lights and a blank background. A movie camera, or a still camera from whose pictures a film could later be made. Every day, every single day, they would prop the baby up before the screen and take a picture. Every day, every single day the same framing and position. They'd have to continue through infancy and childhood, every day, like brushing teeth. Naked. Full body. By the time the child was grown (and rebelled, as she probably would) there would be some thousands of pictures, frames for a movie. String them together and run them at proper speed, and over the course of an hour or so you'd see a child grow. Subtly, unnoticeably from frame to frame, but cumulatively.

Hair and teeth would grow, legs would lengthen, fingers articulate; she'd stand, neck elongating, hair curling and darkening; teeth would go, and come again, changing her face, her character growing too and changing, evident in the face and body. Cuts and bruises would come and go in a moment, a broken ankle in a minute.

Life. Growth. Then what if the kid got interested, or if the parents could somehow force or inveigle the kid into continuing the thing. Then she'd grow older, more slowly but just as surely; breasts would come, and pubic hair; wrinkles, creases, oldness.

Maybe a big belly too. And suddenly two of them.

Or maybe not. Maybe the film would be short, not reach adulthood; stop suddenly, never to be resumed. Lights out. It could end up being not a general story (*Human Life on Earth*) but a particular tragedy.

O lord. O please.

A bright reflection in her window startled her, a car's light's turning in at the entrance. "Well *here* he is anyway," she said, and swung her door open as the doctor's car pulled into its parking space. She got out, waved to the indistinct figure fumbling with his door key, and did not feel the relief she had hoped to feel. She came around the car and reached in to get Sam out. Sam didn't want to come.

"Now c'mon, hon. We came all this way."

"No. Nononono no. I said no."

Hauling her out by main strength then, a bundle of resistance inside her blanket. Stilled by the doctor's voice, who held his door open for them to enter.

"Hi, Sam."

"Hi, Doctor," Rosie said. "Say hi, hon." Rosie trusted Dr. Bock, without exactly liking him; she did though like the way he always spoke first to his patient, liked him for having thought that was important. He went ahead of them, flicking on the piercing white overhead lights one after another through the waiting room to his office.

"So now," he said. Sam glued to her mother would have nothing to do with him. While he washed his hands, he had Rosie describe to him again what had happened; she answered his minutely specific questions as best she could, reduced finally to giving a grotesque imitation of Sam's brief spasms, which made Sam laugh, but brought the moment vividly back to Rosie's imagination.

"Then that was all. She slept."

"Okay. Well, let's take a look."

The lights shone on Dr. Bock's big bald head and his glasses as he bent over Sam. To all his wiles she made no response, and when at last he put hands on her she shrieked. Too young to be cowed into obedience, too old to be manhandled. Dr. Bock did his best, patient except when he tried to look into Sam's ears and she pulled away, knocking his instrument into his glasses.

"Sam! Now *stop*!" Rosie pleaded.

"It hurt!"

"It didn't."

"Did."

While the struggle went on, he asked further questions. Never had anything like this before? Positive? Did she herself remember having things like this, when she was young? No? Mike? Okay.

He let Sam go at last, not exactly finished but apparently satisfied.

"Okay," he said. "She seems to have no indications of anything, flu, chicken pox. Throat. Lungs. All okay."

"All right," Rosie said, uncertain.

"What you look for when something like this happens is an outside cause. If Sam got a spiking fever from say flu or an ear infection, then we could say that very likely what she had was just a febrile seizure."

He smiled at Sam, who was still miffed.

"Febrile seizures are mild seizures brought on by high fevers. A lot of kids get them. Usually there's a family history. Nothing really to worry about. After childhood they almost never recur."

This time Rosie didn't say *All right*. There was more to come.

"But I don't see anything that could have caused the fever. So then what you think is the brain activity itself brought on the fever. This sometimes happens. In other words the seizure caused the fever and not the other way around."

Sam had, unexpectedly, left her mother and gone to stand next to Dr. Bock, looking up frankly into his big face. He put an arm around her shoulder.

"When you say 'seizure,' " Rosie said. "You don't mean that she had. You don't mean like epilepsy."

"Well we don't use that term much any more. There are many different types of seizure disorder. It gives people an inaccurate idea." He looked at her with the grave remote pitiless kindness of an idol. "But yes, epilepsy is what it can be called."

This was it, Rosie knew: this was the source of all the strange darkness that had seemed to fall over her being like passing clouds; it was darkness coming out of the future, from this moment, a land of darkness she had been heading toward all along, which now she had finally come upon, and which had no end.

"I'll give you some basic information," Dr. Bock said, "about what you might be in for, and Sam; but I don't really expect you to remember it all, and we'll go over it again whenever you want to. Okay?"

Later on, when Rosie recalled this night, as she would recall it often, she would find herself once again at this moment, when he said that to her, and she would wonder at it, why he would think she wouldn't remember. She had been erased, like a blackboard, and he wrote on it her future and Sam's; she didn't understand everything he said about seizure disorders, and what she imagined he meant was as hard to recall, and as hard to shed, as an awful dream; but she forgot not a word of what she was told: not even when she tried.

"Now," he said. "What I want to do is to put Sam on a sedative, just a trial course, for six months. There might not be a single recurrence. If there's no recurrence, then we can think maybe it was a fluke. And take her off. Maybe."

Sam, weirdly, had sat on the stool beside Dr. Bock, and laid her head in his lap. Rosie was uncertain she could speak, as though the thick descending dark might clog her throat. "A sedative?" she said.

"Phenobarbital," said Dr. Bock, his hand on Sam's curls.

"O my god."

"Just a very small dose."

Now what was she going to do. Not only must she bear this, she was going to have to say something, she was going to have to do something. She didn't at first believe she would, but the alternative was inconceivable, so she did. She said, tears thick in her throat:

"Well I have a real problem with that."

He lifted his eyes to her, but the light striking his glasses made his look unreadable.

"Well, Rosie," he said. "We don't want a recurrence. We don't. They can be harmless, basically, as I told you. Maybe the majority are. But not all."

"Well," Rosie said. "I just have a problem with giving a three-year-old phenobarbital."

"It's quite well tolerated," said Dr. Bock.

"Uh-uh," said Rosie. "It just has to be no good. It just has to be." How long could she stand poised here, sword raised? Why didn't he back off?

"Look, Rosie," he said. "I'm going to give you a prescription. Tomorrow we can make you an appointment with a neurologist, who can talk to you. But I'm sure he'll tell you the same."

"Can I wait till I talk to him?"

"My advice is not to wait. I want to make that clear."

"Okay," she said. "I hear you," she added, Mike's stratagem, picked up from group, he had often used it on her when he had no way out of replying.

He weighed weary Sam, made some calculations, and wrote a prescription on a pad, telling her how it should be taken.

"First thing in the morning," he said.

She looked at the oblong of paper. His exquisite small writing, odd for such a big ham hand. Phenobarbital Elixir.

Ticket to the underworld. She folded it carefully and put it in her bag. And got all the way back to the car and closed the door before she shed tears, holding Sam, watching the lights go out in Dr. Bock's office.

She's not sick, Dr. Bock said, and she doesn't have to be treated in any special way: but it was impossible not to handle her with fearful care, as though she had become one of those glass animals Rosie had always detested, infinitely breakable; she carried her up the stairs and laid her in her bed, conscious that she was trying not to shake her, for fear she might go off again, like a gun.

There had been a kid in her junior high who had fits. Rosie remembered her, darkly beautiful, she took ballet lessons too, that was the only other thing Rosie knew about her. Rosie herself never saw her have a fit, but they were talked about. Sometimes she fell asleep on her desk. That was the phenobarbital, Rosie saw that now, it must have been. Pale, dark-haired; the teacher gently rousing her, maybe as afraid as Rosie was that she might go off.

She listened to Sam's steady breathing.

What if she were wrong, why should she act like she knew best, what if she hurt Sam by thinking she knew best. Propped on her elbows in her bed in the deep darkness she begged for counsel. Shouldn't she just fill the scrip.

She couldn't.

Steady breathing. A minute pause came after each exhalation, before each inhalation began; Rosie entered into each one, holding her own breath till Sam resumed.

She lay again on the pillow.

Once during her pregnancy Mike came home and told her that he had spent a long bad day, thinking about all the awful possibilities they might be in for, which might demand a lot of sacrifice and extra commitment, and might mean a lot of sadness, a lot of loss; and he said that through the day he had worked through that, and faced it for himself, as he had not before; and he felt readier. She had never done that; she had been keeping all those possibilities far from her, and she had been a little awed and deeply grateful to Mike, though she wondered how he could know what he would be capable of giving up or taking on; and now one of those things had actually maybe possibly very likely happened, and where was he.

She didn't want him here, no, she really didn't, to want him here now would be like making a deathbed conversion, it was beneath her. But she sure wanted someone there. Someone, someone to tell her she was right, was doing the right thing, the wrong thing; was a dope; should wait, shouldn't wait. Someone.

"Mommy?"

Rosie was out of bed faster than she had thought possible to get, and standing foolishly naked beside Sam's bed.

"Mommy I don't feel good."

She was hot again, though not so terribly hot as she had been. "Okay," Rosie said, her heart beating and her mouth dry. "Okay."

Sam kicked back the bedclothes Rosie had put over her. "Mommy."

"Yes, hon."

"My ear hurts."

"It does?"

"Inside."

"It does?"

"Mommy!" Sam laughed at her mother's bewilderment. "My *ear!*" And she pointed at it vigorously, once, again, again.

A nice bright *otitis media,* said Dr. Bock (a little shamefaced, Rosie thought, that he had missed it last night) which, okay, accounts for the fever, frequently we get a spiking fever with the onset of an ear infection; so if we've accounted for the fever, then it's a lot more likely that the seizure was a febrile seizure, and a lot less likely that a seizure disorder is indicated.

Not ruled out though.

No phenobarbital?

Well no. Let's not then. See what happens.

"Well that's nice," said Dr. Bock's nurse, fixing a clown sticker to Sam's sunsuit. "Just as well you hadn't started on the phenobarb. My experience, they won't take you off once you've started. Not till the six month course is up. So good thing."

The morning was brilliant, a hot, clear, happy day, happy. A nice bright *otitis media*.

Like a near-miss dreadful accident, she thought: sailing through without a scratch, inches or seconds from collision; and driving on at a crawl, appalled, newly conscious that at any moment . . . Then gaining speed again.

Should she tell Mike?

On Monday she drove up the Shadow River road to The Woods, having agreed to deliver Sam to her father this one time. Mike had apparently begun a new program of rule-bending. Every now and then he would grow restive or maybe only curious, and try to alter the agreement they had come to about who did what when. Rosie had not had the strength this time to contest.

She no longer liked coming up to The Woods, though.

She had to search for him through the long halls and big common rooms of the old resort, dragging Sam by the hand and extricating her from the attentions of people glad to see a child here. She caught up with him at last in the staff lounge.

"Blue jay," said Sam.

"No," said Rosie. "Woodpecker." All the lounges and common rooms at The Woods were named after forest creatures, a leftover from the resort days. Mike was piling the ingredients for a sort of shake into the blender kept there for the staff: a banana and some yogurt and some sort of gray powder he spooned from a plastic container.

"Hi, Mike."

"Well look who's here." Looking at Sam. He put more items in his shake, fruit juice, honey from a honey bear, a different gray powder from another container. Sam had to be allowed to push the button to make it go, and stared as it foamed and sloshed queasily.

"Want a taste?"

"Yes."

But a taste was enough. Rosie got her an ice cream in a paper cup, sensing Mike's disapproval. It was funny. Most single mothers Rosie knew had to counter Dad's wholesale indulgence of food whims, Dad no good himself at self-control, that being one reason why he was single again usually; but Rosie found it harder than Mike to impose food rules. Funny that Mike could make himself eat or not eat almost anything, even though he wasn't in charge of any of the rest of his wants, the other way around in fact.

"I like mine," Sam said, digging in the phony confection with her little wooden oar.

"I like *mine,*" Mike said.

It had been here, in Woodpecker, that Rosie had first told Mike she wanted a divorce. She'd shoved a bran cake in his face when he made a dumb and smirky remark about her and Rose Ryder, whom he'd been seeing himself. Long time ago.

"So Mike," she said. She stood, her arms crossed before her, unwilling to sit. "How's your research going?"

"Oh," he said.

"What is it, really?" she said. "This special stuff."

"Rosie. I'm not going to go into detail here."

"Well."

"It's about," he said, watching Sam. "Healing. Partly. It's about how much we can do for ourselves by . . . By using methods people have used for centuries but aren't often recognized today as efficacious."

"Like."

"Prayer," he said. He still looked at Sam bent over her ice cream. "Doctors have always known that certain people are able to reverse even incurable terminal conditions. Miracles. Every doctor knows of a few."

"Mind over body."

"Well. More than body. Why restrict it to that. It's documented that there are modes of shaping your personal universe."

"You mean like wishes come true," Rosie said. "Is that what you're talking about?"

"Well. What if they could."

She watched him sip his shake. "Most people stop believing that," she said. "When they grow up."

"Most people," Mike said.

"My friend Cliff . . ."

"O God that guy," Mike said.

"You know Cliff?"

"I know *of* him," Mike said.

"Cliff says reality is dreams checked by physics."

Mike turned on her, as though handed the key to open a mystery to her. "But what if that's not it? What if the physics aren't the last thing, the checking thing? What if dreams really come last, or first, what if they're primary?"

"Well but Mike . . ."

"What if? If they were and we just didn't know it? If they were, wouldn't it be awful to just live not knowing it? Live and die not knowing it was so, that you could have your happiness? That would be hell." He caught fire, and laughed. "That *is* hell!"

She watched him draw in again then, turn away from her and back to Sam; he put his chin in both hands and grinned at her, and she giggled back.

"So how've we been, anyway?" he said.

"Fine," said Rosie. "She had a little thing the other day."

"A little thing?"

Suddenly Rosie wanted to be out of here, and right away; out of this room, out of The Woods. "An ear infection," she said. "It turned out to be. She's better already, actually." They were both touching Sam, Mike's hand on her shoulder, Rosie's on her hair. "She's got the pink medicine, the stuff that smells like bubble gum. It's in the bag." She bent to kiss Sam's cool sticky cheek. "Bye, hon. Gotta go."

Sam gave her, for some reason, you could never tell when one was coming, a long hungry hug, and told Rosie she loved her. Rosie left quickly then, feeling shorn or shriven, as she always did when she left Sam. When she got to the parking lot again and was climbing into the ovenlike Bison, the plump van with *The Woods Center for Psychotherapy* lettered discreetly on it was unloading a bunch of young people like those who had come with Mike to pick up Sam last month, that day, the day Boney died.

She knew now who they reminded her of, cheerful open faces and neat haircuts, short-sleeved white shirts and ties. They were the scary good kids of the Bible club in high school, the kids on the church-camp bus, the kids discharged from cars on Saturday afternoons to spread out in suburban neighborhoods and knock on doors, real nice day isn't it, can I speak to you for just a few moments about something very, very important.

She started the car with a roar, and looked away as they looked toward her.

6

n that August Pierce won his driver's license, and bought a car. In doing so he entered onto a plateau of citizenship and maturity that was at once sobering and elating, and he could imagine how the young must feel, who pass that gateway just at the same time they are going through the big others too, out onto the uplands of adulthood: here is your spear, here are your spurs, your shield.

Pierce's initiation came not only thus absurdly late in life, it was unusual in another way too, having been conducted almost solely by women. Women had given him his rides here and there in his postulant period (the plain paper learner's permit growing limp and tattered in his pocket); women taught him the basics, let him take the wheel under their supervision. He drove Rosie's wagon and Val's Beetle and Beau's family sedan with one or another of the women of that house beside him, who might tramp on a nonexistent brake with an onomatopoeic squeal as Pierce clumsily took a corner. He dinged the Bison on the gatepost at Arcady, having pressed by mistake, he told Rosie, the accelerator instead of the brake pedal. "Gee," Rosie said, "I'd forgotten that was possible."

Women guided him through the license-getting process too. Rose Ryder sat behind him with fingers crossed while a noncommittal policeman put him through his paces. Of course he passed, he had worn a tie, he was a man and a citizen, how could he not be able to drive? And yet he had barely made his way through the three-point turn, and bounced over the curb corner turning into the Registry's parking lot.

Then it was time for him to acquire a car of his own, his first, and it was a woman who offered it, his hatchet-faced neighbor opposite whose glasses-chain swung like mail armor before her cheeks. It was a Steed, simple sturdy car for widows and priests, in two shades of delicate green, sage and celery, with sofa seats and a great agate steering wheel, like a bus. Her sons (she was careful to tell him) had bought her something far better. He had been looking in the papers, and he could have had instead a little acid-green Piranha, like a dodgem car, or a businessman's low-slung black Myrmidon, now spavined and asthmatic. He took the Steed, after getting Spofford (his sole male adviser in the matter) to look under the hood. Not since childhood, not since his old Remington .22, his first chess set, had he felt so rich in a possession.

In it he entered onto the sign-system of driverhood, which had been transparent to his sight before, but which arose around him now, a guide and a puzzle. How had he never noticed before that at every bend in the road there stood a yellow diamond sign, bearing a black arrow pointing in the direction of the turn, and with an appropriate speed posted below? Guided by these he swung his car featly left and right. Other drivers, real drivers as he considered them, seemed to need less help; and at his back he always felt them, impatient, hurrying near.

"Aren't you sort of dawdling?" Rose asked him. "There's a line behind you."

"I'm driving at the speed limit," Pierce said. "That can't be dawdling."

"Oh the speed limit," said Rose. "That's really just a *suggestion*."

He would not drive her little Asp, down inside which they hunkered together, their bottoms inches from the road (he felt the distance imaginatively) and the mystery of the gearshift between them. Mystery: he meant an old special sense of the word, the secrets of a trade or business, the grammar of a skill kept from those outside the guild. For Pierce, as for few others, maybe no others he thought, driving and cars were a female mystery.

"It's easy, really," Rose said, her hand at a stoplight resting lightly on the little trembling herm. "It gives you a lot more control, actually; it's fun. And if you have trouble at first, don't worry. After a while it becomes automatic."

Even as Pierce drove it (rarely on roads more than two lanes wide, never to the city) his car expressed possibility and scope; he rolled the windows down, found a radio station that played music of the Steed's own vintage, and put his elbow into the sun, driving daringly with one hand. Only occasionally did a weird fear come over him, that he should be sitting alone in a car, in its driver's place, moving it himself.

Over the mountain, out of town, along the river road, in September; the plastic plaid of the upholstery hot, and the air cool that blew unhindered through the four big windows.

"Read what it said again," he asked Rose beside him.

"Littleville," Rose said, not consulting the note in her lap. "First left after the gas station. It's miles yet."

Driving hadn't affected Pierce's sense or lack of sense of direction and spatial location. But it had coincided with a crisis that only modern means of locomotion could resolve: Pierce had to find someplace new to live.

"Keep your eyes peeled," he said.

"Ooh yuck," she said. "I hate that expression."

The owner of the Blackbury Jambs building where he lived had decided to turn it into a café and crafts shop. Soon, Pierce supposed, there would be no actual people living in that town, it would be merely facades, all inside would be for sale. In a month Pierce had to be elsewhere, and he had found nothing in town at all suitable. One horrid plastic pine-paneled suite above the smelly kitchen of the Donut Hole. Nice place for a suicide, he'd said to Rose. Why not look farther out, she'd replied, and Rosie said the same. Now that he had the car, he could live anywhere.

"First left," Pierce said, pointing.

"Pierce, that way is right."

"Oh yes."

There was a species of dream he knew, the Finding an Apartment dream, in which he relocated to places more or less satisfactory: dreams filled at once with a sense of settling and of beginning. The new apartment (shifting shape and nature as he inhabited it) always proved to have odd features: free and lavish meals, something loathsome in a drawer, dozens of detached commodes.

"There," Rose said. "Littleville, first left."

Littleville lay along the Blackbury a few miles north of the Jambs, a centerless town really except for an unusual pudding-stone post office and a Baptist church from a model-train village. The cottage that Pierce had found advertised in the Faraway *Crier* lay it seemed on the grounds of a larger estate. This one apparently. Pierce turned carefully in between two stone gateposts of the Arcady type.

"Wow," said Rose.

They followed the drive upward, past fields of unmown grasses tall and heavy-headed as grain, to a big lemony stucco house, somehow soft-looking: the rounded eaves of the roof, maybe, or the plastered chimney-pots, or the arched and heavily molded windows.

"Now *this*," Pierce said.

"Winterhalter," Rose read from a plaque in the form of two symmetrical Scottie dogs. Pierce parked his car next to a yachtlike gold sedan, and they went to the nearest door, which was opened as they approached by a very old man, much shorter than either of them, with a silver pistol in his hand. No in a moment it had become the pistol-shaped nozzle of a garden hose, detached.

"Yes," he said. "Still available. Come in for a minute."

They followed him in. He put down the nozzle on the radiator just inside the door (Pierce would think of it, later, that nozzle, a sign pointing to the trials he was to undergo, which had already been stored up for him even then: but by then there would be hardly anything that did not seem to him such a sign, his mind could not avoid them). And into the big sour-smelling kitchen.

Mr. Winterhalter spoke his part in the plural, so there was undoubtedly a Mrs. Winterhalter somewhere, who used these innumerable pots and pans hanging from hooks, these wooden utensils sprouting from urns. "We rent the place down there for not a lot," he said, "and here's the reason. We go away to Florida in the winter. Who needs the cold. And there are a couple of small things we need done at this place, nothing much, but we like to know there's someone around."

He opened a cupboard door. On hooks inside the door a dozen bunches of keys jangled. Mr. Winterhalter selected a ring that bore an old skeleton and a dull brass Yale key. "We'll need some references," he said to these.

"Oh yes."

"Come on out this way."

He led them out the kitchen door and around to where his car was parked next to Pierce's. "It's small for two," he said, stopping and turning to them."

"Oh I'm not," Rose said.

"Just along for the ride," Pierce said. Mr. Winterhalter seemed to study them for a moment, censoriously maybe; but it was probably only delayed reaction time, information shunting slowly along aged channels into consciousness.

He shepherded them into his car and took the wheel, one of those oldsters Pierce had come to know on the road, sunk inside their enormous cars, heads barely protruding above their dashboards, proceeding at dinosaur pace. "There's some details to explain," he said.

He drove down the drive up which they had come, and then left, along another, humbler drive through the meadows toward a line of trees.

"We're real near the river," Rose said.

"Oh yes."

It was a low, broad little house, the same yellow stucco as the main house, set against the dark line of the trees; obviously it had at one time housed the help. Mr. Winterhalter rolled to a stop before it, and Pierce got out.

He knew this place.

"Listen," said Rose beside him. The river gurgled and plopped, very near. It could be seen through the trees and riparian growth, spreading broadly. Pierce turned to look back up the sloping lawns; past the overgrown lilacs, the house's chimneys and roofs could be seen.

And around back of the cottage, he knew, there was a screened porch; and a little path down through the pines to a dock, a dock where he had tied up a rowboat. Good lord.

Mr. Winterhalter, after a lot of fussing with the lock, now turned the skeleton key in the door and opened it. "Last year," he said, "there was no one here. So it's a little." He stood aside, showing them in with a clawlike hand.

Reversals—day for night, in for out of, invitation for trespass—only heightened Pierce's memory of going through this door, looking up the night lawns to that house. Inside this room then, moonlight lay in rhomboids on the floor, sunlight now. He looked at Rose, who also stood transfixed, her mouth open a little, eyes seeming to see at once what she looked at and the inward sight of something else: but she habitually looked like that, and she exchanged no glance of complicity with him. Could it be she still didn't remember?

"Living room," said his guide. "This furniture you'd be free to use."

Rug rolled in a corner, its head bent up against a wall, a cadaver. This of all places.

"The kitchen."

"Yes."

"You cook? My brother is a chef. Dining room."

"Cook, yes, sometimes." It was in several ways a dreary and damp-spirited little place, inconvenient too. The bathroom was beyond the dining room, and Rose had gone that way, leaving the doors open behind her. Now she opened a door on the far side of the bathroom.

"Oh look," she said. "Secret."

In that age—it would only be clear in looking back on it, from farther on, when nothing was the same, when only in dreams and brief ecstasies could it be remembered as it was—in that age consequences, instead of lying implicit and potential in actions, could sometimes dictate the circumstances which would produce just themselves and not others, like the plot of an old farce.

On a summer night last year, before Pierce had moved from the city to the country, he and Rose had come by boat down the moon-barred river, both thinking the other was someone he, she was not. As they still did now today. They had tied up the little rowboat to the dock, and had broken into this little house, it had taken little breaking; and they had explored, smelling mice and mothballs, bumping into things. And had come at length to this odd bedroom, only enterable through a door knocked into the bathroom wall. *Secret* she had said.

"There's an outside door in that room," they heard Mr. Winterhalter call, who had not followed them here for some reason of propriety or the conservation of energy. "A door out. You'll want to keep that locked."

It was nearly the largest room in the house. Pierce circled Rose's shoulder with his arm, and guided her into it and out of sight of the view through the door.

"You remember," he whispered, embracing her from behind.

"What. What."

They were both looking at an old iron bedstead with brass finials, narrow, penitential, its thin stained mattress still asprawl naked over it. He took her more tightly, his hand lifting her skirt from in front of her though her hands tried to keep it down.

"Don't," he said.

Her resisting hands relaxed; his went inside her pants, searching, while he still held her, his mouth against her neck where the pulse beat. "You remember," he said. "You must."

"Yes," she said. "Yes."

"So it's nice," called Mr. Winterhalter. "There's some things to explain."

With an effort Pierce turned away, left Rose to compose herself; hands in his pockets he came from the bathroom. "Yes?"

"The water," he said. "Come on, I'll show you."

He took Pierce to the last door left unopened. It led to a dank earth-smelling basement. In the haloed light of a dim bulb, Mr. Winterhalter showed Pierce a squat machine, from which black plastic pipes ran in several directions. "The pump," he said. "The water of this house comes from a well. You understand, a well?"

"Yes."

"It's off now. Nobody's here, why run it? But it brings water from the well, and . . . Look here."

He showed Pierce where one of the pipes from the pump ran to a cobwebby window, out through a pane replaced with plywood.

"The overflow. This is very important."

Why was he here? How had he come here? He was not able to pay his full attention to Mr. Winterhalter's anyway weirdly minatory description of the pump's workings. Just because a world-age is governed by certain laws—the iron laws of tragic necessity, or the wooden ones of melodrama, or outlandish, constant Coincidence—does not mean we do not marvel to find ourselves subject to them.

"We'll go up," Mr. Winterhalter said. "I'll show you the rest. The way it works."

Rose stood at the top of the cellar stairs, arms crossed before her, silhouetted by the window light behind her. Pierce climbed stumbling up the ladderlike stairs to where she stood.

"Outside," said the old man.

He took them around to the side of the house and pointed to the ground near the stone foundation. In the yellow grass Pierce perceived a thick black hose, a python disappearing into its hole; it went down into the ground here and then presumably through the wall and into the pump.

"See?" said Mr. Winterhalter. He pointed out the just-discernible line of black piping running through the grass, upward toward the house, into the woods. "Come along. We'll climb up."

Rose didn't follow them as they went up along the plastic pipe, into a little yellow wood, up mossy rocks, the old man breathing hard but not slowing, and Pierce stumbling behind. They came then at length to a beautiful small well-house, its slate roof mossy and its stone sides patched with pebbly concrete.

"Now you see," said Mr. Winterhalter. "Here's your water."

With a hand he invited Pierce to look inside.

"In the winter you let it run," Mr. Winterhalter told him. "You let it run just a little. Flowing water doesn't freeze. It's physics. But just a little. Let it flow too fast, it empties the cistern, the water stops flowing, freezes in the pipe. Not too fast. Not too slow. You'll get used to it."

Pierce looked within, smelled sweet water. Amber reflections over the water's black surface were cast up, marbling the walls and wooden ceiling. A fragment from the well's lip fell with a resonant plunk into the water. It looked bottomless.

When they returned to the little house Pierce saw, through the open door, Rose standing in the dining room, his office or study as it would be, he didn't dine much. She lifted her hand as though to touch the wall, but then didn't touch it; she looked around the room, the house, not as though trying to remember it but as though she might at any moment be told what would happen to her here, and to him; be told, if she paid attention, what the story was to be.

"So it suits you," Mr. Winterhalter declared, breathing hard.

"Yes," Pierce said. "Yes, it really sort of does."

"Could that really be true?" Rose asked as they drove away, Pierce lighter by the amount of a deposit. In his rear-view mirror Mr. Winterhalter still waved, Time's pander, unwitting of course, though even that Pierce would come to doubt.

"Could what be true?"

"About the water. Not freezing, lying out on the ground like that."

"It seemed convincing to me," Pierce said. "Flowing water doesn't freeze." He remembered, with sudden vivid completeness, standing in the bathroom of the bungalow in Kentucky on a winter night and setting the drip of the faucets. Flowing water doesn't freeze. In the bathroom window a ghostly feral face.

In that age the real connections between things—pattern, repetition, inversion, echo—were actually known or sensed at times, but only in odd moments; were come upon as though in the dark, and felt by wondering fingers. What is patent now was hidden then, hard to say, let slip as soon as caught.

They turned at the gate to go out.

"And how in the snow will you get all the way in?" Rose asked. Pierce didn't answer, not having thought of that. Hire plowing. Snowshoe in. It didn't matter. Except that Mr. Winterhalter had locked the door again behind him, no key for Pierce until a lease was signed, Pierce would have turned down that way again now, taken her into that bedroom again, and bent her at last over that sordid bed.

"I'm glad you're by the river though," she said. "I like the water. So much."

"Rose," he said. "That time last year." But he had become just then absurdly afraid, and unwilling to trust his memory, too highly colored suddenly, unlikely. You can't step in the same river twice. The river is not the same. You are not the same.

"Summer's almost over," she said.

A wind had arisen. As though borne on it they drove through the tunnel of roadside trees, whose riddled fallen leaves were swept before them across the asphalt. The road was new-laid, it seemed, for it was deeply black, striped in bright white and dashed with endless yellow oblongs, and it curled through the pale restless woods smartly, purposefully. Pierce, moving his Steed along it, felt his hands turned by the wheel as though the car knew the way of itself.

7

t is a very curious thing:

After the great Armada that Philip of Spain sent against England was defeated, both winner and loser naturally attributed the victory to God. Among the English the story began then to be told which would become a staple of triumphal British History from then on, the story of the wonderful "Protestant wind" that sprang up in the nick of time to save the beleaguered island and its people from the towering galleons and orgulous grandees. *Te Deum* and *Non nobis* were ordered to be sung in churches from Penzance to Scotland. To Thee and not to us O God the victory.

Philip of Spain seems to have agreed, that the victory could not be credited to men's arms and men's ships, even though he had a very different idea of what God had wanted upon this occasion. "I sent them to fight against men, and not against the wind," he is famously reported to have said on hearing of the defeat.

What is curious is that there was, apparently, no wind.

A number of Spanish ships were at length blown by storms against the Irish coast, the survivors becoming incorporated into Irish legend. But that was on the long bitter journey home, after the battle, after defeat. During the days of June when the great encounter raged, the winds were mostly mild, and mostly favored the Spanish. In the dispatches from the ships at sea on both sides sent during the fighting, there is no mention of any great wind, saving or destroying.

What is to be said?

Perhaps there *was* a wind, and it somehow left no trace in the primary records of the time. For if there was no wind, would not the English have preferred to credit *themselves* with the triumph, aided (of course) by God? If there was not a wind, for what reason would Philip have invented one, and given God the blame for the defeat of what was supposed to be God's own Navy?

Or perhaps there really was no wind—until the awesome fortunate power which commentators attributed to it belatedly conjures it up. Only when the myth of the big wind (bringer-in of the new British Empire, blower-away of Spanish hegemony over the old history of the world) settles firmly on the humps of historian's pens does it begin to blow backward from the later time to the earlier, where kings, popes, and ambassadors can feel it, though sailors and ships do not.

There had been a great stillness in the Imperial City of Prague during the whole of the month of May, as the Spanish ships maneuvered in the Narrow Seas and the Prince of Parma prepared his landing-craft and marshaled his invasion forces. The city seemed more beautiful than ever before to the Emperor, the bright buff of its stones, the red cobblestones jewellike, translucent under the dome of blue, the air so clear he could hear laughter rise from the city streets below the Hradschin tower where he sat, the laughter of happy citizens.

This was the year in which his Empire would fall, or be altered beyond recognition. Prophecies made a hundred years ago, but whose roots ran far deeper in time than that, said so, almost clearly, only as darkly as any prophecy perforce must that describes the unlicked bear-cubs of time, still shapeless.

The Emperor (whose horoscope had been cast by Nostradamus) regarded most prophecy as probably true but uselessly ambiguous: as ambiguous as the world whose future it claimed to describe. The only certainty lay in numbers, whose operations every man's reason could agree on. Catholics were enjoined from the practice, but Protestants in the Emperor's employ had combed Revelation, the Book of Daniel, the Book of Isaiah, and certain other books as sacred as these but without canonical standing, manuscripts of which were kept in the carved chests that held the Emperor's treasures.

The computations were growing ever clearer, like frost-writing etching itself on a winter glass. The numbers in Scripture hinted at a series of epochs succeeding one another from the beginning of time, each forming in its turn like a drop at the spout of a clepsydra, forming forming until pregnant with its own fullness it falls, and another begins to form. The next-to-last epoch in the series running from world-creation to world's end had, according to these accumulating and indisputable numbers, ended in 1518, when Martin Luther had defied the Pope, and all Christendom felt the vertigo of freefall. From that time to the Judgment, when the Seventh Seal was opened and the Dragon flew, was ten times seven years. The Emperor had been invited to add up the numbers himself. There was no need. It was self-evident. Fifteen hundred and eighteen plus ten times seven years reached right to this transparent afternoon, clear spherical drop too big to hang any longer.

Then there were the Capuchin friars, busy with prophecies of their own, who also made their secret reports to the Emperor, not on the same days as the Protestant scholars were smuggled in.

The Capuchins (or a certain sect within them, whose members were known only to one another) had for a hundred years and more meditated deeply on the revelation of Abbot Joachim da Fiore. Joachim had long ago determined that the Universe made by God occurred in three parts, just as the Godhead Itself did: the first age was the age of the Father, and the Law was the law of the prophets, an eye for an eye and a tooth for a tooth; the second age, that of the Son, which began when Christ died for our sins and the curtain of the Temple was rent in two, was ruled by the Church and the Law of Love. Last would come the age of the Holy Spirit, when Christ's Church would pass away, unneeded, lovely idea Rudolf thought; then there would be no law, there would be Perpetual Peace, until the stars fell from their spheres and God shut up the world for good.

When would that age begin?

There were those among the Joachimists who already lived in the Third Age, who had withdrawn in their hearts from the superannuated Church and empty sacraments, and lived inwardly free. So the Emperor heard. Free.

His confessor taxed him with listening to heretics, but the Emperor said that heretics could compute as well as good Catholics, and the truths of Scripture are there for all to read, however wrongly they might be interpreted. He did not say, but he remembered well, how his revered father Maximilian had said, before Christendom was rent in two, that all men might be saved by their own lights, the Turks might be saved by their prophet and even the savages of the New World might be saved by their own saviors as we are saved by Christ. Even the airy spirits and other intelligences, the Emperor imagined, might be saved by the precepts of their own religion, whatever it was.

No: they would not be saved, they were of that lucky middle kind who would not be saved or damned, for they would not be judged. Tears rose to the Emperor's eyes.

The tower room from whose windows the Emperor looked out over the city was workroom and study and retreat. Here with his assistants (the three monks and the shaven novice now patiently watching as the Emperor contemplated) the Emperor built and re-built clocks, ground lenses and studied catoptrics, sat up nightlong to measure the stars' movements. The Emperor painted here; his grand-father Charles had once stooped to pick up Titian's brush, but Rudolf learned the art himself, and worked tirelessly (and fruitlessly, he knew it) on his canvases.

He loved clocks, as all the Hapsburgs did; Charles had spent his retirement in the mountains of Spain trying to get all his clocks to chime at the same time. He loved clocks, but he didn't believe in the time they counted.

Time (the Emperor had never had to conceive it in this way, he had found the conception within himself ready-made, he had always felt it so) was like ripples rising in a pond from a thrown stone, the Word of God spoken at the beginning of the world; the difference was that instead of each new rising moment being smaller and contained within all its ancestors, like the ripples in the pond, each moment was larger than all the moments that had gone before, and contained all of them. Time had no motion, only containment; there was no new thing under the sun, for all was contained within every circle.

Which is why astronomers could discern the future in the eter-nally arising circles that the stars and planets made.

So Regiomontanus the astronomer, a hundred and fifty years al-most ago, had glimpsed this awful year (*Octavegesimus octavus mirabilis annus,* '88, year of wonders) and had calculated every *disas-ter,* every astral maleficence (Saturn, Jupiter and Mars conjunct—

right now, this day—in the Moon's cold house) and had written down all their consequences: *Even if all the land and the sea do not fall in ruin, still the world will heave in pain, empires will shrink, great will be the lamentations everywhere.* No astronomer or doctor the Emperor interviewed, and there were many in this city for him to question, could put much better a face on it.

And the English doctor, standing before him, summoning him to listen to angels, and to repent. He would not repent, for he could not believe he had sinned. And now the *annus mirabilis* was come. The whole world knew it. The reformers rubbed their hands with horrid glee, expecting the fall of the Beast, the Whore; the Jesuits set their shaven jaws, expecting angelic hosts in support of their Army. Meanwhile witches flourished, prodigies appeared, and wolves seized children in the streets of villages.

Did they wonder that he withdrew from his audience chamber, refused to go out among the people, kept to his apartment and his tower? Let them wonder.

The English Queen had beheaded the Scottish Queen, dreadful crime, which (he had been told) she had at once repented in tears and rending of her garments, as well she should; she had shut up in prison those who had done the deed (Rudolf saw in his mind a tall man in black). But none of that had saved her from the consequences. Down below in Rudolf's palace, the Spanish Ambassador, the Papal Nuncio and lesser emissaries sat in anterooms or wandered bored and irritable through the map rooms and treasure rooms and libraries, kept waiting for weeks, waiting to give the Emperor the news he already knew: that the navies of his uncle Philip of Spain were on the sea, that the English were about to be overrun; that (for all he knew) the Queen of England was already dead and the gibbets and the stakes erected, the smoke of heretic flesh ascending to God's gratified nostrils. England was far away; anything could be happening.

He had seen the *autos-da-fé* in Valladolid and Seville when he was a boy, growing up in the court of Spain. He remembered the smell. In those days he had been pious, almost saintly, though amid the saints of that court not exceptional; he had attended Mass daily, had served at the altar himself in humble cassock and surplice, and taken Communion. It had struck him in those days as deeply satisfying how the liturgical year was a model or emblem of Christ's life: Winter brought in the Incarnation, Spring the Redemption; in Summer the Holy Spirit descended on the Church at Pentecost, and Midsummer and Autumn recounted the Church's growth and triumph. It was the same with the days of the week: On Monday Christ was born, Tuesday grew in wisdom, Wednesday baptized, Thursday taught and healed, Friday suffered and died, Saturday harrowed Hell, and Sunday, in the miracle of the Bread, rose again.

But every Mass was also the same miracle in even smaller compass: Christ Incarnated in the awesome theurgy of consecration, Sacrificed in the eating and swallowing, passing into the dark and smelly tomb of the intestines, only to be gloriously Resurrected in the transformed heart.

But every Mass (he came with elation to see, it was years ago now, the stern Asturian mountains) was the whole History of the World as well, not simply pictured or rehearsed but having in its center precisely the same miracle, repeated daily throughout the churches of Christendom: Creation Fall Incarnation Passion Resurrection. Acts. End of the World.

Every rising moment contains every older moment within it, contains them all even as it is itself contained in the next to arise. The Emperor Rudolf rested his big jaw in his hand, elbow on the warm stone sill of the tower's window. He had not received the Body of Christ in months.

His tower room was an eagle's ærie; he could overlook the whole broad disc of the earth and the vault of sky like a dish and its cover. Though he knew very well that earth and sky were not like a dish and its cover.

What is that?

The Emperor's eye was drawn to the sky in the East, where low on the horizon a knot of white cloud had thickened.

He gripped the stone balustrade and peered harder into the eastern suburbs. What gathered there? He turned back into the crowded tower room, and muttering began to search amid the papers, clock's bodies, alembics and retorts, fire-gloves, uncut gems, goldbeater's tools, astrolabes and staves, his assistants fluttering before him.

The perspicil. The monks uncovered it for him. Recently constructed by Cornelius Drebble the incomparable. In Flanders (part of his Empire too, though they denied it there) the skilled lens-grinders were trying to do with ordinary lenses and tubes and mirrors what Drebble had done; there were those who would pay a fortune for the secret, but the Emperor had already paid a fortune to keep it for himself.

He had it carried to the window. It was as long as a culverin, its brass barrel chased with scenes of the history of sight: Argus and his hundred eyes, Narcissus and the pool, Moses seeing from the mountaintop the Promised Land.

His assistant fixed the eyepiece, tossed the velvet drape over the Emperor's head. The Emperor bent his eye to the aperture.

There. In the direction of Trebon, where stood the country house of Petr Vok Rozmberk, mighty subject, proud too; there the Englishman Dee and the Scotsman Kelley his creature were now harbored. The Emperor fiddled with the eyepiece but could not make the house itself appear. What were they up to? It seemed that a summer dust devil had arisen near there, only far larger than the little imps of dry roadways. Not big enough to be felt here on the mountain, but growing larger even as the Emperor stared at it.

By evening the eastward sky was dark with cloud, and the Emperor felt the wind on his cheek.

On that night, in a village in the far mountains of Bohemia, a lad was called out for the first time, by a voice calling him from the village street below his window.

He left his bed, and found himself to be in his other form, the same form as the old one who looked up at him from below. He reached the street in a single bound from the window's ledge. No one had seen him leave the house, and he must take care that no one saw him return. They set off together down the village street.

He was little more than a boy in that year; he had not before made this journey, and knew of it only what the old one who ran beside him had told him, in the dark of his barn in the light of day, when he had a form different from that which he now possessed. After discovering that the boy was one like himself and was filled with dread and loathing and confusion, the old one had become his instructor. He had explained to him the strange fate they had both been born to, and the work that befell them in consequence of it, work that the old one had done in the Ember Days of each season these many years; and he promised to run beside the boy when next they went forth, to guide him. The boy looked over at him now: the long panting tongue looped from his grizzled maw, grizzled like his own daytime cheeks; his eyes yellow, but as wet and soft as they always were. All in all he looked comically like himself, himself in the day world.

The street and the shuttered houses they passed were palely bright, as though illuminated by a cold sun, and yet his vision was not as good as it was in waking life: far-off objects were shapeless and unresolved, and leaves and walls had not even the dim memory of color which they have in moonlight—they were gray as tombstones, or stars.

How fast they moved! His heart felt huge within him, pumping stolidly and without effort, like a strong man chopping wood, and the ground fled away beneath his feet. The ripening crops they passed were mown by the night wind passing through their silver ears; he felt a great pride in the standing grain, and yet unconcerned in it, unable to remember how he himself had plowed and sown his father's strips and prayed for their good growth.

The wind was rising.

He had asked the old one: Why do we not tell the people, tell them what we have done for them, how we guard them; wouldn't they love us then, and not hate us as they do? The old one had smiled at his question, and the boy knew the answer now as he sped over the colorless country: knew it in his bloody heart, knew that he was a creature violent and ruthless, who would slay without compunction —a creature like the ferocious armed knights who protected this realm from its enemies, good men whose path the wise did not cross. He almost laughed to think it.

They skirted the cottages of the outlying folk, staying downwind of their stables and their dogs; it was not yet time to raid. Soon they had left the country that he knew, the bounds of his parish; the fields and ways were unfamiliar to him. By the moon he saw they went north and west toward the forested land. The night sped away and yet seemed also to hang changelessly in the gray air, the stars not turning, the moon not going toward its setting.

And there were others on the way now with them. He sensed

them before he saw one, a dark loping shape far off, across the fallow field, at the edge of the forest: he could taste its aliveness, its likeness to himself, with a sense he had not known he possessed. Gone then. And then again with them on the way, drawing closer.

Another caught him by surprise, appearing suddenly almost beside him, a great rufous animal from which the boy-soul just inside him shrank, starting away and toward his protector—but his protector was only another like the red, and just as hideous, as he was himself: and exaltation lifted him.

They came out, the three of them, onto the upland pastures where shepherds summered their flocks. One at least of these shepherds (he knew) was a creature of his kind, and was no doubt on the way with the rest of them this night toward the battle. That was a hard fate, he thought: to be, yourself, inside, the very creature whom you must protect your flock against, the creature they most feared.

In a soft fold of the meadows a little flock had huddled out of the wind, their shepherd with them. The three night-walkers bore down on them behind the tossing trees. The sheep sensed them, and stirred as one animal; in a moment they were running bleating together up the narrow valley, the shepherd with them hurrying the stray lambs with his crook. He could not guard them all, though, alone as he was (his fellows all in hiding, probably, ears big to hear the panicked sheep but too afraid to come out from their huts, not on this night) and it was easy for the three of them to cut out a single lamb, start it from the rest and send it hurrying toward the trees while its fellows fled the other way.

As they closed in on the lamb—he, the grizzled old one, and the red leading them—the shepherd turned to make a stand, crook grasped in his hands and his face set: they could see the teeth in his mouth, the great whites of his eyes. Brave man! They passed around him, and circled the lamb; the little thing had ceased to flee, and stood still, mild and almost patient now, its very mildness starting their bloodlust. The shepherd fled stumbling away. They blessed the lamb, they slew it and ate it.

The boy lifted his bloody head, baptized now, and replete; and the moon's white head looked down on him aghast. Then from somewhere within, from the root of his bony member or from his narrow fundament, there started a noise, a tremor as though his sinews were plucked and sounding. It issued from his throat at last, a cry that made his own rough hair stand up and his back thrill, shaking the bones of his skull and skirling forth seemingly without end. When at last he had done he saw the older ones regarding him with something like fondness; and from far off across the mountain and the valley came an answer, wolf's or man-wolf's.

Now they left the homeplaces of men behind them, the walled towns and tilled fields, the bridges, watchtowers and turnpikes. They climbed up along the bony back of the untenanted mountain, from whose rock outcroppings they could look down on the black and endless bristle of the forest sundered by a twist of river. The giant wind, into whose embrace they seemed to rise, was taller than the mountains, rising to the torn clouds and the moon.

There were many of them now, coming from far places, joining their fellows on the broad invisible way that led toward the battle. The two elders who ran beside him exchanged a look of wonderment, or was it foreboding? This summer's battle would surely be fierce, for the witches too had been summoned in numbers, flocking thither like great nightbirds; as he climbed he heard them in the treetops, alighting to rest, taking wing again to join others passing overhead. In their bags and cloaks, in the belts they wrapped around them, they carried the yield of the year, the ripening grain and the offspring of the herds: bearing it to their lord, who would reward them for their despoiling, for the famine and despair they brought.

But how reward them? he had wondered.. Don't they too have to live on the earth with us, don't they too suffer when the earth is robbed? What reward could be so great as to compensate them, what could make up for the death of the year? God forgive them, the old one said: they are that hungry, that everlastingly hungry, and nothing they can see or touch or taste can satisfy them; they must be always imagining some better food, some greater pleasure, sharper sauce, sweeter fruit than any known, and that's just what they're promised, though they never get it, never, for the Devil doesn't have it to give: he has only his promises.

They came to the throat of a long pass that led downward, to the last valley and to the burned-over environs of Hell, whose sour smell reached them now on the huge wind; there they rested. When they sat to converse, they sat as men did, upright, with their hands upon their knees, looking into one another's faces. Had they been men, they might have taken out a tinder-box, and started a fire for their comfort—but they had no love now for fire.

They talked of the wolf-hunters, out in numbers just now with Imperial licenses to beat the woods and take pelts, on which a high bounty would be paid. Take care, watch well. They gossiped of those they had heard of, who were beings of their kind: how one at least was a prince of the Imperial blood, who in the high castle of Prague was shut up to howl in the deepest dungeon on Ember nights.

They kept their own lore, among themselves, which the waking world didn't know, which they didn't know themselves when they were in the waking world. They told the tale (it was believed among some of them) that on the night of Christ's Nativity there was a great and much-feared wolf in the vicinity of Bethlehem, and when the angels announced the good news of the Babe born, this wolf heard it too, only he was not awed as the shepherds were; and when they had left their flocks to seek the Child, the wolf fell upon their lambs and slew and ate one. When he had done so he felt remorse, for the first time, and didn't know why; and full of grief he fled the flock, and came upon the shepherds who were going toward the manger. He followed them; he saw the Mother there within, and the Child; he saw the shepherds kneeling and offering a new-born lamb. The wolf watched and waited; and when all within the manger were asleep, he crept close. The animals, sensing his presence, began to stir, and the Child awoke, and calmed them; with His mildness He summoned the wolf, who came and laid his muzzle on the hay, to beg forgiveness. And for his sins and the sins of all his kind, the Christ Child that night laid this penance on the wolf: that he and his descendants thenceforth should go into the world of men, and seem in the light of day to be men; only on certain holy nights they would be summoned to be His soldiers, to do battle in the name of the Lamb, and on those nights they would revert to their wolfish forms. And such has been their condition from that day to this, to suffer the hatred of all men, and be known as just only to Him.

So their true nature was the one inside, the hairy nature, and the human form the semblance.

They nodded their heavy heads in assent at this story, heard so often before, and they would have wept too, but they could not weep now. And then one among them lifted his black nose into the air, and caught a scent, and one after another they turned upon their four feet and (heads nodding this way and that, long tongues panting) they set off again.

To be strange within your own homeland.

To go unrecognized; to have allies whom in the light of day you do not know.

To be one thing on the outside, another on the inside; to seem nothing and no one; to be despised and ignored, unseen, and yet to be the one on whom the welfare of all depends, though they don't know it.

In the last battle, the battle that brings in the new age, they would be there; when the children of men run to hide their heads, and cry to the mountains, Fall on us, and to the hills, Cover us. They would be there; they would not hide.

And in the next age, perhaps, they would all be seen for what they were, not the less feared perhaps, but honored justly; and though it might be that heaven was closed to beings of his kind—that at death they would turn again into the earth like the beasts—still while they went among men they would no longer need to hide, they could live whole and not divided: the hidden patent, and the inside out.

In that new time they would not be exiles; they would acknowledge one another in the light of day; they would bear proudly the badge of their fraternity, wear it when (in their bland human daylight forms) they proceeded all together to the altar to receive: in both species too, for they were true Bohemians and Utraquists, they would consume *corporem utraque sanguinem,* both flesh and blood.

The wind still rose. Not only the Bohemian witches were borne on the wind tonight, but the witches of Livonia and Moravia as well, the red witches of Galicia and the witches of the Transylvanian mountains armed with stalks of fennel; witches who had never gone out before rapt into the air and sent on their way as though by the great wind itself. Each one was pursued by a strong pursuer; as many as they were, their enemies were just as numerous, streaking with them eagerly toward Hell-mouth.

He seemed now to have been on the way for a hundred years, to have known for a hundred years what it was to be as he was. He knew that the long rufous one who had run long beside him, with whom he had slain the lamb, was a great captain of their kind—pathfinder, witch-biter, grain-saver. He meant to stay by her in the battle to come at the night's end. He wondered if he would know her if he met her in her other form, a long-armed red-haired housewife at her washing.

He was alone now, out of sight of the others, but knowing them to be proceeding all around him. His heart was huge within him, and far from weary. He thought he knew what the battle to come would be like; he could see the witch it was his fate to pursue and punish, striding on great legs ahead of him down the defiles of Hell: he could see her fearful hungry eye cast back at him.

He followed a dim trail down through the forest, a trail which it seemed his kind had made for their convenience, made by their passing and repassing this way: it glowed faintly in his eye like a snail's track of slime. When the wolf-trap set in the path closed on him, it tossed him into the air with the force of its snapping shut and smashed instantly and for good the ankle of his left foot.

His shocked spirit returned into him shrieking, in the awful knowledge (like the knowledge of the damned soul at death) that he was caught, that he was hurt dreadfully, that he could not free himself and that he was likely now to be captured and to die the death. But what pierced him more, what made him twist and bite in hopeless rage, was the knowledge that by his unwisdom he would miss the battle. The first battle he had ever been summoned to, the last battle it might be, the battle he had been made by God to fight: and he would not be there. He chewed earth and wept. In the air above him his enemies stole on ahead.

It was as though Earth and Nature had finally admitted the force of that argument made against Copernicus, that if the ball of Earth really did roll around always to the East, then we ought to feel a wind blowing continually with awful force, the whole sphere of air set in apparent motion westward by the earth's eastward motion, a wind strong enough to uproot trees, sweep up men and beasts and push them into the sea, slop the sea out of its basin over the dry land. Well here it is.

Or perhaps (Giordano Bruno thought) the earth had only on this day begun her turning, and the slower sphere of air had not yet caught up.

He laughed aloud, bent against the wind. Why does the heart love wild weather, fires, floods and winds, for all that it destroys our works and seeks our lives?

There were still miles to go before he reached the gates of Prague City, and he seemed likelier to lose ground than gain it in this storm. Look at those clouds, dense as haysmoke, black as bear's fur. He had a horrid and exhilarating vision that they might part, and Prague itself and its surmounting castle be revealed riding the wind, uprooted and dropping clods and cobblestones as it went west.

Time to call a halt. He had come down into a huddle of houses, shutters shut, a lost straw hamper being tossed down the street, bumping blindly into walls. There would be no inn here. There was a church, though, and Bruno, tired of batting his stinging eyes against the dust, pushed open the wicket in its door and went in.

It was dark as night inside, for the priest had shuttered the windows; candles and a pitch-pine torch were burning, loose airs toying with their flames. Villagers filled the church, kneeling on the floor, wrapped in shawls and cloaks, black sheep huddled together; now and then a white face looked up from amid them to stare at a sound.

Mass had nearly reached the Consecration. After that, Bruno supposed, they would begin ringing their one sour bell, to scare away the airy dæmons. He raised his eyes: odd the way fissures in the stone fabric of the church, the tower, the roof, amplified sound, making weird harmonies. The dæmon's voice, these people thought, crying for souls. But Bruno knew it wasn't so. The semaphores who are the wind cannot speak.

—*Suscipiat Dominus sacrificium de manibus tuis.* Bruno knelt himself, having already attracted stares, a foreigner, someone to be feared. No doubt they believed too that witches could raise winds. It was perhaps well that he knelt, for this day and this church were soon to be much talked of, in fear and wonder, the reports reaching as far as to the Emperor in Prague, and to the Papal Nuncio, who sent them on to Rome: how when the country priest spoke the words of consecration, turning the wafer to the Body of Jesus Christ, and held it aloft for the people's adoration, the people had seen gripped in the priest's fingers a tabby kitten, who then changed to a stick of elmwood, which changed to a wriggling trout, the priest staring upward with bared teeth and eyes wide, unable to let go; and the trout changed to a live coal shedding sparks, and that to a gray pigeon. The people closest to the altar could hear the flutter of its wings.

The wind blew through that day and the next, moving huge fleets of dark cloud overhead to invade the West. In the Narrow Seas the Spanish captains felt it in their faces, as a man feels the onrush of a wolf at his back the instant before he hears the drumming of its feet. The sky darkened, in the wrong quarter. And they crossed themselves, or swore terribly, or both.

But it blew not only over the length of Christendom; that wind blew right around the world, combing the Russian grasses, whipping up gray foam on the Bosphorus, snapping the Sultan's silken banners, blowing out lamps in Babylon and Cathay. It shook the rope bridges of Peru across which the King of Spain's gold was carried night and day; it closed with driven dust the eyes of Libyan lions, lifted snow from the Caucasus. In Ægypt, as the sands moved like seas, the heads of sphinxes appeared, and the long bodies of fallen obelisks; the stairs of temples ages lost were revealed, leading down; in the sanctuary (the herdsman taking refuge there kneels in awe) the lamps still burned above the altar, and the idol's eyes were open.

In Trebona near Prague where it had first begun, just a little vortex whirling a handful of fallen leaves, it still blew hugely, hooting in the towers of the castle of the Rozmberks and tossing the heads of trees in the park. In an apartment high in the castle the new glass windows rattled in the old stone arches, and vagrant airs stirred the hangings and teased the candle flames. John Dee's wife Jane held her children to her, Katherine and Michael, and sang them a song. Blow blow thou Western wind, the small rain down can rain. On the rich rug that overspread the floor Rowland Dee played with quoits of heavy gold, sophic, wonderful; one rolled away and the cat moused after it.

Above in his tower room, John Dee (at whose command the wind had arisen, who had summoned certain princes of the air by means of a seal which he had cast according to instructions given him) sat before a clouded crystal stone set in a frame on his table of practice. He was looking down into its depths at something he had never seen before, a tiny young woman hiding there.

He asked: Is it the first wind, of which you told us, the wind that will shake down empires?

When she answered he heard, and that for the first time too; heard as though the voice were hers and yet his as well, he could feel the cords in his own throat tremble when she spoke.

—Pity, she said. *Pity a poor maiden, Madimi, who has done all that was asked of her and no more.* Nunc dimittis, *for I cannot stay. Oh pity.*

He understood he had been deceived by her; he had not raised this wind himself for his purposes at all, but had only occasioned it, she had only flattered him to call it his, it had purposes he could not know, it blew where it listed. But was it the first wind of the passage time, and if it was, when would the second, contrary wind arise?

—*Christ Jesus let them not die forever who have done Thee service and blessed Thee and eaten the Bread of Thy Salvation for their sustenance. Let them not go into the night of nothing and be lost.*

—Is it the first wind? Dee asked again. Is it? Answer.

—*He has prepared a place for those who have abandoned the way. They will be cast into darkness and will sleep. Christ let them sleep and not be slain.*

John Dee's hands circled the stone. He would not release her. He said:

—Madam I abjure you.

—*Pity, O pity,* she said, her great eyes wide. *Pity like a naked new-born babe.*

She shivered where she knelt, in the wind that blew also in the place she was. She clasped her nakedness, and tried to draw her flailing gown around her, which the wind wanted. Dee ceased to question her. His heart was full. She was no longer preaching or teaching. She prayed, and prayed not for human souls, but for herself: as frightened as a child on a night of storm, as an orphan of war pleading for her life with pitiless victors, who did not seem to hear.

8

――――

p on Mount Whirligig the wind threshed the aged trees, never cut, of the woods around The Woods Center for Psychotherapy. The center itself—made of wood a century almost ago, and having suffered a lot of weather since—rode out the blow like an old galleon, creaking and moaning to wake the guests (never patients, never inmates) and start their dreads. The flag rope beat the tall metal flagpole rhythmically, ringing like a tocsin.

It was long after lights-out, and the long wooden halls were dark, but an altercation of voices (high and hysterical, calm and low) was taking place in the bathroom at the end of the third floor west. Noise of cascading waters. A door slammed. The pat of bare feet walking swiftly down the hall, and a sort of flying mutter going with them, disappearing toward the stairs, someone following on rubber soles, a whispered entreaty or command.

Somebody had flipped: those awake in their beds listened intently. Disruptions in the night weren't unheard of here, they were discussed in detail at breakfast, who was that up at two A.M.

The somebody appeared next in the odorous kitchen, where a night man found her; when she began to empty the shelves of their contents, big boxes of salt and spices, huge cans of tomatoes and corn and peaches, he found she was too strong to stop, and went for help, waking the second floor east pounding on the resident's door.

It was a true psychotic event, which *was* rare at The Woods. It traveled from the kitchen up to the big game room, having involved

now the third floor west monitor, the therapist whom she had awakened, the night man who found her after the other two lost her, and
the resident *he* had awakened, who was Mike Mucho, doing his
monthly stint. None of them were ready to use force to subdue her,
but they were not having any luck getting her to take a pill, or a shot,
or get back in bed.

They got her to sit quietly for a time, in a conversation area by the
pool table; her face was filmed with pale sweat, her eyes looked from
one to another of them as though trying to determine what sort of
beasts they were. Then, abruptly, she slapped her knees with both
hands and got up, time to be going, and was fighting her way through
their restraining hands (blindly, as through a thicket) when Ray
Honeybeare, dressed in a plaid robe and carpet slippers, appeared
before her.

It seemed to Mike later on a kind of providence that among those
who had been awakened to deal with the girl there was no one
who would want to keep Honeybeare away from her. She stopped
when she saw him, seeming to recognize him as a person, as she
had not the others. He only looked at her curiously, his rumpled
face calm.

Then the show changed venue again, back toward the disrupted
kitchen. She stepped that way deliberately at first, then with reluctance or uncertainty, as though a kind of possessing will came and
departed and came again within her; they all followed, Honeybeare
among them, hands in the pockets of his robe. More lights were
coming on, doors opening, the curious coming to the top of the stair
to look down into the kitchen.

She turned there to face Honeybeare.

Hands still in his pockets, Honeybeare fixed the girl with his
pink-rimmed blue eyes, tiny gems discarded in the ruin of his face.
The wind shook the kitchen windows, and the cedars outside
moaned. He said:

"Tell me your name."

She clamped tight her jaws and raised her head, eyes fierce and
the tendons standing in her neck. Mike Mucho, standing near her,
could smell her fear. Honeybeare said again:

"Tell me your name."

She did: she released it from her mouth, a string of meaningless
plosives; she was shaking with terror or rage or both. As soon as he

heard the name, Honeybeare drew his hands from his pockets, took the girl by her skinny elbows, and staring not at her face but at her breast said in a voice almost too small to hear:

"Leave this woman alone. I tell you. In Jesus' name."

Did the wind rise just then? Mike Mucho would later say it had. He felt himself, and The Woods, Mount Whirligig—all that the world is made of—loosen, and arise and stand in the middle of the air: to be held thereafter in their places only by consent, or by command.

The girl after a long moment ceased to tremble. She seemed to wake, like a child from an attack of night terrors; to coalesce, as herself, in the kitchen pantry amid the spilled food and pots and pans, and to see all these things as she had not before been able to see them; and she began to sob, in grief and relief and embarrassment.

Don't you remember the wind of that late summer, September of 1976, or was it '77, the night it blew so long and so universally? It blew not only in the Faraways and through the open windows of New York and Boston apartments, not only over the eastern sea, plucking up waves, breaking boats at their moorings: it blew countrywide, weather systems connecting one to another like paisleys across the Great Plains (the TV weatherman pointed them out in some wonder to Val and Mama, together in Val's bed with the satin quilt pulled up and the woods alive around them); and it blew out on the other coast as well. Julie Rosengarten knew it, because a phone call from Big Sur woke her after midnight, and she talked about it and its meaning for a while, almost able to hear the singing of the continental wires in her ear, as waves can be heard in a shell.

She was left alone awake, then, when her caller at length hung up after reassurances and long-distance hugs. A siren cried in the sounding tunnel of the streets, and her cats crept closer to her upraised knees. She picked up the phone again, said a number out loud to herself to remember it right, and called Beau Brachman in the Faraway Hills.

Beau had no telephone in his apartment, but the woman who answered downstairs knew he wasn't asleep; no one in the house was, children were crying, people going from room to room to push down windows. She went up the stairs to get him. Julie waited, listening to the distant wakened house.

"Hi."

"Oh, Beau." She pressed the receiver closer to her ear and mouth. "What is it, what is it?"

"I don't know, Julie. You know, sometimes a big wind is just a big wind."

"I talked to Leo," she said. "In California. They felt it too. Beau, Hilary said her amber shattered. She was holding it in her hand, yesterday. It just shattered in her hand." She waited. "Beau?"

"I'm here, Julie."

"I'm scared."

"Can't be scared of change," he said gently.

"Well you can too. I am. I always am."

"If there weren't change . . ."

"I didn't say I didn't *want* it," she said. "Or *refused* it. I don't refuse it. Only, Beau . . ." She lifted her eyes to see the kitchen wall through the door, where a calendar on the wall, livid in a patch of streetlight, just then fluttered its leaves wildly and twisted on its nail. "Beau. I thought if you could just say that word for me. You know."

"You can say it for yourself, Julie. It works even better."

"I can't. I can never remember it. And when you say it."

"All right," he said. "But it's yours too. For you."

"Yes." She waited while Beau seemed to compose himself, and then she received the crabbed and complex word, she could never remember it till she heard it but when she heard, it went into her as familiar as wine. She let it warm her. She said it herself to him, and to her heart. When it had done its work, she could let the wind take her, where, instead of clinging to the branch: she sailed.

"Beau," she said. "I'm worried about Pierce."

"Okay," he said.

"Do you ever see him, do you ever like *tell* him . . ." Beau on the other end was silent, a receiving silence; she was to talk, not he. "He thinks he's so strong. So tough-minded. But he's brittle. He'll break."

"Well it's a hard thing he's doing," Beau said. "Isn't it? At least he's willing. He keeps pushing farther in."

"Where angels fear to tread," Julie said. A lump of grief filled her throat, and tears came to her eyes; unmoored as she was, she was subject to feelings. Fellow-feelings, for those on the way, which meant everyone really: it *was* hard. "I wonder if he knows people worry."

"Oh," Beau said. "It seems to me Pierce wouldn't really believe that people think about him when he's not there."

"Will you watch him?" she asked. "I don't mean . . . But will you?"

He didn't answer for a long time, and she could see his abashing smile, over the hundred miles between them; his smile that might be amused at her for worrying, or at the stumblings of others, who weren't often really hurt, no more than the children he supervised: get up, dust off the pants, hustle on.

"Okay," he said at last.

"Ooh," Julie said, a word like the wind's. "Oooh listen to it now."

Down Maple Street, the maple outside Pierce's building stroked the roof and windows, trying to get in. Pierce had closed the windows of the sunporch, all but one, and at that one his son stood, called from his bed, the narrow white bed on the sunporch, the windowed sunporch.

He turned away at length from the coursing clouds and the night, and went to his father's bed; no room now for him in it. He stood over his father's sleeping form for an indeterminate time naked shivering happy, fed full on all that had happened here. Now he would be succeeded by others, chastening ones and not so kind, not so easily detached either. He bent over his father and kissed his whiskery cheek.

The kiss ought to have awakened Pierce, but did not, not quite; a voice did moan very softly far within, the voice of the smaller Pierce far within, the Pierce who took this kiss, who witnessed this departure. Then his son turned away to the open window, to the night and the wind. He stood for a moment out on the roof in the streetlight shattered by the maple's flailing leaf-shadows, clasping his nakedness, afraid. *Pallidula rigida nudula,* pale little bare little shiverer, no more games for you now; what will become of you, where will you go? Pierce in his dream saw the boy there: and at that his eyes did open, awake and wide.

He sat up after a minute, unable to locate what had awakened him. He swung his feet out of the bed onto the cold floor. He thought it was drink that had awakened him, the economy of drink, knocks you right into sleep but shakes you awake later to even the score; or was it the wind, or the restless stirring of the body beside him, filled with its own dreams, he was unused to a big unquiet woman in his bed, never again would be used to it maybe; maybe he should go sleep in his chair.

He rose carefully, went out to the sunporch, ought to shut that window. He put his hands on the sash, and then thought he would stand there awhile until he was quieter, and then go back to sleep. So he waited for a long time, hollow and open, in the wild pour of air. But his heart was not going to be, could not be quiet: not until it came back again into his breast, not until it returned to him from wandering "those roads to nothingness, where bodies cast no shadows, and mirrors reflect nothing." And he would not sleep again until he woke.

Far away from there (no not so far away, it seemed to Pierce an uncrossable distance but it was short as the wind went, through the Delaware Water Gap, along the wrinkled river, fast following the new Interstate where the great trucks navigated, and up into the mountains) Sister Mary Philomel awoke in her bedroom at Queen of the Angels School.

It was the wide wasteland of the middle night, which she had never been familiar with except in those days (all but forgotten now) when she had lain sleepless and sweated in tummy pain. She seemed to come wide awake all in an instant, not by hesitant dreaming degrees, and she knew there was a reason, though not what reason. What a storm though. She felt the air in her dark room move palpably in sympathy with the air outside.

What is it? she asked the room and the night. Sitting upright in her bed, not conscious of having sat up, she crossed herself and began a quick prayer, her eyes traveling around the long-familiar room, hers for nearly twenty years. Up to the crazed plaster of the ceiling; down the wall over the crucifix and faldstool; across her own feet making tombstones under the gray coverlet; now and at the hour of our death; over the bed's edge to the floor, to where her slippers lay, to where.

She rose by shuddering degrees an inch off her mattress, hands still clasped together, and alighted again: for, right by the bed, so close that she had at first not seen it, stood St. Wenceslaus, her old wormholed boxwood saint, who had been in his accustomed place on the dresser last night when she closed her eyes.

Sister Mary Philomel slid to the edge of the bed, felt for her glasses on the table there, and when they were on looked down at the saint. Crown on his head, scepter in his hand, glue line visible where he had been broken and mended. Him. But on his face a strange constricted needful uncomfortable look not his at all. She looked across the dim rug and up the chair and the dresser to the lace doily where he had stood: the path he had taken to come down and stand by her bed here, a painful impossible journey to have made.

What's wrong? she asked him, not aloud, and bent down to him, her hands on the bed's edge. When she looked at his face thus closely it was clear what the matter was: she put out her hand, and took from the old king's distended jaws the thing stuck in his mouth.

It was a key. The wind bumped and rattled from attic to basement. A small cold brass key.

Thrilling with shivers but unafraid, Sister Mary Philomel threw aside her covers and put her feet out and into their slippers. The saint's face was passive and saintly again and only a little grouchy, as he always had been. When she had lifted him with reverent wonder and set him back in his accustomed place, she put on her robe, and put the little key into her pocket. She stopped at the small square of mirror illuminated by a nightlight and tugged straight her nightcap.

Down she went then through the dormitory, passing between the rows of white bedsteads where twenty girls slept, some as though dead, some in contorted stricken postures, nightgowns rucked up, breathing fast; some moving or muttering dream-slowly. Two, wind-awakened, whispered to Sister as she passed, but Sister hushed them and went on.

Down the narrow back stairs to the second floor, past the rooms where her sisters slept, down the waxed and carpeted broad front stairs (robe rising in a billow on the uprushing night air) to the first floor, where by the wall there stood a great ancient chest, beeswax-blackened, paneled and carved. It had come to Queen of the Angels from the hospital in Bondieu after the expansion there, manhandled by puzzled laborers out of the truck and up the front steps, heavy as lead.

Only when she stood before it did Sister Mary Philomel marvel that she had known, immediately and without question, what the key caught in the poor saint's jaws was meant to open; only when she drew the key out of her pocket did she wonder why she had come instantly to open it. Leave well enough alone, she told herself. Then she knelt on the parquet before the chest, and put the key into its lock.

The vigil lights in their red glasses shuddered; Sister Mary Philomel heard a faroff cry, a cat maybe, or a lost child, or a wind-tormented hinge. When she turned the key she felt a stirring, as though with the turning of the one key all the drawers and compartments within (which no one in her memory had ever seen) also opened one by one in sequence. She had the piercing feeling that she had not simply unlocked something but had started something into life, something that had long expected her, had awaited her, or someone like her, to come and do the proper thing at last.

Just at that time a white Tempest convertible (which had left the Interstate at Pikeville an hour before and driven almost under the windows of Queen of the Angels) passed through the vanished hamlet of Hogback and up and around the next flank of the mountain. Where the wide paved road parted to go up to the old strip mine on Hogback's side, the Tempest chose the other road, dirt, downward; the driver gratuitously cut the engine, and the ghostly car freewheeled silently around a bend through the crunching gravel and came to a halt by the creek's side.

The driver slid across the red upholstery and pushed open the passenger's door; got out. The bridge was the same, she thought, or was a new bridge not different from the old one; she stepped carefully across it on her narrow high heels.

Already she wanted to turn back; she wanted not to have come; but volition was not hers now, and whatever had replaced it within her carried her swiftly surely across the tumbling water and up the path. Past the great boulder, that had never been removed from the premises, left as a sign. The pines above on the mountain had grown, where on more than one night she had slept, long ago, long years ago. Was there a dog under the porch? None woke. She went up to the door; it was unlocked, unlatched in fact, and she pushed it open and went in, leaving it open behind her.

Home. No light but the gray spill of the television, on without sound, small figures in antic distress, swiftly changed for others. By it she saw the spavined couch, and the straightback chair her great-grandfather had made, the Bible laid on it.

She went past it toward the door of the only bedroom, open too. Beneath her feet as she approached the door the linoleum crackled. And the wind like to lift the little place right into the air, up into the treetops.

He was there.

He lay on his back on the mattress, shirtless, his great horny feet apart and one long arm fallen toward the floor. At first she thought he was not asleep, that his eyes saw; but when she came closer (in revulsion and awe but no fear) she could tell that he was absent. The wind wrenched the curtain at the open window.

She did not, or she could not, hesitate, but went to him where he lay; lifted the slack arm up and placed it by his side; pushed her red-nailed hands beneath his back (cold as a corpse, she thought) and pushed. As heavy as a corpse too. She set her feet again, unsteady in heels, and with a tiny bat-cry she rolled the man-doll over on its face. It didn't awaken. It could not.

Now his walking spirit, when at dawn he came back again, could not enter at the mouth from which he had gone out. He was caught outside.

And she turned and left, leaving the door open (he could not now return by it), past the devil's stone and back across the little bridge, this time twisting a heel in a crack. She bent to take off her shoes almost without stopping, then went more swiftly to the white car left waiting by the water's side; and she spurred it away in a spurt of earth and pebbles as the wind called after her aghast.

Oh don't you remember, don't you remember: there will be no record of it except as you remember it. One of the big pines on the knoll at Arcady blew down, shattering right at the hollow in its heart, in which a great beehive had been built; the bees rose in their numbers to meet the enemy, and were scattered. It blew shingles from the stable roof and turned the pages of *National Geographics* piled in the stable's attic; it rattled but could not open the locked door before which Boney Rasmussen had been standing stony and inert since his death in July.

Rosie Rasmussen sat up in bed, awakened by the wind too; or by a sound beyond her room, like an approaching footfall. Something the wind had done, doubtless. Alert and staring at the black oblong of the doorway, Rosie willed whatever it was to go away.

Go away.

But then, just as Rosie grew certain that some presence really was near her, another soft footfall came, and a small figure in white went past her door without looking in.

Oh lord Sam.

"Hon? Do you have to go?"

No she wasn't going toward the bathroom. Rosie got out of bed and went out into the hall, just in time to see Sam turn purposefully and go down the stairs.

Was it true you weren't supposed to wake them, that something awful happened if you did? No that was myth, it sounded when she told it to herself just exactly like something made up, because of the strangeness, because of the fear of, of what.

"Sam," she whispered, not loud enough.

Man listen to the wind.

Sam went down the stairs, holding the thick banister rail, unhesitating, down to the hall. What did she think, where did she think she went. Rosie after her, her neck and shoulders thrilling the way they did when she heard someone's eerie dream. She watched Sam's white nightshirt float down the hall toward the door out. When she reached it she stood on tiptoe and took hold of the knob, meaning to let herself out or the night in.

"No! Sam don't!" Rosie called, unable not to, following fast. "Don't!"

Sam turned from the door. Her body shook violently to see her mother, and the great front hall, and herself there; her eyes were huge.

"What's that?" she said, staring.

Then she shook again, and didn't stop. She fell to the floor before Rosie could reach her. Rosie tried to gather her up, but Sam was twisted rigid, her pupils were rolled away and her teeth clenched, a sort of wild roar coming from her throat.

A storm in her brain, Dr. Bock had called it. Like an electrical storm.

"Oh Christ," Rosie said, trying to hold her. "Oh Jesus." It was just past midnight on the twenty-first of September. The seizure went on for nearly a minute. Forever. "Oh Jesus," Rosie pleaded or whispered. "Oh Jesus. Oh Jesus Christ."

9

___

he heart," Frank Walker Barr said to Pierce Moffett. "It has a history." And he tapped his sternum, behind which his own heart presumably lay.

"Yes?" Pierce said.

"Today the heart is just a pump. A muscle. Liable to failure and needing care. But for centuries it was, really was, the seat of the feelings, interpreter of the world, source of emotional life."

The two walked together along an avenue of attenuated palms, whose high heads indicated an eastward breeze. At the avenue's end a little pyramid stood, guarded by sphinxes painted with cat's eyes and rosebud mouths.

"Once upon a time, of course," Barr said, "the human person was composed differently from the way in which it's composed now. Once, it was made of distinct and incommensurable parts. Soul and body. Body and soul."

"Yes," Pierce said.

"The soul was not material; it had no size, shape, density, weight, none of that. It did have parts, but never mind that for now. The body was all material, made out of the four elements, air fire earth and water, in subtly variable combinations."

Pierce nodded. He took from his pocket and donned a pair of brown sunglasses he had bought on his first trip to the Faraway Hills, in the former age of the world, before the passage time. The sand and sea darkened.

"Now the problem then was," Barr said, "the relation between the two parts. The soul was wholly non-material, and the body was the opposite; therefore how can the soul apprehend the body and the material world? How can the body respond to the commands or aspirations of the soul? What could possibly connect them?"

He lifted a hand to indicate the pyramid ahead, that they should approach it rather than going around. He was a short man who gave the impression of being large, as though he were made of some heavy and powerful matter; yet his step was hesitant, and his arms in their drip-dry shirt were crooked a little at the elbow. He had been old even when Pierce had been his student.

"But of course you don't have to have this problem," Pierce said, who was feeling the onset of familiar anxieties. "You set it for yourself, by dividing up the person."

"Right," Barr said. "The Greeks did that. Setting the problem then to be solved by whoever thought that the Greeks were the last word on everything. Here's what they did eventually: they posited a third thing, *spirit, pneuma* in Greek, a word which had a lot of ambiguous meanings, including *breath*."

Soul, spirit: Pierce said he had been reading those words in old authors and hearing them in church since he was a kid and had never actually understood the difference, if there was one.

"Well," Barr said. "There came to be. You've read Ficino, of course. *De vita coelitus comparanda.*"

"Well, I've read *in* it," Pierce said, blushing hotly, if not in his sun-red face in his heart.

"You know his distinctions, which were perhaps largely his own, but widely influential. The difference between soul and spirit was that spirit was matter, soul wasn't; spirit was an extremely fine, refined, superfine matter, a liquid airy fiery sort of stuff. It flowed all through the body, it was very *quick*, it was hot and it was somehow *shiny* or silvery or reflective, so that whatever the body's senses perceived was reflected in it."

Barr indicated the world, the vegetation, a pair of spiraling butterflies, the people around them who walked barefoot to and fro or gazed out over the sands shading their eyes.

"A sound comes in at the ear," he said. "Or a sight comes in through the eye. It hits the shiny spirit, which is *stirred* by it, heats up with emotion (which is not material). And the soul, which can't perceive matter at all, having no organs to sense it with, *can* perceive reflections, which are immaterial, like light. And so the soul perceives what the body perceives, because it is incised or impressed or reflected in the spirit."

"So I'm not sure what this has to do with the heart," Pierce said. The conversation had begun with Barr's mention of his own, not in good shape he said.

"The heart," Barr said. "Right. You see spirit flowed all through the body. It comprised a sort of second body closely bound up with the physical one, this one."

"The astral body," Pierce said, thinking of Beau Brachman.

"Yes," Barr said. "Exactly. But it was in the *heart* that the spirit was generated, and from which it circulated; and that's where the material coming in through the senses was received and felt."

"Ah," Pierce said. He had begun to perceive the shapes of certain old philosophical difficulties, brought to light by this idea; why people had once said what they had said, done what they had done. Bruno. Dee. "I see," he said, though he didn't, quite.

"Spirit flowed out from the heart and returned to it; partly it was under the soul's control, partly it was subject to the body whose senses it served. The material senses received the data, the data heated up the spirit, the heart synthesized the image from all the senses and the soul perceived in it the immaterial reflection of the object, and considered: is this thing good? Bad? The will (which is part of the soul) could then choose it or reject it."

"Uh huh," Pierce said.

"Take sex," Barr said. "Love rather."

"Uh huh," Pierce said, as though he had known this was coming, which darkly he had.

"You see a person. That person's physical qualities enter your senses. They are reflected in your spirit, which heats up as your feelings awake. The soul looks into this mirror, the spirit, and sees the reflection, and becomes entranced, or doesn't. Love."

They joined a dozen others who had also approached the pyramid and now waited there, some of them old and brown, some of them holding children by the hand, patient in the mild sun.

"She comes in through the eyes," Barr said. "Not her physical person, but the image of her, projected somehow by her own eyes, source of her power to cause love."

"Beatrice and Dante," Pierce said. Sweat had begun to form in a cool band over his forehead. "Petrarch and Laura."

"Remember, the soul, which is the only part of you that can love, can never perceive the body of the other person; it can only see, and love, the *reflection* of the other person in your heart, in your spirit."

"So you don't really fall in love with another person," Pierce said lamely. "Just an idea."

"Not so silly, after all, is it?" Barr said smiling. He took off his straw hat, and wiped the band with his handkerchief. "The Renaissance Platonists pictured the whole personal mechanism differently, but they were no stupider about life than we are."

Now their turn had come. They went up to the wide window and the white counter where oranges were piled in cannonball fashion, small pyramids too; a black youth in a white cap at a rakish angle smiled at them. Arched over his window was painted the word FRESH in bold and convincing letters.

"Large or small?" Barr inquired of Pierce.

"Oh. Small," Pierce said; and Barr held up two fingers to the counterman.

"They use Valencias," Barr said. "I determined that. The best for juice." He gave Pierce a cup of foamy juice and steaming ice that did not seem small at all.

"Another thing this picture could explain or account for," Barr said as they turned away, "was what could go wrong with love, which seems to have gone wrong very frequently then."

"*Amor hereos,*" Pierce said. "Burton talks about it."

"Yes. It was a part of melancholy. Well its etiology was part of this spirit theory. Now watch what happens. Suppose your spirit is a particularly hot, shiny, labile, fluid one. And you see or meet somebody who for all sorts of reasons—the stars mostly—matches perfectly your own spirit's ability to reflect. What can happen is that the image of the beloved can run rampant through the body, carried on the spirit; it can actually become an infection."

"Love-sick," Pierce said. His own heart had begun the steady rapid beat, little hard fist knocking at a cell-door, that had come to be nearly constant, had alarmed him enough to send him to a doctor, a real modern one, who listened and told him to relax.

"The soul ceases to be able to think of anything else, because the spirit can't reflect anything else. The phantasmal reflection of the

other person, let loose in your spirit, takes on a sort of phony auton-
omy. It's not a person, remember—it's a creation of your own—but it
can establish itself as a person. Since the poor soul can think of
nothing else, the phantasm can actually come to supplant your own
subjectivity, so that the phantasm of the beloved is there where you
should be. You have *lost your heart* to her."

"What happens to you?" Pierce said.

"Gone." Barr finished his drink. "If you don't get yourself back,
you die. Can't feed yourself or dress yourself or."

For a moment Pierce felt his knees weaken, and the bright day
darken, and thought he might be about to shame himself and embar-
rass his old teacher by fainting there on the boardwalk.

He would have said that this was not the first case of infection he
had suffered; he would have said that he had rarely in his
postpubertal life not been suffering it, or recovering from it, or seeking restlessly to contract it again. But oh this was different, this case.
The man who walked beside Barr sucking the straw of his juice, who
resembled an old student of Barr's met by strange chance at an out-of-
the-way Florida resort, was in fact a golem no longer operated by
himself, a shell hollowed by something certainly very much like a
fatal disease; and the empty spaces within him filled with awful imaginary things, black matter the sun could not penetrate to.

"So is there," he tried to say calmly, "a cure?" Barr looked at him
curiously, and Pierce smiled down at Barr brightly, just curious. "I
mean if they thought it was a disease, maybe they had a cure. I've
never heard of one."

"They tried," Barr said. "They might put you to bed. Try to get
you to figure it out. Prayer. A vacation amid unexciting surroundings.
And in some cases there was spontaneous remission, of course."

Certainly there was. Had Pierce not survived the process himself,
and not once only, but more than once? Weaker but not dead, not
yet.

This time, though.

"I," he said, and Barr waited. "I."

He stopped then, and turned as though to look out over the
miniature beach (man-made) and the vanishing cloudscape. But it
was really to turn his still-smiling but (he could feel it) alarmingly
unwell face away from his old teacher. He experienced the madman's
awful bind: having to ask for help, from people who cannot conceive

the spiritual difficulty you're in; and realizing that they can therefore give you no help; and so sinking deeper into darkness before their kind puzzled faces.

Smart whole ordinary people who could not imagine what had become of Pierce. Beau and Rosie Mucho and Spofford, when he had tried to explain, a child in the grip of night terrors, comforted by big safe grownups, a child who knows that grownups are beyond all such fears, which makes him even more afraid and alone. Of course they found it hard to believe, or to sympathize. Pierce himself found it hard to believe, dreadfully, wholly unlikely; his self, from whatever gray cold noplace it had been remanded to, looked back on Pierce in helpless and amazed dismay.

He walked with Barr up the beach road past the souvenir stands and food stalls, back to the iron grille of Barr's hotel. They both remarked again on the coincidence, coming upon one another here of all places, each as far from home as the other, and Barr said Small world; but Pierce had actually ceased to be surprised by these vatic encounters, any more than the errant knight is surprised to encounter the hermit in the wide forsaken forest, just the hermit he needs to meet. No Pierce was not surprised; it seemed to him that from now on he must probably meet his old mentor and guide at every hopeless juncture of his journey, or if not him someone just like him; and yet still he did not know to ask the question that would free him, or even that there was a question that could be asked.

Christ let him not die of it, he thought as he walked back to his mother's place: that would be so futile, so shaming, he would never be able to hold his head up among the dead.

"She was working at a psychotherapy center," Pierce told his mother. "And that's where she fell in with this. Group."

They sat together again at evening on the marina deck of the little motel that Winnie owned a share in. The winter air was mild.

"It's called the Powerhouse International," Pierce said, and gave a strangled chuckle. "The *Powerhouse*, yes. A quasi-Christian sort of Bible cult. They specialize in healing, at least the elite does. They claim a big success with mental patients."

Winnie shook her head, dismayed.

"I think an old lover of hers got her into it," Pierce said. He could see them, the operatives of her newfound faith, the nightbirds roosting open-eyed in his inward darkness: Mucho the tool, Ray Honeybeare the torpid sorcerer; and farther behind them, somewhere in the Midwest where the cult had its home and temple, the cult's founder and head, the prophet-dragon, who appeared Oz-like in videotapes to instruct his followers and inductees. Rose had described the sessions; she said she thought Pierce would find them really interesting.

"A lot of people in cults get over it," Winnie said. "You think they get swallowed up and never come out. But a lot do."

Cults were everywhere then, or seemed to be, gingerbread houses appearing on the path into which the young especially were tempted by the thousands. Cults were passage-time creatures, perhaps, compound monsters amazed at their own sudden new powers; or they were hopeless refuges to rush to in the upheaval of time, as passengers on a sinking liner rush to the uptipped stern, to cling together there; or they were symptoms of social or psychic distress that had always been there, and had only come to be noticed, or re-noticed. Or they were none of these things. Anyway Pierce had had fatidic dreams about them often in recent years, dreams of being in the power of one or another, as had many other sleepers; but till now he had always been able to tell he was dreaming.

"They believe they can alter the world in certain ways. Not just healing. They can, you know, get things through prayer. Find lost things. Have what they want."

"Oh for Pete's sake."

"If you ask for bread, you won't get a stone. Jesus said."

He had tried to tell Rose, calmly, *openly,* that he had a long history with this religion, had given it a lot of thought, not only its premises and dogmas but its passion too. *But you're not a Christian, Pierce,* she'd said to him, surprised. *You're a Catholic.*

"If they still let you see her," Winnie said. "You're supposed to be understanding, and not judge, and not get hysterical. I've read this. That just drives them deeper in." She laughed a little, and looked at Pierce sideways. "Can you do that?"

"I haven't," Pierce said. No he had raged at her, a furious village atheist, forgetting all his wisdom, his new infinite God at the infinitesimal heart of things; in inexplicable horror watched her fall helplessly asleep beneath their spell, though she laughed when he described it that way. Raged at himself, too, appalled at his unkindness, his lack of tact and tactic. He had gone, effectually, nuts, without knowing in the least why. He wasn't going to tell his mother that he had himself seen miracles, small ones, small elisions or alterations in time or matter, meaningless mostly but terrifying: the small undeniable signs which in a dream mean that reality is not as you have assumed it to be.

Well maybe he hadn't seen miracles. It was *as though* he had seen them, so exactly as though that he could not dispute them. He lived daily now in a world of as-though. Maybe not he alone either, maybe the distinction was failing everywhere in the world, metaphors imploding, tenor subsumed in vehicle.

He tipped back his chair with a foot against the deck's rail. Overhead great birds sailed the evening, winging with slow beats into the west, legs trailing behind. Rose Ibis, his bird book said, birds wholly unrelated to the Old World ibis sacred to Egypt, and to Ægypt.

"In Kentucky," he said. "That orphan girl we took in that time, when you were gone?"

"Yes."

"She believed in a secret gospel," Pierce said. "That her daddy figured out. About the end of the world."

"She did?" Winnie regarded him in amazement, that he should recall such a thing; she herself kept few useless memories.

"The devil threw this big rock at her daddy's house," Pierce said.

"Oh yes?"

"To keep him from telling the news. That the end was coming. So his own troops I guess wouldn't lose heart. Who knows."

"Those people," Winnie said.

That's what this felt like, Pierce realized: it felt like sitting on the steps of the dogtrot, in the summer of the end of the world, unable to save Bobbie, fending off from his inhabited heart the darkness she seemed to will herself into. No it didn't feel like it, it *was* it, as though it had never ceased.

But he knew now that nothing ever happens once, everything reoccurs as the cycles swing, each cycle is exactly like the last in another form, each age too no doubt; like one of those novels where all the characters are avatars of mythic personages, their commonplace acts reproducing all the turns of an ancient story, their names too echoing the old originals, though even that they don't recognize; thinking they are inventing their lives even as they are driven here and there by unsleeping Coincidence, obliged to carry it all out, down to murder, down to madness, before the last page.

"Pierce?" Winnie said. "Are you okay?"

He realized that for some time he had been bent over in his aluminum chair, pressing one hand against his chest.

"Are you in pain?"

"No. No." He tried to straighten up, look normal. "I keep thinking my heart is somehow damaged. But no, don't worry, the doctor says no."

"Not broken?" Winnie said, and put her hand on his. "Isn't it funny that's where you feel it. Just as though."

Yes just as though. What transfer from head to heart, from organ of knowing to organ of circulation, made possible this awful hurt in the middle of his bosom? Why here of all places? "It used to be," he said, "that people did believe it would break. And kill you."

"Well people still think that today," Winnie said. "A lot of people do."

"Well sure," Pierce said. "These concepts never really go away. In fact this book I am now writing."

He ceased speaking then, and his heart ceased its tapping in astonishment. The evening slowed, for an instant, to a halt.

Good god he had found it.

The heart in his breast swelled to sudden great size with understanding, and Pierce let out a cry, or a sob; and then he went on sobbing, emptying it of tears, though it seemed not to shrink at all.

He had found it. He had promised he could find it and he had.

What thing is it that we inherit from the distant past that has survived, unchanged, from the way things used to be? What is the one thing that has not lost its older nature or its powers?

Boney had wanted it to be an Elixir that would keep him alive forever. But it wasn't.

It had been within him, of course it had, all along; it had been within Pierce, was within everyone, always there right in our own backyards, well known to everyone too except the fool who goes out in search of it. It isn't even possible to think or talk without invoking it, referring to its powers and its reasons; whatever the surgeons find and handle when they crack the chest, everyone knows what it is, what work it has to do: it is there that the dry sticks of perceived reality are transformed into meaning, for the soul to feed upon. Even surgeons know it.

The heart. The heart yes in the bosom, for where else is it, it's no metaphor, it's *here, here, here,* and Pierce struck his own thrice. Here where the power was, and is, and always has been: just where magic said it proceeded from.

"Oh, son," said Winnie. She rubbed a forefinger beneath her nose, and sniffed. She took his hand again. "Oh damn it all."

He had just come upon the end of his book. His ridiculous sobs modulated to a mad shriek of laughter. Yes his *book.* Worse than never having come upon it at all, he had come upon it now, the surprise ending of his book, now when he was certain that he could never, ever write it.

He was to lose everything, mind as well as heart, occupation too; it was all to be taken from him. The big payback, and he supposed he well and truly deserved it. Out of cursed restless Saturnian boredom and longing he had hurt his own magic heart, abused it fatally in the search for thrills to animate it, and it had finally gone haywire, shrunken and contracted in his bosom, and would no longer do its work, would do nothing but pump his poor blood, and sob.

As the winter night fell in the North the temperature dropped; on television he and Winnie and Doris, Winnie's partner and companion, watched people in overcoats and galoshes bending into the snowy wind of northern cities, or hopelessly shoveling out their submerged cars. Pierce thought of the storm enveloping his little shuttered house at the end of its by now erased drive. Twice since winter began, the water coming into the house had begun to freeze, and twice he had freed the plastic pipe of ice before it was too late. Now he wasn't there.

Snow and bitter cold were apparently general all over Europe too, snow drifting deep where it usually frosted lightly, and falling in big theatrical flakes on Mediterranean towns that had rarely seen it at all, where children held up their hands to be visited by the tiny beings, who vanished when they alighted. Commentators said it was perhaps the advancing edge of a new cold phase, the return maybe of the

Little Ice Age of the seventeenth century, when the river Thames had frozen solid every year, and festivals were held on the ice.

All was still and mild on Winnie's key, and on the waters of the cove beyond the motel's little marina. A tall heron stood on one leg in the sawgrass, asleep with its beak beneath its wing. Pierce could have seen it, silhouetted against the silver water, if he had lifted his head to look out.

He lay awake on his damp pillow looking instead up into the ceiling tiles, which seemed to make faces, squarish pocked flat-hatted desperadoes squinting at nothing.

The heart, Julie, the heart. Isn't that something? The last magic engine persisting unchanged, still able to do wonderful things, Julie, if you want to dare to try them; terrible things too.

Magic is love, Julie. Love is magic. And hadn't she known it all along? The best kind of surprise, the one you could have guessed, the one you had known and yet hadn't expected. Though what Julie meant by love was surely not the awful winged *ker* that had covered Pierce; the heart she would think of wasn't the fearsome synthesizer of binding images cultivated by potent Saturnian melancholics of the Bruno type.

Bruno—ah it was clear now, very clear—had actually been trying to contract this disease of the heart, *amor hereos,* on purpose: allowing his own subjectivity to be overthrown, exiled, killed, replaced by a phantasm of the beloved, who would rule in his stead. Only his beloved wasn't a fleshly woman but the Goddess Diana: self-created image of the universe of which the heart and brain and self were all products. After he had fashioned in the erotic heat of his heart's workshop an image so gorgeous, so incandescent, that he could not but fall in love with it, he was going to undergo death in the replacing of his own consciousness with it: with a spiritual cognate of the whole wide world, all inside himself then as well as outside, and at his command. He would become a god.

Nut. Misguided nut. Let him get to Rome, and explain this to the Inquisition. Then he would find out where the real power lay, in which god's hands.

Pierce's heart had again begun that horrid tiny rapping at his ribcage.

When in the course of a dreadful night he had told Rose Ryder that he was afraid he had become unable to write the book he had promised to his agent and to his publisher, was going to have to abandon it maybe probably, she'd said *Well anyway it was all falsehoods, Pierce*. All falsehoods. He hadn't bound her with his spells at all, and now she had found stronger magic than his.

Oh jeez just let them not hurt her. Just let her not be hurt.

Maybe if he got up now and called her; told her how sorry he was for the way he had acted, and how he would try now to really understand, really.

No she would be sound asleep for sure, and not glad to be wakened. Sleep, peaceful sleep, was one of the benefits promised to believers.

Sweet dreamless sleep.

What he could not have expected, what he would not ever have thought possible: that his old God, miserable deistical structure compounded of bad metaphysics, scholastic quibbles, absolute claims subscribed to by absolutist child's logic, should suddenly come alive, factitious but animated, stirring like an eyeless lump of foulness in a dream; seeing through his evasions and casuistries just as Sam had seen through his old effrontery; alive, potent, immune to excuses, and claiming for his own the woman Pierce had hidden in his house.

And he had had nothing to fight for her with, no sword, no shield, they were lost, gone, broken; his soul wasn't pure either. He had had nothing but argument. He had entered into rational argument with her, about her God's existence, the truth of her Book, the claims of her hierophants, entered into argument as into a wood of tearing thorns that closed immediately behind him.

Hypnerotomachia.

Nor did it do any good; he could hurt her with his relentless hacking, make her weep, but couldn't shake her heart from the one good great thing (she said) that had ever taken hold of it. It was only himself he convinced, arguing even when she wasn't present, all by himself daylong, nightlong, not moving from the chair where he formulated his case: until at midnight or dawn his speaking mouth froze in horror, and he realized that for hours, for days, he had been living in *their* universe, and staring at *their* God, giving him only more life by his discourse.

Where was it that Barr said, was it in *Time's Body* or another of his books, that in the religious history of the West old gods are always turning into devils, cast from their thrones into dark undergrounds, to be lords over the dead and the wicked? It had happened to the old Titans when the Greek sky-gods came, it had happened to the *dives* of Greece and Rome in turn and the Northern gods too, who became horned devils for the Christian to fear.

And now look, the wheel turns, Jehovah becomes the devil. Old Nobadaddy, liver-spotted greasy-bearded jealous God, spread over his hoard of blessings like the Dragon, surrounded by his sycophants singing praises, never enough though: Pierce could see him, when he closed his eyes, reigning in his dark and fuliginous heaven. Also when he opened his eyes. He wondered if in the end he would see nothing else forever.

Winnie said: *I don't understand why you don't just drop it.* And he hadn't understood himself, and now he did.

In the little cabin by the Blackbury they had conspired together, she and he, to forge a hieroglyph of Love in the shape of her (multifoliate Rose) in his spirit, by the alchemical power of Eros. Now it could not be evicted, it was nothing but an image but it was ruling in *his* heart in *his* stead, while she went on living the tragicomic real life from which they had at first extracted it.

Weird, because the story they had built between them in the little bedroom by the river was all about how she was to surrender her throne to him.

Oh, come back, come back, soul, self, how was he ever to find his way back, by what awful journey, to the empty throneroom of the heart?

He wished he could weep.

Hermes, he prayed, old devil, god of binding and unbinding: release me from this spell I've caught myself in. I'm not so smart, I thought I was so smart, I'm not. Bruno: You got me into this, come to me now if you can, teach me how to take back the magic I started. You bastard.

He lay still and tried to believe there might be help for him if he could believe in help, but there was none. And why should there be.

No the only hope was to ride it out; to make it over somehow unkilled into the next age, the new world, when the loathsome and beautiful creatures of the passage time will disinvent themselves, gone with the wind. All that he saw and felt now (gripping the edges of his motel bed, tasting the sweat on his lip) would maybe become plain madness then, a simple mental or moral mistake. Understandable.

Curable. Maybe there would be a pill he could take. A calm clinic, he could see it clearly; the nurse entering, and on her tray the glass of cool water, and a pill, rose-colored, divided in half by a tender groove.

O world stop spinning. Like a ball in a roulette wheel seeking for its resting place.

It might be years, though, it might be decades from now. He would have to keep himself alive till then, make his way across this wild waste, alone too, not even Good Deeds to go with him, for he had never done any; he could not remember one, not one.

Just let him not cease hoping for it to come to be, the new world. Let him not cease longing, or it might not come; its coming into being might depend upon his longing, his willingness to want it still.

He sat up. It was no use lying in the dark. If there were something to read. But he was afraid of the books he had brought with him, history books, magic books. Falsehoods. He wished he had brought Enosh, just one volume, to be by his side.

When he got home, he decided, he would call Rosie Rasmussen. He would tell her he was ready to go to Europe now, ready to fill out his application, whatever; that he was ready to go soon. A different sky, a long vacation; something to look for there too, and a reason to look for it: an *apotropaic,* gorgeous black word, something to fend off this evil. He felt in his pants pocket for his smokes, and lit one, though he knew that meant he was now awake till dawn. He sat in his shorts on the edge of the bed, the ashtray between his legs, and his back bent with the weight of the succubus that clung there, his own cunning work, made in the smithy of his own heart, which now was shut and could make no more.

But meanwhile, meanwhile: from somewhere in the Realms of Light, wasn't help on the way?

Had not a messenger already set out, tiny messenger, infinitesimal at first, but surely much grown up by now? Traveling outward or inward, through æon upon æon, with a message just for Pierce?

Well he had got lost; had got lost more than once in fact, had been distracted, led astray, sent off in the wrong direction or even backward, wandering in spheres of confusion and forgetfulness, delayed over and over, unconscionably, fearfully delayed, as by the twists of a plot, an old farce plot. Now, even as the hoary powers of the old age of the world shuffle offstage, their work still undone (it was never to be done, never would or could be done, has not been finished ever in any age so far) he, or is it she, stands at the border of some vacant and evanescing circle, trying to remember where she, or is it he, was headed, toward what place, with what word for whom: fretting like the traveler pacing the midnight station who suspects that the last train has gone.

But will she come in time? Oh yes just in time; whenever she comes is just in time; when we have despaired for the thousandth midnight of any such a one ever coming from anywhere, she will arrive, in a tearing hurry, breaking into or out of the last spheres of air, fire, water, earth as though throwing open the successive doors of a long corridor, down which she rushes, her hair streaming and her brow knit, her hand already beside her mouth to call into the ear of our souls *Wake up.*

AUTHOR'S NOTE

In the preceding volume of this series of fictions I acknowledge my debt to many writers, thinkers and historians from whom I have learned, principally the late Dame Frances Yates.

To that list I wish now to add, for the particular contents of this book, some further thanks: to Harry Caudill (*Night Comes to the Cumberlands*) for reminding me of much I had forgotten and explaining much that I had not understood; John Bossy (*Giordano Bruno and the Embassy Affair*); Gerald Mattingly (*The Armada*); Carlo Ginzburg (*The Night Battles*); R.J.W. Evans (*Rudolf II and his World*). I have drawn on the researches of Piero Camporesi, Caroline Walker Bynum, Caroline Oates and Ernan McMullen. Thanks also to L.S.B., Jennifer Stevenson, Thomas M. Disch, John Hollander and Harold Bloom.

Above all to the late Ioan Couliano: for *Eros and Magic in the Renaissance,* from which I have taken much, but for far more than that, I offer gratitude and grief. *Quæ nunc abibis in loca; nec ut soles dabis iocos!*